FORREST REID

Tom Barber

Young Tom
The Retreat
Uncle Stephen

❀❀❀❀❀❀❀❀

INTRODUCTION BY

E. M. FORSTER

PANTHEON BOOKS

NEW YORK

AUTHOR'S NOTE

Chronologically the stories dealing with Tom Barber run in the following sequence—*Young Tom, The Retreat, Uncle Stephen*—though actually they were written in the reverse order and each is complete in itself. All the characters except Roger, Pincher, and Barker are imaginary.

Young Tom was first published in England, in 1944; *The Retreat*, in 1936; *Uncle Stephen*, in 1931, revised edition in 1945.

LIBRARY OF CONGRESS CATALOG CARD NUMBER: 55-10277

MANUFACTURED IN THE UNITED STATES OF AMERICA

CONTENTS

CONTENTS

FORREST REID
(1876–1947)

Forrest Reid's major creation is now presented for the first time to America. He has also been slow to gain recognition in Great Britain. Neither in England—a country he never greatly liked—nor in his beloved Northern Ireland was much notice taken of him in his lifetime. He belonged to no clique and did not know how to pull wires or to advertise himself. His reputation spread slowly, and much more by word of mouth than by press reclame.

After his death a change took place. In particular his own great city of Belfast awoke to his worth, and paid honour to one of the more eminent and more reticent of her sons. In 1952 a plaque was unveiled to him on the four-roomed house where he had lived during his latter years: not a bad little suburban house—I have often stayed there —not squalid, but not of the nature of a shrine. The Lord Mayor of Belfast attended in state, the Vice-Chancellor of Queen's University came, the Irish Academy of Dublin sent a distinguished representative, the Governor of Northern Ireland congratulated and we were making the proceedings as august as we could contrive, when a regrettable interruption occurred. A car tooted. Off dashed the police on their motor bikes to discover the tooter. They returned with smiles on their faces. It had been a little girl who had been left in the car by her papa while he attended the unveiling, and she had got bored.

Forrest Reid would have enjoyed this interruption far more than all the homilies to which we treated him. Childhood and youth and their spontaneity were to him the essentials, the Wordsworthian starting point to which, however old we get, we must return. The tooting of a little girl—or rather of a little boy—is constantly heard in his novels—a horn of elfland, interrupting the pompous noises of grown ups. I do not mean to say that he is a whimsical writer. He is indeed an extremely serious one. And he is an extremely careful one, who paid rigorous attention to his art. But he does introduce the

7

supernatural. It flits through his pages—gone as quickly as summer lightning sometimes, gone as quickly as the thunder clap when young Tom spoke the Word, but it never leaves the pages as it found them. The glimmer of the inexplicable gets attached to the certainties of youth.

Tom Barber, the hero of this trilogy, is Forrest Reid's most important creation. The books describing his career were composed in reverse order—*Uncle Stephen* came first in 1931, *The Retreat* in 1934, and *Young Tom* in 1944—and I have sometimes thought this unusual sequence of composition, this moving back towards origins may have brought extra strength. The books have puerilities and longueurs in them—no admirer would deny it—but whatever happens Tom himself is never a bore. He is not a very mischievous boy or a very good one or very clever or very stupid, or a professional charmer: why does he hold us so? Through his honesty. He shares the honesty of his creator. Tom faces up to things, however alarming they are, and even when he is told that they do not exist. It is natural in his childhood that he should speak to animals—most children do this, and he does it so naturally that the animals reply. Later on they become silent, but they have taught him to have commerce with intangibles, and at the end of the trilogy he grapples with that most intangible of all things—Time—and makes it talk sense.

He has also commerce with good and evil. Forrest Reid had a strong ethical strain in him: his Protestant forebears saw to that. What he sought, though, was not moral principles which often lead to cruelty and stupidity, but "a sort of moral fragrance." He tells us something about this fragrance in his remarkable autobiography *Apostate*. The evil personages in *Tom Barber*—except indeed the Japanese ghouls—are never emanations of Hell. Even the bad magician is sad. Even Henry the cat, though he does all the harm he can and is fiendishly clever, can be made to feel a fool. Even the serpent in the Garden of Eden has a heart. Towards the end of the trilogy the ethical sense deepens, the ethical pronouncements wear thinner and thinner. Uncle Stephen, the white magician, is close, and his influence permeates. Deverell, the young poacher, the Lion in the Way whom Tom encounters at dusk, could be classed as evil if classification remained. Tom escapes and rejects Deverell for the cold clean Philip. But in that rejection there is love, adolescence has brought comprehension. And Philip has in his turn to be re-jected and to be annihilated.

Beyond adolescence maturity begins and Forrest Reid was not interested in maturity. His characters are all young or in attendance on youth. So although his setting is realistic, and the lovely Ulster countryside and less lovely Ulster interiors are faithfully delineated, his population is specialised and some would say monotonous. There will always be readers to whom this unusual writer will not appeal. I remember Virginia Woolf giving him a trial and then turning him down. I recommend him to those who care for the spirit I have indi-cated above, and who like to see that spirit expressed in sensitive prose.

I first met him in 1911. He dedicated his next book, *Following Darkness*, to me: a lovely book it is.[1] We kept in touch for the rest of his life. Occasionally he came over to England for the purpose of playing croquet—he was a croquet champion—more frequently I went over to stop with him, and with his friends, and with his dogs. These last were important, as readers of *Tom Barber* will con-jecture: dogs were the companions, the rescuers, the testers of char-acter. People who were bitten by dogs had no one to blame but themselves. He lived exactly as he liked—not Bohemianly, for he did not care for Bohemianism. He had a fine collection of books; he wrote a standard monograph on the *Illustrators of the Sixties*, and various other works, besides about a dozen novels. He had just enough money, from his sales, and from other sources, to support him. He had begun his career as a clerk in a Belfast tea-warehouse, an old-fashioned establishment to which he always looked back with affection. To quote from *Apostate:*

> When one's life, or the greater part of it, is passed in certain fixed conditions, is not the pleasantness of those conditions more important than the distinction of paying a super-tax? If I had been chained all day long to a desk I should have been unhappy: as it was I was happy. My mental growth was not checked: on the contrary, my mind expanded more rapidly and freely than it had ever done before; I did not acquire elderly and methodical habits, the spirit of boyhood was left un-touched. I had been brought into contact with ordinary rough-and-tumble life, but I had not been caught in the wheels of a machine.

[1] Rewritten by him as *Peter Waring*.

After leaving the tea-warehouse, he went to Cambridge and took a degree there. Cambridge made no impression on him whatever. His heart was in his own country, and nearly all his novels take place in Northern Ireland and draw their beauty from its beauty.

E. M. FORSTER

Young Tom

or

Very Mixed Company

✸✸✸✸✸✸✸✸

What call'st thou solitude? Is not the Earth
With various living creatures, and the Air,
Replenished, and all these at thy command
To come and play before thee? Knowest thou not
Their language and their ways? . . . With these
Find pastime.

Paradise Lost

PART ONE

THE FRIENDS

1: "TAKE your hands out of your pockets and don't stand there dreaming," had been Daddy's farewell words. Spoken in a distinctly impatient voice too, so that Tom, while he waved good-bye and watched the car receding down the drive, felt both surprised and annoyed. Yet these same words when pronounced by Mother (as they usually were about fifty times a day), never annoyed him in the least. Coming from Daddy—who didn't even practise what he preached—and above all coming in that irritable tone, they were quite another thing; therefore, having withdrawn his hands in token of obedience, Tom felt justified, immediately afterwards, in putting them back again. True, this gesture of independence was largely directed at William, whose self-righteous and reproving gaze he perceived to be fixed upon him. William said nothing, but he shook his head pessimistically before proceeding with his work. William was clipping edges—and no doubt clipping them very neatly —yet Tom didn't see why that need make him look so dourly conscious of possessing every virtue—all the less attractive ones at any rate. He ought to have looked like Adam (see *Paradise Lost*—Mother's recollected version of it), and he didn't. In fact, Tom could imagine some thoughtless young green shoot, filled with an ardent zest of life, wriggling excitedly up through the brown soil, catching one glimpse of William's sour countenance, and hastily retreating underground again.

The strange thing was that nothing of the kind happened. If anywhere, it was in Tom's own private garden that plants exhibited signs of nervousness. The struggle for life there was bitter in the extreme, and not a few had given it up as hopeless, while the survivors hung

13

limp and melancholy heads. Turning to this questionable oasis now, he could not help feeling that last night's attentions had only increased its resemblance to a violated grave, and he stooped to pull out a weed, and to press down the earth round a recently transplanted orange lily. The officious William was watching him, of course, and very soon came his grumpy counsel: "You let them alone, Master Tom, and don't be always worretin' and pokin' at them. Plants is like men; they can't abide naggin' and fussin'. . . . When I was a wee lad, no bigger'n what you are now, I'd have had that patch lovely."

"So *you* say!" Tom retorted, though a sense of justice presently compelled him to add, "Well, maybe you would."

For though William might be a cantankerous, disageeable old man, for ever grousing and complaining, all his surroundings—flowers, shrubs, paths, and lawn—were undeniable and brilliant testimonials to his efficiency. On this morning of the last day of June the garden was looking its very best—a wonderful blaze of colour—and deliberately Tom inhaled its fragrance—the varied scents of stocks, roses, mignonette, and sweet-briar—all mixed together in one aromatic medley.

It was going to be very hot later, he thought; for even now, early as it was, he could feel the sun pleasantly warm on his bare head and neck and hands, and penetrating through his grey flannel jacket and tennis shirt. Two young thrushes were swinging up and down on a slender prunus branch as if it were a seesaw. He tried to draw William's attention to them, but William, continuing his slow methodical progress with the edge-clippers, would not even look, merely grunted. That was because he thought birds received a great deal too much encouragement in this garden: if he had had his way he would have shot them, like Max Sabine, or else covered up everything eatable with nets.

The abundance of birds was partly due to the glen beside the house, and partly to the fact that Daddy took an interest in them, hung up coconuts for them, supplied them with baths, and fed them all through the winter. Tom liked birds too, but he very much preferred animals. Doctor Macrory, to be sure, had told him he would like penguins, because penguins were much the same as dogs, came when you called them, and allowed you to pat them on their broad solid backs—good substantial thumps, which they accepted in the proper spirit. But he had never seen a penguin except a stuffed one in Queen's University Museum, and even Doctor Macrory thought they might be troublesome to keep as pets unless you happened to be a fishmonger. . . .

Suddenly there was a tapping on the window behind him, which he knew, without turning round, to be a signal from Mother. The signal was to remind him that he was supposed to be on his way to the Rectory, where he did lessons with Althea Sabine, under the supervision of Miss Sabine, who was Althea's Aunt Rachel, and the Rector's sister.

But there was no hurry; in fact he didn't know why Miss Sabine wanted him at the Rectory at all this morning, for she had set them no lessons. This meant that the long summer holidays had already begun; and whatever she had to say to him she might just as well have said yesterday. Anyhow, it would be for the last time; since he was going to school after the summer.

That had been decided at Miss Sabine's own suggestion. She had called specially to talk the matter over with Daddy and Mother, and apparently her report had pleased them, though what she had actually said he did not know, except that she regarded him as "quite a talented little boy." He would not have known even this had not Mother let it out inadvertently, for to himself Miss Sabine had always expressed her approval in a very brief and dry fashion. Yet somehow he liked her dryness, and liked doing lessons with her; and though she had never told him so, and never showed it openly, he knew she knew this and that it pleased her.

Miss Sabine kept house for her brother, there being no Mrs. Sabine. Poor Mrs. Sabine, indeed, was so much a thing of the past that Althea had once told him her mother had died before she was born. Tom had puzzled over this, having heard of a similar phenomenon in the case of a sheep who had been struck by lightning. But Althea had not mentioned a thunder-storm, and delicacy had prevented him from doing so either. Mother, when he repeated the story at home, declared it was all nonsense. . . .

A second and more imperative tap on the window at this point interrupted his meditations; so he left William and the thrushes, and proceeded on down the short drive as far as the gate, where he found Doctor Macrory's Barker waiting for him.

The gate was shut, but Roger or Pincher would easily have found a way in; it was just like lazy old Barker not to bother. "Take your hands out of your pockets and don't stand there dreaming!" Tom told him sharply, but Barker only wagged a stumpy tail.

It was largely his fashion of mooching along, never in a hurry, never excited, never demonstrative beyond a tail-wag—which he made as brief as possible—that gave Barker his sluggish and slouchy appearance. He was the most phlegmatic and independent dog Tom had ever met. Of course, he was old—older even than Roger, the collie from Denny's farm, though he too was well on the other side of middle-age—and much older than Pincher, the Sabines' rough-haired fox-terrier. Indeed, he was old enough to be Pincher's great-grandfather, Tom supposed. All three were his friends, and spent a considerable portion of their time with him. It was their sole point of union, however, for they never dreamed of associating together in his absence. Meeting them occasionally on his daily rounds, Doctor Mac-rory would stop to discuss the "Dogs' Club," as he called it, and question Tom as to their several breeds—a joke which had begun to pall slightly, though it was still received with invariable politeness. They might not be show dogs, Tom thought, but he couldn't see why it should be less aristocratic to be descended from a lot of ancient families than from only one. This view Doctor Macrory himself admitted to be reasonable. And after all, it was his own dog Barker who required most explanation, though you could easily see he was an Old-English sheepdog from his face, his big clumsy paws, and his rough woolly coat of several shades of grey, both in colour and texture remarkably like the hearthrug Mother had made last winter for the study. The three were as different in temperament as they were in their coats. Pincher was restless, for ever getting into scrapes, excitable, and possessed of a sort of primitive, errand-boy sense of humour, vulgar and extremely knowing. Roger was emotional and demonstrative; swift, graceful, lithe; with a tail like a waving ostrich plume. Roger was Tom's darling, and they could sit side by side for a long time with their arms round each other, immersed in a warm bath of affection, while Barker regarded their sloppiness with indifference, and Pincher with impatience. . . .

All the same, it was Barker who was at the gate now, and he wanted Tom to come down to the river. He nearly always did, for that matter, however busy you might be with more important things. "Can't you see I'm going to the Rectory?" Tom asked him; and Barker looked disappointed.

This, Tom felt, was understandable, for it was just the right kind of morning for the river, and certainly not one to be wasted indoors. The myriad voices of Nature were calling—whispering in the trees that overhung and cast deep pools of shadow on the sunlit road—calling more loudly and imperatively from bird and beast and insect. Everywhere was life and the eager joy of life. The very air seemed alive, and from the earth a living strength was pushing upwards and outwards—visible in each separate blade of grass and delicate meadow flower no less than in the great chestnut-tree standing at the corner where the road turned.

From the tangled hawthorn hedge, though its bloom had fallen, came a fresh, cool, green smell. Unfortunately Tom and Barker, tramping along the dusty highway, were on the wrong side of it. On the other side, as they both knew, far more was happening. On the other side was a ditch, where, in a jungle of nettles, vetches, and wild parsnips, young thrushes and blackbirds and sparrows would be hiding. A rook flying out of the chestnut-tree cawed a greeting as he passed over their heads. Two white cabbage butterflies, circling about each other in their strange fashion, flitted across the road and were lost to sight. Barker, pausing by a stile, again mentioned the river.

"No," said Tom emphatically; and after a moment, as a somewhat feeble consolation: "Anyhow, what would we do?"

"Fish for stones," Barker replied promptly.

But Tom had guessed he would say this, and remained unmoved. "Yes, *you'd* fish for them, and I'd sit on the bank and get splashed all over with mud and water."

Barker said no more, not really being importunate. It was strange, all the same, that this fishing for stones should so appeal to him. It had no charm for the other dogs; they never even attempted it; yet Barker could spend happy hours merely dragging stone after stone from the river bed, and dropping each one carefully beside Tom for the latter to arrange in a heap. It was a dirty job, too, because the river bed was soft, and Barker would emerge from it, a large stone in his mouth, and his face so plastered with mud as to be unrecognizable. He must at the same time have swallowed quantities, besides getting it into his eyes and nostrils; yet this did not seem to trouble him, and he would go on as long as Tom's patience lasted. What the latter couldn't understand was why he should have to be present at all. There was nothing to hinder Barker now, for instance, from going down to the river by himself, and spending the rest of the morning fishing for stones; yet Tom knew he wouldn't; and he was right; Barker accompanied him as far as the Rectory gate, and then turned and trotted off at his customary pace, unvarying as the wheels of a clock. But he went in the direction of his own home, not of the river.

2: THE Rectory hall door was open when Tom reached it, so he walked straight on in without ringing the bell. In the dining-room, where they did lessons, he found both Miss Sabine and Althea seated at the table, snipping off the tops and tails of gooseberries. Mother thought there must be foreign, probably Spanish, blood in the Sabines, which was what made them all so vivid-looking. At breakfast this morning she had said so, and also that there was something masculine about Miss Sabine's whole style and appearance, due partly, perhaps, to the way she dressed. Tom, however, could see nothing masculine about her, unless it was that Miss Sabine looked big and strong and had a tiny black moustache. In every way she suggested strength—strength of character, strength of mind, strength of purpose. Her skin was almost swarthy, her hair jet black, and when she was really angry, as he had seen her on one memorable occasion with Max, her eyes literally flashed.

"Good morning, Tom," she now greeted him, in her firm deep voice; while Althea said "Hello!" and giggled.

Tom returned Miss Sabine's "good morning," but took no notice of Althea, whose habit of giggling at nothing displeased him. Althea, at any rate, was vivid enough, with cheeks like apples, and her hair hanging down in sleek black pigtails. At the moment, however, he was much less interested either in her, or in Mother's discoveries, than in a row of brand-new books, with brilliant bindings and gilt edges, spread out in the middle of the table. Having cast a rapid glance at these, he determinedly looked away, and coloured when he saw Althea watching him with a kind of sly amusement. It was very like her, he thought: she was always amused when you found yourself in some delicate situation and didn't quite know what to do. Not that she was a bad kid on the whole. There was at least nothing mean or treacherous about her, as there was about Max. . . .

"I expect you've been wondering, Tom, why I asked you to come back this morning," Miss Sabine said. "It was simply because those books didn't arrive till after you had gone yesterday, though the man in the shop promised faithfully to send them out in plenty of time. I want you to choose one as a small memento; or perhaps I should say a prize, for of course it is really that."

Tom's blush deepened, and Althea began to hum a little tune, so that he could have kicked her. Nevertheless he managed to jerk out: "Thanks awfully, Miss Sabine."

"Well, you'd better have a look at them," Miss Sabine observed, since shyness seemed to have reduced him to immobility. "You mayn't like *any* of them, for I could only guess; so if there's some other book you'd prefer instead, I hope you'll tell me."

After this she tactfully resumed her gooseberry-snipping, nor did she once glance at him while he was making his choice.

The first book he took up was Macaulay's *Lays of Ancient Rome*, the only volume he had already rejected in his mind. But Althea, who had *no* tact, was still covertly watching him, and he turned his back upon her.

There were more than a dozen books to choose from, and Miss Sabine must have gone to some trouble in selecting them. Here were *The Talisman* and *David Copperfield; Huckleberry Finn*, and *The Golden Treasury* bound in leather; *Tom Brown's Schooldays, Westward Ho!, Grimm's Fairy Tales, King Solomon's Mines*, and *Treasure Island*. Each attracted him; but he already possessed a tattered copy of *Grimm*, and the attraction of *The Talisman* and *Westward Ho!* was somewhat faint. *The Golden Treasury*, moreover, was poetry, though if it had been Edgar Allen Poe's poetry he might have taken it. As it was, he lifted each book in turn, glanced through it, and looked at the pictures if there were any. But this was an act of politeness pure and simple, for very quickly he had made up his mind that the choice lay between two books only—*Nat the Naturalist*, by George Manville Fenn, and *Curiosities of Natural History*, by Frank Buckland. He would have decided on the latter at once had it not been in four volumes—First Series, Second Series, Third Series, and Fourth Series—therefore it might seem greedy to choose it when all the others were in one volume only. True, the *Curiosities* volumes were less sumptuously bound, and had neither gilt nor olivine edges. If you took them individually, they looked less expensive than the others, and it suddenly occurred to him that very likely they *were* to be regarded as separate books, so he lifted the first and said: "I'd like this, please."

"Well, I think you've made an excellent choice," Miss Sabine agreed, "though I haven't read it myself, and picked it out just because I thought from the title it might interest you."

"But—but——" Tom stammered, for Miss Sabine had drawn all four volumes towards her and was now preparing to write his name in them. Pen in hand she paused, glancing up at him.

"I meant—I thought—there'd be only one," Tom mumbled in confusion.

Miss Sabine smiled: she understood perfectly. "Oh, that's all right," she assured him, looking at him very kindly, and dipping her pen. "They go together: they *are* only one." And she began her inscription, quite a lengthy one, or so it seemed to Tom, for her writing was very large and black, and sprawled over the whole yellowish end-paper.

"And now," she said, pressing down the blotting-paper, "there you are. You certainly deserve all four, and if you do as well at school as you have always done with me, I don't think they'll be the last prizes you'll get."

Tom thanked her once again, beaming all over with a pleasure that lit up like sunshine his plain, freckled, blunt-featured face, and greenish-grey eyes. At the same time he wondered what Althea had got, but did not like to ask since the others had not mentioned it.

Nor, though she accompanied him as far as the garden gate, did Althea mention it when they were alone. "Max is going to camp," was all she told him. "He didn't want to, but his form master or somebody wrote to Dad about it, so he won't be coming home just yet." Then, as Tom received this information in silence: "I suppose you're not interested. . . . I forgot. . . . You don't like him much, do you?"

"No," Tom said.

The remarkable frankness of his agreement did not appear to trouble Althea. "Why?" she asked, without the slightest hint of resentment.

"Because I don't," Tom answered.

Althea was silent for a minute or two, as if mentally turning over this response. He could see, nevertheless, that what she was really searching for was an excuse for pursuing the subject. "I don't think you ought to dislike him," was the very feeble one she eventually found. "I mean—to keep it up in that way. It's wicked."

In spite of his annoyance, Tom laughed. "Do you think he likes *me*?" he said.

"I don't know. I never asked him. But that shouldn't prevent you from setting a good example."

"Yes . . . ?" He looked at her closely. "Why are you sticking on all this? You don't go in much yourself for setting good examples."

"I can't: I've nobody to set them to," Althea sighed. But curiosity once more prevailed, and she said: "I suppose it has something to do with the Fallon boy—James-Arthur."

Tom flushed hotly. "You can suppose what you like," he retorted, and would have left her abruptly had she not caught him by his jacket.

"Don't be so huffy! I only said I *supposed* it was that. And if you want to know why, it was because I heard Max talking to Dad about it, and telling him you oughtn't to be allowed to be friends with a farm boy. . . . So you needn't get in a temper as if it was *my* fault. . . . Aunt Rachel heard him too, and ticked him off for being such a snob."

But Tom by this time had shaken himself free, and with a brief "Good-bye," he made his escape, leaving Althea standing at the gate gazing after him.

3. WITH the four precious red volumes under his arm he hurried down the road, eager to display them at home. But when he reached the church, a squat little grey stone building with a square tower, he paused. The door was wide open, and he remembered he had never been inside on a weekday, when it must be more interesting, or at any rate different. On Sundays he had to sit in a pew from which he could see little except the upper parts of the congregation, and the whole of Mr. Sabine in his white surplice. Even the stained-glass window was at the opposite side from where he and Daddy and Mother sat, so that he had never been able to examine it closely. This was his chance, for though somebody of course must be inside, it would only be Mrs. Fallon, James-Arthur's mother.

He swung himself over the low, moss-lined wall, and crossed the grass between green graves and dark cypress-trees. Sure enough, Mrs. Fallon emerged at that very moment, carrying a bucket of slops, which she emptied on to the grass. She was obviously not expecting visitors, for her petticoats were extremely tucked up, revealing quite a lot of grey woollen stocking above two stout black boots, large enough to have been James-Arthur's own. Also her head was tied up, like a dumpling, in a blue duster with white spots.

"Good morning, Mrs. Fallon," Tom said, approaching her from behind, so that Mrs. Fallon, who had neither heard nor seen him, jumped.

"Good gracious, Master Tom! You give me quite a turn!"

"Sorry," he apologized. "I didn't mean to. May I go in to the church, Mrs. Fallon—just for a few minutes—unless you've finished and want to lock up?"

But Mrs. Fallon hadn't finished. "You're welcome, dear," she told him, "and if it's the tower, the door's not locked, you've only to push it."

Tom thanked her. "It was really the window I was thinking of," he explained, "but I'd like to go up the tower too."

"You'll not be fiddling with the bell-rope, then, will you, like a good boy?"

He promised, and went in, followed by Mrs. Fallon, who had re-filled her bucket from a tap beside the porch.

He went straight to the stained-glass window, through which the sun was pouring, casting warm splashes of coloured light on the whitewashed pillars and on the floor and opposite wall. The window showed an old man wading across a river, carrying a small boy on his shoulders. The man, with his white beard and his staff, Tom knew to be Saint Christopher, and the small boy to be Christ. He also knew that Christ was growing heavier and heavier all the time, though of course the artist could not show this in his picture.

He admired the window for several minutes, trying to remember how the story had ended: then he drew closer that he might read the tablet below, which said that it had been put up by loving grand-parents in memory of their grandson, Ralph Seaford, who had died at the age of ten years, and was buried with his parents and infant sister in the churchyard outside.

"It's all very sad, isn't it?" Mrs. Fallon called out cheerfully from the chancel steps, where she was on her knees scrubbing them. But it did not sadden Tom; he only wondered if Ralph Seaford had been fond of the story of Saint Christopher; which in turn led him to won-der what kind of boy he had been. At any rate the old people must have thought a lot of him. . . .

Speculating as to whether Granny in similar circumstances would have put up a window to *him*, he crossed the church, and passing behind the pulpit opened the door leading to the tower. It was not a high tower, and a narrow, winding flight of stone steps soon brought him to a kind of loft, or small square room, in the middle of which the bell-rope hung down stiffly like a giant's pigtail. There were little windows—or rather slits in the wall, for they had no glass—which let in a certain amount of light; and far above, in the dusk beneath the rafters, he could see the bell itself.

The tower and the bell reminded him of a poem which had got Althea into endless trouble while they had been learning it. This was because she could never say "bells, bells, bells, bells, bells, bells, bells," without giggling; and that was only seven times, and once or twice it came oftener. Miss Sabine used to get furious, and Tom, too, had thought Althea very silly: for the repetitions were part of the tune, and the tune was part of the poem. He himself liked it, and had even tried to sing it. Unsuccessfully, it is true; because for some strange reason it wasn't that kind of music. He could sing it a little in his mind, but he couldn't sing either it or *The Raven* out aloud; though when nobody was listening he could and often did sing *Annabel Lee*. All these poems, he was well aware, had been chosen to please *him*; but that was Althea's own fault, because she either never would, or never could, say what she liked. . . .

He gazed up at the bell, hanging motionless and silent beneath the dark rafters framing the roof; and while he did so, slowly it began to take life—the life of a great sleeping, dreaming bat. Yet it was iron—an iron bell—

> *Every sound that floats*
> *From the rust within their throats*
> *Is a groan.*

Tom felt a sudden desire to awaken just one of those groans, but he remembered his promise to Mrs. Fallon, so instead began to repeat the poem, at first into himself, but presently in a chant that grew louder and louder.

> *And the people—ah, the people—*
> *They that dwell up in the steeple,*
> *All alone. . . .*
> *They are neither man nor woman—*

They are neither brute nor human—
They are Ghouls:
And their king it is who tolls;
And he rolls, rolls, rolls,
　Rolls
　　A paean from the bells!
And his merry bosom swells
　With the paean of the bells!
And he dances and he yells;
Keeping time, time, time,
In a sort of Runic rhyme,
　To the paean of the bells—
　　Of the bells:
Keeping time, time, time,
In a sort of Runic rhyme,
　To the throbbing of the bells—
Of the bells, bells, bells—
　　To the sobbing of the bells;
Keeping time, time, time,
　As he knells, knells, knells,
In a happy Runic rhyme,
　To the rolling of the bells—
Of the bells, bells, bells:
　To the tolling of the bells,
Of the bells, bells, bells, bells—
　Bells, bells, bells—
To the moaning and the groaning of the bells.

The potent magic of that Runic Rhyme had by this time created a kind of intoxication through which he distinctly saw a queer little ancient face surmounted by a pointed cap peeping down at him. It was old, old, old; and it peeped, peeped, peeped—peeping down. It was king of all the people; they that dwelt up in the steeple——But at night?

Tom ceased; suddenly silent at the interruption of another voice.

"Come down, Master Tom. Whatever are you doing up there?"

"Nothing," he shouted in reply. "Just looking."

"Well, it's a queer kind of looking you can hear all over the church. Come along now: I've finished, and I want to lock up."

Mrs. Fallon's tones, though primarily expostulatory, were also distinctly curious; and when he joined her at the foot of the staircase she inspected him with a hint of suspicion in her eye. "You've been up there these twenty minutes or more," she told him; "and there's not a thing to be seen unless it would be a few bats, and you don't see *them* except when they're flying out at night."

"There weren't any bats," Tom admitted. "I mean, I didn't notice any. But it's so dark under the roof there might be hundreds."

"What were you doing then?" Mrs. Fallon persisted. "Not writing your name, I hope—which is what I've known to be done. . . . Names and dates—Roberts and Sarahs—with maybe a heart drew round them, or some such foolery; as if a church was a fitting place for the like of that."

"Still, people get married in church," Tom reminded her. "Anyhow, I didn't write anything: I was just looking at the bell and—thinking."

He gathered up his books, which he had left in one of the pews, and followed by Mrs. Fallon, walked on down the aisle. In the porch he managed to give her yet another surprise, though all he said was; "Could I have the keys, Mrs. Fallon? I mean, would you lend them to me? I'll bring them back to you first thing to-morrow."

Mrs. Fallon gasped—or pretended to. "Well——!" Then she recovered. "And what might you be wanting with the keys, if I may ask?"

"I'd like to come back here by myself. I'll promise not to touch anything or do any harm, and I'll leave them in with you to-morrow morning."

Mrs. Fallon had already thrust the three keys—one large and two smaller—into a capacious pocket, as if she feared he might grab them and run. "Keys!" she said severely. "What would Mr. Sabine think? It's him you'd better be asking for the keys if you want them. Run along home now, like a good boy, and don't be talking your nonsense."

4. MRS. FALLON no doubt spoke metaphorically; nevertheless, for a good part of the way, Tom obeyed her literally, having suddenly remembered that Mother had specially asked him not to be late, as Daddy would be coming home for lunch.

He strongly suspected that he *was* late, and when, hot and breathless, he burst into the dining-room, suspicion became certainty. He was later even than he had feared. "How often——" But at sight of his flushed face, shining eyes, and the four crimson volumes he dumped down triumphantly on the table between her and Daddy, Mother checked the well-known formula of rebuke at word two. "It's my prize," Tom said, and she looked nearly as pleased as he did himself.

"What—*four* books!" she cried. "Well, I never!"

"It's really only one book," he explained excitedly—"in four series. She had a whole lot of books for me to choose from—*Tom Brown's Schooldays, King Solomon's Mines*—oh, heaps and heaps!"

Mother laughed. "So you chose this! If ever there was a little 'curiosity of natural history', I fancy I could name him without much difficulty. . . . No, dear," she hastily added, "I don't mean that, and I'm sure they're most interesting." She turned to the inscription in the first volume and read it aloud, while Daddy took possession of the second.

"It's a prize," Tom whispered to Mary, who had come in, bringing his lunch, which she set before him with a cautionary, "Mind the plate, Master Tom, it'd burn you."

Automatically he advanced an experimental finger, and then began to eat—a somewhat complicated performance, since while doing so he had at the same time to keep a watchful eye on Daddy and Mother, so as not to miss any impression the prize might be producing upon them. Mother's impressions, it is true, were conveyed audibly, by little exclamations and occasional comments and citations, but Daddy required closer observation because he remained silent.

"Who *was* Frank Buckland?" Mother presently asked. "Or should I say who *is* he?"

"He was a naturalist," Daddy replied.

"Yes, I gathered that much myself; but I thought you might know a little more."

"So I do," Daddy answered. "He was Government Inspector of Fisheries, and a popular writer—a kind of journalist-naturalist. It was he who started *Land and Water*, a weekly paper of the same type as *The Field*."

"Miss Sabine says he was like Darwin," Tom put in, but Daddy received this with a non-committal "Hm-m . . . ! Darwin was a scientist of the same school as Huxley, and Frank Buckland certainly wasn't that. He was the old-fashioned type of field-naturalist, much more like White of Selborne. . . . But he was a well-known figure in his day, friends with all the keepers in the Zoo, who sometimes sent him smaller animals when they were sick, to be nursed back to health. For that matter, what with monkeys and other pets, his own house must have been very like a zoo in miniature."

"Wasn't he married?" Mother asked, which seemed to Tom an irrelevant question.

"Your mother is thinking of the zoo, Tom. . . . I don't remember whether he was married or not, but if he was, we'll hope the lady shared his tastes, for I've an idea there was an aquarium too."

"I'm going to keep an aquarium," Tom announced, and Mother sighed.

"Yes, I thought that would be the next thing. If you do, you'll keep it either in the garden or the yard. All those creatures sooner or later develop wings, or at any rate become amphibious, and I'm not going to have a lot of nasty insects flying and crawling all over the house."

"Only the beetles get wings," Tom assured her, "and I'm not going to keep beetles; because Max Sabine did, and they killed his sprickleys and ate bits out of them."

"Horrid!" Mother shuddered. "I can't think why boys invariably want to do unpleasant things."

"But it was the beetles," Tom expostulated; and the remark about boys somehow switched his thoughts back to Mrs. Fallon and the stained-glass window. "Who was Ralph Seaford?" he asked.

Mother gazed at him in unfeigned astonishment. "What on earth put Ralph Seaford into your head?"

Daddy, too, looked perplexed; so he had to tell them of his visit to the church, and even then got no satisfactory answer. "Ralph Seaford was just a little boy," Mother said. "The Seaford grave is in the churchyard: you must have seen it often."

"Yes, but what happened to his father and mother? Why didn't *they* put up the window?"

"His father and mother were dead. They were killed in a climbing accident—out in Switzerland. The rope broke, or something. . . . I'm not quite sure what happened."

"I can't say I remember any question of a rope breaking," Daddy put in. "It was never really known *what* happened. They had done the same climb several times with a guide, and it was not considered a particularly dangerous one. . . . This time they did it alone, and it was supposed that one of them may have slipped, and the other fallen in attempting a rescue. Something of the kind at any rate. . . . The boy, Ralph, was only a year or two old at the time, so his grand-parents took him to live with them at Tramore."

"At Granny's house?" Tom exclaimed in surprise. "Did you know them?"

Daddy shook his head. "The old people were still living when we first came here, but they both died within that year: Doctor Macrory says they never got over the loss of their grandson. . . .

"After that," Daddy went on reminiscently, "some people called Dickson came to Tramore, but only for six months or so; and the house then stood vacant till Granny took it."

"Against everybody's advice," Mother supplemented.

"Why?" Tom asked; for he liked both the house and the grounds round it; and now the knowledge that it had once belonged to the Seafords lent it an additional interest.

"For one reason, because it's far too big for her," Mother replied. "Certainly nothing would induce *me* to live in a house with a lot of locked-up empty rooms—and servants don't like it either."

But Daddy thought Granny was right. "It's not really such a big house," he said, "and she pays remarkably little for it: the garden alone is worth the rent."

Mother disagreed. "It doesn't come to so little by the time you've paid the wages of two maids and a man. Especially if you're a person like Granny, who gives them all far too much."

Daddy laughed. "Possibly. . . . But if it pleases her, that surely is the main thing. Can you imagine her living happily in a poky little villa with no garden to speak of, and one maid to look after every-thing?"

"I can imagine her living perfectly happily with us," Mother said, "and it's what I've always wanted her to do."

Daddy shrugged his shoulders. "I think it's much wiser to let people decide these matters for themselves. They're naturally the best judges of what suits them."

"Not always; and it's really only because she hates the idea of part-ing with any of her possessions. Of course, there wouldn't be room for all her furniture and china and things here——"

"There certainly wouldn't."

"But at least she'd have company. . . . Which reminds me," she went on, turning to Tom, "that she wants *you* to spend a few days with her, now you've got your holidays."

At this sudden and unexpected development, Tom's face grew rather glum. "Days!" he echoed without enthusiasm. He had already made several plans which could only be carried out at home—including this brand-new plan of an aquarium.

"I thought you were so fond of Granny!" Mother reproached him.

"But there's nothing to do there," he responded dolefully. "Granny never does anything, and there's nobody else. . . . Besides," he added, "I can't very well leave the dogs."

It was a perfectly genuine excuse, and he couldn't see why Mother should look displeased, yet she did. "Of course the dogs are a great deal more important than Granny," she said; and since this mild sarcasm elicited no denial; "Surely you can go for a week-end at least! How would *you* like to be left all alone by yourself from morning till night!"

"I'd like it all right," was Tom's artless rejoinder, which, though it made Mother look graver still, drew a characteristic chuckle from Daddy.

A moment's reflection, however, suggested that a week-end meant primarily Sunday, and after all, it didn't much matter *where* you were on Sundays, so he changed his mind and asked, "When?"

Mother's face cleared. She made a rapid calculation. "Let me see. To-day is Tuesday. You could go on Friday or Saturday."

Here Daddy intervened. "He can't go on Friday. I called to see Mr. Pemberton this morning, and he wants him to sit for an examination on Friday."

"An examination!" Mother cried. "When he's not even at school yet!"

"This is for the boys who will be going after the summer. It gives him some idea of how much they know and in what form to put them. . . . In the present case, the very highest, I should think, judging from those four splendid volumes now before us!"

Glancing at Mother, Tom saw that though Daddy had spoken jestingly some such idea had crossed her own mind, therefore he hastened to nip any hopes she might be entertaining in the bud. "There'll be far older boys than me there," he told her; but instead of corroborating this, Daddy questioned it. "Most of them will be younger," he declared. "Some only eight or nine, and you're eleven. Anyhow, I should think you'd be graded according to your ages."

Tom at once switched on to another track. "Does it matter if I don't do well?" he asked; and was relieved when Daddy answered,

"Not in the least," before Mother had quite time to get out, "Of course it matters." Unfortunately she also said: "I'm sure you *will* do well."

He sighed, for that was just the difficulty. And Miss Sabine would be surer still. He looked up to find Mother's eyes fixed upon him with an odd expression, half amused, and to that extent reassuring. Daddy had ceased to be interested and had taken a sheaf of papers from his pocket.

"Well, we needn't discuss what is still in the future," Mother concluded, rising from the table. "And don't look as if all the cares of the world were on your shoulders: Daddy has just told you it doesn't matter how you do. I don't quite know why—but there it is." She passed behind him, laughed, and stooping down, kissed him on the top of his head.

5:    THE cares of the world, however, slipped from him like Christian's Burden, as he left Daddy to his papers and went out into the garden. The more immediate care was to find a suitable place for an aquarium. As for the aquarium itself, there was an old bath up in the loft which he thought might do, so he went round to the yard and climbed the ladder to have a look at it. He knew, of course, that to be really satisfactory an aquarium ought to be made of glass. He had seen a picture of one, and it stood on a kind of trestle, and was square, with glass sides through which you could see all that was going on within. Max Sabine had used a goldfish-bowl, but that would be much too small for what he wanted. Anyhow, he hadn't got one, so the bath would have to do.

He dragged it out now from its corner for inspection, and removed a festoon of cobwebs. The enamel inside was cracked, and the outside was coated with rust, but that didn't matter so long as it didn't leak, and he could see no holes when, with some difficulty he tilted it up against the light. He had already evolved a plan which seemed quite practicable. He would dig a trench beside the shrubbery, just deep enough to contain the bath, and in this way turn it into a little pond, with the upper rim of the bath flush with the soil, or perhaps an inch or two above it. . . . Only he wished it was deeper. Then it would be exactly like a natural pool, with the grass growing round it.

All this would require to be done very neatly and accurately, the sods cut out and the edges trimmed with a sharp spade. The best way would be to place the bath upside down on the grass, and get somebody to sit on it to keep it from moving while he cut round it: after that the rest should be easy.

Unfortunately, he would have to ask William to help him to get it down. And William would grumble, being made that way. But if he let him grumble for a while, and didn't answer back, in the end he might do what was wanted. Tom had reached this point when a sudden doubt arose in his mind. It had nothing to do with the construction of the aquarium; that was all settled; but when it *was* made, wouldn't the dogs use it? They had got into the habit of taking it for granted that whatever he did was done for them, and Barker, especially, could never resist water in any shape or form. In imagination, Tom could see him now, slopping about in the middle of the aquarium, perhaps lying down in it, and at any rate scaring all its legitimate inhabitants to death. Stray cats, too, from Denny's farm, where there were swarms of them, might fish in it at night. The glen was their usual hunting-ground, but he was sure they visited the garden as well; in fact he had often heard them; and fish were to cats what water was to Barker. . . .

He wished he knew some other boy who was interested in aquariums and would help him. As it was, there was only Max Sabine, his enemy, whom he disliked more than ever after what Althea had told him, though he had always known he was slimy and treacherous. If only James-Arthur wasn't kept so busy at the farm he would have been the very person. . . .

Undecided, he descended from the loft and came round again to the front of the house, where he found Daddy seated patiently in the car, waiting to drive Mother into town. Tom stood by the door, and as soon as she appeared asked if he might come too, though he already knew she had an appointment with the hairdresser and after that was going to have tea at the McFerrans', where Daddy was to call for her a little before six to bring her home. But his request was merely formal, and having watched them depart, he fetched the croquet-balls and a mallet from the hall and began a solitary game, blue and black against red and yellow.

Now of all games, croquet is the least amusing when played alone. Tom began this one with every intention of finishing it, but "whether skill prevailed" (which was seldom) "or happy blunder

triumphed" (infrequent also) it was equally dull, and after ten minutes or so he gave it up and returned to the house to get his yacht.

Between the cloak-room door and the grandfather's clock stood a
big oak chest in which the croquet and tennis things, with a few of
his more personal belongings, were kept. Here was his yacht, and he
lifted it out, gazed at it, and put it back again, taking a much smaller
boat instead—one he could easily carry tucked under his arm. Then
he set off for the river, visiting on his way the raspberry canes to see
if any raspberries were ripe. He found only two or three rather dubious specimens, but he ate them, before taking the path through the
shrubbery, at the end of which was a green postern door where two
walls of the garden joined. Passing through this door, he was immediately above the glen, on the top of a high steep bank thickly carpeted
with dark glossy bluebell-leaves. In spring, this bank was a feast of
brilliant colour, but there were no flowers now, except here and there
the small white flowers of a few wild strawberries. A narrow path
bordered by nettles ran along the top of the bank, but Tom clambered down to the stream and followed that.

The slender trees were nearly all either larch or birch or hazel, and
the sun, glinting between them, was the colour of old silver. He now
began to realize how hot it was—actually hotter down here in the
shade than it had been up above in the open sunshine, for the air was
heavier, almost stagnant. The birds were silent; a low droning murmur, which accompanied and mingled with the splash of water,
proceeded from smaller winged creatures.

Gradually the banks of the glen widened out as Tom neared its
entrance, and presently he emerged into a flat meadow-land. Here
the stream was broader and shallower, flowing between beds of
flowering rushes. In winter, after a rainy spell, this land became a
swamp; and even now, though dry enough, it was soft as velvet beneath his feet. The whole meadow was flooded with brilliant sunlight, but in the distance everything melted into a bluish-silver haze,
composed of air and cloud and sky.

A solitary tree grew in the meadow—an oak. It must once have
been a giant, for though now its branches were sadly dwindled, the
girth of the trunk was immense. Tom knew it well, because Edward,
the squirrel, lived here. It was quite hollow, and many of the branches
had broken off and fallen, though those remaining still put forth
leaves and, at the right time of the year, a crop of acorns. The boughs
were so brittle that it was a dangerous tree to climb, but James-

Arthur had climbed it, and said the trunk was quite hollow and looked just like a huge chimney; so that if you were to slip and fall down inside you would never be heard of again, but would gradually starve to death, unless somebody passing by happened to hear your cries. . . .

Leaving his boat by the stream, Tom ran over to the oak and whistled, but apparently Edward was not at home. He knew Tom's whistle quite well, and if he had been there he certainly would have peeped out on the chance that a few nuts had been brought to him. Tom had in fact brought him some biscuits, only there was no use leaving these, as, what with mice and other creatures, it was most unlikely they would still be there when Edward came back. . . .

Half-way up the trunk, a bat hung motionless and asleep, with his dark wings neatly folded. Tom had never before seen one sleeping right out in the open, and he wondered whether he ought to awaken him or not. He must be a very young and inexperienced bat, or he would have known that the cats from Denny's were always prowling about, and might easily come as far as this on the chance of picking up a baby rabbit. On the other hand, he couldn't be reached except by throwing a stick or a stone, and he was sure bats were very easily hurt. He returned to the stream therefore, and picking up the boat, continued on his way. . . .

At the end of the meadow was a deep ditch, with thickets of brambles on one side and a steep bank surmounted by a hedge on the other. In the hedge were more brambles, and a tangle of wild roses now in full bloom and stretching wide their pink and white petals to drink in the heat. But the ditch was dry, so in spite of the thorns that caught at his jacket and tried to hold him, Tom was able to wriggle his way through, emerging on to the tow-path between two bends of the river, whose winding course could be traced by the trees on the farther bank.

Kneeling at the water's edge, he fixed the rudder of his boat to steer a slanting course to the opposite shore. When it was nearing land he would cross over himself by the lock gate, which, though out of sight, was not more than fifty yards beyond the nearer bend. But it was a bad day for sailing boats. A languid puff of air caught the sails for a moment or two, and this, with the push he had given it, carried the boat out towards mid-stream, where it began to drift slowly with the current. Tom followed it along the bank till it reached a clump of water-lilies; yet, though it only brushed them, in the lack of wind this was sufficient, and there it remained—"as idle as a painted ship upon a painted ocean."

He searched for a stone to throw at it, because it was not even entangled, and beyond this one snag had a perfectly clear passage. But there were no stones big enough to be of any use, so he sat down on the bank, since there was nothing else to do.

The broad shining lily-leaves cast black shadows on the water. The yellow flowers were as usual half closed, and a dragon-fly was dreaming on one of them, his blue enamelled body glittering in the sun. In a very few minutes Tom was dreaming himself. He didn't really care whether the boat worked loose or not, for toys had never interested him much. When he got a present of one he would play with it for a shorter or longer period, but that first experiment over, he would put it away and very seldom think of it again. The model yacht, for instance, had been a present from Granny on his last birthday, and after a single trial had rarely been removed from the chest in the hall. If Granny had given him a monkey, now—as he had himself suggested—or indeed anything alive—but a model yacht! He was glad, at all events, that he had left it at home to-day, for it didn't matter a straw whether this other old boat were lost or not. . . .

Suddenly he heard a faint splash on the opposite side of the river, and instantly boats were forgotten. He knew what *that* was, and next moment fancied he could see the very small head, and certainly could see the ripple in the water behind it. Daddy had told him there were no real water-rats in Ireland, but there were at least plenty of rats who lived near the river and appeared to be more or less amphibious. This one was swimming straight across to him. Perhaps he had not seen him, and would change his direction when he did; yet on he came, nearer and nearer, and soon it was quite clear that he was making directly for Tom, for his black little beads of eyes were inspecting him very sharply indeed. In another minute he had scrambled out of the water and up the bank, where he sat down and proceeded to comb his whiskers.

Tom had an impulse to dry him with his pocket handkerchief, only he thought the rat perhaps liked being wet, and at any rate, with his short fur, the sun would dry him in no time. Then he remembered something much better—the biscuits he had brought for Edward—most attractive-looking biscuits, with pink and white sugar on the top. He put his hand in his pocket and fumbled; but alas! when he fished the biscuits out, they were in a sadly broken condition and all mixed up with sand. That, of course, must have happened when he was getting through the hedge, squirming his way through on his stomach.

Luckily the rat did not seem to mind. One by one he took each piece of biscuit in his tiny hands and nibbled it quite nicely. Not that this surprised Tom, for he knew rats, like squirrels, had better table-manners than most animals. It was really because they *had* hands, he supposed; since without hands, table-manners must be rather a problem.

"I was glad to see you had no dogs with you to-day," the rat said presently, and Tom noticed that he was careful not to speak with his mouth full. "So I thought I'd seize the opportunity, for it's not often you're without them."

"No," Tom replied.

"Which is a pity," the rat went on, "because it must greatly narrow the circle of your friends."

This hadn't occurred to Tom before, yet when the rat mentioned it he felt that very likely he *was* associated with dogs in the minds of other animals. "You see," he hastened to explain, "I'm very fond of them: we're old friends."

"Lovers, I should call it," the rat answered unsympathetically. "At least so far as the one with the brush is concerned."

"The brush?" Tom repeated, momentarily puzzled. "Oh, you mean his tail. . . . But it's not a brush: it's far more like a big feather."

"Well, a feather-brush," the rat said.

"That's Roger," Tom told him; "and you'd like him. At least if you could once make friends with him you would: and I'm sure you could if I was there."

"The little one's the worst," the rat went on dispassionately.

"Pincher?"

"Yes, I dare say he'd be called that. . . . The old lazy one's the best."

"Barker?"

The rat seemed amused. "Ridiculous names, all of them," he sniggered, "but then they're ridiculous creatures. What, if I may ask, is your own name? Squeaker, perhaps?"

"Squeaker's much more like yourself," Tom retorted indignantly, for whatever his table-manners might be, the rat's politeness appeared to end there. "I don't squeak."

"You're squeaking now," the rat said. "And anyhow, don't lose your temper."

"I haven't lost my temper; but I think you might be a little more civil—especially after gobbling up all the biscuits."

To his surprise, the rat took this quite well. "I enjoyed the biscuits," he admitted, looking rather ashamed. "Didn't I thank you for them? At any rate I enjoyed them very much indeed. One often hears of such things, but seldom sees them. You may be surprised to learn that I'd never tasted a biscuit before in my life. . . . And please don't misunderstand me," he continued, delicately removing a crumb from his whiskers. "It's universally granted that you're a most agreeable little boy—much above the average. Indeed, I may say that you're regarded as practically unique. We all think that. Your actual name, however, has caused a good deal of dispute and conjecture. You're usually referred to as the Child, or the Boy, or Freckles, or Snub Nose, or——"

"You needn't go on with the list," Tom interrupted him. "My name is Tom."

"And a very good name too," the rat declared encouragingly. "The best names, as I'm sure you've noticed, are always in one syllable—like Rat, Mouse, Frog, Bat, Horse, Pig, Cow—and now we can add Tom."

"And Dog, and Cat, and Owl," Tom was continuing, but the rat looked displeased. "I don't think we need include those," he said coldly. "There are exceptions to every rule."

"There are a jolly lot to yours," Tom agreed. "What about Squirrel? You can't possibly object to him. And Badger, and Otter, and——" But whether Rat would have objected or not he was never to learn, for at that moment they both heard the tramp of approaching footsteps, and in a flash Tom was alone.

The tramp, tramp, tramp, was made by heavy boots, and in time to a martial tune, which in spite of elaborate variations Tom recognized as "Onward Christian Soldiers." Next moment the Christian Soldier himself appeared round the bend of the river, waving his banner, a towel.

"Where are you going?" Tom demanded, for it was only James-Arthur from the farm.

"Goin' for a dip," James-Arthur replied. "Oul' Denny let me off." Then he saw the boat. "You've got her well stuck there! Sure, what was the use of tryin' to sail her a day like that? She'll be there now till night unless you go in for her."

"I can't go in for her," Tom answered, "and you know I can't."

James-Arthur reflected, for he did know it.

"*You* can swim," Tom said. "You're a good swimmer."

"Not so bad," James-Arthur confessed modestly. "An' if you like come along with me, I'm just goin' down below the weir."

"If you bathed here you could get the boat," Tom said pointedly.

But James-Arthur only scratched a flaxen poll and shuffled his feet. He was, however, a most good-natured boy, and presently he murmured doubtfully; "I wouldn't like, Master Tom."

"Why?" Tom asked. He knew, of course, that the water below the weir, where the current was strong, was much cleaner and fresher, but he didn't see why James-Arthur couldn't go in here first.

James-Arthur nevertheless, continued to look worried. "Well— someone might come along," he explained. "It'd be all right for a wee lad like you; but if I was to take off me on the bank here someone might come along."

"You said that before," Tom told him. "What matter if they do come along? You're only a boy yourself."

James-Arthur shook his head, though clearly wavering. "Ah now," he mumbled, "sure you know it wouldn't be the same at all. They might be making a complaint. I'm sixteen, and bigger'n you—about twiced—an' it might be a woman too."

"It won't be anybody," Tom returned impatiently; for this bashfulness seemed to him extremely silly. He himself, like most small boys, was perfectly indifferent to nakedness. "I've been here for hours," he went on, "and there hasn't been a soul, except a rat—not even a barge. . . . Anyhow," he wound up persuasively, "I'll promise to keep watch; and I'll shout the moment I see anyone, and you can stay in the water till they've gone by."

Yet even with this assurance James-Arthur did not look too happy. In his mind there was evidently a conflict going on between a sense of propriety and his liking for Tom. In the end, but with obvious reluctance, he gave in; and sat down on the bank to remove his boots and socks. The rest did not take him long, for it consisted only of a dirty ragged old pair of flannel trousers and a grey flannel shirt.

James-Arthur was as fond of the water as Barker, and now, while he stood up on the bank in the sunlight, he slapped his sturdy thighs in pleased anticipation. Even at this early date of summer his body was sunburnt, and in Tom's eyes he somehow did not look naked. He had simply emerged from his soiled and much-patched clothing like a butterfly from a chrysalis, and the contrast between his fair hair and the golden brown of his body and limbs appeared to the smaller boy as attractive as anything could be. In fact James-Arthur, merely by divesting himself of his clothes, had instantly become part of the natural scene, like the grass and the trees and the river and the sky, and the dragonfly asleep upon his water-lily. Tom told him how nice he looked, and, while James-Arthur only smiled and said he was a queer wee lad, it was easy to see that secretly he was not displeased.

Anyhow, he plunged in, rescued the boat (which was the main thing), and then swam quietly about for a bit, very much in Barker's manner.

Watching him, Tom felt more and more tempted to go in too. "Is it cold?" he shouted.

"Naw; it's not cold:—how would it be cold, and the sun on it all these days?"

Tom, nevertheless, felt pretty certain that *he* would find it cold. Yet James-Arthur appeared to be enjoying himself so much that he made up his mind and hurriedly undressed.

"Wait now," James-Arthur called out. "Don't be comin' in without me. There's deep holes—plenty of them—would take you over your head in a minute."

He swam to the bank, and gingerly Tom stepped into the water. At the edge it rose hardly above his knees, but a single pace forward and he was floundering in one of those very holes, from which James-Arthur rescued him, spluttering and gasping.

James-Arthur laughed, but Tom, as he tried to spit out the far from crystalline water he had swallowed, saw nothing to laugh at. "Lie flat on your belly, Master Tom. Don't be afeared: I'll keep your head up."

Having complete confidence in his instructor, Tom obeyed; but as he had suspected it *was* cold, except on the surface.

"Easy on, now," James-Arthur encouraged him. "Take your time, an' go slow. You've watched the frogs many's a time: try an' kick your arms and legs out what they do. . . . That's fine now: You'll be the great swimmer yet."

And when they came out he made Tom take the towel, while to

dry himself he used only his flannel trousers. "How did you like it?" he asked, with a broad grin.

"It was very nice," Tom temporized. "At least, I think perhaps I'd get to like it."

"Course you would," James-Arthur said.

"Only," Tom added, wrinkling up his nose, "I've got a smell, and it's pretty strong—the smell of the water."

"Ah, sure that's nothin'. A bit nifty maybe till you get used to it, but it'll pass off in the course of the evening."

"I hope so," Tom said, for he didn't think James-Arthur realized the full potency of the "niftiness." "I saw your mother this morning," he went on. "She let me go up the tower."

"Ay, she was tellin' me so; an' that you were wantin' the keys off her. . . . But I'll have to leave you now, Master Tom. Oul' Denny only give me half an hour an' it's more like an hour I've bin."

He caught up his towel, gave Tom an amicable slap on the shoulder, and departed—once more to the strains of "Onward Christian Soldiers."

6: TOM sat on alone. He had been very happy a few minutes ago, but now that James-Arthur was gone he felt sad. He thought he would like to be a farm boy at Denny's, working every day with James-Arthur; instead of which he was going to school, and all he knew about school was what Max Sabine had told him, obviously with the view of showing what an important person he was there, which Tom didn't for a moment believe.

Cloppity clop! Cloppity clop!

He looked up, and saw a big grey barge horse approaching. Next minute the barge itself came into sight, the rope slackening as it rounded the bend; then suddenly tightening again, rippling through the water and throwing up a shower of spray. A man was walking beside the horse; another man was at the tiller.

Tom drew back to be out of the way. He was prepared to nod to both men and return their greeting, but beyond an indifferent and somewhat surly glance, neither took any notice of him, and they and the horse and the barge passed on just as if he were non-existent, presently disappearing from view round the next bend. Why couldn't they have said something? Then he too would have walked beside the horse and kept the man company for a little way, and perhaps told him about bathing. . . .

He had stooped to lift his boat, when suddenly he was sent staggering nearly on to his nose by the impact of a warm heavy body against the middle of his back, while simultaneously two big paws were planted on his shoulders. It was Roger, who had come up silently behind him. He was always playing these tricks—more like a boy than a dog—and immediately Tom's cheerfulness was restored. Roger licked his face, so he licked Roger—but just once, because he had been told it was a disgusting thing to do. It couldn't be disgusting, however, unless there was somebody there to be disgusted, and at present there was no one.

"Well, I suppose *you'll* want to bathe now!" Tom said, adopting an elderly manner. "But it'll be only one dip and then out, for it must be time to go home. Where have you been, and how did you guess I was here?"

Roger, instead of answering, began to bark and jump about him, rushing to the edge of the bank and back, slewing round his head, and making it very clear in every way what he expected Tom to do. But there were no sticks on the tow-path, and bits of hedge were far too light to carry any distance. In the end, Tom seized his boat by the mast, and pitched it out as far as he could. Before it had even left his hand, Roger leapt into the water, making a tremendous splash, calculated to scare Rat out of his wits if he were still lurking in the neighbourhood. As he watched him swimming smoothly and swiftly, Tom wished Roger had come sooner, for then he could have had a race with James-Arthur. They had very different styles of swimming, and James-Arthur declared that even in a short race across the river and back Roger wouldn't have a chance; but if James-Arthur used the breast stroke and gave Roger half a minute's start Tom wasn't so sure. . . .

The boat was floating on its side when Roger reached it. He made a grab at the hull, but it was too big for him to get a proper grip, so he bit on the mast and sails and struggled along that way—though not without difficulty, to judge by the growls and snorts. He couldn't be really angry, of course, but it sounded as if he were, and Tom hopped about shouting encouragement mingled with laughter. It was an ex-

tremely wrecked-looking boat which eventually was dragged up the
bank and dropped at his feet. He didn't care. "Good dog!" he said,
hastily stepping back to avoid a shower-bath. "And now I *must* go
home: I was late for lunch, and you should have come sooner if you
wanted to bathe." He picked up the wreck, and they returned by the
route James-Arthur had taken.

As it happened, he needn't have been in such a hurry; in fact he
had been waiting on the doorstep for nearly half an hour, and Phemie
had twice appeared to remark that the dinner would be ruined, before the car drove up with Daddy and Mother. "I know we're very
late," Mother called out through the window. "I expect you're starving and Phemie is furious, but it couldn't be helped. . . . You'll find
a parcel on the back seat which you might take into the house. It's a
book Granny ordered; and it cost five guineas, so be very careful
with it. Why she should want to spend a fortune on a huge tome
about Chinese art is best known to herself."

"Japanese, I expect," Daddy amended.

"Well—Chinese or Japanese—five guineas seems to me an absurd
price. It nearly took my breath away when the man told me."

"Special publications of that kind are always expensive," Daddy
said. "The pictures very likely are printed in facsimile. . . . What
is the correct name for a book of that size?" he suddenly asked Tom,
who stood clasping it in his arms.

"A folio," Tom replied learnedly. "May I look at it: the string's
untied."

"Did *you* untie it?" Mother questioned suspiciously, but added;
"Perhaps—if you're very good—after dinner. . . . Only you must
promise to take the greatest care and your hands must be spotless."

"They're spotless now," Tom informed her. "I've been bathing."

Mother might have inquired further into this unexpected disclosure
had not Phemie at that moment again appeared in the doorway, her
countenance this time suggesting that there were limits even to *her*
patience. So it was not till they were safely seated at the dinner-table
that he was able to embark on a fuller description of his adventures.
Mother was not enthusiastic about the bathing part, and made him
promise not to do it again without first getting her permission, and
never to do it at all unless James-Arthur was there to look after him.
But she was amused by the behaviour of the rat, and thus encouraged,
Tom in the end produced a few specimens of their conversation.

Mother maintained that all rats were horrid, and some of them evidently most conceited; while Daddy went on quietly with his dinner and did not appear to be listening. This, as it turned out, was a delusion, for suddenly he said: "It seems to me Miss Sabine was definitely right, and that it's high time you went to school."

There followed a pause, before Mother replied rather dryly; "If rats choose to talk to Tom, I can't see how that is any concern of Miss Sabine's."

"Yes—*if*," Daddy agreed.

A faint flush rose in Mother's cheeks. "Judging from all accounts, school doesn't appear to have particularly improved her own nephew," she said.

The matter dropped there, for Daddy returned no answer, and during the remainder of dinner Mother too spoke little, and then merely on the dullest matters of fact. By the time they rose from the table it was well after eight and within half an hour of Tom's bedtime.

Daddy, who had so effectually, if perhaps unintentionally, thrown a damper on the conversation, now followed his usual custom and went out to potter about the garden, while Mother retired to the kitchen to discuss household matters with Phemie. Tom, alone in the study, vacillated between the rival attractions of *Curiosities of Natural History* and Granny's book. It might be better to choose Granny's, he decided, since very likely she would either send or call for it tomorrow; so placing it carefully on the table, he drew up a chair and began to turn the pages.

Daddy had at least been right about the pictures; they *were* coloured, and most of them were queer—some of them very queer indeed. There were birds and animals, and pre-eminent among the latter was a superb tiger, with his head lowered and an extraordinary expression on his face. Whatever might be true of rats, it was at least quite clear that *he* could talk, and also that he could come alive and spring right out of the book if he wanted to. Tom was fascinated by this picture, yet at the same time wasn't wholly sure that he would have liked to have it hanging above his bed. . . . That is, unless he could make friends with it first. . . . Then it would be lovely. . . . "Puss—puss," he whispered, as a preliminary endearment.

But there were men and women, too, and they were equally strange—even the more ordinary ones—with their slanting eyes and pale, mask-like faces; to say nothing of the demons, bogeys, and magicians. Mother, entering unnoticed, found him absorbed, with flushed cheeks and very bright eyes, while a single rapid glance at the picture he was studying showed her how foolish she had been not first to have had a look at Granny's book herself. She gently drew it away from him, and he relinquished it without a word: nor did she say anything except that he could come for a little walk round the garden with her before going to bed.

He was surprised, for a glance at the clock told him it was already past his bedtime, but he asked no questions, and they went out together into the evening twilight. The garden was dreamy and still; pleasanter, because cooler, than it had been all day. Daddy, surrounded by a halo of moths, was doing something with his sweet peas, and looked up to greet them. Then he stooped to capture an imprudent snail, while Tom and Mother passed slowly on, her hand resting lightly on his shoulder.

She talked gaily of any topic she thought might at once distract and tranquillize his mind, but all the time she was secretly reproaching herself. For she had seen his face as it was raised from Granny's book, and though a tendency to walk in his sleep appeared to have little connection with any immediate or discoverable cause, Doctor Macrory had strongly urged that there should be no pre-bedtime excitements. Of course it was most unreasonable to feel vexed with Granny, when the fault was entirely her own; nevertheless she *did* feel vexed; and determined to have a look at the other pictures after Tom had gone to bed, in the hope that they might prove more innocent than the horribly malevolent and lifelike demon he had been poring over when she had discovered him. One good thing was, that his nocturnal peregrinations nearly always took place early—before she and Daddy had retired. To-night she would sit up later than usual, and must be sure to leave her bedroom door open, which occasionally she forgot to do.

7. YET, had he guessed her anxiety, Tom could have told her that there wasn't the slightest danger of his walking in his sleep, and this for the excellent reason that he had a plan which necessitated lying awake. True, a most important part of

the plan had been defeated by Mrs. Fallon's refusal to lend him the keys, but he could still pay a midnight visit to the church, even if he could not go inside. Therefore it was in a way disappointing to find he no longer very much wanted to pay this visit. The attractiveness of the adventure had curiously waned with the waning of daylight, and at present he was positively glad that Mrs. Fallon had been so scrupulous. With the keys in his possession, he might have felt it his duty to make use of them, whereas now—supposing he went at all— he need only look over the wall from the road. . . .

But that "supposing" was nonsense: of course he was going: he had said he was, and though nobody had heard him and therefore nobody knew, to back out at this stage would be none the less to funk it—at the thought of which the lines of his mouth grew remarkably obstinate.

In fact it seemed hardly worth while undressing—except that Mother occasionally came in to see him after he was in bed, and she would be sure to notice if he still had his clothes on. Besides, with such an exploit looming before him, he wasn't in the least likely to fall asleep, and to make doubly sure, he would lie and think about his aquarium. Then, when all the house was quiet, he would start.

Once snugly in bed, however, he felt less adventurous than ever, though not a bit drowsy. He lay on his back, his eyes wide open, thinking first of his aquarium, and then of the examination on Friday, when he would see a lot of boys he had never seen before. Even if there were only a few, there might still be one with whom he could make friends. At least, that was always what happened in school stories. In the very first chapter—or if not in the first, at any rate in the second—the hero always found a chum; and, though he would have liked to be, of course he wasn't really James-Arthur's chum. James-Arthur, when his work was over, went about with boys of his own age, and now and then—which was more surprising— with girls. . . .

Mother evidently wasn't coming, but she had done what was much the same thing, she had gone to the drawing-room and begun to sing. It was for him, he guessed, or partly for him, and she had left the door open so that he might listen, for she knew that this was what he liked. He himself could sing most of her songs, and did, not only at the piano but all over the house. When Miss Sabine was there he was invariably called on to perform, but not when there was only

Doctor Macrory, because Doctor Macrory, like Daddy, couldn't tell
one tune from another.

> *I remember all you told me,*
> *Looking out where we did stand,*
> *While the night flowers poured their perfume*
> *Forth like stars from—"*

The song Mother was singing was called "Edenland." The tune
had a waltz rhythm, which the accompaniment accentuated, so that
it seemed to swing round and round inside you, rising at the end of
each verse to a climax before dying away. In silence Tom's body
moved now with this mounting climax——

> *And the path where we two wandered,*
> *And the path where we two wandered,*
> *Seemed not like earth, but Edenland,*
> *Seemed not like earth, like earth,*
> *But Edenland.*

Mother sang song after song, picking out his favourites——

> *I think of all thou art to me,*
> *I dream of what thou canst not be,*
> *My life is filled with thoughts of thee,*
> *Forever and forever.*

Actually it should have been "My life is cursed with thoughts of
thee," but Mother has crossed out "cursed" and written "filled"
above it. . . . He hoped she would sing "When Sparrows Build";
but these were the introductory bars of "My Dearest Heart," also a
favourite——

> *All the dreaming is broken through,*
> *Both what is done and undone I rue,*
> *Nothing is steadfast, nothing is true,*
> *But your love for me, and my love for you,*
> *My dearest, dearest heart.*

There were three verses to Arthur Sullivan's song, and when it
was finished, Mother was silent for a long while—so long that he

began to think she must have stopped altogether. But he was wrong; she hadn't; and now there came at last what he had been waiting for——

> *When sparrows build, and the leaves break forth,*
> *My old sorrow wakes and cries,*
> *For I know there is dawn in the far, far north,*
> *And a scarlet sun doth rise;*
> *Like a scarlet fleece the snow-field spreads,*
> *And the icy founts run free,*
> *And the bergs begin to bow their heads,*
> *And plunge and sail in the sea.*
>
> *O my lost love, and my own, own love,*
> *And my love that loved me so!*
> *Is there never a chink in the world above*
> *Where they listen to words from below?*
> *Nay, I spoke once, and I grieved thee sore,*
> *I remember all that I said,*
> *And now thou wilt hear me no more—no more*
> *Till the sea gives up her dead.*

* * * * *

> *We shall walk no more through the sodden plain*
> *With the faded bents o'erspread;*
> *We shall stand no more by the seething main*
> *While the dark wrack drives o'erhead;*
> *We shall part no more in the wind and the rain,*
> *Where thy last farewell was said;*
> *But perhaps I shall meet thee and know thee again*
> *When the sea gives up her dead.*

After that, he did not know how many more songs Mother sang, for he must have fallen asleep in the middle of one of them, and when he opened his eyes the night was gone, the sun was shining in at his window, and somewhere down below, Roger was barking. In a trice Tom was out of bed and hurriedly dressing. Out in the garden Roger greeted him with effusion, tore wildly round the lawn in a circle, and then, with Tom after him, raced on to the gate.

It was a lovely morning—cloudless, cool, and fresh—the air extraordinarily clear. But it was impossible to keep up with Roger, who dashed on ahead, and quickly was out of sight round the bend of the road. Well, he could just come back again, Tom thought, and slackened his pace to a walk. It was only then that in the hedge, a few yards farther on, a door he had never before noticed was suddenly pushed open, and a girl looked out and beckoned to him. Tom did not know her, had never seen her before, and he stood gazing at her without either advancing or retreating. It was not that he was shy of strangers as a general rule, but this girl was so different from anybody he had ever met, or expected to meet, that he forgot his manners. For one thing, her skin was smooth as ivory, and pale yellow: for another, she had narrow dark eyes set obliquely under thin, slanting eyebrows; and her sleek black hair was drawn tightly back and rolled up on the top of her head. Her mouth was extremely small; her nose was rather long, and curved down to a point, almost like a parrot's beak. Her dress was equally unusual, for it was gathered about her in loose voluminous folds that appeared to cling to her without any visible fastening. Moreover it was brilliantly blue and green and white, sprinkled all over with embroidered flowers, and she carried in her left hand a little fan. Certainly she was attractive, in a strange exotic fashion that seemed to him about three-quarters human. But this first, somewhat dubious impression lasted only till she spoke, when he immediately regained confidence; for her voice was beautiful—low and clear like a wood-pigeon's—as she invited him to come in and look at her garden.

She spoke and smiled so pleasantly that he couldn't very well refuse, though really he wanted to go after Roger, who hadn't returned, which was most unlike him. But he need only stay a minute or two, she told him; a single glance would show him what the garden was like; couldn't he spare just a moment?—and her eyes glinted oddly over the fluttering fan.

Still doubtful, yet by no means incurious, Tom followed her into the brightest, gayest garden he had ever beheld—composed entirely of flowering shrubs, with vivid emerald-green patches of smooth short grass, stone terraces, and tiny ponds; while in the midst of all was a stone house, carved and ornamented like a huge ivory casket, and surmounted by a tower. He thought it very wonderful—that at least was his first reaction; his second, perhaps, that the garden was too perfectly arranged and elaborately ornamental to be really *his* kind of garden. And the house, with its carved dragons and delicate arabesques and tracery, was equally artificial. But he could hardly tell her this, though quite evidently she was waiting for his opinion. So he expressed a thought suggested by the numerous little ponds and pools: "What a lot of aquariums you could have!"

He feared it might not be quite the remark she expected, yet she seemed pleased, and agreed at once. "Yes, goldfish, and silver fish, and water-lilies. . . . Only now you *are* here, you must come in and be introduced to my brothers. They are just going to have supper."

For an instant, at the sound of that incongruous last word, the whole garden seemed to flicker like a candle-flame in the wind—to flicker and go out. Or did it?—for he was walking up the path with her, they were entering the house.

There, in a big bright room with many windows, the three brothers were already seated at the table, but they were much older than he had expected—short, fat men, nearly naked too, with yellow faces and thin drooping black moustaches. And protruding slightly beneath each moustache were two pointed walrus tusks, very sharp and cruel-looking. That they were magicians, Tom recognized immediately, and he did not like their appearance at all. Nor, for that matter, did he now like the strangely sly and altered smile with which the girl was watching him. He had seen a cat watching a bird just like that, and with a sinking of the heart he felt he had better go away at once, and said so.

Since he had entered the room the brothers had not opened their lips nor even looked at him, but now one of them spoke, in a smooth, expressionless voice—"Isn't it too late to think of that?"—and instantly Tom knew it *was* too late, and that he would never leave that house alive.

He made an effort to reach the still open door, and none of them moved or spoke, merely watched his struggles. For he could do nothing; all the strength had gone out from him, and his feet seemed to be glued to the floor. But at that moment, just as he realized that he was indeed lost and helpless, there came from far, far away, yet distinctly audible in the silent room, the sound of a dog barking.

Though infinitely faint and distant, nevertheless it was Roger's bark, and it had an instantaneous effect on the inmates of the room. The eyes of the seated brothers slid round quickly towards the windows, the power flowed back into Tom's limbs, while the girl gave him an evil look and said contemptuously "Now, I suppose, he must get his chance."

Tom hated her. He hated her even more than he hated the magicians; because it was she who had decoyed him in and betrayed him. And though she seemed so young, that, too, must be an illusion, she must really be an old hag, as old as her brothers, and all four probably had made many a meal off tender and juicy small boys whom she had entrapped—serving them up whole, very likely—and in their skins—like baked potatoes.

All the same, his courage had revived with his strength, and above all with the certainty he now felt that Roger, wherever he was, had missed him, had divined his peril, and was at this moment trying to get back to him, to break through whatever magic barrier of intervening space the magicians had created by their spells.

He was to have a chance, they had said: but what kind of chance? They soon told him, and he was relieved; indeed now felt very little alarm. All he had to do was to climb the three flights of steps, which would bring him out on to the roof of the tower, before the girl—who would start level with him—had climbed them three times. True, the trial also was to be repeated three times; but with such an enormous start surely he had nothing to fear.

And it turned out to be even easier than he had expected. At the given signal, a sharp blow on a gong, they both started together from the hall, and though she was certainly quicker than he, and to gain the roof he had to hoist himself through an open trap-door, yet he had done so, and come out on to the square stone platform at the top, before she had half finished her second ascent. Looking over the parapet, he now saw far below him, not the wonderful garden, but a wide, bare landscape—stretching out and out—with, on the extreme edge of it, yet nevertheless *within* it, a tiny black spot which he somehow knew to be Roger.

Well, that was over, and it had been nothing; he wasn't even out of breath, he wouldn't mind a dozen such races. So it was in a spirit of complete confidence that he started on the second trial. This time he did not exert himself so much—or was it, perhaps, that the girl exerted herself more? for he was a little startled when she actually passed him on her second ascent before he had reached the roof. Looking again over the parapet, he found that the landscape had greatly contracted, and that Roger was quite close—close enough to bark an excited recognition, with frantic waggings of his whole body. Tom called down to him, and braced himself, this time in dead earnest, for the final contest.

That second trial had awakened him to the danger of over-confidence, and in the third he was determined to take no risks. At the very stroke of the gong he raced up the steps as hard as he could, but his opponent's feet seemed to be winged. At the beginning of the second flight she passed him on her way down, her robe streaming behind her, so that he felt the wind it made; and near the top of the third flight she passed him on her second descent. Still, all he had now to do was to scramble through the trap-door on to the platform. But half-way through he stuck, and, though he struggled and twisted, his limbs seemed suddenly to have gone dead. She was still far below, but she had turned, and was once more coming up, approaching rapidly, with a sort of terrifying, screaming noise—not human, not even animal. Another effort brought him through the trap-door, all but one foot. He squirmed and wriggled over on to his stomach, he was nearly free, another twist would do it; and with that—at that last fateful moment—he felt just the tip of her long finger touch the sole of his shoe. He kicked out with his whole strength, but though he felt the full impact of his kick reach her, and she fell back and down and down, her finger still adhered to him, spinning out, thinner and thinner, longer and longer, like a spider's thread. There came a dull thud from below as her body reached the hall, and Tom struggled to his feet. But all was changed. It was blackest night, and he could see nothing. Roger, the very house itself, had disappeared; and the platform was shrunk to a single stone, upon which he stood poised dizzily above an infinite gulf. For two or three seconds he maintained his balance—horrible, agonizing seconds—then he crashed over and down. . . .

His own scream awakened him. He seemed to be in bed. . . . Yes, he was in bed, and now here was Mother; he heard her in the passage; and next moment his door was opened and she had turned on the light.

"Good morning," he said, managing a rather feeble little chuckle. "I suppose I disturbed you."

"It's all right," Mother answered quietly. "I hadn't gone to sleep or I shouldn't have heard you: you didn't waken Daddy."

"It was just a dream," he explained. "I dreamt I fell off a tower. You must have heard the flop."

Mother took no notice of this small joke, but she sat down beside his bed.

"Is it very late?" he asked.

"Not very. I don't really know. . . . I was reading. . . . Your prize, you see," and she held it up. "Would you like me to read to you for a little now?"

He signified assent, and turned over on his side, away from the light. Presently he shut his eyes; and when he opened them again it was morning, and down in the hall Mary was ringing the breakfast bell.

8: "NOW boys, you've just ten minutes more, and then I shall collect the papers."

Tom, looking up at these words, encountered the passing glance of Miss Jimpson who had spoken them and who had presided over the examination from the beginning. Miss Jimpson smiled ever so little, therefore he immediately smiled back. She was nice-looking, he thought, and far younger than he had imagined schoolmistresses ever were: quite grown-up, of course, but not really much more than that: he hoped he would be in her class. That her name was Miss Jimpson he had learned when Mr. Pemberton, the headmaster, had come in a short while ago to see how they were all getting on.

There were fourteen other boys in the class-room besides himself, and their names had been called out in alphabetical order, though they were not now sitting in that order, Miss Jimpson having allowed them to choose their own seats. Tom knew none of them, but the majority appeared to know one another. From time to time he had scanned them with interest, wondering if he would like them. Macfarlane, the boy directly in front of him, had the appearance of an industrious and rather worried sheep. Macfarlane had begun to write from the very moment the papers had been handed round, and he had never stopped writing since. Tom himself had stopped only too frequently, but the whole experience was so new to him that he

couldn't help watching the others. The boy beside him—Pascoe by
name—was the most out-of-the-ordinary-looking. His sturdy body
and tow-coloured hair were indeed ordinary enough; what made
him look different was simply a very small, prim mouth, and the
unusually wide space between two extremely serious blue eyes.
Twice he had turned and caught Tom's speculative gaze fixed upon
him, and the second time he had stared back with so severe an expression that the latter feared he must be offended. Thereupon a big
boy seated some distance away, who had observed this brief and silent
passage, winked, and then wrinkled up his nose in signal of the con-
tempt and disgust with which Pascoe was to be regarded.

This boy, Brown, in spite of being the biggest boy there, evidently
had exhausted all he had to say about the questions in the first half
hour, which left him free, and obviously prepared to welcome any
form of distraction. True, shortly before Miss Jimpson's warning that
time was nearly up, he had had a further industrious period; but this
had lasted only about five minutes, and from the movement of his
hand, Tom suspected that art, not letters, was engaging him. Returning to his own labours, he had not written more than two or
three lines when a tightly-rolled-up paper ball struck him on the
nose before falling on the the desk in front of him. The daring of
this act nearly took Tom's breath away. Instinctively his first hasty
glance was to see if Miss Jimpson had observed it, but Miss Jimpson
was looking out of the window in absent-minded contemplation of
her own private thoughts. Very stealthily, therefore, he unfolded the
paper and smoothed it out, conscious all the time that Brown was
watching him. It was, as he expected, a drawing—an extremely vulgar one too—representing, he supposed, the artist's impression of
Pascoe. Not that it was in the least like him, but underneath it was
scrawled: "The silly little fool next you"; and below that again,
"What's *fierté*?"

"Pride," said Tom aloud, without thinking, and everybody
looked up.

Miss Jimpson, recalled from her daydreams, spotted the speaker
at once. "You mustn't talk, Barber," she told him, but not very
sternly. "You did say something, didn't you?"

"I didn't mean to," Tom stammered, covered with confusion.

Miss Jimpson said no more, but several of the smaller boys looked
slightly shocked. Not so Brown; who merely grinned broadly and
gave him another wink, which Tom was much too shy to return.

The ten minutes having elapsed, Miss Jimpson now descended from the platform where she had been seated, and began to collect the papers. Everybody was ready for her with the exception of Macfarlane, who continued to write till she had practically to wrest his papers from him, and even then he seemed to relinquish them almost tearfully. "How could he have so much to say?" Tom marvelled. "He *looked* stupid enough!"

Anyhow, the exam was at an end, and Miss Jimpson, returning to her desk, with a few words dismissed them, saying they would meet again when school reopened, and that in the meantime she hoped they would all have very pleasant holidays.

Somebody, Tom felt, ought to have replied to this, but instead there was only the scuffle and noise of a hasty exodus, in which he joined, hanging a little behind the others. Out in the playground a general comparison of notes at once began. In this he was too shy to take part till Brown hailed him, gave him a playful poke in the ribs, and remarked genially, "Thanks for the tip, Skinny. . . . Not that it'll do much good."

Brown, in fact, appeared to take the examination very lightly indeed, and his own participation in it as being more in the nature of a joke than anything else. Quite soon he mounted his bicycle, and with a farewell, "See you in September, Skinny," rode away. The effect of his friendliness on the other hand remained; and though one tiresome result of it was that everybody thenceforth addressed him as Skinny, Tom found himself, so to speak, introduced and accepted.

Meanwhile, in the shrill babel of conflicting opinions, of confident assertions and flat contradictions, it was extremely difficult to judge how he had done in the examination. On the whole, he thought, pretty well, for the paper had suited him, being designed primarily as a test of general knowledge, whereas he had feared there might be a lot of arithmetic. One of the questions, for instance, had consisted simply in a list of five longish words, which you had to bring into five sentences of your own composition. He had enjoyed doing this, though like everybody else, except a red-haired boy called Preston, he had been floored by the word "frugality." Preston was the only one who had known what "frugality" meant— which just proves how much there is in luck, for *he* knew merely because there happened to be a picture called "The Frugal Meal" hanging above the mantelpiece in his dining-room at home. It was a Dutch picture, Preston said, and showed a Dutch family sitting down to a very skimpy-looking dinner. The sentence he had written was: "Since there was very little to begin with, and the parents each took two helpings, the children's meal was naturally one of great frugality."

This was considered pretty good, but Preston's cleverness was speedily forgotten in a general comment on the "squinty" behaviour of the parents, until it was discovered that actually there was nothing in the picture to justify the statement that they had taken two helpings. That was entirely due to Preston's own imagination. "Shows what you'll do when you've kids yourself," Haughton said, and everybody laughed.

Further ragging ensued, with the result that Preston, whose temper seemed uncertain, suddenly got mad. "How *could* it be in the picture?" he shouted, his face as red as his hair. "Lot of damned silly little fools! Here, give me back that paper, Skinny, or you'll get a punch in the jaw."

Skinny, who was no warrior, and as a matter of fact had been guilty of only one very mild witticism, hastily returned the paper, which Preston thrust angrily back into his pocket. A little later they all dispersed, singly or in groups, until only Pascoe was left. Pascoe, like most of the others, had a bicycle, but he walked beside Tom, wheeling it, and it was perfectly clear that he wanted to make friends. Tom himself felt no particular desire either one way or the other, but Pascoe was the only boy who had not called him Skinny, and moreover he now declared his intention of accompanying Tom part of the way home, which settled the matter. Pascoe, in fact, seemed very nice, though rather alarmingly serious, so that if you ventured on a joke you had subsequently to explain it to him, a task dreadfully calculated to reveal its true feebleness. Before long, nevertheless, several points in common were discovered; such as that neither possessed any brothers or sisters, that Pascoe thought an aquarium would be a jolly good scheme, and that, when Tom had finished with it, he would love to read *Curiosities of Natural History*. "I'm going to be a scientist, you see; very likely a naturalist. Only at Miss Wallace's, where I was at school till these hols., there was nobody to teach science. What are you going to be?"

Tom wasn't sure; he hadn't thought much about it; and changing the subject, he asked what Miss Wallace's had been like.

"Oh, all right," Pascoe replied half-heartedly; adding, after a pause: "Brown was there."

Somehow the tone in which this was uttered suggested that Brown was not among its happier memories, so Tom tactfully refrained from further questions, and it was Pascoe himself who proposed: "Couldn't we make the aquarium together? It would be better sport than doing it alone, and it could be at your place; I can easily ride over on my bike."

"I haven't a bike," Tom admitted, "so if you're sure you don't mind——"

"We'll need a net," Pascoe interrupted him. "I'll get Mother to make us one."

"So will I; we ought each to have one. . . . They'll need to be strong, too; so that the sticks won't bend when they're full of water. . . . When will you come?"

Pascoe considered. "I'll come to-morrow. Mother can make the net to-night."

This being arranged, he was on the point of turning back towards his own home, when Tom suddenly remembered he was going to Granny's to-morrow. It was a nuisance, for any other time would have done just as well, but it had been definitely settled. "I can't," he said, "I've got to go and stay for a week-end with Granny. But I'll be coming home on Monday."

"Well then——"

"Only I don't know what time; so it'd better be Tuesday."

"All right: I'll ride over first thing after breakfast, and I'll bring the net and a collecting-bottle. . . . Not if it's pouring rain, of course."

"Come anyway—if it's not too bad. There's heaps of things we can do inside. I've a sort of playroom up in the loft. And you needn't bother about bringing a bottle; Phemie has tons of glass jam-pots. . . . Besides, we'll have to fix up the aquarium itself first. I want to have it like a pond, and we'll need to dig a place for it."

"See you Tuesday then," Pascoe said, with one foot on the pedal. "And promise you won't begin to do anything till I come."

9: SHORTLY after lunch, by arrangement, Doctor Macrory called to drive him to Tramore. Stretching out a large left hand, he opened the door of the front seat, and Tom, who had been waiting all ready in the porch, deposited a leather bag and Granny's book on the floor. He had just got in himself when Mother, evidently not expecting so rapid a departure, hastily emerged from the dining-room. "Well, I must say you're in a great hurry to be off! Am I not even to be allowed to say 'How do you do?' to Doctor Macrory? Granny ought to feel flattered. . . .

"It's extremely good of you to take him," she went on, coming to the window of the car; but the doctor said he had to visit a patient who lived in that direction anyhow, so no question of goodness was involved. "And I'll collect him for you some time on Monday afternoon," he added. "It'll probably be latish, but I don't suppose that matters."

"Of course it doesn't matter," Mother replied, "though there's nothing to prevent Edgar from collecting him, as you call it."

"Only that it would be several miles out of his way, and won't be out of mine: so you'd better tell him."

"If I do, may I tell him also that you'll be dining with us? You can, can't you?"

"Thus we see how infallibly virtue is rewarded," Doctor Macrory observed to Tom, as the car turned out on to the main road, and the latter leaned from the window to wave a last farewell. . . . "And now I want to hear all about yesterday's doings. To begin with, how did the examination go?"

"Very well, thank you," Tom replied.

Doctor Macrory chuckled. "That's good; but tell me a little more, won't you?—how it all struck you, what happened, and what the other boys were like."

Tom, at no time addicted to taciturnity, at once proceeded to do so. If it had been Daddy to whom he had been giving his account, it would have passed through a half-subconscious process of selection and elimination, based upon what he felt Daddy would or would not wish to hear, but with Doctor Macrory he never felt the need of this. So, as they drove between the summer fields, past farmsteads and an occasional wooded dingle, he gave him a minute description of everything and everybody, which he only broke off to utter a sudden "Oh!"

—as the car swerved violently, the front mudguard narrowly missing a small child who had rushed out of a cottage in pursuit of a hen.

Doctor Macrory said "Damn!" and a moment later: "Did we get the hen?"—but Tom, gazing out behind, was able to assure him that both hen and child were safe.

"Well," said the doctor, "I'm afraid I interrupted you. You were telling me about the other boys. Brown I can't be sure of—there are so many Browns; but Preston, I fancy, is Bob Preston's son; and Pascoe quite certainly must be connected with the wine people—whole-sale and retail—in Arthur Street. . . . In which case I was at school with his father."

"Do you get your wine from him?" Tom asked politely.

"I get my whiskey from him," said Doctor Macrory, "so I suppose the answer is in the affirmative. . . . To return, however, to the main question—have any plans been made yet about what you're going to do at school? What subjects, I mean. Of course there'll be the usual subjects: what I really want to know is whether you're going to begin Greek. . . . You see," he went on, as Tom looked surprised, "I've been discussing that matter with your father, who doesn't quite share my views upon it. To me it is most important, but I'm not at all sure that my arguments convinced him; so a word from you yourself might not be out of place—in fact might settle things. What do you think?"

Tom had done a little, a very little Latin with Miss Sabine, but his classics ended there, and he didn't know what to think. In his uncertainty he suggested that there mightn't be anybody to *teach* Greek. At Miss Wallace's, for instance, where Pascoe had been, there hadn't been anybody to teach science; yet that was what Pascoe was most interested in, because he was going to *be* a scientist.

"Possibly he is," Doctor Macrory answered; "but unless I'm singularly mistaken you're not: Greek for you every time. . . . And of course there'll be somebody to teach it. . . . Science too, for that matter; though my own recollection of science at school is that it consisted largely in making fireworks and bad smells. . . . I really mean what I say, Tom, about learning Greek. I haven't met Master Pascoe, but the fact that you and he propose to make an aquarium together doesn't mean that science is at all likely to be in your line. You haven't that type of mind. If you're interested in natural history, it's only because, like the Greeks, you're fond of animals—which is a spiritual quality, and has nothing whatever to do with science."

Tom listened: he was in truth an excellent listener, as could be seen now from the thoughtful expression on his face. Doctor Macrory, noting that expression, may have wondered what he was thinking about, though he did not press him further.

It was indeed some little time before either of them spoke again, but at last, gazing out across the sunlit landscape, Tom said softly: "I'd like to learn Greek: I liked that book you lent me."

"Then you'd like their own writings still more. When you're a little older you must have a shot at your Uncle Stephen's book. There may be a good deal in it you won't understand, but you'll get something."

"I didn't know he had written a book," Tom said.

"Well, he has; and a good one."

Tom wondered why it had not been mentioned when Mother had told him other things about Uncle Stephen. Perhaps she didn't know about it, or had forgotten; but this seemed hardly likely. He pondered the singular lapse for some time before he asked: "Have we got it? Has Daddy got it?"

Doctor Macrory sounded his horn and slowed down to pass a flock of sheep. "I doubt it. It's not in your father's line; and unfortunately I don't possess a copy either."

"Is it in my line?" was Tom's next inquiry, for he found this matter of "lines" most interesting, though at the same time somewhat puzzling—puzzling to him, that was; Doctor Macrory appeared to find no difficulty.

The doctor smiled. "Very much, I should say; but not at present. It's a great mistake to read a book before you're ready for it. . . . I suppose you think I'm talking nonsense; but to start off with, you must remember that there's a bit of him in you—of your Uncle Stephen, I mean. Like dogs and other animals, we're all made up of bits of our ancestors, and his father was your great-grandfather, and his brother was your grandfather, and his niece is your Mother."

Tom was impressed. "That makes a whole lot," he said, "not just a bit."

Doctor Macrory's glance again rested upon him, with an oddly re-flective expression. It quite often did, Tom had noticed, proving that he was really interested and not just pretending to be; which was one reason why it was so much easier to talk freely to him than to Daddy.

"It does sound rather a lot—put in that way," the doctor admitted. "But the bits are discontinuous, you know; the only direct source is your great-grandfather."

"Is there anything about Orpheus in Uncle Stephen's book?" Tom asked after another pause. "In the book you lent me there was, but only a little."

"I'm afraid I don't remember: it's a good many years now since I read it. . . . I know there's a great deal about Hermes in it. Are you particularly interested in Orpheus?"

Tom hesitated. "It's just what it said about him in that book of yours—that when he played his music, all the animals and birds followed him and wanted to listen."

"And you'd like them to follow you?"

Tom laughed. "Of course I know it's only a story. Still, it *could* have happened, couldn't it? And there might be something about it in Uncle Stephen's book; because it says in your book that maybe it was Hermes who gave him his lyre."

"Does it? I'd forgotten that too. It's usually supposed to have been Apollo." He drove on for a while in silence. "I'm afraid I can't manage a lyre," he next said; "but since we're living in modern times, how would you like to experiment with a more modern instrument—the kind of pipe bird-charmers use, or used to use? I've a notion I've got one put away somewhere, if I can only lay my hands on it."

Tom coloured. "Do you mean——" he began, and abruptly stopped.

"Do I mean a present? Yes—that was the idea—if I can find it."

"But——"

"You won't be depriving me of anything. I've never used it in my life, and am never likely to. Whatever its effect on birds, I doubt if it would charm patients. It was merely given to me as a curiosity."

"Thanks most awfully——" Tom was beginning, when the doctor interrupted him. "And here we are! Do you think you can manage if I don't take you right up to the house? I'm rather behind time, I'm afraid; and if I go in I'll have to pay my respects to your grandmother, which will mean another five or ten minutes. That bag doesn't look very heavy."

10:

TOM walked up an avenue over-arched by trees. It was not a particularly tidy avenue: indeed it badly required weeding at this moment, and he decided that he would perform that service for Granny to-morrow. With a hoe and a wheelbarrow it might be rather fun, and would at least help to pass the time, for to-morrow would be Sunday. If Mother were here she would certainly object on this very ground, but he had an idea that Granny's objections, if she had any, could be overcome. There was a saying employed by Phemie on such occasions, "The better the day the better the deed," and though really all it meant was that you intended to do what you wanted, it might work with Granny.

On the other hand, she probably didn't care a straw whether there were weeds in the avenue or not. Out of doors, she left everything to Nature, or what amounted to Nature, Quigley, who, with his wife, lived in the lodge, and was supposed to be her gardener. Both Mother and Daddy strongly disapproved of Quigley, and were always at Granny to get rid of him. They pointed out that he was lazy, incompetent, neglected his work, and imposed on her in every way he could. But of course Granny knew they had the irreproachable William in their mind's eyes, and to everything they said merely replied that she liked Quigley, and thought *he* liked *her*.

In fact, Granny had her own ideas, and was not easily influenced by other people's. Everything at Tramore was as different as possible from the garden at home. Granny didn't go in for flowers, therefore there were no flower-beds; and the only flowers were those which themselves wanted to be there; such as snowdrops, primroses, daffodils, and bluebells—all of them spring flowers and now over. Daddy didn't even approve of the Tramore grass, and again laid the blame on Quigley, because the sickle-shaped lawn in front of the house was thick with moss. William, he said, would have got rid of the moss long ago, but Quigley appeared to encourage it. Beyond the lawn, on every side, grew a green and tangled jungle. . . .

The house itself was covered thickly with creepers, so that looking at it from a little distance it appeared to sink into and be half lost in the leafy woodland behind. Granny preferred it like this, and so did Tom. In the late autumn and winter doubtless it presented a somewhat forsaken and neglected appearance, so that if it were not for the thin grey threads of smoke curling up from its irregular chimney-stacks, you might almost think nobody lived there; but on a summer afternoon, dreaming under a deep soft blue sky, it had a rich and drowsy beauty, profoundly peaceful. . . .

And here, like Mariana in her moated grange, lived Granny. Tom had learned the poem about Mariana for Miss Sabine, and, as with most of the poems he was fondest of, had found its counterpart in real life. Naturally it was only the "moated grange" itself which was a counterpart, for Mariana had been young and most unhappy, whereas Granny was old and remarkably lively: still, the picture and the music were the same——

All day within the dreamy house,
The doors upon their hinges creak'd,
The blue fly sung in the pane; the mouse
Behind the mouldering wainscot shriek'd,
Or from the crevice peer'd about.
Old faces glimmer'd thro' the doors,
Old footsteps trod the upper floors,
Old voices called her from without.

It was lovely. Daddy, to be sure, had said that Miss Sabine's taste in poetry seemed to be very nearly as morbid as Tom's own—when *he* was a boy, he had been given such things as "Ye Mariners of England," and "How they Brought the Good News from Ghent to Aix," to learn. This had made Mother laugh. "But you didn't enjoy them very much, dear, did you?—though they *were* so stirring; and Tom at least likes his." And since Daddy returned no answer: "I think it's wonderful how Miss Sabine always knows what he *will* like. It's very clever of her, and certainly makes his lessons much easier and pleasanter."

"Oh, they're a nice pair!" Daddy had grumbled; but Tom knew he really thought a tremendous lot of Miss Sabine.

The outer door of the house was open, so he did not need to ring the bell. He turned the handle of the inner door and entered the hall, which was square and had a fireplace in it, making it look like a room. Here he left down his bag, and went in search of Granny. He knew where she always sat; and there he found her—in the big panelled drawing-room, with its bright chintzes and soft grey carpet, and the cabinets where she kept her collection of china. Granny herself, sitting so quietly among her things, was not unlike some delicate and fragile object surviving from an earlier period. She looked, somehow, as if nothing had ever happened to her. Her tranquil, gentle face, with its faint wild-rose colouring; her white hair; her slender hands; even her knitting—were all singularly in keeping with the porcelain cups and plates and vases she was so fond of. A fantastic notion crossed Tom's mind that Granny was growing more and more to re-semble her things. The yellow sunlight, filtering through curtained windows, awoke the dragons on a Chinese screen behind her to a fiery life; the whole room was flooded with magic light and colour; a single silvery note from a small clock on the chimney-piece chimed the half-hour.

But Granny—who could not have heard his arrival or she would have been out in the hall to meet him—at once became very human indeed, as she got up quickly from her chair to kiss him welcome. "Tom darling, it's so nice of you to have come. Does Rose know you're here? Perhaps you'd better touch the bell. I wasn't quite sure when you would arrive."

Granny was always a little extravagant in her endearments, as in-deed, according to Mother, in everything else; but when there was nobody there Tom didn't mind this; and at all events she didn't bother you about such matters as going to bed on the first stroke of the clock, or keeping your hands in your pockets, or eating between meals—in fact she would have fed him from morning till night if she had had her way.

He produced his parcel. "Here's your book, Granny: Mother got it in town; and there's a lovely tiger in it."

"Thank you very much, dear. Doctor Macrory brought you, I suppose. Your mother rang me up last night to tell me he was going to."

"Yes; but he only came as far as the gate. . . . Where's Dinah?"

"Dinah is in the kitchen with her kittens. Perhaps you didn't know she'd had kittens?"

Tom was immediately interested. "Why don't you have them in here?" he asked.

"It's too soon yet: their eyes aren't even open. Rose says they're just like little rats. But the next time you come——"

Tom interrupted her. "Do you mean to say you haven't even *looked* at them, Granny? Kittens aren't a bit like rats. They've got fur, and whiskers, and everything. Rats are naked when they're born."

"Well, that's what Rose says," Granny answered meekly; and as the door opened, "Oh Rose, I did ring for tea, but perhaps you wouldn't mind bringing in Dinah's basket: Master Tom wants to see the kittens."

"I'll get it myself," Tom cried, jumping up. "How many are there, Rose?"

"I'm sure I never counted them," Rose replied with an air of supe-riority. "Nasty crawling little things! Cook says there *were* five; but she gave three of them to Quigley to be drowned."

Tom regarded her coldly. He did not approve of affectation, espe-cially of Rose's kind—just as if kittens were far beneath her. "Then if there were five, and three have been drowned, you ought to be able to tell how many are left," he said.

He knew this wasn't a proper way to speak, and Rose, maintaining a lofty silence, evidently thought so too. All the same, it was what she deserved, so he left her there, and ran out to the kitchen to get the basket.

Dinah was in it with her children, but Dinah, too, behaved stu-pidly. The moment he lifted the basket she hopped out, with a distinctly irritated mew. She very soon altered her tone, however, to a more humble and plaintive one, as he carried the basket back to the other room, while she followed closely on his heels. This anxiety was extremely silly, and he told her so. If *he* couldn't be trusted with kittens, he would like to know who could! "Nobody," poor Dinah replied; and since she had already lost three, her pessimism was per-haps excusable.

Not that she appeared to suspect him of wishing to steal the kittens; from the tone of her mews it was more as if she feared he might break them by letting them drop; and she got back into the basket the moment it was deposited on the hearthrug. She didn't remain there long. Tom took the whole family out and lay down on the hearthrug himself, curling as well as he could round both cat and kittens till all felt warm and furry—and very soon purry, too; with a rough tongue, intended for a kitten, occasionally passing over the back of his hand.

From these domestic felicities he was summoned by Granny to come to the table and have tea. At home there would have been a reminder to go and wash his hands first, and Granny received due credit for being sensible and unfussy. She got yet a further good mark for having remembered that he was specially fond of potted shrimps and hot freshly-baked shortbread. Dinah, though unused to any but kitchen meals, also was comforted with a few shrimps, and a saucer of milk—a good deal of which she splashed on to the carpet.

"Granny, have you got Uncle Stephen's book?"

Granny, who had been beaming benevolently at nothing in partic-ular—merely in a sort of general amiability—shook her head. She seemed not even to have grasped the importance of the question, for

she went on pressing food upon him as if he were never to expect
another meal.

"But Granny, you *must* have. Grandpapa was Uncle Stephen's
brother, you know."

Granny, continuing to beam, again shook her head.

"Do you mean to say he *wasn't* his brother!" Tom cried, both incredulous and indignant.

At this Granny pulled herself together. "No, dear, of course he
was his brother; but your Uncle Stephen was ten years younger than
Grandpapa, and for a long time lived abroad. Then, when he came
back to this country, he shut himself up at Kilbarron, where he has
lived ever since. Grandpapa *did* write once, asking him to pay us a
visit, but we never even got a reply—so naturally that ended the
matter."

"Why don't *you* write, Granny?"

Granny laughed. "Perhaps I shall. And tell him he's got a nephew
who's most anxious to meet him."

Tom pondered a moment. "Will you write to-night, Granny?"

But Granny had either exhausted or been exhausted by the subject.
"Is this your mother?" she asked, "or is it Doctor Macrory? It must
be either one or the other."

"It was Doctor Macrory," Tom admitted, "but mother told me
about him too. She thinks I take after him."

Granny seemed amused. "Since she never set eyes on him in her
life, that at least does credit to her powers of imagination; but I
should have thought Doctor Macrory would have had more sense."

Tom was disappointed, though at the same time not convinced.
After all, he had much more faith in Mother's judgement than in
Granny's, while Doctor Macrory was by far the most sensible person
he had ever met. For a minute or two he remained silent, and then
asked; "Would you mind if I went all over the house, Granny?"

Granny, if she appeared to be slightly puzzled by this abrupt di-
gression, at least had no objections. "Of course, dear, you can go
over the house. Why not?"

But the very promptness of her agreement made Tom doubt
whether she had understood what he meant. "I mean now," he explained. "I mean the locked-up rooms in the east wing. I've never
been up there except once, when there was a spring-cleaning."

At this a sudden light dawned, and Granny looked slightly annoyed. "If you're still thinking of that book," she declared, "I *know*

it isn't there. Why are you so unbelieving? There are no books there except a lot of rubbish—old school-books and magazines, and perhaps a few yellow-backs."

"Yes, Granny; but do you mind if I go up?"

"Whether I mind or not," Granny told him, "I think you're an extremely persistent little boy, and I hoped you had come to see me."

Tom sighed. "So I have, Granny. . . . I'll be seeing you all this evening, and to-morrow, and part of Monday. We can play backgammon after dinner—or even draughts."

The "even," though entirely unpremeditated, was not lost upon Granny, who could not help recollecting that draughts had figured not infrequently as an entertainment on similar occasions in the past. He was certainly a very odd little boy, but she was much too old and too fond of him to be offended for more than a moment. "Run along," she said, "since you're so bent on it. . . . Tell Rose to give you the key of the door at the top of the stairs: all the other doors are unlocked."

11:    TOM did as she told him, though he would have felt more comfortable if she hadn't made those remarks about his persistence. After all, Granny *did* forget things; he had often heard her say she would be forgetting her own name next; and simply because he wished to make quite sure didn't mean that he was unbelieving. Very likely she hadn't been up in the empty rooms for ages, and even if she had, she wouldn't have been looking for Uncle Stephen's book. In fact she didn't seem to take the least interest in either Uncle Stephen *or* his book. That it wasn't downstairs, Tom himself was certain, for there were only two bookcases downstairs and he had gone over their contents heaps of times. Nor had it taken long: Tramore wasn't a booky house: Daddy had ten times as many. . . .

The staircase rose from the hall, first in a single broad flight with very wide shallow treads, and then branching to right and left in two narrower flights terminating in and connected by a railed gallery. The closed rooms were in the east wing—the old nursery quarters, Granny said—and the locked door through which you reached them was at one end of this gallery. It was a queer arrangement, Tom thought, but there were unnecessary doors all over Granny's house, just as if everybody had wanted to live as separately as they could from every-body else; and of course, if it were kept open, you mightn't notice the door. He opened it now, and after a moment's hesitation shut it behind him. It was lighter here than it had been in the hall or on the stairs, because the doors of all the rooms were wide open and their windows unblinded. Not that there were really many rooms—only four, and one of them was a bathroom. It was in the biggest—perhaps the old nursery—that he found the books, and a single glance told him that Granny had been right about them. They were arranged on a couple of hanging shelves and were just such a worn-out, tattered collection as you might find in the fourpenny box outside any sec-ond-hand bookseller's. She had even overrated them, for there were only three yellow-backs, the rest were railway-guides, hymn-books, spelling-books, geographies and grammars, with some bound volumes of magazines. Granny certainly would be able to say, "I told you so," or "Perhaps you'll believe me next time." At least that was what most people would have said.

The inference, indeed, was plain—Uncle Stephen hadn't given Grandpapa his book, and Grandpapa hadn't bought it. For that mat-ter, nobody seemed to have bought it—not even Doctor Macrory—and Tom felt more in sympathy with Uncle Stephen than ever.

He went over to the window and looked out. From up here you got a much better view than from the rooms downstairs, and he opened the window and leaned over the sill. Beyond the lawn, the ground took a slight dip downward, and then rose again to the sky-line. It would be a splendid place for animals, he decided. You could have all kinds of animals here, and Granny hadn't even a dog—no-body but Dinah and her two kittens. He began to make plans of what he would do if he were Granny. First, he would build a very high wall all round, so that there could be really wild animals, like those they have in zoos. Next, the dogs would have to be taught not to chase anything—which would be easy enough with Roger and Barker. He would have snakes, too, in spite of Saint Patrick. Only with so many animals to take care of he would need somebody to help him, and as Quigley would be no good he would get James-Arthur from Denny's. . . .

Tom could not have told what it was that at this point made him suddenly look round. He had heard no sound of footsteps—con-sciously he had heard no sound at all—nevertheless, standing in the passage just outside the door, was a boy watching him—a boy of about his own age, or perhaps younger, dressed in a dark blue jersey and shorts. He was standing in the full sunlight, and possibly had been there for some time, though the moment Tom looked round he hastily retreated and was gone. Tom himself was so taken aback that for a minute or two he simply stared at the empty doorway without moving. Who was he? Either Cook or Rose must have sent him up; and probably it was Cook, for he knew she had nephews, though he had never seen them. It was pretty cheeky of him all the same—to steal up on tip-toe like this, and then run away. . . . Unless he had suddenly turned shy. . . . And perhaps he hadn't run away; perhaps he was only hiding, in a kind of game. To make sure, Tom crossed to the door and peeped out. Yes—he was there—but now he was in the doorway at the end of the passage, and as before, the moment Tom caught a glimpse of him he disappeared. . . .

It evidently *was* a game, yet Tom felt half annoyed as well as puzzled. "If he imagines I'm going to run after him, he's very much mistaken," he said to himself. "He can either go or stay as he pleases."

Then, while he stood there, uncertain what to do next, he began to think. . . . If this had been Cook's nephew, wouldn't Cook herself have come up to explain, to perform some kind of introduction? Besides, he somehow didn't look like Cook's nephew—or at least what Tom would have expected Cook's nephew to look like. . . . Did Granny know any boys? If she did, he had never heard of them; and anyhow, she, too, would either have come up with the visitor or have called Tom down. It certainly was very queer; the boy's behaviour even more so. . . .

There he was again—he had come back—but this time he lingered, perhaps because Tom had not followed him. He was not in the sunlight now, yet surely there was a light, a kind of brightness, that seemed to be in the air behind him and all round him. A sudden memory was stirred in Tom's mind. He knew neither how nor whence it had come, but it was there, and held him hushed and spellbound. That other boy—Ralph Seaford—this was where he once had lived —this was his home—Tramore. With nearly the whole length of the passage between them, Tom remained motionless—hardly startled— not really frightened at all, for the boy was smiling at him, half timidly, half doubtfully, yet as if he wanted very much to make friends. There was an interval before Tom smiled back, but in the end he did, seeing which the boy's smile instantly deepened, and step by step he drew nearer, coming very slowly down the passage.

"I know who you are," Tom said, hardly above his breath. "At least I think I do."

There was no answer, and, though the boy was close beside him now, Tom somehow knew that if he stretched out his hand it would touch nothing, that he was near and yet not near, there and yet not there.

Side by side they returned to the room where the books were. No sound passed the boy's lips, nevertheless Tom was as sure as if he had said so that he wanted to be with him, to play with him, that this was why he had come. Somehow the thought was oddly pathetic, and awoke an immediate response. Only what could they play at? If they had been at home it would have been easy enough; he could have set his railway going—which he rarely did for himself—he could have shown his yacht, or built a house with his bricks: but here there was nothing except a lot of dusty antiquated furniture and household odds and ends—boxes and trunks, either empty or packed with old clothes, old bills, old letters—for Granny seemed never to destroy anything.

Presently his glance fell on a pile of ancient *Graphics* on the floor by the window. These might at least be better than nothing. So lifting an armful on to the table he sat down and began to turn the leaves, pausing at the full-page pictures, while the boy leaned forward to look too, his hand seeming to rest on Tom's shoulder although Tom could feel no pressure there.

Tom talked about the pictures, because it was easier to talk aloud. Yet he had no idea whether his companion could hear him, or simply understood him without words. The sense of communication at any rate was there—vividly there; and by and by even the feeling of strangeness was lost. The sunlight slanted across the room; and the rustle of leaves, and the gay careless music of birds, floated in through the open window. Now and then Tom glanced at the face that was so close to his, and always, when he did so, it broke into a smile—happy and strangely trusting. . . .

Time slipped by unnoticed; the shadows outside were lengthening. At last, breaking in upon them unexpectedly, came the deep and distant notes of the hall gong. It was meant for him, Tom knew, a reminder that he must get ready for dinner; and he also knew that if he neglected the summons a very cross Rose would soon appear to fetch him. "I must go," he whispered, yet with a feeling of compunction. He really did feel distressed, for the small figure beside him looked infinitely forlorn and lonely the moment he had spoken the words. But he had understood, and he stepped back at once. "I can't help it," Tom went on: "I'll come again if I possibly can; though I know Granny will think it very queer and ask questions, and, and—— Good-bye." Deliberately he averted his eyes, and without another look or word ran out of the room and along the passage and down the stairs. . . .

At dinner, Granny had an unusually quiet guest beside her. Before long she noticed it. "What are you dreaming about?" she asked, half amused, and half curious. "I suppose you'll say 'nothing,' but you might at least tell me what you found upstairs to keep you there for two hours. I very nearly sent Rose up to see. It can't have been the books."

"No," Tom answered, in a rather subdued voice. Actually he had forgotten all about the books.

"Granny——" he began presently, and stopped, leaving her to wait expectantly while he stared at the opposite wall.

Granny, however, was not unaccustomed to such pauses, and allowed him to take his own time. He did, and in the end decided it would be better not to say what he had been going to say. Instead, he told her that he had liked it upstairs, and had been looking at pictures in the *Graphic*. "I didn't finish them," he added, so that he might have an excuse for a second visit.

Unfortunately Granny, in her innocence, at once upset this stratagem by replying that she would tell Rose to bring them down to the drawing-room after dinner.

12:    LATE on Monday afternoon, Doctor Macrory "collected" him as he had promised, and they drove home together. On the way, the doctor told him he had been unable to find the bird-call, adding that he now didn't think it would have been of much use even if he had—was not, that is to say, the kind of thing Tom wanted. "At any rate, I consulted a friend of mine who's a great bird man, and he said the only instruments of the sort he had ever seen were of German manufacture and purely mechanical—each one separately designed to reproduce the mating call of a different bird. There wouldn't be much fun in that, would there? and I expect mine must be the same. What *you* want is something on which you can play—if not like Orpheus, at least like the shepherds in Theocritus—something more in the nature of Pan-pipes; and I imagine the nearest modern instrument to that is a mouth-organ, so I got you one. . . . It's there," he went on, nodding towards the shelf in front of Tom's seat, upon which lay a small parcel wrapped up in brown paper.

Tom opened it, a little disappointed, but only momentarily, for after all he had never possessed a mouth-organ. "Thanks most awfully," he said; and from time to time during the remainder of the drive he blew a note or two, though very softly, in case these experimental sounds should not be pleasing to the doctor.

No one was in sight when the car turned in at the gate, but they had not arrived many minutes—in fact he had only had time to go into the house and be kissed by Mother and come out again—when Roger appeared. Roger had missed him a lot, it seemed. At least twice every day, Mother said, he had come over from the farm in search of his friend, and had looked so disappointed at not finding him that she herself had gone out to talk to him, because she thought he deserved it for being so faithful. Tom thought so too, and their first greetings over, sat down on the lawn to pet him. It was strange that dogs should be so much more trustful and easily made happy than human beings. Roger demanded no explanations or apologies; he simply turned over on to his back, waving his four legs absurdly in the air, pretending to be a puppy. Tom rubbed his chest and tumbled him over, now on this side and now on that, while Roger growled and bit and rolled his eyes, which was all part of the puppy game; and when the sound of the gong interrupted them, he followed Tom into the cloak-room, where he sat watching him while he washed his hands. After that he would have gone out as usual to wait on the lawn had not Tom given him a whispered signal from the dining-room door.

This was a "try-on," as James-Arthur would have said, and Daddy immediately spotted it. "Go out, sir!" he commanded sternly, and Roger, with drooping head and tail was turning to obey, when Mother—melted it may be by his air of dejection—came to the rescue. "Oh well, perhaps for once!" she murmured, and clever old Roger, needing no more, instantly stretched himself beside Tom's chair. Here, knowing he was only there on sufferance, he kept so still that all might have been well, and his presence very soon forgotten, had not Tom surreptitiously given him a spoonful of soup. Roger accepted it, but with so resounding a thump of his tail on the floor that naturally it attracted the attention of Daddy, who this time rose ominously from the table.

"Come on, sir; out you go!"—and before anybody could utter a word of protest, poor Roger was hustled from the room, and the door shut with what was very like a bang.

"Disgusting!" Daddy continued, returning to his seat. "Feeding him with the same spoon you're using yourself!"

Doctor Macrory smiled one of his barely perceptible smiles, while Mother looked reproachfully at the offender as much as to say, "Now you've put *me* in the wrong!" And to relieve the situation she went on aloud; "You haven't told us yet how you got on at Granny's. Did you give her her book?"

Tom glanced furtively at Daddy, but Daddy's countenance had not relaxed. "Yes," he replied; and after a pause: "Some of Granny's other pictures are like that—like the pictures in the book."

As it chanced, he could not have hit on a more fortunate remark, for it straightway turned the conversation to Granny's collections of Oriental prints and china, which Doctor Macrory declared he envied her. Granny, he said, must have a wonderful flair, and not only that, but have been uncommonly lucky as well.

"As a matter of fact, it was really Father who collected them," Mother said, "and at a time when such things were much easier to find and much less expensive than they are to-day."

"But Granny helped him," Tom put in loyally: "she told me she did."

"For my part," Mother went on, ignoring Granny's advocate, "though the china is very nice, I must say I prefer European pictures" —which led to an animated discussion between her and Doctor Macrory as to whether it is possible to appreciate pictures of completely different kinds even supposing they are equally good.

The Doctor thought not, "for the simple reason that for us as individuals they never *can* be equally good. I remember visiting an exhibition of early Dutch masters and trying my hardest to wax enthusiastic over a picture of a hare by Jan Weenix—supposed to be the gem of the collection. Which, in a way, I dare say it was. Only all the time I couldn't help wondering why he should have wanted to paint a dead hare hanging up by its feet when he might just as easily have painted a living one. . . . It was the same with several of the other pictures; the painting was marvellous, but the subject appeared to be a matter of indifference—whether it was a madonna or a child with diarrhoea."

Daddy, who on principle never agreed with Doctor Macrory, here found a few words to say in favour of the child with diarrhoea. It struck Tom as a rather strange topic to choose at dinner-time, but the argument was academic, and as it proceeded became more and more metaphysical, and less and less comprehensible so far as he was concerned. It was the kind of argument, however, both Daddy and Doctor Macrory loved, and it lasted so long that dinner was practically over when Phemie, very red in the face, abruptly terminated it by bursting into the room.

"If you please, ma'am, will you come and speak to Mary. I can't do anything with her, and she's going on the way you never heard the like—crying and sobbing about a ghost she says is upstairs."

"A ghost!" Mother repeated feebly, staring at Phemie in bewilderment. "What kind of ghost?"

At this both Daddy and Doctor Macrory laughed, but Phemie was nearly choking with bottled-up indignation. "You may well ask!" she cried, "and it's what I asked myself, for it might be a whole regiment of them from the noise she's making. But sure it's only the ghost of a little boy, up in Master Tom's room. . . . She says she won't sleep another night in the house, and——"

Mother rose with a sigh and followed Phemie to the kitchen, while Daddy observed, "One of the lesser domestic felicities which you, Doctor, as a bachelor, I presume have to forgo." Then, with a twinkle in his eye, he turned to his son: "You must have brought the ghost with you, Tom, from Granny's."

It was an ill-timed joke if ever there was one, and Tom tried vainly to hide his discomposure. Little did Daddy know how true his words were, or he might not have spoken them so lightly! With a mumbled apology he rose abruptly from the table, but Daddy immediately asked; "Where are you going to?"

He hesitated guiltily, avoiding the two pairs of eyes he now felt to be fixed upon him. At last he stammered: "I'm going upstairs to—to look."

"Sit down," Daddy told him quietly, "and don't be silly. She probably saw a curtain flapping, or something equally terrifying"—and he actually cracked a walnut and pushed the decanter in the direction of Doctor Macrory, who appeared to be equally unperturbed.

Tom sat down, but it was only with the greatest effort that he remained seated. The possibility of any such development as this had never crossed his mind. He had found no opportunity before leaving Granny's to pay a further visit to the closed rooms: or rather, there had no longer *been* any closed rooms; for the very next day Granny herself had gone up to inspect them, with the result that she had suddenly taken it into her head to have them tidied up, cleaned out, the floors scrubbed, and even the woodwork touched up with fresh paint, so that from then on either Quigley or Mrs. Quigley had been in constant possession. This, so far as ghosts were concerned, had effectually ended the adventure; and pondering on it quietly and at leisure Tom had even come to be half persuaded that it was his own private adventure—by which he meant that other people, had they been there, would have seen nothing. . . .

Yet now Mary had seen. . . . Only, why Mary . . . ? And why, above all, here at home—miles away from Tramore . . . ? And *what* had she seen?

Meanwhile Doctor Macrory and Daddy had once more taken up their interrupted discussion, but they broke it off the moment Mother returned, and all three looked at her, Tom with round anxious eyes, the other two in a sort of amused inquiry. Mother herself was less amused than vexed, though she veered oddly between the two as she recounted what had taken place. It appeared that she and Phemie had managed between them either to cajole or bully the unfortunate Mary into a more reasonable, or at any rate a more submissive frame of mind. Mother had taken the line that there was no ghost, that it was all nonsense; Phemie, accepting the ghost, had dwelt scornfully on its diminutive size. "It's asking the mistress's forgiveness you ought to be, Mary Donaghy, instead of roaring and rampaging round the house, the way it might be Doctor Crippen or some of them ones was after you!"

Tom did not smile. Phemie may or may not have used those words, but Mother only repeated them because she thought they were funny. Her own description of poor Mary was very far from bearing them out. "There she sat, the tears streaming down her face, though if I told her once I told her fifty times, 'There are no such things as ghosts.' "

"That surely was a rather rash statement," Doctor Macrory observed. "According to the great Milton, 'millions of spiritual creatures walk the earth unseen, both when we wake and when we sleep.' "

"Yes, unseen," Mother retorted, and Daddy asked curiously: "What actually does she say she *did* see?"

"Oh, she now admits she only *thought* she saw something—a little boy—standing by the window—and he was gone next moment. . . . It's a pity he *did* go, for it's chiefly that which seems to have frightened her."

But at this point Tom ceased to listen. The preoccupation of the others gave him the opportunity he had been waiting for, and slipping quietly away, he ran upstairs to his own room. He opened the door precipitately, but whatever he may have expected to find he did not find; the room was empty, and empty it remained, though he waited on for some time.

He did not know whether this was a good sign or the reverse, but at least there was nothing he could do about it. Perhaps the trouble was over and might not happen again; and since he could not stay up here indefinitely, and did not want to rejoin the others, who would still be talking about it, he decided that he might as well go down to the kitchen and get some bread-and-milk for his hedgehog.

There, however, the sight of Mary renewed his uneasiness, mingled now with a sense of irritation. For she was seated in a chair in a lax and mournful fashion, very much as Mother had described her, suggesting something between a sagging bolster and Watts's picture of the abandoned Ariadne. Even if she *had* seen Ralph, Tom thought impatiently, what was there to make such a fuss about? and he cast a sidelong and unsympathic glance at her. Phemie, too, every time she looked in Mary's direction, emitted a disdainful sniff.

Leaving them to settle their own troubles, Tom went out into the garden and down to the hedge at the foot of it. Roger must either have grown tired of waiting or been offended by Daddy's treatment of him, for he had gone home. Everybody, Tom thought, seemed to be at cross-purposes and at variance with everybody else, and it was all most stupid.

He sat down under the bank, close to a deserted rabbit-hole, and gave a low call, which he repeated at intervals until Alfred peeped out. Then his mood instantly changed, and misgivings were forgotten. Alfred had brought a friend with him to-night—either that, or he had acquired a wife. At any rate they both shared the bread-and-milk—Alfred boldly and confidently—the wife, if she *was* his wife, at first timidly. They had odd little faces, with tiny black eyes, small ears, and long, sensitive noses; and in spite of their very short legs they could climb up and down the bank and across Tom with surprising agility. He hoped they would soon have a family, for he had never seen very young hedgehogs, and they must be dear little things. Alfred had only come to live in the rabbit-hole that spring, or at any rate had only been discovered then, and by the stupid William of all people, who had found him on the croquet-lawn, half-way through a hoop, and been frightened to touch him. Luckily Tom had not been far off at the time, and had lifted him out of danger in spite of William's warning that his spikes were poisonous. William had wanted to kill him with his spade, which was just like William. He insisted that hedgehogs ought to be destroyed, that they devoured eggs and young birds, and carried away apples on their spines, though this last was so obviously untrue that you wouldn't have thought even he could have believed it. Daddy, fortunately, soon put a stop to that nonsense, and told him they were the most useful things you could have in a garden, and got rid of far more slugs than any of William's own contrivances. At which William had moved off, muttering to himself, and of course still firmly convinced that he knew better. . . .

"Tom! Tom!" It was Mother calling to him—to go to bed, he supposed. He didn't want to go to bed, but since Alfred and his wife had now finished the bread-and-milk he lifted the empty dish and returned slowly to the house.

Mother was waiting for him on the lawn, and half involuntarily, while he walked beside her, he asked the question he had very nearly asked Granny. His mind, indeed, was at present so full of it, that he asked it just as if they had already been discussing the matter. "Suppose there was a boy who wanted very much to play with another boy, *could* he come back? I mean—I mean, do you believe he could?"

It was only after he had uttered the words, and seen Mother's purposely blank expression, that he realized they had *not* been talking. "I'm afraid I don't understand," she said. "Could who come back? And come back from where?"

"I don't know," Tom answered doubtfully. "From—from heaven, perhaps."

Mother, after studying his face for a moment, abandoned subterfuge. "This, I suppose, is Mary's work! Phemie's also, for she at any rate ought to have known better. I was extremely angry with both of them."

"But how was it Phemie's fault?" Tom expostulated. "How could she help about Mary?"

"She could help bursting into the room the way she did—before Doctor Macrory too. What was to prevent her from calling me out and speaking to me in private? Only they never consider anybody but themselves. And as for Mary! I could have smacked her—great stupid lump—sitting there moaning and groaning over nothing! Probably some trash she'd been reading—about ghosts and murders and——"

"Mary reads love stories," Tom thought it only fair to point out.

"Well, it's the same thing," Mother rather wonderfully replied: "never anything sensible. . . . Now, I suppose, we'll be treated to a similar scene every time she has to go upstairs by herself in the dark."

"It wasn't dark," Tom again pointed out. "And," he added, "if you're thinking of me you needn't worry, for I don't care a straw."

His words, or more perhaps the tone in which they were uttered, must have had the right effect, for Mother, while seeming slightly surprised, also appeared considerably relieved. She gave him a long look, and then suddenly smiled. "No—I don't believe you do," she declared. "Well, I'm glad you're such a sensible boy. . . . People of that class are always superstitious—terrified if they hear a death-watch beetle, or break a looking-glass, or dream of a hearse."

This at least cleared the air for the time being: nevertheless, later on, and up in his own room, Tom half wished Ralph *would* come, if only that he might be warned of all the trouble he had made. And just before he fell asleep he fancied he *did* see him, but in a half-dream, between sleeping and waking. "You must stay in Granny's house," he whispered very gently—"in your own house—or go back to—to wherever you really come from. . . . I'm sorry, but you can see for yourself what happens when you don't. It would be all right if there was only me, but I think other people—*some* other people—like Mary—can see you too—and they're frightened. They can't help it, I expect. . . . They don't understand. . . . Do, please, go back."

13: TOM, Roger, Barker, and Pincher were all in the garden next morning when Pascoe, armed with a fishing-net and waders, arrived. As his approach was heralded by a good deal of ringing of his bicycle-bell, naturally the three dogs, unaccustomed to such spectacular entrances, hastened to assist him to dismount; which he did precipitately, eliciting a cry of anguish from Barker, upon whose paw he had descended, and yelps of delight from the excitable Pincher, who had grabbed him by the jacket.

"I say—call your beastly dogs off, can't you!" Pascoe shouted, for Pincher, relinquishing the jacket, had now got hold of the handle of the fishing-net, and in the tug-of-war that followed, the bicycle clattered to the ground.

"What are you laughing at?" Pascoe screamed. "If he gets the net he'll tear it to pieces! Let go, dash you!" But Tom had already caught Pincher by the scruff of the neck, and a monitory smack brought him to order.

"It's your own fault," he said, "for kicking up such a row. If you'd come in quietly like anybody else it wouldn't have happened. . . . Anyhow, they're not my dogs; they're only friends."

Pascoe, however, had already recovered his natural calm, and was now studying the canine bodyguard with a thoughtful expression. He seemed to be pondering something, with the result that presently he turned his gaze upon Tom himself, and pronounced solemnly: "If I were you I'd keep them here for a while."

"Keep them?" Tom echoed, bewildered by this sudden change. "Do you mean all the time? How can I keep them when they're not mine?"

"You could borrow them," Pascoe replied, "and I'll tell you why. I was going to warn you in any case, so that you could let your people know."

A pause ensued, which was broken in the end rather impatiently by Tom. "Well—why *don't* you warn me? Is it something you're too scared even to mention?"

"No it isn't," Pascoe retorted, "and I've a good mind now not to tell you."

"You needn't if you don't want to: I don't care."

Since this was obviously untrue, Pascoe took no notice of it. "It's a man," he said slowly. "He's hanging about outside, and he was staring in through your gate when I came along. He didn't know I was watching him, but I was. . . . Because I guessed from the way he was behaving what he was really up to. . . . He was reconnoitring."

"Reconnoitring?" Tom was becoming more and more mystified. He could see that the word was intended to be impressive, and he knew what it meant of course; but he associated it with military tactics, which didn't seem to make sense here.

"They always do," Pascoe went on darkly, "before they break into a house. It's to get the exact position of everything fixed in their minds, so that they won't make a mistake if there's an alarm and they have to make a sudden bolt for it."

Tom was now gazing at him open-mouthed, which appeared to afford Pascoe a gloomy satisfaction. "You mean he was a burglar? But how could you possibly tell?"

"Because he was in disguise," Pascoe answered. "He was disguised as a tramp."

This, somehow, was a little *too* much, and Tom recovered his equanimity. He was extremely curious, nevertheless, and wanted to learn more, so he only said: "He must have known you were there."

"Naturally, in the end, he did; seeing that I got off my bicycle and spoke to him."

"You——" There flashed across Tom's mind a picture of Pascoe's attitude when Brown had approached him in the playground, and Brown was a good deal less formidable than a burglar. The corners of his mouth twitched, but he repressed a temptation to laugh. "What did you say?"

"I asked him if he knew where you lived. I had to have some excuse, so that he wouldn't suspect I had penetrated his disguise."

"And *did* he know where I lived?"

"He *said* he didn't, but he gave me a very queer look, and then began to tell me a lot of lies—that he was out of work and just looking round in the hope of getting some kind of job, such as clipping hedges or sawing wood; that his wife was sick, and that they had five children and were expecting a sixth; and that the eldest was a boy about my age and very like me in appearance, though of course not so good-looking."

"Why 'of course'?" Tom asked.

"Well, I'm only telling you what he said," Pascoe returned huffily. "If you don't want to hear I can stop. . . . Later on, he said something about his *six* children, and it was then I saw it had been all lies."

"I don't see why," Tom objected. "He may have been counting in the expected one"—but Pascoe dismissed this objection as too frivolous for notice.

"I pretended to believe him, and told him I was very sorry and hoped he would soon find work. Then he thanked me and said he wished there were more people like me in the world. He said he was sure my father must be very proud of me, and my mother too, for they had every reason to be: and in the end he asked me for the price of a pint."

"Goodness!" Tom exclaimed. Again he wanted to laugh, but instinct warned him that if he did he would hear no more.

"I asked him how much the price of a pint was," Pascoe continued gravely, "and he told me sixpence. But I expect my asking him may have raised his hopes, for when I said I hadn't got sixpence, nor indeed any money at all, he suddenly turned nasty, and wanted to know what I meant by wasting his time. In fact he called me two very bad words, which I think I'd better not repeat, though I dare say you've heard them before."

"I didn't ask you to repeat them," Tom replied; and since Pascoe appeared to have concluded his story he took him to the spot he had thought of for the aquarium, and from there up to the loft to see the aquarium itself.

The loft was a long, low, whitewashed room, lit by a skylight and by a broad window facing the cobbled yard. They climbed up to it from the interior of the motor-house by means of a board with footholes in it, at the top of which was an open trap-door. Its only furniture was a plain solid kitchen table and a couple of chairs, but Pascoe's attention was immediately caught by the railway spread out on the floor, and it was with some difficulty that Tom drew him from this to more important business. "There it is," he said, pointing to the bath, "and what we've got to do is to get it down. I've tied ropes round it, because we'll have to lower it out of the window; the trapdoor's too small."

Even with the window pushed up as high as it would go, it looked as if it might be a narrow squeeze, though, as Pascoe observed, if it had been possible to get the bath into the loft, it must be equally possible to get it out again; and he examined the ropes himself, testing each knot carefully in spite of Tom's repeated assurances. Fortunately the window-ledge was level with the floor, so there would be no hoisting to be done, for the bath was an old-fashioned iron one and remarkably heavy. They pushed it nearly half-way through the window, where it remained poised. "We'd better stand well back," said the prudent Pascoe. "And jolly well mind what you're doing, because it'll give the most frightful jerk once it gets over."

"We can't both stand back, or how are we to push it?" Tom objected, and they were still discussing the problem when Phemie came out into the yard and saw them.

"What are you at now, Master Tom?" she cried in alarm. "Don't you push that bath another inch, or you'll be down after it. . . . Do you hear what I'm telling you . . . ? Wait—I'm coming."

They waited, and Phemie hurriedly crossed the yard and disappeared inside the motor-house. Next moment they heard her laboriously climbing the footboard, for the holes were far apart, and Phemie was stout and hampered by her skirts. Presently her head and shoulders emerged through the trap-door, and they both rushed to her assistance. "Get out of me way," she snapped at them, "I can manage better by myself."

Manage she did, though with much puffing and blowing; and the moment she recovered sufficient breath she began to scold them both impartially, regardless of the fact that she had never seen Pascoe before. Tom tried to explain why they wanted to get the bath down, but she continued to speak her mind, while Pascoe gazed at her with solemn blue eyes. He seemed surprised at Phemie's extremely frank remarks, but Tom wasn't, and moreover knew they wouldn't prevent her from helping them, and that with this powerful aid the job of lowering the bath would be child's play. It was at any rate successful, for there was not even a bump when it reached the ground. "Thanks awfully, Phemie dear," Tom said affectionately, while Pascoe expressed a more reserved gratitude.

The task concluded, Phemie recovered her good humour. "We'll help you down," Tom assured her, but the proffered aid again was refused, though this time more graciously. "Run on now, the both of you—and don't be waiting in the garridge eether, for I know I'll be a sight, with them steps near a yard apart." So they left her, and hovered discreetly just outside the door till she had accomplished the descent. "She's frightfully decent, isn't she?" Tom whispered to Pascoe. "Of course we could have got it down by ourselves in the long run, but it was decent of her all the same, and it saved a lot of bother."

Possibly Phemie overheard these commendations, or guessed them; at all events she continued her good offices by helping them to convey the bath—balanced on the largest wheelbarrow—to its destination. There she left them, amid a shower of renewed thanks. "She's as strong as a horse," Tom murmured in admiration, as he gazed after her broad back. "She's got arms like the Japanese wrestlers in

Granny's picture. She broke the kitchen range one day when she was cleaning it, and *it's* solid iron."

This feat—much, if less appreciatively, commented on at the time by Mother—had greatly impressed him, but Pascoe received it absent-mindedly, for he was thinking of the aquarium. The dogs had already examined this in their own fashion.

"We'll get a spade—two spades—and the thing William uses for cutting edges—it's as sharp as a knife."

They ran to the tool-house, accompanied by Roger and Pincher, while lazy old Barker stretched himself alongside the upturned bath, knowing very well they would soon come back.

"We'd better use the wheelbarrow," Pascoe deliberated, "and put the sods and earth in that. It'll save time and won't make a mess of the grass all round."

Tom agreed; and Pascoe, with the edge-cutter, began at once to outline the cavity they had to dig. He did this with the greatest skill and neatness, as if he had been accustomed to such jobs all his life. Indeed, the superiority of his workmanship was so patent that Tom soon left all the nicer part to him, and even William, whom curiosity presently brought along to see what mischief they were up to, emitted a grunt of approval.

Pascoe alone was not satisfied. "What we need is a beetle, to pound the bottom firm and hard; and a spirit-level too, if we're to get it really right."

"I'll get the——" Tom was beginning, when to his amazement William interrupted him with, "Bide you where you are"; and stalked off.

"He's gone to get them!" Tom marvelled. "At least I believe he has. I bet he wouldn't have got them for me."

He was still pondering on this strange phenomenon when William returned with both beetle and spirit-level. These he handed to Pascoe: to Tom he merely gave instructions to put them back in the tool-house "when the young gentleman has finished with them." After which, he left them to their labours, the most difficult of these being to graduate the slope of the sides to fit the shape of the bath.

It took time, but they both worked hard, and had practically completed the task when Mother came out to invite Pascoe to stay to lunch. "Well, I must say," she exclaimed, "you've done it very neatly! I wonder how much of the neatness is due to—— You haven't told me your friend's name yet, Tom."

"Pascoe," said Tom, who had told her dozens of times.

"I don't mean that. You can hardly expect me to call him Pascoe."

This left Tom at a loss, for he had never thought of any other name. It turned out, too, to be an extremely footling one—Clement—though that of course wasn't Pascoe's fault.

Before she went, just to give Mother an idea of how spacious the aquarium was, Tom decided to put all three dogs in it together. "Look, Mother!"—and he called them.

Mother looked; so did Pascoe; both standing back in order to give Tom and his dogs a free field. The obliging animals immediately approached, wagging their tails. Standing in a row and regarding him with affection, they listened attentively to what he told them; but for all that, they paused on the brink. Tom was surprised. "Don't be so silly," he said; and to prove the aquarium was all right, got into it himself. The dogs watched him benevolently—Barker sitting down to do so—and Pascoe and Mother began to laugh.

If they hadn't laughed Tom might have abandoned his attempt, but now he was determined. So, apparently, were the dogs, though they evinced the greatest good nature, and Barker, who was perhaps growing bored or absent-minded, offered a paw. Tom tried first persuasion and then physical force, but neither availed. He might lift them in, but while they permitted this with a touching docility, they jumped out again so quickly that still there was never more than one in at a time, and Pascoe, when called upon to help, proved useless. Very nervously he lifted Pincher, choosing him because he was the smallest; but at the first growl he hastily set him down again.

"I think you'd better leave them, dear, and come in and get ready for lunch," Mother said. "They evidently don't like it."

"Wait just a minute," Tom begged, but Mother had waited quite long enough, and since she now left them and returned to the house, there was no point in continuing the demonstration.

"I wonder *why* they won't get in?" Tom murmured, puzzled. Pascoe suggested that it was because they were stupid, but to this Tom shook his head. "Well—the next thing, I suppose, is to get water; and we'll have to carry it in cans, for the hose wouldn't reach half-way."

Pascoe, who with his hands in his pockets was contemplating their morning's work, did not at once reply, and when he did, it was to say that that wasn't the next thing. "If you fill it with water now, you'll only have to empty it again."

"Why?" Tom asked, for he was impatient to see what it would look like. There could be no denying that it still closely resembled a bath; but by planting moss— Or perhaps stones, with rock plants, would be better. . . .

"I went down town on Saturday afternoon," Pascoe continued— "to the library; and looked up aquariums in the Encyclopedia; and you ought to make a gravel bed at the bottom, and plant water weeds in it to keep the water pure. Real aquariums have running water, but it says the other will do; and snails help too. If the water isn't kept fresh it gets an awful smell and all the things die. But it doesn't do to change it; that's just as bad; so we'll plant weeds and get a lot of snails."

Tom felt a little annoyed that he hadn't thought of looking up the Encyclopedia himself. He also felt, or was beginning to suspect, that his part in the aquarium was going to be a secondary one—that of assistant to the more efficient and thorough Pascoe. Not that he really minded. Pascoe wasn't like Max Sabine; there was nothing bossy or superior about him. "We'll get gravel from the stream in the glen after lunch," he said; "and we'd better go in now, for I have to look after the dogs' dinner."

Later, when they were seated at the table, it became clear to him that Mother had taken a liking to Pascoe. Somehow this faintly amused him, he didn't know why. He himself thought Pascoe was jolly decent, but at the same time there were certain things about him that made it quite easy to understand Brown's attitude. Boys like Brown were bound to think him a bit of a squirt, and once or twice during the morning Tom had not been wholly exempt from this feeling himself. For one thing, Pascoe sometimes talked—was talking now for instance—in the most frightfully grown-up way; never raising his voice or getting excited; never interrupting, though Mother sometimes took a long time to say what she wanted to say, because this usually reminded her of a lot of other things which she had to deal with before getting back to the main thing, so that now and then she had to ask you what that was.

Daddy never interrupted her either, but it wasn't the same. He simply sat there with a look of resignation on his face, as different as possible from Pascoe's polite attention. Anyhow, Mother was growing more and more pleased with him. She hoped he would be able to spend the rest of the day with Tom, because she and Daddy were going out after tea and wouldn't be back till fairly late in the evening.

There wouldn't be any regular dinner for them, but Phemie would see to it that at least they weren't starved.

"High tea," Tom thought; and it would be good fun having it by themselves. He would pour out. Mary of course would want to, but he wouldn't let her. It was disappointing, therefore, when Pascoe said he must go home soon after lunch, because he was being taken into town to get a new suit of clothes. He promised, on the other hand, to stay as long as he could, and this so positively that it caused Mother to reverse her invitation. She now thought he ought to be home by three o'clock at the latest, since Mrs. Pascoe might have a number of things to do in town, and he certainly oughtn't to keep her waiting.

"That means we'd better put off getting the gravel till to-morrow," Tom said. "But I can show you the stream now; there's tons of time for that."

Out in the garden, he collected the dogs and took Pascoe through the side door leading to the glen, where they all scrambled down to the water's edge. Here they followed the stream, through chequered sunlight and leafy shadows, noting where in its broken course there were beds of fine sand and gravel. "We'll have to bring buckets, and it'll take a good many journeys, for we won't be able to carry more than a half a bucketful at a time, gravel's so heavy. . . ." Suddenly he broke off. "Oh, don't let Pincher drink or he'll be sick! Pincher! Pincher! Good dog . . . ! Now stay there or you'll get a smack. . . . He always *will* drink after his dinner, and it gives him indigestion, and then he's sick. It doesn't matter so much at home, because later on he eats it up again, but here it would all be wasted."

Pascoe looked disgusted, and Tom thought he must be terribly sensitive, for he himself could see nothing disgusting about it. To rectify matters, he hastened to explain what actually happened. "It's quite clean: it comes out exactly the way it was when he swallowed it— perfectly smoothly—just the way meat comes out of a mincing-machine. And it's only his dinner: you wouldn't notice the slightest difference really, except that it's perhaps a bit more mixed up and in the shape of a sausage."

"Oh for goodness' sake!" Pascoe exclaimed. "You'd make anybody ill the way you talk!"

"I wouldn't," Tom answered indignantly. "If you're so easily made ill you won't be much good as a scientist."

"It's nothing to do with science," Pascoe returned disdainfully. "I'm not going to be a vet."

Meanwhile Roger and Barker had been splashing up and down the stream—particularly Barker. Except in an occasional pool the water wasn't deep enough for swimming, but they both liked wading, and nosing about after fugitive scents. "We'll not bring them when we're collecting," Pascoe muttered, "or we won't get a thing." He sat down on a fallen tree-trunk and Tom sat beside him. "I don't know that this stream will be much good anyhow," Pascoe went on—"not nearly so good as a pond, or even the river. We want tadpoles for one thing, and there are none here."

"There are spricks though," Tom said, "and I know a pond where there are plenty of tadpoles. There are little eels, too, in the river—whole shoals of them—and they're quite easy to catch if you don't frighten them."

"We'll get some, but we chiefly want tadpoles, so that we can watch them changing into frogs. In a book called *Pond Life* it says there's a kind that turns into newts, but I don't expect you get them in this country. They're quite common in England, but you never get anything in this country: it's the worst possible country for naturalists. . . . Look!"

The last word came in so vehement a whisper that it would have been a hiss had it contained a sibilant. At the same time he had grabbed Tom by the arm and was staring up at the opposite bank of the glen. Tom, momentarily startled, also turned in that direction, and saw between the trees—about twenty yards away and at the very top of the bank—the figure of a man watching them. "It's him," Pascoe whispered. "*Now*, what do you say?"

Actually Tom said nothing, it was Pincher who gave tongue. He remained where he was, however, pressed against Tom's legs, and the other dogs didn't even bark. Nevertheless, the man, who could only have been there for a minute or two, retreated out of sight.

So absorbed had both boys been in planning, making, and discussing their aquarium, that it had driven every other thought out of their heads and they had forgotten all about the burglar. But now even Tom could not help thinking there might be something in Pascoe's idea. They sat in silence till the latter, still speaking in a whisper, asked: "Why has he been lurking about all this time? What has he been doing—or do you think he's been away and come back again?"

Tom couldn't imagine; it certainly looked queer; though he still had not quite adopted Pascoe's sinister view. "He may have been over at Denny's—doing some job—and they may have given him his dinner: they're very decent—especially Mrs. Denny."

"It's taken him a long time to eat it then," Pascoe replied. "But perhaps now he's seen the dogs he'll clear off permanently. . . . I wonder if he knows your father and mother are going out for the evening."

"How could he know?" Tom exclaimed. "I didn't even know myself. And if he was really spying, as you say, he must have seen the dogs before. Anyhow Phemie and Mary will be there; and I thought your idea was that he was going to break into the house in the middle of the night."

Nevertheless, Pascoe's last remark suggested to him a scheme, which he determined to put into practice. If nothing else, at least it would be good fun; and he might never have the opportunity, or at any rate so good an excuse, again.

"If I were you," Pascoe was saying, "I'd tell your mother before she goes out. I'd come with you myself, only I ought to be going home. It must be precious near three o'clock already, if not after it."

He got up as he spoke, and Tom and the dogs accompanied him to see him off. "I'll come over to-morrow," Pascoe promised, and finally, before mounting his bicycle, he repeated still more urgently his advice about telling Mother.

14: TOM waited until Pascoe was out of sight before turning away. But he did not go back to the house, he followed the road for some fifty yards till he reached a five-barred gate. This he climbed, and was in the fields.

The cool breeze which had freshened the morning had now died down, and the hot sun brought out powerfully the heavy drowsy scents of whin and meadow-sweet. It was a lazy, sleepy afternoon, Tom thought. And in harmony with it, he himself felt agreeably lazy, as he loitered along the deeply-rutted cart-track skirting the outlying fields of Denny's farm. These stretched away on his right, while on his left was a broad ditch with a high bank topped by a tangled hedge of hawthorn, honeysuckle, and briar, broken at intervals by trees—ash, willow, or oak—and by rough grey boulders stained with moss and lichen. The dogs plunged in and out of the ditch, which was at present dry, innumerable plants having drawn up its moisture—vetches, cow-parsley, ragged-robin and foxgloves. The ferns and ivy, which would gradually darken as summer advanced, were still vividly green; and the leaves of the trees had a similar freshness—narrow oval willow leaves, serrated oak leaves, shining beech leaves, and cool delicate ash sprays. A cawing of rooks floated from the direction of the farm-house half a mile away.

The dogs were hunting, but in a desultory fashion, and they raised nothing. Suddenly Pincher disappeared down a cavernous rabbit-hole. Tom had known he would, for every time they passed that way the same thing happened. The hole had been abandoned long ago, and Pincher must have known this, but it possessed an irresistible fascination for him, and by frequent excavations he had so widened the entrance that now it would nearly have admitted Tom himself. The pertinacious Pincher had even managed to turn a corner, so that only his tail and frantically-working hind-legs were visible amid the showers of sand he scattered behind him. Tom, standing above the hole, could hear his fore-paws scratching underground, and wondered how he prevented the sand from getting into his eyes. He must keep them shut, he supposed, for it never did; and then, through the noise Pincher was making, he heard very faint little squeals. *Something* alive was there—something much smaller than a rabbit—and he tried to get Pincher to come out.

But this was difficult, and before he had succeeded in gripping him, Pincher emerged backwards of his own accord, holding in his mouth a wretched little mouse, whom Tom hastened to rescue. He was too late; the mouse appeared to be dead; and yet Tom, examining the tiny body closely while he stroked it with one finger, could discover no wound. The mouse *might* not be dead, for he remembered once rescuing a young thrush from a cat, and the thrush had lain unconscious just like this, yet after a few minutes had suddenly recovered and flown away. Perhaps the mouse too would recover, though mice were much more easily killed than birds, and Pincher was rough and clumsy, not in the least like a cat.

He lifted the body and laid it on the grass under some dock leaves where he could keep an eye on it and see that Pincher, who had been very good about giving it up, did not return to have another look. The dogs at first waited with him, but presently, knowing he would not go home without them, wandered on. They still kept to the bank, because it was pitted with innumerable rabbit-holes, and though the inhabitants of these at the first alarm had all scuttled into safety, everywhere enticing smells were calling for investigation.

Tom, left alone, retreated a few yards into the deep green meadow, which looked cool and inviting, though actually he would have found it cooler in the ditch itself. Lying on his back, he gazed up through the tall feathery grass at the sky, and nibbled a leaf of crimson-seeded sorrel. Now that Daddy and Mother were gone out for the evening, he thought it would be pleasant to stay here till the moon rose, and wished he had brought some provisions with him, and also his mouth-organ. He plucked a clover-blossom and tried to suck out the honey, but the quantity he could extract was so small that it left no more than a faint ghost of sweetness on his tongue. . . .

It was very still—so still that when he listened attentively he could hear stealthy movements in the unmown grass all round him, where a hidden life was in full activity. Perhaps this activity ceased at night, but just now there was an extraordinary busyness, as if all these minute creatures were intent each on his own private work—getting food, looking after eggs, bringing up families—and hadn't a minute to waste in idleness. A very big beetle—broad, polished, and black as ebony—climbed on to the back on Tom's open hand, clutching it with sharp little feet, as if with the friendliest intention. A bumble-bee alighted on the tuft of clover from which he had plucked his flower, and like the beetle, he looked enormous—which was strange, seeing that the mouse, who was really much bigger than either of them, had looked extremely small. Perhaps, when you came to consider them, most things were strange, Tom thought. It was strange, doubtless, that he should feel sure that the bumble-bee was a very simple and good-natured person, and the beetle affectionate—for this latter feeling was produced entirely by the grip of his tiny feet. No, not entirely; because there was no reason why the beetle should have climbed on to Tom's hand unless he had wanted to be friends. . . .

He began to grow drowsy, and the endless summer murmur whispered in his ear, "Sleepy-head, sleepy-head, go to sleep." An orange-tipped butterfly, wavering past, hovered for a moment above him, as if uncertain whether or not to alight: from the far side of the meadow came the peculiar wooden "crake—crake" of the corncrakes calling to one another; and once, from still farther off, he heard the harsh cry of a heron. By and by he heard the movements of what must be some quite large animal in the grass, and cautiously raised himself to look. A hare had come out on to the cart-track not more than three yards away, so that when he raised his head, Tom could clearly see his nostrils working. He tried hard, by wishing, to make the hare come to him, but instead he suddenly bounded across the ditch and was gone. . . .

Tom had forgotten all about the mouse, and must have been lying there dreaming for quite a long time before he next remembered him and went to look. The mouse, too, was gone. . . .

Well, that was a good thing at any rate. The mouse now would be able to tell his wife and children of the terrible adventure he had had. Tom could imagine him repeating the story again and again until the mother mouse said, "You've told us that before, dear," when he would relapse into offended silence. . . .

The bumble-bees must have their nest under the twisted roots of that old thorn-tree, where they were flying in and out. It was a good place, the entrance being hidden by a bramble-bush. Close by, under a flat mossy stone, there must certainly be a colony of ants, for he could see several on the stone itself. He partially raised it, and there they were —plunged instantaneously into commotion, scuttling off in every direction with their precious eggs, which must be saved at all costs. It was extraordinary how every creature, down to the very smallest, immediately knew what to do in an emergency. Their efforts might not always be successful, but they never failed to grasp the one chance of success.

Was it cleverness? Frogs, Pascoe declared, always came back to spawn in the pond where they had been born as tadpoles. When they grew up into frogs they scattered over the countryside, but they always came back to spawn in their own pond, though it might be half a mile or a mile or even two miles off. How did they find their way . . . ? And the three swallows' nests under eaves of the stables at home—every year the same swallows came back to them. Distance did not to seem matter. They did not have to search about, but came directly, unerringly, like a needle to a magnet. It couldn't be cleverness; cleverness wouldn't help in the least. Miss Sabine said it was instinct, and instinct, she said, was inherited memory; but she had been unable to tell him why swallows had inherited a memory so good that it could guide them all the way from Egypt to the exact spot in Ballysheen where their nests were. He didn't believe it was memory at all. Mother's view, that they had simply been created by God with a special gift, seemed far more satisfactory, though it didn't explain how the gift worked. . . .

Here was old Roger back again. That was like him. Tom had known he would be the first to come back, just to make sure that all was well. Roger was a good dog, "lovely and pleasant in his ways," like Saul and Jonathan in the Bible: though Saul hadn't been so lovely and pleasant when he had thrown javelins at David. Pincher would be the next to come: both Roger and Pincher would search for him a long time rather than go home without him.

Barker wouldn't. At least he might or he mightn't—it all depended on whether he got bored or not. If he got bored he would be just as likely to trot quietly home by himself. Tom could never tell how much Barker liked him, and there was no use asking him, for he wouldn't say. . . .

He whistled, and at the third or fourth whistle Pincher came bursting through the hedge, evidently having been hunting on the farther side. But still no Barker. It was getting late too, so Tom turned slowly homeward, though he didn't care for this way of doing things, and paused every few yards to repeat his whistle. But he might have saved his breath, for, as he had half expected, the very first object to meet his eyes when he turned in at the gate was Barker himself, reclining peacefully beside a croquet-hoop. Why did he behave like that? Tom couldn't understand it. Yet neither could he accuse Barker of having abandoned the party, for he hadn't, he was waiting for them here, and the very way he rose now, with a friendly wag of his stumpy tail, showed an untroubled conscience. Tom sighed, and thought how different Roger was—and even Pincher. He brought the whole lot of them into the house to keep him company while he was at tea, and though Mary shook her head, he knew this was merely perfunctory and meant nothing. What was much less perfunctory was her exclamation, "Well of all——!" followed by an eloquent silence, when she came in later to clear the table. Yet there was really nothing to exclaim at, except that, so far as food was concerned, a clearance had already been effected. Mary shoo'd the replete and torpid Pincher out of her way, remarking while she did so that Master Sabine had called early in the afternoon.

Tom's face darkened. He pushed away his plate and pushed back his chair. "What did he want?" he asked petulantly. He had known, of course, that Max would be coming home very soon, but he had forgotten; and in sudden anxiety he added; "You didn't tell him about the aquarium, did you?"

Mary replied that she had told him nothing. "It was the mistress he was talking to; and he only stayed a wee minute anyhow, so perhaps it was just a message he brought."

Tom was only partially reassured. The aquarium belonged exclusively to himself and Pascoe, and he wasn't going to have Max butting in so long as he could keep him out. He could make an aquarium of his own if he wanted one, and he determined to tell Pascoe to-morrow that under no circumstances was Max to be encouraged.

Calling the dogs, he went out to make sure that everything was as he had left it, and also to pass the time till he could put his plan for the night into action. It was really quite a simple plan—or at least it would be if only Mary and Phemie would take it into their heads to go for a walk. But with Mother and Daddy both out he supposed there wasn't much chance of this, and he daren't overtly suggest it for fear of arousing suspicion. He *had* mentioned to Mary what a beautiful evening it was, yet even that had drawn from her a suspicious glance. It was pretty rotten when you couldn't make a remark about the weather without being credited with ulterior motives. . . .

Anyhow, the initial step, which had consisted in giving the dogs a good solid meal that would last them till morning, was safely accomplished: the second—which was to smuggle them secretly up to his bedroom—would be much more ticklish, for here the slightest hitch would prove fatal. Roger and Barker he thought he could count on, but he was not so sure of Pincher. It might be better to explain the exact scheme to them beforehand, since after all you never knew—or at least Tom never knew—how much of what you said they understood.

So he sat down on a bench under the study window, and got all three dogs before him in a row. Then, very slowly and distinctly, he told them his plan. They listened—Pincher, as usual, cocking his head on one side to do so—and at the conclusion all wagged their tails in approval. So far so good; the plan appeared to have been passed unanimously: on the other hand it had yet to be put into action.

Twilight was drawing on. The new moon, like a slender silver bow, had risen in a fading sky, and pallid moths were flickering in ghostly flight above the rose-bushes. Two or three bats wheeled round the trees, uttering faint yet shrill squeakings as they seized their prey. Not every ear could catch that high note, but Mother's could, and so could Tom's. Presently, breaking in on the quietness, came the noise of the gate opening and closing, and a few seconds later he saw the Sabines' maid approaching up the drive. This was better luck than he could have hoped for, and most cordially he returned her "Good evening" as she passed on round to the back of the house. She must have come, he guessed, to see Phemie and Mary, and being well acquainted with the conversational powers of all three, he knew he could now take a whole regiment of dogs upstairs without attracting attention.

It might, nevertheless, be just as well to seize the opportunity at once, while the going was good; so he gathered his flock around him and cautiously approached and opened the hall door. The flock followed with equal caution—in fact not only behaved, but looked, so extremely like conspirators, that it was quite clear they must have understood his lecture. Noiselessly all four ascended the stairs, but it was not till they were safely in his own room that Tom at last breathed a sigh of satisfaction. So did Pincher, who immediately jumped on to the bed, though the others, better-mannered, remained standing on the floor. Then Tom remembered that he hadn't drunk his glass of milk, which he must do, or Phemie and Mary might think he was still out and go in search of him. Telling the dogs therefore to be good, he ran downstairs, hastily swallowed the milk, and left a pencilled scrawl beside the glass to say he had gone to bed. . . .

When he returned to his room Roger and Barker, influenced no doubt by Pincher's bad example, were now also on the bed, while Pincher himself had found an even more luxurious resting-place on the pillow. It was extraordinary how quickly they had grasped the situation and made their preparations for the night. All the same, these preparations would have to be modified. "I suppose I'm to sleep in a chair," Tom said sarcastically, "or on the floor"—but the only effect of his irony was a partial unclosing of eyes, and a faint movement of tails in drowsy acquiescence; nobody budged.

Tom undressed, put on his pyjamas, and knelt down to say his prayers. These consisted of a short prose prayer and a hymn; but Barker, who was nearest, kept snuffing at his hair in a most distracting way, so he hastily finished and rose from his knees.

"How do you expect me to get in?" he asked, as he stood beside them. "Here Pincher, you come off that pillow at any rate!—and you'd better all get down for a minute."

They did so, Roger and Pincher at once, Barker more reluctantly and with an audible grumble. But Tom wasn't going to have any nonsense of that sort and gave him a shove. Then he slid between the sheets, settled himself, patted the counterpane, and next moment was nearly smothered under an avalanche of dogs.

By degrees, however, after some pushing and pawing, all found suitable places, and for a while peace reigned. Yet, though the dogs appeared to have fallen asleep almost instantly, Tom, for some reason, had never felt wider awake, and moreover it seemed a pity, in fact a positive waste of this golden opportunity, to go to sleep so soon. Down below, he heard Phemie and Mary coming out of the kitchen with their visitor, and from the fact that shortly afterwards he heard them closing the hall door and coming out into the garden, he guessed that they must have seen his note, and now intended to walk back with her to the Rectory. He listened to the sound of their receding voices and footsteps, and a few seconds later to the distant clang of the gate. They were gone—probably for an hour at least—a fine chance for Pascoe's burglar if he had known—and if he actually existed. . . .

But as yet it was much too early for burglars, whether real or imaginary: certainly things couldn't have worked out better. The dogs, to be sure, appeared to have settled down for the night, but that could soon be altered. In the grey cold light of the quarter-moon their slumbering forms were dimly visible—Roger and Barker on either side of him, Pincher down near his feet. Therefore the first thing to do was to make rats of his feet—rats moving stealthily beneath the bedclothes.

"Rats!" Tom said aloud, and Pincher trembled, cocking one ear out of dreamland, but otherwise not stirring.

"Rats!" Tom said again, and at the repetition the rats themselves made so vigorous an upheaval that Pincher could no longer ignore them. He raised his head, but at the same time he yawned. Very well he knew that these were no true rats, but only Tom's feet. Still, since it seemed to be expected of him and a game was always a game, he made a pounce. After that there was no more sleep for anybody, even the sedate Barker joining in the hunt.

The rat hunt was merely a prelude—designed to remove constraint and set things going; the next item was choral singing. Tom himself had taught them this, only hitherto it had been practised out of doors; within four walls it was infinitely more telling. The volume of sound was indeed remarkable. What it was all about—that is to say, the precise subject of the song—he had never been able to discover; though that it was in essence religious, a sort of hymn to some great invisible spirit—Universal Pan very likely—seemed indicated by its fervour. Yet to-night Tom was inclined to a more secular interpretation. True, he still couldn't make out the exact words, the din was too great, but with a little assistance from his imagination he could fancy them going something like this, the influence of Pincher being unmistakable, especially in the last lines:

> *Who's got a bone for Barker?*
> *Who's got a bone for he?*
> *A comic old dog and a larker,*
> *Most excellent companee:*
> *So who's got a bone for Barker,*
> *A juicy Be Oh En Eee?*

> *Who's got a bone for Pincher?*
> *A bone with a bit of meat.*
> *Bad luck to the one that would stint yer*
> *O' things for to drink and to eat:*
> *So who's got a bone for Pincher?*
> *Who wants for to give him a treat?*

> *Who's got a bone for Roger?*
> *Roger's the pick of the lot;*
> *An honest old dog, not a dodger;*
> *So fish out a bone from the pot.*
> *Is it deaf that you are, y'ould cod yer—*
> *Bones is bones, whether cold or hot.*

* * * * *

"Tom!"

The door had opened, the light was on, and Mother stood there, her face and whole attitude expressive of mingled consternation, astonishment, and displeasure. A profound silence ensued. The dogs hung their heads and looked guilty; Tom looked *very* guilty; and Mother—a most unexpected apparition, for she ought to have been miles away—paused, as if to allow this accumulated sense of guilt to sink well in. . . .

They must have come home early! Had Daddy heard the noise? He could hardly help hearing it, though evidently he had driven the car on round to the garage, leaving Mother to deal with the situation.

She proceeded to do so, while the culprits gazed at her, mute and conscience-stricken. "You're an extremely naughty boy! We came back early because Daddy has a bad headache, and this is what we find! Phemie and Mary both out; and you with the dogs on your bed, though you know very well you're not allowed to bring them upstairs. Just look at that counterpane! Not only filthy dirty, but with a great rent in it!"

Tom looked, and could not deny that the counterpane had suffered, though till Mother had turned on the light he had not been aware of it. The rats, he supposed—Pincher was always so careless! But he had never been told not to bring dogs up to bed with him; possibly because nobody had ever dreamed that he would do so. Still, the fact remained, and he hastened to point it out to Mother. Instantly she asked him; "Did you think I would allow you to bring them up?"—a question admitting of only one answer.

On the other hand, he had had a special reason to-night, which made all the difference, and he proceeded to relate the story of the burglar.

She listened, yet though he tried hardest to impart to it something of Pascoe's impressiveness, it did not appear to be impressing Mother. Instead of comment, when he had finished she simply asked a further question, which, if answered truthfully, would nullify everything he had said. "Did you really think a burglar was going to break into the house?"

"I—I—I thought—perhaps Pascoe thought so."

It sounded feeble—very, very feeble—and he knew it. So, from their dejected attitudes, he gathered, did the dogs. "In that case, why did you let Phemie and Mary go out?" Mother said. "And why didn't you tell me about it before *I* went out?"

"Pascoe advised me to tell you," Tom put in eagerly.

"Yet you didn't. Why?"

"I—I thought——"

Mother waited rather grimly, and then answered for him. "Yes; you thought that if you didn't it would be a good excuse for keeping the dogs with you."

Since this was the exact truth, Tom could only try to look injured.

"Well, they're going home now at all events," Mother continued firmly. "And I'm very much disappointed: I thought I could have trusted you."

"But it's so late," Tom pleaded.

"It's not a bit late," Mother replied; and after a further look at the counterpane added ominously: "I don't know what Daddy will say to all this!"

Tom didn't either, and remained silent until he murmured with deep feeling, "Poor Daddy! Don't you think it might make his headache worse to be worried—I mean, if you told him?"

This sudden sympathy, instead of mending matters, appeared to have precisely the opposite effect. "Don't be a little hypocrite," Mother answered sharply. "Much you care about Daddy's headache! And at any rate he knows already: we heard the noise before we ever reached the gate. Come, Roger and Barker: you've got to go home. That's all your friend has done for you."

"And Pincher?" the friend ventured, in the infinitely forlorn hope that Pincher might be left.

But Mother was adamant. "Pincher is included with the others," she said, and Tom watched her leave the room, taking the three dogs with her.

PART TWO

THE ENEMY

15: TOM expected Pascoe to make at least some allusion to the burglar when he next appeared; but no,
not a word. This was annoying. "I thought you were so anxious!"
he reminded him sarcastically, but Pascoe remained unruffled.

"So I was," he said, "till I saw it was all right."

"How did you see it was all right? Even if he *had* come, I don't
suppose he would have burned the house down. I don't believe you
ever thought he was a burglar at all."

"I did; and he was. . . . Where are the buckets?"

"In their skins. You got *me* into a nice row . . . ! Just because I
took the dogs up to my bedroom as you told me to do."

"I never," Pascoe cried indignantly. "What I told you was to
warn your mother."

"So I did too—afterwards—and she says you invented the whole
thing for your own amusement."

"You saw him yourself," Pascoe returned loftily. "Why are you
trying to put it all on to me? The next time I see burglars prowling
round your house I'll jolly well let them do what they like."

Tom was unmoved by this threat, and they were still wrangling,
though with perfectly amicable feelings, when the last thing either
of them expected happened; the burglar himself appeared, actually
walking up the drive, boldly and in broad daylight. He even had
the cheek to grin and wink the eye of an old acquaintance at Pascoe,
who naturally gave him a freezing look in return. Tom laughed, his
sympathies had now veered round to the burglar, who looked precisely what from the beginning he had claimed to be, an "out-of-work"
in search of a job. In order to clinch matters he ran in to tell

97

Mother, and was still further tickled when she came out, talked to the burglar, and eventually called William to see if he could find something for him to do. William then took him in tow, and both went around to the yard.

Pascoe had watched all this coldly from a distance, but disappointingly made no comment when Tom rejoined him. Instead, he remarked, "We're wasting time," with the air of one whose patience, though great, is not inexhaustible. "He's as obstinate as a mule," Tom thought, yet not without a certain appreciation, as they collected the buckets and went down to the stream.

While they worked, toiling to and fro between the stream and the aquarium, his cogitations shifted from the burglar to Max Sabine. It was three months now since he had last seen Max, but he gladly would have extended the period indefinitely. True, there was no particular reason why he should expect him to-day, except that he had called yesterday—on the pretext, Mother said, of looking for Pincher. Nevertheless Tom felt sure he *would* come. . . . That is to say, supposing he could find nothing better to do—his visits had always been contingent upon this. Certainly the fact that they had quarrelled violently on their last meeting would not deter him. . . .

The quarrel had not been altogether for the reason Althea supposed. That, indeed, had been the climax, but there had been several unpleasant incidents before the James-Arthur episode had finally opened Tom's eyes. Max might think he had forgotten, but he hadn't: he had made up his mind last April to have nothing more to do with him, and his determination remained unchanged. It seemed, therefore, the moment to warn Pascoe. He had already done so more or less, but it could do no harm to be a little more explicit. "Of course he mayn't come," he wound up, after a brief summary of the situation—"but if he does, don't be letting him interfere, which is what he'll want to do."

Pascoe had set down his bucket, glad of a temporary rest, for they were both by this time wet and weary. "What's he like?" he asked.

Tom with difficulty concealed his irritation. He had already told Pascoe what Max was like, and he now added pointedly: "He's like Brown, only far worse." Not that he himself had the least feeling against Brown, but because he knew from past experience that Max's first aim would be to try to establish an understanding with Pascoe, and he thought this would be the best way to guard against such an alliance. Unwarned, Pascoe was far too simple to realize Max's cun-

ning: in fact, if left to himself, he would be a lamb in his hands, because for all his cleverness Pascoe was really as innocent as a baby,
and Max could be most ingratiating.

They worked all morning without interruption, and by lunch-time
the aquarium was finished, filled with water, and ready to receive its
destined inhabitants. Pascoe, having conscientiously repeated a message from home to the effect that Mrs. Barber wasn't to allow him to
be a nuisance, again accepted an invitation to lunch, during which
meal Mother had a lot to tell them about the new man, who evidently
had poured out all his misfortunes to her. His name was Patrick Keady,
and according to Mother, or rather according to the story he had told
her—for she was going to make further inquiries before accepting it
as gospel—he was a most domestic and virtuous character, out of
employment through no fault of his own, and, like other unskilled
labourers, finding it very difficult to get a fresh start. At this point
Tom couldn't resist glancing at Pascoe, expecting to see him looking
a little abashed; but not a bit of it; Pascoe, prim and demure as ever,
returned the glance with his usual calm and steady gaze. The extraordinary thing was that Mother did not appear to have identified her
protégé with their burglar, or else, since this seemed scarcely credible,
was deliberately avoiding that aspect of the subject in order to spare
Pascoe's feelings. She needn't have worried, Tom could have told her;
there was a sort of "Time-will-show" expression on Pascoe's face,
which plainly indicated that he still held to his first opinion.

As soon as he got him alone, Tom tried to reason with him, pointing out the wretched nature of the evidence which was all he could
produce in support of his prejudice; but he had scarcely begun when
he broke off abruptly, for at that moment he caught sight of Max.
Instantly his face clouded. "Here he is!" he ejaculated in a rapid undertone, while Max, in a self-possessed and leisurely fashion, got off
his bicycle, leaned it against a tree, and strolled towards them across
the grass.

They watched him, themselves motionless and silent, but their
guarded attitude did not appear to embarrass the visitor. "Well, well,
well!" he explained jocularly, approaching the aquarium. "What's
all this?"—just as if it wasn't perfectly obvious what it was.

Max had grown a lot in the past three months—or at any rate Tom
thought so. In contrast with Pascoe and himself he looked tall and
languidly elegant; but then of course he was nearly four years older
than they were, and had always been given to plastering his hair and

trying to make himself look like an illustration in an American magazine. He was supposed by most people to be very handsome—just because he had finely-moulded features, a clear olive skin, and dark sleepy eyes—but Tom disliked his appearance, and particularly dislike his thin-lipped mouth, which he thought unpleasant and sneering. Pascoe meanwhile stood staring at him, as if seeking a resemblance to the notorious Brown—a resemblance certainly not there, Brown being anything but languid, and his dimpled, smiling countenance reflecting at all times an inveterate good-nature.

"It's our aquarium," Tom muttered unwillingly, wishing they had started out at once to collect their specimens, instead of lingering over lunch, discussing Keady and other things with Mother.

Max's smile was the patronizing one of a fully-fledged adolescent schoolboy among kids. He kicked the brim of the bath and remarked: "What's the good of an aquarium with nothing in it? D'you keep it for washing the dogs? Here, Pincher!"—and he threw in the skin of the banana he was eating.

It was no doubt a very mild offence, and coming from anybody else Tom would not have resented it, but now he flushed angrily and grabbed Pincher by the collar before he could move, while Pascoe cried: "Don't!"—and proceeded to fish out the banana skin with his net.

Max turned at the word, as if discovering for the first time that Tom was not alone. "Hello!" he said, raising his eyebrows. "Where did *you* spring from?"

Pascoe blushed, but Tom replied for him. "He didn't spring from anywhere: it's you who sprang. And if you didn't see him till now your eyesight must be defective."

It was an unpromising beginning, and Max, though not in the least disconcerted, evidently decided to alter his tone. "Sorry," he apologized: "I was only ragging."

Tom said nothing, but Pascoe quite unnecessarily began to explain that they had only finished the aquarium that morning, and hadn't had time to stock it yet.

To Tom's secret disappointment, Max immediately dropped his air of superiority and became all friendliness and good humour. "Let's get some things now," he proposed. "What about the mill-dam? It used to be a good place."

The artless Pascoe at once responded to this change of manner. "We didn't think of the mill-dam, did we?" he said to Tom. "I didn't

even know there was one. We might have a look at it first—though
the book says a pond's the best. Still, a mill-dam might have fish in it"
—and to Tom's annoyance he clearly accepted the idea that Max was
going to help them: in fact Pascoe was behaving in exactly the way
he had been cautioned not to.

"There's a pond there too," Max continued. "At least, it's not far
off: I'll show you."

"I can show him," Tom interrupted pugnaciously. "I told him
about it yesterday"—for this was his tadpole pond, which he had
been reserving as a special surprise. "I suppose you're going for a
ride," he went on, though he supposed nothing of the sort.

Nor, apparently, did Max, who merely answered; "No; I think I'll
come with you."

Tom was silenced. He knew Max understood him perfectly, but he
also knew that (with Pascoe so conspicuously failing to back him up)
this would make no difference. Nevertheless he persevered. "We've
only got two nets," he said; and this hint also being ignored, he added
disagreeably: "Of course, you can carry the bottles."

It was *meant* to be disagreeable, and drew indeed an expostulatory
glance from Pascoe; but Max only gave him a peculiar look—not at
all pleasant. "Thanks," he drawled, after a deliberate pause. "I think
I'll only superintend. . . . You might fall in, you know."

The last words were obviously spoken in mockery, but Pascoe—
who really was behaving most stupidly—took them seriously. "The
mill-dam, do you mean? Is it deep?"

"Awfully deep," Max replied, "with slimy, slippery sides. If you
can't swim, to fall in would be certain death." Then, as Pascoe swallowed this like a glass of milk: "They fished out a man's body last
winter, and the eels had eaten his face off, so that they never would
have found out who he was if a detective hadn't discovered a masonic
sign very faintly tattooed on his chest."

"On his chest!" Pascoe repeated in an awed tone.

"Well, you wouldn't have had it on his——"

"Oh, come on," Tom broke in irritably. "Can't you see he's only
stuffing you up?"

He lifted a net and one of the glass jars as he spoke, and they were
about to set off when Pascoe suggested that they should leave the
dogs behind. "They'll only go splashing about and frightening everything, the way they did yesterday in the stream."

Max glanced sidelong at Tom. "Good idea," he agreed. "We can either leave them here or send them home: they won't mind, and it doesn't much matter if they do."

"Well then," said Pascoe, preparing to start; but abruptly he paused.

For Tom had made no movement to accompany them, but stood there, sullen and hostile, his face black as a thundercloud. "I think you and Max had better go together," he said stiffly to Pascoe; "I'm going with the dogs." And immediately he called them to him, which was hardly necessary, seeing that the faithful creatures were already there and hadn't the slightest intention of leaving him.

Pascoe looked alarmed. He had spoken on impulse, but now he realized his mistake, though still not understanding why Tom should be taking it like this. After all, it wasn't *his* fault that Max was there, and if it came to that, Tom had been just as much to blame as Max for any unpleasantness there had been. However, it was Tom who was his friend; so he said hastily; "We'll bring the dogs"—to which Max added lightly, "The more the merrier."

On this they set off, though, with the exception of Pincher, the only person who appeared to be particularly merry was Max himself, who did most of the talking, and seemed quite unconscious that all was not well. True, he addressed his remarks entirely to Pascoe, but this, in the circumstances, perhaps was not unnatural.

They went down to the river, and crossed by the lock gate to the opposite bank. But for Tom the whole expedition had lost its charm, and he now wished that Max and Pascoe *would* leave him; even his interest in the aquarium had vanished. When they reached the pond the first thing he did was to offer his net to Max, saying he didn't want to fish, and would take the dogs along the river bank and give them a swim.

Max needed no pressing; he simply said "Thanks," and accepted the net; but Pascoe, gazing at Tom dubiously, seemed uncertain what to do. That was his own fault, Tom thought, and he left them, returning to the river, and following it down past the weir to the saw-mill.

This was an ancient and rather primitive construction of rough grey stones, between which bright-green hart's-tongue ferns and crimson valerian and crane's-bill had taken root. They had not only taken root, but had flourished so vigorously that the mill itself appeared to be either emerging from or returning to Nature. In the shadows of its archway the great water-wheel revolved slowly and ponderously with a rumbling noise that made the walls tremble; and from the roof of the arch, in a perpetual twilight, grey stalactites hung down. The water was black as ink, except where it was splashed by the wheel and rose in white showers against the semi-darkness of the cavern beyond; but all around, everything was cool and fresh and green, and Tom, feeling injured, sulky and resentful, lay down in the shade of an ash-tree to brood over his wrongs. Pincher immediately sprawled across his middle, while Roger sat up beside him, and Barker went for a solitary bathe, swimming slowly round and round the dam, occasionally scrambling out to shake himself (when Tom could distinctly hear his ears rattling), but very soon plunging in again. He did all this most solemnly, and yet clearly he was enjoying himself in his own quiet fashion, not troubling his head about what the others did or thought, content if they cared to share his amusement, and equally content if they didn't. . . .

Gradually Tom's mood altered. The rumble and plash of the huge wheel, monotonous and musical, had a tranquillizing effect upon him —lenitive, almost palpable, soothing as oil or balm. Stretched on his back, with his face upturned to the sky, he could not see the wheel; therefore in his imagination it became a living and benevolent monster, guardian of the river and of this green shade. Why were animals —even fabulous and imaginary ones—so much closer to him than human beings? He no longer felt cross, yet neither did he feel the least inclination to rejoin Max and Pascoe. It was they who eventually rejoined him—or rather one of them, for Max, it seemed, had soon grown tired of collecting tadpoles, and suddenly recollecting something much more important he wanted to do, had gone back to the house to get his bicycle, leaving Pascoe to carry the nets and both jam-jars. Pascoe, with a jar in each hand, and the nets tucked under his arm, looked none too pleased by this desertion; but to Tom it was not at all surprising—was in fact just the kind of thing he would have expected from Max.

Pascoe set his burden carefully down on the grass, glanced at Tom with a shade of anxiety, as if not quite certain of his ground, and after a pause asked; "*Are* there any fish in the dam?"

"I don't know; I didn't look."

Another and more prolonged silence followed, and again it was broken by Pascoe. "What were you in such a bait about? I wouldn't have said not to bring the dogs if I'd thought you'd mind. I only meant while we were fishing."

"I know. It wasn't that really. At least it wouldn't have been if he hadn't been there."

"But you were mad with *me*; and I don't see what I had done."

"You didn't do anything. I warned you beforehand what would happen: it's always the same when there's more than one boy there. He makes them quarrel with each other, and he does it on purpose. I told you he had tried to do it with James-Arthur and me, only he didn't succeed. If you'd been alone, or I'd been alone, he'd have been quite different."

"I don't like him much," Pascoe admitted, glancing at the jam-jars.

"He says he has a rook-rifle," he pursued slowly, after another interval, "and that shooting is better sport than making an aquarium. . . . He says he's shot lots of things—birds and rabbits, and a cat. His father gave him a rifle for a birthday present, and thinks there's no harm in shooting—that all healthy-minded boys like it, and that if they don't they must be morbid or something. . . . He offered to let me have a try."

Tom appeared indifferent. "Are you going to?"

"No."

It sounded decisive, yet the word was hardly out of his mouth before the conscientious Pascoe began to fidget uneasily, evidently fearing more might be attached to it than he had actually meant. "It's not that I wouldn't do it," he said, "or that I think shooting's wrong, but——"

"But what?"

"I thought he thought it would annoy you if I did, and that that was really why he offered to let me."

16: AWAKENING in the early morning, Tom had heard the sound of distant drums, but in a minute or two he had dropped off to sleep again, and it was quiet when he awoke once more and this time definitely. Breakfast, he knew, would be earlier than usual, because of the general holiday. It was strange how everything felt so differently on different days. There was a Saturday afternoon feeling, a Sunday feeling, a Monday morning feeling, and there was certainly a twelfth of July feeling. While he was dressing he again caught the far-off beating of drums. William would be walking, and meals would be informal and picnicky, because Phemie and Mary would be getting most of the day off. In the early afternoon Pascoe was to come over, and he and Tom were going to the field to watch the procession. Daddy and Mother might be going too, and there would be speeches—Max's father, who was a great Orangeman, would be making a speech: the field chosen for this year's meeting was only about a mile from the Rectory.

After breakfast he filled a pocket with cherries and went down to the hollow oak to give Edward the squirrel a twelfth of July treat. The whole countryside was deserted, for, except those whom domestic duties confined to the house, and the very smallest of the children, the entire village, dressed in its Sunday clothes, had gone into town holiday-making, though most of them would return in the afternoon in the wake of the great procession.

Tom crossed the meadow and stood beneath the oak. "Edward!" he called, and from the gnarled upper branches a sharp little face with cocked ears and bright eyes peeped down, just to make sure it was the right person. Then Edward descended, leaping swiftly and lightly from branch to branch till he was on a level with Tom's head, when he paused, waiting to see what had been brought to him.

Tom produced a cherry, and Edward, sitting up alertly, took it in his hands. But being rather greedy, and having caught a glimpse of the store from which this was only a sample, he nibbled it hastily and threw it down half finished. "Here!" said Tom; "that won't do. If you're going to be so wasteful I'll eat them myself." As an example, he lifted the rejected cherry and finished it slowly, while Edward watched him and presumably felt ashamed. After that, they divided the remainder between them, though Edward got very much the lion's share, Tom only eating one now and again to keep him company. There were a few nuts to wind up with, but these Edward carried off one by one to his secret store-room. Finally he perched on Tom's shoulder and allowed himself to be scratched and stroked, till the sound of a voice hallooing from a distance made him spring back into the tree like lightning.

The voice was Pascoe's, and Tom answered with a shrill whistle. Pascoe, still invisible, could be heard scrambling up the bank of the glen, and next moment Roger, who must have picked him up somewhere, burst into the open. Pascoe was not so quick, but very soon he also emerged, waving a small flag, and with an orange lily in his buttonhole. "What are you doing? I've been hunting for you all over the place."

"I was feeding Edward," Tom replied. "You told me you weren't coming till the afternoon."

"I know, and I didn't intend to; but Mother thought if I was riding over I'd better start while the road was clear. . . . Who's Edward?"

"He's a squirrel, and lives in this tree: but you've frightened him and now he's hiding. He'd soon come down, all the same, if Roger wasn't there."

Pascoe gazed up through the branches. "What were you giving him?"

"Cherries. . . . Nuts too; but he puts those away. He's got a storehouse where he keeps acorns and beech-nuts and things like that for the winter. . . . I made a storehouse myself—to keep biscuits in—under a tree in the glen; but Barker and Pincher found it and ate the biscuits, though they were in a tin box. I suppose the lid must have come loose."

"You blame everything on Barker and Pincher," Pascoe said. "How do you know it wasn't Roger? He's with you far more than they are."

"Yes, but he wouldn't; he's got a frightfully sensitive conscience and that makes him different from the others."

Pascoe turned a somewhat sceptical eye on Roger. "He wouldn't know it was *your* storehouse. . . . How could he? And if he didn't, I don't see where the conscience comes in."

"He *would* know. As a matter of fact they all knew; because they were with me when I made it. And Barker and Pincher went straight back that very afternoon and dug out the things and ate them."

"But you didn't *see* them do it," Pascoe argued, "you're only guessing."

"I didn't actually see them," Tom admitted; "I never said I saw them. But who else would do it?"

"Roger."

Tom gave a shrug of impatience. "Haven't I just told you Roger wouldn't—because of his conscience."

Pascoe pointed out that because Tom told him a thing didn't necessarily make it true. "If you're so sure about it," he went on, "you must have seen him some time when he *had* done something he shouldn't. Therefore his conscience can't always keep him from doing things."

"Oh, there's no use talking to you."

"Not if you can't talk reasonably. To hear you, you'd think Roger was perfect—a kind of angel."

This was a new idea, and struck by it, Tom did not reply. He, too, surveyed the dog with a conscience, who finding himself the centre of so much attention, wagged his tail and planted his forepaws against his friend's shoulders. "An angel could take any form he wanted to," Tom murmured dreamily. "Roger might be an angel without anybody knowing—a guardian angel. . . . So might Ralph."

He awoke to find Pascoe's gaze—remorseless as an arc-lamp—fixed searchingly upon him. "Who's Ralph?" Pascoe demanded.

"Nobody," Tom answered. . . . "Just a name I saw."

But Pascoe was not satisfied. "If he's just a name it's queer you should have mentioned him! I suppose you mean you don't want to tell me. Is he somebody you're not allowed to know?"

This was so very likely to be true that Tom couldn't help laughing, though he stopped at once when Pascoe began to look offended. "I would tell you about him, only I know you wouldn't believe."

Pascoe said no more, but there was a cloud on his brow which showed what he thought. Tom, for that matter, disliked reservations and secrecy himself, only he was quite sure Pascoe *wouldn't* believe. He might be credulous where burglars were concerned, but that was different. Burglars belonged definitely to this world—were very much solid flesh and blood, whereas——. On the other hand, he didn't want to seem distrustful and uncommunicative, so he compromised by telling the beginning of the story, without mentioning his adventure at Granny's and its sequel. "Ralph is Ralph Seaford. . . . He died when he was a boy, and there's a stained-glass window put up in memory of him in the church. That's how I know his name. His people used to live in Granny's house—Tramore—but they're all dead."

To his great relief he saw that his words suggested nothing to Pascoe beyond their literal meaning. Indeed, Pascoe seemed disappointed. "I don't see why you couldn't have said so at once, then," he grumbled, "instead of making a mystery about it. As it happens, people when they die *don't* become angels. Angels are quite different; they've never been human. So if the window has a picture of an angel, it only means that they hope this boy has gone to heaven."

He paused for a moment, and then pursued cynically "Everybody when they die is supposed by their relations to go to heaven. . . . If you were to judge by all the stuff you read on tombstones you'd think the other place didn't exist."

For Tom it didn't, or rather it didn't interest him, his conception of it being so narrowly cut and dried as to discourage all imaginative speculation, whereas heaven was simply crammed with possibilities. "Do you think there'll be animals there?" he asked, and to his surprise Pascoe, who rarely laughed, gave an odd little chuckle.

"In heaven? Since Roger came from there, I suppose he'll go back again. . . . Which means," he went on, "that you'll have to be jolly careful if you want to be with him instead of with Barker and Pincher."

It was the first joke Tom had ever known him to make, but, though he thought it quite a good one, he pursued his own fancy. "Mother does. . . . She thinks there will be animals for people who wouldn't be happy without them. And the sea will be there for the same reason —for people who are fond of it. . . . Stop!"

The last word was really a cry of alarm, called forth because Pascoe, with the end of a branch, had suddenly begun to poke among the withered leaves gathered in a hole, and Tom knew what else was there. But his warning came too late. Like the imprisoned jinn in the *Arabian Nights* story, a cloud of bees seemed literally to *flow* out, and next moment the air was filled with their angry buzzing. It was no time for hesitation, and Tom and Pascoe took to their heels. Down into the glen they plunged, down the bank and across the stream. Up the other bank—tripping, slipping, and stumbling— trying to beat off their savage assailants, and above all to shield their faces—while Roger barked and raced on ahead. It was not on him, it was on the two boys, that punishment was falling. Utterly reckless of their own lives so long as they could plant a sting somewhere in the enemy, the bees pursued them to the very hall door, and even as Tom slammed it behind him he could see a bee crawling in Pascoe's hair, and feel one or two who must have got down his own back and beneath his shirt. "Come on!" he cried. "We'll have to take off all our clothes. I'm stung in about sixty different places, and there are some still walking about, I can feel them."

Nor had he greatly exaggerated. Up in his bedroom, when they had pulled off their shirts and turned them inside out, they found several bees still alive. Now that the attack was over, Tom began to laugh, but Pascoe seemed not far from weeping, for though both were about equally stung the effect upon him had been much more severe. Upon Tom it had been no more than the stabbing of a number of little red-hot needles; the pain, though sharp, was superficial.

Pascoe, on the contrary, where the stings had entered was already beginning to swell up in surprising little lumps, so that Tom, alarmed by the spectacle presented, opened the door and shouted for Mother.

"Wait!—wait!" Pascoe cried irritably. "Wait, can't you, till I get on my trousers!"

"Wait!" Tom echoed, for Mother was by now half-way upstairs. She must have heard the clamour in the hall, and from broken phrases and exclamations have guessed what had happened. Holding the door very slightly ajar, Tom kept her outside on the landing while he explained the situation. "Have you got them on yet?" he called back over his shoulder, and a muffled affirmative being returned, Mother was then permitted to enter and administer first aid.

Pascoe, trousered indeed, but otherwise unclothed, lay face downward on the bed, and there was no doubt he was pretty badly stung. Having done all she could, Mother finally suggested that he might like to go home—a remark which, more than any of the remedies she had brought with her, had an excellent effect both as stimulant and restorative. Pascoe didn't want to go home. He very rightly didn't see what good missing all the fun was going to do his stings, so Mother hastened to reassure him. It was only that she thought he must be feeling very sore and uncomfortable, in spite of the splendid way he had taken it—making so little fuss, when most people would have been moaning and groaning.

"He's like the Spartan boy and the fox," Tom put in, paying his tribute, and these timely blandishments clearly brought their measure of consolation.

Lunch revived the Spartan boy still further, for as Tom had expected, he proved to be exactly the kind of boy Daddy liked, and the appreciation was mutual. The meal concluded, they waited till Mother was ready, and then all four set out to walk to the field. Daddy had suggested driving, but Mother had thought not, as there was bound to be a crowd, quite apart from the procession. "Poor creatures!" she sympathized, "beating those big drums and carrying enormous banners on a day like this! They'll be utterly exhausted, and the field will be like a fiery furnace, with not even a tree to give the slightest shade!"

"The greater the discomfort the greater the glory," Daddy reminded her. "Also, a certain amount of refreshment, I imagine, will be produced from hip-pockets."

This, so far as Mother was concerned, was an unfortunate suggestion. "I hope not," she murmured doubtfully. "I'm relying on what Mr. Sabine said—that every year sees an improvement in that direction."

More by good luck than calculation, they had timed their departure accurately, for the shrill sound of fifes, soaring above the deep roll and pounding of drums, was already audible in the distance when they emerged on to the main road. Mother and Daddy hurried on, in order to reach the field before the procession, while Tom and Pascoe, who wished to watch it passing, climbed on to a bank.

And here it was—the first banners swinging and dipping round the bend of the road, brilliantly purple and orange in the sunlight. At the same moment the leading band, which had been marking time by heavy drum-beats, suddenly burst into its own particular tune, and Tom, carried away on the wings of the infectious rhythm, raised his voice in song:

> Sit down, *my pink and* be *content*,
> *For the cows are in the clover.*

They were the words he had learned from James-Arthur, and whether right or wrong they fitted into the tune; but Pascoe, less excited, nudged him violently in the ribs to show him he was attracting attention. All the same, it *was* exciting—each band playing its special tune, which, as the players drew closer, disentangled itself from all the other tunes, till it became for a minute or two the only one, and then, passing on into the distance, was itself lost in the next and the next and the next—a constant succession. The big drums, crowned with bunches of orange lilies, were splotched and stained with blood from the hands of the drummers, whose crimson faces streamed with sweat. . . . It was great! Flags waved; musical instruments gleamed and glittered; the drums pounded; the fifes screamed! Yet in the midst of all this strident Dionysiac din and colour, the men and boys carrying the great square banners, or simply marching in time to the music, looked extraordinarily grave. It was only the accompanying rag tag and bobtail who exhibited signs of levity, bandied humorous remarks, and threw orange-skins—the actual performers were rapt in the parts they were playing in a glorious demonstration, which, if secular, had nevertheless all the bellicose zeal and earnestness of a declaration of faith. The very pictures on the banners were symbols of that faith. "The Secret of England's Greatness"—in other words, Queen Victoria presenting Bibles to kneeling blackamoors, passionately grateful to receive them—was a subject second in popularity only to King William himself. It told a story, it expressed an ideal— or if not an ideal at any rate an immovable conviction. . . . And there, marching along and helping to carry a banner, was the other, the more familiar William, yet not quite the William of every day. Tom screamed his name at the top of his voice, but William, who must have heard, took no notice.

"Don't!" Pascoe said, glancing uneasily to right and left.

"Don't what?" answered Tom impatiently.

"You're dancing up and down: everybody's staring at you."

This was purely a figment of imagination, for nobody was paying the least attention to them, but Pascoe seemed to have a morbid dread of publicity.

The procession took nearly three hours to pass, and they waited till the end before themselves adjourning to the field. There the speeches had begun, but they were not interested in these. They wandered through the crowd; they listened to Mr. Sabine for a few minutes; they saw Max and avoided him; and they had begun to feel that the best of the show was over when Tom's arm was grabbed from behind. "We've been looking for you," Mother said. "Daddy and I are going home and you'd better come with us: I'm sure you've had enough of all this; *I* certainly have. Besides, you must be hungry; we had lunch so early."

It was what they had been thinking themselves, so they complied at once, and began to thread their way through the crowd, Daddy and Pascoe leading, Tom following with Mother.

"Did you see James-Arthur?" he questioned eagerly. "He's with his girl."

"What girl?" Mother answered. "And don't talk like that."

"Like what?" Tom said; and then: "Why?"

"Because I don't like it—especially coming from a little boy."

"Well—anyhow she's Nancy from the Green Lion."

Mother laughed. "Such nonsense! I suppose she was asking him how he was enjoying himself. Nancy used to be the Sabines' maid, and I should think must be old enough to be James-Arthur's mother."

17: "I WONDER how long this is going to last?"
Mother said, pausing with the coffee-pot in her hand,
but addressing nobody in particular, as she gazed out next morning
through streaming window-panes at the soaked and dripping garden.
"I should have thought it might have rained itself out by now: twice I
woke up in the night and it was coming down in a deluge. It's extraordinary the luck they always have for their procession. Just imagine if
it had been like this yesterday!"

Tom imagined it, and Daddy said: "The rain will do a lot of good:
in fact if it keeps on all day I shan't be sorry; the garden needs it.
. . . Unfortunately the glass seems to be on the turn again."

He got up as he spoke to give it a further tap, which suggested to
Tom how much better an arrangement it would be if the barometer
affected the weather instead of the weather the barometer. "Then
we could fix it so that it would never rain except at night."

"Wouldn't that be rather unfair to some of your nocturnal
friends?" Daddy reminded him, and after a prolonged and impartial
consideration Tom was afraid it would.

Supposing such an alteration could be made, Alfred for one
wouldn't like it. Nor would the owls who lived at Denny's, nor the
rats who lived by the river. Perhaps, then, things were better as
they were. Yet it was an interesting question, and he began to
ruminate on how his proposed amendment would go if put to the
vote in a parliament of beasts. Cows and horses and dogs would vote
for it, and of course wasps, bees, and butterflies; but frogs and ducks
probably would vote on the other side, and cats and bats certainly
would. Field mice would be for, and possibly indoor mice against. As
he kept on enumerating the ayes and the noes he was impressed by
the diversity of taste among Earth's children, and the wonderful
impartiality with which she looked after them all. She had no favourites—as he feared in her place he would have had—a hippopotamus,
a blackbird, and a boy were equally pleasing to her, equally provided for, equally her sons. From which it most clearly followed
that none had a right to interfere with or rob the others of *their*
rights.

Having discovered this truth, he immediately tried to communicate it, and was surprised when Mother told him he would find it
expressed in the very first chapter of Genesis, when the various
creatures are brought to Adam that he may name them: but Daddy,

whose gaze had been fixed upon him throughout his struggle to find the right words, here interposed. "I don't think that's quite what he means:"—and on Tom's confirming headshake—"it goes further than that. The Edenic doctrine is autocratic, whereas Tom's is based on an ethical conception of the greater democracy."

"I'm afraid I don't know what the greater democracy is," Mother said.

Daddy knew, however; and though from his choice of such long words Tom suspected that he was not taking it seriously, he could see at the same time that he had perfectly grasped the idea. "It means," Daddy went on, "a social community in which you and I and Tom, and squirrels and hedgehogs and dogs and mice, all have precisely equal rights to freedom and happiness—the communist ideal, in short; with this important difference, that it is to be extended to the non-human races. . . . Therefore, no more animal circuses and shows; no more shutting up in zoos; and, if we are to be absolutely consistent, I'm afraid no more——"

Daddy, turning a quizzical glance upon his son's falling countenance, deliberately left the last word unspoken, but Tom had already seen that this was the end of the aquarium. . . .

At least so far as fish were concerned: luckily there was nothing in it at present except tadpoles, and an aquarium must be just as good a place as any other for tadpoles to develop into frogs. Pascoe would grumble, no doubt, but it couldn't be helped. . . .

Lost in thought, he sat staring at the opposite wall until Mother brought him back to the present with a start. "Tom dear, *do* get on," she urged him patiently. "It may be raining, but I don't see that that is a reason for our spending the entire day at the breakfast-table."

"I've finished: I've practically finished," he hastily mumbled, swallowing the last mouthfuls of toast and marmalade, and gulping down the remainder of his coffee.

"Is Clement coming this morning?" Mother asked him.

"Pascoe, do you mean? I don't know. I suppose he'll come if he's not frightened of the rain." He rose from his chair. "If he does come, I'll be up in the loft."

He went out through the back quarters, and in the kitchen found Mary alone. There had been no repetition of Mary's psychic experience; indeed she appeared to have recovered from it so completely that Tom felt she was now in a position to give him a detailed account of what she actually had seen. He would know at once if she had seen Ralph, and it was a question which interested him intensely. Unfortunately Mother had strictly forbidden him to allude to the matter in any way, and had even extracted from him a promise that he wouldn't. So except in the extremely unlikely contingency of Mary herself broaching the subject, he supposed he should never really know the truth. . . . With this, an alternative occurred to him, and he wondered why he hadn't thought of it sooner. It would be perfectly simple to take Pascoe to Granny's, and when there take him up to the closed wing. Whether anything would happen or not if he *did* do so was another matter.

He opened the back door, crossed the yard, and climbed up to the loft. The rain was still coming down, though no longer violently, but in a persistent drizzle that seemed half water and half mist. It was a fine, nearly noiseless rain, though all around there was a steady dripping and trickling from eaves and spouting, and in spite of what Daddy had said, it did not look to Tom in the least like clearing. The light was dim, and the little wind there was, instead of breaking the clouds, seemed to be gathering and melting them together, till they were less like clouds than a thick grey veil spread out to hide every glimpse of the sky. Yet there was no chill in the air; it was quite warm; which perhaps meant that the veil was not really very thick and eventually would be drawn up by the sun.

In the meantime it was not unpleasant, and he sat down on the floor by the open window. He watched the raindrops run along the edge of the roof, swelling rapidly as they united to form larger drops like crystals, which trembled for a moment on the brink before splashing down on to the cobble-stones below. The continuous trickle and splash made a kind of music, and presently he took his mouth-organ from his pocket and began softly to play an accompaniment. Like Orpheus, he was working a magic, but of a different kind, for the swallows flying in and out under the roof did not stop to listen to him. It was a dream magic, and beneath its spell the song of the rain acquired a more personal note, till at last out of the mist a little grey old man with a weak and tearful voice materialized. Yet not completely; his speech never passed into actual words; and his form remained fluid and nebulous, dissolving when Tom tried to look at him closely, and drawing together again when he half shut his eyes and breathed into his mouth-organ. If it had not been for his so lachrymose appearance Tom might have suspected this strange old man of mocking him, but his tearful eyes had far too melancholy an expression for that, and even his long nose was mournful. His grey hair, too, was long and thin and dank, and hung straight down like his drooping hands, which seemed all pendulous fingers. But his wavering shape was growing ever more uncertain and transparent, fainter and fainter, till suddenly a golden shaft pierced him through, and without even a sigh he vanished. His world was vanishing also— curling up, evaporating—as if the sun were a dragon and had put forth a great fiery tongue that wound about it, lapping it up, and leaving only at the edges a few diminishing wisps of white drifting vapour.

When it was quite gone, Tom descended the ladder and came round to the garden, which he found transformed, like some garden in an Arabian tale after a shower of precious stones. Everything was soaking wet, and from each leaf and blade of grass the light in all the colours of the spectrum was refracted as through a prism. He gazed up at the sun between nearly closed fingers, because an angel lived there. The angel's name was Uriel, but Tom had never been able to discover him, and he did not see him now. Roger found him thus engaged, and soon afterwards Pascoe arrived—both very wet, for Roger had come across the fields and through the glen, and Pascoe must have left home while it was still raining.

The latter looked uncomfortably hot, which was not surprising, seeing that he was encased in a sort of shining black cocoon, composed of waterproof trousers, cape, and hat. "I wish I'd waited till it was fine," he grumbled, wheeling his bicycle into the porch. "These beastly things may keep out the rain, but they make you nearly as wet as if they didn't: my shirt's sticking to me."

"What's in the parcel?" Tom inquired, glancing curiously at a brown-paper parcel, oblong in shape and of considerable size, which was fastened to the carrier of the bicycle.

Pascoe unstrapped it. "It's things for making a kite," he said— "just some laths and linen. I didn't know it was going to clear up, so I thought we might as well make a kite."

Tom had never possessed, nor even seen a kite, and he thought Pascoe's plan a good one, though it had a drawback. "What about Roger?" he said. "I mean, if we're going to work all morning up in the loft, he'll find it very dull, and he can't get up by the foot-board. . . . I've tried carrying him, but it's no use; he struggles like mad and he's frightfully strong."

Pascoe frowned. This perpetual fuss about Roger seemed to him exaggerated, and in any case a nuisance. He liked dogs himself, but he liked them sensibly. What is more, he was convinced that if Roger had been a human being Tom would have shown no such compunction about leaving him. Nevertheless, he considered the problem, while they walked round to the yard.

Beneath the loft he paused thoughtfully, gazing up at the window before entering the motor-house. Here he paused again. "We ought to be able to arrange something," he murmured, while Tom, who had the greatest confidence in his friend's practical ingenuity and inventiveness, said "Yes," and waited expectantly.

"It'll have to be a lift," Pascoe deliberated, "but that shouldn't be difficult; and the best place to put it would be exactly under the trap-door, so that the foot-board will help to keep it from tilting."

"He'd jump out," Tom said.

"Well, that's his look-out. All the same, I bet if he's really anxious he'll soon pick up the idea, and one of us can stand below for the first trip or two. After all, he's a sheep-dog, and you can teach a sheep-dog anything. . . . Where's William?"

"William!" Tom repeated. "What do you want William for?"

"I don't. It's just that to do the thing properly we ought to have a winch or something, for the rope to go round."

Tom was less ambitious. "We can pull him up without a winch," he said; for he could see that Pascoe presently would be wanting a bell for Roger to ring. "Anyhow, William's not here; he's recovering from yesterday."

This, as he knew, was a gratuitous libel on the strictest of tee-totallers, but Pascoe, who had begun to hunt among a pile of wooden boxes and cases, was too busy to notice it. Very soon he found what he thought might do, and dragged it out. "There's just about room for him if we take off the lid and knock out the partitions; and it's got handles we can tie the ropes to. As a matter of fact it's an old wine case, which is why it's so well made."

Tom was dubious. "He'd never stay in that, and if he jumped out when it was half-way up he might hurt himself. Dogs' legs are very easily hurt; they're different from cats'."

"Just as you like," Pascoe replied. "I believe he'd be all right, but if you're nervous we'd better wait till we can get a basket or something we can shut him into. . . . Only," he added, "if we're going to make the kite this morning, we'll have to begin soon."

"Of course we'll make it," Tom gave in. "Roger'll have to stay down in the yard."

This was all Pascoe wanted, and he lifted his parcel. "If you can borrow a pair of scissors for cutting out the linen," he said, "I think I have everything else."

"Won't you need paste? There's a tube of seccotine in my tool-box, but seccotine makes your fingers stick to everything."

"I'm going to use nails," Pascoe said. "I brought some with me—specially small ones. My father has a workshop, you know."

Tom didn't know, but it now appeared that Pascoe's father was an expert carpenter. "He made a lovely cabinet for Mother's birthday, and the drawers slip in and out as smoothly as if they were sliding on butter. He says himself that that's the best test of good workmanship: in cheap modern furniture the drawers never work properly. . . . When you're getting the scissors, get some old newspapers and string too. You may as well be making the tail while I'm making the kite."

Tom departed on these errands, and when he returned Pascoe was already up in the loft, where he had cleared the table and unpacked his materials. Tom watched him for a minute or two, as he laid out and secured the framework of the kite; then, Pascoe having shown him what to do, he himself set to work on the tail, cutting the newspaper into strips and rolling these into solid wedges, which he knotted at regular intervals on the cord.

"Make them thick," Pascoe warned him, "and it'll need plenty. If the tail isn't heavy enough the kite won't fly steadily, but dive about all over the place, and very likely get smashed on the ground."

"I know—I know," Tom muttered, for if making the tail was not difficult, neither was it particularly interesting—all the interesting work was being done by Pascoe, who having completed the frame and laid it on the tightly-stretched linen, was now drawing on this the shape to be cut out. He seemed to be quite as good at making kites, Tom thought, as he had been at making the aquarium; clearly the example, or the lessons of Pascoe senior had not been thrown away. But he must have a special gift as well—inherited very likely—just as *he*, according to Mother and Doctor Macrory, took after Uncle Stephen. In that case, he suspected, Uncle Stephen wasn't a carpenter. Nor was Daddy, who couldn't be trusted even to fix a blind, Mother said, without making it ten times worse than it had been before. . . .

All the same, he would have liked to know rather more particularly just in what way he *did* take after Uncle Stephen. Nobody had explained this, and Granny seemed to think it was all nonsense. Tom didn't believe it was nonsense, and felt extremely curious about Uncle Stephen—though there wasn't much chance of his curiosity ever being gratified, unless by some miracle Uncle Stephen should become curious about *him*. . . .

These reflections were interrupted by Pascoe, who without looking up from his work suddenly asked; "Did I tell you I saw Max on the road?"

"No," Tom answered, in a tone which indicated he had no desire to pursue the subject.

"Well, I did," Pascoe said, "and he had his gun. Imagine going out shooting on a morning like that—though of course it was clearing up by then. . . . I'm going to use seccotine after all—just to finish things off."

Tom took this as a signal that he might get up to inspect the progress he had made. It was a big kite Pascoe had designed—about three feet by two. "The square ones are the best," he said. "The others may look more ornamental, but they never fly so well."

"*I* think it looks great!" Tom declared.

So perhaps did Pascoe, though he replied modestly that it was too soon to judge. "Wait till we see how she goes. It all depends on the balance—and the belly-band may have to be altered, though I *think* it's all right."

"Will we be able to fly it this afternoon?" Tom asked.

"Not unless you buck up with the tail. You're taking a deucy long time over it."

But this Tom took to be merely a cautionary remark: he was pretty sure that Pascoe had every intention of flying the kite that afternoon, and during lunch the conversation was devoted exclusively to his and Daddy's earlier flyings. Daddy thought that Chinese boys had kites shaped like boxes, which didn't require tails, but he was unable to tell Pascoe where he could find a description of how to make one. He admired *their* kite, and so did Mother and Phemie and Mary, to all of whom Tom displayed it, while Pascoe remained quietly in the background.

The best place for a trial, they decided, would be Denny's fields, where they could get an open space without trees. So they set out, still chattering eagerly as sparrows about the kite, and taking it in turns to carry it. "You can try it first," Pascoe said, which—seeing that it was he who had thought of it, and made it, and supplied all the materials, including a ball of whipcord—was jolly decent of him. On their way they came upon James-Arthur: and James-Arthur, forsaking a cart he was loading with turnips, joined them to witness the start. Roger and Barker of course were there; but Pincher wasn't: ever since Max's advent Pincher had become an infrequent visitor, though he came as often as he could escape.

Pascoe now held up the kite and instructed Tom what to do. "Run as hard as you can against the wind, and we'll soon see if she's all right."

She was. A fair wind was blowing down the field, and as Tom ran into it the kite rose behind him, and once it had reached a certain height did all the rest itself. It rose nearly straight, and as rapidly as he could let out the cord. Then, each in turn held it, so as to judge of the strength of its pull. The only disappointing thing was that neither Roger nor Barker showed the slightest interest —indeed actually turned their backs and looked the other way: Pincher would at least have barked. . . .

Presently it was so high up that it floated against the sky like a seagull. It could mount no higher now unless it broke free, for the cord had run out. So Tom and Pascoe sat down on the damp grass and gazed up at it, while James-Arthur returned to his work.

"I bet Roger or Barker couldn't hold it: I bet it would pull them up."

"Of course. I bet it would pull up even a small boy; or if it didn't, at any rate he'd have to let it go."

"Let's send up messengers," Pascoe said.

He straightway produced a dozen messengers from his pocket, evidently prepared beforehand, for they were circular discs of thick white paper with a nick cut at the side so that they could be slipped over the string. It was the strangest thing, for the messengers, caught by the wind, rose right up till they reached the kite itself, yet they wouldn't fly up at all if you just flung them loose into the air. Tom had never before even heard of messengers, and asked Pascoe if he had invented them. But he hadn't, and thought probably it was Chinese boys who had. The messengers were better fun than the kite itself, but they were quickly exhausted. After that, just holding the string became rather a bore, so they crossed the field and tied it to the top bar of a gate, while they played, for lack of anything better, a game of cocks and hens.

"I suppose that's why kites went out of fashion," Pascoe presently remarked.

"Why?"

"Because there's nothing more to do once they're up in the air. Daddy says all the boys flew them when he was a boy; and there was a particular season for them, and for tops and marbles. But none of the boys have them now. Even James-Arthur had never seen one."

"Neither had I—except in a picture."

"That's what I mean. They're not much use really, except for the sport of making them. I wonder where I could find out how to make a box-kite?"

"They're as good as boats anyway," Tom declared. "There's nothing to do with them either, except watch them."

Pascoe agreed. "It was really Daddy who wanted me to make a kite—I expect just because he used to fly them himself. The first time I made one he helped me with it. . . . Here's your father, too; come out specially, I suppose, because *he* used to have one."

It was true, for there he was, approaching from the far end of the meadow, which at any ordinary time would have been a most unlikely place for him to take a walk. Pascoe's brow was puckered slightly, and he said slowly; "I wonder what they'd do if they were left all alone with tops and marbles, and it was the proper season. . . . I mean, if there was nobody to watch them. I bet they'd play, if they were sure no one would ever hear about it."

"I don't believe Daddy would," Tom answered loyally.

"Not even if it was the season?" Pascoe murmured, which made Tom glance at him suspiciously; but Daddy had already hailed them, and they ran to meet him.

18:   TOM wished Pascoe would come home again. He had been away now for over a fortnight, staying at the seaside with some aunt or other who lived in Donegal, and a picture-postcard received that morning, mentioning that he was bathing every day, and hoping Tom was well, said not a word about when he expected to return. Also there was another reason why Tom had found the postcard unsatisfactory. Pascoe had been so very particular about leaving his address and getting him to promise to write (which he *had* done, quite a long letter, all four pages of a sheet of notepaper), yet this brief scrawl was the sole communication he had got in reply—nine words, two of which were Pascoe's name.

He wouldn't have minded this had he only sent a postcard himself—which was all he would have sent had not Pascoe made such a fuss about letters. But he had not only made the fuss, he had even invented a special cipher in which the letters were to be written, so that if they fell into the wrong hands they would be unreadable by anyone who didn't know the code. And the cipher was so extremely complicated that even with the code before him it had taken Tom hours to write his first page. After that, he had abandoned it; and Pascoe hadn't bothered to use it at all. . . .

Another and much queerer thing was that he had wanted Tom to make a compact by which they should solemnly bind themselves by a "blood oath" to continue to be chums after school recommenced. Tom had said of course they would continue, but he hadn't seen any necessity for the shedding of blood. Why, he had asked, should school make a difference? Pascoe, however, seemed to think it might, and this distrustful attitude had struck Tom as very strange until it occurred to him that Pascoe appeared to have made no friends at his previous school. He had gathered this in the first days of their acquaintance—not just from Brown's remarks, which probably were prejudiced—but from one or two let drop by Pascoe himself, though these had made little impression at the time, and later had been forgotten. The "blood compact" reminded him. It was as if Pascoe feared Tom might find somebody at school he would prefer for a special chum, though how a compact was to prevent this was hard to understand. In point of fact Tom already knew somebody he would have preferred—James-Arthur—but naturally he kept this to himself, nor could he see how it made the slightest difference in his friendship with Pascoe, which was of another and more practical kind, consisting largely in doing things together, or making things—like the kite and the aquarium—for Pascoe took no interest in ordinary regulation games such as tennis or croquet. After one or two unsuccessful trials, Tom had abandoned these as hopeless; but there was no doubt, though he might be a dud at orthodox games,

Pascoe was jolly good at planning unorthodox ones—or rather schemes—and at carrying them out. So it was not surprising that in his absence Tom should miss him, and find himself now and then at a loose end. Occasionally he played a game of croquet or tennis with Mother; and every day with Roger and Barker he went over to Denny's on the very improbable chance of finding James-Arthur doing something at which he could help; but this was all. . . .

By far the best of these days had been that of the mowing of the great meadow, when in the evening he had ridden back to the farmhouse on Apollo, one of the solemn old carthorses. True, Apollo was so big, or else so preoccupied with private meditations, that he never seemed to know whether Tom was on his back or not, but pursued his way, or halted to sample some attractive specimen of vegetation, just as it pleased him. On this particular evening he had stopped to drink from a well, and in spite of coaxings and expostulations had drunk so much that he had got broader and broader till it was like balancing yourself on a cask. Tom, to be sure, may only have imagined this increase in bulk, for at no time were his legs long enough to obtain a proper grip, but the fact remained that when one of the men gave Apollo a playful smack with his open hand, and Apollo, surprised at this unexpected treatment, broke into a lumbering trot, Tom had slid gently off behind. Then everybody laughed, including James-Arthur, but they soon set him up again.

It had been a good day, and in the general atmosphere of rough friendliness he had felt very happy. He had eaten his supper that evening in Denny's kitchen, and afterwards walked home with James-Arthur. "Would you like me to fetch the owl?" James-Arthur had asked. "Just you watch and I'll bring him in a minute."

They paused in the deepening twilight by some beech-trees, and now James-Arthur locked his hands together and blew between his upright thumbs, producing a "Hoo, hoo, hoo, hoo, hoo!" He next mimicked the squeak of a mouse—once, twice, thrice—at irregular intervals—and soon after, sure enough, there was the owl, floating soundless as a ghost above their heads.

"You can always bring him," said James-Arthur, "but he won't stay when he sees it's only us."

Tom was filled with admiration, for this was far better than any artificial bird-call, and James-Arthur promised to teach him how to do it. They walked on, while the moon, large as a harvest moon, rose up over the trees and threw their shadows and the shadows of

the trees on the silvered grass. James-Arthur had his arm round
Tom's shoulder. He often walked like this, though only when there
was nobody else there. Yet in spite of the intimacy thus created, he
always called him "Master Tom," never just Tom, which would
have shown that they were really chums and was what Tom would
have liked.

19: ONE morning, a few days after the arrival of Pascoe's postcard, he was in the garden stretched full
length on the grass in what to most people would have seemed an extremely uncomfortable position for reading; nevertheless Tom was
reading, and with profound interest, a work Doctor Macrory had
lent him. This was *The Library* of Apollodorus, and Mother, who
had glanced through it, thought it a most extraordinary choice on
the doctor's part. In some amusement she had turned the leaves
of the two learned-looking volumes, with their Greek text printed
on one page, and Sir James Frazer's English translation on the page
opposite. Yet at the same time she could not help feeling pleased, for
it showed that Doctor Macrory, who was a very intelligent man,
must think Tom no ordinary little boy, and, since she certainly
shared this opinion, she was content to leave the rest to be tested
by experiment. As a matter of fact the doctor had made no mistake:
the tales Apollodorus had to tell of Greek gods and heroes, though
he boiled them down to their bare bones, as it were—presenting them
without embellishment, and in the somewhat sparse and dry manner
of an historian concerned only with plain facts and not at all with
their imaginative treatment—Tom found as absorbing as those of
Grimm or Asbjörnsen. More so, in a sense, because he could not help
feeling that what had once been accepted as truth might *really* be
true, or at any rate partly true; while as for the imaginative treatment, he could supply that himself. He supplied it, indeed, so lav-
ishly, that though separated in time by nearly two thousand years,
he and the ancient Greek mythologist became collaborators—a result
all the more easily reached because Apollodorus made not the slightest attempt to criticize or explain his material. The only stumbling-
block lay in the pronunciation of a good many unfamiliar names,
and since Tom tackled these in the boldly sporting manner of Mr.
Silas Wegg, it was a very minor one.

He had reached the story of a little boy Glaukos, who while
pursuing a mouse, fell into a jar of honey and was drowned (though
a little later restored to life by a medicinal herb brought by a kindly
serpent), when suddenly he heard a low whistle, and glancing up,
saw James-Arthur at the gate. He was surprised, for James-Arthur
had not often visited the house, and that he should come at such an
hour, when naturally he ought to be working, made it more surprising still. James-Arthur waited at the gate, but he did not open it, so
Tom jumped up and ran to see what he wanted. He was standing in
the road, looking grave and rather troubled, and in his arms was a
squirrel—a dead squirrel.

For a moment there was silence; then James-Arthur said: "I
brought him, Master Tom: I thought maybe you'd wish to have
him: he's yours—the one you made a pet of, that lived in the big
oak-tree in the meadow. . . . Now he's dead. . . . Young Sabine
shot him."

Tom had turned very white, and James-Arthur shuffled his feet
and looked uncomfortable.

"I think maybe he didn't know he was yours," he went on, in a
gruff, awkward attempt at consolation. Then abruptly and with
a complete change of manner he added: "But he must have known
he was tame, for you can see he shot him from quite close—dirty
bastard! He was always that anyway."

Tom took the small body in silence. He looked down at it as
it lay limply in his arms. The eyes were filmed and half closed, the
little hands, once so quick to take nuts and cherries, were closed
too, and a trickle of blood had smeared and matted the thick red fur.

"I thought maybe you'd wish to have him," said James-Arthur
again; "so you could bury him in the garden."

"Thank you."

James-Arthur looked at him and did not seem to know what more
to say. "I can't stop, Master Tom, for I have a cart waiting . . . but
I'm sorry."

"Yes," said Tom. And after a pause he added; "I know you are."

He brought the body into the garden, holding it close to him.
He kissed the soft fur and his face puckered, as if the tears he had
kept back were on the point of falling. But suddenly a wave of
furious anger swept through him. He carried Edward up to the
loft and laid him gently on the table. For a minute or two he stood

motionless, his face still white, but his mouth now firmly set; then he descended the ladder and set off for the Rectory.

He had no definite plan of action in view; certainly it was not Max he was in search of, for he knew he could do little or nothing even if he did meet him: nevertheless his mind was filled with hatred and the desire for revenge. Not that he believed an interview with Mr. Sabine would achieve anything. A few perfunctory words perhaps, and an expression of regret, but that would be all; he had no expectation that Max would be punished. The first momentary thought of getting James-Arthur to give him what he deserved he had abandoned also, for that would only be to create trouble for James-Arthur himself—possibly serious trouble, both for him and his mother, if Mr. Sabine took the matter up, as he would be sure to do. Tom didn't know much about Mr. Sabine, but he knew the gun had come from him—Max himself had told Pascoe so—and that he approved of his shooting.

Uncertain what he should do, yet his mind seething with passion, he hurried along, meeting nobody on the road; and when he reached the Rectory and rang the bell it was Miss Sabine he asked for. The maid—Phemie's and Mary's friend—invited him to come in, because Miss Sabine was busy in the kitchen making jam, and he might have to wait for a minute or two. Tom muttered that he would wait where he was. He had heard Althea's voice in the distance, and did not wish to talk to her just now. Besides, in the brief space occupied by this exchange of words, he had caught sight of Max's gun leaning against the hat stand, where it had evidently been left temporarily; and in a flash he had made up his mind. The maid departed to tell Miss Sabine he was there, and five seconds later Tom was scudding down the garden path and along the road, with the gun in his hand.

He made directly for the river, and once or twice glanced back over his shoulder, but nobody was following. Nevertheless it was not till he had reached the tow-path that he paused to draw breath. He stood motionless now, with the gun in his hands, as if for the first time he had begun to realize what he had done, and what it must lead to. The moment the gun was missed, though this might not be till Max himself missed it, the whole thing would be clear to everybody. That, however, did not matter, was indeed just as he would have wished, for the secret destruction of the gun would somehow have been nothing. He lifted it by the barrel and brought it down

with all his force on the path; but either the ground was too soft,
or he was not strong enough, for it did not break, nor did he try
again, but flung it out into the middle of the river, where, with a
splash, it sank.

Tom stood watching the ripples spreading out in a widening
circle, yet feeling no relief beyond a momentary satisfaction. What
he had done was useless, altered nothing, could not bring Edward
back to life. It was a poor kind of revenge too; but the right kind,
which would have been to fight Max and hammer him till he sobbed
and begged for mercy, was beyond his power. Walking back to his
own house, he felt more and more depressed. Nor could he now tell
anybody—not even Mother—to whom he naturally would have
gone for sympathy. He had an impulse to seek out James-Arthur
and tell *him*, for he would know at once from James-Arthur's manner
whether he thought what he had done a rotten as well as a futile
thing; and by the time he had reached home and climbed up once
more to the loft, he had begun to wish he had not done it, and then
again to be glad he *had* done it. He cried a little as he stroked Edward's soft fur and placed his body in a box—with a straw bed for
it to lie on—and presently took the box down and buried it in the
shubbery. He marked the spot where he would put up a stone with
Edward's name on it when Pascoe came back. Edward was nothing
to Pascoe; Pascoe had never even seen him: but he would help,
and make everything neat and orderly—and more than ever, Tom, in
his unhappiness, wished he was there now.

20: DURING lunch he was so silent that Daddy asked
him what was the matter. He returned the answer
usually given in these circumstances, but he could see that, whatever
Daddy might think of it, it did not convince Mother. She kept on
glancing at him, and in the end asked him if he had a headache.
Why a headache? Tom wondered gloomily, but he tried to look
more animated. He was quite well, he repeated, yet, though Mother
did not press him further, he knew this was only because Daddy
was there, and not because she was satisfied. To set him at his ease
she began to talk of other things—chiefly of the visitors she was

expecting for tea that afternoon. Tom listened with a wandering attention. He could have informed her that he too was expecting a visitor—but one who probably would inquire for Daddy. . . .

He escaped as soon as he could, seizing the opportunity while Mother was giving directions to Mary, and ran out into the garden, where, like Adam and Eve, he took refuge in the shrubbery. Here before long he was discovered by Roger, who with his usual cleverness grasped the situation at once, and here they both skulked out of sight, while keeping a sharp watch on the approach to the house.

The visitor Tom was expecting would arrive, he was sure, long before Mother's friends; and of course it might be only Max, in which case Tom would immediately come out into the open. On the other hand, it was far more likely to be Mr. Sabine. Max was bound to know—for, if he hadn't known before, James-Arthur would certainly have told him—that the squirrel he had murdered was Tom's pet; and he would guess from this at least part of the truth, and tell the rest of his family—particularly his father. Well— let him! Tom didn't care. Only he wished that whatever was going to happen would happen soon. . . .

Very likely Miss Sabine was one of the visitors Mother had invited to her tea-party, but *she* would say nothing; at any rate not till she got Mother alone. For that matter, Miss Sabine might even be on his side—to some extent at least—certainly it wouldn't be for love of Max if she wasn't. Mother might too—he wasn't sure— but Daddy he felt certain wouldn't. . . .

Roger was very quiet, evidently perfectly content to sit like this, with Tom's arm round him, as they had sat so often before. Roger had beautiful brown eyes, very loving and trustful. Roger was thinking mysterious doggy thoughts, and he sat bolt upright, in which position his head was exactly on a level with Tom's own. . . .

They had been waiting now for nearly an hour, he supposed— which was strange surely, since Mr. Sabine's object, if he *were* coming, would be to catch Daddy before he went out. It began to look as if after all nobody were coming, and cautiously Tom ventured forth from his hiding-place, and stood thinking. Perhaps he ought to take just one peep down the road before going over to Denny's to consult with James-Arthur. But at the very moment of reaching this decision he saw the tall dark figure of Mr. Sabine at the gate, and for an instant they stood thus, face to face, not more than ten yards apart.

Mr. Sabine's hand was on the latch, but before he had spoken a word Tom turned tail and fled back into the shrubbery, and from the shrubbery down into the glen. It was hardly the behaviour of a hero, nor was it calculated to placate Mr. Sabine, whose voice could be heard in the distance calling after him. Tom, however, was already scrambling down the steep bank of the glen and had no intention of obeying the summons. What he had anticipated had happened, and oddly enough in a way he felt glad, for he knew that everything would now come out, so that when he returned to the house he would at least know what to expect. . . .

He clambered out of the glen and pursued his course straight across country. He had no idea where James-Arthur was or what he would be doing, but leaving the matter to Roger, very soon he found him digging potatoes in a field, and luckily he was alone.

Tom began at once, and James-Arthur, the sun streaming down on his flaxen head and open blue shirt and bare arms, stood motionless leaning on his fork, while the story was poured out. As it proceeded, Tom from time to time glanced at him anxiously, but James-Arthur kept his eyes fixed on the ground, and it was impossible while he did so to guess what was passing in his mind. He did not speak once until Tom reached the point where he had thrown the gun into the river, and then he only said: "It's a pity you done that, Master Tom."

Tom stopped abruptly. "Why? Why is it a pity? I'm very glad I did. It's what he deserved."

"It is," returned James-Arthur laconically.

"Then why is it a pity? I don't see any pity about it."

James-Arthur spat on his hands, which were broad and powerful, and plunged his fork energetically into the ground. But it was a solitary plunge; he left it there; and proceeded to wipe his hands on his dirty corduroys. "It'll maybe get you into bad trouble if they find out," he answered.

"They've found out already," Tom told him. "Mr. Sabine was going up to the house when I left."

James-Arthur scratched his head in silence, and Tom immediately said: "Don't; your hands are all earthy." But this was involuntary, and because James-Arthur's hair was exactly the colour of very ripe oats, and looked as if it would show the slightest mark: next moment he returned to the matter he had come about. "Did you tell Max it was my squirrel?" he asked.

"I did, an' I told him how much you valued it, an' what I thought of him. But sure he had it destroyed before ever I come up. . . . It was the shot that brought me."

"What ought I to do now?"

James-Arthur scratched his head again, till remembering Tom's expostulation, he smiled sheepishly. The little boy's admiration had always puzzled and amused him, though it pleased him too. "You wouldn't go back—would you?" he suggested after a pause.

Tom was surprised. "Back where?"

"Back to your own house. . . . I mean before Mr. Sabine's gone. . . . It's just so they wouldn't think you might be hiding."

Since hiding was precisely what he *was* doing, Tom couldn't quite grasp the point of this remark. "You mean they'll think—Mr. Sabine will think—I'm frightened of him?"

"Ay," said James-Arthur slowly: "if he seen you, it'd maybe look like that."

Tom hung his head and began to kick at a lump of earth. "Of course he saw me," he muttered, but said nothing further till he felt James-Arthur's arm slipping round his shoulder in the old way. This, for some mysterious reason, had the alarming effect of making him want to cry, and also, in return, to put his arm round James-Arthur; but fortunately he was able to quash both impulses, and presently to ask in his normal voice: "What do *you* think?"

"Well, it's only natural you'd be a bit scared," James-Arthur thought. "I wasn't meaning that. I was only meaning—if so be you could keep from showing it too much—to oul' Sabine anyways."

"I'm not scared of him," Tom answered. "It's not that. It's——"

"What is it, Master Tom?"

"It's because they'll want me to tell him I'm sorry—Daddy will— and I'm not going to. I hate Max and I'd kill him if I could."

James-Arthur shook his head reprovingly. "Now, now, that's foolish talk, for you wouldn't do no such thing—because you're not that sort, an' never will be. If you were, you wouldn't be sorrowing over a dead squirrel at this moment."

"I'd hurt him anyway," Tom said; "and badly too, so that he'd remember it for a long time. You don't believe me, because you think I'm soft."

"No," James-Arthur replied. "I think you're tough enough in plenty of ways—other ways—a heap tougher than young Sabine I dare say. But I think you're soft-hearted, because I've seen it."

"I'm not," Tom denied.

James-Arthur smiled. "I don't mean anything you wouldn't like," he said. "But anyways it wouldn't hurt you—would it?—just to say you're sorry. Whether you are or not, it's only two words, an' it might make a lot of difference—though I suppose the oul' lad'll be lookin' a new gun."

Strangely enough, until James-Arthur mentioned it, this thought had never entered Tom's head; but now he instantly saw that the first thing Daddy would do on learning the truth would be to offer to replace the gun. It was sickening, hateful, unfair. Max had done a rotten, cruel thing, and in return he would get a new gun and carry on just as before; while Edward, who had never harmed anybody or anything, would never again be able to peep down from the branches of his oak-tree, to gather and stow away his winter stores, to come down at the sound of his name, and sit on Tom's shoulder and be stroked and petted. . . .

When he raised his head it was to find James-Arthur looking at him very kindly. "Now don't you be taking on so, Master Tom. I wish I'd hit that young scut a clout on the head myself, an' if you were a bit nearer his match I'd tell you to leather into him an' break his jaw. But the way it is, it'd be no good."

Tom said nothing, and James-Arthur went on consolingly: "Troubles happen, but in the latter end they pass. So if they ask you to, just you say you're sorry, an' in a day or two it'll all be forgotten."

Then Tom at last found words. "I *won't*," he replied, his mouth closing obstinately. "They can keep on and on, and punish me in any way they like, but I'll never tell either Mr. Sabine or Max that I'm sorry, and I'll never speak to Max again."

21: WHEN he got home William was cutting the grass on the croquet-lawn—probably on purpose, so that he might pounce on him at once. "The master's been lookin' for you all roads," he called out sourly. "Ever since Mr. Sabine come."

Tom halted irresolutely. "Is Mr. Sabine still here?" he said.

"He is not then; they give you up. An' if you ask me, he wasn't lookin' too pleased eether when he left—whatever you may have bin doin' to the gentleman."

Without replying to this insinuation, Tom thrust his hands into his pockets and walked on, assuming an air of nonchalance he was far from feeling. Through the open drawing-room windows floated the sound of mingled feminine voices, telling him that Mother's tea-party was still in full swing.

He went straight to the study, but outside the door paused for nearly a minute before opening it. Daddy was writing at the big leather-covered table near the window, and at the sound of Tom's entrance he glanced up; then, seeing who it was, sighed and laid down his pen. To Tom's surprise he did not look angry—merely rather bored at the interruption, and at the same time half amused.

"Won't you sit down?" he asked politely, as his son lingered uneasily by the door; and Tom, uncertain what to make of this most Daddyish reception, sat down in the nearest chair.

Daddy removed his glasses and inspected him for a moment or two without speaking. This accomplished, he pushed back his chair, sighed again, stretched his legs, and said in the resigned accents of one embarking on a tedious duty: "I presume you already know that I've had the pleasure of a visit from Mr. Sabine—and why. He mentioned your encounter, and also that at sight of him you ran away. . . . I, unfortunately, was not in a position to do so."

The last words may or may not have been intended to reach Tom, whose sharp ears nevertheless caught them. It certainly was a most unexpected beginning, and a little more hopefully he began to wonder what really could have happened. Daddy still did not enlighten him. "That was a very ill-mannered thing to do," he went on, "and I must add, not at all like you. Yet when I ventured to say so to Mr. Sabine, he not only assured me that you had seen him, but that he called after you several times, and you took no notice. Naturally he arrived here in a somewhat heated mood—which I hope may account for the suspicions he expressed—and still clings to, I'm afraid."

"Did he tell you Max had shot my squirrel?" Tom asked in a low voice. "He shot Edward."

Something woebegone in his attitude must have struck Daddy, for he dropped his semi-ironical tone and answered quickly and kindly; "Yes, he told me so; but that Max had no idea the squirrel was a pet of yours when he shot it—which I'm sure is true."

"I don't believe it's true," Tom burst out. "He knew he was tame anyhow, because he shot him from quite close. He's always shooting things, and Mr. Sabine allows him to."

Daddy waited a moment before going on. "You see, Tom, it's like this: very few people quite share your feelings about animals. It may be unfortunate, but it is inevitable, because we are all born with a limited number of sympathies only, and yours, in that direction, happen to be unusually strong. I did my best to explain to Mr. Sabine how you felt about such things, but it would have been very much better if you had been there yourself, instead of taking to your heels as if you had done something you were ashamed of."

Tom gazed at him half incredulously, for there was a note in his voice, as he uttered this very mild reproof, far more friendly than angry.

"You think I did right?" he stammered.

"I don't think you did right to run away—which never helps anything—but I certainly think you had a much more legitimate grievance than Mr. Sabine, and I told him so."

Tom drew a deep sigh and murmured, "Thank you, Daddy."

"So that when you return the gun, or tell Max where you hid it, I imagine the apologies will be on the other side. In fact, taking everything into consideration, I think it will be sufficient if we send it back by William—unless you actually wish to have an interview with our reverend friend."

Tom's face fell. In one second all his newborn confidence came toppling to the ground, and he saw that if Daddy had taken his part it was due to a complete misunderstanding. He believed Tom had taken the gun, but no more than that, as indeed might have been guessed from his remarks about Mr. Sabine's suspicions. "I can't return it," he whispered.

It was strange, but Daddy still seemed not to comprehend. He merely looked puzzled. "Why?—why can't you return it? I don't suppose you've hidden it in such an inaccessible place that you can't lay your hands on it."

"I threw it in the river," Tom said; and those few words sufficed to change everything.

It was not that even now Daddy looked angry; but what was worse, he looked profoundly disappointed.

"So Mr. Sabine was right after all!"

"Yes," Tom said.

There followed a silence, which seemed to last for hours before

Daddy spoke again. "That, I'm afraid, alters the position. Don't you think it was a rather spiteful revenge to take?"

Tom did not answer, and Daddy went on: "Stupid too—since you must have known I should have to replace the gun."

"I didn't," Tom broke in eagerly. "I mean, I didn't think of that till James-Arthur told me you would."

"And what else did James-Arthur tell you? What does he think of the whole performance, for I suppose you talked it over?"

Tom's eagerness died. "I think he——I think he thinks the same as you."

"Did he say so?"

"No."

Daddy sat there, as if he were turning over this last response in his mind, though Tom had not intended it to convey more than a bare negation. "If," he began at last, and speaking less sternly—"if Max had shot the squirrel knowing it was yours, I shouldn't blame you perhaps—at all events not so much. But he didn't; he did it in ignorance; which makes all the difference. . . . Don't imagine I approve of what he did: on the contrary, I think he must be an unpleasant boy; but that is not the point, nor does it justify your action. At any rate, the fact remains that I parted with his father on far from cordial terms; with the result that now I shall have to take you over to the Rectory and we shall both have to apologize."

Tom had been staring at the carpet, but when Daddy paused he once more looked up. For a moment, though his lips moved, no words came. Then; "I won't," he brought out in a low but extremely stubborn voice. "I'll say I'm sorry to you—about having to buy a new gun—but I won't say it to either Mr. Sabine or Max."

It was his nervousness, no doubt, that made it sound so openly defiant. None the less, it *had* that sound, and Daddy, who hitherto had been leaning back in his chair carelessly twiddling an ivory paper-knife, suddenly sat up straight, and Tom saw that now at all events he was genuinely angry. "I can't take you over there this evening," he said coldly, "because it is Wednesday, and Mr. Sabine will be conducting the church service, and possibly have other business to see to afterwards; but I shall take you over tomorrow morning."

"I won't go," Tom repeated.

"You certainly *will*," Daddy answered. "And in the meantime

you had better go to your room, and remain there till you have
learned to speak more respectfully."

22:

TOM left him without a word.

In his own room he sat down on the side of the
bed to think things over. The situation was at any rate definite and
clear, and in one respect he was perhaps glad to be condemned to
solitary confinement, since somehow it made it easier for him to
keep to his resolve. Possibly, therefore, it would have been more
satisfactory still had he been followed and locked in, though of
course it was none the less imprisonment because this formality had
been neglected.

His broodings were interrupted by the sound of voices, and he
went to the window to watch Mother's departing guests. A little
later he heard Mother herself coming upstairs, and turned round
expectantly, but she passed his door without even pausing, and
went on into her own room. Did she not know, then, what had
happened? Or had Daddy told her he was to be left to himself
till he showed signs of penitence, and promised to do what he was
told? Very likely nobody would be allowed to come near him—
except perhaps to bring him food, for even Daddy would hardly
try to starve him into compliance. If he did, it wouldn't succeed;
and he pictured himself fainting with hunger yet still defiant. . . .

He stood listening, for Mother was moving about in her room,
getting ready for dinner. He could have gone to her there, and it
was not so much obedience to Daddy's orders as an odd kind of
pride that prevented him. Presently the gong sounded and he heard
her again passing his door, this time going downstairs.

Well, he could be equally determined, and somebody must come
soon unless they *were* going to starve him—either Phemie or Mary—
he hoped Phemie.

This hope at all events was realized, indeed more than realized,
for shortly afterwards Phemie came in beaming, and with an air of
being so completely on his side that for a moment he thought she
was going to kiss him. She carried a tray, too, on which was not
only an ordinary dinner, but what looked very like a special treat
in the shape of macaroons, of which, as she well knew, he was

particularly fond. Even in the midst of his troubles he could not help feeling gloomily tickled, for he strongly suspected the macaroons to be spoils pillaged from Mother's tea-party. This surmise, as he learned later, was correct. Connecting his disgrace with Mr. Sabine's visit, Phemie had formed her own view of the situation, and had expressed it openly and with vigour. "Shutting up the poor lamb all alone there!—just because of old Nosey Sabine! Him and his Orange sash, and a face would turn the milk inside a cow! I never could abide him, and I wonder the Master would be heeding his complaints—as like as not a pack of lies invented by his own brat!"

Phemie's championship was the more striking, because in ordinary circumstances she herself was by no means slow to point out Tom's faults and call him to order. At present you would think there had never been even a passing tiff between them, and that from infancy he had been the apple of her eye. She set down the tray on a small table, hoped he would enjoy his dinner, and noticeably made no allusion to the macaroons. "And if you want any more," she told him, "or anything else, just you ring the bell and eether Mary or me will answer it."

She had taken jolly good care he wouldn't want more! Tom thought, as he surveyed the ample repast provided; but he promised, and when he had finished his meal, took a book from his shelf and lay down on the bed.

It was no use, however: he found it impossible to fix his mind for more than a sentence or two on what he was reading, and by and by a sudden shower beating sharply against the pane took him once more to the window. Outside, the aspect had changed; a light breeze had sprung up and the sky was dappled with floating shreds of cloud. One very dark cloud, purple-black in colour, and in shape resembling a gigantic bird floating on widespread wings, was drifting towards the horizon. It was from that cloud the shower must have come, and Tom decided it was like a condor, though all he knew of condors was derived from a cheerful little lyric by his favourite poet:

> *Flapping from out their Condor wings*
> *Invisible Woe!*

But at the sound of the opening door poetry was forgotten, and he wheeled round, expecting to see Phemie again, come this time to clear the table. It was not Phemie, however; it was Mother; and unlike Phemie she looked very far from smiling, with the consequence that his first instinctive movement towards her was checked abruptly. At the same time a mood of obduracy, even of antagonism, which Phemie's friendliness had temporarily dispelled, was revived. Why need she look like that? After all, he had been guilty of nothing so very dreadful! And with his back to the window he stood watching her guardedly, waiting for her first words.

Mother's first words hardly sustained the impressive effect of her entrance, being not in the least what she had intended to say. This was due to the spectacle of the neglected dinner-things, which at once prompted the irresistible question, "Why hasn't Mary come to clear away?"

Tom said he didn't know, but his relief was immediate. With the quickness of perception common to small boys, he divined that if Mother really were taking his behaviour so much to heart her attention could hardly have been distracted by a dinner-tray. Therefore he permitted his own features to relax to something hovering on the verge of a smile, though he still remained where he was, and more or less on the defensive.

Meanwhile, since her distraction had been only momentary, and the result of a strong natural objection both to untidiness in general and to Mary's habitual carelessness, Mother's face had reassumed its former expression. Or very nearly, for Tom was conscious of a subtle modification, as if she had decided to abandon severity and to try persuasion instead. "I came to tell you it is bedtime," she began, "and to ask you to promise to be a good boy and do what Daddy wishes."

It was mildness itself, and Tom's tongue flickered for a moment over his lips, for this was a kind of attack he found far more difficult to meet than either scoldings or reproaches. Nevertheless he steeled himself against it, and returned her gaze unwaveringly. "I'm afraid I can't do that," he said.

Why couldn't he? poor Mother seemed to wonder; for the very quietness of his reply stressed alarmingly its obstinacy, so that having looked in vain for some sign of yielding, she at last turned away. It was against Daddy's advice that she was here at all; he had strongly urged that in the meantime she should hold no communication with the offender; but men were so stupid, and, anyway, he had never understood Tom. "Why are you so headstrong?" she asked gently. "I'm not; but I'm not going to tell lies."

Mother waited a moment before she tried again. "It wouldn't be a lie," she said. "It wouldn't mean——" But in fact she didn't quite know what it would or wouldn't mean—beyond the restoration of peace, since Daddy insisted on it. What weakened her position still further was that she herself felt very far from amicably disposed towards Mr. Sabine. If Daddy were angry with Tom and wished to punish him, she didn't see why he couldn't have given him a smacking and have done with it, instead of insisting on what to her own mind seemed a quite unnecessary apology to Mr. Sabine. Really it was Max who deserved the smacking—an odious boy, and the direct and sole cause of all the trouble. She used to think Miss Sabine was inclined to be hard on Max, but now she fully agreed with her, and his father was just as much, perhaps even more, to blame. How, at any rate, he could reconcile it either with his conscience or his position as a clergyman to encourage his son to go about shooting harmless squirrels, she couldn't imagine! She would never feel the same again towards Mr. Sabine. She had told Daddy so, and a great deal more; but Daddy had pointed out that Tom wasn't being punished for being kind to animals—as she seemed to imply—but for deliberate disobedience; and that to pass this over would be fatal, and the worst possible thing for Tom himself in the long run. Daddy had actually told her not to kiss him good night unless she found him penitent, and she was quite sure that the first question he would ask on her return would be whether she had done so or not. But Tom was as much her son as his—a great deal more so if it came to that—and really there were limits——

At this juncture she caught sight of the macaroons, which had been saved up to eat in bed. There they were now, beside the pillow, and it was just like his innocence, she thought, not to have tried to hide them—as Max no doubt would have done. The macaroons were Phemie's handiwork, she guessed, for the stupid Mary never would have ventured on anything so daring. Or so kind, she added— mentally registering a good mark to Phemie's credit, while at the same time deciding not to see the macaroons. She did kiss him, too; justifying this departure from Daddy's injunctions by telling him to say his prayers, and that she hoped in the morning he would be a better boy. . . .

One effect at least, if not the desired one, her visit produced; and this was to impress on Tom how difficult it was going to be to keep up his present line of conduct. In the morning the battle with Daddy would begin all over again. . . . That is to say, if he were still here in the morning. . . .

Slowly he removed his jacket and hung it over the back of a chair. If he were *not* here—if he were at Granny's for instance. . . . He put his jacket on again, and sitting down on the side of the bed began thoughtfully to nibble a macaroon. . . .

Dusk slowly gathered in the room while, little by little, his plan took shape. He need not go downstairs—which indeed would be risky on account of Mother's open door; and to-night she might listen specially. In the ordinary way he would have *had* to go down, if only to get his shoes; but he had come straight from the study to his own room without removing them, and though he had since put on a pair of slippers, the shoes were still there—luckily half concealed beneath the bed, so that Phemie had not noticed them. Neither had Mother, or she herself would have taken them away, as she had taken the tray; and it was most unlikely he would have any further visitor to-night.

Everything favored his project. He had given no promise to Daddy, which was fortunate, for of course a prisoner on parole was bound by honour not to attempt to escape. He could climb down easily enough by the drain-pipe, and even if he fell part of the way it was no great height, and would be on to a flower-bed. Only he would have to wait till the house was perfectly quiet; and it wouldn't be safe to lie down on the outside of the bed, for he remembered his old plan of visiting the church at night, and how it had come to nothing because he had fallen asleep and slept till morning. . . .

Suddenly he heard the sound of Daddy's voice, and it appeared to be coming from immediately below his window. The dogs must be there too, and have been waiting patiently all this time, for Daddy was telling them to go home. Tom rushed to the window to look. Yes; both Roger and Barker were there; and he longed to make a signal but dared not. They were paying no attention to Daddys' orders, which rapidly became more peremptory, so that in the end Roger reluctantly began to move away. Barker, however, did not budge. He was lying at the edge of the lawn, and when Daddy, losing patience, pushed him with his foot, he growled. Tom couldn't actually hear the growl, but he could see it, and anyhow

he could have told there was a growl from Daddy's immediate outburst of indignation. He even lifted a pebble from the drive and
threw it at poor Barker. At this final insult Barker indeed got up,
yet still he did not run away, but retired slowly and with dignity,
leaving Daddy, Tom thought, looking both undignified and absurd.

It was another proof, if he had needed one, of the faithfulness of
animal friendships, and in his present mood it not only consoled him
but strengthened him in his determination. He would go. . . .

How long would it take him? He had never walked the whole way
to Granny's, and though of course he had often driven, it was very
hard to judge of distances when you were in a car. It couldn't, he
thought, be more than seven or eight miles—possibly less—and at
any rate it didn't much matter when he arrived, since, at the soonest,
Granny and everybody else would have been in bed for hours. . . .

It was too dark now to read and he dared not turn on the light. He
would just have to sit in the darkness, doing nothing, till it was time
for him to start.

23: ON that night of all nights it was just like Daddy to
sit up later than usual, but at length Tom—who for
the past hour had been dozing fitfully in his chair—now sleeping,
now waking—heard him coming upstairs. The time for action was
drawing nearer, and a strange thing was, that as it did so it became far
more difficult to wait. He decided that if he drew down the blinds
he might perhaps risk turning on the light, since sitting on tenter
hooks like this made it impossible to gauge the passage of time,
whereas, if he were to read say forty pages of Apollodorus or Frank
Buckland, that would be practically as good as a clock, and by then,
surely, Daddy would be asleep.

Doggedly—and taking in nothing of what he read—he went
through with his task; after which he shut the book, put on his
shoes, and carefully drew up the blind. He leaned far out over
the sill, and the sweet fragrance of the stocks below his window
rose to him through the night, friendly and reassuring. There was
no moon, yet it was not really dark. He could make out the different
constellations, shining clear and bright in the grey vault of the sky
amid the twinkling of countless unknown stars, and through the

pale glimmer they shed the trees rose black and solid, as through a milky sea. In this ashen half-light, so unlike the light of day, shrubs and bushes assumed fantastic shapes, and the trees seemed to stretch out beckoning arms, stirring softly in the wind, whispering with the whisper of innumerable leaves. Tom put one leg out of the window, and sitting astride the sill, leaned sidelong till he could reach the drain-pipe. This he grasped firmly before drawing out the other leg and clambering down. It was really quite easy, easier than he had expected, for the thick tough creeper gave plenty of support to his feet, and he accomplished the descent almost in silence.

The adventure had now begun, and once out on the road, with the gate closed behind him, his sense of it so entirely took possession of his mind that all else was forgotten. He was no longer running away; he was conscious only of freedom and of being at large in a strange nocturnal world he had never before explored.

He walked on steadily, soon leaving the more immediate and familiar surroundings behind him. The loneliness did not trouble him, though he would have liked Roger as a companion; but only for the sake of his company, not because he had any fears. He felt, in fact, both exhilarated and excited. A light breeze was blowing, but its coolness was merely pleasantly fresh, and it was behind him.

He must have walked two or three miles before a drop of rain fell. It was an uncommonly big drop, and it splashed on to his bare head so unexpectedly that he stopped and looked up in surprise. Somehow he had never thought of rain, yet now he saw that a black wall of cloud had overtaken him and as it advanced was extending rapidly on either side, eclipsing the stars and threatening soon to cover the whole sky. It would only be a shower, he hoped; indeed the large size of the raindrops and their warmth encouraged this view; but it would be a heavy plump while it lasted, and since there was what appeared to be a wood, or plantation, a little beyond the hedge on his left, he determined to seek shelter.

It was not really a wood, Tom found, on coming up to it; not much more than a thicket, composed for the greater part of laurels and rhododendrons; but crouching under these he was completely protected—at all events for the present and till they should be soaked through. Fortunately he had reached it in the nick of time, for the rain now came down in a torrent, like a thunder-shower without thunder, and heavy enough to have drenched him to the skin in a few minutes had he been out in the open. He wriggled in closer to the heart of the thicket, for the ground, though soft, was dry, and composed of a loose vegetable mould. Here he was snug enough, and the combination of the hour, the place, and the sound of the rain pattering on the broad leaves above him, created a sense of solitude such as he had never before known. It was as if, so far as human beings were concerned, he had the whole world to himself, and yet this feeling, though very strange, was by no means unpleasant. On the contrary, it was happy, it was dreamily peaceful, and mingled with it was also the feeling that another and lovely world was near—so near that a sign, a message, possibly a visitor from it, seemed on the point of breaking through. Crouching there, hidden in his leafy den, a hushed and expectant eagerness shone out through his eyes as clearly as a light shining through a window: he was himself, at that moment, half boy, half spirit. . . .

But the rain was nearly over; most of it at present was dropping from the bushes, not from the clouds; and like some small nocturnal animal, Tom crept forth from his shelter.

The cloud-bank had passed on, uncovering once more the starry vault above it, and there once more, far far away in the remoteness of space, were his old friends, the Great Bear, Orion with his belt, the chair of Cassiopeia.

Back on the road, he resumed his tramp, and kept it up for a long time with no noticeable slackening of pace, though he was beginning to feel tired, and sometimes sat down on a low wall or on a bank of stones to rest.

He must be a good many miles from home now. Gradually, too, the surrounding fields were becoming greyer and objects more distinct as the sky lightened. The stars were fading in the twilight of approaching dawn, and presently they disappeared altogether, and a crimson flush swept up above the eastern horizon. This was followed swiftly by a golden shaft of light, and then by the whole edge of the sun's flaming disk: the new day was here.

But Tom's journey was ended, for he had reached Granny's. He passed through the gate and up the avenue to the sleeping house amid the first twittering of drowsy birds. It would be still some hours, he knew, before the servants made an appearance, and there was nothing to be done in the meantime but sit down on the doorstep and wait. He was on the point of doing this, when he remembered that in the open yard at the back of the house there was a dog-kennel, and a very large one, though Granny had never possessed a dog, and the kennel dated back no doubt to ancient Seaford days. It had been specially built, too, for not only was it bigger than usual, but also—supported on four thick squat legs—it stood some inches above the ground and was covered with waterproof sheeting, while, apart from the customary dog's entrance, the entire front was made to slide backwards and forwards along grooves, so that it could be cleaned out more effectively. Of course it must be a long time since it *had* been cleaned out, and it was sure now to be dusty and cobwebby. But Tom wasn't afraid of dust and cobwebs, and if he curled himself up, there would be at least sufficient if not plenty of room. The idea—bringing with it an immediate vision of Roger and Barker, both probably at this moment fast asleep in their kennels—appealed to him strongly. Three minutes later he had put it into execution.

24: HE had rolled up his jacket to make a pillow, and he was so tired that after a while, in spite of the hardness of a bare wooden floor and the discomfort of his narrow quarters, he fell asleep, though it was not a sound sleep, and the unbolting of the back door woke him at once. Peeping out, he saw that it was Rose coming to get coals from the coalhole, and at any ordinary time he would have enjoyed giving her a start. Now, however, he did not feel much in the mood for playing tricks, and merely said softly: "I'm here, Rose."

Nevertheless, Rose uttered a half-stifled scream and dropped her shovel, though she still clung to the bucket. The scream brought Cook, and they both stood stock-still, side by side, gazing in mute astonishment at a rather sheepish Tom, who—feeling cold, stiff, and at a low ebb generally—emerged with some difficulty from his unusual bedchamber.

Cook recovered first, or at any rate first found words. "My sakes! In the name of goodness what's happened to you and where have you been? Just look at the state of him!" And they both looked, which really was not surprising, for you can't burrow in loose earth under laurel bushes, and sleep in disused dog-kennels, without accumulating a certain amount of grime, and Tom had accumulated more than he realized. His hands and knees were black, his face was streaked with dirt, and there were cobwebs in his hair. As for his clothes——! But Cook made a sudden grab at him, caught him by the shoulders, and hurried him on into the house without further speech.

A fire was roaring good-temperedly in the kitchen range, and he held out his hands to the genial blaze, seeing which, Cook drew forward a chair and plumped him into it. "What the mistress will say I don't know!" she began. "I'm going to make her morning tea now, for she likes it early, and it's gone seven."

She stood over him, as if uncertain what to do next, while Rose, who had returned with her coal-bucket, also hovered near. Both, Tom saw, having got over their first consternation, were now consumed with a burning curiosity, yet at the same time they seemed worried—Cook especially. "You look just about worn out," she commiserated, "which I'm sure is little wonder." Turning from him, she shook her head dubiously before proceeding to make tea in two pots—one for the present company, he supposed, and one for Granny.

"What am I to tell her?" the more lackadaisical Rose murmured, casting an uneasy glance at the tray Cook was preparing.

The question was not addressed to Tom, but it was he who answered it. "You needn't tell her anything," he said. "I'm going up myself, and I'll tell her."

This brought Cook round to him again for a further inspection. "You can't," she declared peremptorily. "Leastways, not till I've cleaned you up a bit first."

She had poured him out a cup of tea, which he drank, and then began munching biscuits from the tin. The tea revived him, and he drank a second cup; while all the time they watched him as if he were Edward or Alfred eating nuts or bread-and-milk. "I'll clean myself afterwards," he mumbled, with his mouth full of biscuit. "I'm going to speak to Granny first. What's the good of waiting—when she'll want to see me anyhow. . . . Besides, there's nothing to tell—except that I'm here, and arrived too early, and got into the kennel."

"You mean to say you've been walking all night—and by yourself —and all those miles!" Cook exclaimed, while Rose simultaneously put in a feeble "Well I never!"

But this wonder-struck attitude was beginning to pall on Tom,

and he answered impatiently: "Of course I've been walking all night.
How do you think I got here if I didn't walk . . . ? Sorry!" he
added next moment, a little ashamed of his irritability; and when
Rose lifted the tray to carry it upstairs, he followed her—though
he lingered outside on the landing until he heard her announcing in
awe-stricken tones, "Master Tom's here."

Granny was sitting up in bed, and he ran forward to kiss her
before she had time to speak. She didn't behave like Rose and Cook,
and he had known she wouldn't. Certainly she looked astonished,
but she didn't gasp or stare or throw up her hands, nor did she
seem to mind his being dirty. "I've run away, Granny," he whispered
impetuously into her ear. "I had to, because Daddy wants me to
say I'm sorry to Mr. Sabine and I won't. Max killed my squirrel,
and I took his gun and threw it in the river, and——"

But Granny was saying "Ssh—ssh," and he stopped, while she
spoke to Rose, who having deposited the tray on a table beside
the bed, still lingered near the door. "See first of all that he gets
a bath, Rose. You might prepare it now: I suppose the water's hot. . . .

"And after that you're to go straight to bed," she went on, turning
to Tom. "You can tell me everything later; but not another word
now. By the time you're undressed, Rose will have the bath ready,
and the moment you come out of it you're to go to bed and to sleep
till I call you. Rose will make up the bed while you're having your
bath, and she can take away your things and clean them. . . . Be
a good boy, now, and do as I tell you. We'll have plenty of time to
talk afterward, so meanwhile just show me how good you *can* be."

She smiled, gave him a pat on the hand and a friendly little push,
and in return, determined to obey literally, Tom departed without
one further syllable, going to the room he always slept in, while
Rose went to the bath-room, where he heard her turning on the taps.

He undressed slowly, giving the bath plenty of time to fill. But
it was very pleasant to get his soiled clothes off, and still pleasanter
when, having made his way to the bath-room, he was lying soaking
in the warm water. He allowed his limbs to relax deliciously.
Stretched at full length, he lay quite still, with his eyes closed. All
the same, it wouldn't do to fall asleep, which he began to feel might
easily happen if he wasn't careful. . . .

Presently there was a knock on the door—Rose again—this time
to tell him she had made his bed and was taking his clothes down to
the kitchen to see what could be done with them. Rose must have

recovered, for her voice sounded admonitory and slightly aggrieved. Later she would leave the clothes on a chair outside his door, she said, where he would find them when he got up. Tom thanked her drowsily, and getting out of the bath began to dry himself. This finished, he opened the door about two inches just to make sure the coast was clear before scuttling across the landing to his bedroom.

There, the first thing he did was to look to see if Rose had stuck a hot jar in his bed, and of course she had. He removed it. As if anybody wanted hot jars—particularly in the middle of summer! But it was always the same at Granny's: she herself actually liked two! Raising the bedclothes, with a little sigh of satisfaction he slid naked between the sheets, and before he had quite decided what he was going to think about was wrapped in a slumber too deep for dreams.

It was Granny who awakened him. She did not come in, but merely tapped on the door, and when he answered told him lunch would be ready in a few minutes. Tom yawned and stretched himself luxuriously. He felt warm and extremely comfortable. All the tiredness and stiffness had passed out of his bones, and the boy who presently ran downstairs to Granny was very different from the weary and travel-stained one who had visited her a few hours earlier.

"Well, you look 'slept' at any rate," was the old lady's rather dry comment when he entered the room, feeling not only "slept" but quite recovered. She inspected him with an air of strict neutrality, as of one temporarily reserving judgement. "And now," she went on, when they were seated at the table, "you'd better give me *your* version of this escapade."

He did so, omitting nothing, nor had he only one listener, for during the progress of his story Rose found so many pretexts for lingering in the room that in the end Granny had to tell her, "That will do, Rose; I think we have everything we want."

So Rose had to clear out, though with such obvious reluctance that Tom thought it rather unkind of Granny. He understood her reason, all the same, when having waited till the door was closed, she said: "I've been talking to your mother on the telephone. I rang her up as soon as I could to tell her you were here, and fortunately I got her in time. . . . I mean, they hadn't yet missed you, as only the servants were down. Otherwise, I imagine, she would have been even more astonished and more upset than she was—which is saying a good deal. . . . Suppose, for some reason she had gone to your room in the middle of the night and found you weren't there! How could she possibly have known where you were or what had happened to you?"

"I'm sorry," Tom murmured repentantly. "I know I ought to have left a note or something, and I would have if I'd remembered."

Granny herself knew he would; therefore all she answered was: "She told me she would be over in the afternoon, probably by teatime."

It was enough for Tom, however, who had not contemplated such rapid action. It altered indeed the entire prospect, and he turned two startled eyes on Granny's mild though at present distinctly noncommittal countenance. "Then—Daddy will be coming too," he faltered.

"I don't think so," Granny replied.

"But he will," Tom persisted. "How can she come without him? She can't drive the car, and there's nobody else."

Granny guessed what he was thinking, and for a minute or two deliberately allowed him to go on thinking it before she said quietly: "I told her I should like to keep you for a few days, and in the end she agreed that this might perhaps be best—if she could persuade your father to consent to it. She said she would ask him, at any rate, though she very much feared he would insist on your coming home at once."

Tom listened with a clouded and brooding expression on his face. Past experience enabled him to picture the scene only too clearly— Mother's proposal, Daddy's reception of it, Mother's reply, and the ensuing arguments and discussion—much more suggestive of a conflict of wills than of "persuasion."

Granny noticed the worried look in his eyes, but mistook its origin. "She rang me up again—about two hours later—to tell me Doctor Macrory was going to drive her over, and that she would bring whatever things you required."

"That means Daddy's furious," Tom said darkly.

Some such suspicion had in fact crossed Granny's own mind— particularly since, in the later communication, her son-in-law's name had not been mentioned. So she replied: "Well, if he is, it ought to show you what comes of being self-willed and disobedient. Other people, who are perfectly innocent, have to suffer for it."

"But Granny; I told you exactly *everything* that happened, and *you* didn't seem so very angry!"

"That's not the same at all. In your father's position I dare say I should have been. And now he'll very likely feel offended too. . . . Which, in all the circumstances, I must say doesn't strike me as surprising."

Tom sat in silence, frowning. The silence was prolonged, for Granny, perhaps again on purpose, forbore to break it. At last he said: "Maybe I'd better go home."

To his surprise, this sudden and belated compliance had far from the anticipated effect. Granny, in fact, asked him quite sharply: "Do you mean by that you are now willing to apologize to Mr. Sabine?"

"No," Tom muttered.

"Then perhaps for once you'll allow other people to decide what is the best thing to do—and nothing can be decided until your mother comes."

25: LUNCH over, Tom went out to talk to Quigley, who, whatever his shortcomings as a gardener, possessed one great advantage over William, in that he was a most sociable person. So they pottered about together, Tom following like a dog close on Quigley's heels, while they kept up a familiar if broken stream of conversation. Among other things, they discussed William himself; Quigley in a mock-serious vein, and illustrating his appreciation of that irreproachable person with several anecdotes, which if not strictly veracious, were at least new to Tom and amusing. Thus the time passed till they heard the sound of the approaching car.

Tom had left the gate open for it, and a few seconds later it swept up the drive, bringing not only Doctor Macrory and Mother, but also a most unexpected Pascoe, whom he had supposed to be still far away in Donegal. The usual bustle of alighting ensued—accompanied by greetings of various kinds—an embrace from Mother, a friendly "Hello!" from Pascoe, and a slap on the back from Doctor Macrory—in the midst of which Granny appeared at the top of the steps to welcome her visitors.

Mother looked worried, and as if she very much wished the others

weren't there. But, backed up by Tom's verbal asseverations, an
anxious inspection persuaded her that outwardly at least he was none
the worse for his adventure, and just at present there was no opportunity for more. Pascoe had dragged out a suitcase, which Tom took
from him, and they all moved together towards the house, with the
exception of Doctor Macrory, who refused to come in, but promised
to return later in time for tea and to take Mother home. With this
assurance the doctor got back into his car, and they waited to see
him start—Mother and Granny on the doorstep, the two boys
close beside him on the drive; so that after leaning out to wave *au
revoir* to the ladies he was able to catch Tom's eye, and by a wink
convey a private message that all was well.

At least this was how Tom interpreted it, and he was about to
follow Mother and Granny into the house when the latter suggested
that he should leave down the suitcase for Rose to look after, adding
that she and Mother wished to have a little chat together, and that in
the meantime he might like to entertain his friend by showing him
the garden and the grounds. . . .

Nothing loath, for Doctor Macrory's signal had had a most cheer-
ing effect, Tom deposited his burden. "Come on," he said gaily to
Pascoe; and as soon as he got him alone: "When did you get back,
and how did they manage to pick you up?"

"I got back yesterday," Pascoe replied sedately, "and I rode over
to your house after lunch to-day. They were just starting when I
arrived, so your mother told me where you were and asked me if
I'd like to come with them."

"I suppose that means you'll have to go back with them," Tom reflected. "It's a pity you didn't ride over on your bike: then you could
have stayed all evening. . . . I must say," he went on, "you didn't
write many letters—considering all the fuss you made about getting
me to write!"

Pascoe admitted the truth of this. "I meant to—honestly: but somehow or other I was always prevented—or else I was too sleepy—or
——. Anyhow, we needn't bother about that now: tell me what's
happened."

The expression on Tom's face, which prior to these words had be-
tokened a remarkable revival in his spirits, immediately altered. All
the troubles and difficulties, from which the arrival of the car and its
occupants had temporarily distracted his thoughts, now came back
with a rush, and he wondered how much Pascoe knew—if indeed he

really knew anything and were not merely trying a shot in the dark?
"Why?" he asked warily. "What makes you think something's
happened?"

Pascoe shrugged his shoulders. "Because I know it has."

Tom looked at him, but gained no information from the calm gaze
which met his own. "Did Mother say anything?" he questioned
doubtfully.

"Not to me: I don't suppose she would before Doctor Macrory.
All the same, I knew at once that something must be up."

"I don't see why," Tom muttered, far from pleased. Of course
sooner or later he would have confided in Pascoe, but just at present
he was sick of repeating the same story again and again, and this
persistence made it inevitable. To get done with it as quickly as possible, he produced a bald and much abbreviated account, to which
Pascoe listened without comment. Tom didn't care. In fact he was
rather glad Pascoe said nothing—even if it meant that like everybody else he disapproved. For by now he felt so weary of the whole
thing that all he wanted was to forget it. Perhaps it was this that
brought back to memory an old plan, which recent events had thrust
into the background of his mind. Certainly he could have no better
opportunity than the present for putting it into practice, and it would
at least save him from having to talk about Mr. Sabine and Max. Not
that he himself felt in the right mood. Very definitely he didn't, but
that couldn't be helped; and besides, it was what Pascoe would feel—
if he felt anything at all—that mattered. At all events he might as well
try the experiment and see what happened. . . .

"Let's go in," he proposed, turning back towards the house.

Pascoe made no movement to follow him. "I don't think they want
us," he said dubiously. "Your grandmother practically told us she
didn't."

"Oh, Granny won't mind: why should she?" And since Pascoe, in
spite of this assurance, still hung back: "I don't mean to *them* of
course, if that's what you're thinking. I mean upstairs—to a part of
the house Granny doesn't even use. It's been shut up ever since she
came here."

But Pascoe, possibly failing to see how this constituted an attraction, continued to hesitate. It was obvious that he would very much
prefer to explore the grounds outside, and that only his status as a
visitor prevented him from saying so. "Oh, all right," he finally gave
in, but with such a marked absence of enthusiasm that at any other

time Tom would have abandoned the project. Now, however, Pascoe's unwillingness was ignored; he was led indoors; Tom got the key; and they ascended the stairs together to the disused wing.

Yet nothing was going right. Conscious of Pascoe's latent antagonism, Tom already felt discouraged, and it was with but the faintest echo of his former thrill of expectancy that he unlocked the door at the end of the passage. Pascoe, still hankering after the sunlight and the unexplored grounds outside, clearly felt no thrill whatever; nor, as he rather sulkily followed his conductor, did he try to conceal his dissatisfaction at being dragged upstairs—apparently to gaze at three or four abandoned rooms, with nothing in them except some more or less dilapidated furniture and a few mouldy old books. Pascoe very obviously was bored, and notwithstanding all efforts to the contrary, his unresponsiveness and complete lack of interest were producing a more and more damping effect upon Tom himself. There, in the window, was the table, with the pile of *Graphics* still open upon it; outwardly, in spite of all the dusting and scrubbing, little was changed since he had been here last; yet in an inner and spiritual sense everything was changed. The beauty and the wonder and the sense of haunting were gone; he even began to see it all as Pascoe saw it—an abandoned room, some more or less dilapidated furniture, and a few mouldy old books. He turned, and a question hovered on his lips, but died unspoken as Pascoe asked bluntly; "Is this *all?*"

The accentuation of the final word completed what had been nearly accomplished without it. "Yes," Tom answered. "We'll go down."

His abrupt and unexpected acquiescence—perhaps because it *was* unexpected—seemed to produce more effect than his earlier eagerness, for it was with a quite genuine curiosity that Pascoe now glanced at him. "Why were you so anxious to bring me up, then?" he said. "You *were*, you know, though now you seem to have changed your mind."

Tom turned away. "I thought you might like it," he replied.

"Like what? What is there *to* like? I don't believe you thought any such thing. You had a particular reason, and now, as usual, you're making a mystery about it."

"Well, I haven't any longer," Tom said, "so it doesn't matter. . . . There's the gong," he continued with relief, as the sound came up to them, faint and muffled, from the hall below. "Doctor Macrory must have come back, so we'd better go down."

The interruption was welcome. His proposed experiment had faded out so flatly that it could not even be said to have ended, since it had never begun. Or rather, what had faded out was his own enthusiasm, his own responsiveness. His present reaction almost amounted to a feeling of disillusionment, and as they retraced their steps along the passage, and he locked the door behind them, he half made up his mind never to open it again.

To come downstairs was to come at once into a comfortable pro-saic world where, if nothing was particularly enthralling, all was safe and familiar. Mother, Doctor Macrory, and Granny had already be-gun tea when he and Pascoe entered, Granny presiding at the table. The sunshine streaming through the open windows made the room attractively gay, but it was gay also with that general atmosphere of cheerfulness and geniality which this most informal and conversa-tional of meals seems particularly to promote. Moreover, whether by previous arrangement or not, evidently it had been decided to regard Tom's visit to Granny, not as the result of home complications, but as a perfectly ordinary one. Granny herself made this doubly clear, when, after urging Pascoe to try Cook's slimcakes, she invited him to stay for a day or two to keep Tom company.

For some private reason this appeared to amuse Doctor Macrory. "What about the Dogs' Club?" he suggested. "That is, if you want to do the thing really in style. I think I can accept so far as Barker is concerned."

It was a very transparent joke; nevertheless Mother, knowing both Tom and Granny, thought it prudent to intervene. "I fancy if she has two gentlemen to look after her that will be sufficient."

Tom and Doctor Macrory laughed, but Granny had never heard of the Dogs' Club, and Pascoe saw nothing to laugh at. Granny had turned again to him, this time to inquire if they had a telephone at home. "If so, you could ring your mother up after tea. That is, if you think you'd like to stay."

Pascoe thought he would like it very much, but on the other hand, supposing he got his mother and she gave him permission, wouldn't he still have to go home first to get pyjamas and other necessaries; and he had left his bicycle at Tom's house.

"I'm sure Tom can lend you all you need for to-night," Granny declared. "And you can get anything else to-morrow."

Doctor Macrory, with his customary good nature, endorsed this view. "His best plan will be to come with us now in the car. I'll have to be going in a few minutes anyhow. Then he can ride back here on his bicycle, and I dare say you'll forgive him if he's a little late for dinner."

Mother alone, for a moment looked doubtful: but seeing Pascoe getting up to put Granny's suggestion into execution, she left her misgivings unspoken, and after a brief hesitation said: "In the meantime, while Clement is telephoning, I think Tom and I will take a stroll in the garden. You'll find us there when you're ready to start."

She rose from her chair as she spoke, and Tom followed her, not surprised, for he had known she would want to speak to him by himself before leaving, but wondering a little what she was going to tell him.

She began at once. "I saw Miss Sabine this morning: in fact I had a long talk with her. I don't know whether you realize what a good friend you have in Miss Sabine. Nobody could have been kinder or nicer about this whole unfortunate business than she was, and I think you might do something in return—something to please her, to please Daddy, and to please me."

Tom desired nothing more than to please Miss Sabine and to please Mother; about Daddy he felt less keen. "What do you want me to do?" he asked.

"To write a little note to Mr. Sabine; that is all."

Tom hesitated, his face clouding. Mother might pretend it wasn't much, but she must know it meant abandoning his whole position, and admitting he was wrong when he wasn't. "To tell him I'm sorry?" he muttered unwillingly.

"Yes. Remember this is entirely between ourselves: I purposely said nothing to Daddy about it in case you might refuse."

He waited a moment, Mother's hand on his shoulder. He felt that by putting the matter in this way she was somehow imposing on him, but he knew she would be deeply hurt if he were to tell her so. All the same, he could not help looking at her reproachfully before, with a faint sigh, he submitted. "All right," he said. "But I won't really be sorry—I mean in the way he'll think—not about him and Max."

Mother did not press this point: she drew a breath of relief. "I'm sure if you write the note and show it to Granny before sending it, you will be doing what is right, and will never regret it afterwards."

Tom was very far from sure, but since he would be doing it to please Mother and Miss Sabine, not Mr. Sabine or Max, and since he could make the note extremely cold and formal—in fact thoroughly unconvincing—he promised; nor was there time for much more before the others appeared, and Mother, Doctor Macrory, and Pascoe got into the car.

Tom and Granny saw them off, standing side by side; and when the car had disappeared and they had re-entered the house, he told Granny of his promise. She, too, seemed relieved, and between them, and with many consultations and fresh starts, they proceeded to compose the momentous letter, not without some chuckles from the old lady, though Tom could see nothing funny in his efforts to keep his word to Mother and at the same time not to encourage Mr. Sabine to imagine he had really changed his mind or regarded him with anything but the most frigid and distant politeness. The task was difficult, but Granny, entering into the spirit of it, was very helpful; and the rough draft at last completed, he copied it out, addressed the envelope, and left it on the hall table for the postman to collect.

26: GRANNY was much surprised when after dinner her guests, instead of going out to the garden as she had expected them to do, suggested playing a game of Pelmanism, or, as they called it, Twos. Still, if that was what they wanted she was quite agreeable, and anyhow, after last night's performance, she had decided to send Tom to bed early. Granny, however, entirely mistook the situation, and this because she knew nothing of a private consultation in which the question of her own entertainment had been very carefully weighed. It never crossed her mind that the game of Twos might have been proposed for her benefit, nor did it subsequently strike her that, with her rather dim old eyes and their remarkably bright ones, it was, to say the least, surprising that she should win. Nevertheless, win she did; and the game over, and the card-table put away, good-nights were said—with final injunctions from Granny that there was to be no dawdling, and no talking after they were in bed.

But such instructions are received as a matter of course, as part of a conventional formula, and enter in at one ear straightway to go out at the other. Once in bed, Pascoe had a number of things to relate about his visit to Aunt Rhoda in Donegal, and from these, by easy transitions, the conversation drifted, first to their present visit, and next to Tom's previous visits at Tramore. Following on the activities of a very crowded day, the darkness and stillness and sense of comfort and privacy induced a mood of confidence, and without being questioned, without indeed remembering his earlier uncommunicativeness, Tom found himself telling Pascoe why he had taken him up to the deserted wing, and what had happened there on a former occasion. The story came at first fluently, but, as it proceeded, more and more brokenly and with increasingly longer pauses, though Pascoe continued to listen attentively—so attentively that he made neither a movement nor a sound to interrupt it. Even after it was finished the silence still persisted, and it was only then that Tom, growing suspicious, discovered him to be sound asleep.

He was not offended; he had been talking really, towards the end, as much to himself as to his companion; and now he felt too drowsy to wonder at what point Pascoe had ceased to hear him. That, he would learn to-morrow, and in the meantime he was content to lie in dreamy contemplation of a world shifting uncertainly between recollection and imagination. Nor was he surprised to see, amid drifting scenes and faces, Ralph himself standing between the window and the bed. By that time, too, he must have forgotten Pascoe, or surely he would have awakened him, whereas all he did was to murmur sleepily; "Why have you come?"

The voice that answered him was faint and thin as the whisper of dry corn. "I don't know. I don't think I have come. I don't think this is real. . . . Or perhaps I can only come when you are dreaming, for I think you are dreaming now. . . ."

There was a silence—deep, wonderful, unbroken—as if all the restful murmuring whispers of earth and night were suddenly stilled. . . .

"Listen!"

Tom listened, but somehow Ralph was no longer there; and far, far away he could hear the sound of waves breaking, and surely he had heard that low distant plash before—many times perhaps, though when and where he had forgotten. Next moment the darkness vanished, and he had a vision of a wide, curving beach of yellow sand, where children were playing in the sunlight at the edge of a timeless sea. They were building castles on the sand, and their happy voices reached him—gay, innocent, laughing. Vision or memory, the scene brought with it no feeling of strangeness, only the sense of returning to a lovely and familiar place, which would always be there, though at times it might be hidden from him. . . .

The dark blue water stretched out and out under a golden haze, till it met the softer, paler blue of the sky. That happy shore he knew— and it was drawing closer, it seemed very near, already less dream than reality. For he could feel the warm sun on his hands and face, and he had to step back quickly as a small wave curled over and broke, melting and hissing, in a thin line of foam at his feet. . . .

November 1942
October 1943

The Retreat

or

The Machinations of Henry

'There's tempest in the sky'
The Three Little Kittens

THE RETREAT

Happy those early days, when I
Shined in my angel-infancy!
Before I understood this place
Appointed for my second race,
Or taught my soul to fancy aught
But a white, celestial thought;
When yet I had not walked above
A mile or two from my first Love,
And looking back—at that short space—
Could see a glimpse of his bright face;
When on some gilded cloud, or flower,
My gazing soul would dwell an hour,
And in those weaker glories spy
Some shadows of eternity. . . .

HENRY VAUGHAN

PART ONE

1. AN old man, clad from throat to silver-buckled shoes in a wide loose-sleeved black robe, stood at a window peering out into the darkness. His silken silver hair fell in one long smooth lock over a high narrow forehead; his face, minutely lined, was fine as a cameo, and his skin the colour of an ancient parchment. The ears were very slightly pointed, the nose strong and straight, the mouth small. The hand that grasped and held aside the black curtain was fine too, and though time had wrinkled it and revealed the blue veins running up into the wrist, it had not spoiled its shapeliness.

The old man looked frail and wasted, as if his body were no more than a dry transparent husk through which the flame of life shone bright but heatless. He was like one of those delicate skeleton leaves one finds in some sheltered hollow in the woods—desiccated, perfect in form, yet so fragile that when one holds it up against the sun the light shines through. His dark still eyes had a tranquillity of detached contemplation rather than of amiability, for beneath their abstraction glittered the latent energy of a cold and formidable will. "Tib—Tib——" he called. "Tibby—Tibby." But the world outside was dark and frozen, the latticed window shut, and he called so softly that it was little more than a murmur. Then he let the curtain drop back soundlessly into its heavy folds, and returned to a carved high-backed chair by the hearth. . . .

It was late—very late—some hour between midnight and dawn— and a strange, precarious silence filled the room. On a stool, blotted in the shadow of the chimney corner, with eyes that a moment ago had been closed in slumber, but were now glinting and watchful, sat a slim boy of twelve or thirteen, also dressed in black. He had fallen asleep there, he did not quite know when, but it must have been several hours ago, and he guessed that his master either thought he was asleep still, or more likely had forgotten him.

He was a peculiar old man: the boy had begun to fear him. What was he doing now for instance, and for what or whom was he waiting? Did he sit up every night like this, in that straight-backed chair, with its green threadbare velvet cushion? It would be better for him if he were to say his prayers and go to bed, for though by no means exceptionally pious himself, the boy had been brought up in the Catholic faith, and he remembered uneasily that since he had entered the old man's service they had never once been to mass, nor had a priest crossed their door. At first he had fancied that his master himself must be a kind of priest, but now he held another view. He was no priest—of the true church at any rate—nor was that mysterious sign of two interlocked triangles, drawn in gold on the white marble table, a Christian symbol. The boy comforted himself with the reflection that Tibby at least was gone, and the hope that he would never come back. . . .

He wished he had not fallen asleep, but that nearly always happened after he had been looking at the pictures in the black polished stone. He tried to remember the pictures, but he could not—he never could—and the stone itself was gone, locked up once more, he supposed, in the cabinet where his master kept it. He wished he had gone to bed, wished he could summon up energy to go now; but a kind of languor held him, mingled with curiosity and a vague expectancy, for surely his master was not sitting there in mere idleness, though what his purpose could be was hard to imagine. If it were not that no visitors ever came, the boy would have thought he was expecting a visitor now. And it *might* be that: it was just possible that the old man was not so solitary as he seemed to be. The boy slept soundly in a little room in the other wing of the house: if someone were to come in the night he would know nothing of it. Only, to crouch here forgotten was almost like hiding, almost like spying; perhaps he should make a movement, a sound. Yet he did neither. . . .

In the great bare room three of the four walls were hung with moth-riddled, perishing tapestries, at present only dimly visible even to the boy's keen young eyes. The lamplight, he thought, must have grown weaker while he slept. It floated towards, but no longer quite reached, the outer edges of the room, so that the walls remained in an equivocal shadow that was neither light nor darkness. And next moment it seemed to him that the light was not so much failing as being thrust back by this shadow, which was condensing in certain places, and very slowly gaining ground. At the same time he became conscious that the temperature of the room had sunk, as if the windows had been stealthily opened to admit the icy air from outside. But he knew this could not be so—knew the windows were fast. Besides, the black velvet curtains which hung before them had never once stirred.

The old man's head had begun to nod forward on his breast, but now abruptly he sat up. None too soon, it seemed, for the flame of the lamp had begun to wink ominously. Yet it must have been the cold which had aroused him, for his eyes had been shut. As he stood up his face was angry and impatient. He went to attend to the lamp, though what he did to it the boy could not see, because the old man's back was turned to him. He could only see that his hands hovered about it and that when they lifted the flame lifted also. Then, still with his hands outstretched, he stepped forward slowly, muttering incomprehensible words, and the shadow retreated before him, and the darker cloudy patches melted away.

The boy was less surprised than he would have been some months ago, but he hurriedly drew a cross upon his breast and whispered a Latin prayer he had been taught. Once more the lamp burned brightly, and now, in the increased light, all the objects the room contained were clearly visible. They were not numerous—a few chairs, a cabinet whose tall black doors somehow suggested the wings of a sleeping bat, a tripod surmounted by an empty brazier, two tables, and some shelves of books. The floor was bare, and at one side of the immense open hearth stood what appeared to be a kind of furnace built of brick and surmounted by a cone. The larger of the tables was drawn between the windows. It was square and massive and littered with oddly shaped vessels of copper and crystal. On the smaller table, the white marble table in the centre of the room, there was nothing but the burning lamp.

The old man returned to the hearth and cast on more wood. As he did so the boy could see his lips moving, though they made no sound. The wood was dry and soon broke into a flame. Golden jets of light spurted beyond the radius of the lamplight, licking up against the tapestried walls, flickering and darting, like the tongues of serpents. They had a curious effect, beautiful and fantastic, for at one moment there was only a veil of trembling shadow, and at the next a stiff and formal landscape peopled with ghostly figures leapt into view—all the more lifelike because the figures and the trees visibly moved. The boy, however, knew the origin of this movement, and that it was not of his master's making. It was natural: he had seen it happening in the daytime. Every room in this crumbling half-dilapidated house was full of draughts, and it must be only such a draught now, passing between the wall and the hangings, which caused them to ripple and to swell.

Again he began to feel drowsy, and again he closed his eyes. Suddenly he opened them to find that he was alone. At once his sleepiness vanished. The lamp was still burning, but the fire had ceased to blaze and was sunk to a hot red glow. The boy had never been alone in this room before, and he glanced nervously about him with quick yet stealthy movements of his head. It was here that his master carried on his secret labours, and always when he left the room he locked the door behind him. The boy stepped swiftly across the floor, for the thought of being shut in was not pleasant, but the key was in the lock, so his master must be coming back. With that a spirit of inquisitiveness seized him: it was his chance to examine and explore, and he might never have another. The alchemical apparatus he did not dare to touch, but might there not be simpler instruments of magic—cloaks of darkness, flying broomsticks, wishing-caps—he knew not what? He had never seen the doors of the cabinet opened for more than a moment or two, when his master had opened them to get out the shining black stone. But in those moments his quick eyes had caught glimpses of the interior—of dried herbs and chafing dishes, of crystal phials and a rod of hazelwood that was perhaps a wand, of a sickle-shaped dagger and a sword. He knew the exact uses of none of these objects except the stone, but the cabinet was large and deep, its interior dusky enough to hide many secrets, there must be other things, and perhaps the purposes of some of them could be grasped. He resolved at any rate to take a peep, for this key too was in the lock. Nevertheless, when he tried the door, it would not open.

And all at once the boy was afraid. Why had he been left alone like this? Was it a trap? A minute ago he had felt bold, excited, adventurous; now he was abruptly transformed into a coward. He had heard no sound, nothing appeared to have happened, nothing was changed except himself. He still stood by the door of the cabinet, but he no longer thought of opening it. An icy presentiment of horror gripped coldly and woefully at his heart, his blood chilled, his breath stopped, for he knew with every nerve of his body that the visitor his master was expecting had arrived—had at that very moment entered the house. Only what visitor? He had no name, no identity, and he had given no warning of his approach. The boy stood paralyzed, listening intently. He listened, and presently it was as if every part of him had become merely one wide quivering ear. He heard now many faint sounds in remote closed rooms—sounds, in this room, that had hitherto been inaudible—the frost drawing patterns on the window pane, a spider weaving his web. . . .

And then he heard a louder sound—clear though still distant— knock—knock—knock—in the lower part of the house. Knock— knock—knock—it was drawing nearer, it was mounting the stairs, it was at the end of the passage. The boy's wide eyes were fixed in terror on the door. He might still have time to lock himself in, only he knew this would be useless: when the knocking reached it, the door would open slowly and inevitably, as to the Hand of Glory.

That last dreadful summons on the door itself would be worst of all. Better to avert it, better to go to meet it, and he sprang across the room and flung the door wide.

Instantly his fear was gone. He half laughed, half cried, in the sudden wonderful uprush of relief, as there stepped across the threshold no hideous phantom, but the loveliest little creature he had ever beheld. It was a deer—still far too young to have horns—with dark soft eyes and smooth dappled coat. And those four small delicate hoofs it must have been that had made the knocking which had so frightened him. It had sought him out, was actually in the room, bringing with it a kind of wild fragrance of the woods. It had come to look for him, this little messenger without a message, for as he put his arm round it and began to stroke it, it turned and they walked together down the dark passage and the darker stairs, and along another passage leading to a side door which stood ajar.

The boy pushed open the door; but the winter and the night were gone. Gone like a dream—gone and, almost before he had taken two steps, forgotten. The old man was forgotten, the room forgotten, the house forgotten. There was nothing—nothing but a world of gleaming sunshine—a world of cool green leaves and running water. . . .

Tom opened his eyes in the darkness. His heart was still thumping, but he had a feeling of gladness. It must be the middle of the night, he realized, or very early morning, for the tree whose leaves were brushing softly against the window pane was hardly distinguishable. As usual before getting into bed he had pulled up the blinds, always carefully drawn down by Mary, and now as he grew wider awake he stared out through the dim square of glass into a penumbral world. Not a sound could he hear except when the branches stooped to stroke the window. And then, soft and far, a rounded melodious note was repeated twice. It was the old grandfather's clock in the hall conscientiously striking the hour, but Tom liked to fancy that it was calling to him, for it was a nice old clock, and he had persuaded himself that there was, if not an actual friendship, at least a sort of secret understanding between them. . . .

He had been dreaming, and he perfectly remembered his dream; but the strange thing was that though it had been pleasant and happy it seemed to have left a shadow on his mind. Had there been an earlier dream which he could not recall? He remembered trees, and sunlight dancing on a stream, and a deer. He had been in a kind of narrow valley with a stream flowing through it; and it was spring. But what had happened earlier? Or had anything happened? If not, why was he in a perspiration, and why had he kicked off his bedclothes as if he had been struggling against a nightmare? There had been *something*—something frightening—though it seemed silly to say so when it had left not a trace behind it. Unless this in itself were a trace! For there had been a series of similar awakenings—three at least he could remember in the past fortnight—and always that feeling of having escaped only just in time. But escaped from what? The merest hint, Tom thought, and the entire thing would come back to him but that hint was withheld. When he tried to break through the intervening blank he could not, and the struggle was even physically painful, as though a band were being pressed tighter and tighter round his brain. It was as if he were pushing against a void, and the strain grew so acute that he felt as if a spring in his mind were on the point of snapping. The instant he relaxed his efforts he had a feeling of relief. He would not try to remember, and to dismiss the whole thing still further from his mind he sat up in bed and sang in imagination the tune of "Who is Sylvia?"

When he lay down again he still felt a little shaken and exhausted, but he turned on his side and shut his eyes. This was the right treatment, for very soon he felt comfortable and drowsy. Perhaps some day an instrument would be invented for recording people's dreams. It did not seem to Tom at all impossible, nor even much more wonderful than when Mr. Holbrook put a black shining disk into a wooden box and presently Caruso, who was actually dead, began to sing to you. That, again, wasn't very different from the *Arabian Nights* story of the fisherman who unsealed the stopper of a brass

jar and released a genie who had been shut in the jar ages ago by King
Solomon. . . .

Tom must by now have been very drowsy indeed, for through his
closed eyelids he saw a great dark camera, shrouded with mysterious
black curtains or doors that were somehow like the wings of a sleeping
bat, set there beside his pillow, waiting to photograph his dreams.
He was just wondering if bats really could see dreams, and in that
case if owls and cats could, when he heard a light scratching on the
panel of the door. He knew what *that* was in a moment, and after
waiting till it came again slid out of bed. He opened the door and
stopped on the threshold to tie the cord of his pyjamas, while faint
little mews, scattered like grace notes through a rich purring, rose
out of the darkness, and the black plump body of Henry rubbed and
pressed against his legs.

Henry must have come to watch his dreams, but since he wouldn't
be able to talk about them afterwards, that wasn't much use. It would
have to be a person—a person with second sight, Tom decided,
though he didn't quite know what it was you actually saw when you
had second sight. He knew that there *was* such a thing, however,
because Mother's grandfather had been "gifted" with it. It had always
run in the Collet family, Mother said, and she ought to know, because she was a Collet herself. In fact, though when she had married
Daddy she had been obliged to take his name and become a Barber,
she still seemed to prefer being a Collet. Tom made these reflections
standing spellbound like Apollonius of Tyana, though for a less
protracted period; then, the meditation completed, he shut the door
and hopped back into bed.

Next moment Henry was on the bed too, plucking with his front
paws at the counterpane, and continuing to purr.

"Stop!" said Tom, for he knew Henry was pulling out threads—
indeed he could hear him doing it—giving little picks that made a
noise nearly as loud as raindrops. He was the most frightfully destruc-
tive cat, and had ruined Daddy's leather arm-chair by stropping his
claws on the back of it.

Henry stopped picking, but he continued to move about the bed
until he had found a hollow that suited him. Then he curled himself
up and began to purr again, but now much more softly. Tom lay
listening to him. It was a queer sound, he thought, and Henry must
make it somewhere at the back of his nose. Tom puckered up his
own nose and tried, but it wasn't very good. He could make a noise,

but not that kind of warm, broken, comfortable noise. It was easier
to mew, and indeed he could mew quite well, though Henry pretended not to recognize it. He mewed now, while from the garden
outside came the first chirps and twitterings of early birds. The early
worms, Tom supposed, would now be burrowing in all haste back
into the tennis lawn. He mewed again, and there was no twittering.
"I've frightened them," he said for Henry's benefit, but Henry did
not reply.

2.   WHEN Tom next opened his eyes it was broad day-
       light and the sun was shining. But after listening for
a minute or two he knew it must still be pretty early, for he could
hear none of the domestic sounds which usually began about seven.
He rather liked those early-morning sounds—Phemie's violent assault
upon the kitchen range—which always seemed to be resisting tooth
and nail—and Mary's more circumspect movements in the dining-
room and study. Phemie, Mary, and William composed the indoor
and outdoor staff, and Phemie and Mary were sisters though you
never would have guessed this to look at them. Phemie—whose full
name was Euphemia—was several years older than Mary, and bossed
her like anything. Both were Roman Catholics, while William was a
Protestant and an Orangeman, and walked with an orange-and-purple
sash over his shoulder on the twelfth of July. Phemie had been
crossed in love many years ago, and now hated men though she didn't
mind boys. She had a loud voice, muscles of iron, and a temper which
Mother said all cooks inherited from the cook in *Alice in Wonderland*.
Nevertheless, Tom preferred her to Mary, though he preferred Mary
to William, who was the gardener, and lived with his wife and family
in a cottage not far from the old Ballysheen graveyard, about a
mile away.

All this district was Ballysheen, and Doctor Macrory said there had
once been a church near the graveyard, though nothing was left of
it at present except a few stones. And even the loose stones had nearly
all been carted away at one time and another to build walls and byres
and cottages. For that matter, Doctor Macrory said there must long
ago have been another house—a big house—where Tom's own house

now stood. It had disappeared completely, and was not mentioned in any local history, but the builders had discovered traces of it when they were laying the foundations, and Doctor Macrory himself had poked about while the digging was going on. Doctor Macrory was very much interested in things of that sort. By profession he was a physician, but his hobby was archaeology, and he had written several pamphlets on the subject. Tom hadn't read the pamphlets, but he had seen them, Daddy possessed them, and they were bound in green paper, with Celtic designs.

All Daddy's friends were scientific, which, according to Mother, accounted for the narrowness of their views, their lack of imagination, and the irritating way in which they pooh-poohed anything they couldn't understand. It was queer that Tom's friend Pascoe should be scientific too, because Tom, Mother said, took after *her* family, and was a Collet.

On the other hand, she had one day told him that he got his brains from Daddy, though they were a different kind of brains. This seemed a little complicated, and became still more so when in answer to his question as to *how* they were different, she discovered that the person he really took after must be Uncle Stephen, of whose existence Tom had not till that moment heard. So sometimes he was a Collet and sometimes he wasn't; it depended a good deal on the humour Mother happened to be in, and whether she was pleased with him or not.

In one particular, however, she rarely varied her opinion, and this was that neither he nor Daddy possessed as much practical sense as a child of six. Six was Mother's favourite age; it was always a child of six who would have known better than to say or do whatever it was that Tom or Daddy might have said or done; and when Tom pointed out that you can't remain six for ever, she laughed, and replied that if he and Daddy hadn't it was only because they were five. This appeared to worry her more about Tom than about Daddy, though there were occasions when it had the contrary effect, and then she would kiss him. But Tom himself knew that he was different from Daddy, who was never in a hurry to do things, and never got heated or excited no matter what happened, whereas both Tom and Mother did. He wondered if Uncle Stephen did: it was natural to wonder about a person you resembled and who was so mysterious as Uncle Stephen. He couldn't make out what Mother thought of him. He didn't believe she *knew* much about him. Yet he hovered there somehow in the background, a distinctly romantic figure. Once, ages ago, he had asked her if she would rather have Uncle Stephen than Daddy, which had annoyed her a little, though afterwards she had repeated it as a joke. . . .

Henry some time during the night must have moved down to the foot of the bed, where he now lay asleep, curled up in a black circle. Tom felt a lazy inclination to pet him, and called "Puss, puss," but it produced no effect. So he raised his feet under the bedclothes, making an uncomfortable hill. Still Henry did not budge; only he gave Tom a long secret look out of green slits of eyes before closing them again. That was like him: he never did anything unless he wanted to do it himself. It had been a most peculiar look too, Tom presently thought; just as if Henry knew something about him—something faintly discreditable. Tom believed he did know things. Only why had he looked like that? It wasn't on the whole a friendly look—rather the reverse—though it certainly suggested that there was some kind of understanding between them. The more Tom considered it the less he liked it. There wasn't *any* understanding between them. Henry knew nothing about him except what everybody else knew, so he had no right to pretend that he did. Tom raised his feet again, this time higher, lifting Henry up in a kind of loose, sprawling crescent, so that he looked as if he had either no bones or else were dead. Yet even then he wouldn't move. He merely opened his mouth, showing a tiny scrap of pink, and emitted a faintly irritated mew. He had suddenly become an ordinary cat again.

He had no business to keep changing about like this. Ordinary cats didn't. Therefore, by the rules of logic, Henry couldn't be an ordinary cat, whatever he might pretend. Pascoe had produced electric sparks from him, though of course that didn't prove much, except that he was crammed with electricity. But Henry did things on his own account—queer, very nearly magical things—when he and Tom were alone together in the house. Before the others, even before Pascoe, he put on an innocent expression, as if he had never done anything more thrilling than to lap up a saucer of milk. But when only Tom was there it was a different story. Then he no longer troubled to look innocent. It seemed to be Henry's opinion that Tom didn't matter, and just to show this he would start off by making the whole house queer. He had done it yesterday evening when they were alone and Tom was at his lessons. Henry had walked to the study door and scratched on it—his usual sign that he wanted to be let out. Then, when the door was opened, he had strolled slowly on down the passage as if he were going to the kitchen, while Tom, pondering, had stood watching him as far as the corner. Yet when he had turned back into the study again and shut the door, there Henry was—on the hearthrug, washing his face, just as if he had never left the room at all. Meanwhile, the things in the study had changed their places: Tom's *Latin Grammar*, which he had left open on the sofa, was now on the floor, closed, and the frame with his photograph in it had been moved forward from the other photographs—he was sure that if it had been like that before he must have noticed it. It was strange—very strange. And if it came to that, who *was* Henry, and where had he come from? Nobody knew. He had simply walked through the open back door into the kitchen one afternoon about a month ago, and Phemie had immediately decided that he had come to bring her luck and mustn't be turned away. That was all nonsense, of course, as even Phemie soon knew. The very next day she had upset a pot of boiling water and scalded her foot. But *why* had Henry come? He was a full-grown cat, sleek and lithe, with a coat like black satin: anybody could see he had never been hungry or homeless in his life.

And certainly he hadn't troubled himself to bring much luck to poor Phemie! She had broken a teapot and a vegetable dish on the day after the scalding, and Henry had ceased to be a kitchen cat. His next move had been to wile himself into the good graces of Daddy. This had been accomplished easily—merely by following Daddy about the garden and jumping up on the arm of his chair. Daddy tried not to look flattered, and said nothing; but every time Mother said—and she said it about five times a day—"Henry's *devoted* to Daddy!" it was easy to see he was as pleased as Punch.

Tom knew better. The devotion was mere policy. He could prove it. Henry wasn't in the least interested in games with string, for example. They bored him. Tom had tried him again and again, and he had simply yawned or turned his back. Yet if Daddy dangled a piece of string or waved his handkerchief, Henry immediately crouched and quivered and pounced.

That wasn't how he behaved with Tom. Once, when he was sitting alone in the drawing-room at dusk, tired of reading and too lazy to get up and turn on the light, Henry had actually begun to play the piano to him. Only a note or two—very, very softly, and really rather beautifully—for it had sounded more as if the piano were singing in its sleep than being played. Tom had liked it, and so most surely had Henry; but did ordinary cats play the piano?

Then there was the matter of the tennis balls, more mysterious still, because this time Henry hadn't been there. And mind you, Tom himself had put the tennis balls away in their cardboard box, and put the box on the oak chest which stood beside the cloakroom door. Yet he had hardly been in the cloakroom a minute before he heard a bouncing noise in the hall, and, running out, found the tennis balls, all six of them, rolling over the carpet in different directions, with nobody to roll them, nobody near them.

When things like this happened, you couldn't help beginning to wonder why. And they had happened pretty often of late, usually in the evening. They didn't frighten you, perhaps—in fact they were rather exciting—but they did give you a queer feeling of uncertainty, as if nothing was quite what it seemed, and things like tennis balls, or photograph frames, or pianos for that matter, were a good deal more alive than they had any right to be. It was Henry's doing, of course, and he knew that Tom knew it was. He knew and didn't care—which was probably the meaning of the strange look he had given him just now. What Henry's green eyes had said was: "*I* know, and *you* know, that there's something most unusual going on in this house; but the others don't know, and if you tell them they won't believe you. That's why it doesn't matter about you, and why it wouldn't matter if you did tell. They'd only make fun of you—especially that daddy of yours, who thinks you're queer enough as it is."

"He doesn't think me queer," Tom contradicted, but without much conviction; and Henry didn't even bother to open his eyes. This annoyed Tom, so he continued with more spirit: "Anyway, you'll get down off the bed." And he jumped out himself and pushed Henry on to the floor.

It was a poor argument, and he felt a little ashamed, so he picked Henry up again and set him once more where he had been. "You needn't start purring," he told him. "I only did that because I don't approve of bullying: I still think you're pretty awful."

Saying which, he took off his pyjamas, and stood in a patch of sunlight, letting the sun stroke his naked body with its warm breath. He liked it, and liked the feeling of the carpet under his bare feet. Henry, seeing him up, jumped down from the bed and began scratching at the door, but Tom watched him unsympathetically. "Why don't you go?" he asked in a cold voice. "It's too much trouble to do a magic, I suppose. Go on—vanish! *I* won't be surprised."

In spite of this sarcasm, Henry merely lifted his voice in a very unmagical mew, so Tom had to open the door for him. Then he went to the window and looked out into the garden. The garden was bright with its first dewy freshness, and as usual there was a squabble going on among the birds. Of all the quarrelsome creatures! And they were supposed to be so angelic. Probably it was the row they were kicking up which had attracted Henry, who, as Tom was well aware, could get out by jumping from the bath-room window-sill to the roof of the coalhouse. Yes, there he was, gliding between the bushes like a black panther. But the birds saw him also, and with a sudden whirr of wings rose in a cloud. The birds detested Henry, and had every reason to do so, for he hunted them from morning till night. Often he got one too; an absent-minded bird had no chance whatever with Henry: Tom could quite understand their feelings. . . .

A flat lawn with a sagging tennis net in the middle of it stretched in front of the house. All round this lawn were flower-beds and trellises festooned with rambler roses. On the left was a line of trees, and on the right a border of flowering shrubs—syringas, azaleas, rhododendrons—just now a splash of brilliant colour. Tom could smell the perfumes that drifted from them, and he could smell the roses and the grass. Suddenly he wanted to be out there.

He put on a shirt, a pair of grey flannel shorts, stockings, slippers, a jacket. He knew he should have taken a bath, or at least washed properly, but all he did was to pour a little water into a basin and give a perfunctory dab or two at his face with a sponge. He was on the point of leaving the room when he remembered his prayers and knelt down by the bed. He had two prayers—one in prose and one in verse. The poetry prayer he always said last. Both were short, but they included, Mother told him, everything he really needed. They left out of account, none the less, a lot of things he really *wanted*—a bulldog, a donkey, long trousers, hairs on his legs, a bicycle, not to miss catches at cricket, and not to be called "Skinny." Sometimes Tom added these items, sometimes he omitted them. In spite of past failures he put them all in to-day, like a Christmas or a birthday list, where one leaves the final choice to the giver.

He ran downstairs, put on his shoes in the kitchen, emptied the biscuit jar in the dining-room (it was nearly empty, anyway), and went out through the side door into the garden.

It was a fairly large garden, walled all round to the height of some five feet, but not too large to be looked after by one man. Tom thought at first of marking the tennis court, the lines of which were rather faint, till he remembered that it was William's day for cutting the grass. That altered matters. If William found the court freshly marked he would make this an excuse for leaving it alone—"not liking to interfere with Master Tom's work." William was splendid at excuses, and, like Henry, so plausible, that though actually the most frightful slacker, he was regarded by everybody as a model of industry. "Slow but sure," Daddy would say of him; or "Hurried work's usually scamped"—things like that, when it ought to have been: "William does as little as he can, and never anything you ask him." Only it wasn't easy to tell exactly *how* slow William was, because through long association with the garden he had acquired a kind of protective colouring and his movements were veiled. If you merely glanced at him as he stood with a hoe or a spade in his hand between two bean-rows or stooping over the cabbages, he produced an illusion of activity, but if you watched him closely, as Tom had done, this illusion vanished, and a curious affinity between William and the sundial emerged. Not that Tom would have cared, if he hadn't been such a grumbler. But he bemoaned his lot every time you spoke to him, so that you'd have thought he was a slave driven by Egyptian taskmasters. He wouldn't, for instance, be in the least grateful if Tom were to cut the grass for him now: he'd just accept it as a matter of course and point out how it might have been done better.

Tom had reached this point in his summing-up of William when the hall-door opened and Mary appeared, carrying a long-handled brush with which she began to sweep out the porch. The instant she caught sight of the figure on the lawn she stopped. "What are you doing there, Master Tom?" she asked in a tone of suspicion and disapproval.

Tom was amused. "Admiring the view," he replied; at which Mary gave a sniff—inaudible, but perfectly perceptible even from that distance. She took no further notice of him, however, from which he deduced that she regarded his remark as cheek.

As a matter of fact the old house *did* look rather nice, he thought. There was honeysuckle climbing up one side of the porch, and clematis climbing up the other, while ampelopsis spread over the walls. Also he liked the oriel windows and red-tiled roof and irregular chimney stacks. Not that the house was really old, having been built by the people from whom Daddy had bought it; but it had been designed from the beginning to have an old-fashioned appearance— warm, comfortable, and homely—and it really *had* been that kind of house until Henry had begun to play tricks with it.

Still, Tom couldn't stare at it for ever, even to impress the suspicious Mary, so he took a path through the shrubbery, which terminated in a small green postern door set in the angle where the south and west walls met. This door was locked at night, but the key was always left in the lock, and next moment Tom was outside the garden, on the high bank of a glen thickly carpeted with long green spiky bluebell leaves, and overgrown with larch, hazel, and birch trees. The glen was long and very narrow, as if at some remote volcanic period the earth had split asunder here. A stream ran through it, which never dried up even in the hottest summer, and Tom scrambled down to it, because the walking was easier there. He saw a squirrel and stopped to look at him; he disturbed a hare who had come down from the meadows and at Tom's approach fled up to them again. He followed the stream, jumping from side to side of it, and as he proceeded the steep banks of the glen gradually grew shallower, till at last the ground was level, and only a field of meadow grass bright with buttercups lay between him and the river. In wet weather the ground was soft and boggy here, so that cows sometimes sank up above their knees and had to be hauled out by ropes, but just now it was firm enough. Anyhow, Tom knew every inch of it, and passing lightly between two beds of yellow irises, and scrambling through a hedge, reached the towpath.

"Shall I bathe or not?" he was asking himself, and the question was difficult to answer, for though he wanted to be able to remark at breakfast that he had had a bathe in the river he wasn't really fond of cold water, nor even sure that it agreed with him. "I'm afraid a lot of things don't agree with me," Tom mused. "I'm quite easily made ill." And he particularly wished not to be ill just before the exams, because he was rather a dab at exams, though not such a dab as Pascoe. But he really knew far more than Pascoe did, only the kinds of things he knew weren't so useful. Besides, he was hopeless at mathematics.

He stood with his greyish, greenish eyes fixed doubtfully on the water, while the wind made little whisperings and songs as it swept over the rushes. Then he knelt down to try the temperature with his hand. This experiment elicited a sigh; nevertheless, after the briefest hesitation, he divested himself of his clothes and stepped cautiously into the shallow water at the edge. Why was it, he wondered, that he should think of leeches and eels at such a moment, instead of darting silver fish? But he did think of them, and dreaded at every step lest he should put his foot on something soft and fat and slimy which would move. He took only three or four steps and then stood still, not much more than knee-deep, among a patch of dark broad glossy leaves. He splashed a little water over himself, wetting his dim brown hair, and this was the bathe.

Buzz! A large bumble-bee, after some preliminary fussing, alighted on Tom's shoulder and began to walk down his body, which looked very white among the dark leaves, though his hands and neck and freckled blunt-featured face were sunburned. The bee tickled him, but not unpleasantly. He was a very handsome bee, with an air of importance, and his black and orange velvet coat was rich and splendid. He looked so important, indeed, that Tom fancied he must be a Mayor or an Alderman at the very least. People like Daddy (who was a professor), and Doctor Macrory (who was an archaeologist), and Mr. Holbrook (who taught music), hadn't at all such an important air. This was the kind of affluent, pompous bee who would be a Member of Parliament, or a City Councillor, and whose wife would open Sales of Work.

Tom poured more water over his head—to make sure that it would look sufficiently wet at breakfast—and while he was doing this an old grey horse came plodding along around the bend of the river. A rope was attached to the horse, a barge to the rope, and there was a man walking by the horse's head, and another man standing at the helm of the barge, steering it. The man who was walking was on the farther side of the horse, so that he did not notice Tom, but the steersman spied him at once and bawled out at the top of his voice: "Hi, Joe, here's a water-lily!" This caused Joe to lean a beery stubbly face over the horse's back, and it also drew a laugh from him. They were really very rude! Tom thought.

But there was not much time for thinking and he would have done better to have acted. "Look out for that bloody rope!" he heard the steersman shout. "What the——"

Tom heard no more, for just then the rope reached him and he was swept off his feet—splash!—on the flat of his back. He emerged spluttering, spitting, choking, and very angry. The horse had already passed him as he floundered to the bank and scrambled out. It was lucky, Tom thought, that he had been so close to the bank, or the barge might have gone over him. Much they would have cared even if he *had* been drowned! He would have liked to tell them his opinion of them, but it was the bargemen who shouted remarks. These were derisive and indecent—eked out by much raucous laughter. The man who was leading the horse was not even funny: the steersman was— a little. The old grey horse, unaware of the accident, was the only respectable member of the trio.

Tom dried himself, partly with his pocket handkerchief, and partly with his trousers. But he never remained cross for long, and before the barge had disappeared round the next bend he had ceased to be either angry or shocked. After all, it had been his own fault. With a little presence of mind he could easily have avoided the rope, and the bargemen couldn't possibly have stopped the barge. So he finished dressing and trotted happily back to the house.

3: THE bell had rung and Daddy and Mother were already at the breakfast-table when Tom appeared. He kissed them both and sat down.

"What have you been doing to your hair?" was Mother's expected question.

"It's only water," Tom replied. "I had a bathe."

Mother rose beautifully to this. "A bathe!" she repeated incredulously.

"Yes," said Tom, "in the river."

"But why?" Mother, after all, was less impressed than he had hoped. In fact she was looking at him in quite the wrong way. "Is this some new fad?" she went on, though Tom had no fads at all. "I've told you before that I don't think it's safe for you to bathe in the river—particularly by yourself. You might easily step into a hole that was out of your depth. It's just the sort of thing you *would* do."

Tom's light and airy manner had to be abandoned. "I want to learn to swim," he protested. "And I can't learn on dry land."

"You can't learn without somebody to teach you," Mother said, "and there's nobody now James-Arthur's gone. Besides, you'll have plenty of opportunities in the holidays, and it's much easier to learn in the sea than in fresh water. Everybody knows that rivers are dangerous."

They were far more dangerous than she imagined, Tom reflected, but he kept this to himself. "It isn't dangerous if I stay close to the bank," he argued. "Lots of boys bathe in the river."

"Not alone," Mother answered, "and not boys like you. There are just as likely to be holes near the bank as anywhere else. The bed of a river isn't like the seashore: one minute you may be in three feet of water and the next in ten."

"I doubt if he was in three feet of water," Daddy here interposed. He had been glancing at the newspaper, but he now gazed over the top of it at his son. "I should put it at eighteen inches in spite of those dripping locks."

This guess was so very nearly accurate that Tom blushed. It was like Daddy to take that tone, he thought, and he had half a mind to tell him how nearly drowned he *had* been!

For that matter Mother did not seem too pleased at the interruption either. "You surely don't approve of his bathing by himself!" she said to Daddy. "Suppose he got caught in the weeds. In some places the river's thick with them, and even if he could swim, you know what Tom's like!"

"Yes," said Daddy playfully, "I know what he's like. Probably it was a naiad or an undine who enticed him in. I can't imagine anything less attractive overcoming his natural distaste for cold water."

Tom smiled, but only from a sense of duty. He knew that Daddy was alluding to an adventure he had had when he was smaller, and had then been foolish enough to talk about. He wouldn't be so foolish now, nor was he going to be drawn into the trap.

"*Was* it a water-nymph, Tom?" Daddy went on teasingly. But Tom merely smiled again and remained discreetly silent.

Mother, to the surprise of both of them, suddenly came to his rescue. "It's rather strange that you should want to encourage him, Edgar, considering the attitude you take up at other times about such things!"

Daddy looked taken aback—indeed quite startled. "How am I encouraging him?" he asked. "And what attitude do you mean?"

"Your usual attitude," Mother returned. "I understood that you disapproved of fairy tales and thought they did a lot of harm. I've certainly heard you say so."

"Only when people believe in them," Daddy answered mildly; "and Tom, we know, has long since passed that stage."

"Still," Mother persisted, "if he told you that he *had* seen a water-nymph you'd be annoyed with him."

Daddy did not reply, but he looked at Tom for sympathy, which the latter withheld. It served him jolly well right, Tom thought: perhaps he wouldn't be in such a hurry to butt in another time; and he met Daddy's gaze with serene and slightly derisive eyes.

This had the effect of making him come to his own assistance. "I don't quite grasp, my dear, the precise object of this attack. It can hardly be that you yourself have seen a water-sprite. At least, if you have, you've kept remarkably silent about it."

"Yes, that's what I mean," Mother said quietly. "It must be so comfortable to be able to feel like that."

"Like what?" Daddy asked, not looking too comfortable.

"To be so sure about everything that you can afford to be indulgent and ironical."

"But——" Daddy protested, half laughing.

"I don't mean about water-nymphs especially," Mother went on, "though they'll do as an example. They can't exist, we know, because their existence isn't recorded in scientific books and you yourself have neither photographed nor dissected one."

"Who's being ironical now?" Daddy asked meekly. "The scientist is as open to conviction as most people, I expect; and if he demands a little more evidence than some it's because it's his job not to take things on trust."

"It may be his job," Mother returned, "but if nothing was taken on trust life would be a very poor affair."

"Very," Daddy agreed. "I'm only suggesting that trustfulness may be combined with common sense—and that all witnesses aren't equally reliable."

The last words were intended for him, Tom supposed, and Mother perhaps thought so too, for she asked after the briefest pause: "What exactly do you mean by that?"

Daddy glanced up quickly. "But surely, my dear——!" he exclaimed in a tone of deprecation. Then, as Mother only waited, he gave a little shrug. "Let us put it this way then, for the sake of argument. If Doctor Macrory were to tell you that a water-nymph haunted the river, it would be a rather different thing, wouldn't it, than if the news came from Tom?"

"No, it wouldn't," answered Mother without hesitation; and since Daddy merely opened and closed his mouth soundlessly, while his eyes expressed a kind of wonder: "Why should I believe Doctor Macrory rather than Tom?" she asked sharply.

Daddy sighed. "That's not the point," he murmured. "It's not a question of veracity or inveracity. We'll suppose that neither of them would deliberately tell a lie. Still, there would remain several reasons for attaching more weight to Doctor Macrory's evidence than to Tom's. A: he has a trained mind and a trained eye, which Tom hasn't. B: neither his friends nor his enemies could describe him as imaginative. C: he's a shrewd and far from impressionable man, whereas Tom is only a small boy, and one, moreover, with a distinct taste for the marvellous."

"Yet Tom has very good sight," Mother interrupted before Daddy could get on to D, E, and F; "much better, I should think, than Doctor Macrory, who has to wear glasses. And we were talking about seeing things."

"Yes, yes," Daddy assented, at the same time taking up the newspaper in token of surrender. "Fortunately he hasn't seen anything in the present instance," he added, "so we may dismiss the argument as hypothetical."

Clearly this was funking it, and Tom guessed from Mother's face that she thought so too. At any rate she wasn't going to dismiss the argument, nor abandon her advantage. "You'll admit, I suppose, that William Blake was a genius?" she said; and Tom could see, though he didn't know why, that if Daddy answered "Yes," he was going to place himself in a corner.

Yet he made the admission: he seemed to have reached a stage when he would admit nearly anything; and immediately afterwards he put a question of his own. "Much as we might like to regard Tom as a genius, we haven't up to the present found any particular grounds for doing so, have we?"

He said it quite pleasantly, and even with a conciliatory smile which included not only Mother but Tom. Nevertheless, it was an error in judgement, and he might have known that. Tom knew it at all events; for whether Mother believed he was a genius or not, she certainly wasn't going to allow other people to deny that he was. "I'm

not talking about Tom," she said, but in a way which plainly showed
she was thinking about him. "I'm talking of somebody whom you admit to be a man of genius, yet whose every statement both you and
Doctor Macrory would dismiss as absurd—too absurd even to be
worth a moment's consideration."

This was odd, and Tom couldn't help popping in with "Who was
William Blake?" though directly afterwards he remembered, for
they had learned one of his poems at school last term—*Tyger Tyger
burning bright*. And straightway he ceased to pay attention to Daddy
and Mother, and began instead to say the poem softly over to himself.

> *Tyger Tyger burning bright*
> *In the forests of the night,*
> *What immortal hand or eye*
> *Could frame thy fearful symmetry?*

He liked it better than any other poem he knew. . . . Except perhaps
Ulalume—and he repeated what he knew of that also, but as he had
never learned it he could only remember little bits here and
there. . . .

When he once more listened to what Daddy and Mother were
saying, it was to find that the conversation had lapsed into trivial remarks about roses and William, so he brought it round again to the
other William by a variation on his original question. "What was
William Blake like?" he asked.

He was really curious to know, or at least to hear some of the
statements which Daddy and Doctor Macrory would have dismissed
as absurd. He had an inkling that perhaps *he* wouldn't find them
absurd; Mother evidently didn't; though it was never so easy to tell
what Mother thought as it was to tell what Daddy thought—or at
least to be sure that in the meantime she wouldn't have thought
something else.

It was Daddy who answered him, with just the slightest lifting of
one eyebrow. "He was very like your mother in his opinion of scientists," Daddy said cautiously. "In other respects a good deal of light
is thrown by the only recorded remark of Mrs. Blake: 'You know,
dear, the first time you saw God was when you were four years old,
and He put his head to the window and set you a-screaming.' "

There was a mewing at the window at that moment, and Tom
turned round quickly. But it was only Henry, and he got up to let
him in. He opened the window, and of course Henry entered as

slowly as possible, just to keep him standing there. It was easy to see that he was doing it on purpose, for he paused when he was half-way through, and made no further movement.

"Come on, hurry up!" cried Tom impatiently, giving him a push.

Henry at this actually uttered a word which shocked Tom, even though he didn't quite catch it. At the same time he alighted on the floor with an extraordinary thud.

"Good gracious!" Mother exclaimed. "You'd think he was a ton weight!"

"It's his sins," said Tom darkly. "It's a wonder he can jump at all."

He came back to the table and for a minute or two sat wrapped in thought. "Daddy!" he said abruptly, and then paused to think again. But Daddy was staring at him, so he completed his sentence. "Did God really look in at the Blakes' window?"

"Never you mind about——" Mother began, but abruptly checked herself. And just as well, too! for he was sure she had nearly said "Never you mind about God." She changed it, however, to "Never you mind about the Blakes. You're slow enough as it is."

Tom glanced round at the clock on the chimney-piece, for it was his music morning; but there was loads of time, so he made a secret sign to Daddy to answer his question. But Daddy wouldn't: he might argue with Mother, but he would never go against her in practice. For this reason it was much more useful to have Mother on your side than Daddy; in fact it was no use having Daddy at all unless you had Mother too, though if you had Mother without Daddy you very soon got him also.

Tom pondered over this, and also over the Blake family, while he pursued an intermittent course with his breakfast. His progress was slow; he was invariably the last to finish. And this wasn't because he had a large appetite. It was because he couldn't help stopping to think. With the consequence, Mother said, that meals, which for other persons were intervals of relaxation, for her were the most arduous tasks of the day. Instead of enjoying them she had to spend her whole time in waking Tom up and goading him into swallowing each mouthful: he had been less trouble in the days when he was fed with a spoon.

This of course was an exaggeration. Mother was very prone to that. Really she exaggerated most frightfully, though she objected when Tom did. And what was the use of asking him why he couldn't be like Daddy and talk and eat at the same time? She knew it was

Uncle Stephen he was like, not Daddy. Anyhow, the way she put it made it sound as if Daddy talked with his mouth full.

He thought of the barge and wondered how far up the river it had got by now. He thought of his accident, and the narrow escape he had had. It grew narrower and narrower the more he considered it, until at last it seemed to him that only by a miracle had he been plucked from the closing jaws of Death. He felt a strong desire to describe the miracle, but on the other hand he was sure that it would make Mother more nervous than ever about his bathing in the river —might make her definitely forbid him to bathe there again, which at present she had forgotten to do. . . .

"Tom!" Mother cried so suddenly that he jumped. Hastily he swallowed a mouthful of toast, with the result that he choked and then had a fit of coughing. But instead of being sorry for what she had done, Mother only said: "Well, I haven't time to sit here all morning!" and got up from the table. Daddy followed her, which left Tom all alone; so he got up too, though he hadn't really finished, and very likely would feel faint and ill through starvation long before lunch time. But it was their fault: he wasn't going to sit on eating by himself. He collected his school books from the study, got his cap from the cloakroom, and went out.

The sun was much hotter now than it had been before breakfast, and the shadows were deeper. The wind, too, had died, and the dew had been sucked up from the grass. Henry had come out, and with his back turned to Tom was sitting on the path under the study window, playing.

Or at least he seemed to be playing—a quiet and absorbing game —so absorbing that he did not look round or stop at the sound of footsteps. What was this game? Tom felt bound to investigate. It *looked* harmless enough, though of course you never could tell. Henry was playing it with his right paw only—giving little taps and scratches at the gravel. Suddenly Tom became intensely interested, for he saw that each of these seemingly careless scratches left a mark on the path. Henry wasn't playing: he was drawing!

Tom stood perfectly still, while Henry continued to draw, though he must have known he was being watched. Perhaps, however, he knew who was watching him, for he had ears so sharp that he could hear a leaf falling or a butterfly passing behind him, and might easily have recognized Tom's tread. He gave a final touch, and, still without looking up, slowly rose and pretended to yawn.

But Tom took no notice of him; he was too intent on something else; and this something was a figure traced there on the black gravel path. Just a few simple lines, yet certainly a diagram; and Tom stared down at it. Not that there was any need to stare, for it could not have been more clear to him if it had been drawn in thin lines of flame. There flashed across his mind the recollection of a description Daddy had once read to him of certain horses who had been trained to solve arithmetical problems by tapping out the answers with their hoofs. They were German horses, and Daddy had said there was probably some trickery behind the experiments, though the most careful observation had failed to detect any. But Henry hadn't been trained: this was his own work: One thing was sure; he must get Daddy and Mother to look at this marvel immediately. And then, as if he had spoken aloud, and just as he was on the point of rushing back to the house, the figure was suddenly broken and scattered into a shower of gravel, while Henry's powerful hind feet scored it across and across, sending the small grains flying.

Tom was raging with him. He had destroyed the whole thing and now nobody would believe in it. "Bad cat!" he said angrily, but Henry began to rub against his legs, arching and lowering his back. He pressed his sleek flattened head into the hollows above Tom's rather meagre calves, where the skin was bare above his stockings; he curled his elastic body half round them, and from the suddenness and lavishness of these caresses Tom immediately felt sure that a third person must have appeared upon the scene. He was right, for there was Mother, leaning out of her bedroom window, and of course she wanted to know what he was doing.

He wasn't doing anything, Tom replied; adding that Henry had just made a drawing on the path. Yet for some reason this answer did not satisfy Mother, nor did she show the least interest in the drawing. On the contrary, she told him that he was a very naughty boy, and that if he didn't start for school at once she wouldn't allow him to go out in the afternoon. Also she said that she was going to tell Daddy. As if that mattered! Besides, she never did tell—at least not things of that sort, things that might get him into a row. And anyhow he was going to tell Daddy about the drawing himself.

But here was William, and Tom realized that he must be later than he had thought. He would have to run, and even then he wouldn't be in time. He couldn't possibly be. Yet it wasn't his fault,

for if he had had a bicycle he could have done it easily. Practically
everybody else in the school had a bicycle: boys who were far
younger than he was. Pascoe had had one for nearly two years, and
Brown was allowed to drive his father's car. At least he said he was,
and even though, coming from Brown, this was almost certain to be
untrue, still it proved——

4: IT proved nothing at all, Tom knew, though he had
used it as an argument when trying to make Daddy see
how far less indulgent he was than the average parent. The argument
had failed, because Daddy seemed to have no wish to resemble the
average parent, though he had often expressed a desire for an average
son. And Mother was nearly as bad. Tom had pointed out to her how
much less freedom he had than other boys; Pascoe, for example, who
was allowed to do all sorts of things; Pascoe's father had complete
confidence in him. But it appeared that Mother had complete confidence in Pascoe also: *he* didn't go about dreaming; he was practical
and reliable; the kind of boy who was bound to get on in the
world. . . .

Tom jogged along the dusty road, growing hotter and hotter, till
at the end of half a mile, just when he should have been getting his
second wind, he found himself with no wind left at all, and relapsed
into a walk.

On most mornings he got a seat in the car and was deposited at the
school gates, but on Tuesdays and Thursdays he had a music lesson
with Mr. Holbrook at nine o'clock, which was too early for Daddy,
so he had to make the journey on foot. He could do it comfortably
if he left the house at twenty past eight, but something nearly always
cropped up to delay him. And Mr. Holbrook, though he usually was
late himself, now and then was punctual, on which occasions he expected Tom to be punctual too. This was unreasonable, perhaps, but
Mr. Holbrook wasn't a reasonable person—quite the opposite. On the
other hand he was a very pleasant person—particularly if he happened to like you—for he had favourites, and you precious soon
found out whether you were one of them or not. Tom saw nothing
wrong in this; he was sure that in Mr. Holbrook's position he would
have had favourites himself: indeed, what was the use of liking people

if you didn't show them that you liked them. Besides, it made everything more likely and interesting. You never knew beforehand what kind of lesson you were going to get. That is, if you happened to *be* a favourite: the others, he supposed, knew well enough. In Tom's case it meant that he was allowed to choose his own songs—except when he chose something too difficult—and also that quite often after school he was invited to Mr. Holbrook's house to listen to the gramophone. Mr. Holbrook would put on records and tell him about singers and operas (he went abroad every year to listen to operas; that was how he spent his holidays), and he would describe them, and play little bits on the piano, and it was all highly enjoyable. Tom had never heard a real opera—in fact he had only once been inside a theatre, when Mother had taken him to see *Peter Pan*—but through these fugitive glimpses, in which Mr. Holbrook supplied the scenery and the story and piano impressions of the orchestra, while famous tenors, sopranos, and baritones sang the principal airs, he had acquired a remarkable erudition, and an enthusiasm which nearly equalled Mr. Holbrook's own.

A most agreeable feature of it, too, was that being Mr. Holbrook's "star artist" aroused jealousy in nobody. *Nor* antagonism. Tom had felt very doubtful before the last Christmas concert, for instance, of the prudence of standing up to sing "Vio che sapete" in Italian. It had seemed to him that it would be wiser to sing it in English. But when he had revealed these timidities to Mr. Holbrook, the latter had grown so impatient that argument became impossible. And as it surprisingly turned out, he need not have been afraid; nobody—not even Brown—had accused him of putting on side. On the contrary, for the two nights of the concert—which was always repeated and always crowded with parents and visitors—he had found himself, if not exactly popular, at least an important person; and though by the beginning of the next term everybody else had forgotten this, it had been very pleasant while it lasted. Since then, having heard them first on the gramophone, he had learned two other Italian airs—Tosti's "Serenata," and the "Spirto gentil" from *La Favorita*. Daddy, who didn't really care for music at all, wondered why Mr. Holbrook couldn't teach him sensible songs, and even Mother, who used to sing herself but had lately given it up, thought the last choice a little odd. Fortunately it had the advantage of an easy accompaniment, she discovered; for at home Mother played his accompaniments, though Tom could sing better when Mr. Holbrook played.

These meditations were interrupted rudely by a sudden shout behind him. "Hi! Skinny!"

Tom, who would have liked to take no notice, wheeled round at the offensive name.

A boy on a bicycle had ridden out on to the road through a garden gate—a large and burly boy with red cheeks, smiling mouth, dark hair and dark eyes. At least he seemed to Tom large and burly, though actually he was only thirteen. But Brown was an out-sized thirteen and much the biggest boy in the school. Mother thought him handsome, she was always praising his looks: Tom thought that if he had been differently dressed and carrying a flat basket he would have looked exactly like a butcher's boy. He was not only big, but he was as strong as a bull, had legs as thick as columns, and was forever wanting you to feel his muscles. "Hello, Brown!" he replied.

Brown zigzagged slowly on for a few yards and then hopped off his bicycle. "Done your algebra?" he asked.

"Yes," said Tom. "Have you?"

Brown walked beside him, still smiling. "Well, as a matter of fact I haven't," he said ingratiatingly. "And the worst of it is, I've promised to play cricket. So I wonder if you'd let me copy yours? Do you mind?"

Tom hesitated, while his face grew distinctly glum. His algebra was invariably wrong, and he knew from past experience that identical mistakes in two separate copies of work were apt to lead to further investigation—particularly when one of the copies happened to be Brown's. But Brown, though perfectly aware of the reluctance, was not an easy person to discourage. "No," said Tom at last, in a tone of resignation, "I don't mind."

Brown ignored the resignation. "Thanks awfully, Skinny," he said. "I'll give you yours back in plenty of time. You're going to Holbrook, aren't you?"

"Yes," said Tom.

"Well, I'll give you a lift as far as the cricket field if you get up behind."

Tom still hung back, however; not that a lift wouldn't be most useful, but because he felt he had been weak in the matter of the algebra. "I say, Brown," he began uncomfortably.

"Yes," said Brown, waiting.

"Nothing," Tom muttered.

Slowly he unfastened his schoolbag and produced an exercise book.

Brown, with much more expedition, seized it and stuffed it into his jacket pocket. "Thanks," he said again—this time rather carelessly—and immediately remounted his bicycle. "Jump up," he cried, and Tom got on to the backstep.

Brown to impress him began pedalling like mad. The road was up-hill, and though the hill was gradual it was long. Tom could see Brown's face getting redder and redder; he could hear him breathing, and he could even feel the heat exuding through his thick body. "Silly ass!" he reflected, yet not without appreciation of Brown's powers. It couldn't be easy to carry a double load up that hill.

When they reached the playing-fields he got down and Brown too dismounted, trying hard not to appear puffed. Together they walked over the beech-shadowed grass, Brown wheeling his bicycle and Tom thinking of the algebra. Thanks to the lift, however, he was now in no hurry; indeed he had several minutes to spare. This reminded him of his grievance against Daddy. Besides, if he had had a bicycle he wouldn't have met Brown.

He wished he could get his exercise book back again. There was nothing to hinder Brown from doing the sums himself, except that he wanted to play cricket. "I say," he once more began dubiously. "Are you going to write them out in ink?"

Since Miss Jimpson insisted upon ink—as a precaution against last-minute copying—Brown merely gave him a half-compassionate look.

"Because," Tom went on more firmly, "if you are, I hope you'll be careful. You know the row she kicks up about blots, and the paper's so thin you can't scrape them out. It's as thin as gauze is."

"As thin as blazes, you mean," Brown rejoined lightheartedly; but he didn't promise to take any precautions.

That was like him, once he'd got the thing, and Tom's annoyance increased. "Did you bring me those stamps?" he asked suddenly, for Brown had turned aside and was proceeding towards the bicycle shed. "What stamps?" he inquired, disappearing into the shed.

He knew very well what stamps; Tom had reminded him about them every day that week. He followed him now, though without much hope. "The stamps you owe me," he said, "the two Mauritius stamps."

Brown looked surprised. "Mauritius stamps?" he repeated, as if he had never heard of Mauritius stamps before. Then he added calmly: "I don't know what you're talking about." And having fixed his bi-cycle, he emerged from the shed, still followed by Tom.

"You do!" Tom exclaimed indignantly. "I gave you three Cape of Good Hopes, and one of them was unused."

"That's because it was a forgery," Brown returned quickly. "You can be sent to jail for passing forged stamps; it's just the same as passing forged banknotes."

"You can't," said Tom. "And it isn't a forgery. If you think it is why won't you give it back to me?"

"Because I don't want to get you into trouble," Brown answered kindly.

Tom's face darkened. Pascoe had warned him to have no dealings with Brown, but Pascoe was always warning you about something, and always so sure he was right that it only made you more determined not to take his advice. "You promised me two Mauritius stamps," he repeated gloomily. "You promised to bring them the next day."

"That was before I knew you had committed a crime," Brown explained. "Anyway, I haven't got any Mauritius stamps."

"Then you told a lie," said Tom.

"I didn't. I said I'd bring you two Mauritius stamps—perhaps."

Brown was looking him straight in the eyes with the utmost candour, and Tom knew he could do nothing. "You didn't say 'perhaps,' " he muttered.

"I did. You mayn't have heard me, but that's because you weren't listening. I said it like this." And Brown repeated the sentence, yet even now, though he strained his ears, Tom could not catch the last word.

"It was the same as a lie," he declared. "And you're the same as a thief."

Brown suddenly grabbed him by the wrist. "Look here, Skinny," he observed softly, while at the same time he screwed Tom's arm round till he was completely helpless, "all this sounds to me uncommonly like cheek."

"You're a cad," Tom gasped, twisting his body sideways to ease the strain on his arm. "You attacked me when I wasn't expecting it."

Instantly Brown released him. "Expect it now," he said, "because I'm going to attack you again."

Tom hastily retreated—an instinctive precaution which Brown's immobility made all the more ignominious. He simply stood there smiling. "I'm not going to attack you, Skinny," he said; "you're beneath it. And besides, you were quite obliging about the algebra. See you later."

With that he strolled off, whistling, while Tom gazed after him. He would never get his stamps, he knew, and he never would be able to retaliate. Words meant nothing to Brown, and physical force was out of the question. He couldn't stand up to Brown for two minutes, and even if he had the courage to attempt it there wouldn't really be a fight: Brown would merely twist his arm again, or sit on him till he surrendered. It was queer that Brown should be so invulnerable, and in most ways successful, because actually he was a stupid person. He had never been able to get beyond the third form and he was always at the bottom of that. But he was cunning, and you couldn't exactly say he knew nothing, since he knew everything that you weren't supposed to know. Really he was as stupid out of school as he was in it, yet for some reason he was successful—and popular—more popular than Tom, and infinitely more than Pascoe. It was hard to understand why.

Suddenly he remembered that the school clock had struck while Brown was twisting his arm. This was annoying, for it meant that though he had arrived in tons of time he was none the less going to be late. There was precisely the same rush and fuss as if he had only arrived that moment. He tore on to the school, clattered up the stairs, and hurried down a passage. He could hear the piano thundering and crashing, which meant that Mr. Holbrook must have been waiting a good while. He opened a door at the extreme end of the passage, and entered.

"Late, of course," Mr. Holbrook remarked without ceasing to play. "Out of breath, of course. Too hot to do anything for the next quarter of an hour. Wasting my time, wasting your own time, wasting your father's money. If you have any excuses don't make them. Take off your jacket; sit down in that chair; and don't move or speak till you can do so without panting."

These words came in a kind of sing-song through the music, so that Tom immediately knew it was all right. He followed Mr. Holbrook's instructions to the letter, except that he said he was sorry.

He didn't know what Mr. Holbrook was playing, but he liked it. Moreover, it was very pleasant in the music-room, which seemed particularly cool and shadowy after the bright sunshine outside. And Mr. Holbrook wasn't in the least like Brown. The windows were wide open, and Tom sat quiet as a mouse.

Mr. Holbrook played for perhaps five minutes, but at last he got up, lit a cigarette, and motioned to Tom, who perched himself on the edge of the music-stool and plodded through a few scales and exercises. He was really no good at the piano, because the drudgery of practising bored him, and he shirked it whenever he could. Mr. Holbrook knew this as well as he did: in fact Tom at the piano bored them both. He wondered if Mr. Holbrook was supposed to smoke cigarettes while he was teaching: he didn't believe he was, though he always did it. Tom's hands looked very brown on the black and white keyboard, and in spite of the cooling process his fingers stuck to the notes. After a very unsatisfactory performance Mr. Holbrook sighed, pushed him off the music-stool without a word, reseated himself, and played three or four chords. "Sing," he said, and Tom, standing beside him, began to sing.

This was the part of the lesson he enjoyed. He even enjoyed singing scales and exercises nearly as much as songs; and he sang up the scale now, while Mr. Holbrook thrummed chords in unison. The treble voice sounded through the room, filling it, clear and fresh as a blackbird's. It gave Tom pleasure; it gave Mr. Holbrook pleasure— you could tell from his face, and also from the way he played the accompaniment. This indeed was why Tom loved singing to him. He liked singing to other people too, but not in the same way; and there were a few people, such as Daddy, whom he couldn't sing to at all unless he forgot they were listening. Nearly without a break Mr. Holbrook's chords and arpeggios dissolved into the opening bars of a melody, his eyes slid round for a moment towards the singer, while he gave a little backward jerk of his head, the customary signal.

It was a curious, and probably to Mr. Holbrook quaint, example of unconscious mimicry, for every shade and accent, every rise and fall, every lingering glissando, even the plaintive twang on the "ahimè—ahimè!" before the repetition of the tune, was a faithful echo of the Caruso record. The emotion, the tone, the expression, were in fact to Tom simply a *part* of the tune, as were the words, of whose meaning he had only a loose and general impression derived from Mr. Holbrook's free paraphrase. It was not Donizetti's "Spirto gentil" he sang, but Caruso's interpretation of it, and he would have found it more difficult to alter that interpretation than to learn an entirely new air.

Nevertheless, the emotion remained, etherealized, rarefied, translated out of actuality into terms of pure music. "Bravo!" cried Mr. Holbrook, smiling, and then repressing the smile. He played a few more notes, softly and low down in the bass, before he added to himself: "It's a pity."

But Tom had heard him, and Mr. Holbrook, divining that he had heard, wheeled round on the music-stool. "I only mean that it's a pity there isn't more of you," he said: a remark to which Tom made no reply.

Mr. Holbrook smiled at him again, and the smile seemed to come mostly from his round horn-rimmed and very expressive spectacles. He continued to gaze at Tom, and then with a kind of impatient gesture he ran his hands through a thick shock of reddish hair, making it stick straight up till it resembled a field of corn at sunset. "I see you don't understand me," he went on. "It's not your height I'm referring to: it's your shape, your build, the skeleton inside you. That won't alter, and it's what is so important. Do you know what you ought to look like? A small prize-fighter. And you don't, do you?"

"No," Tom replied.

"Well then," returned Mr. Holbrook half-petulantly, "we needn't talk about it."

But it was he who had begun the talking, and he oughtn't to leave it just like that. "Why?" Tom ventured after a pause. "I mean, why do you want me to look like a prize-fighter?" He tried not to show it, nevertheless he couldn't help feeling discouraged and disappointed. He supposed Brown would have been more to Mr. Holbrook's taste.

Mr. Holbrook said: "You've got it all wrong. I'm only thinking of your voice—the voice that is going to come when your present voice breaks. There should be lots of room for it—the more room the better."

"Perhaps I'll get bigger," Tom suggested more hopefully.

"Of course you'll get bigger," Mr. Holbrook declared. "You're quite big enough," he added inconsequently.

"I'm not," said Tom. "I've only grown an inch in the last year."

"An inch is plenty," said Mr. Holbrook, "though two might be better—particularly if they were in the right direction." He described a circle in the air, indicating the direction he meant. Then he laughed. "I don't believe you do understand me. This is what I mean. You've got a voice, and a sense of rhythm, and what is very much rarer, a sense of pitch. That's why you don't sing your notes on either the upper or the lower edge of them, but bang in the middle. And certainly you've got the temperament. All that's lacking is the chest measurement, lungs of leather, and vocal chords of I don't know what, but apparently something only to be found in Italy. It doesn't matter now, but unfortunately a boy's voice is only at its best for about a year or eighteen months, and yours was at its best six months ago. With any luck you'll be all right for the concert next Christmas, but I'm afraid that must be your last appearance. I'm not going to let you force your voice and ruin it. At the first sign of strain you stop singing. . . . And now——"

The lesson continued: certainly there was no sign of strain at present. In the midst of it, and unexpectedly as usual, the bell clanged out its tiresome summons. Mr. Holbrook took no notice of it except to twitch his nose. Tom, for his part, was quite willing to stay on: Pemby might grumble, as had often happened before, but he couldn't do anything. Still, when they came to a pause, he thought he'd better mention that the bell had gone.

"I know—I know," said Mr. Holbrook impatiently. "You don't imagine I'm deaf! We ought really to change our hour, only I suppose you like to be free in the afternoons. We can't discuss it now at any rate. Run along, and if Mr. Pemberton says anything unreasonable tell him that I kept you."

5. WHEN he entered the classroom, Pemby, who was Mr. Pemberton the headmaster, had finished calling the roll. He glanced up, said "Barber—music-lesson," and put a tick opposite Tom's name. Tom sat down beside Pascoe, in the back row, near the door.

It was an English lesson: they were doing Elizabeth's reign; and Mr. Pemberton, embarking on a favourite subject, proceeded to give an account of the Elizabethan theatre. He spoke of Marlowe and of Shakespeare; of the strange fashion dramatists had in those days of working on a play anonymously and in collaboration; of Stratford-on-Avon, and of boy-actors. He seemed quite keen about it all, and though his enthusiasm was not nearly so personal and catching as was Mr. Holbrook's about operas, Tom was interested.

But presently there came a push from Pascoe's knee, accompanied by a whispered: "Did you bring him?"

Pascoe was a sturdily built, intelligent-looking boy, with tow-coloured hair, an unusually wide space between his blue eyes, a small prim mouth, and an expression of innocent severity. Tom, still listening to Mr. Pemberton, merely shook his head.

"Why?" Pascoe whispered. At the same time he drew from his pocket a small cardboard box with a perforated lid, and opened it under the desk.

Tom took no notice. Anyway he knew what was in the box without looking.

Next moment he got a much more violent nudge, this time in the ribs and from Pascoe's elbow. "Shut up," he muttered, moving farther off.

But he couldn't help giving just one glance through the tail of his eye. On the desk in front of Pascoe was a large smooth green caterpillar, obviously an athlete, and in the pink of condition. Tom felt the sting of temptation. The caterpillar raised his head to have a look round, and Pascoe hissed: "I bet he beats your champion."

The caterpillar stared Tom straight in the face, as much as to say: "There now!" but still he would not yield. Only he watched, which was perhaps much the same thing.

The caterpillar, with undulating back, proceeded to explore his new surroundings, and Tom couldn't deny that he was a very fine specimen. Secretly, too, he had begun to feel doubts about the champion, who yesterday had seemed distinctly out of form. Maybe it was only that he was overtrained, though Pascoe had hinted that he was approaching his chrysalis days. Tom's hand stole to his pocket.

The opportunity was golden—at any rate as golden as you could expect in the middle of class. For Mr. Pemberton, blind as a bat always, was at present gazing out of the window, lost in the tragic fate of Kit Marlowe. His pupils, respecting his reverie, had begun to busy themselves with such soundless occupations as noughts-and-crosses and the folding of paper darts. Tom opened his cardboard box and tumbled the champion, a black "Hairy Willie" of the name of Charles, out on to the desk.

Immediately Charles curled himself into a tight ring and pretended to be dead. Pascoe sniffed contemptuously. "He's a funk," he whispered. "Anyway, he's done: I knew he couldn't last."

"He's not done," Tom whispered back. "He's resting. It's because it's so hot, and he's handicapped with all that fur. Yours is naked."

The green caterpillar, having now reached a sunken china inkpot at the top of the desk, was bending down over its dark and mysterious well. Tom was instantly reminded of the story of Narcissus, but Pascoe said: "Gracious, he's drinking the ink!" and hurriedly removed him to a place of safety. He drew a chalk line on the desk opposite Tom, and another one opposite himself. This was the racecourse, and the distance between the lines was about two feet.

"What's your's name?" Tom whispered.

"James," whispered Pascoe.

Tom was impressed. "That's queer," he said, but Pascoe, who was sometimes rather slow at seeing things, did not grasp the significance.

"It means that they're both of royal blood," Tom whispered. "Stuarts." He lifted Charles Stuart and set him on his chalk mark. Pascoe's James was already on the other chalk mark, held back, straining on the leash as it were. For the races were always now cross races: that is to say, Charles's starting point was James's winning post, and vice versa. This had been found to be the best plan, and the competitors might be guided on a straight path by their owners. Pencils were used for the purpose, though pushing was strictly barred. Otherwise, as experience had proved, the race in moments of excitement was apt to degenerate into a kind of table-hockey—particularly towards the finish.

"You're not to push," Tom warned.

"*You're* not to push," Pascoe retorted sharply.

Then both breathed a simultaneous "Go!" and their eyes grew round with suppressed eagerness.

Charles and James, probably filled with despair, started off at top speed. After proceeding for some inches, however, in this reckless fashion, it apparently dawned on them that their lives were not in danger. Their pace slackened; they sniffed the air; presently they paused to consider what all the fuss was about. Where were they? Charles and James raised questing heads—James, no doubt, seeking the green cold smoothness of cabbage leaves; Charles the darker aromatic shade of nasturtiums. But there were no cabbages, no nasturtiums, only a deeply scored and ink-splashed wooden desk. Charles and James were temporarily discouraged. Still, beyond this there *must* be cabbages and nasturtiums—soft damp brown earth and a green twilight where one could rest and eat and sleep in peace. Meanwhile there was an arid desert to be crossed—yellow, dry, unknown —possibly dangerous, and certainly unpleasant. Nor could they proceed with their customary freedom. Ever and anon, when they attempted to strike out a more promising trail, a bar of wood descended out of the sky and pushed them back. To Charles the experience was not new, though he had never been able to explain it. Still, he had traversed this desert before—whether in reality or in a nightmare was uncertain. To James the adventure was entirely novel, and the first time the pole barred his progress he attempted to climb it. But only to be shaken off, while Tom whispered indignantly: "You jerked him four inches at least," and hastily drew a new winning post for James.

"I didn't," Pascoe glared, but there was no time to argue, for just then James and Charles met.

This was bad management perhaps, though who could have thought it would have mattered! And James indeed would have passed by had not Charles prevented him. Charles hesitated, reared up, blocked the path, and finally, yielding to a delirious and unsportsmanlike impulse, embraced James. So, at least, Tom said: Pascoe said he attacked him. Whatever the motive, the effect was disastrous, for James immediately turned round and hurried back as fast as he could to his starting place. A fierce altercation ensued—recriminations, denials, threats—in the midst of which Mr. Pemberton awoke out of historical reverie to the fact that something illicit was going on at the back of the room. So did everybody else, and craned round to have a look; but Mr. Pemberton breathed "S—sh!" and raised a hand for silence. In the hush that followed he advanced a few steps on tiptoe,

peering shortsightedly at the offenders, who instantly, by some
mysterious telepathic warning, became aware of what was happening.
They were far too cunning, however, to make a movement, for they
knew much better than Pemby did the range of his vision, and that
from his present distance he couldn't possibly see James and Charles.
But they looked up in innocent surprise when, after continuing to
peer vainly, he suddenly stretched out a long forefinger of accusation. "Pascoe and Barber; Barber and Pascoe. Always the same pair:
gabbling away like two old market-women—distracting the attention
of the other boys—turning the hours of fruitful study into hours of
unprofitable gossip. Pascoe and Barber will each bring me tomorrow
morning the first part of *The Rime of the Ancient Mariner* written
out neatly in ink."

So that was that—eighty-two lines, as Tom despondently noted
after a stealthy reference to his poetry book.

And the morning dragged on, growing ever more close and sultry,
till by twelve o'clock it had become positively breathless. Everybody
felt it: all the windows were opened wide; but the air that drifted in
might have been coming from a furnace. Three more classes to go;
then two; then at last only one. . . .

It was in this final session that Tom—that shining light of scholar-
ship—was obliged to make an ignominious descent from the first
form to the third. He hated this—hatred being shoved among a lot of
kids—and wished he could leave out maths altogether. What was the
use of wasting time over subjects in which he never made the
least progress!

Over the third form Miss Jimpson presided, and with the exception
of Brown it consisted of boys younger than Tom—several of them
two years younger. But Brown was a permanent adornment, and he
never would have been promoted even as high as the third if it hadn't
been that at the age of thirteen he couldn't very well be left among in-
fants of eight or nine. Tom knew that Miss Jimpson longed to get rid
of Brown, and looked forward to next term, when he would have to
leave because he would then be fourteen. His placidity, his impervi-
ousness to either reproaches or sarcasm, and more particularly his
habit of lounging back in his seat with his hands in his pockets, got
on her nerves and had an effect upon the whole class. More than once
she had lost her temper and referred openly to the shamefulness of
Brown's position. But Brown had only smiled pleasantly, and now

she ignored him as much as possible. Brown indeed was perfectly content with his position, which he knew would be reversed the moment the bell rang. He was neither ashamed, nor did he bear malice when Miss Jimpson ticked him off: but then, even when he was bullying smaller boys or fighting bigger ones, Tom had never seen Brown looking anything but good-natured. His mouth curled naturally into smiles, and he actually had dimples.

To-day Tom saw at once that Miss Jimpson was in no mood for nonsense. Both her appearance and her voice suggested that she found the temperature trying. She went straight to the blackboard, chalked up a geometrical figure, and instead of legitimate A's and B's and C's, proceeded to decorate it with K's and L's and M's, always a bad sign. To Tom, whose one hope was in his memory, the substitution of these different letters would, he knew, be fatal. Fortunately Miss Jimpson, instead of calling anybody up to the platform to do the proposition, gave it to the whole class to write out in their scribblers. So Tom put the A's and B's and C's back in their proper places and set to work.

But he had begun to feel very tired and drowsy. Perhaps it was the result of getting up so early after a pretty restless night, or perhaps it was just the effect of the day—not so much the heat really as the lack of air. Anyhow, he could hardly keep awake, let alone concentrate on geometry. Sleepy far-off sounds reached him through the open windows, and he couldn't help trying to disentangle them. The motionless shadow of a tree, silhouetted on the pale lemon-coloured wall beside him, made him think of trees. Slowly and unresistingly, as if drawn by an invisible thread, his spirit floated out through the window and over the tops of elms and beeches. Only the avenue did not come to an end at the school gates as it ought to have done, but stretched on and on till at last it reached the river. And from the river it reached the garden, where William was pottering about in his shirt-sleeves, and Henry was blinking in the sun. Tom saw Henry quite distinctly. He was sitting on the path, and presently he stretched out his right paw. Idly Tom drew with his pencil on the white sheet of paper before him what Henry was drawing on the black cinder path. Then his pencil seemed to stop of itself, and he saw that he had completed a figure. This was strange. It was very like the figure Henry himself had scratched that morning on the gravel, and not in the least like the figure on the blackboard. Yet he supposed it too could be made to prove something by the addition of A's and B's and C's.

Suddenly he jerked himself straight: he must actually have dozed off, for Miss Jimpson had her eyes fixed on him, and he knew that next moment she would call him up and discover that he had written only the first line of the proposition, and even that with the wrong letters. And how dark it had grown! Through a yellowish twilight he gazed at Miss Jimpson as some fascinated thrush might have gazed into the green eyes of an approaching Henry. Not that Miss Jimpson usually was alarming: indeed, Tom had always liked her—in spite of the fact that she taught mathematics. Yet now for some reason he had an acute feeling of suspense. It was as if Miss Jimpson had suddenly acquired talons and a ravening hunger, with a power to leap the whole length of the room and strike surely. Tom felt a kind of squeal rising in his throat, though he made no sound. And then—without remembering, without knowing, without thinking—he spoke the word. . . .

Instantly it happened. There was a sudden rushing noise, a blinding glare, and an explosion that shook the whole building. In the brief pandemonium that followed it was somebody else who screamed, not Tom. The wind whirled through the room, scattering papers, circling in a kind of vortex, as if trying madly to force an outlet through the ceiling. Crash! That was the blackboard—either the wind or Miss Jimpson had knocked it over. Tom sprang to his feet in an ecstasy of excitement. It seemed to him that the darkness was thickening at the centre, concentrating in a spiral twirling column, through which there blazed down two white eyes of fire. He called out something—or a voice called out near to him. Everybody had jumped up: the room was in a tumult. And next minute the whole thing was over, passing as abruptly as it had begun. But the behaviour of Brown was most astonishing of all. He was actually standing on the form, clapping his arms, like wings, against his sides, and making the most extraordinary bird cries.

"Brown!" called Miss Jimpson hysterically, and Brown himself seemed suddenly to awaken to realities. He hopped down from the form, looking for once, Tom thought, rather disconcerted. One of the smaller boys had begun to weep.

"Don't be silly, Donnelly!" snapped Miss Jimpson with a touch of temper. She had made a rapid recovery and now proceeded to control the situation. "It's all over," she declared, "whatever it was. A most unusual thing to happen—in this climate at any rate—but due of course to some atmospheric disturbance. A kind of small cyclone, I suppose, such as they often have in the tropics. I must say I've been half expecting something of the sort all morning. . . . And now, will the end boy in each row kindly gather up the papers on the floor. The others keep their seats."

Since Tom was not at the end of a row, he remained seated. Nevertheless, what had happened was so remarkable that Miss Jimpson did not insist on an immediate resumption of the lesson.

"Was it a cloudburst?" Saunderson asked, and Miss Jimpson temporized. She glanced out of the window and saw only one heavy patch of cloud in a vividly blue sky.

"Well," she hesitated, "something of that sort, no doubt; though I don't suppose there can be a cloudburst without rain. But some kind of electrical disturbance at all events, which will probably clear the air. As I say, in tropical climates such sudden storms are quite common, and nobody thinks anything of them."

Miss Jimpson spoke in her most confident and businesslike tone, yet her explanation was not entirely successful, for little Donnelly piped up in a voice still broken by woe: "It was in the room. I saw it. It came right in through the window, and there was a man in it."

"A man in it?" Miss Jimpson repeated briskly. She hadn't the least notion what the child was talking about, but in the circumstances felt it better to reassure him. "What do you mean, Donnelly?" she went on, smiling, yet kind. "As I tell you, the whole disturbance was caused by the meeting of two opposed electric currents in the air. Surely you can understand that! Just like a railway collision. It was the collision which produced the flash, the thunder, and a sort of air storm. In fact it was just the same as an ordinary thunderstorm except that there was no rain. . . . And of course it happened more suddenly and was over more quickly."

"But I saw him," said Donnelly unhappy.

Miss Jimpson's voice grew a shade firmer. "You mustn't talk nonsense, Donnelly," she said. "There was no 'him,' as you call it, to see. You were startled—as indeed we all were—and when one's frightened it's very easy to imagine things."

"I saw him," Donnelly repeated obstinately.

Miss Jimpson paused, and seemed on the point of losing patience, but laughed instead. "What was he like, Donnelly?" she asked. "I suppose you can describe him since you saw him so clearly. You'd better tell us, because none of the rest of us saw anything."

"Yes, I *can* describe him," Donnelly replied unexpectedly and rather defiantly. "He was all hunched up, with a cloud round him, and he had a dark cross face and white eyes."

"I saw him too," Tom felt tempted to put in; only everybody had begun to laugh at Donnelly, and Donnelly himself had turned as red as a poppy. Tom didn't want to be laughed at, and above all he didn't want to be questioned.

"I saw him too," he suddenly said.

Miss Jimpson looked at him coldly for about half a minute. Then she remarked: "In that case, Barber, you'd better write out for me fifty times: 'I must not try to make myself interesting by telling fibs.'"

"But I did," Tom persisted.

"A hundred times," said Miss Jimpson.

She was awful, Tom thought, and for two ticks he'd bring the whole thing back again.

Only, *had* he done it? There was the figure drawn on his scribbler; he looked down at it; but he had *said* something, too. It had been only a single word, and now it was gone: he couldn't remember anything except that it had begun with an A and that the next letter was Z. At least, he was almost sure it was. Az—Az—what? He mumbled over imaginary words beginning with "az," but knew they weren't right, and indeed nothing happened. *Could* it have been only his imagination? But in that case how had young Donnelly seen it? And he had seen more than Tom had!

Meanwhile, though he tried to avoid looking at her, he kept on catching Miss Jimpson's eye, and Miss Jimpson's eye was witheringly sceptical. She had no right to look at him like that, Tom felt, or to accuse him of telling lies; though somehow it was really her remark about trying to make himself interesting which rankled most. He never tried to make himself interesting—at least very seldom—and certainly he hadn't tried then, he hadn't wanted to speak at all. There she was again! Why couldn't she look at Donnelly? Just because Donnelly had said it first she didn't bother about him. Maybe, however, it was because she had repented and was filled with remorse. Only she didn't a bit look as if she was filled with remorse, though you never could tell, and Tom resolved to wait on after school to give her a chance of apologizing. Also of cancelling his imposition. He had now a couple of impositions to do, and all because of Pascoe and Donnelly. Yes, he would wait.

On the other hand, he wanted very much to question Donnelly as to what exactly he *had* seen. Perhaps Donnelly would wait too—outside. He scribbled a brief note, folded it, wrote Donnelly's name on it, and passed it to the boy in front of him. Anxiously he watched the surreptitious progress of the note from hand to hand until finally it reached its destination. He watched Donnelly opening it and reading it. For a minute or so nothing happened. Then, to his intense surprise and indignation, Donnelly, instead of writing a reply, simply turned round and made a face at him. Tom was furious. That miserable little squirt, who blubbed every time he missed a question, and in winter came to school wrapped up in so many mufflers that he had practically to be unpacked! He felt a violent uprush of the most Brown-like impulses. He contorted his face into an expression of frightful pugnacity, but Donnelly seemed merely to find it funny and screwed up his face too. Then he nudged the boy next him, who turned round and grinned. Tom had only partly recovered from these insults when the bell rang.

With the first note of the clapper Miss Jimpson's head disappeared behind the raised lid of her desk, and it was not till the scuffling and noise of escaping pupils had died into silence that it emerged again. Then she gazed across the empty room in surprise. "What are you waiting for, Barber?" she asked.

It wasn't a very easy question to answer, and Tom's mumble failed to enlighten Miss Jimpson, who, moreover, betrayed no sign at all of wishing to apologize. "Come closer," she said. "I can't hear what you say."

So Tom got up, and in some confusion advanced to within a foot of the raised platform upon which were Miss Jimpson, her desk, and the blackboard.

"Come up here," Miss Jimpson said, "and don't look so scared—I shan't eat you."

Tom climbed the three steps and stood beside her. Still he did not speak, and Miss Jimpson, who was tying exercise books into a bundle, suddenly smiled at him. "Well," she asked, "what is it?"

Tom swallowed hastily. "I wasn't telling lies," he answered. "I did think I saw something."

Miss Jimpson looked at him calmly, and whether it was because school was over or not, she seemed much more approachable than before. Also, Tom thought, she looked rather pale and fagged, and a wisp of dark hair had come loose and fallen down over her left ear. "We all saw something," she presently observed. "We saw that it got quite dark for a few minutes, and we saw a flash of lightning."

"It was a part of the darkness," Tom told her.

Miss Jimpson unexpectedly placed her two hands on his shoulders, and her eyes were now bright and friendly. "Tell me this, Tom Barber," she said. "If Donnelly hadn't been scared out of his wits and imagined all that nonsense, would *you* have said a word?"

Tom was obliged to confess that he wouldn't.

"Well then?" pursued Miss Jimpson.

"All the same I did see it—think I saw it, I mean. . . . Smoky— with two eyes."

Miss Jimpson looked very hard into Tom's own two eyes before she answered. "This is very absurd. And especially coming from a comparatively big boy like you."

Tom did not deny its absurdity, and Miss Jimpson herself, after a brief reflection, appeared to recognize that that was hardly the point. "You really *weren't* telling fibs?" she resumed.

"No," said Tom.

Miss Jimpson once more pondered, and she looked rather nice while she was doing so: she was really quite pretty, Tom decided. "In that case, what do you suggest ought to be done about it?" she asked. "By me, I mean?"

Tom told her what he thought should be done. "I don't think I ought to get an imposition," he said.

"I don't think so either," Miss Jimpson agreed. "So we'll wipe that out."

"Thank you, Miss Jimpson," Tom replied. "Thank you very much."

Miss Jimpson laughed. She had finished tying up her bundle. "Let us hope there will be no more thunderstorms," she declared. "They seem to affect our nerves. We were all of us a little upset."

"Especially Brown," Tom couldn't help reminding her.

"Yes, Brown," Miss Jimpson echoed, frowning a little. She glanced at him questioningly, as if struck by a sudden suspicion. "I don't quite know *what* came over Brown," she murmured doubtfully.

But Tom's candour was apparent. "Neither did he," was all he answered.

Miss Jimpson looked relieved. "I thought at the time he didn't," she said; "otherwise I should have had to take more notice of it."

"Do you think——" Tom began, and then stopped. "They were bird screams he was making," he went on after a pause. "Like a macaw."

"A macaw!" Miss Jimpson repeated wonderingly.

"Yes—a kind of parrot."

But Miss Jimpson, for some unknown reason, now appeared to be less interested in Brown than in Tom himself, and it was upon him that her gaze was fixed in reflective scrutiny. "You're a very strange boy, Tom Barber, "she murmured. "And I believe even much stranger than you allow anybody to suspect. Is that right?"

"I don't know," said Tom.

"What do they think about you at home?" Miss Jimpson continued. "Not that it matters much, because it's sure to be wrong."

"Why?" asked Tom, gravely.

"Oh, I don't know—except that it usually is. At any rate," she added, "I feel that a cup of tea is what we both need to restore us to perfect sanity. If you were to invite me I know I'd accept."

This frankness put Tom in a distinctly awkward position, and he blushed. "I'd like very much to invite you," he stammered. "But you see I—I'm afraid I couldn't pay for you—nor even for myself."

"That *is* a difficulty," Miss Jimpson admitted. "Wait for me in the porch all the same. . . . I've only to put on a hat and won't keep you more than three minutes. But I simply *must* have a cup of tea, and I hate sitting in a teashop by myself."

6: SO five minutes later Tom and Miss Jimpson were walking down the road together under the lime trees. Miss Jimpson looked even nicer in her hat than she did without it: Tom felt quite pleased to be walking with her. Then he remembered that he ought to be on the outside of the pavement, and changed his position.

"Where are we going?" he inquired.

"I suppose to Nicholson's," Miss Jimpson thought. "It's the nearest place and probably at this hour we'll have it all to ourselves. The room upstairs is rather nice if you can get a table at the window; but I expect you've been there before."

"Only once," said Tom. "With Mr. Holbrook. . . . We had ices."

What a thing to say! He could have kicked himself. And he had said it in such a clear voice too—like somebody announcing a hymn. Miss Jimpson would think he was awful! Anybody would, for that matter! And covered with confusion, he determined that he wouldn't accept an ice even if she offered him one.

"We'll have ices," Miss Jimpson said. "That's a splendid idea, but I must have tea too."

It wasn't a splendid idea; it was the very reverse; yet if he told her now that he didn't care for ices it would be a lie. The whole thing had been spoiled just by that one unfortunate speech. "I didn't mean —" he protested.

"Here we are," Miss Jimpson said, not listening to him, but passing under the striped red-and-white awning into the shop, so that he could only follow her as she walked straight on through it and up the stairs at the back.

The stairs led to a bright sunny room on the first floor, containing half a dozen small white-clothed tables; and, to add to his embarrassment, the very first thing he saw was Brown seated at one of these. He was indeed the only person there, and Miss Jimpson nodded to him and smiled, while Brown smiled back and stared at them, though without ceasing to absorb refreshment. It was like him to come here and gorge himself in solitude. Tom could see from the two empty dishes that it was his third ice he was finishing. He had always more money than anybody else, and he spent practically the whole of it on grub. Miss Jimpson passed on to a table placed in the bow-window, and as Tom was following her, Brown stuck out a treacherous foot over which he came to grief.

"Sorry, Skinny!" Brown whispered, abstracting the last remains of his ice with a red and flexible tongue; but Tom, whose face was now the colour of Brown's tongue, ignored the apology and hurried after Miss Jimpson.

He sat down opposite her and refrained from glancing round, though he could hardly help doing so when he heard Brown pushing back his chair. He listened to his footsteps crossing the room, and a moment later clattering down the stairs.

Well, Brown was gone—that was one comfort—and he breathed more freely. All the same, he wished Brown hadn't been there at all, for he knew the sort of story he would make of it. He would accuse Tom of being Miss Jimpson's pet and of sucking up to her: it would be all over the school to-morrow, with additions and embellishments of the kind that Brown thought funny. If he did try to be funny, Tom determined that he would jolly well remind him of the ass he had made of himself, standing up on the form flapping his wings.

You would have thought after such an exhibition he might have kept quiet for a bit, but he seemed to have forgotten about it already. Other people wouldn't have forgotten, though; no fear of that: and it was the first time within Tom's memory that Brown had placed himself in a position when he could be ragged. . . .

Only there was nobody to rag him. Tom's brief elation sank as he remembered Brown's powers of retaliation. He knew very well that even if he had the courage to attempt it, it wouldn't come off. You can't rag people like Brown. For one thing, they don't care, and for another, Brown would rather like it, because it would give him an excuse to resort to physical measures, which he would pursue happily until Tom apologized.

Still, he was glad that Henry had tried to turn Brown into a bird. He hadn't succeeded, but he had at least made him look a fool. Henry almost deserved a saucer of cream for that. Unless Brown *really* had done it on purpose; and somehow, in spite of Miss Jimpson's doubts, it now seemed to Tom that this was more likely to be the truth. Anyhow it was what he would say and what the others would think. Besides, Miss Jimpson secretly, Tom thought, had let it pass because she didn't much care about tackling Brown, and after all, everybody had been making a row. To connect it with Henry was nonsense. *That* part, he knew, he was just pretending, in order to make it more exciting and mysterious. And he felt a sudden inclination to talk to Miss Jimpson about Henry. It was rotten that he couldn't. But she would think he was either mad or else silly. That was the worst of it. He wished he knew somebody like the Blakes to whom you could talk about such things. The only possible person Tom had was Pascoe, who wasn't really possible except in the sense that he never repeated what you told him. As for believing, or half believing, or even *pretending* to believe (which was really all that was necessary), Pascoe was no good at all. He was too literal, too matter-of-fact, too like the celebrated child of six.

The temptation to experiment on Miss Jimpson was strong, and Tom very nearly yielded to it. Was there the slightest chance that she was less commonsensical than she looked? Spoon in hand, he gazed at her over his strawberry ice. Should he throw out just one cautious hint and see what happened? But he knew what would happen, what invariably happened, and since she had already said that she thought him strange, there didn't seem to be much use in making her think him stranger. In his uncertainty he kept on glancing at her until suddenly he perceived that she had noticed this and was evidently puzzled by it. So he looked out of the window instead, watching the people passing on the opposite side of the road.

"If I weren't practically sure that I know them already," was Miss Jimpson's not very original remark, "I might be inclined to risk a penny."

Tom turned round from the window. How could she possibly know them? She didn't, of course, but he had better make certain. "What was I thinking?" he demanded.

"That I ought to have passed the age for ices," said Miss Jimpson. "Nothing but disapproval can explain that frowning brow." Then, rather curiously, she asked the point-blank question: "How old do you think I *am*, Barber? Or Tom; for I'm going to call you Tom now that we're alone."

Tom hesitated—not because he couldn't give a pretty good guess at Miss Jimpson's age, but because he knew most people preferred to be thought younger than they were.

Miss Jimpson smiled at the hesitation. "Come on," she insisted gaily, so he told her the truth. "Thirty," was Tom's estimate.

Miss Jimpson laughed. "Well, precious near it," she confessed, "though it wasn't what I hoped you'd say. . . . But age is a variable thing, don't you think? I mean so far as one's private feelings about it are concerned. There are days when one feels eighteen and days when one feels eighty."

"I've never felt as old as *that*," Tom replied. "It must be very queer."

"Queer isn't the word for it!" declared Miss Jimpson. "But tell me this, Tom: how many brothers and sisters have you?"

"I haven't any," Tom answered in surprise.

"I thought not; and that partly explains it."

"Explains what?" Tom questioned her, for he thought that Miss Jimpson was talking a little wildly.

"Explains you," said Miss Jimpson. "It means that all your home life must be different: different from that of boys like Brown, I mean. If nothing else, the family conversation is sure to be different. In your house I expect it's real conversation."

"Isn't there real conversation in the Brown family?" Tom wondered.

Miss Jimpson pushed a plate of cakes towards him. "I think it's most unlikely that they all sit dumb," she replied. "But by real conversation I meant an exchange of ideas."

Tom pondered this in silence. He didn't know the Brown family except by sight, but he knew that Brown had three sisters and two brothers, and that Brown himself came somewhere in the middle, and that they all looked very much alike. "Daddy and Mother exchange ideas," he suddenly decided. "They were exchanging them about the Blakes this morning."

Miss Jimpson looked mystified. "The Blakes!" she repeated. "What Blakes?"

"The William Blakes," said Tom. "About God looking in at the window. Daddy doesn't believe He did, but Mother does."

Miss Jimpson recognized the William Blakes. "That's just what I mean," she said. "The Browns would be talking about the Smiths or the Atkinsons."

Tom didn't see why they shouldn't be talking about the Smiths and Atkinsons, but he asked: "Is this a real conversation we're having now?"

Miss Jimpson considered. "Yes, I think so," she replied. "At any rate, it's the beginnings of one: it's not just gossip. Have another ice."

"No, thank you," said Tom.

"Then you'll have a cup of tea," and she poured it out, leaving him to add the milk and sugar himself. "What do you and Mr. Holbrook talk about?" she asked.

"Usually about music," said Tom. "I don't think we exchange ideas."

"Such nonsense!" cried Miss Jimpson. "I'm sure you do. Does talking about music interest you?"

"Yes," Tom answered. "You see," he explained, "when I go to his house we play the gramophone, or he plays the piano—and it's only in between that we talk."

Miss Jimpson saw, and she looked out of the window for a minute or two without speaking. "He told me you were fond of music," she then said.

Tom was surprised. Somehow it always surprised him to find that he had been talked about in his absence. It gave him a slightly ghostly feeling too—as if he had been there and not there at the same time. Yet he hadn't this feeling when it was he himself who talked. He had been talking about Mr. Holbrook and Mother and Daddy and Brown, and it hadn't seemed at all ghostly, which was strange, because really it ought to have been just the same.

"I'm afraid I'm *not* very fond of music," Miss Jimpson was saying, and Tom thought her face had clouded a little. Not clouded exactly, for she didn't look cross or anything like that; in fact she was smiling. But something was different—or perhaps it was just that she was thinking.

"I've tried to pretend I am," Miss Jimpson went on, "but it was simply because I hate missing things, and naturally that is no good. When I was in Milan last year I sat through two operas at the Scala and was bored stiff the entire time."

"Gracious!" cried Tom, but hastily added: "Perhaps they weren't good operas."

"They were," said Miss Jimpson grimly. "They were even supposed to be specially good—with Toscanini conducting. Mr. Holbrook was disgusted with me."

"I don't see why he should be," Tom declared gallantly.

"Neither do I," Miss Jimpson agreed. "Particularly since I went, if not entirely, at any rate very largely, on his account. But men are like that—most men, Tom; not you, as you're just shown."

"I shouldn't worry," Tom told her kindly. Then: "Who was singing?" he naturally inquired, but Miss Jimpson immediately sat up and gazed at him.

"Don't!" she exclaimed. "I thought you were different, but I see you really aren't!"

Tom was surprised. "Why?" he asked.

"I treasured up the programmes for Mr. Holbrook," Miss Jimpson continued, ignoring the interruption, "so that he could read the names of the singers for himself—and, incidentally, to prove that I'd been there at all. You'd have imagined that would be sufficient, wouldn't you? But merely because I couldn't *remember* the names when he asked me, he was more irritated than if I hadn't gone."

Tom's private opinion was that it *had* been pretty slack of her, though he only said: "Yes, he wouldn't like that; he'd think it showed that you weren't really interested. Surely you can remember now."

"I can't," Miss Jimpson snapped. "And I don't want to. Why should I remember the names of people who annoyed me. And that's all they did—the principals even more than the others, because they made more noise. And it was all so perfectly idiotic! Imagine a priestess of the Druids, dressed in what looked to me like a white ball-dress, standing under an oak tree——"

"That was Rosa Ponselle," Tom put in immediately, "and the opera was *Norma*, and she was singing 'Casta Diva.' "

"Heavens!" cried Miss Jimpson.

"Well, it *was*," said Tom, a little impatiently. "I know, because Mr. Holbrook told me about the oak tree, and that nobody else sings that part. He's got a record of her singing 'Casta Diva,' and I've heard it; it's lovely."

"I'm not doubting you," Miss Jimpson said meekly. "I was only thinking what an apt pupil he'd got. It's not much wonder he thinks such a lot of you."

Tom wasn't sure whether she meant this or not, but he thought she did, and blushed.

"I'm going to slip in one morning and hear *you* sing," she told him. "Do you think Mr. Holbrook would mind?"

Tom wasn't certain about Mr. Holbrook, but he knew he would mind himself. If Miss Jimpson felt that way about a person like Rosa Ponselle, she must be as bad as Daddy, and he didn't want to sing to her. Nor could he see why she should want to listen. "I think you'd better not," he said after a pause.

But Miss Jimpson didn't pause for a second. "Why?" she demanded. "Do you mean he *would* be annoyed?"

"He might be," Tom answered guardedly. "It's better not to risk it." And he looked more guarded still.

"I'm perfectly prepared to risk it," Miss Jimpson returned rather sharply. "And at any rate you could find out, couldn't you?"

"Yes," Tom murmured, though it was not a promise. But he felt that the ground was tricky, and that they'd better get off it as soon as possible; so, with a sleek, black, green-eyed phantom in his mind's eye, he asked her if she were fond of cats.

Miss Jimpson was dubious. "I like them better than canaries or white mice," she compromised, "and I haven't to get up and go out of the room if a cat happens to come into it. But no, on the whole: dogs every time for me."

"I used to have three dogs," Tom said sadly. "At least, they weren't mine exactly. I mean, they didn't really belong to us; they had their own homes; but they went about with me everywhere."

"And what happened to them?" Miss Jimpson asked.

"Roger was poisoned. He must have picked poison up somewhere in the field, and when he got home, though we did everything we could think of, it was too late, and he died before the vet arrived. . . . Barker is dead too. He was getting very old and blind and a motor-lorry ran over him. . . . Pincher I expect is all right: he was a young dog. But he belonged to the Sabines, and when Mr. Sabine got another church, and they went away, they took Pincher with them."

"That's the worst of having pets," Miss Jimpson said. "You get fond of them, and then something happens. Or even if it doesn't, their lives are so short, so much shorter than ours. I had a dog once myself, and when he died I was so upset I made up my mind never to get another one."

"You could get a pet tortoise," Tom said doubtfully. "They live for ages and ages."

"I dare say, but what good would that be? It wouldn't care a straw about you: you might as well have a pet cabbage."

Tom sighed. "We've only got a cat," he said, "and I don't think he cares much either. . . . I've wanted to have a bulldog ever since I can remember, only Daddy won't let me."

He looked up to find Miss Jimpson regarding him closely. "What other things do you want?" she asked, and the suddenness and unexpected aptness of her question caused him to gaze at her in consternation.

He did not attempt to answer, but he couldn't help thinking, and he was profoundly thankful that Miss Jimpson couldn't read his thoughts. Just imagine if he had been obliged to give her the list of wants he had gone through that very morning! Especially the hairs on his legs! He looked so embarrassed that Miss Jimpson must have guessed something was amiss, for she hastily put another question: "What kind of cat is it—a Persian?"

"No, just an ordinary cat," Tom answered with relief; though truthfulness compelled him to add: "At least, he's not quite ordinary. He's a black cat and his name is Henry."

"Does he do tricks?" asked Miss Jimpson innocently. "But of course cats don't: they're too aloof and superior for that."

"They *do*," Tom couldn't help replying, in a tone both dark and emphatic. "Only they don't do dogs' tricks, and they do them to please themselves, not because they've been taught."

He saw, however, that Miss Jimpson wasn't really attending, she was doing something to her hat. "Well, you must tell me about Henry's tricks another day," she said. "What I want you to tell me now is whether I've got a smut on my nose or not. I feel that I have, though I can't see it. . . . And then we must go."

Tom inspected her carefully. "You haven't," he said.

"In that case——" And Miss Jimpson rose from her chair.

They both got up. "Thanks awfully," Tom was beginning, but Miss Jimpson pushed him along by his shoulders and they descended to the shop, where she paused at the cash-box, while Tom went on to the door, where he stood waiting. Then, out in the street, they said good-bye, and Miss Jimpson went one way and he the other.

7: TOM walked home through the afternoon sunshine. He was a rather pottering walker, given to standing and gazing at anything that happened to catch his attention, whether it were a dog, a street musician, a furniture van being unloaded, or merely somebody clipping a garden hedge. This was not because he was an idler, but because so many things interested him. His mind was as easily stirred as the river sedges, and when it was deeply stirred his bodily activities were sometimes temporarily suspended.

As a rule this did not matter, but there had been disastrous exceptions. Yesterday afternoon, for instance, when having gone in to bat at the tail end of a practice game supervised by Mr. Poland, suddenly he had been so much struck by the appearance of the bowler that he had made no attempt to defend his wicket. In a dream he had stood there—and the awakening had been rude. One couldn't have believed that people would be so nasty about what was really nothing—or at any rate very little. Tom had never been called so many names in his life. Even the opposite side had joined in, though they ought to have been pleased, since it was to their advantage; while Driscoll, the bowler in question, had been angriest of all, seeing in the subsequent explanation (dragged out by Mr. Poland) a reflection on his personal appearance, whereas Tom had actually been thinking how nice he looked.

But of course he couldn't tell them that: it would only have made matters worse: and now, as he pursued his way homeward, it was Miss

Jimpson who occupied his thoughts—chiefly because of the remarks she had made about wanting to hear him sing. Tom couldn't quite believe in this desire, or at least that it had not behind it a motive which had nothing to do with music. Miss Jimpson didn't care for music: she had said so: she had said that she had only gone to those operas to please Mr. Holbrook. Wasn't it very likely, then, that her new plan had been made with the same object? A sudden suspicion dawned upon Tom. Why should Miss Jimpson be so keen on pleasing Mr. Holbrook unless she was fond of him? A romance it was. And this hypothesis was no sooner born than he saw that it explained everything and must be true. At the same time it struck him as pretty thick! That is to say, the excuse of the singing lesson struck him as pretty thin! And mightn't it have had something to do even with the tea and ices at Nicholson's? This illumination of Miss Jimpson's secret designs gave Tom a shock. Clearly she wanted him to help, and, though he felt a certain sympathy with her, he wasn't sure that he could go quite as far as that. He would first have to decide whether she was worthy of Mr. Holbrook, and next find out what were Mr. Holbrook's private feelings in the matter. Indeed the whole thing must be considered carefully—possibly discussed with Mother—before he took any active step.

Tom turned in at his own gate feeling important and influential—as was only natural, with Miss Jimpson's happiness hanging on his decision. He saw nobody in the garden nor in the house, though he could hear Phemie whistling in the kitchen, a sure sign that Mother was out. He flung his books down on the study table and went back to the garden.

There was nothing to do unless Pascoe happened to turn up, which he hardly expected, for they had made no arrangement. Still, Pascoe often rode over: it took him only about ten minutes on his bicycle, whereas for Tom to go to *his* house meant at least half an hour's walk. He chose a suitable spot and stretched himself comfortably in the shade. . . .

Once Brown had come—uninvited, and of course simply out of curiosity. He had stayed most of the afternoon, all the same, though he had never repeated his visit. For that matter, Tom didn't want him to repeat it. Pascoe was different: Pascoe would come up into the loft where the railway was laid down, but the only games Brown cared for were games you played with a bat and a ball, and he was far too good at them—or Tom too bad—for it to be much fun playing

with him. He wished Pascoe *would* come, because he wanted to talk
to him and find out how the electric storm had affected the rest of
the school. Besides, they could dam the stream—an engineering feat
planned several days ago, but planned by Pascoe, so that Tom daren't
attempt it without him.

Pascoe was a queer chap, he reflected. For one thing, he hardly
ever laughed. It wasn't that he was gloomy or melancholy or bored,
but merely that jokes didn't amuse him. He disliked, too, even the
mildest form of ragging. He went about everything with a kind of
intense concentration of purpose, just the way ants do. Nevertheless,
it was rotten having nobody. . . .

Tom lay on his back and looked up into a cloudless blue sky. He
could hear the leaves rustling on the apple trees behind him when a
breath of wind passed, and presently a pigeon flew out of the weep-
ing-ash near the summer house. A couple of swallows were wheeling
over the lawn, flying very low, which was supposed to be a sign
of approaching rain, but Tom didn't believe it was going to rain.

Where had William gone to? He must either have concealed himself somewhere in the shrubbery or else have gone in to the kitchen
to have tea. Tom considered whether it would be worth while going
to the kitchen, but he had already had tea with Miss Jimpson, so
instead he got up and strolled round the house to a cobbled yard at
the back. Here were what had once been stables, though at present
they were used partly as a garage, and partly as a kind of tool-shed,
containing a carpenter's bench, the lawn mower, and all William's
gardening implements. Above was a loft, to which you could climb
by a board with foot-holes in it. This loft in former days had been
a hayloft, but hay being no longer required, it had been cleaned out,
whitewashed, and given over to Tom for a playroom.

He had used it a lot at one time, and he still used it when Pascoe
came. Its attractiveness, however, had waned of late, and it was only
because he had nothing else to do that he climbed up there now.

It was quite light in the loft, for there was not only a skylight, but
also a large window facing the yard. The room was long and low,
with a sloping roof which left plenty of space in the middle, but at
the sides slanted down to within three feet of the floor. The only
furniture consisted of a couple of kitchen chairs, and a solid deal table
littered with papers, chalks, a box of paints, a pair of scissors, and
other odds and ends. From the rafters hung crinkled Chinese lanterns,
and on the floor were the railway lines, with their stations, signal

boxes, and tunnels. A toy yacht fully rigged, and a Meccano erection which Pascoe had built weeks ago, stood near the wall.

A broad band of sunlight, filled with myriads of tiny floating specks, streamed in through the dusty glass. On the whitewashed wall hung a burglar's black cloth mask with eyeholes cut in it, a coloured portrait of Abraham Lincoln and his young son, a scabbard without a sword, and a cracked and tarnished mirror. Also a map of the garden and the immediately surrounding country—chiefly Pascoe's work—and two charcoal silhouettes, one of Pascoe and one of Tom, traced over their actual shadows.

All these familiar details Tom took in with a rather bored glance. He pulled the window up, stretched himself on his stomach on the dusty floor, and supporting his chin between his hands, stared out into the sunshine.

After some ten minutes of this, during which his mind had become very nearly a blank, he heard the sound of the wheelbarrow and leaned farther out. From where he lay he could see William, but William could not see him unless he chanced to glance up. Tom therefore had a view of William as William was when he believed himself to be alone, and at once he became interested. William wiped his forehead with a spotted and very dirty pocket handkerchief and muttered some remarks to the wheelbarrow. Tom strained his ears to catch what he was saying, but failed. A very one-sided conversation this, as William himself appeared to realize, for he sighed loudly, sat down on the barrow, and took out his pipe. Tom had never seen William fill that pipe, and he didn't fill it now; he merely struck a match and held it between his hands over the bowl: nevertheless he lit the pipe, and puffed a cloud of dark blue smoke into the air. This proved that the pipe was a magic one, always filled with tobacco, and, since William was certainly not a magician, it must have been given to him by an ancient crone in return for some service—carrying her bundle perhaps, or giving her a share of his lunch. It followed therefore that William had two older brothers who had been less obliging, and the question was what *they* had received from the crone. Nothing very nice, of course, but possibly amusing. Tom leaned as low down as he could, and shouted "William!" at the top of his voice.

The effect was remarkable. William, seated on the wheelbarrow immediately below the window, jumped several inches. And he was very angry indeed. "What's ailin' you?" he snarled. "You might have more manners than to be yellin' in people's ears. It's time you were learnin' somethin' instead of behavin' like the young street-boys that knows no better."

Tom apologized. "Sorry!" he said. "I was only going to ask what happened to your brothers."

"Brothers!" William growled, stuffing his pipe back into his pocket as he got up.

"Yes, brothers," said Tom. "*Your* brothers. Are they dead?"

"No, they're not dead," returned William sourly. "Because they never was born." And he grasped the shafts of the barrow and moved away, still muttering under his breath about manners and education.

It was like being at the theatre, for William was no sooner gone than Henry appeared on the scene—silently, discreetly—stopping every few steps with one black paw lifted in the air. If ever anybody looked bursting with plots and secrets, it was Henry at that moment, and Tom watched him from his hiding place, careful not to make a sound. It was quite good sport, this. It was moreover a kind of proof that life actually did go on when you weren't taking part in it—a truth sometimes hard to realize. Should he startle Henry the way he had startled William, or should he continue to watch him? While he hesitated Henry himself reached a decision, and instead of proceeding further sat down where he was, stuck one hind leg up in the air like a post, and began to perform a complicated toilet. Somehow this had the effect of breaking a spell. . . .

Tom turned his head quickly at a sound in the room behind him. It had been made by a mouse, he was sure, and he didn't want mice up here: they would run over everything, leaving tracks and nibbling holes. He rose from the floor and walked on tiptoe on the table whence the sound had come. Such a litter of stuff! He'd have to clear it all up one of these days and burn most of it. He stood contemplating the jumble. Right on top were several large sheets of white cartridge paper. He remembered bringing them up the last day Pascoe had been here, along with the scissors and *The Boys' Own Toymaker*. Pascoe was good at making things—very neat and clever with his fingers—and the *Toymaker* gave heaps of models. You drew the outline on paper, leaving dotted lines in certain places. Then you cut out the pattern and folded it at the dotted lines and it was a house, or a windmill, or a cart, or an arm-chair, and would stand up on the table—or at least it would if Pascoe were the designer. For more complicated models you had to cut out several pieces and use gum, but this was a bother.

The scissors attracted him, being a large and special pair which Mother used for cutting out, and he was surprised that she hadn't missed them. For Mother was as clever at making things as Pascoe, and that very summer had made Tom two pairs of white linen trousers which were just as good as if they had been bought in a shop. Now he came to think of it, it was quite possible that she *had* missed the scissors, for he'd borrowed them when she wasn't there. He'd better take them down with him when he was going.

Meanwhile, they looked very sharp and efficient: in fact, in conjunction with the cartridge paper, they invited immediate use. Only he didn't want to make toys: he'd cut out a portrait. He knew what Pascoe, who had gone shares in buying the paper, would say—that it had been bought for a special purpose and was jolly expensive and oughtn't to be wasted. Still, Pascoe had used a sheet of it himself to make their map, so Tom felt entitled to one, and slipped a brown thumb and two fingers through the large bright rings. He had no clear image in his mind to start with, beyond a human silhouette, but if this happened to suggest a likeness to anyone he knew, it would be easy afterwards to make the necessary trimmings and alterations. It reminded him of the days when he had been quite small and had spent hours in cutting out, though then he had only been allowed to use newspapers. This was much better, for the paper didn't bend or crumple, and the blades cut through it with a crisp sharp sound. They worked very smoothly, Tom found—almost of their own accord—and cutting out must be either a great deal easier than drawing or else he was much better at it, for something far more satisfactory than any of his pencilled efforts was emerging. It was a man, Tom already saw—an old man, he fancied—just the head and shoulders—life-size. The clear profile was really quite striking even if the rest was a bit dicky. Tom at all events was pleased with it, and resolved to keep it to show to Pascoe. He rose, placed the portrait standing against the back of the chair, and retreated a few steps to admire it.

And with that—though bafflingly, because no name suggested itself—he felt that it did remind him of someone—someone he had seen either in actual life or in a picture. But he could get no further than this, though several fugitive impressions passed through his mind. . . .

Suddenly he heard the mouse again, and this time it was actually in one of his railway tunnels. That wouldn't do: there was probably a whole family of them, and he must set a trap. He crossed the room and clambered down the footboard with the idea of borrowing a trap from Phemie. But as he passed through the stable door into the sunlit yard, he spied exactly what he needed, in the person of Henry.

The problem was how to get Henry up into the loft. He was still seated in the middle of the yard, but he had now finished washing, and, with his back turned, appeared to be contemplating the chimney-stacks. It was going to be jolly difficult to get him up, Tom reflected, for Henry had a distrustful nature and would be deaf to coaxing. It could never be managed by the footboard. Henry would struggle like mad even if he didn't actually use his claws. A ladder was the thing, because Tom could climb a ladder and keep at the same time a firm grip on Henry, whereas, for the footboard, he required to use both his hands. There were a couple of ladders in the shed, and the small one would do. He dragged it out and propped it up against the open window, which he could shut once he got Henry safely inside. True, there was always the other way out, and no trap-door covering it; but he didn't think Henry could get down by the footboard.

Meanwhile, attracted by the noise, Henry had turned round and was watching him. His interest was very languid, however; nor did Tom's "Puss, puss—poor puss!" perceptibly deepen it. It was this air of complete indifference, habitual with Henry unless he himself wanted something, which Tom found so irritating. It annoyed him to be treated as if he were an inanimate object, and it removed any scruples he might have had against the employment of force. Slowly he approached Henry, and it was not till he had actually passed that he suddenly swooped down and grabbed him.

Instantly Henry was in action. His hind legs kicked against Tom's body like powerful steel springs, his front claws dug into the sleeves of his jacket; but after one mew he struggled in silence and in vain. Up the ladder they went, Henry squeezed nearly flat under Tom's arm, and Tom's fingers tightly grasping the scruff of his neck. In at the window he was thrust, and the sash quickly pulled down, leaving him a prisoner till morning.

At least that was the plan when Tom slid down the ladder and stood listening. Not a sound. This seemed odd, unless Henry had fainted. "Perhaps I'll bring you some milk later," Tom called up, but there was no reply.

Tom still stood listening. He wished he didn't suffer such frightful pangs of conscience every time he committed an assault on Henry, for he knew he hadn't hurt him a bit, except possibly his feelings. All the same, this silence was surprising, for Henry had a powerful voice and it wasn't in the least like him to submit without a protest. He could hardly have found his way down by the footboard so soon, either, though perhaps it would be better to make sure. So Tom looked inside the stable. Henry was not there. Indeed, unless he jumped it, Tom didn't see how he was going to get down that way, and the height was about ten feet.

But perhaps Henry was keeping quiet because he had already smelt the mouse or heard it, though somehow this seemed improbable too. It would be far more in keeping with Henry's character to allow the mouse to escape, since he hated doing things under compulsion. Tom waited a few minutes longer in the hot sunshine, and then the desire to know what Henry really was up to became irresistible. Stealthily he re-climbed the ladder, and stealthily he raised his head till he could peep in.

Henry was there—yes; but what on earth was he doing? Not bothering about mice, that was clear. Actually he was walking in a sort of semicircle backwards and forwards in front of one of the chairs, and every time he brushed against it he arched his back and his tail rose stiffly in the air. Through the shut window Tom naturally heard no sound, nevertheless he could have sworn that Henry was purring. It was in fact exactly as if he were playing a kind of ceremonial game, the point of which was to pretend that somebody he liked very much was sitting in the chair. Yet the only thing in the chair was Tom's paper man, who had fallen down, and was now lying flat on the seat.

More and more solemn and amazed Tom's face grew, as he stared at this performance with round unblinking eyes. And then abruptly it ceased; Henry walked away from the chair and straight up to the mirror, before which he began to posture. And somehow, with this, Tom's curiosity was satisfied; he felt he had seen enough; and without waiting for further developments scrambled down the ladder so rapidly that he was within an ace of falling.

Once safely on earth, he felt a little foolish. Suppose Pascoe had been there to witness that hasty descent! But of course if Pascoe had been there nothing would have happened. His mere presence would have prevented it. Pascoe had an effect on his surroundings very like that of a powerful arc-lamp: at the sight of him cocks crew and phantoms vanished in despair. If the worst came to the worst, Tom could always threaten Henry that he would give him to Pascoe. That would teach him! That would put an end to his magic!

Yet the rational explanation was that Henry simply had been amusing himself—with the mirror! "Mirror, mirror, on the wall"— the wicked queen questioning her mirror in the story of Snow White —it might have *looked* like that, but it wasn't really. On the other hand he rather regretted having ever begun to pretend things about Henry. It had been silly, or at least it would be silly to go on pretending. In the beginning it *had* been a make-up, and it just showed you that Daddy really was right about such things. Now of course he was sensible again, but even now it would have been a comfort to have known Henry as a kitten, or at least to have known somebody who had known him. In that case his advent wouldn't have so closely resembled the arrival of the Raven—from the Night's Plutonian shore. As it was, there seemed to Tom to be a marked resemblance, though Henry hadn't come tapping at a window, but merely mewing to Phemie.

In the midst of these uneasy cogitations he heard the sound of the car, and next moment it came into view, with Daddy driving. Tom ran to the doors of the garage and pulled them open, while Daddy drove cautiously in, for he was not in any way a very dashing person.

"Well, what have you been up to?" Daddy asked, when the car was safely parked and he had got out of it. "And what's the ladder doing there?" he continued, stopping to look at it.

"I put it there," Tom said. "I put Henry up in the loft because I heard a mouse."

Daddy gazed dubiously at the window. "Are you going to keep him there?" he inquired. "He won't like that."

"No; I think I ought to let him out," Tom agreed. "I think if I open the window he'll be able to get down if he wants to. Would you mind waiting just a minute, Daddy, till I do open it?"

"Waiting!" Daddy repeated. "Why?"

You'd have thought he might have done what he was asked without questions, but he didn't, it wasn't his way, and Tom gave him a reproachful, not to say an indignant, glance. "I just want you to wait, that's all," he answered. "I nearly fell down the ladder the last time."

Daddy seemed about to speak, and his expression was slightly puzzled, but in the end he said nothing. However, he waited—which was the main thing—while Tom climbed up and opened the window. Henry was there, meek as milk of course, and even allowed himself to be carried down perched on Tom's shoulder.

As they crossed the yard in this fashion, Tom opened a conversation. "We had a cloudburst at school to-day," he told Daddy. "Did you have one?"

"I saw a flash of lightning," Daddy said, "and I heard a peal of thunder. But that was all."

"And Brown stood up on the form and flapped his arms and called out like a bird," Tom continued. "He did it because of the electric currents."

"The electric currents?" Daddy murmured, apparently not grasping the connection. "You mean he gave himself an electric shock?"

"No—the electric currents in the air," Tom explained. "Miss Jimpson said it was that."

"I see," said Daddy, but Tom was quite sure he didn't see and wasn't even trying to see.

"I had tea with Miss Jimpson at Nicholson's," he went on.

"That was nice," Daddy said. "And very kind of her. Had you managed by any chance to get a sum right, do you suppose?"

"No," Tom replied; "she just asked me—socially."

"Oh, socially!" Daddy echoed. "Well, I want to speak to William before he goes, and I think you'd better clean yourself up a bit. You look as if you'd been rolling in the dust."

8: DADDY was writing a letter; Mother was darning socks; Tom sat at the other side of the table over his lessons. In spite of the array of books, he was not doing very much, she noticed. He was not even looking at them, but was sitting with his head slightly on one side, which showed that he was thinking. Mother paused in her work to watch him. He looked pale; he looked tired; she was glad that the holidays were so near. A plain little boy, she supposed most people would call him—at any rate stupid people. Perhaps he *was* plain, with his freckles, his blunt features, his dull leaf-brown hair that needed cutting. And in his eyes was a listening expression, not unhappy exactly, yet extraordinarily sad.

She had seen it before, only somehow never before had it so struck her. Why should he look like that? He wasn't unhappy. He was different, she knew, from the ordinary run of small boys—perhaps even more different than she thought—but she knew he was happy, he had everything to make him happy, and that expression didn't mean what it seemed to mean. Suddenly she told him: "I think you'd much better put away your lesson books and go to bed."

Tom did not answer. He didn't want to go to bed, though he was very tired, and his eyes were heavy, and he didn't feel very well. He tried to persuade himself that he didn't feel ill either—just vaguely uncomfortable and headachey—symptoms which had become much more marked after dinner, but which had been hovering in the background all day. He braced himself to look more lively, and Mother repeated her words.

"It's only half-past eight," Tom mumbled, turning a page. He knew this didn't deceive her, but he hated admitting that he wasn't well. It seemed so silly, besides leading to all kinds of fuss and questions, and he'd be all right in the morning.

"You hardly touched your dinner," Mother continued. "And you know you're not really working now. I expect it's the heat, or Miss Jimpson's ices, that have upset you."

Daddy, who in the ordinary way would have noticed nothing, of course at this began to gaze at him too. "Do you hear what your mother says?" he asked.

The question annoyed Tom, for naturally he had heard what Mother had said; he wasn't deaf. But this irritability was only another symptom, and he swallowed it down and answered in a subdued voice: "The exams begin in a day or two."

"There won't be any exams if you're ill," Mother remarked quietly.

That was nonsense, he could have pointed out. Still, he knew what she meant, and his mind, refusing the effort of concentration on his work, sought relief in pondering over the difficulty of saying anything which was not at the same time both true and untrue. Mother's statement was untrue, because there certainly would be exams whether he took part in them or not; yet in another way it was true, because there would be no exams for him if he were in bed. Similarly Henry, now lying curled up asleep on the sofa, would be speaking the truth if he said that mice were delicious; yet if Daddy were to say "Mice are delicious," they would all not only disbelieve him but get a most frightful shock into the bargain. No sooner had this example arisen in Tom's mind than it passed from the abstract to the concrete, and an unpleasant picture was conjured up of Daddy crouching over mouseholes, quivering and silent, with eyes floating and shining with greed. . . . He sighed and pushed away his book. "It's because it's so hot and stuffy," he said petulantly. "I wish I could sleep out in the garden in the summer-house."

"I don't think you'd find that very enjoyable," Mother replied; "and if you leave your door open you'll get plenty of air. Think how nice it will be next month at the seashore."

"Yes," Tom sighed again, for next month seemed very far away.

"And it's not nearly so hot as it was," Mother went on. "At least, not so oppressive." But she was still watching him doubtfully, and presently she said: "I hope you haven't got a temperature!"

So did Tom, for temperatures were the bane of his existence. He was pretty sure he *had* one, too, or was going to have one. It was so stupid being like that! Anything in the least out of the ordinary upset him. Not that there *had* been anything out of the ordinary. A hot day—what was that! Nothing at all events to make you ill.

"If you like," Mother said, "we'll go out for a little walk in the garden—for half an hour. That is, if you'll promise to go straight to bed without dawdling the moment we come in."

Tom promised, and Mother put away her work. He followed her into the hall, where she wound a sort of scarf thing round her shoulders, so light that it couldn't really make the least difference. Then they went into the garden.

The walk didn't amount to much, for they merely sauntered along the paths and up and down the lawn, while Mother stopped every now and again to smell flowers. She was very fond of smelling flowers, and she could even smell things that to Tom were quite unsmellable, such as stones, and water, and the sun baking the bricks of the house.

A greenish translucent glow still lit up the sky, and against this a few small birds were wheeling in delicate noiseless curves and patterns, as they chased the moths. Tom's first impression was of something extremely graceful and pleasing, till all at once it struck him as horrible. "They're catching them!" he exclaimed in a shocked voice.

"They're eating them!" And he began to clap his hands to frighten the birds away.

"Insects are their natural food," Mother observed calmly. "They're not being cruel."

"But it's awful!" Tom cried in anguish. "They're swallowing them alive!"

Mother put her hand on his shoulder and gave it a little squeeze. "You mustn't think of things in that way," she said. "You're far too sensitive, and you must try to get over it. That isn't the way to look at things. I don't suppose the moths even know that it's happening."

"It's our fault," Tom went on, unconsoled by Mother's philosophy. "We oughtn't to put nets over the fruit. Then they wouldn't want moths."

Mother at this gave him a shake, almost as if she were trying to wake him up. "Now you're getting into one of your silly moods," she declared.

But Tom refused to be shaken into comfort. "I'm not," he said. "And it isn't silly."

"It's silly if you allow it to worry you," Mother told him. "Because you can't alter it. It's the way the world's arranged, and if you don't accept it you'll never be happy. Besides, it's necessary, or there'd be a plague of insects."

"It isn't necessary for *us*," Tom argued gloomily. "We could live very well on vegetables and things."

"Not so well as you imagine," Mother replied. "As a matter of fact it would be extremely troublesome—especially in winter, when there are very few vegetables."

This might be true, yet it did not satisfy Tom. Nor merely because it was true did that seem to him to make it good, and he said so. "In the Garden of Eden," he went on, "everybody must have lived on vegetables. I mean all the animals—even animals like lions and tigers."

"Probably there weren't any lions and tigers," Mother thought. "The savage creatures, I expect, lived outside the Garden."

"The snakes didn't," Tom reminded her.

"Snakes were different then," Mother said. "They must have been quite different, because we're told that the serpent was more subtle than any beast of the field. So no doubt they were tame and gentle too, and only afterwards became what they are now."

Tom thought this a prejudiced view—prejudiced in favour of humanity. "I don't see that they're any worse now than we are," he said. "If it comes to killing things, I don't expect they're as bad." But Mother's words had called up a picture in his mind which temporarily distracted his thoughts from the callous terrestrial plan. "What happened to the Garden of Eden, do you think?" he asked.

"You know what happened," Mother answered. "It's all explained in the first chapters of Genesis."

"There's very *little* about it in the first chapters of Genesis," Tom replied. "You're told practically nothing, except that the Garden was there, and that, after Adam and Eve were driven out, it was guarded by angels. So unless something happened to it later, it must be there still."

"The place where it was of course is there still," Mother agreed, "but not the Garden itself: that disappeared long ago."

"Why?" Tom demanded. "How do you know? It may still be there—hidden by magic."

But Mother did not find this a profitable subject to pursue; she thought more was to be gained by thinking and talking about the New Testament.

Tom wanted to talk about the Old. "It's true, isn't it?" he said, knowing that this would place her in a difficulty.

"Yes," Mother answered, "all the Bible is true."

"Well then, I think the Old Testament is more interesting," Tom declared.

But he could see that Mother didn't approve of this opinion, though she didn't actually say so. "The New Testament is more important," she distinguished carefully. "I mean to people living at the present time, because it contains the actual words of Christ. The other is important too, but its importance is more or less only an historical importance. It describes things that happened a long time ago, and naturally such things haven't a great deal to do with *us*."

"All the same, they were interesting things," Tom persisted. "The Flood, and Jacob's ladder, and the Witch of Endor, and Lot's wife, and Balaam's ass, and Jonah in the whale, and Moses turning his rod into a serpent—they're just like the *Arabian Nights*."

"They're not in the least like the *Arabian Nights*," Mother contradicted, "and it's very wrong to talk in that way."

"Wrong!" exclaimed Tom in astonishment. "Do you mean wicked?"

"Yes," Mother said. "You know the *Arabian Nights* stories are fairy tales, and that the Bible is God's word."

"But I only said it was *like* them," Tom protested.

"And I say it isn't like them," Mother answered. "Nor is that the proper way to read the Bible—picking out bits here and there—especially the bits you seem to have picked out—just because they happen to contain marvels."

"How ought I to read it?" Tom asked.

"The Bible was written to teach us how to live properly," Mother continued, "and to reveal the truth. It isn't like any other book."

"But I didn't really pick out those bits," Tom said, after a brief pause. "They just happen to be the bits I remember."

"Yes, and that shows they were the bits you liked. Otherwise you wouldn't have said that the Garden of Eden might be hidden by magic. You said that because you *wanted* to think so. There is very little in the Bible about magic, and when it is mentioned at all, it is condemned as wicked. If the Garden of Eden had been hidden, it would have been hidden by God."

"Yes, that's what I meant," Tom hastened to assure her.

"It isn't what you said, then," Mother told him. "God isn't a magician."

"N——o," Tom hesitated. He couldn't quite grasp the point, however, nor in what consisted the apparently so great difference between miracles and magic. But he was willing to leave this unchallenged, for his interest really was in the Garden itself. "You see," he went on, reverting to his original thought, "the flood would only flood it: it would still be there when the water drained away. . . . Do you mind if I tell you what I think really may have happened?"

Mother for a moment looked as if she did mind, but suddenly she smiled and said, "No."

"I'm not cross," she added; "it's only that these things aren't the same as fairy tales: they're true, and I want you to realize that."

Tom was relieved, and told her that he did realize it. "I think," he went on quickly, "that just before the flood came the Garden sank down into the earth, and then, after the rain had dried up, it rose again. You see, it would have been a pity to spoil a place like that. And I think all the animals who were in it—— No, I don't—what I really think is that the flood wasn't allowed to touch it at all. A magic wall—I mean a barrier suddenly rose up all round it, with watch-towers on which the guarding angels stood, waving their swords. . . . Square watch-towers," he added, his eyes narrowing till they were nearly shut. "Then Noah, if he looked out from the Ark across the water at night, would see the moving lights of the swords, but he wouldn't know what they were. It would be all dark, all black water, except for the red moving flames on the towers—the swords of the Cherubims. Even if a little bit of the Cherubims was lit up by the swords, they would still only be like shadows, standing with their faces hidden in the clouds."

"Well," said Mother, abandoning theological discussion and pressing her cool hand against his cheek, "it's time we were going in and time you were going to bed."

But Tom didn't want this at all: he wanted to talk; and the hour and the place were somehow just right, if only Mother would be right too. "Don't let's go in yet," he pleaded. "It's far nicer out here and I feel better already. Besides, there's the moon."

"What has the moon got to do with it?" Mother asked. "You're a little humbug. And anyhow I must go in, because I'm being eaten alive by midges."

She did not insist on his accompanying her, however, and he sat down on a bench outside the study window. The midges did not trouble him, and a light wind had sprung up and was whispering its plaintive sighings in his ears. Daddy, who was always too busy to sit in the dark, or even in the twilight, had turned on the light in the study, and it streamed out through the uncurtained windows. It had a quite different effect, Tom noticed, from daylight. The shrubs in its immediate radius were vividly and metallically green, but they suggested the brightness of a painted scene in a theatre, and behind this the trees assumed dark listening shapes, and the bushes were like crouching Sphinxes and Chimeras. Where the light fell, it created a superficial illusion, a glittering enchantment; but beyond was the great world of nature—profound, real, and living.

Then, in the study, Mother drew the curtains, and the enchantment vanished. The trees drew closer, while the great white moon, like a pale floating water-lily, rose higher above them. Tom had an impression of drifting up to meet it, of drifting above the tree-tops. And looking downward thence he could see the shadowy garden and the house, and a small human figure with a white face sitting on a bench. Higher still, so that now he could see the silent coils of the river and the foaming whiteness where it rushed over the weir, and the dark tangle of woodland on the farther bank. The sense of actual levitation was much more real, much less dreamlike, than it had been that morning when he had sat half asleep in school. Now he could see the grey fields, intersected by dark lines that were the hawthorn hedges. It was

the country Pascoe had mapped, but soon Tom left it behind him. On
and on he voyaged, over hills and lighted towns and open country,
until at last below him he saw a wide dark stretch of water and knew
that he had reached the sea. A white line marked the breaking of the
waves against black cliffs; and where it curved in a long slender bow
he knew there was a beach.

Miles and miles away he was, and yet a step on the gravel, and
Daddy's voice, reached him across all that distance, and brought him
at terrific speed back into the waiting empty body on the bench.
"You're to come in, young man," Daddy announced. "Your supper
is ready; and after that, bed."

Tom got up at once, for the moment Daddy spoke he realized that
his feet and lower limbs were cold. His body was not much warmer,
yet his head felt very hot. He did not mention these symptoms,
though they struck him as remarkable and most likely dangerous.
For if his blood was circulating properly, how could there be all
these different temperatures? Meanwhile Daddy's hand, placed beneath Tom's armpit, impelled him firmly towards the house.

9:    TOM opened his eyes with a feeling that somebody
        had called his name. It was uncommonly dark, and
without raising his head from the pillow he could see two tiny green
lamps outside the window. The lamps appeared to be suspended in
mid-air some eight inches above the sill, and shone with a bright
steady glow. It was quite half a minute before he understood what
they were: then he knew that Henry was watching him. . . .

Why, Henry must have clambered up somehow by the creeper,
yet evidently not with the intention of coming in, for both windows
were open. He must have climbed up for some other purpose, though
what that might be Tom could not imagine, and he softly called:
"Puss—puss!" Instantly the green lights disappeared, and he heard a
rustle of leaves, followed by silence. . . .

Tom was perplexed. Not that he objected to Henry being on the
window-sill; it was only his secretiveness that seemed strange. He
didn't believe Henry had had any purpose at all beyond that of making himself mysterious, and with this he dismissed him from his
thoughts and tried to go to sleep again.

He shut his eyes, but it was no use. His pillow was hot and uncomfortable, and he also was hot and uncomfortable, though only a sheet and a counterpane covered him. There were peculiar little noises, too, going on all round him, and they were very like voices. They came from everywhere—from under the bed, from the ceiling, from the windows, from the pictures, from the wardrobe, from the washstand —and they grew every moment more eager and confused, as if a discussion were being carried on and everybody were talking at once. In such a babel how could he go to sleep? Yet the voices didn't really say anything, were only sounds, little cries and chirps and squeaks, not human at all.

And with that, quite distinctly, he heard three words: "Follow the light."

Queerer still, he was neither startled nor particularly surprised, though he sat up and listened. It had been a very small voice certainly, and the moment he sat up it stopped speaking, in fact there was a general silence. Tom could be quiet too, however, and presently, as if reassured by his stillness, the same small voice spoke again, evidently from somewhere behind the washstand. "Follow the light," it said; and this time there could be no mistake; for a ray of light, not much thicker than a whipcord, actually darted across the room about three feet above the carpet, so that the end of it passed straight through the keyhole.

Tom did not hesitate an instant, but sprang out of bed and opened his door. He was just in time to see the ray of light gliding forward like a thread of elastic pulled by an invisible hand: next moment it had stretched round the corner at the end of the passage, and he hurried after it, passing the open door of Daddy's and Mother's room and reaching the wide landing above the staircase. Down into the hall the thread of light went, and down into the hall Tom pursued it. Then, just as he reached the last stair, the grandfather's clock began to clear its throat, and the sound brought him up abruptly.

For it was not the same sound as the clock ordinarily made, or else Tom's sense of hearing was not the same. It seemed to him now that the wheezing noise was trying to make words, trying to tell him something, trying to attract his attention. He stood still, and "Don't go! Don't go!" the old clock choked and gasped, but the words were indistinct and he could not be sure that he had heard them aright. If the warning had been repeated, or if he had been quite certain that it had *been* a warning, he might have heeded it, but there was a sudden break in the sound, and a brief silence, followed immediately by two slow clear notes striking the hour. The deep mellow chime floated out and died away, and with this the clock's power of speech died too. It appeared to Tom that for just a few seconds the tall wooden figure quivered slightly, but when he touched it, half expecting to find in it some lingering vibration of life, it had stiffened once more into immobility, and its round placid old face was sunk in its customary repose.

But the silver thread remained, and it passed through the keyhole of the hall-door, showing that the track it marked led outside the house. The door was a heavy mahogany one, locked and chained, nevertheless Tom had no difficulty in unchaining it and in turning the big iron key. He slipped back the latch and swung the door wide; and maybe the door too tried to warn him, but its voice had been drowned in oil, and it could make no sound, only turn on its hinges and let him out into the night. Tom followed the guiding thread. It led him through the soft darkness, and the cool air was pleasant, though his feet were naked and his pyjamas thin. The flowers were shut in sleep, but the garden was filled with sweetness strengthened by a heavy dew that lay on everything, deep as a shower of rain. And the night already was more a veil than a curtain; not really night, but only a shadow which would be lifted in another hour.

The light passed round the house, and Tom, turning the corner after it, saw at once whither it was leading him. Merely to his play-loft, and he crossed the yard on the cobblestones, while out of the shadow a black shape emerged, purring and rubbing dew-soaked fur against his legs. The thread of light ran up the wall like a silver vein of mushroom spawn: it passed through the window of the loft, but more than that Tom could not see.

The ladder was still there, however, propped up against the wall, and he put a bare foot on the lowest rung. And then once more something checked him, this time something within himself, a faint and vague premonition of danger. Yet he climbed up—mounting more and more slowly—and now he saw that there was a dim light in the loft, pale and phosphorescent, hardly so powerful as the light of a candle. And in fact no candle was burning, the light had no visible source—unless it issued from that fantastic figure seated in a chair beside the table.

The head and shoulders of this figure were distinct: the rest was barely a suggestion. Yet, while Tom looked, the faint diffused light trembled and drew in, giving a more realistic appearance to the whole shape, and brightening as it contracted. It had less substance than a vapour, but it was very slowly assuming the nebulous outlines of a human form, through the upper portions of which the flat paper portrait he had cut out that afternoon was still visible. And the materialization took place so gradually, and the process was so strange, that Tom, watching it, was more curious than alarmed. Besides, it was only paper after all, and one quick tear across, he felt, would be sufficient to destroy it. There was at any rate nothing to fear: that phantom had no sensible reality. It was too feeble to produce a sound or a touch: it was no more formidable than a breath on frosty air, or a reflection of moonlight in water. And already, as if exhausted, it was dimming again, and far more rapidly than it had brightened. Then Tom suddenly felt himself grasped from behind, and next instant he was lifted down and set upon the ground, while the hands that had seized him still held him, and Daddy's voice kept repeating firmly but gently: "It's all right: don't be frightened: I'm here with you and we're out in the yard; but now, I think, we'll go back to the house."

Tom said nothing at all, and he did not move. He was not frightened, he merely felt confused and somehow half asleep, conscious of very little more than that Daddy was speaking to him.

"It's quite simple," Daddy was saying. "You were dreaming, you see, and in the middle of your dream you got up and came out here. We heard you—or at least Mother heard you—unchaining the hall-door. So she woke me up and I came down to look for you."

Tom still listened without seeming to hear; but he was perfectly docile, and allowed Daddy to lead him back across the yard. Then suddenly he asked a quite pertinent question—"Did she think it was burglars?"—and Daddy answered: "No, she thought it was you; and *I* thought it was her imagination until I found the hall-door open. The rest didn't take very long."

After this neither of them spoke again till they came round to the front of the house, which was at present all lit up. Then Daddy called out: "I've got him—safe and sound";—and Mother was there in the porch, in her dressing-gown, and with a warning "S—sh!" upon her lips.

"Don't make a noise," she whispered, drawing Tom into the hall. "We don't want to wake Phemie and Mary. . . . Where did you find him?"

"In the yard," replied Daddy cheerfully. "Half-way up a ladder. The ladder was one he had put there himself this afternoon. I had to lift him down and that's what wakened him. But it's all right, and he's wide awake now—or very nearly."

Tom said nothing, and Mother stooped and kissed him. She kissed him twice, and smiled, but rather anxiously. "He's only half awake," she murmured. . . . "I thought he had outgrown it. It must be more than a year since it happened last."

"Since what happened last?" Tom questioned dreamily; for everything now seemed to him strange and unreal, and this conversation as strange as all the rest.

"Since you came marching down into the study with your eyes wide open," Mother said, "and—— However, this isn't the time to discuss it," she went on. "You must get back to bed as quickly as possible. It's a blessing it's such a warm night. Perhaps you won't catch cold after all."

"It's far more likely that I will," Daddy observed, but Mother took no notice. She hurried Tom upstairs, packed him into bed after drying his feet with a rough towel, and put an eiderdown quilt on top of him.

All this Tom submitted to in silence: only the quilt drew a protest from him. "I can't," he remonstrated plaintively. "I'm burning!"

Mother put her hand on his forehead and then reluctantly removed the quilt. She sat down beside the bed. "Now go to sleep," she told him. "It's all my fault; I should never have allowed you to sit out in the garden with the dew falling."

"But I've sat out hundreds of times," Tom expostulated.

"Not when you weren't feeling well," Mother said. "I should have had more sense."

Nevertheless she seemed a good deal less anxious now that she had got him safely into bed, and it was Tom himself who began to feel a little worried by what had happened. He still wasn't at all clear about it, and the few words Mother had spoken in the hall, before she had suddenly checked herself, seemed particularly mysterious, referring, as they evidently did, to something that had occurred in the past— something which both she and Daddy knew about but had never before mentioned. "Why shouldn't my eyes have been opened?" he began. "I mean that time when you say I came down into the study."

Mother, he thought at first, wasn't going to answer: however, in the end changed her mind. "Because you were sound asleep," she said. "Just the way you were to-night. Only then we hadn't gone to bed."

Tom was less satisfied than ever. It was the first time he had heard of this sleep-walking, and that in itself was peculiar. He hated half-explanations. Besides, if he *had* been asleep to-night when he came downstairs, then he must have been asleep before that; which meant that the voices, the thread of light, the figure in the loft, even Henry on the window-sill, had all been nothing but a dream. Yet in that case how was he ever really to be sure when he was dreaming and when he wasn't? "How often did I come down to the study?" he asked dubiously. "More than once?"

"Now, Tom, I'm not going to talk any more," Mother answered. "I want you to go to sleep—and you've all to-morrow to ask questions."

But he knew that to-morrow she would find some fresh pretext for putting him off. "I can't go to sleep like this," he complained. "I'm far more likely to go to sleep if you tell me about it first."

Mother looked at him and hesitated. "I *have* told you," she said, "all that there *is* to tell."

"Oh, Mother dear!" Tom protested.

"But what do you want to know?" she asked, half laughing. "There's no *secret!* I never saw such a boy for weaving mysteries and romances out of nothing!"

"I want to know about walking in my sleep," Tom replied. "Did I do it more than once?"

"Once!" Mother exclaimed. "Once a night would be more like it." Then, as he lay gazing at her with a frown puckering his forehead, she resigned herself to the inevitable. "It was like living in the house with a small ghost," she said, "and I got so accustomed to it that I used to look at the clock if you were a few minutes late. Luckily it didn't have to be midnight; between half-past ten and eleven was when we expected you, and it never occurred twice in the same night. As soon as you had had your little perambulation, that ended it, and you were all right till morning. Now, are you satisfied?"

Tom lay pondering. "How long ago was it?" he asked.

"Three—no, it must be more than three years ago. At least, that was when it started and when it was really bad. Later it became less frequent, and in the end we believed you had outgrown it. Doctor

Macrory always said you would. And so you have, really; to-night's performance was an exception and only happened because you weren't very well."

"Why didn't you tell me before?" Tom questioned suspiciously.

"I don't know—except that Doctor Macrory thought it might be better not to."

"You weren't even going to tell me now," Tom reproached her, but he was too much interested and too curious to dwell on that aspect of the matter. "It was queer," he went on, "that I didn't wake when I came down to the study. I woke up to-night the minute Daddy grabbed hold of me—that is, if I was really asleep."

"We didn't grab hold of you," Mother said. "We were always very careful. And now——"

But Tom interrupted her. "What did I do?" he asked.

"Nothing," Mother answered. "You were as good as gold. You used to open the door and come into the room—that was all. As I say, exactly like a little ghost. You took no notice of us, and when we'd turn you round, back you'd march to bed again without the least trouble."

"But didn't you speak to me?" Tom still pressed her. "Why didn't you? Are you sure I was asleep?"

Mother sighed. "That's the worst of telling you anything! There's never an end to it. You know *yourself* that you must have been asleep, or you'd remember about it. *You* sometimes spoke, but we didn't."

"And can't you remember anything I said?"

"No, I can't," Mother answered. "You didn't talk to us at all, you didn't even know we were there. . . . There's nothing wonderful about it," she added, "lots of people talk in their sleep now and then. I dare say most people do."

Tom turned on the pillow so that he faced her. "Weren't you cross?" he asked.

"Cross!" Mother repeated uncomprehendingly.

"Well, it must have been a nuisance if it happened so often."

"Oh, I see! No, I wasn't cross."

After that he lay quiet for so long a time that she began to think he must have dropped asleep, when suddenly he said: "I'd like you to sing to me."

She was accustomed to abrupt changes of mood, but this one was more surprising than usual. "Sing!" she exclaimed. "That would be a nice thing to do at this hour of the night—and wake up the whole house!"

"You need only hum," Tom coaxed her. "That won't wake anybody."

His face was flushed now—even his forehead—and when she put her hand against his cheek it felt hot and dry. She didn't know precisely what lay behind this odd request, but she could guess perhaps, so she began to sing in hardly more than a whisper, and instantly he smiled. This made her want to kiss him, but she was afraid it might disturb his drowsiness if she did, so she sang on, in the lowest voice she could produce—lower even than her speaking voice. And outside in the garden other voices presently were raised, though it was barely dawn. But by this time she could hear him breathing and knew that he must really be asleep.

10: TOM wasn't ill at all—at least nothing to signify —though Mother insisted on getting Doctor Macrory to see him, and Doctor Macrory, just because he had been called in, wrote a prescription and kept him in bed. He was sitting up, with several pillows behind him, on the afternoon of the third day, when Mary opened the door and announced Master Pascoe. Master Pascoe thereupon entered, and from the foot of the bed gazed at the invalid commiseratingly.

Tom put down his book and said: "Hello!"

He had not expected this call, and for some silly reason its first effect upon him was to make him feel embarrassed. This was partly due to Pascoe's attitude, which was exactly that of a visitor at the Zoo. He kept on staring as if the bars of the bed were the bars of a cage, till Tom at last advised him to go down to the study and get the field-glasses; then he stopped.

"I only wanted to see how you were," he apologized. "You don't look too bad. What's the matter?"

"Nothing. . . . Just I wasn't well."

Pascoe seemed satisfied with this diagnosis, and came round to the side of the bed. He had a parcel in his hand, and in silence he proceeded to remove the string and paper, revealing within the outer wrapper yet another paper—a paper bag—while Tom watched the performance with curiosity.

"I got you these," Pascoe explained, "because I thought they'd be strengthening, being filled with wine."

Tom, still more surprised, expressed his thanks.

"They're wine gums," Pascoe continued. "I don't expect you've ever tasted them before."

"Why?" Tom asked. "I mean, why shouldn't I have tasted them? Are they expensive?"

Pascoe, being a truthful boy, hesitated. "As a rule I expect they are," he compromised. "But these weren't—so very. . . . I mean I got them more or less a bargain."

"Oh," said Tom, noncommittally.

"It was for the very queer reason, too, that they had been in the shop for some time."

To Tom, however, the reason appeared quite comprehensible, though he did not say so, Pascoe's eyes being fixed upon him.

"Of course, that only makes them better," Pascoe pointed out, "because wine improves with age. In fact it isn't really good till it *is* old. Everybody knows that."

"The man in the shop can't have known it," Tom mentioned guardedly.

"No. People like that don't drink wine; they only drink beer or stout. Anyway it wasn't a man, it was a woman, and Daddy says women are never judges of wine."

Tom did not dispute the opinion. Pascoe's father, he knew, was a wine merchant; in fact generations of Pascoes had been in the wine trade—Pascoe, Wine Merchants, established 1802—he had seen the place often, down town—dark but attractive-looking—old-fashioned—with a low doorway, low windows, and a brown dusty interior within which, amid casks and flagons and cobwebby bottles, somewhere lurked Pascoe senior, rubicund and genial, though Tom had never actually been introduced to him.

Still, wine gums weren't just the same as wine, he thought; they must consist of a variety of materials, not all of which would be improved by keeping. Meanwhile Pascoe junior placed the open bag on the counterpane between them, and since he could hardly refuse, Tom rather gingerly selected a specimen and began to chew it. It tasted better than he had expected, for viewed in the mass the wine gums looked distinctly unappetizing, with a tendency to coalesce, even to liquefy; but taken singly they proved not so bad—sticky and soft and sweet—eatable at any rate. "Thanks awfully," he repeated. "It was jolly decent of you."

Pascoe did not deny the decency. He too helped himself, and then sat down beside the bed, after which, amid fragmentary talk, they munched the wine gums for some time.

The bag indeed was more than half empty when Pascoe pronounced these astonishing words: "We'll stop the minute we begin to feel the effects. It doesn't matter with you of course, but I have to ride home."

Tom's jaws slowly ceased to work as he turned an uneasy gaze upon his friend. "What effects?" he asked, with a dawning consciousness that he had begun to feel them already.

"We may get tight," Pascoe replied, "with any luck."

Tom was startled. That Pascoe, of all people, should express such a desire, was bewildering. It must be inherited. It detracted too, he couldn't help feeling, from the generosity of the gift, reducing it at once from an act of sympathy to a mere experiment of dubious disinterestedness. Anyhow, he didn't see why Pascoe need smack his lips in such a fashion, and told him so.

"I'm tasting," Pascoe said. "You always make a noise like that when you're tasting."

"I don't," Tom contradicted, "and it's pretty awful! You don't eat your meals in that way, I hope."

"No. You don't understand. I don't mean ordinary tasting. You only taste like this with samples—when you're trying a new wine. I've seen Daddy doing it heaps of times. Sometimes you spit the wine out again."

"Well, you needn't do that here," Tom exclaimed quickly. "It's disgusting enough as it is."

Pascoe was not offended. "All right," he said; "I wasn't going to." And with that he stopped tasting, or at least stopped making a noise. "The exams began to-day," he presently observed. "I did rather well in the maths papers. Have another wine gum."

"No, thanks," Tom muttered, turning his head round towards the window and lying very still. His voice, too, had acquired an unusual, muffled sound, and something in his aspect—a slight haggardness, a peculiar hue perhaps—appeared to strike Pascoe, who leaned forward, looking at him hopefully. "Do you feel—" he was beginning, when Tom with a sudden upheaval of the clothes half scrambled, half tumbled out of bed. On his knees he groped frantically beneath it, and then, before the solemn eyes of his visitor, was painfully and emphatically ill.

Pascoe, quickly retreating, watched the catastrophe from a distance. "Hard luck!" he murmured.

But Tom, with the sweat trickling down his forehead, and his hands clutching the counterpane, could not answer for some time. "It's your beastly wine gums," he at last managed to gasp, hurt and annoyed by the calmness of Pascoe's tone. "You'd better ring the bell," he added, getting back shakily between the sheets.

Pascoe crossed the room, but at the chimney-piece he paused in thought. "What are you going to say?" he inquired.

"I'm going to say I've been sick," Tom answered impatiently. "Unless you want to take it away yourself."

Pascoe didn't, so he rang the bell, and immediately afterwards announced: "I think I ought to be going."

"All right," Tom answered coldly, for he knew well enough why Pascoe wanted to go, and indeed Pascoe himself made no secret of it. "Your mother will think it was my fault," he explained.

"So it was," Tom replied.

"I couldn't tell that *this* would happen," Pascoe murmured deprecatingly. "I really thought they might buck you up a bit. Honestly I did. That was why I got them."

"You got them to see if they'd make us drunk," Tom told him. "And you jolly well waited till I'd made myself ill before you mentioned a word about it."

Pascoe's gaze was still fixed upon him. "You're surely not going to tell her *that!*" he expostulated.

"I'm not going to tell her *anything*," Tom answered. "Because for one thing she's out." And with this he shut his eyes and kept them shut till Mary appeared in the doorway. Then he opened them and looked at her. "Mary, I've been sick," he said.

Mary, who had actually brought them up tea, hastily set down the tray. With unerring instinct—though possibly helped by the sight of the paper bag—she at once grasped the situation. "My goodness, Master Tom, what rubbish have you been eating at all? I'd have thought you'd have had more sense!"

So for that matter would Tom, and he did not defend himself; but Pascoe detected a reflection on the quality of his gift. "As it happens, what he was eating was perfectly harmless," he interposed loftily. "And people are never sick unless they require to be."

Mary gave a kind of snort. "Oh, indeed!" she retorted. "It's well there's somebody that knows everything! Of all the conceited little brats!" And she flounced out of the room, bearing with her the evidence of calamity.

Tom chuckled feebly, but Pascoe's face was crimson. "She oughtn't to be allowed to speak like that," he spluttered. "You ought——"

"How can *I* help it!" Tom interrupted. "I expect she and Phemie were in the middle of their tea when the bell rang, and it's not the sort of job anybody likes at such a time. You were jolly lucky that she didn't box your ears."

He chuckled again, and Pascoe stalked to the door with a frigid "Good-bye."

"Good-bye," Tom called after him. "Thanks for coming."

Pascoe stopped. With his hand on the door-knob he stood wavering. At last he turned round. "I *may* come to see you again or I may not," he pronounced doubtfully.

"If you don't," Tom reminded him, "you won't be able to dam the stream."

Pascoe instantly returned to the bedside. He particularly wanted to dam the stream, and had even planned the construction of a new channel. Anyhow his exit was all spoiled by Tom's indifference, so it was with a complete return to affability that he asked: "When do you think you'll be well enough?"

"I don't know. In a day or two. At the moment I believe I'm going to be sick again."

"Oh, here!" Pascoe remonstrated, drawing hurriedly back.

"Well, I can't help it," Tom grumbled, though he was still half laughing. "I feel rotten."

"I'll tell that woman," said Pascoe. "And I dare say I'll come to-morrow."

This time he really did go, and a minute or two later Mary reappeared. "I'm most frightfully sorry, Mary," Tom apologized humbly. "It was a false alarm."

But when he was alone again he shut his eyes and lay quiet. He was glad Pascoe had gone, for he wanted to lie still, without talking to anybody. In a little while he might begin to read, but just now it was more comfortable to lie thinking. Pascoe's visit had reminded him of

school and Miss Jimpson, and that his absence must have interfered
with her plans concerning Mr. Holbrook. Not that he could really
have helped her much. Mother, to whom he had imparted his impressions of Miss Jimpson's romance, had told him it was all nonsense and
that he was on no account to say or do anything. She had been very
positive about this, and for some reason not particularly pleased. . . .

Dash it all, he might have talked to Pascoe about the holidays!
Those beastly wine gums had put it out of his head. Pascoe usually
spent his holidays with an ancient aunt who lived in the Manor House
at Greencastle in Donegal, and it was to Greencastle that Tom and
Mother and Daddy were going—to an hotel there. Of course he had
already told Pascoe this, but they hadn't had time to discuss is properly and there were all sorts of questions he wanted to ask. However,
he was pretty sure Pascoe would come back to-morrow. . . .

He wondered if he would see much of Pascoe after the holidays.
Not nearly *so* much, anyhow, for Pascoe, like Brown, was leaving at
the end of the term, and at his new school he would be a boarder.
Tom half wished that he was leaving too, though he dreaded changes.
Still, he would have to leave fairly soon in any case, and it might as
well be now—Daddy had even suggested it, but had somehow let
the matter drop. On the other hand he would like to stay on till after
the Christmas concert, and he would hate saying good-bye to Mr.
Holbrook: there were difficulties both ways. . . .

Presently he took up his book. He did not open it, but holding it
in his hands still lay thinking. The book didn't interest him, it was
stodgy and dull—a story of the Peninsular War, and war stories
always bored him. There was a book downstairs in the study, however, which did interest him, and he felt suddenly tempted to go and
get it. The temptation was strong, and it was undisguised, for Tom
knew very well that it was temptation. He had discovered this book
some weeks ago, quite by chance, on the top shelf of a locked book-
case, and had first been attracted by the queer pictures it contained.
These had to do with magic, but not the kind of magic described in
fairy tales. This was utterly different, and, whether true or false, was
propounded seriously, while the magicians mentioned were persons
who had actually lived—Nicholas Flamel, Schroepffer of Leipzig,
Cagliostro, Doctor Dee and others—wizards and alchemists, evokers
of spirits, searchers for the Elixir of Life and the Stone of the Philoso-
phers. The book told of black magic and white magic, of the doctrine
and rituals; it explained ceremonies and symbols, it described experi-

ments. Tom had kept his discovery to himself, feeling sure, before he
had read many pages, that though this book must belong to Daddy,
Daddy certainly would forbid him to read it. He *had* read it however; there could be no going back on that. He had not only read it
but pored over it, and at present he wanted to pore over it again. Yet
in another way he didn't, because he knew that he would hide it under the bedclothes the moment he heard Mother coming in, and that
was rotten. Besides, there were things in the book—— He didn't quite
know what some of them meant, though he could guess vaguely, and
that, somehow, helped to keep them in his mind. It might have been
this book, too, that had first made him begin to think queer thoughts
about Henry.

What he didn't understand was how it could have come into
the possession of Daddy. He could understand Daddy's borrowing it,
and glancing through it perhaps, out of curiosity, but not keeping it.
For one thing, he wouldn't believe a word of it: in fact it was exactly
the sort of stuff that would irritate him most, with its fantastic statements unsupported by proof, and its mysterious hints at secrets that
must not be fully revealed. Of course, Daddy might have bought it
with a lot of other books at an auction, or it might have been given to
him. It was at any rate a strange book for him to have; and Mother,
Tom was sure, would think it wicked.

Abruptly he decided that he wouldn't look at it again. Yet still he
didn't feel happy. There wasn't much virtue in so late a resolution
—nor much use either, since his memory could now supply all that
his imagination needed. He felt that perhaps he ought to tell Daddy
about it: he felt that he wasn't quite what either Daddy or Mother
believed him to be. And that was to put it mildly! Anyway, he resolved that he wouldn't look at the book again, or, if he could help it,
think about it. . . .

This determination brought him relief, and gradually his mind
emptied and stilled. His feeling of sickness, too, had completely
gone; he felt now only languid and comfortably drowsy. The soft
summer murmur floated in to him through the open windows. The
afternoon sounds, the afternoon silence, were different from the
morning, he thought—or was it only the light that was deeper? He
would think of pleasant things. Mother said Donegal was lovely.
That was easy to believe, but Mother had never been in the particular
part of Donegal they were going to, so had been unable to give
him any details. He lay making pictures of the sea; and behind the

pictures he called up, and washing through them, was a low endless music, for he could not look at even imaginary waves without also hearing them. . . .

"Well, have you had a nice sleep?" Mother was home again, and bending down over him with her hat still on, so that she must only this moment have come in.

"I suppose so," he smiled.

"And are you feeling better?"

"Yes, a great deal better, Mother dear." And this was true: half an hour's sleep had revived him marvellously. But he knew from the way she had spoken that her inquiry had merely been a general one, and that she had heard nothing about the wine gums. Probably she had come straight upstairs without seeing Mary.

"That's good," she said. "Would you like to get up? I don't mean now, but after dinner. I shouldn't think it would do you any harm to get up for an hour or two then."

"I will," said Tom. "Have you just come in?"

"A few minutes ago," Mother answered. "It's nearly half-past six. What have you been doing?"

"Nothing much," said Tom. "Pascoe was here for a bit. What have *you* been doing?"

"Interviewing Mr. Pemberton part of the time. I think we'll try to get away as soon as we can—perhaps early next week—and I wanted to explain things to him."

"But will Daddy be able to go next week?" Tom inquired.

"I don't know; we'll talk it over this evening." She sat down on the side of his bed.

"Where did you meet Mr. Pemberton?" Tom asked, after a moment.

"I didn't meet him, I called at the school."

"But——" His brow puckered a little.

"I saw your friend Miss Jimpson too," Mother went on, "and had a talk with *her*."

This was getting serious, and Tom's face reflected his anxiety. "You didn't mention what I told you, I hope?"

Mother looked at him curiously. "About her troubles? No: she struck me as being a singularly heart-whole young woman, and quite capable of attending to her own affairs."

Still he wasn't completely reassured, for he knew Mother had a

habit of saying whatever came into her head, without caring a scrap
to whom she said it. "What *did* you talk about?" he persisted.

"Chiefly about you," Mother teased him. "Miss Jimpson seems
very fond of you."

Tom blushed. "Oh!" he muttered, taken aback. He waited for
her to tell him more, but she didn't, so he was obliged to ask: "What
did she say?"

"That she thought you were a dear little boy, though at the same
time rather peculiar."

Tom blushed again. He didn't believe Miss Jimpson had said
that—at least not just so plump and plain, nor in those words. "Did
you tell her I wasn't?" he demanded, for Mother had another of
her pauses.

"No, why should I? I entirely agreed with her."

Tom glanced up quickly, and then for a little lay silent. "Did
you talk for long?" was his next question.

"Not very; a quarter of an hour perhaps. Much can be said in
a quarter of an hour." She still smiled down at him, and then suddenly
asked: "Why are you so suspicious? What do you *imagine* I may
have said to her?"

"I can't imagine," Tom murmured doubtfully; "that's just the
trouble."

He became conscious that Mother was looking at him with an
ironical expression in her eyes, and he turned away. "Would you
rather people *dis*liked you?" she said, but he made no reply. He
knew that she knew he hated people to dislike him, and indeed
next moment she proved it by adding: "So you see!"

She stooped down and Tom put his arms round her neck.

"Why are you such a silly?" she whispered.

He didn't know why, and he didn't know that it *was* silly. Pascoe
he was sure, would have hated to be thought a dear little boy, and
still more to be called one; and though he hadn't any particular wish
to resemble Pascoe, neither was there any need to be sloppy. He
wondered if he *was* sloppy? He was afraid it looked very like it—
sometimes. Secret sloppiness didn't so much matter; at all events you
couldn't help it; but open sloppiness was another thing, and the
difficulty was to keep it secret—at least with people like Mother,
who didn't pay the slightest attention to what you said, but went
bang behind your words to what they outwardly denied. He felt
very contented now, for instance, though there was no doubt that

she was petting him. In fact it was pretty awful, and she herself of course was quite shameless. But then, he liked it, and she must have guessed that. He sighed, and thought of the reserved and austere Pascoe. Also he thought that he wasn't a "dear little boy," and perhaps he ought to tell her so. He wasn't particularly little to begin with, and, though he might be dear to Mother, that wasn't what either she or Miss Jimpson had meant. What they had meant was something quite different, and it wasn't true. It might be true in some ways—at least he hoped it was—but it certainly wasn't in all.

PART TWO

11: THE house was to be shut up, though William of course was to look after the garden as usual. But Phemie and Mary were going to stay with their own people near Downpatrick, and this had created the problem of Henry. Henry had no people, or none that anybody knew about, and obviously he couldn't be taken to an hotel. It was decided therefore to leave him, like the garden, to William, until Phemie at the last moment thought he would be more comfortable at Downpatrick. Why, nobody quite knew, and Mother was doubtful if Henry would want to go; but Phemie was sure he would. She made ready a travelling-basket, and after all, though everyone had forgotten about it, she had a kind of proprietary right in Henry, he was *her* cat, or at least it was she who had first opened the door to him. So that was settled, and it was remarkable how confident Phemie was, even going the length of showing the basket beforehand to Henry, who glanced at it and yawned. "You see, Master Tom, it will be quite easy."

Thus speaking, Phemie placed the basket on the kitchen table, with a sort of "this-is-how-we-do-it" air, like a conjuror about to perform a trick that has never yet failed.

"Wouldn't it be better to shut the window?" Tom suggested, but Phemie ignored his advice. She smiled and shook her head. Then she approached Henry, who having recently finished a plate of fish was in a lethargic mood, and allowed her to lift him in her arms and set him standing up in the basket. True, she had to hold him there, but his struggles were perfunctory, there was really nothing more to do except to get him to lie down so that the lid could be closed and fastened. That was a simple matter, and to accomplish it Phemie, still smiling complacently, laid a large flat hand on the middle of Henry's back. Tom at this point breathed "Look out!" but Phemie pressed firmly and at the same time tried to pull down the lid. It was only then that Henry awakened to her intention. His whole body stiffened; he neither spat nor swore; but he drew one lightning

243

incision about two inches long down Phemie's wrist. There was a
scream; the basket was knocked flying; and Henry, like a black
streak, disappeared through the kitchen window.

Phemie wept, which in so strong-minded a person struck Tom
as disappointing. It struck Mother in the same light, for there was
nothing to cry about, though the scratch was a nasty one and had
to be treated with iodine. After that nobody pretended to have any
further qualms about leaving Henry behind; William was told to fix
up a bed for him in the wood-shed; and though it was practically
certain that Henry would occupy another bed, of his own choosing,
human duties were felt to be fulfilled.

Henry in the meantime was gone, and after such behaviour you
wouldn't have expected him to reappear till the house was shut and
the coast clear; yet actually he turned up half an hour later, when
Phemie and Mary had departed to catch their train. Daddy and
Mother were still upstairs, but the luggage had been brought down
and packed into the car, and Tom was merely waiting in the hall
when Henry strolled in through the open front door just as if nothing had happened. He walked straight up to Tom, his tail in the air,
and began to rub against his legs, purring loudly. "No," Tom scolded,
rejecting these overtures. "You're a bad cat and I don't want you.
You can have the house to yourself since you're so determined; but
it will be the outside of it."

He had no sooner said this, however, than it struck him as pre-
mature. Nothing was more probable than that Henry would contrive
to find a way into the house if he wished to. Just now he seemed to
be very affectionate and anxious to make friends, but hadn't he
already achieved the first of his purposes, which simply was to be
left behind?

And Henry, between Tom's legs, purred louder and louder,
rolling up his eyes sentimentally. There weren't any whites, but if
there had been, nothing else would have been visible, so Tom looked
into the "greens" and pondered. There must be something behind all
this—some object—and though he failed to guess the object, he
sat down on the floor and absentmindedly began to stroke Henry,
without realizing that he was doing so.

Henry arched his spine and gave a tiny guttural cry from the back
of his throat. It was really quite a touching picture of the emotional
interval before bidding farewell; and also, Tom felt, it was a direct
invitation to him not to go with the others, but to change his mind

and stay on, when he and Henry would have the house to themselves.

"I must be getting frightfully suspicious," he thought. And, "We're a nice pair!" he added to Henry. "Though it's mostly your fault and I'm not just going to let you have it all your own way."

At these words Henry hid his face, thrusting it against Tom's jacket, while simultaneously the grandfather's clock struck eleven, and Tom couldn't help thinking there was warning in its voice, and, when he looked up, in its kind old face also. It was a clock of the highest principles—anybody could see that—and he turned Henry round so that he might get an object lesson. But Henry didn't look—wouldn't look—which in itself was a bad sign. The clock, Tom decided, ought to be wound up the very last thing, so that for eight days at least, even if Henry did succeed in breaking in, the house would have a proper guardian. The only drawback to this scheme was that he had been strictly forbidden to wind it: Daddy always wound it himself; and there wouldn't be the least use in trying to explain the present situation to Daddy.

He *would* wind it. He hesitated only for a moment, then quickly crossed the hall, opened the case, and proceeded to do so—after which he felt better. He listened to the comfortable ticks, and each tick assured him that the clock was pleased and would try to keep awake as long as possible. "I believe he will, too," Tom said; and to Henry: "Now—he'll tell me everything that happens while we're away, so you'd better be careful!"

"And goodness knows what he's up to at this moment!" he concluded aloud, for he had merely been going over all this parting scene in memory; actually Henry and the clock were far away; Tom, Daddy, and Mother had been in Donegal for more than a week now, staying at the Fort Hotel at Greencastle; and at the present moment he was climbing the hill to Glenagivney.

Or not exactly that, because he had come to a temporary halt, and for the last five minutes had been sitting on a stone bridge resting. The climb was a long one, and the hill—though the other afternoon when they had driven over in the car it had seemed nothing—this morning had proved to be one of those wearying and deceptive hills whose summits retreat at the same rate as you advance, so that you always have another final stretch in front of you. Tom's jacket was slung over his left arm, a luncheon basket was on the bridge beside him, and the day, as he reflected, beating off the flies with his handkerchief, was about the hottest day he could have chosen for his excursion.

Not that he really had chosen it, or for that matter been given any choice. He wouldn't be here now if he hadn't received a post-card from Pascoe to announce that Pascoe himself would be arriving to-morrow, and would be staying with Aunt Rhoda till the end of the holidays. That had settled it: it must be to-day or never.

Yet when he had mentioned his plan, giving the reason why it would have to be carried out at once, it had called forth unfavourable comments from both Daddy and Mother. Also untrue and unjust, for it certainly didn't imply, as they appeared to think it must, that he wouldn't be glad to see Pascoe or didn't want his company. It only meant that on his last visit to Glenagivney he had felt very much attracted by the place, and had decided that he would like to re-turn to it some day by himself. He didn't know exactly why he wished to do this, though it was partly because it had seemed so secluded and deserted, even with Daddy and Mother there, that he couldn't help imagining how completely solitary it would be if he were alone. It would be strange; it would be exciting; it would be an adventure; possibly he mightn't like it as much as he expected, but far more probably he would. . . .

Yet that was not all—was not even the chief thing. Only the chief thing could hardly be expressed even to himself. It was—wasn't it?— a feeling, ever so deeply and mysteriously alluring, that there was just the remotest, just the faintest chance that he might meet some-body. This, in a way, perhaps appeared contradictory; but it wasn't really—not with the kind of meeting, the kind of person, he had in mind. Possibly there *was* no such person—outside dreamland—but possibly there was, and *if* there was, then this place was as close to dreamland as solitude and loveliness could make it. Naturally, how-ever, he couldn't tell Daddy and Mother such things, though he had often thought them and sometimes dreamed them. Anyhow, by coming alone, he didn't see what harm he would be doing to Pascoe. . . .

He listened to the stream trickling far down below him, under the road. He began to print his name on the stone, but the point of his pencil broke. He had rested long enough, he must be getting on, and he slid down from the bridge and caught up his jacket and basket.

The road was thick with dust and so steep that in places horses and donkeys had to draw their carts from side to side in a zigzag track. Here and there it was actually solid rock, which must make it frightfully slippery in winter, especially for the small feet of the donkeys. Tom's own feet were big, and so were his hands. He ought to have pointed this out to Mr. Holbrook, for it might be a hopeful sign. . . .

On either side of the road stretched the heather, purple and brown and dark olive-green, with black patches where the turf had been cut. There were no trees, but only the wide gentle curve of the hill rounded against the sky, very simple, and somehow soothing.

Now that he had left the bridge and the stream behind him, he wished that he had taken a drink while he still had had the chance. He had been a long while on this road, partly because of donkeys who weren't working and therefore had time for a little gossip, and partly because of stones in his shoes. Every time he got a stone in his shoe he sat down on the bank, and every time he sat down on the bank he found it hard to get up again. It was so hot, with that cloudless sky and not a vestige of shade, and he very much doubted if carrying his jacket was really a good plan. The grasshoppers made as much din as if they were being broiled on frying-pans. He wished that he hadn't brought a basket at all, though at the time, when Miss Forbes had suggested it, he had been pleased. Already he had examined the contents. It contained a thermos flask, a bottle of milk, a knife, a spoon, a cup, cake, sandwiches, bread, biscuits, cheese, bananas, sugar, butter, salt—and some of these things were pure luxuries, he could have done quite well without them.

The sun was almost directly overhead and so fiery that if you looked at it through your fingers it was like a solid ball of white flame. Well, he must be near the top now—and—yes—here it was! And there down below him, though still some distance off, was the sea.

It looked intensely blue under a glittering haze of light. It looked as if it were absolutely unvisited and unknown. The descent on this side was much shorter and steeper than the hill he had just climbed, and the country was greener, being mostly pasture land. There were two or three white cottages, but he saw no human beings anywhere.

Near the bottom of the descent, the road, which had been growing narrower, branched off sharply to the left, and became a grassy track, winding between thick fuchsia hedges to the entrance of a rocky gorge, from which rose a low murmurous noise of water. Where the hedges were broken, Tom caught a glimpse of high grey rocks threaded with silver streaks. Under the shadow of the hedge the grass was thick and long, and the golden pollen of the buttercups brushed off on to his shoes. There was a pungent scent of wild vegetation everywhere—quite different from the heavier, sweeter scent of a garden—and some of the fields were so white with daisies that they looked as if they were deep in snow.

"I'm going to rest here," Tom made up his mind, "and get cool again." So he lay down in the grass under the hedge—lay on his back as close to the hedge as a half-hidden ditch would allow—and after the hot glare of the sun it was like being in a green twilight.

"This would be a good place to camp out," Tom thought.

It would be easy enough to do it, too—with Pascoe. Pascoe was what old Pemby called a resourceful boy. He had mended the spring of Pemby's gate for him one afternoon, while Pemby himself had stood watching and beaming through his glasses. Tom also had looked on, and not been resourceful. In that respect he took after Daddy, who, according to William, "had no hands." "The master has no hands," William had explained confidentially to Tom; and this after poor Daddy had spent nearly half an hour trying to adjust the lawn mower. "I'm not sure that it's much better than it was, William. Perhaps *you* can find out what's wrong." William had merely stood silent and supercilious, and the moment Daddy was gone: "The master has no hands," he had said. "These learned people's all like that."

Pascoe had hands, and if a tent could somewhere be borrowed he would be sure to be able to rig it up and do the other necessary things. Yet in spite of his resourcefulness Pascoe wasn't the companion Tom imagined as sharing his adventure. He wasn't like him in any single way: which was indeed easy to see, for at that moment the companion appeared.

He had scrambled through a gap in the hedge, and when he saw Tom he stopped short as if in half a mind about scrambling back again—a very ragged boy, with bare feet, no jacket, and rents in his shirt and trousers through which his skin showed. He had hair the colour of the bleached ears of wheat, and the brightest eyes Tom had ever beheld.

While he stood hesitating, neither advancing nor retreating, Tom sat up. Then the boy, though still keeping at a distance of two or three yards from him, sat down facing him. He had a home-made fishing-rod in his hand, which he laid on the grass beside him, and a basket filled with damp dark watercress. He gazed at Tom in alert stillness.

There was something in this fixed gaze that Tom found unusual. It was not rude, but it was very much interested, and the interest was of an oddly impersonal kind, just as if he were confronted with an experience entirely new to him. But they couldn't sit staring at each other for ever, and to break the silence, and because he could think of nothing else to say, Tom pointed to the watercress and asked: "Where did you get it?"

"Down there," the boy replied, without removing his gaze from Tom's face. "There's plenty in the stream. Fishes, too, if you can catch them." He lifted off the top layer of watercress and revealed beneath it three speckled trout. "You could cut a willow rod that might do."

Tom shook his head. "I haven't a line, or a hook, or bait."

"I've a line," the boy said, "and the bait's only wor-r-rms."

He pronounced the last word slowly, and put so many "r's" into it that Tom thought he must be Scotch. But the rest of his speech wasn't Scotch. Besides, dressed as he was, he must be a native, a farm-boy very likely, belonging to one of the thatched cottages Tom had passed a quarter of a mile back, for there were no others between this and the sea. He decided to ask the boy if he lived here, and was very much astonished when he answered "No."

After this he began to laugh, and when Tom wanted to know what he was laughing at, he said "At you," and instantly became grave.

The strange thing was that Tom didn't feel a bit offended by this speech, it merely quickened his curiosity. "Why?" he questioned. "Because I asked you where you lived? I don't see anything funny in that!"

"No," the boy agreed, "it wasn't funny." Yet he said this, too, in an unusual way, as if he were only accepting Tom's word for it; and he still kept on looking at him inquiringly. "I don't know what 'funny' is," he presently added. "I was really laughing for practice."

This was a very strange boy, Tom thought. A little astray in his wits probably—only his eyes, his whole face, seemed to deny that. And he just sat there, without speaking again, but watching Tom intently and looking rather lovely. It was queer, but he *was* lovely—really lovely: his beauty seemed to shine through his rags, and he sat with a most peculiar lightness, like a butterfly poised on a leaf.

"Where *do* you live?" Tom tried again, and the boy, without turning, waved his hand.

"Over there," he said; but the gesture was vague, and might have included the whole sky and sea. Tom, at any rate, could make nothing of it.

Neither could he very well go on asking questions; it would be better to mention something about himself; so he did this, and told where he was staying and about his walk that morning, and ended by telling his name.

"I have a name," the boy at once replied; and when Tom asked him what it was, he said: "Gamelyn."

Tom repeated the syllables to himself. He had never heard the name before, and it might be either a Christian name or a surname. "That's only one of your names," he said aloud. "What's the other?"

Then the boy answered: "I have no other."

Tom said nothing except "Oh!" After that he sat thinking. The bright clear eyes were still fixed upon him, and now he shrank a little from their light. Surely it had increased! Not a word had Tom uttered, nevertheless the boy answered just as if he had spoken: "I was sent to you. I am what you asked for."

"I didn't ask for anything," Tom denied, but his voice had a quaver in it, and it was with an effort that he went on more firmly: "I don't think I can wait here any longer. I must go down to the sea."

Then the boy smiled at him and immediately his uneasiness vanished.

"Why did you say that?" he asked. "I mean about being sent to me. It wasn't true, was it? How could you have been sent to me?" Yet it might be true, he reflected; he might have been sent from one of the cottages.

The boy shook his head. "I was sent because you wanted me. I was told to come. *Didn't* you want me?"

There was a pause before Tom's reply came, very haltingly: "I don't know. I don't know who you are."

"I'm an angel," the boy smiled. "*Your* angel. You must have imagined me and wanted me. You must have imagined me very strongly, because if you hadn't I couldn't have come."

A still longer silence followed, and then Tom muttered unhappily: "I imagined a boy."

"I'm a boy," the angel said—"the boy you thought of."

"You're not," Tom answered. "It was a human boy I thought of."

As he spoke the last words it seemed to him that the figure before him quivered and grew less distinct. The voice too was now hardly more than a sighing of the wind. "Once—twice—a third time—and then no more. . . ." But Tom could not be sure that he had really heard these words, and now that it was too late he cried out: "Don't go away. . . . Don't. . . ."

There was no boy—no angel—only a vanishing brightness in the air, soon indistinguishable from the sunshine.

Simultaneously there sounded a music as of the chiming of innumerable tiny bells. It came from the fuchsia flowers above his head, and it was wakening him, though he tried not to awaken. But something else was awakening him also—a touch, a warm breath on his hair. Abruptly he opened his eyes and found himself staring straight into the long narrow face of an inquisitive old goat.

12: GO away!" said Tom sharply, and the goat, who had been bending down over him, was momentarily startled, and backed several paces. There she paused to size Tom up. This did not take long, and, the result being reassuring, she approached again.

She had managed to uproot the peg to which she was tethered and it trailed after her at the end of a rope. Tom distrusted goats. Moreover this particular goat had a sardonic gleam in her eye which boded little good. He would have retreated had it been possible to do so, but it wasn't, and the goat realized this. It may have been sheer playfulness, but suddenly she rose half sideways on her hind legs in an extraordinary fashion, and Tom, without an instant's hesitation, rolled backward into the ditch.

Luckily it was dry, so he got only a few nettle stings. But the goat, surprised by his abrupt disappearance, advanced to the edge of the ditch to see what had happened. Once more they stared at each other face to face. Then—and actually leaning over him to do it—

she began to pluck sprays of ivy from the bank on the other side. "This really was the limit!" Tom thought. "Only what could he do?" and she showed no sign of moving on. He was obliged to crawl along the bottom of the ditch on hands and knees, encountering further nettles and brambles, while the goat, quite regardless of the trouble she was causing, continued her meal. Then, to crown all, when he judged it safe to clamber out again, she immediately gave chase, so that he had to take to his heels.

The pursuit, it is true, was brief, and on the goat's part not very serious, but it was none the less alarming to Tom. Besides, he had left his basket behind and didn't see how he was going to retrieve it. The goat, he felt sure, still had her eye on him. Without the least inconvenience she could watch his movements and continue to eat at the same time. It was most annoying. Perhaps if he were in his turn to attack—to advance boldly and with loud shouts—— But he didn't think so: a peace-offering would be better. Only the rich greenness of the lane seemed to make any additional offerings rather superfluous. Everything she could possibly desire was there already and within easy reach. The lane was a kind of caprine Paradise. All she had to do was to stretch her neck and she seemed jolly good at that. The grass was long and juicy; the hedge was full of honey-suckle, ivy, and convolvulus; there were pollard willows above her, and cow-parsley and wild strawberry plants under her feet. There was also deadly nightshade, Tom perceived, but nothing was deadly to goats. She was now sampling some furze prickles. Still, an offering was his best chance, so he chose vetches as being easiest and quickest to gather, and collecting a large bunch of these, intermixed with willow-tops, and holding the bunch at arm's length before him, he returned.

The goat seemed surprised to see him. It was as if they were meeting for the first time. She gave conventional little bleats of astonishment as he approached. What a dear little boy! And so kind! Where *had* he got all those lovely things? Surely they couldn't be for her, and really they were far too pretty to eat! She took jolly good care all the same to gobble them up as quickly as possible, and in the process made them sound so crisp and succulent that Tom felt half inclined to try a mouthful himself. He cast the remains of his bouquet at her feet, lifted the basket, and this time walked away with dignity.

He had come out of that rather cleverly, he thought. A resourceful boy—like Pascoe! Only there was never anybody to *see* his resourcefulness, or to be impressed by the way he managed things. . . .

As he proceeded, the sound of a stream grew louder, and another turn brought the whole valley into view. Tom scrambled down to the water's edge. The stream splashed its way swiftly, the stony channel narrowing in places to form miniature rapids, and again widening out into sandy pools. In several of these pools he found watercress.

His dream, driven out of mind by the encounter with the goat, was thus brought back to it, though he couldn't remember the boy's name. A queer name—beginning with an "L." But he wasn't a boy, he was an angel—*his* angel—which meant, Tom supposed, his guardian angel. The only names of angels he could think of were Michael, Raphael, and Gabriel, and it hadn't been any of these; nor, he thought, like them. And was it true that he had imagined an angel before he fell asleep? He was sure it wasn't, though certainly he had been thinking of somebody to camp out with—somebody not like Pascoe. This seemed unkind, but then Pascoe *wasn't* his ideal friend, and there was no use pretending he was. On the other hand, an angel wasn't his ideal friend either, no matter how nice he might look. An angel wasn't right at all, Tom felt: he couldn't be a friend; he was at once not enough and too much.

In the meantime he might as well have his lunch before going any further. Sandwiches usually made you thirsty, and the stream water would be pleasanter to drink than tea out of a thermos flask. So he unpacked his basket, ate a few sandwiches and a banana, and when he had finished took a deep drink. The water was brownish in colour, but clear and cold. Probably it contained iron, in which case he'd better have another cupful, for iron was a tonic, as he knew, having been ordered it after more than one illness by Doctor Macrory.

He repacked his basket and followed the stream down to the shore. Here it became shallower and wider, flowing in several channels, and though it still ran swiftly its voice was lost in the roar of the breaking waves. For a while Tom threw pieces of wood into the current and watched them being carried out to sea, but presently he tired of this amusement and began to walk along the beach. The place *was* as lonely as he had imagined it would be. Perhaps even lonelier, for it seemed to him almost like an undiscovered world. Or an abandoned world maybe—with that black broken hull of a boat half buried in the sand. "The world will be like this," Tom mused, "when all the saints have been caught up into the air."

No sign of a human being: not a soul could have been here to-day; the only marks on the long brown stretch of sand were the thin strange footprints of sea-birds. The entire crescent of the bay must measure more than two hundred yards, and it was shut in behind and at both ends by cliffs which rose nearly perpendicularly to a height of some hundred and fifty feet. These cliffs were covered, but not densely covered, with grass, through which fragments of grey rock thrust forth. The sun was still well above them in spite of Tom's loitering, and the tide must be nearly at its lowest ebb. When it was full, the water would reach almost to the foot of the cliffs, he supposed, because except at the edge the sand was not white and powdery, but brown and smooth.

And it was the most fascinating shore he had ever seen. Below the unbroken stretch of dry sand, the lower, ridged sand was strewn with rocks of many colours—bluish, pink, and every shade between light and dark grey. It was as if in some remote past these rocks had been thrown up by an earthquake; and the water churned between them, and ran up the beach in foam. There were glittering pools and delicate seaweeds—seaweeds moss-green, and seaweeds more brightly green than grass; seaweeds branching like coral and coral-pink; seaweeds brown and purple. There was very little of what he knew as wrack, but there were seaweeds, clinging to the lower flatter rocks, with long smooth slippery blades that were exactly like the razor-strop hanging up on the door of Daddy's and Mother's bathroom. He supposed that all these weeds really had their own individual names, like land weeds, though people just called them vaguely sea weed. It would be interesting to make a collection of them—with Pascoe. Something caused him to add this little tail to his thought— something very like a precaution, though he wasn't sure what the precaution was against. Perhaps an angel. He glanced round, but saw nobody. . . .

The pools were fascinating. They were like small lagoons. There were tiny fishes in them, and crabs, and other creatures. Tom wondered how they managed not to be carried out by the tide. He took off his shoes and stockings, but some of the pools were deeper than they looked, so he took off his trousers as well. He explored the pools for a long time. He'd have bathed, only perhaps the bathing here was dangerous. Anyway, secretly, he much preferred paddling.

Many of the rocks were stained and patterned curiously with beds of minute mussels, purple and black. The colours were clear and beautiful. He stood watching all this vivid sea-washed beauty and listening to the waves. He could have listened to the waves for hours without tiring. Their sound was like no other sound, though the wind in a wood might sometimes remind you of it. He thought he liked the sea better than anything, but it was really the sea running up the sand or breaking against the rocks, really the music of the sea, that he liked; for when he was out in a boat he didn't much like it—in fact it soon bored him. But when you were on the shore it was different, and the sound hid away everything else, and was like an endless lullaby. . . .

Gamelyn, his name was. It didn't begin with an "L" after all. . . .

A small and very tickly green crab was walking over Tom's foot. He drew his foot out of the water with the crab still on it, and then turned to look back at the cliffs. He wondered if he could climb them. "Not that I'm going to," he added prudently, "and perhaps get stuck half-way up."

Several sheep had come to the edge and were looking over. Somehow they made the whole scene less lonely. It wasn't exactly as if they had been human beings, but it was very nearly the same, whereas the seagulls hadn't made any difference at all. This was puzzling. . . .

The cliff was in shadow now, and there was a line of shadow along the shore at the foot of it. Mother had lent him her watch. It was a wrist-watch—a rather silly little thing and a very distant relation indeed of the clock he had left in charge of the house— but still it told you the time, and what it said now was four o'clock. He wished he had a spade so that he could dig channels between the pools, but there weren't even any big shells. Suddenly a dark round head rose out of the water to look at him. "That's a seal," said Tom, and remembered having read somewhere—but it might only have been in a fairy story—that seals are passionately fond of music. If they are, he thought, they must get precious little of it except what the waves make. So he sang to the seal, and the seal really did seem to listen, though he wouldn't come out of the water.

It was lovely singing here: it was like singing with an orchestra. "What I'd like most of all," Tom decided, "would be for all animals and all birds, and even all fishes and insects, to want to be friends with me. And they would too," he thought, "if they only knew. Some do know—some dogs and donkeys—but there are so many that don't. It would be fine to be friends with a seal." And he began an adventure in which the seal came close to the rocks and took him for a ride on his back. He imagined Daddy and Mother and Pascoe and Miss Jimpson and Brown—a whole crowd of people—standing on the shore in amazement. Nor was it really so impossible. It would have been quite possible, and even quite easy, if things had been just a little different—if animals could speak in a human language, for instance. . . .

He wondered if ships ever came into this bay. He hadn't seen one, but he supposed they must. . . .

"Was this the face that launched a thousand ships?" Pascoe had made a mess of that; he had said "boats," and been offended because Pemby had talked for five minutes about how the change of one word could rob a line of all its character. "Ships," Pascoe had amended. "Silly old ass," he had added under his breath. "Steamers, rafts, canoes, barges." And though Tom had appreciated the wittiness of this, he had felt all the same that Pemby was right. There *was* a difference, though he didn't know what made it, and Pemby hadn't explained. But "ships" meant more—meant masts and yardarms and great white sails, and even a lookout man at the bow, shading his eyes with his hand—and a wide, heaving sea.

It was rather mysterious: he wished Pemby *had* explained it. . . . But perhaps he ought to be going home soon. He had enjoyed himself frightfully, though he wouldn't object at present if a fisherman or somebody were to come down to the bay, or even appear at the top of the cliff. It had begun all of a sudden to be a little *too* lonely. He put on his trousers and walked back along the shore, while the seal accompanied him, or at any rate swam in the same direction. Tom followed the track of his own footprints, but they somehow looked now so solitary on that deserted beach that they gave him a queer feeling and he was not sorry to reach the end of the bay.

Here he had another meal, to fortify himself for the homeward climb. Also another drink out of the stream—more iron. The basket was lighter and Tom heavier when he began to toil up the ascent. He reached the place where he had gone to sleep, but the goat was no longer there. . . . Yes, this was the exact spot—where the grass was crushed—and that was where the angel had sat. A sudden thought made him stoop lower and examine the ground carefully. It showed no superficial marks, but actually Tom was not looking for marks, he was looking for a sprig of watercress.

But there was nothing. He sighed faintly and resumed his journey. When at last, plodding stubbornly, he reached the beginning of the wider road over the hill, there was a cart loaded with green rushes drawn across the way, and beside the cart was a man with two dogs. Tom was glad to see all three of them, and as the man wished him good evening, he thought he might stop to talk with him, and pat the friendly sheepdogs. The conversation lasted while the man finished his pipe, but Tom talked most, for the man hadn't much to say. He was a good listener, however, and Tom made a lengthy and circumstantial story of his rambles. The goat was in it, and so was the seal; only the angel was not mentioned. Then he told the man about Daddy and Mother and the expected Pascoe. Henry came next, but this was because the man asked him if he had a dog of his own. And the dogs pricked up their ears, Tom fancied, at this point, listening with far more attention while he was describing Henry's antics than they had shown before. "Well, I'm afraid I must be going," he concluded at last, quite reluctantly, "but I'll very likely be back with my friend soon; in fact I'm sure to be."

"That's right," the man replied, "I'll keep a lookout for you."

13: HE arrived home, tired and dusty, to find Daddy and Mother entertaining visitors. To Tom they were not interesting visitors, and when after dinner they were taken out for a drive, he was quite content to be left behind, though he had nothing particular to do. But he did not want to do much, feeling a good deal more tired than he would admit, and for a while he sat on a bench watching a very noisy and hilarious game of golf-croquet which was being played by two young men and two girls. All four were staying at the hotel without adding to its attractiveness, Tom felt; and while he watched their game his actual thought was that they were awful! So presently he climbed up on to the battlement and stood with his back to them, gazing over the parapet.

Below him the gound dipped and rose again, forming a narrow ravine which ran on to the sea. On the opposite side of this ravine, and on a level with the Fort, were the grey ruins of a castle. The castle had been built in 1313, Daddy said, and little remained of it now except the lower walls, and here and there the fragments of a spiral staircase. The floor was solid rock, however, though partly coated with grass; and looking through a broken archway, her pale mild face turned towards him, Tom perceived a sheep reposing in solitude.

He waved his hand and smiled (he was getting to know quite a number of animals), and the sheep bowed. There were plenty of rabbits moving among the rocks and bracken down below, but the sheep appeared to be the sole proprietress of the castle, a white and woolly chatelaine, gazing out with the prudent inquisitiveness of her race. She somehow had an exclusive, old-maidish appearance, and Tom wondered if that ever happened with animals. Rather prim, she looked, but affable—quite different from those girls anyhow, who were certainly bent on not remaining old maids.

The sun was sinking, and the rich warm flood of light, filling empty spaces and washing crumbling stones, had a curious effect of spiritualizing the scene. From the precise spot where he now stood, Tom two or three times a day had looked across at this castle—also he had climbed up and explored every inch of it—yet never before had it suggested to him anything beyond itself. Now its altered aspect awakened a vague stirring in his mind, as if a submerged impression were trying to force its way upward to consciousness; but unsuccessfully, for it produced in him only a dim sense of being reminded of another scene, a place still unidentified, but which he had at some time visited, though he could not tell when. Yet it ought to be easy, he felt, for he knew very few ruins—Inch, Greyabbey, Bonamargy, Dunluce—he could remember no others. And then suddenly he knew that it wasn't a real place at all he was thinking of, but only a place in a dream—that queer dream which he was convinced had been repeated several times, though it still obstinately eluded his waking efforts to recall it. He saw, too, that even the fancied resemblance was an illusion. There was no resemblance; the house of his dream had not been like that. Moreover, it had not been near the sea, and the ravine itself had been different, a kind of wood, a kind of glen—like the glen beside his own house at home. . . .

The glen at home! Could it be? The thought brought him up with an abrupt little shock of discovery. But it was true, though it seemed very strange that recognition should only have come now, and in so roundabout a fashion. On the other hand his dream-house had not been like the house at home either, and certainly it had been the castle, perched up there with the steep drop beside it, which had set him pondering. Surely he ought to be able to remember everything now. But he could not: it was just as baffling as ever. Only that one brief glimpse of a vanishing scene—as if he had entered a theatre at the very moment when the curtain was descending—and then—Henry scratching at his bedroom door. . . .

Tom turned round, and immediately perceived that he must have been gazing at the castle for a long time. The croquet players were gone, yet he had not heard them going. It was latish too—he could feel that—though perhaps not more than half-past nine or ten. At all events Daddy and Mother had not yet returned, and since the moment they did so he probably would be sent to bed, it might be just as well to move a little further off while he had the chance.

He came down from the battlement, and passing round by the kitchen quarters and through the vegetable garden, descended a rough path to the shore. The falling dew had made the grass slippery and enticed crowds of snails from their hiding-places. Tom, careful not to tread on these adventurers, walked along a beaten track, with bracken on either side of him and the rocky shore below. He climbed a stile and skirted the wall of the Manor House, where Miss Pascoe lived. It was a low stone wall, scarcely three feet high on Tom's side, and almost level with the strip of green sward within. The garden stretched at the foot of tall rocks, which were split here and there into narrow crannies suggesting the entrances to secret caves. It was a brilliant garden in the daytime, but the colour was draining out of it now. And behind house and garden and rocks there rose steeply a dark plantation.

An overflow of flowers from Miss Pascoe's garden bordered the path along which Tom was walking. Some had even seeded themselves close to the shore—white, yellow, and purple foxgloves, and Saint-John's-wort with its yellow flowers and green and deep-crimson leaves. At the end of the wall the ground widened out on both sides and the coastline was broken into a series of small bays, each with its smooth sandy beach. The tide was full or nearly full, and Tom scrambled out as far as he could over the lichened barnacled rocks, till the water was lapping at his feet. The thickly crusted rocks were the colour of tarnished silver, and up the numerous channels between them the water swelled and sucked backward with a hollow melancholy sound.

The sun had vanished nearly an hour ago behind the hill Tom had climbed on his way to Glenagivney, but it was still reflected in the clouds, and the reflection was mirrored in a crimson track, almost the colour of blood, across the tumbling sea. On the opposite shore, soft as a pastel drawing, the hills were outlined in dark slate-blue against a paler sky.

The light was fading fast.

The Manor House, large and square and white, had become like a phantom house glimmering against the black background of the wood. Further along was the grey mass of the Fort, with the round Martello tower, at the foot of which was a stone staircase leading to Tom's bedroom (for he had a private staircase all to himself), and further still was the castle. Up the faint blue sky there rose a heavy column of cloud, like a genie escaping from a jar. Cloud upon cloud, the sky was strewn with them, loose and floating, those underneath tinged to gold, those nearer earth grey or faint mauve, with deep translucent wells between them of pale pea-green and silver-blue. But on the farther shore darkness was descending like a curtain, blotting out the pattern of the hills; and a peculiar mystical happiness had descended upon Tom—dreamily peaceful—almost ecstatic—for it was only remotely related to this world.

14:   HE had been right about that at least; undertaken with Pascoe the walk to Glenagivney became quite different. Pascoe, with a specimen-box and a press he had manufactured for drying flowers, turned an idle excursion into a scientific expedition. He had even brought a botany book with him, borrowed from Daddy, whom he had consulted, and who had given him a sort of introductory lesson on how to use the book, while Pascoe all the time had hung on his words with a rapt interest and attention that ought to have been flattering. It had made Tom, at least, think how extremely satisfactory a son Pascoe would have been for Daddy; and this in turn made him wonder what kind of father would have found *him* satisfactory.

Not one like Daddy, he was afraid, though perhaps sharing the same tastes and interests was less important than he imagined. It couldn't be the only thing, at any rate, for he and Pascoe shared very few, and it didn't prevent them from being friends. They were much happier now, for instance, going this walk together, than either of them would have been with any of the other boys they knew, and yet each probably was getting a quite different kind of enjoyment from it. Pascoe was busy collecting flowers; Tom, though he too plucked a flower occasionally, was really thinking all the time of what had happened on his last visit here. It was in this very lane that he had dreamed of his angel, and in this lane that he had met the goat. *She* certainly had not been a dream, and he kept a lookout for her, wondering if she would remember him. The lane, however, proved to be empty of goats and angels alike.

"Let's get over to the other side of the hedge," Pascoe suggested. "It looks as if it was mostly heather there, but we may find some small flowers, and anyhow I want to press the ones we've got while they're fresh." So they jumped the ditch, crawled through a gap, and picked their way on stepping-stones across a shallow stream.

They were now on the edge of the ravine above Glenagivney Bay. Here and there, marking the track of the lane, a few slender half-grown trees grew, chiefly birch and willow, but all the open ground was rocky and deep in heather—dry, brittle, and fragrant. Tom sat down among it; Pascoe, who had work to do, sat on a stone.

"I love this place," Tom thought, expressing the immediate feeling of contentment that flowed in to him through all his senses. What stretched before him was a kind of pageant of summer at its height— an intensity of heat and light, of colour and growth and movement, filled with low stirrings and secret calls. The sea was visible when he sat up; indeed, though considerably below them, it was quite close as a bird would fly. Then, when he lay back in the heather again, it disappeared, and looking up he saw nothing but a bluish quivering haze that veiled the deeper blue of the sky.

Pascoe at once got busy. He opened his tin specimen-box and un-screwed his press, between the boards of which were a dozen sheets of blotting-paper. Tom admired the neatness with which he manip-ulated his flowers. He must have a very delicate sense of touch, for his fingers seemed never to bruise anything, never to fumble or make a slip. Watching him, Tom felt a momentary desire to assist, but knew that he wouldn't be allowed to do so, and relapsed again into laziness. The slope on which he lay supported him at exactly the right angle for comfort; in spite of the buzzing and humming, no flies molested him; and the fairhaired Pascoe, with his mouth pursed up and an intensely serious expression on his whole countenance, looked somehow both amusing and attractive. "Would you be surprised if we saw an angel?" Tom asked him, but it was the kind of question Pascoe evidently regarded as merely symptomatic, for he neither stopped working nor answered.

"The worst of botany books," Pascoe presently remarked, "is that unless there's a coloured picture, or you happen to know the name of the plant already, they don't help you much. That is, if you're a beginner. Your father told me I might find it a bit complicated at first."

It was at this moment that a large woolly dog joined them.

Neither of them had seen him approaching; he hadn't been there a second ago, and now he *was* there—that was all. Probably a sheep-dog of sorts, though he bore a marked resemblance to a bear, for his eyes were small, his muzzle blunt, and his unusually thick blackish-grey coat, to which a long streamer of goose-grass was attached, seemed to contain the accumulated dust of a lifetime.

He sat down facing Tom and Pascoe, nearly closed his eyes, and opened his mouth sufficiently to allow three or four inches of pink tongue to protrude. His breath came with the quick, panting sound of a small gas-engine, and his tongue dripped slowly drop after drop of moisture on to the ground. Pascoe, looking up from his work, frowned thoughtfully at him in silence. Then he said, with what was rather like a sigh: "There's no doubt it's much easier to identify animals than flowers."

Tom supposed it was, though at the same time he was finding some difficulty in regard to this particular specimen. "You mean you'd know he was a dog?" he pondered.

"Well, wouldn't you?" Pascoe replied; "and yet there's far more difference between him and lots of other dogs than there is between you and a monkey."

"Thanks," said Tom, while he continued to study their visitor.

"I didn't mean you in particular," Pascoe explained. "I meant *us*—humans beings. What breed would you say he was?"

"That's just what I've been trying to make out," Tom murmured doubtfully. "He *isn't* so easy to identify. I don't think he's any breed at all. He's just Dog. He looks to me like the first dog."

"Yes, he does rather," Pascoe agreed. "And I expect they were all the same once, like pigeons. I think that's pretty clever of you."

Tom was pleased, for Pascoe did not often pay compliments. He tried to be clever again. "I think I know his name," he said.

Pascoe looked at him sceptically. "What is it?" he asked.

"Bruin," said Tom, though the moment he had said it, it struck him as feeble. "Bruin! Bruin!" he called.

Yet marvellous to relate, he had guessed right, for a bushy heavy tail immediately thumped the ground. Tom was delighted. "I nearly always know dogs' names," he added imaginatively.

Pascoe did not answer, but suddenly he called out: "Chrysanthemum! Chrysanthemum!" and the tail once more thumped recognition.

Tom changed the subject. "Anyhow, he's joined us," he said. "And he's going to stay with us all day. You can see that." And indeed Bruin, or Chrysanthemum, or whatever his name was, did show every sign of intending to remain.

"Go home, sir!" ordered Pascoe, but this time it didn't work, and Tom murmured: "Shucks to you!"

"It's no good," he went on; "he's just friendly and frightfully determined. He knows quite well we're having a picnic, and he knows we can't do anything if he makes up his mind to stay. He'll eat most of the sandwiches too: dogs like that have awful appetites. I bet he could eat a whole leg of mutton."

"I bet he won't eat *my* sandwiches," replied Pascoe simply.

He began to screw up his press, and Tom waited till he had finished before rising to his feet. "Well, what about going on?" he then proposed. "It'll be nicer down at the sea."

They picked their way back to the lane, the woolly dog preceding them, looking round over his shoulder every few seconds as if encouraging them not to lag behind.

For some reason this air of leadership began to displease Pascoe, who wasn't particularly fond of animals. Tom merely found it amusing, and Pascoe's attitude amused him also.

"It's because he's so beastly full of himself," Pascoe grumbled. "Besides, I know he's going to be a nuisance. Just look at him! You'd think he was taking charge of us! It's what *he* thinks, anyhow. For two ticks I'd turn round and go the other way."

"So would he," Tom answered gaily; "you won't get rid of him like that, and we want to get down to the shore."

There was something in what Pascoe said, all the same, and the nearer they drew to the sea the more urgent became Chrysanthemum's signals. For an oldish dog he was behaving very oddly. He kept running on ahead and then running back again, showing all the time more and more excitement. Tom half expected to be grabbed by the jacket at any moment, and though this didn't actually happen it came as near to it as possible. Pascoe deliberately slackened his pace.

"He *is* leading us!" cried Tom with sudden conviction. "I wonder what's the matter!" For he had read about Saint Bernards, and other philanthropic dogs, organizers of rescue parties, inveterate humanitarians. Yet it seemed hardly likely that there could be any question of a rescue here, unless somebody trying to climb the cliff had sprained an ankle or fallen.

"There's nothing the matter," Pascoe told him. "Don't take any notice; he sees he's impressing you. If you stop taking any notice of him he'll soon get tired."

But Tom was doubtful, and he ran down the last slope and on to the beach, where he waited for Pascoe, with Chrysanthemum jumping round him in the most extraordinary fashion.

It couldn't be a rescue, however, for there wasn't a living soul in sight. Besides, Chrysanthemum never so much as glanced at the cliff, but devoted all his attention to Tom. In another minute Pascoe had joined them.

The tide was out and they walked at the sea's edge till they reached the end of the bay. Here, on a flat rock, Tom put down the basket and Pascoe his botanizing paraphernalia.

"What *is* the matter?" Tom exclaimed again, all his curiosity returning as Chrysanthemum began to dig wildly beneath the very rock they had chosen. He showered the sand out in a thick storm, and in a very short time had scraped a hole about a foot deep. "He'll soon be in Australia," Tom murmured, but he had begun to feel a share of the excitement himself, half hoping for romantic developments—a big brass-bound box—even a little one would do.

"Perhaps it's a smuggler's hiding-place," he suggested to the less impressionable Pascoe. "Do you think it could be? Or it may be treasure out of a wreck."

"It's much more likely to be a dead body," returned Pascoe gloomily, and this unpleasant view was somehow so plausible that it instantly dispersed Tom's dream of treasure-trove.

He wished Pascoe had kept quiet: he wished they had gone to the other end of the bay. Side by side they stood watching Chrysanthemum, who was now so plastered with sand as to be more like some unclassified marine object than a dog. The hole he was making grew deeper and deeper; at any moment a stiff dead hand or foot might gruesomely appear.

"I wish we hadn't come," Tom whispered. "Do you think it would be wrong for us to go away?"

"No, I don't," returned Pascoe emphatically, "and I'm going." He lifted up his own personal belongings as he spoke, and Tom lifted the basket.

"We're not the police," Pascoe went on. "It's none of our business to go hunting for corpses. And if there *is* a corpse, it must be of somebody who was murdered."

This also seemed a logical conclusion: Pascoe would make a very good detective, Tom thought. So they retired nearer the cliff and chose this time a rock above high-water mark.

The curious thing was that Chrysanthemum, after a single parting glance at his unfinished labours, immediately joined them and began fresh excavations in the new spot.

They were equally vigorous too, and Tom, though he was several yards off, got a shower of sand in his face. Yet in spite of being half blinded he felt relieved. "It's all nonsense!" he cried. "There can't be dead bodies all over the place. It's not a cemetery."

Then he tried an experiment. He lifted a stone and threw it. Chrysanthemum instantly ceased digging and raced after the stone with deafening barks. At last they'd grasped what all along he had wanted, and from that moment he jumped about them and barked without ceasing. The rocks reverberated. It was a marvel how one dog—even a big one—could make so much noise. There was little question now of sea-music and lonely shores. Nothing less like his last visit could Tom imagine.

"He's going to spoil the whole thing," he said, beginning to share Pascoe's opinion. "We may as well give it up and go somewhere else. We can try up there on the cliff. If we get further away from the sea he may stop barking, and he won't be able to dig."

"I'm not going away from the sea," Pascoe declared obstinately. "I'm not going to let any dog upset my arrangements. What's more, I'm going to bathe before lunch."

"He *has* upset them, whether we like it or not," Tom replied; but when Pascoe began to undress, he did so also, and they ran down to the water's edge. The blue sea glittered in the sun, and big rounded waves came tumbling in, foaming past the rocks and hissing up the smooth brown sand. Chrysanthemum bathed with them: that was to be expected. But it didn't matter much; it was only surf-bathing anyhow; for even quite close to the edge the waves were as high as their shoulders and carried them for yards up the beach. Chrysanthemum was swimming most of the time; Pascoe tried to swim; but Tom waited for the waves, sitting in the shallows and letting them lift him up and sweep him on with squeals of delight, leaving him stranded high and dry. It was fine sitting on the sand in ten inches of warmish water, with bubbles of spray melting on your legs. Presently Pascoe came into the shallows too; and then Chrysanthemum—they were all together now. Pascoe looked extremely naked beside Chrysanthemum, whose coat was as dense as, and much longer than, a sheep's. Chrysanthemum was really a good name for him, though Tom knew it had been chosen by Pascoe as the most unlikely he could think of. But really it was much better than Bruin, which was stupid. The kind of chrysanthemum that has long loose petals, Tom decided. For the hair of his coat, mixed with sand and sea, was hanging down now in tangled clusters exactly like petals.

"I don't see why we need dress," he said, burying his feet in the sand. "Not a soul ever comes here, and it's more interesting to have no clothes on; it makes you behave differently."

"It doesn't make *me* behave differently," Pascoe contradicted, "and you always behave as if you were naked."

This remark puzzled Tom. It sounded as if it ought to have a meaning, and perhaps it had—yet he couldn't discover any. He gazed at Pascoe in uncertainty.

But Pascoe was doing exercises—touching his toes without bending his knees. "Are you hungry?" he asked. "We'll not dress if you don't want to."

"Middling," Tom thought, abandoning the question of nakedness. "But I'll get hungrier when I begin. I always do."

"Then let's have our grub," Pascoe said, "because *I'm* starving."

The unpacking of the basket was of absorbing interest to Chrysanthemum. With a slowly moving tail he sat down about a yard from Tom and directly facing him. To Pascoe he paid no attention whatever. "How does he know?" Tom wondered. "He heard him saying things, of course, but he can't have understood. It's very mysterious how they know. They must get thought-waves or something." He held out a sandwich of ham and brown bread. Chrysanthemum leaned forward and the sandwich disappeared. It was exactly like posting a letter.

Tom looked at Chrysanthemum and Chrysanthemum looked at Tom. The pendulum movement of his tail seemed as automatic as if he had some clockwork arrangement inside him. "After all, he's not as big as I am," Tom mused, "and yet it takes me two minutes, I should think, to eat a sandwich." He glanced at Pascoe half guiltily as he offered another, but Pascoe was feeding as hard as he could, his jaws working as regularly as Chrysanthemum's tail. "You're a silly to give him all your lunch," he remarked with his mouth full. "He's probably better fed than we are; at any rate he's about twice as fat. I'm not going to give him *any*thing—not so much as a crumb."

He had said this before, and Tom didn't care. Besides, it wasn't true that Chrysanthemum was fat. He wasn't any fatter than Pascoe himself; they were both about right, and Tom wished he was the same.

It was strange, nevertheless, how Chrysanthemum had divined immediately whence the source of blessings would flow. He never so much as looked at Pascoe until the latter offered him the shell of a hard-boiled egg. "I wouldn't do that," Tom advised. "You might want it later."

Pascoe had begun on the tomatoes, which were overripe and inclined to spread; in fact they *had* spread—there was tomato on his chin and on the tip of his nose—but this didn't trouble him, nor did Tom's sarcasm. "I don't want him," he replied, "and I'm not going to encourage him. You didn't want him yourself a few minutes ago. It's only weakness now, and because you're silly about animals. I suppose you think *I'm* being stingy."

Tom didn't think so; he knew Pascoe was acting upon principle. But then he didn't share the principle and had begun to like Chrysanthemum; how could you help liking anybody who was so friendly!

He mentioned this, but Pascoe said it was only cupboard friendship.

"It began before he ever *knew* there was any grub," Tom declared. "It began the moment he found us."

"Which was the moment he sniffed the basket," Pascoe replied. "You said yourself he knew we were having a picnic."

"Even if he did," Tom argued, "I don't see that it makes any difference. He came because he wanted our company, and he wouldn't go away now if we stopped feeding him: he wouldn't say a word; he would still be friends."

Pascoe went on eating, unmoved.

Luckily Chrysanthemum didn't care for tomatoes, so Tom had his full share of these. During this course Chrysanthemum disinterred a long-deceased crab, which he crunched and swallowed with apparent relish. "The eggshells were at least fresh," Pascoe pointed out dispassionately. "It just shows you what he's like." But Pascoe didn't understand Chrysanthemum any more than he understood Tom. Tom and Chrysanthemum understood each other. And in the end Pascoe *did* give him a sandwich, though he was careful to explain that it was really to Tom he was giving it.

They had left enough for a second if smaller meal, and now they repacked the basket. "What do you want to do?" Tom asked: but Pascoe had eaten too much to be immediately energetic.

"Nothing for a bit; then either bathe again or else dress and explore along the top of the cliff. What would *you* like to do?"

Tom had no special wishes, so this programme suited him well enough. Clothes were arranged as pillows and Pascoe went to sleep almost at once. So did Chrysanthemum, with his heavy damp head on Tom's stomach—selected after several trials as being the only really soft spot in his body. Tom did not feel sleepy—only lazy and content to lie on his back and listen to the waves. Besides, he didn't want to go to sleep; it was too pleasant lying here like this; and the pleasantness somehow included everything—Pascoe and Chrysanthemum—the sea and the sun and the earth. He thought of his angel, but very lazily, and the angel reminded him a little, though only a little, of a boy who had once spoken to him at a party, and whom he had never seen again. Eric Gavney his name was—quite a big boy. He went to the school Pascoe would be going to after the holidays, and to which Tom himself would be going, he supposed, next year. . . . If not sooner; for there had been some talk of that recently—chiefly, he thought, because Daddy and Mother seemed to have an idea—a quite ridiculous idea—that Pascoe looked after him, and that it would be better if they were to go together. . . .

It was queer—this getting to know people. Sometimes it made a difference, though usually it didn't. Three years ago he hadn't known Pascoe. And there was Chrysanthemum, lying with his head on Tom's stomach—and yesterday neither of them had had the least suspicion that the other existed! When he went to his new school he would get to know a whole crowd of boys whom he now couldn't even imagine, though they must all be alive and doing something at this very moment. With some of them he might become friends: with

one he might become great friends—have the kind of friendship he
sometimes dreamed of: not that he would ever drop Pascoe. He
couldn't conceive of happiness without friends; they were much
more important than anything else, he thought; and even the earth
he would have liked to be as nearly human as possible. Though human
wasn't exactly what he meant: Chrysanthemum, for instance, wasn't
human. What he meant was more just having feelings and the power
to communicate them—a capacity for friendship. . . .

Pascoe wasn't like that, he knew. As a matter of fact Tom was the
only boy with whom Pascoe ever associated. Of course, Tom didn't
associate a lot with other boys either; but he would have liked to, he
couldn't feel indifferent in the way Pascoe seemed to feel. He didn't
really dislike Brown, for example. At the present moment he couldn't
think of a single person he disliked. True, the present moment was
hardly to be relied on, for he was in a peculiar mood—a rather sloppy
mood, he fancied—one at any rate in which he felt capable of finding
passionate romance in limpets and beauty in a woodlouse. . . .

And the waves curled over and ran up the sand; and a little puff of
wind came from the sea and moved in Pascoe's hair. . . .

A long time elapsed.

"Wake up!" cried Tom at last, for it looked as if Pascoe and Chrysanthemum would lie there for ever.

Pascoe opened his eyes, but very drowsily.

"It's getting late," Tom told him. "You've slept for hours."

The sun had indeed dropped visibly, but at the same time it was
moving round the side of the cliff, which was lit up now where before it had been in shadow, while the whole sea lay in a rippling
glory. Chrysanthemum was the first to move; sleep had refreshed
him and he began to dig. Pascoe jumped up with a shout and ran
down to the breaking waves. Pascoe was knee-deep in the Atlantic.

And it began all over again. Pascoe's voice was raised in a tuneless
chant; Chrysanthemum's voice was raised: Tom, though he squatted
in the shallows as before, joined in the chorus; the cliff's edge was
lined with interested sheep. They plunged in and out till they were
cold; they ran along the sand till they were hot; they threw stones
for Chysanthemum; they dressed and ate everything that remained
in the basket.

"We ought to be going home soon," Tom supposed regretfully,
for he didn't want to go home, and suddenly realized that he was

feeling very tired. He might have been wiser, perhaps, to have had a sleep like the others.

"We'll go now," Pascoe said, "and then we can collect more flowers." He gathered up the botany book, the specimen-box, and the drying-press as he spoke. "If we could only make *him* carry something," he added, with a glance at the unencumbered Chrysanthemum. "I don't suppose he's ever done a stroke of work in his life."

"I don't suppose he has," Tom agreed, "though he *may* work for a shepherd, and this may be just his day off."

The walk back he found very heavy going, for the tide had come in a long way and they had to plough through soft sand. Pascoe and Chrysanthemum seemed to find no difficulty.

When they reached the stream he explained about its tonic quality, which he had forgotten to do before, and Pascoe said there *might* be something in it, though Tom's deduction, made from the colour of the water, was unscientific. At any rate all three drank from it—Tom and Chrysanthemum close together, Pascoe higher up.

"You can get a most frightful thing from dogs," Pascoe mentioned when they stood up again—"a thing that grows on your liver till it kills you. It's quite common among the shepherds in Scotland, because they allow their dogs to eat off the same plates as they use themselves. I'm sorry I didn't remember about it sooner, though it's very unlikely you'll get it. He *was* below you, wasn't he?"

"Yes," said Tom rather faintly.

"Then that's all right; you're safe. I wouldn't have told you, only it's just as well that you should know in case you ever get a dog of your own."

They had begun the ascent through the now familiar scene, though in the evening light all the colours were deeper. The fields of still un-ripe oats were vividly green, but the hay was already cut and stacked. Pascoe—who always seemed to be a few yards ahead—did not find many new flowers, and Tom found none. On the other hand, he lingered to watch half a dozen black bullocks standing dreaming in the shade, knee-deep in long grass, their tails alone moving, switching away the flies. He knew it was partly an excuse to rest, and Pascoe, he was afraid, must have guessed this, for he stopped at once, and asked him if he were tired. Tom didn't answer, because he wasn't sure whether Pascoe was tired or not. Then this struck him as stupid, so he said he was, and sat down on the bank with his arms round Chrysanthemum.

Pascoe sat down also. "I am too," he declared, but he couldn't be so very, for he immediately began to work with his flowers. Pascoe was very nice in ways like that, Tom pondered dreamily; lots of boys would have boasted that they weren't tired even if they were. But Pascoe wasn't like that, and he was the only boy who never called him Skinny. . . .

He could have sat there for a long time just thinking such thoughts; he could even have gone to sleep, and would have liked to do so; but in a few minutes they resumed their journey. The last faint sound of the waves had been left behind, but there was a constant ripple of hidden water near. At length they emerged out of the lane and the smoother road across the hill began—bare, and without hedge or bank or wall. Before them was an unbroken outline, as of an immense curving bronze-green barrow—smooth, naked, and dark against the evening sky. On either side the turf bogs stretched, rich and sombre covered with heather and sprinkled with bog-cotton. Greener beds of moss and flowering rushes showed where the land was soft and treacherous, while the light caught an occasional gleam of stagnant water. At wide intervals, and branching off at right angles from this ascending road, cart tracks diverged across the heather. These tracks were firm yet soft under foot, being composed really of powdered turf, and they were grey in colour, except where a darker patch showed that a stack had recently been removed.

Suddenly Pascoe gave a little squeal and stood still.

"Good!" murmured Tom, immediately subsiding.

"Look!" cried Pascoe, grabbing him by the arm and pulling him to his feet. "There they are! I'd forgotten all about them."

Tom looked obediently, but saw only a couple of turf-cutters, with their carts, far away across the bog.

"I'm sure it's them," said Pascoe eagerly. "I don't see Kerrigan, but I'm sure those horses are Blossom and Welcome."

"Blossom and Welcome?" Tom repeated, unenlightened.

"Yes—Aunt Rhoda's horses. . . . Kerrigan was to come over with the two carts this afternoon for turf."

"Oh," murmured Tom, beginning to understand.

"We'll not have to walk home after all."

"Good!" said Tom again.

They had got so used to the company of Chrysanthemum that it was only at this point that they realized he oughtn't to be there, and that they must have passed his home long ago. Immediately a new problem was raised, altering everything.

"He picked us up away down near the sea," Pascoe said, "and that must be where he lives. What are we going to do about it?"

Tom didn't know. But he knew that, stuffed with grub and after hours of friendship, Chrysanthemum wouldn't want to leave them.

"*You'd* better tell him to go home," Pascoe said. "It's really you he's following, and he won't take any notice of me."

Tom said nothing, but he gazed back down the hill. He was pretty certain that he couldn't do that climb over again. "Go home," he said to Chrysanthemum, but he didn't say it in the right way. It sounded weak, more like a suggestion that he might have made to Pascoe himself, and as such Chrysanthemum considered it, with his head on one side and an amiable expression on his face. He wagged his tail.

"Oh, well," said Pascoe good-naturedly, "I suppose we'd better keep him and bring him back to-morrow."

So, with Chrysanthemum still of the party, they set out across the bog, striking a diagonal line to the nearest track.

The horses and carts and the figures of the two turf-cutters were clearly silhouetted against the sky, but it was not till they were quite close that they perceived a third man, for he was reclining on the ground on the farther side of one of the carts, leaning his back against the wheel and smoking.

"They haven't done a thing, of course," Pascoe murmured in an undertone, "except take out the horses and stand there yarning. They're always like that: Kerrigan would sit there talking till to-morrow morning."

Certainly nobody was working at the moment—or looked like beginning to work. Blossom and Welcome were browsing on such scattered tufts of grass as they could find among the heather; Kerrigan was talking through a haze of tobacco smoke; and the two turf-cutters, leaning indolently against the stack, were also talking, while at the same time they watched the approaching trio. The whole scene had an atmosphere of leisureliness that fell in marvellously with Tom's own mood and inclinations: he felt quite ready to sit down and join in the conversation, or at any rate listen to it.

"Shall we go or stay?" Pascoe continued to whisper. "Kerrigan doesn't really want them to hurry. They haven't even taken off their coats, and we may have to wait for hours."

"I'd rather stay," Tom whispered back. "Does it matter?"

But Kerrigan at this point must have discovered what they were discussing, for he took his pipe from his mouth and called out: "Now sit you down, Master Clement, and take your ease. A rest will do you good, and the mistress will know rightly where you are."

"We didn't promise to be back at any particular time," Tom put in persuasively. "I'll stay if you will."

Meanwhile the turf-cutters were being greeted as old friends by Chrysanthemum. "And where might you have picked up Mrs. Reilly's Mike now?" one of them asked. "Sure it's two desperate dog-stealers you have there, Kerrigan, an' you'd do well to keep a watch for the police when you'd all be riding home together in the light of the moon."

This was a joke, and a good many others followed, during which Tom noticed with relief that Pascoe had become absorbed in the botany book. He himself began to stroke the soft cheeks of Blossom and Welcome: Blossom dappled-grey, and Welcome chestnut-brown; both wearing stockings. He had always felt a particular liking for carthorses with stockings: the stockings seemed somehow to add to their powerfulness. Blossom and Welcome were solid as mountains, and Tom thought far more attractive than slender highly-strung thoroughbreds. They moved slowly and ponderously, and looked as mild as old-fashioned nurses. He could even imagine them answering advertisements, and putting in "fond of children" at the end. But he was really very tired, and seeing that the turf-cutters, so far from be-ing spurred to activity by the arrival of Pascoe and himself, had now actually sat down, he followed their example, and stretching himself on his back in the smoky clouded purple of the heather, listened to the slow lazy talk. Pascoe had produced a pocket-lens and with his penknife was performing some kind of botanical dissection; Chrysan-themum was searching for rabbits; Blossom and Welcome continued to nose about for provender; while Kerrigan and the turf-cutters smoked and pursued a desultory conversation interlarded with hu-morous yarns. Everyone was doing exactly what he wanted to do, Tom reflected, and not interfering with anybody else; and this seemed to him to be exactly the way life ought to be conducted. . . .

Kerrigan and the turf-cutters had drifted into reminiscences of supernatural visitations and warnings, suggested by Tom's account of the fright Chrysanthemum had given them when he had first be-gun to dig. They were chiefly tales of hearsay—one leading to another—but they all had a local background, being the experiences of friends or relations, and the cumulative effect was persuasive. Pascoe probably was the only sceptic present. . . .

It was Chrysanthemum's tongue licking his face that made Tom open his eyes. And astonishingly he found that everybody was ready to go home. The turf-cutters were putting on their coats, the carts were loaded, Pascoe was on Welcome's back, and Kerrigan, knocking out the ashes from a last pipe, asked Tom whether he would like to ride on one of the loads or on horseback.

Horseback, he decided, feeling now quite rested and energetic; so he was up on Blossom, and slowly the journey home began.

Probably he would have been a good deal more comfortable sprawling on top of the load, but nothing would have induced him to make this change. Pascoe had begun to sing—his usual kind of tuneless song—and the two turf-cutters walked with Kerrigan beside the carts till they reached the road. There they said good-night, and with Chrysanthemum, turned back towards Glenagivney.

Kerrigan didn't know what time it was. Neither did Pascoe, and neither did Tom, for to-day he hadn't Mother's watch with him. But it wasn't moonlight, though a wraith of a moon was in the sky. Far below them was the grey shadowy sea, and across it—a sign that it must be fairly late—the revolving lights had begun to flash their signals.

15: TOM and Pascoe, after a religious discussion, had decided to read the whole Bible through, chapter by chapter, from Genesis to Revelation, but it was Pascoe to whom it had occurred that this spiritual effort might be turned to material advantage. And strange to say, mentioned in a carefully thought-out letter to the wine merchant, it *had* actually produced a postal order for five bob, though Aunt Rhoda, perhaps because she seldom went to church, would only go the length of half a crown, and even that in the unsatisfactory form of a promissory note payable on the accomplishment of the task. Fired to emulation, Tom had tried what *he* could do, but either he lacked Pascoe's adroitness or else possessed the wrong kind of parents, for Daddy had simply looked at him and sighed, while Mother, with a wretched sixpence, had given him a lecture on the ignobility of seeking pecuniary reward for good actions. It appeared that there were even specific warnings in the Bible against this very plan of Pascoe's—texts about serving two masters, about God and Mammon. Pascoe, Mother seemed inclined to think, was serving only one master, and that one Mammon; whereupon Tom instantly, though it was their first encounter, had a clear vision of this Mammon—called up out of Limbo by the mere sound of his name—a sort of debased demi-god, with a large stupid face, a fat smooth dark-grey body, and a dirty tail. He didn't like the looks of Mammon at all.

But as yet the reading had not progressed very far; the first three chapters of Genesis, subtracted from the grand total of chapters in both Old and New Testaments, leaving so large a number that it became a question as to whether Aunt Rhoda oughtn't to pay interest on her half-crown. In the meantime there had been much to argue about. Tom remembered talking of these very chapters with Mother, in the garden at home, on the evening preceding his sleep-walking adventure, but Mother hadn't got nearly so much out of them as Pascoe. Pascoe—by means of logic and pure mathematics—had actually deduced, not the area indeed, but the exact shape of Eden. He went over the proof with Tom. It was quite clear, wasn't it, where the Tree of Life stood? You were told that bang off: it stood in the middle of the Garden. But the Bible, you were also told, was absolutely true, and the only absolute truth is mathematical truth.

"I don't know whether it is or not," Tom said, feeling all the same that Pascoe was about to produce something remarkable.

"Well, you ought to know," Pascoe replied. "Everybody else knows; all mathematicians at any rate."

"Miss Jimpson?" Tom suggested.

"Miss Jimpson!" Pascoe echoed pityingly. "Miss Jimpson isn't a mathematician. She knows just about enough to teach a few kids." But he added: "You needn't mind my saying that, because maths, of course, isn't your subject. You're good at other things, and nobody can be good at everything."

"All right," said Tom, leaving Pascoe to proceed with the argument.

"I suppose you admit that the only mathematical figure which has a centre is a circle?" was the next question.

Tom thought of a square and a triangle, but did not mention either.

"You do admit that?" Pascoe went on. "Well then, since we're dealing with absolute truth, which is mathematical truth, and since we're told that the Tree of Life was planted in the centre of the Garden, it follows that the Garden must have been circular in shape."

"There were two trees," Tom objected after he had recovered a little. "There was the Tree of Knowledge as well as the Tree of Life, and I don't see how they both can have stood in the same spot."

"No," said Pascoe, "they didn't; and you aren't told that they were both in the centre; you're only told that the Tree of Life was."

Tom had no further arguments, and indeed ever since then he had pictured Eden as Pascoe described it. "It's a huge circle," he said to himself now, after he had blown out his candle. And having decided this, he thought for a minute or two of Chrysanthemum, and then of the ride home. But very soon his mind slid back again to Eden, which had always interested him, and had been made by Pascoe more interesting still.

Why, for instance, when forbidden to eat of the Tree of Knowledge, had nothing been said to Adam about the Tree of Life? Pascoe had a theory explaining this also, though he admitted himself that it was not based on such pure reasoning as the other, and therefore could be regarded only as a probability. His theory was that there was no *need* to warn Adam against tasting the Tree of Life, because the Tree of Life was invisible to him until after he had eaten the apple of knowledge. Then, of course, his eyes had been opened, just as Siegfried's ears were opened when he tasted the dragon's blood. And this really was frightfully clever, for it exactly bore out what the Bible told you—that as soon as Adam had eaten the apple, or whatever it was, God had begun to be frightened that he might find the other tree and eat one of its apples too. "They were both magic trees," Pascoe expounded, "therefore one of them might easily have been invisible. Only their magics were different. The Tree of Knowledge showed you things and taught you things; the Tree of Life had the same power as the pillar of fire in *She*. . . . Not," he added, "that I believe at all in either of them."

The last words were a disappointment; in fact they left Tom distinctly annoyed, for he had been on the point of accepting these conclusions. But Pascoe was always giving you surprises like this, and he looked at him reproachfully. "You've just *said* that the Bible is absolutely true," he grumbled.

"I didn't," Pascoe returned. "I said people *told* you it was absolutely true; and I said that if it was, then it must be mathematically true. In my opinion it's neither the one nor the other."

"Then you're an agnostic," Tom declared. "Or an atheist," he added more thoughtfully, struck by what would ultimately happen to Pascoe. "Daddy, I don't think, believes it all," he presently admitted, "though he won't argue about it. But Mother does: she told me so."

"A lot of it's nonsense," Pascoe replied. "Just as much nonsense as the story of Saint Columba learning to read by swallowing a cake with the letters of the alphabet printed on it. You don't believe *that*, do you?"

"No, I don't," said Tom, "and I never heard of Saint Columba."

"Well, a lot of the Bible stories are just as silly."

"Who told you about Saint Columba?" Tom asked suspiciously.

"Aunt Rhoda told me. And she says the lives of the saints are crammed with things like that."

"The lives of the saints aren't in the Bible," Tom pointed out. "And anyhow I don't think the Tree of Life is silly at all."

Pascoe looked at him. "Why are you fixing so specially on the Tree of Life?" he said. "There were two trees."

"I don't know," Tom confessed. "Except that I saw it and not the other one. I mean I saw it for a minute when you were speaking about it." He paused to pursue a private cogitation. "*Can* you see a thing if it isn't real?" he wondered aloud. "I mean, could you see an oak tree in your thoughts if there never had *been* an oak tree? Where would the thought come from? Not that this was like an oak tree. It had flat leaves of a kind of silvery grey, and nearly white on the under side. They were big leaves too, for the size of the tree, which wasn't really a big tree; and they moved very easily—not with the wind, but as if they *wanted* to move. The trunk was smooth, and like the trunk of a birch, only thicker, and——"

"Oh, stop!" cried Pascoe, almost choking. "You're about the biggest little——" He left the rest unspoken, but Tom had no difficulty in supplying the word "liar."

"It's queer that we should always call each other 'little' when it comes to disputes," he thought, pulling the bedclothes up under his chin. "And it's queer the way Chrysanthemum dug in the sand. . . . I wonder how Henry would like it if I brought Chrysanthemum home with me? Not at all, I suppose. I wonder what Henry's doing at this moment, and if the clock has stopped yet? . . . I wonder if I could really bring Gamelyn again?"

But this was a proposition he could test, and it brought him up abruptly. "He *said* three times," Tom pondered. "Or anyway I thought he did. . . . Which means of course now only twice. . . . He had fair hair, but not so fair as Pascoe's, which is practically white.

"Fair hair," he murmured sleepily. "I like fair hair best." And then, somehow, there was a window open to the dawn—a garden, and birds singing endlessly. Another voice, a human voice, but not really Tom's voice, though he was making it come out of him and it sang— sang ever so much better than Tom could sing. . . .

Suddenly he was wide awake.

"I think I *will* try," he determined, sitting up in bed. "Just where that streak of moonshine is."

And even as he said so, the moonlight quivered and Gamelyn was there.

Like and unlike the boy in the lane; but this time not in any disguise, really an angel.

He certainly *had* altered. He looked even nicer than before, though he was now such a big boy that Tom felt qualms about having called him. He had better explain how it had happened, find an excuse. "I'm afraid I didn't *really* need you," he apologized. "I was just trying——" And then he was silent.

The angel waited: he did not seem to understand. For all that, Tom still felt that he had done wrong. The angel was a guardian angel and at present Tom had nothing to be guarded from, in fact he had brought him for no reason whatever—at least no serious reason. If only he were a real boy! He looked so like one, and Tom so wished he was one! The angel watched him with bright steadfast eyes, like pools with the sky mirrored in them: his body was silvered by the moonlight, and he had no wings. "This is the second time," he said. "Let us go."

"Go where?" Tom answered.

He slid out of bed nevertheless, and stood in his pink striped pyjamas on the floor. The angel had opened the door, and now beckoned to him before passing on down the stone staircase. It was very like a picture Tom had seen of Saint Peter escaping from prison, and next moment they were out on the grass.

The angel climbed on to the ramparts and Tom climbed up beside him. The ruins of the castle were clear in the moonlight—everything was marvellously clear. Down in the ravine he could see the rabbits playing.

And if anybody should happen to be awake, he suddenly remembered, and should happen to glance out of a window, both he and his naked companion would be plainly visible. But at that moment Gamelyn caught his hand and their flight began.

It was so swift that Tom felt and saw nothing—so swift that he seemed only to have drawn his breath once before they were standing in a hollow misty land between mountains. Or at least he thought they were mountains, though they might only be gigantic clouds, for it was very dark, and through the darkness there leapt streaks of scarlet flame. Presently his eyes grew more accustomed to the gloom, and peering through it, he could make out two immense shadowy forms moving rapidly and soundlessly backward and forward. In the right hand of each was a long thin scarlet flame that wheeled and darted, cleaving the mist this way and that; and Tom knew that these were the flaming swords, and that those grey shadowy forms were the sentinel cherubim; but they were of colossal proportions, and in the dim light he could not see their faces.

A voice whispered in his ear: "Not much chance of getting in that way!"

Tom answered "No," for he felt scared, and also surprised. The voice somehow did not sound right—sounded far less like the voice of an angel than the voice of a boy.

"Don't be frightened," the voice went on. "They don't see us, and even if they did we could get away. They never leave the garden and they're not nearly so close as you think."

This was a comfort at any rate, though Tom would gladly have been further off still, and presently he said as much.

"I thought you wanted to get in," the voice answered. "It can be done."

"I don't think we ought to try," Tom murmured uneasily. "I don't think they want us to try."

He had never, indeed, felt surer of anything in his life, and the boldness of Gamelyn implanted another misgiving, and this time one which awakened not only opposition but reproach. "It's very strange," he said, "that you should talk like that—seeing that you're supposed to be my guardian angel. I'd have thought you'd have tried to keep me *out* of mischief—especially dangerous mischief like this. Are you sure you're an angel at all?" And he turned to Gamelyn suspiciously.

But there was no reply: no Gamelyn.

And this was natural, because for a second or two he was sitting on the bank of the river at home, though he had hardly time to realize it before he was back again in the hollow misty land; and it was not the river at home that was rushing in an inky blackness beneath him.

"That is the way," Gamelyn pointed, "if you have the courage and will trust me."

Tom sighed. He hadn't much courage, he thought; but he had a great deal of trust, so perhaps it came to the same in the end.

"Put your arms round my neck and hold tight," Gamelyn whispered, and Tom obeyed him. He gave just one tiny cry, barely audible, but which he couldn't quite repress, as they plunged down. . . .

Down—down—down—through the soft black rushing water. They sank like stones, and Tom held his breath. But if you know *how* to hold your breath it is quite easy, he found, and he felt no discomfort at all. He simply didn't breathe out any of the breath he had drawn in, and therefore everything remained just as before, and he could have gone on for hours. Actually, they weren't a very long time under water, and it wasn't cold—perhaps because they were moving so quickly. For when he came to the surface again no mountains or cherubim were in sight, and he was in broad sunshine. Gamelyn, too, had disappeared, so Tom scrambled out on to the bank— alone in Eden.

But if it was a garden, it was a garden grown wild, and was far more like a wood, though there were plenty of flowers. And birds and butterflies and bees. Animals, too, for that was a giraffe over there, nibbling the tops of some shrubs. Tom sat down to collect his thoughts, and it was not till he felt his seat gently rising and sinking beneath him that he found he had sat down on a hippopotamus. The hippopotamus was reclining on his side in a bed of purple irises, and seemed so comfortable, that though Tom scratched him under his ear—always the best place—and scratched his hardest—he only opened one small eye and closed it again.

So this was where Adam had lived! Tom stood up to take stock of his surroundings. But here on the river bank, even when he stood on the hippopotamus, he was too low down to see much. The right spot would be that hill, or mound, about two hundred yards away—and there was something else about the mound which caught and riveted Tom's attention.

It rose in grassy smoothness to a height of some fifty feet—green sward all the way up till you reached the very top; but on the top, in conspicuous isolation, stood a tree. Tom gazed at this tree with round and ever more credulous eyes. No tempter was there to beguile him; he had no such excuse as had been found by his greatest grandmother; the dire result of the Fall can never have been more convincingly illustrated than by his instantaneous resolve: "If there are any apples on that tree, I'm going to have one." And he had no sooner reached this determination than he set off at a run.

Climbing the mound did not take long, and in another minute or two he was standing under the dark-green spreading branches, peering up eagerly between them. Yes, there were apples, early as the season was. But before he could take a further step, with a loud whirring noise, ten times more startling than the rising of a pheasant, a great white bird, surely some kind of albatross, flew out, uttering a strident metallic cry. Tom got a terrible fright, which was only natural. "It's so silly for a big bird like that to build in a tree!" he exclaimed half angrily. And it was a nuisance, too, for now if he were to climb the tree, the albatross would very likely think he was going after her nest, and might attack him. What was he to do? For though he could see that there were lots of apples, they were all on the upper branches where he could not reach them. And they looked small and unripe. The tree itself, he felt sure, was not the Tree of Life, but the Tree of Knowledge. Still——

There! she *had* come back, and was standing watching him, not more than five yards away. "I'd better not climb, but throw a stick," said the prudent Tom. "She can't very well object to that!" Luckily there were several good-sized sticks lying about.

So he chose the largest, and taking careful aim—and trying not to think of the albatross—he flung it as hard as he could at the nearest clump of apples. Instantly there was a commotion in the brushwood below, and a large shaggy dog—the born image of Chrysanthemum—came tearing up the hill to retrieve it.

But not before a shower of little apples had come pattering down on Tom's head and shoulders, rebounding thence on to the grass. The dog, having brought back the stick, dropped it at Tom's feet, and then backed a few paces, where he stood, with his red tongue lolling out and his eyes rolling affectionately. The albatross also watched, but she made no movement. It was really not a bit like the Bible—or at least not very.

Tom picked up an apple. "Hard as a board!" he muttered; and indeed it was. It had a thick wrinkled rind, too, and when he forced his teeth through this, he found the inside very dry and bitter. He screwed up his face, for the apple tasted worse than the worst medicine, and he could hardly keep from spitting it out. But he got it down at last, and then stood waiting for some mysterious change to take place within him.

Nothing happened. Once he had actually swallowed the apple its bitterness vanished, but that was all. No fresh knowledge dawned upon him; nothing new about either good or evil; his mind was precisely what it had been before. "I'd better test it," Tom decided, only it was difficult to think of a satisfactory test. "I wish I had an algebra here," he whispered to himself; "then I could have tried a sum and I'd soon have known."

As he stood puzzling his brains the shaggy dog came sidling up to him. He caught a flap of Tom's pyjama jacket between his teeth and gave it a little shake to attract attention. After which he said shyly: "I'm the first dog. I'm Dog."

Tom instantly remembered his theory about Chrysanthemum. Pascoe had thought it clever at the time, and now it was confirmed— Dog's words confirmed it—and it occurred to him that perhaps everything in the Garden was the first of its kind.

"I'm the first dog," Dog said again. "My name's Dog."

"I know, I heard you," Tom replied.

"You wouldn't have heard me if you hadn't eaten the apple," Dog reminded him; and from the sound of his voice Tom was afraid his feelings were a little hurt.

Hastily he patted Dog's head. "That's quite true," he told him. "At least, I'd have heard you, of course, but I wouldn't have understood you."

"Now I'll be able to understand Henry too," he thought, "and not just pretend I do."

Meanwhile the albatross had waddled over to them. "Here he comes!" she scolded, and in so pugnacious a tone that Tom instinctively stepped back a pace. But it wasn't with Tom she was angry. "Look!" she cried, giving him a nudge with her wing, so that the tip of a feather narrowly escaped his eye.

"Don't," said Tom peevishly.

The albatross apologized, but at the same time she stretched her right wing out to its full extent, till it almost covered him. It was the first time Tom had ever been taken under a wing—literally at all events—and he struggled to free himself. "I can't see anything when you do that," he muttered in excuse.

"Well, keep close to me, and don't let him fascinate you," the albatross said. "Keep as close as you can."

Tom did as he was told—partly because the albatross seemed to be really uneasy, and partly because he felt a little nervous himself. For a large and beautiful serpent, his long sinuous body burning in the sun, was leisurely climbing the mound. His colour, except for some jet-black markings, was more brightly green than the grass, and his raised, flattened head was swaying slowly from side to side as he advanced, with jewelled lidless eyes fixed upon them.

Neither Dog nor the albatross spoke a word, but Tom could feel them, one on each side of him, quivering with diapproval. Yet the serpent showed no sign of hostility, nor did he seem embarrassed by the marked silence in which he was received. "Well, Adam," he said softly, in a low pleasant voice, "so you've come back at last, and without Eva."

Tom felt very absurd. Really it was ridiculous! He had always pictured Adam as at least middle-aged even thousands of years ago; and now to find himself actually mistaken for him!

"I'm not Adam," he answered, turning away.

"Not in the least like him," snapped the albatross. "Quite different in colour, shape, and size. No more like him than a wren is like me."

She drew still nearer to Tom, and so did Dog, though goodness knows they had been near enough before. All three were now as firmly united as the ace of clubs, but the serpent merely coiled himself round them, and with his head raised to the level of Tom's face, gazed straight into his eyes.

"I didn't really think he was," he murmured in a voice that had a kind of sleepy music in it. Tom had never before heard a voice so beautiful—so caressing and persuasive. "I didn't think he was—in spite of those ridiculous things he's got on." He touched the ridiculous things with the tip of his forked tongue for only a second, yet the albatross ruffled all her feathers. "If he's not Adam," he went on, "why is he wearing them?"

"They're my pyjamas," Tom answered, blushing; while the albatross muttered "Manners!" loud enough for everybody to hear.

But the serpent paid no attention to her. "Take them off," he said to Tom, and seemed to expect him to do so.

"I won't," Tom replied, astonished at his own boldness.

"Why not?" said the serpent. "They're very ugly."

Tom looked down at them with diminishing confidence. They certainly *weren't* particularly beautiful. Mother had bought them at a cheap sale, and compared with the albatross's soft plumage, and the serpent's enamelled skin, and even Dog's rough fur, they looked both gaudy and common. "Do you really want me to?" he asked in a wavering tone. "I mean if you——"

"Of course," said the serpent. "What are they for? Why shouldn't you look nice?"

"Why indeed!" Tom thought. But aloud he said: "I don't know that I *will* look nice. . . . It's not that I *mind* taking them off. Only ——" He proceeded to do so, however, and felt that they were all watching him with the liveliest interest, not excepting the albatross, in spite of her remark about manners.

He pulled off the jacket slowly, and then the trousers, and there followed a pause in which nobody expressed admiration. It was just as he had anticipated; he was a disappointment; and he sat down on the grass, resigned but sad.

"You're far too thin, poor child!" cried the albatross fussily; and now that Tom was naked she appeared more than ever bent upon mothering him.

This seemed to arouse a latent jealousy in the serpent. "Don't coddle him," he sneered. "He's a boy, not an egg."

The albatross trembled with annoyance. She rose threateningly, and Tom was afraid there was going to be a battle. But the serpent was either too cautious or too lazy, and to Tom's relief the dangerous moment passed. The temper of the albatross remained ruffled, however, and when, with those snowy pinions closely enfolding him, Tom couldn't help fidgeting a little, she gave him a peck and said quite sharply: "Sit still!"

Tom repressed a squeal. It hadn't really been a very hard peck, but on the other hand she had a beak of iron, and he certainly didn't want a second one. So he sat as quiet as he could, and it was more with a view to effecting an escape than anything else that he presently made a suggestion. "Now that there are four of us," he ventured timidly, "we might have a game of something perhaps."

"Why so?" inquired the albatross, and Tom indeed had no particular reason to offer. "Making up a four you know," he explained rather feebly. "It was just the words that put it into my head."

"The child has very little sense," the albatross observed. "It's kinder to take no notice."

"I'll play a game with you, if you like," Dog whispered in Tom's ear, but the albatross overheard the whisper and her wing pressed tighter than ever.

"He doesn't want to play games," she snapped. "He's tired. If anything, he ought to have a sleep, and in the meantime we'll sit as we are."

Dog did not insist. There was something very nice about Dog, Tom thought. Though he mightn't be as clever as the other two, or have so strong a character, you felt at your ease with him, which you didn't quite feel with either the serpent or the albatross. Dog was like the Rock of Ages: he evidently hadn't changed in one single quality since the very beginning; so that knowing successive generations of dogs was really just knowing Dog.

"It seems strange that nobody is asking questions," remarked the albatross inconsequently. "I suppose it is because the child is extremely well-mannered—either that or else unusually shy."

Now Tom had been thinking of a question at that very moment. Unfortunately it was an extremely personal one, having to do with the loss of the serpent's legs, so in spite of this encouragement he still hesitated to ask it. The albatross broke the ice herself. "What is your name, child? I expect you have a special name, like Adam and the angels."

"Tom is my special name," he said.

"Tom!" they all repeated, and it had a curiously different sound coming from each. Dog turned it into a short sharp bark; with the albatross it sounded more like a cry, plangent and harsh; with the serpent it had a low breathing sound that was half a love word.

And then suddenly a most pertinent question occurred to Tom, and he asked: "Does God ever walk in the Garden now?"

Possibly he had said the wrong thing: it very much looked as if he had. The serpent's eyes glittered; the gaze of the albatross was fixed on a point so remote that Tom wouldn't have been surprised to learn that her home was at the South Pole. Only Dog remained untroubled as ever. "I don't think so," he answered cheerfully. "I've never seen him." Then he added, with a sort of quaint innocence: "Sometimes I bark at the angels and their swords."

Tom could quite believe it. All the same he thought it was brave of Dog, and said so.

Dog looked pleased. "They take no notice," he remarked modestly. "Besides, I keep on our side of the hedge. It's just for something to do, and because there's nobody else to bark at, but it'll be different now you've come; I'm very glad you've come."

Tom was sorry to disappoint Dog, but he felt he ought to mention that he was only paying a visit and wouldn't be staying long. . . . Though how on earth he was to set about going home again, he had as yet no idea.

"Of course he won't be staying," chimed in the albatross, in her possessive domineering way. "I'm going to take him to the sea in a few minutes."

"Then your nest *isn't* in that tree," Tom exclaimed, "and I needn't have been frightened to climb it after all!"

"Do I *look* as if I would have a nest in a tree?" the albatross replied impatiently. "Use your wits, child."

"I *am* using them," Tom retorted, for he was getting rather tired of being treated in this fashion. "And it's ridiculous of you to talk of carrying me. You couldn't possibly do it even if I was only half as big as I am."

The albatross looked as astonished as if a linnet had attacked her. "Well I never!" she cried, spreading out her wings like great white fans and taking a few leaps from the ground as though to show him. Tom felt that perhaps he had spoken too impulsively, and to change the subject he asked her where she *did* live.

The albatross settled down again, but he wasn't sure that she had entirely forgiven him, for it was rather coldly that she answered: "I live beside the Pacific Ocean."

"Near the top of a cliff," Dog supplemented.

"The highest cliff," continued the albatross. "If you were there you could look out over the water all day long. And when there was a storm you would see waves as high as that tree, rolling in and bursting and thundering up the rocks. At night you would watch the clouds scudding across the moon, and listen to the howling of the wind, and perhaps see a great ship foundering."

"I don't want to see a ship foundering," Tom told her.

"Don't you?" said the albatross, surprised. "Why not? It's most exciting. There's nothing so exciting as a good shipwreck, with plenty of screaming and struggling. And in the morning at sunrise you fly over the place where the ship sank and search among the floating wreckage and dip down to the green waves and let them carry you along, up and down, up and down—like the rocking of a cradle—with nothing but the sea all round you and the sky above you for miles and miles and miles."

"I couldn't do any of those things," said Tom quietly, "because I can't fly. And I can't even stay in the water for more than a very few minutes without getting benumbed."

"Benumbed!" repeated the albatross. But she was really so moved by her own picture of the joys of the sea that she had hardly listened to him. "I must be going," she cried restlessly. "I only looked in—I don't remember why."

"Only birds and fishes *can* get in or out," Dog whispered to Tom. "The rest of us have to stay here."

The albatross now stood with her head lifted and her eyes fixed on the sun. She stretched out her wings, beat them twice, and then, seemingly without an effort, rose into the air and glided away over the tops of the trees, higher and higher, till she was only a minute white speck in the sky; and finally that speck too vanished.

"And she never even said good-bye!" Dog marvelled. "After all the fuss she made about you too!"

Yet with the disappearance of the albatross he himself seemed to find that they had talked long enough, for he yawned, and presently dropping his head down between his outstreched paws, closed his eyes.

And all this time the serpent had been looking at Tom. It was as if he had been waiting for this moment, as if he had anticipated it, for now he drew his green coils in a little, and his narrow head found a pillow on Tom's legs, while his eyes remained bright and wakeful.

"You are the youngest thing here," he breathed, "and I am the oldest. I am older than Dog and the albatross, older than Eden, older than the earth."

"I don't think I can be the youngest, surely," Tom replied, having just seen a very small squirrel peeping down at them between the leaves.

"You are the youngest, because nothing has been born here since the gates were shut. Nothing has been born and nothing has changed."

"But you said just now that birds and fishes could get in," Tom reminded him dreamily, for the serpent's voice had a strangely lulling influence.

"*I* didn't say it; Dog said it. Birds and fishes might find a way in, but nothing that was not here at the beginning could live in this air."

"The albatross," Tom murmured.

"The albatross is Albatross and was named by Adam."

"Then is Adam himself still alive?" Tom questioned wonderingly.

"No. But on the other creatures there was no curse, only upon Adam and me. Besides, old age came on very slowly here, not at all as it does with you; and sooner or later most of the animals and birds and creeping things ate the berries of the Tree of Life. After that they remained for ever as they were."

"Is that a secret?" Tom asked eagerly. "I mean, can I tell about it when I go back? I'm sure nobody else knows, and it may be frightfully important." Not that he could quite see the importance, but he was sure it would cause a sensation and possibly make him famous. Not only scientists like Daddy, but people like bishops and Dean Inge—— And then an objection occurred to him. "How is it that *I* can live here?" he asked. "I wasn't here in the beginning and yet the air hasn't done me any harm." He drew in a deep breath to prove it.

"Didn't an angel bring you?" said the serpent softly. "I too am an angel."

"A fallen angel," Tom very nearly reminded him, but luckily checked himself in time.

The serpent looked sad, which made Tom feel sympathetic. He began to stroke the smooth glittering coils. Then the serpent raised his head and pressed it tightly against Tom's cheek. Fallen angel or not, Tom had begun to like him. "I never cared for Eva," the serpent whispered, so close to Tom's ear that it was like the murmur of a sea-shell. "That was the cause of it all."

Tom, who had no great affection for Eva himself, was neither surprised nor shocked, only interested. "What had she done?" he asked.

"I don't know really that she had done anything," the serpent answered plaintively. "You see, she didn't need to do very much, she was a misfortune in herself. Everything was so much nicer before she came. Afterwards Adam grew different. It was because she didn't really care about anybody *except* Adam, though at first, to please him, she pretended that she did. And before long she got so great an influence over him that he could see only with her eyes and think only her thoughts. Of course he didn't know this. She would ask his advice, she would consult him, she would look at him with eyes full of admiration, but all the time really she was making him say and do exactly what she wanted. And he was flattered and pleased and weak and foolish, and he thought there was no one like her."

"Nor was there," the serpent presently resumed in a more sombre tone. "Poor old Dog was the first to find the difference, though he was too simple to understand what had caused it. Eva, in a way, was simple also. I knew exactly the depth of her intelligence, and it exasperated me to see Adam hanging on her words."

"How deep was it?" Tom inquired curiously.

"A dewdrop would be an ocean in comparison."

Tom could not help fancying that there must be some personal feeling here, but he did not say so. "Adam's must have been still shallower," was what he said.

"So far as she was concerned Adam's didn't exist," the serpent replied. Then he paused, but soon went on sadly: "It was at no time remarkable, but before Eva came there was at least enough of it to make conversation possible. We used to talk in the evenings—Adam and I—when it was coolest and pleasantest. It was rather like talking to Dog, but Adam wanted to learn, he took an interest in most things, and I became very fond of him. Later he was interested only in Eva, which made his conversation monotonous. To her, however, this seemed natural and right: she wished to have him wholly to herself, and when he came to talk with me—as he would still do sometimes, though more and more rarely—she would find an excuse for calling him away. There would be something she wanted done, something she must ask him about, something she must tell him. Failing this, she would come with him, and that was worst of all. Picture it—little Tom! Since she couldn't be ignored, everything had to be reduced to the plane of her interests. Adam would sit silent, listening to her. I would be silent too. And she would babble on. But, unlike Adam, I used to think, when I wasn't too bored to think anything, how sweet it would be to wring that soft little neck. Anyhow, it was all utterly changed from what it *had* been. And then one day, when Adam was doing something or other she wanted him to do, I thought of a plan to get rid of her. I knew it needn't be elaborate; I didn't think it would be difficult; as a matter of fact I decided only to remind her that this tree was forbidden. There was no need to do more, no need to persuade her to taste an apple. If I had tried to persuade her she might even have refused. So I simply watched—watched her eating it—taking silly little bites so that I could hardly keep from pushing the whole thing down her throat. This I know was mere impatience, and when she had finished I no longer felt any grudge against her, and was even prepared to be friendly with her. I knew she would be banished from the Garden, and Eva as a memory would be not unpleasant. What never for a moment occurred to me was that she would run straight off to Adam and get *him* to eat an apple. Perhaps I ought to have guessed, but I imagined she would keep the whole thing secret, if not for her own sake, then for his."

"I've eaten an apple," Tom could not help interrupting.

"Yes, I saw you; but they've lost most of their power now."

"Oh," said Tom, a little regretfully. "They're like musk, I suppose. You know how the smell of musk has gone." Then he asked: "Has the Tree of Life lost its power too?"

"Do you wish to live for ever?" the serpent questioned him.

Tom hesitated. "I don't know. . . . Yes, I do. I do wish it."

"It only means for ever in that body," the serpent said. "It would be a foolish choice. You will live for ever as it is, though it will not always be the same life. But that is better."

"Do you think so?" Tom pondered doubtfully.

"Much better," said the serpent. "How do you know that your present life will not become a burden to you? I could show you lives you have already lived, and I don't think you would wish to return to them."

"Tell me about them, you mean," Tom corrected him. "You couldn't show me."

"Show you," the serpent said.

"But how?" Tom argued. "If a thing is past it isn't any longer there. You can't show me the snow house Pascoe and I built last winter. I could show *you* a photograph of it if I was at home, but the house itself isn't there."

"Where is it then?"

Tom wondered. Where *was* it? Where was anything you didn't happen to be looking at? "I suppose," he said, puckering up his forehead, "I suppose it has gone into the invisible world."

"There *is* no invisible world," said the serpent.

"But that can't be true," Tom answered, frowning still more. "Lots of things are invisible. Sounds are invisible—and smells."

"There *is* no invisible world," the serpent repeated.

Tom made no reply, and presently the serpent continued: "There are degrees of perfection in the organs of vision—that is all."

It was a puzzling doctrine. But then, many things were puzzling, and it was not the first time that something rather like it had occurred to Tom himself. At all events, even if it wasn't true, he couldn't prove it wasn't. He remained silent until he said: "You mean that all that has happened *is* still there."

"Yes; all that has been; all that is; all that will be. Time is an illusion. Shut your eyes and look."

Tom shut his eyes, and, as he did so, he felt the air filling with the serpent's peculiar odour, felt the serpent's coils twining about his naked body like a climbing plant, felt the serpent's face pressing, smooth cheek by cheek, against his own. There was a minute of dizziness—a blank—and then he was in a large bare stone room hung with black curtains and decaying tapestries. Or was it he? A boy was in the room, waiting beside an old man clad in a white woollen robe, with a wreath of leaves upon his silver hair, and a short naked sword at his feet. The old man was shredding herbs into a chafing-dish poised above a lighted brazier, and a blue smoke wound up to the roof. There was a white marble altar with strangely shaped alchemi-cal vessels upon it, and the boy, who was Tom and yet not Tom, knew the names though not all the purposes of these vessels, and he heard the old man muttering as his hands moved like fluttering pigeons above the chafing-dish.

"To-night, half an hour after midnight, the great work will be ac-complished," he muttered. But the boy had heard those words before, and he knew the old man's hopefulness, and he thought: "The great work will never be accomplished. He has been saying that for years. He was saying it before I was born. He will be saying it when he is dying. Always it has failed, something has gone wrong before the appointed time was reached. And I think it was well for me perhaps that this happened. I do not like to leave him, because he has been kind in his way, and he is old and lonely; but I will leave him before the hour strikes." He could hear the wind in the dark trees outside, and a black cat, crouching beyond the magic circle drawn upon the floor, watched him with fierce green eyes. Then the boy thought, as he had lately come to think, that the cat was an evil spirit, for he knew that the old man was a wizard. "The cat will try to keep me from escaping," he thought. "He is here for both of us. Why else should he have come? But my master does not know this. Or if he knows it, then the cat is his familiar spirit. I am not sure which is true, but I am sure that it is time for me to leave him—now while I am still able to do so."

The smoke drifted slowly through the room, and as it spread out, the different objects it touched began to waver and to lose their substantiality, and the mirror behind the altar became clouded. There was no light now except from the fire burning in the brazier, and this fire glowed and dimmed as if it were a living creature breathing. The air grew sensibly colder, and the boy felt an increasing lassitude in all his limbs, and a numbing drowsiness that weakened his will. And suddenly there came a knocking on the heavy oak door. The old man did not hear it, for he had begun his incantations in a louder voice. But the cat heard it and growled angrily. His fur bristled, his tail switched from side to side, his eyes glared and he looked as if he were about to spring. Then the knocking came again—louder, louder, louder. The cat sprang; it was tearing at Tom's doublet—trying to reach his throat. It had grown large and heavy; it was shaking him. Tom gasped, choked, cried out—and suddenly he was back in his bedroom at the Fort, with Pascoe standing over him in the sunlight, his hands still grasping Tom's shoulders.

"Goodness, you're hard to wake!" Pascoe exclaimed. He had a towel and a bathing suit, and he looked very "early-morning" and energetic. "I'm going to bathe before breakfast," he said. "Down below the castle. Do you want to come?"

But for a moment or two Tom could not answer. "What time is it?" he then asked weakly. "And how long have you been here?"

"About an hour," Pascoe said, "shaking you as hard as I could. It's after eight, but there's still plenty of time if you hurry up."

Tom heaved a deep sigh, though it was a sigh of relief and he disguised it as a yawn. He stretched himself under the bedclothes and smiled. "I've had the queerest dream," he couldn't help beginning, but Pascoe would not listen.

"Are you coming or not?" he asked impatiently. "When I say there's plenty of time I don't mean there's time to waste. You can talk about your dream on the way."

Tom would rather have talked where he was. He didn't particularly want to bathe—the water would be as cold as ice at this hour —only still less did he want to go to sleep again. But he could see that Pascoe wasn't in the mood for dreams: he seldom was, for that matter. "Yes, I'll come," he said, making up his mind. "But I'll not dress. I'll put on a coat and come as I am."

16: LEANING over the stern of the boat, Tom dabbled his hand in the water and wished that the holidays were not so nearly over. Pascoe was in the bow among the lobster-creels—which contained more wrack than lobsters, for the haul had been a poor one—and old Danny McCoy was rowing, with little dips of strokes, and chewing a plug of tobacco. Tom and Pascoe had rowed round from the harbour to the lobster-pots; Danny was bringing the boat back. . . .

Only three more days for *him*—though Pascoe would be staying longer. But on Saturday Tom would be going home—Mother had actually suggested going on Friday—and two weeks later (it had all been settled in an extraordinary hurry) he and Pascoe would be going to their new school.

Not that Tom had any apprehensions about that, and he was still to keep on his music lessons with Mr. Holbrook. . . . Mr. Holbrook might now be engaged to be married. At any rate there had been plenty of time: it seemed to Tom ages since that afternoon when he had sat with Miss Jimpson in the teashop.

He gazed down idly through the water. The boat was passing over a shoal of jelly-fish. He had never seen a lot of them together like this before, and he hoped they were drifting out to sea. Possibly jelly-fish served some useful purpose—Mother said everything did—but he doubted it, and in a swarm they looked repulsive. Ambiguous creatures at the best, on the border line between two kingdoms, hardly more animal than vegetable. Pascoe said they could move in any direction they pleased, by a process of suction and contraction— Pascoe was always interested in how things worked—but to Tom it looked as if they merely drifted on the current or the tide, trusting to encounter a bather. . . .

Danny rowed on in silence. The only sound was a cloppity noise— like little slaps—made by the sea against the bows of the boat. Pascoe had taken a small book from his pocket and was reading it. It was called *Spinning Tops*, but, in spite of this rather gay title, was in reality a scientific primer. Pascoe was unique—absolutely single-minded; Tom couldn't imagine anybody else who would bring *Spinning Tops* with him when going out on a lobster hunt. . . .

He listened dreamily to the cloppity clop. The sea was lovely. When he grew up he wouldn't live in a town or near a town, but by the sea. Danny McCoy shifted his plug of tobacco from the left cheek to the right. Why did he do that? Danny's brown hands, rough and wrinkled as oak-bark, tugged at the oars with little jerks that had not much weight behind them. He was a strange old man—"touched," people said—and Tom had once seen him the worse for drink. But he had been told that two pints of stout could produce this effect on Danny, and anyhow, even when drunk, he was never objectionable. He might stagger a bit, and talk to himself out loud, but that was all, and it did not happen very often. He lived alone in a thatched cottage at the end of the village, and the country people said he was odd because he had been "away" when a boy. This meant, Tom knew, that he had been taken by the fairies. He was burning to question Danny on the subject, but had been cautioned against doing so. The old man never spoke of his experience himself, and got angry if anyone else alluded to it.

Daddy, of course, said it was all nonsense—at least the fairy part of it. This, and one or two similar tales which Tom had picked up, Daddy said were the inventions of ignorance and superstition embroidering on what probably were ordinary cases of hysteria. Pascoe was equally incredulous, but Tom himself had seen a young man—Sam Grogan—who had been chased for more than a mile by a ghost. Along the high road, too! He had been on his bicycle, and riding as hard as he could, yet the ghost had only given up the pursuit at the edge of the village. Outside the Post Office Sam had fallen off his bicycle exhausted. He had been taken into the Post Office by several friends—for it was a spot where most of the boys and young men gathered in the evenings—and somebody had brought him a drink from Casey's public house opposite. Tom had not only seen Sam Grogan, but he had also seen and talked to one or two of those who had assisted him, had seen the bicycle, had seen Casey's public house, had been in the Post Office—had seen everything in short except the actual ghost, and *it*, save for Sam's first impression of a tall shadowy figure approaching through a gap, nobody had seen. But its screams had been bloodcurdling, and it had screamed the whole time it was chasing Sam—screams of murder.

Tom felt tempted to ask Danny's opinion of this story: he felt particularly tempted to ask him what he thought of Port-a-Doris. For Tom had recently visited that lonely little shut-in bay and had not liked it. To say he had not liked it was indeed a mild statement of his feelings. He had hated it. He had felt uncomfortable the whole time he had been there. Port-a-Doris had seemed to him ugly, gloomy, and

sordid, which was remarkable, since it was a kind of show spot, and
supposed to be most picturesque and romantic. You got to it through a
little tunnel in the rocks. There was nothing but a narrow stony
beach, the sea, the black rocks, and a high sloping grassy cliff. Yet
while everybody else was exclaiming how charming it was, Tom had
got an impression of something sinister and depressing. It had been
a most unpleasant feeling, as if a cloud of ugliness, gloom, and evil,
were pressing down upon his mind. And—which was stranger still—
the ugliness was the same kind of ugliness he had seen once in a crude
woodcut Brown had brought to school, showing a man, in a squalid
bedroom, hacking with a razor at the throat of a half-naked woman.

What produced this sense of ugliness, and why should he alone
feel it? It had not been there for Daddy or Mother or Pascoe. Pascoe
had bathed, and while he was still in the water two young lovers had
come along to look for cowrie-shells on the beach. Mother in the end
had got quite cross with Tom because he couldn't help suggesting
every now and again that they should go away. They had brought a
tea-basket with them, and though at last she had given in to his persistence, she had said that she would never go on another picnic with
him. And Tom loved picnics. But not picnics to Port-a-Doris. . . .

While he was thinking these thoughts he kept his gaze fixed on
Danny's face, and old Danny rowed in meditative silence. His eyes
were nearly shut, but what you could see of them was greenish-grey.
He wore an old blue jersey; his hair was white; his face and throat
were mahogany brown. And myriads of little crinkles, fine as threads,
radiated from the corners of his eyes. Tom liked these, perhaps because they showed more clearly when the old man smiled. His smile
made you smile back again, and, though his teeth were very much dis-
coloured, it had all the engaging innocence and immediate friendliness of a baby's.

The sea dropped in glittering showers from Danny's dipping oar-
blades. The blades themselves were hardly wider than the clumsy
shafts. There was a gurgle of water under the floor-boards of the boat
when she tilted, and the mast and the rolled-up patched sails lay along
the bottom under the seats. Danny rarely sailed her except when he
went out fishing at night or across to Magilligan. Perhaps a little
smuggling went on. Pascoe was sure there was a great deal, which
was why Danny had not invited them to go out with him at night,
in spite of several pretty broad hints. The hints had been dropped by

Pascoe, but Tom hadn't bothered, because he was sure that anyway he wouldn't be allowed to go. . . .

The shore glided slowly past: the Manor House glided past; the Fort was gliding past, when Danny rested on his oars and gazed up at it. Pascoe went on reading, but Tom looked up too, though only for a moment, because really he was watching the old fisherman's face. "Strange things do be on the sea at night," Danny pronounced slowly, "and strange things on land. I've seen a light rising out of the sea like a thousand holy burning candles, and I've climbed the hill to Glenagivney and seen a glory of saints and angels in the sky."

"I've seen that too," Tom said, and the old man looked at him kindly.

"You're living up there," he went on mildly, nodding his head towards the Fort. "And I seen a strange sight there too—not so long back."

"Yes," Tom answered softly.

"It was a night it might be two or three weeks ago when I seen it," Danny went on.

"From here?" Tom asked. "From the sea?"

But Danny shook his head. "That night I wasn't on the sea. It was from up yonder—from the castle. I'd been resting my bones there in the early evening, and sleep came on me, and when I woke the moon was up and throwing a light you'd see clearly by it to read a book. But the sight I'm tellin' you of was two figures on the battlement, and one might be like yourself in your night clothes, but the other bigger —and the big one was in his pelt. The little one was ordinary like, but the other had a shining round him that was more than the shining of the moon. Maybe you'll be thinking I had a drop taken, and maybe I had before I lay down. But it had passed off, and I was as sober then as I am now. I didn't offer to rise up from where I was, and I didn't stir hand or foot unless maybe it was to cross myself. Not that there was danger for me or anyone in that shining boy, and him with the beauty of an angel of God. I just looked for while you'd be holding your breath, and then they was gone."

Beyond the old fisherman Tom could see Pascoe, but Pascoe had not even stopped reading.

"I'll take you in here," said the old man pleasantly, "and it'll save you the walk round from the harbour."

He put the boat in close to the rocks, and Tom and Pascoe jumped ashore. But even when they were alone Pascoe made no comment on

Danny's story, though he must have heard it. On the other hand, he didn't know what Tom knew, for Tom had not told him his dream. Interrupted at the time, he had never told it later, so perhaps there wasn't really very much for Pascoe to say.

17: ON the level ground above the rocks they separated, and Tom climbed the path to the kitchen garden of the Fort. He was dining at the Manor House that evening for the first time, and Mother had told him that he must put on a clean shirt and collar and his Sunday clothes—a black jacket and light grey trousers. Miss Pascoe, it seemed, would expect nothing less, though Tom was sure, from the odd glimpses he had caught of her, that she wasn't the kind of person who cared at all about dress. She rarely went outside her own garden, and she must be as old as the hills, being not really Pascoe's aunt but his father's.

Dinner was at seven o'clock and Pascoe himself opened the door when Tom arrived. He gazed at the immaculate attire without comment, but also, Tom felt, without approval, his own appearance being precisely what it had been an hour ago when they had stepped out of Danny McCoy's boat.

"You're in plenty of time," he said. "Aunt Rhoda's having a bath."

Tom, a little disconcerted by this frankness, murmured that he was sorry. "I mean," he explained, "if I'm too early." He *was* on the early side, he knew, and Mother had warned him that he would be. But he hadn't thought it mattered, and anyway Pascoe's greeting ought to have been different.

Pascoe was still taking in the details of the Sunday clothes, when a stout florid gentleman, in a crumpled grey flannel suit, descended the stairs, whistling. He, also, cast a glance at Tom, and then immediately turned to his son. "Now you just run along and dress properly to receive your guest," he said. "This is a civilized country and *somebody* must keep up appearances."

"Come in, come in," he went on breezily to Tom, shaking hands in such a manner as to propel him at the same time into a large, low-ceilinged room. "Run on now," he repeated over his shoulder to the motionless and reluctant Pascoe. Then, shutting the door, he turned to Tom with what was remarkably like a wink, and said: "He'll blame this on you, I expect."

Tom, from the last glimpse he had had of Pascoe's face, thought it very likely, but he couldn't help it and didn't very much mind. He looked about him curiously. This was the drawing-room, he could see, and it contained a frightful lot of furniture—cabinets with glass and china in them, high-backed chairs, and round polished tables. There was a black woolly hearthrug of the kind he liked to lie on, a grey patternless carpet very soft underfoot, a grand piano, an ornamental gilt clock flanked by Dresden china shepherds and shepherdesses, a beautiful Japanese screen in four panels, and a sprinkling of Yorkshire terriers.

"Seven of them," said the wine merchant, who had been closely following Tom's gaze. "Companionable little beasts. Usually find one or two of them on your bed in the morning. There *were* eleven, but she screwed herself up to parting with four. . . . You wait," he went on, with a quick glance at the clock. "It's now ten minutes to seven. You just wait!"

Naturally he would wait, Tom thought; and it seemed to him a strange thing to say, seeing that he had been asked to dinner. But the wine merchant continued to look at the clock as if it held some secret. He had not invited Tom to sit down, and they were both standing facing the chimney-piece when there arose a remarkable though distant noise, as of demons struggling in a cataract. "The bath water," said the wine merchant, cocking an ear. "You'll find this a house of surprises. Makes the deuce of a row, doesn't it! Whole place needs going over from chimneys to drains—particularly the drains—only she won't listen to advice. . . . By the way, we've not met before," he suddenly recollected. "Better introduce ourselves."

"I know who you are, sir," Tom said politely.

"And I know who you are. Call it a draw, and start at scratch. . . . Six minutes now."

It seemed to Tom that the wine merchant was a most unusual person, and especially surprising as the father of Pascoe. Of course Pascoe was unusual too, but not in the same way—not nearly so genial and off-hand.

"You're Clement's great friend, aren't you?" the wine merchant said. "At least, his *only* friend, which mayn't be quite the same thing. I'd ask your opinion of him only I don't believe you'd tell me."

Tom didn't tell him, and the wine merchant hardly gave him an opportunity before he added: "You're having great times, I understand. It's just the place for that. I had great times here myself when I was a boy, and I wouldn't mind having them over again. . . . Three minutes more."

His gaze was still glued to the clock, and Tom found himself staring at it too, though without the faintest comprehension. Even the companionable dogs seemed infected by the mysterious expectancy, for they had gathered round, with their seven little faces lifted.

"Ah!" murmured the wine merchant at last, raising both hands to his ears as the first silvery note of the chiming hour floated out. But one note only was audible, for with that there arose from the seven Yorkshires such a nerve-shattering acclamation as Tom had never heard in his life. They stood in a crescent before the chimney-piece, their heads thrown back, their lungs expanded, and the din while it lasted was appalling. It was all over in less than a minute, however, leaving Tom slightly dazed. The wine merchant withdrew his fingers from his ears, laughed briefly, and looked at him with rueful, comical eyes. "She's trained them to do it," he said apologetically. "Miss Pascoe, I mean."

Tom drew in a breath. "Trained them!" Then, recovering, he added half incredulously: "Every time the clock strikes?"

"Yes," the wine merchant sighed. "Every time. It's their star turn —and there used to be eleven of them."

"Eleven!" Tom echoed.

The wine merchant nodded. "They only do it if they're in this room, you know; but then they usually *are* in this room, except at night. Still, it's a comfort that they don't do it for other clocks. There are clocks all over the house, you see—even in the bathrooms—and few of them agree about the time."

"But how very——" Tom was beginning, and then stopped.

The wine merchant's eyes met his in a glance of complicity mingled with warning. "Unusual—eh?" he suggested. "I'd call it that —till you get home at any rate. The old lady likes you to be surprised, but not anything more. Not a word of criticism, remember: the dogs are sacred. I asked Clement if he had told you about them, and he said he hadn't."

These last words were enlightening; they explained to Tom why he had been brought into the drawing-room with such eagerness. Pascoe's father, he was beginning to think, must be rather an anxiety for Pascoe the son. Perhaps that was why he had not been introduced before, though Pascoe had been on familiar terms with *his* people for ever so long. "No," he said, "he didn't. Maybe *he* wanted me to be surprised too."

The wine merchant looked at him. "D'you think so?" he murmured. "Hardly in his line, I should say. Not the sort of thing he approves of—though he holds his tongue about it because he and his aunt are as thick as thieves. . . . Clement—you know—that was *her* idea. He was Edward at the font—called after me—only better not mention that I told you. The old lady when she began to take an interest in him wanted him to be called after *her*. Difficult, naturally, but luckily she had a second name, Clementina, for if she hadn't she'd have done her best with Rhoda. She's an old lady of character, you see, and what she wants she usually gets."

"Well," Tom exclaimed, "I don't think she'd any right to make a change like that. He's your son, not hers, and I expect you'd have liked him to be Edward."

"Ssh!" the wine merchant cautioned, for there were sounds outside the door, and next moment it opened to admit Miss Pascoe herself, followed by her grand-nephew in the unaccustomed elegance of an Eton suit. The Yorkshires rushed tumultuously to greet their mistress, and, more or less entangled in the group, Tom was introduced.

Aunt Rhoda was a slight, small, and wiry-looking old woman, visibly of extreme energy both of mind and body. Tom had hitherto seen her only from a distance and through bushes, digging in her garden; on which occasions she had been wearing a kind of purple tam-o'-shanter, top-boots, and a very short skirt. She was now wearing a wig, though not with any attempt at deception, since obviously it had been chosen as a compromise between the age she felt and the age she actually was. The wig was piebald, and the small wizened mobile face beneath it reminded Tom irresistibly of a monkey's. The dark, observant eyes, younger than the wig and ever so much younger than the wrinkles, increased this resemblance. And perhaps the strangest thing about it all was that Tom did not think Miss Pascoe ugly. The standard might be simian, but the effect was sympathetic and attractive. She was dressed in black, with a lot of soft black lace at her throat. Her hands, yellow and dry as parchment, were even more wrinkled than her face, but they flashed with emeralds and diamonds, for she wore at least half a dozen rings. She welcomed Tom in the most gracious manner—not without a hint of ceremony —and they went in to dinner, one of Miss Pascoe's jewelled claws resting lightly on the wine merchant's sleeve.

Tom got a nudge in the ribs from his own partner. "What did you want dressing yourself up like that for?" Pascoe whispered. "Now we'll have to sit in the drawing-room all evening, I suppose—looking at picture-books."

"I didn't dress myself up," Tom whispered back.

"You did; you've got on your Sunday things, and that's why I was made to put on mine."

"They look very nice," Tom told him, but Pascoe answered with disgust: "Oh, for goodness' sake! . . . I'd all the stuff ready for a bonfire, too. All the garden rubbish for months and months, and a lot of stuff that's been there for *years!* I got Kerrigan to dump it all over the wall this afternoon, and it's there waiting, about as high as a haystack. You told me you liked bonfires."

"So I do; I love them," Tom replied.

But this muttered conversation was interrupted by the wine merchant's voice, raised from the dining-room: "Come on—come on—you two. What's keeping you out there?"

So they entered, and took their seats, as if no dispute had arisen, both looking very proper and well behaved.

All through dinner Tom received constant attentions from the Yorkshire terriers, who gradually converged in an ever closer circle about his legs. Every time he put his hand down it was met at once by a tongue or a cold damp nose. But nobody minded his feeding them: Miss Pascoe indeed was clearly pleased, and passed him tit-bits from her own plate. In fact it was the nicest dinner-party Tom had ever been at. Both Miss Pascoe and the wine merchant seemed to like him, and were interested in all he said. Not politely interested, but really interested, so that he couldn't help feeling he was a success. In this congenial atmosphere he expanded happily, for it was never difficult to make him talk, though it might be easy enough to shut him up. He talked now—talked quite a lot.

After dinner they returned to the drawing-room, leaving Pascoe's father over his port. But almost immediately he joined them, coffee was brought in, and the wine merchant lit a cigar. Tom, anxious to hear the next performance of the dogs, had looked at the clock the moment he had entered the room. But they had sat so long over dinner—which had been late to begin with—that the hour was past, and he saw he would have to wait until nine. The dogs, indeed, were perfectly aware of this themselves, and seeking the more comfortable chairs, they scattered themselves about the room in attitudes of repose. After one wavering glance at the hearthrug, Tom sat down on a straight, tall, very high-backed chair, probably valuable, and certainly uncomfortable. The Yorkshires had been wiser or more experienced, for Tom's was a chair in which you could only sit bolt upright and look and feel like a graven image. But having once made his choice, he didn't like to change it.

"I hear from Clement that you're a very good singer," Miss Pascoe said to him; "much better than any of the other boys."

"What about going out?" Pascoe immediately called from the window, but was as quickly squashed by the wine merchant.

Tom, himself, thought the interruption rude: Miss Pascoe took no notice of it whatever.

"I should very much like to hear you sing," she went on. "Don't fidget," she suddenly told her nephew, turning round so sharply that Tom was reminded of the albatross. "Clement, I'm sorry to say, takes no interest in music, and has no ear. He must get that from his mother's side, for all our family were musical."

"Mother does like music," Pascoe contradicted. "She likes military bands."

Miss Pascoe ignored this reply. "We were a large family," she continued, lapsing into reminiscence, "and my father had us all taught either to sing or to play some instrument. What he liked best himself was chamber music—trios and quartettes for strings and piano. I used to play the piano parts, and I sang a little too. But my youngest sister sang really well. Her voice wasn't big enough, or perhaps she might have become a professional. But she was sent to London, to have lessons from Tosti."

Tom was at once interested. "I learn from Mr. Holbrook," he said, "but I know one of Tosti's songs—'Serenata.' "

Miss Pascoe had risen from her chair. "The great drawback to living in a place like this is that one has no opportunity to hear music."

"Couldn't you get a gramophone?" Tom suggested, watching her as she went to the piano.

"I don't care for gramophones," Miss Pascoe answered.

Tom was surprised, and wondered how long it was since she had heard one. "Mr. Holbrook says the recording is ever so much better now than it used to be," he ventured, "and it goes on getting better and better."

"I dare say it does," Miss Pascoe agreed, "but even if the records were perfect they could still only repeat themselves, and that's what

I don't like. Every shade of expression coming always in exactly the same place. . . . I wonder now if there's anything here that you know." She opened a box of music and began to rummage amongst it. "My fingers are rather stiff, I expect, but I ought to be able to manage an accompaniment if it's not too difficult. Unfortunately the only songs I have are those my sister used to sing when she was a girl. If I'd thought of it sooner I'd have got you to bring your music with you."

"I couldn't have," said Tom. "We didn't know there'd be a piano in the hotel and didn't bring any music."

"Well," said Miss Pascoe, "just have a look through this, though it's hardly likely that you'll find anything." She brought him a volume bound in limp dark-blue morocco, with the initials "A.F.P." stamped in gilt letters on the front cover.

Tom took it on his knee and turned over the pages, glancing at the words more than at the notes.

"List, pilgrim, list! 'tis the harp in the air."

"The green trees whispered low and mild."

"Stay, stay at home, my heart, and rest."

All were unknown to him, forgotten drawing-room ballads, much more old-fashioned even than Mother's songs, and the paper was quite yellow. Yet, as he turned the leaves, a faint music seemed to float out into the air, thin and ghostly, like the tinkling notes of a musical-box.

"Say, must ye fade, beautiful flowers. . . . Stars of the earth, why must ye away? Stars of the earth, why must ye away?" Absent-mindedly he glanced over it, till something familiar in the rhythm arrested his attention. He looked then at the notes, and, though his ability to read music was rudimentary, he knew these notes, and turned back to the title and the composer's name on the front page. The title was strange to him, but the composer was Donizetti, and, in small letters underneath, the title Tom knew was given, with the name of the opera, *La Favorita*.

"I know this," he cried, strangely pleased by his discovery, which was like the finding of an old friend. "Only I don't know these words. But the music's the same."

"Let me see," said Miss Pascoe curiously, as she stooped over his shoulder.

"Mr. Holbrook made me sing it in Italian," Tom continued; "but

I don't think this is a translation. In fact it can't be; it doesn't mean the same thing at all."

"Dear me," murmured Miss Pascoe, "what an accomplished little boy you are!"

Tom blushed. "It's not that," he protested hurriedly. "It's just that Mr. Holbrook likes the sound of the Italian words, and so I learn them off by heart."

Miss Pascoe had taken the book from him. "Of course!" she exclaimed abruptly. "It's from an opera. . . . The tune was a favourite with my father, and he used to play it on the fiddle. . . . Do you think you can remember *your* words?"

"Oh, yes," said Tom. "It's the last song I learned."

The wine merchant was puffing at his cigar in friendly silence; Pascoe was silent too; and Miss Pascoe smiled at Tom. "Shall we try it?" she asked, returning to the piano. "But I'd better just run over the accompaniment first to see how it goes."

Tom complied at once, and leaving his chair, crossed the room to stand beside her.

Aunt Rhoda's beringed hands looked strangely ancient and withered on the ivory keys, he thought, but she needed no glasses to read the music, and she played quite well. Not with the careless assurance of Mr. Holbrook, naturally, who could improvise an accompaniment if he didn't know the right one, but certainly better than Mother.

Pascoe came over from the window to get a closer view of the performance, and Tom frowned at him to go away. He wished Pascoe wasn't in the room at all, because, though he didn't mind in the least singing to Aunt Rhoda and the wine merchant, Pascoe made him nervous. Especially when he came so near and stared solemnly like an owl. Tom frowned again, but it had no effect.

Meanwhile Aunt Rhoda played the four introductory bars. "Now," she murmured—just like Mr. Holbrook.

Tom moistened his lips with the tip of his tongue, opened his mouth, and then suddenly spluttered: "I can't if you keep on staring at me."

These words were not addressed to Miss Pascoe; nevertheless the accompaniment stopped as abruptly as if they had been. "Come away, Clement," called the wine merchant from the other side of the room, and Pascoe obeyed. The accompaniment began again.

Tom tried to think he was singing to Mr. Holbrook. He shut out the others from his mind; shut out the room; shut out everything but the sound of the piano—plaintive, soft, and clear. There was just the slightest pause, and then:

Spirto gentil. ne' sogni miei brillasti un dì,

ma ti perdei, fuggi dal cor. mentita speme,

larve d'amor. larve d'amor. fuggite insieme. larve d'amor!

He loved the sound of it—caressing and sad—the floating, liquid curves of sound, lingering like a pattern drawn on the air; then melting away. . . .

"You sing beautifully, dear, and perfectly in tune," said Miss Pascoe when he had finished, her hands still resting on the keyboard. "Doesn't he, Edward?"

"Like a lark," the wine merchant agreed, relighting his cigar, which had gone out during the performance.

Tom felt flattered and pleased. He thought he had sung well, and he would have liked to go on and sing better still, with such an appreciative audience, but Pascoe approached and drew him firmly by the sleeve towards the door. Tom had to go; anyway it was most unlikely that he knew another of Miss Pascoe's songs; he was very lucky to have found even one.

Pascoe led him into the hall and closed the door behind them. "Come on up," he said. "I'm going to change, and then we'll light the bonfire."

They went up to his room, where Tom sat on the bed, while Pascoe hastily removed the Etons and got into his everyday clothes. He had two boxes of matches, one of which he presented to Tom; and as they ran downstairs Tom could hear Miss Pascoe still playing over softly the air he had sung.

The moment they opened the hall-door the sound of the waves

reached them, but the evening had clouded over, and a gusty breeze was blowing from the sea.

"There's the stuff," said Pascoe, pointing to two heaps of garden refuse—one of them much larger than the other. "We'll light the small one; it's as dry as timber; and pile on the other by degrees. You light this end and I'll light that."

They wasted a few matches in their hurry, but soon a thin blue smoke, accompanied by a light crepitating noise, rose waveringly into the air. The foundation, however, was so dry and inflammable that almost at once it burst into a blaze. The danger was that it might burn itself out too rapidly, but there was a pile of fir-cuttings, and these caught too. Using the pitch-forks which Kerrigan had left for them, Tom and Pascoe built up their pyre, working as hard as they could, while the flames rushed up, licking the air and dropping round them in scarlet flakes. Then, before they knew what was happening, a gust of wind swept the flames backwards, and with a rushing, roaring sound, their whole store ignited. A clear blinding sheet of golden flame leapt at them, and so quickly that they had barely time to jump back. There was no more stoking to be done, everything was burning at once, and for a minute or two, even to Tom, it was rather terrifying.

Pascoe was in an agony. "I hope the old wall doesn't go!" he cried, beating with his fork at descending showers of sparks, while Tom stood rooted to the spot in a kind of trance. The whole house was lit up—and the shore, and the rocks, and the edge of the sea.

"You're doing nothing!" screamed Pascoe, who was still making desperate and futile efforts to keep the surrounding bushes from catching, though the heat was too intense for him to get near the actual fire. Tom beat out a few sparks, but it was useless, they could do nothing, and he dropped his fork. He retreated a few paces, and then stood still, lost in a rapture that was dreamy yet exultant. Through it, after a while, he became dimly aware of other figures, other voices, than Pascoe's—the wine merchant's, Aunt Rhoda's—and all the voices sounded excited, and the wine merchant's angry. But Tom was only half conscious of them, like far-off sounds heard in a dream. The growing brambles and furze-bushes had caught now: it looked as if the whole shore would soon be ablaze. And the shifting uncertain wind swayed the fire sometimes towards him, and sometimes away. Through the smooth, rushing sound there came numerous explosions; blazing fragments fell; and showers of sparks floated far and wide like burning rain. . . .

The fire seemed to have divided Tom from the Pascoe family. It had thrust them back to an immense distance; they were no more than gesticulating marionettes. They were outside his world, but the fire was in his world. He heard the seagulls crying, and a startled rabbit ran almost over his feet. The whole world was burning, with bright wings of flame that rushed up the sky, while far above Tom's head, pale and remote and spectral, a white moon hovered like a gigantic moth, appearing and disappearing as the clouds drifted across it.

The red flare reached no further than the foam at the edge of the sea, but it was still increasing, and the flames were still mounting higher. Kerrigan and another man had now appeared, and they and the two Pascoes were exerting every effort to keep the fire from spreading through the garden inside. But Tom did not notice this till a dense cloud of white steam suddenly hissed up. Then he saw what was happening; they had turned on a hose; and in a minute or two the enchantment was ended. To Tom it was like the slaying of a beautiful great beast. The beast—a dragon—still heaved its rosy coils here and there, but they were dying rapidly, and as they died they sank back in an ashen grey. Soon only smoke and cinders and steam were left—charred black branches and sodden ashes—while the vanished colour-notes of dim green and bronze crept back into the evening landscape.

Then, and not till then, did Tom really awaken to the disaster. At the same time he felt his arm grasped and shaken; and an angry voice almost sobbed into his ear: "Why didn't you help? There's going to be the most frightful row about this. All Aunt Rhoda's ramblers are burnt, and the trellises with them."

"Are they?" said Tom, beginning to feel a little scared. "I don't think they can *all* be burnt."

"All that were on this side of the garden," Pascoe wailed. "She's pretty mad about it, I can tell you, and Daddy's worse. You'd better go home. There's no use your saying good-night to them; they saw that you didn't do a thing."

Tom shook off Pascoe's hand. He hadn't done much, he knew; but what *could* he have done? He made a detour, with Pascoe gloomily following him, and then scrambled over the low wall into the garden. The remains of the fire had been beaten down, but the flattened mass of embers still glowed dangerously when the wind swept over it, and Kerrigan was still plying the hose. Tom walked straight up to Miss Pascoe and the wine merchant, who watched his approach in silence. He didn't know what to say, and, since nobody else spoke, in the end he held out his hand to Miss Pascoe, murmuring involuntarily: "Thank you very much for a pleasant evening."

The wine merchant coughed, and Miss Pascoe replied rather grimly: "I'm glad you enjoyed it, though I suppose we ought to thank you and Clement for the chief entertainment."

"I'm sorry about the garden," Tom said uncomfortably. Dusk hid the full extent of the ravages, but he could see that they had been considerable.

"Yes, we're all sorry about that," the wine merchant put in; and for a moment or two they stood looking at each other—Tom with very grave and serious eyes.

"It was an accident," he said.

"But it made a fine show—eh? Clement, I'm afraid, will have to be more careful in future about the pleasures he arranges for his friends. Something a little less Neronic perhaps."

Miss Pascoe's dark eyes, very bright in the small wizened face, had been all this time fixed on Tom in a close scrutiny. "Do you know, I believe the child was hypnotized!" she now abruptly exclaimed. "He *was!* You can see it!" She gave a sudden little cackle of laughter which astonished everybody, though it drew a sigh of relief from the depressed Pascoe.

"Come in," she cried, grasping Tom's arm tightly. "You must have some supper before you go home. The men can look after the wreckage." And she drew him towards the house, leaving the wine merchant and Pascoe to follow.

"Are you really sorry?" she questioned, peering at him curiously; "because I never saw anybody who *looked* more rapt in enjoyment. Tell me the truth, please; it's the least you can do."

"I'm sorry *now*," Tom told her. "I'm very sorry about your garden. But at the time I don't think I was sorry. I mean I *did* enjoy it."

"Well, you gave *me* something to enjoy when you sang to me," Miss Pascoe answered, "so perhaps we'd better leave it at that."

"Would you like me to sing again?" Tom asked her.

Miss Pascoe laughed quickly. "Yes, I would," she said. "I'd like you to sing that song again before you go. Then you'll be able to tell your mother that the evening was a complete success." She gave his arm a sudden squeeze that was almost a pinch as she spoke; adding however, with just the faintest sigh: "She'll require all the assurance you can give her, I expect. That is, if she happens to look over my wall to-morrow morning."

PART THREE

18: A PECULIAR thing was, that though it had several times occurred to Tom that he might be asked to stay on at the Manor House after Mother's and Daddy's departure, and return with Pascoe at the end of the holidays, this evidently had occurred to nobody else. Or perhaps it had, and they didn't want him. At any rate, whatever the cause, no invitation had been given; yet the wine merchant was gone, and even if he had been still there, there must be heaps of empty rooms.

Nor was it much good, he found, trying to make the most of his last two days. They weren't days at all; he had no sooner got up than it was time to go to bed again. Possibly these days contained, as usual, twenty-four hours, but it was difficult to believe it. Time was a cheat. If you watched the hands of the clock you could hardly see them moving, but the moment you turned your back and got interested in anything they simply raced. Breakfast—a bathe—and then the clatter of the lunch bell to announce that the day was half over. And always a melancholy feeling that there were only so many hours more; with gaps—great empty blanks—to be deducted for sleep.

On the last night of all, as he looked out of his window before getting into bed, he saw that it had begun to rain. Not heavily, but a feeling of gathering rain was in the air—the weather was breaking. And then, with a sudden pang of conscience, Tom realized the frightful selfishness of his thought. He couldn't help the thought, but he could make amends for it by adding a special petition for fine weather to his prayers, and he did this, leaving the rest to Providence.

When he awoke the sun was shining brilliantly. Part of his prayer at least had been answered, if not the Aunt Rhoda part. The whole place was looking its best, and the knowledge that he would be leaving it in another hour or two added to its attractiveness. He dressed and went downstairs. He almost wished that they were starting at once, for he had a feeling of restlessness, which nevertheless wasn't in the least like the restlessness he had felt when they were leaving home. It had no excitement in it: he merely felt unsettled. . . .

At breakfast both Daddy and Mother were fussy. Practically all the packing had been done overnight; only the last few things remained to be put in; and directly the meal was finished Mother went upstairs to do this while Daddy waited to pay the bill. Tom went out into the garden.

He expected Pascoe, but no Pascoe appeared. Presently the luggage was brought down and stowed away in the car. This was too sad to watch, so Tom hung over the wall and looked down at the sea. He imagined Pascoe running in at the last minute with an invitation from Aunt Rhoda. That would be a real answer to his prayer—far more to the point than all this sunshine. "Come along, Tom, and get your coat on," Daddy called out; while Mother asked, as he slowly approached: "Are you sure you've left nothing behind you?"

Yes, Tom was sure. He put on his cap and his overcoat. Here was the lunch-basket—a good big one—for they were going to picnic by the roadside. Then came the last good-byes, shakings of hands, prognostications for next year—which might or might not come true, and anyhow were cold comfort—and he took his place beside Mother in the seat behind. The door slammed; more waving of hands; Daddy started cautiously, yet for all that managed to uproot a croquet hoop with the left back wheel as he turned the sharp corner through the gateway.

But it was better now that the journey had begun. Strange, however, that Pascoe hadn't turned up. He had said he would: he must have overslept himself. Tom pictured him enviously, with the whole long summer day before him—nearly a fortnight before him. Lucky Pascoe! And there he was, racing down the road, waving and shouting! Tom waved, so did Mother, but Daddy wouldn't stop. How pleasant it would be if by some miracle Daddy and Mother, like Saint Paul, were suddenly to be converted, change their minds, and decide to stay on for another week. Only it was too late now, he supposed: their rooms would have been taken. . . .

They drove on—past the Post Office—through the village—past Danny McCoy's cottage—nothing before them now but the empty road.

"Well, so far so good!" Daddy remarked, with what seemed to Tom an unnecessary air of joviality.

The statement wasn't even true, so he found a faint pleasure in contradicting it. "I've forgotten my bathing things," he said.

The car slowed down. Tom knew he had been pretty careless, but somehow his mood was not apologetic. "And I particularly *asked* you if you'd got everything!" Mother exclaimed. "Besides going through all your drawers myself."

Bathing things weren't usually put in a drawer, Tom thought, but he kept this to himself. "I know," he said. "They weren't in my room; they were on the garden wall, drying. And I've left my racquet up in the tower; and the tennis balls are there too, and my tennis shoes."

Daddy laughed, but Mother didn't. She told him he was the most provoking boy she had ever met, adding in a tone of resignation: "I suppose we'll have to go back." Daddy turned the car.

This time he didn't bring it in to the Fort, but waited at the side of the road, and Tom had to run on by himself and make his collection. The place was deserted; everybody had disappeared— gone golfing, or bathing, or whatever the morning's programme might be. He wouldn't think about it: it was too depressing. He got his things and returned to the car.

The second start was accomplished without spectators or good wishes. Tom had a flat sort of feeling, as he scrambled back into his seat, that the Fort and all connected with it belonged to the past.

He was not in a talkative mood; neither was Mother; and Daddy never talked while he was driving. Mother made an occasional re- mark, but only of the kind to which you answered "yes" or "no" out of politeness. Nor were they even remarks about the recent holi- days, but about home matters, about Phemie and Mary, and the hour of arrival. Tom leaned up against her, snuggling into the most com- fortable position he could find.

The journey was uneventful, and even on the barest and straightest stretches Daddy demonstrated clearly that he was not one of our Speed Kings. "Step on it!" Tom urged him, but the request was re- ceived and intended merely as a mild little joke. They were not a motoring family; Mother probably came nearest to it of the three.

Towards one o'clock they began to look out for a suitable place to have lunch—eventually drawing up in a lane. It proved, however, to be less suitable than had at first appeared, for they had scarcely un- packed the basket before the car was surrounded by an audience of released schoolchildren. "They all look so hungry, too!" Mother ex- claimed, torn between compassion and a desire for privacy. "Give that little girl a sandwich, Tom."

"If they're hungry, it's only because it's their dinner time," Daddy said unsentimentally. "They're perfectly ordinary, well-nourished, greedy children."

Mother, nevertheless, insisted on distributing cake and bananas to those she fancied—a most unfair arrangement, Tom considered—for obviously there wasn't enough to go round, and he could see the little boys were getting nothing. He gave the last banana to a boy of his own size.

During the second part of the drive he felt pleasantly sleepy, and it was only when Mother began to recognize landmarks that he sat up and looked out. They were within a few miles of home now, and as the road grew more and more familiar Tom's alertness increased. Soon they were within walking distance, and a few minutes later the car slackened speed before turning in at their own gate. The journey was over.

And there was William—there was everything in fact—looking exactly as if they had never been away. William had cut the grass, too, and marked the tennis court, which was surprising. All the windows in the front of the house were open.

Mary must have been on the look-out, for she was at the hall-door before Tom could scramble from the car. Mother and Daddy were slower. Then Phemie appeared, and William began to take out the luggage. Mother went straight on into the house, but Daddy, William, Mary, and Phemie collected bags and suitcases before following her. Tom brought up the rear, carrying Daddy's golf-clubs.

The first thing he did on entering the hall was to look at the clock. It had stopped. He left the golf-bag in the cloakroom and came out to have another look. Yes, it had stopped—and at three minutes to twelve. "Three minutes before midnight," he added darkly to himself, though he knew it was just as likely to have been three minutes before noon. And it didn't really matter anyhow; all that mattered was that from three minutes to twelve on a certain day or night the house had been left unguarded.

Everybody else had gone upstairs carrying luggage; Tom was left alone in the hall. He had wound up the clock once before and he determined to wind it again. But he must act swiftly, before Daddy came down: the clock might have something to tell him in private. He opened the door; he wound the clock and started the pendulum; then he stepped back and looked inquiringly at the round mild face. The clock regarded Tom with an air of recognition, but it said nothing. It really *did* look different from the way it had looked a minute ago. Its ticking, too, seemed laden with unconfided secrets. If only it would hurry up, for time was so important! Here was Tom back again! it ticked; and doubtless it would be as well that he should know what had taken place during his absence—certain things, certain doings, more than odd. At any rate he would be able to judge of that for himself. The clock cleared its throat and——

Of course Wliliam must appear and spoil everything! Down the stairs he came clumping, and didn't pass on, but stopped beside Tom. "You've set her going again, Master Tom," he observed. "You weren't long!"

"It's not 'her,' it's 'him,' " answered Tom rather crossly, as the clock discreetly struck twelve in the perfectly conventional manner of ordinary clocks. William waited till the last note had sounded. "No," he then said, "clocks is always 'her'; same as boats. You haven't moved the hands: it should be eight minutes past four." He had spoiled everything anyway, Tom thought, and he was sure the opportunity would never occur again. It *couldn't*; he didn't know why, but he felt sure that it couldn't. This had been the one chance, and it had been wasted.

Meanwhile Daddy's head appeared over the banisters. "Leave that clock alone, Tom. How often have I told you not to touch it!"

"I just wound it up," Tom explained guiltily, "just to save you the trouble."

But he sighed directly afterwards. There must be a doom upon this house. He had only been back about five minutes, and already he had told a lie and begun thinking in the old way. "Where's Henry?" he asked William gloomily.

"I've hardly set eyes on him, Master Tom; not since yous all left. He's taken to running wild, though he comes home for his food and it's always gone in the morning. Once or twice I got him sleeping up in the loft when I'd left some boards that he could climb up by, and one evening, after dayligh' gone, I see him along the loanin' that takes you up by the old churchyard. There's a wheen o' rabbits there and he'd likely be hunting them."

"I just thought he wasn't here," Tom answered, frowning. "I knew it the minute we arrived."

William reassured him. "Oh, he'll be back, Master Tom; you needn't fear that. He'll know when the family gets home: cats always knows."

"If he knew, he should have been here to meet us," Tom said.

"Give him time, give him time," William muttered. Then with a renewed sense of social requirements: "Did you enjoy your holidays, Master Tom? I suppose you'd be bathing three and four times a day."

Tom gave him a quick look. "I bathed once a day," he replied suspiciously, for William before now had been known to attempt a joke.

And even that, he reflected, as he accompanied William out on to the lawn, was an exaggeration; there had been coldish days when he hadn't bathed at all.

He did not stay with William, but began a tour of inspection which brought him to the yard, and eventually up to his play-loft. Everything seemed undisturbed, from the cobwebs to the mice—for a tell-tale rustle reached his ears. His paper man was still there, lying on the floor. But he was no longer spotless, he was marked all over with Henry's footprints. Tom stood looking down at him, and then, moved by a superstitious impulse, lifted the paper and tore it into fragments. He was about to throw these fragments away when a second thought occurred to him. He climbed down the ladder, made a little heap of paper on the cobblestones, and lit the heap with one of Pascoe's matches. "Why had he done this?" he asked himself, as he watched the paper burning. . . . All the same, he knew the answer.

He returned to the house, for it must be nearly tea time, and went on up to his own room. Mother and Daddy were still in *their* room, and through the not-quite-closed door he could hear them talking. Tom sat down on the side of the bed.

He was perfectly *certain* that Henry had been in his room. All was as he had left it, except that his suitcase was on the floor and the windows were as wide open as they would go. Also there were clean sheets on the bed, clean pillowcases, clean pyjamas, clean towels—everything was spotless, and yet he knew Henry had been here—and not once only, but repeatedly, perhaps every day.

Suddenly Mother appeared in the doorway. "Where have you been, and why aren't you getting ready for tea? Mary says she found your room in an awful state. Birds must have got into the chimney. The grate was full of soot, and there was even soot on the carpet and on the bed, though how it can have got *there* is a mystery. Anyway, the chimney will have to be swept. I told Mary to telephone about it, so if you hear unusual sounds in the morning, you'll know what they are."

"It wasn't birds, it was Henry," answered Tom, with complete conviction.

Mother laughed; she even called out the joke to Daddy.

But Tom could see nothing to laugh at. "Birds don't build nests at this time of year," he told her; "and a bird wouldn't get on to the bed even if it did come down the chimney. Besides, it would have been there for Mary to see, it isn't very likely to have found its way *up* again!"

"It may have been an old nest," Mother answered rather wildly. Then, noting his expression: "At all events there's no need to look so worried about it. What's the matter? Why are you looking so glum? Surely it's not because we're home again. You didn't expect to stay on at the Fort for ever!"

"No," said Tom, "of course not."

"And if Pascoe got staying longer, he didn't *come* till after you did."

"It's not that," cried Tom, repudiating indignantly such a suggestion. "As if I cared how long Pascoe stayed! It's nothing to do with Pascoe."

"What has it to do with then? Why won't you tell me—instead of scolding me?"

Tom smiled. "Well, I will tell you. . . . Whisper."

Mother bent down her head, and he first kissed her cheek, and next put his mouth to her ear. Then he blew.

"Don't!" cried Mother, who particularly disliked this trick and had told him so before. She gave him a push, half annoyed and half relieved. "You're a little humbug," she said. But her voice sounded reassured, and Tom himself, a minute or two later, was whistling and singing while he washed his face and hands.

19:    THOUGH he could only extract a sort of half-promise from Mother that she *might* play tennis later on if she didn't feel too tired, Tom put up the net, cleaned the balls by rubbing them on the back of the doormat, and begged Phemie to be punctual with dinner because the evenings were getting so short. Then he changed into his white flannels, hoping that this would make it more difficult for Mother to refuse.

She didn't refuse, in spite of Daddy, who seemed to want her to, and asked in the most dubious tone: "*Are* you going to play? I should have thought you'd done enough!"

"So I have," Mother replied, "but I don't expect it will kill me."

Tom was pleased—though not with Daddy naturally. As for Mother, he couldn't see what she had done except sit in the car and afterwards unpack, both of which he had done himself. He hustled her out as fast he could. "Rough or smooth?" he called.

"Rough," Mother said, "and don't be knocking the balls over the wire netting or else I'll stop."

"I must play my ordinary game," Tom replied; and Mother said: "That's not anybody's ordinary game, and it's when you're fielding the balls that you usually do it. So remember I've warned you!"

Tom promised to be careful.

They played two sets, Mother winning the first easily, because Tom found that he was off his game. While announcing this he couldn't help wondering what one's game was? *His* appeared to be something that happened about twice a season. He won the second set however—not without suspicions. He didn't often win—except against Pascoe, who was putrid—and in spite of the bad light, which certainly was in his favour, he didn't feel that his performance had been brilliant. "Of course I was trying," Mother assured him, but he didn't believe she'd been trying very hard. She could be quite good when she liked, and used to play in tournaments before she was married. He balanced his racquet on the end of one finger—a sign that the tennis was over. "Why are people who are rotten at games called rabbits?" he asked her; but she didn't know why.

There must be a reason, all the same: or at least there must have been a reason the first time the term was used. Tom began to let down the net, his mind still running on the question of rabbits, and how they could have earned their unathletic reputation. Why rabbits any more than hedgehogs? Rabbits were rather lively as a matter of fact; he'd watched them himself, in the evenings, from the battlements of the Fort. Besides, the only game *any* animals played was tig, which required no skill. Except cats, perhaps, who played a sort of one-sided socker if they could get a ball, and were obviously good at it—quick as lightning. . . .

He imagined a very small tennis court, with a low net, and four rabbits contesting a final. All round were the spectators—a motley gathering—not only rabbits, but ducks, squirrels, seagulls, several fox-terriers, a bulldog, and a polecat. The babel of encouragement was amazing. . . .

Mother, who was watching him and waiting patiently, at this point asked: "What is the problem?"

Tom finished his task and straightened himself. "Nothing. Only a tournament," he explained. "The bulldog was the umpire and they didn't dare to dispute any of his decisions. When he thought a rally had gone on long enough he just said 'Out!' and they had to stop."

"Well, come along," Mother murmured, without seeking further enlightenment.

But at supper, and apropos of nothing, she suddenly declared: "I've been thinking it over, and I've made up my mind that it would be the greatest mistake possible to send Tom as a boarder. It wouldn't do at all."

Daddy was so taken by surprise that he nearly spilled his tea. "But, my dear!" he expostulated, "it's all settled. And he's only to go as a weekly boarder, which means that you'll have him at home on Saturdays and Sundays. Mr. Rouse was particularly urgent about it. Actually, what he would like is to do away with day-boys altogether: he told me so. Besides, it's not as if Tom would be going to a school where he knew nobody. Pascoe will be in the same House with him."

"Pascoe isn't Tom," Mother answered briefly.

Daddy couldn't deny this, so he put the matter from a different angle. "There's the distance to be considered," he pointed out, "and the time it would take. Going to and from school, Tom would have to travel twelve miles every day—and right through the centre of town."

"Of course he'll have his dinner at school," Mother said, "and most of the way he'll be in the tram. . . . I don't pretend it's ideally convenient," she added, yielding the point, "but the only alternative would be for us to move."

"Or for Tom to go as a weekly boarder," Daddy repeated. "It's really a concession on Mr. Rouse's part to allow him to come home for the week-ends; the other boys only get the half-term holiday, and that's all Pascoe will be getting. . . . Also," he went on, "Tom would have to catch two trams, which means an extra delay, and there's the walk from our house to the terminus."

"I know," Mother admitted. "As I say, it's not ideal. We'll have to wait and see how it turns out. But he needn't always go in the tram. On fine days he could ride to school on a bicycle, and in that case he needn't go near town. If he went by the road under the Castlereagh Hills it would be just as short—probably shorter. I suppose you'll have to speak to Mr. Rouse about it at once, but I shouldn't think he'd raise any difficulties. . . . At all events," she added firmly, "even if he *is* silly about it, it can't be helped. We're certainly not going to send Tom as a boarder simply because Mr. Rouse wants to do away with day-boys. For one thing the idea's absurd. As if the people living round about the school—some of them within a stone's throw of it—are going to send their sons as boarders because of Mr. Rouse's fads!"

Daddy sighed. "I've spoken to him already, as you know; and it's a little late in the day to go back on arrangements that have actually been made."

"Made by you and Mr. Rouse," Mother reminded him. "*I* never approved of the plan."

"You agreed to it at the time, when we first talked it over."

"You mean I was bullied into it," Mother corrected.

"Bullied!" poor Daddy exclaimed.

"Well, argued—it comes to the same thing: I never liked the idea or no arguments would have been necessary. And as for being too late to change—that's nonsense. People must have time to think things over. If Mr. Rouse doesn't want to take Tom as a day-boy he needn't, but I suppose I know more about my own son than he does. . . . However, if you like I'll speak to him myself: it might be better if I did."

"Why?" Daddy inquired, raising his eyebrows.

"Well, I only mean if you don't care to do it."

"If anybody is to speak to him," Daddy said in an offended voice, "I should think I'm the proper person."

"I think so, too," Mother at once agreed. "I merely suggested doing it myself because I'm not in the least in awe of Mr. Rouse."

"Neither am I," Daddy replied.

"I should hope not!" said Mother.

This left Daddy silent, but he looked neither convinced nor pleased. "He'll think it most peculiar," he presently began again, evidently thinking so himself—"as if we didn't know our own minds."

"Perhaps," Mother murmured. "But I don't see really that it matters very much *what* he thinks. He'll have nothing to do with Tom after their first interview."

"I don't mind trying it," Tom at this juncture put in obligingly.

It was a pretty safe speech, of course, and he knew this or perhaps he wouldn't have made it. Mother took no notice of it whatever, but Daddy immediately chirped up. "You see!" he said.

"Yes, I see," Mother answered dryly. And there, for the time, discussion ended.

Tom really was extremely pleased—especially about the bicycle. The only drawback to the plan was in relation to Pascoe. It was a bit rough on Pascoe undoubtedly, and he'd have to write and tell him at once. Most of Tom's own nervousness about going as a boarder had been removed by the knowledge that Pascoe would be going too, and Pascoe might have had similar feelings. On the other hand he mightn't; certainly he'd never expressed them. Pascoe was about the least nervous person Tom knew. In his own way he was just as tough as Brown—tougher in fact, for Brown, Tom suspected, would cut a much less dashing and self-confident figure if he happened to get among boys different from himself, whereas nothing could alter Pascoe. The lucky thing for Brown was that there always *were* boys like himself, and always a majority of them.

Mother's sudden decision, none the less, puzzled him. He knew she would get her own way in the end, but, like Daddy, he felt that Mr. Rouse might be annoyed. And he couldn't imagine what had made her change. It couldn't be because of anything he had said to her, for he had accepted the fact that he was to go as a boarder without protest, and had even, in more optimistic moments, thought he might like it. At any rate the prospect hadn't troubled him much. Not really —not deeply. He had always known that if he *dis*liked it—that is to say, if he was actually unhappy—neither Daddy or Mother would force him to stay on.

The mystery behind Mother's change of plan, however, was a good deal less important than the change of plan itself, and it was in a very contented frame of mind that Tom went up to bed. Soon Daddy and Mother came up also, but he did not hear them, for by that time he was sleeping peacefully.

Another hour or two passed, and perhaps now the sleep was not so peaceful. A watcher—a guardian angel—Gamelyn—might have noted that every now and again he stirred uneasily—might have heard something broken and uneasy in his breathing. Presently his face began to twitch, and then his hands. Something louder than a sigh, yet not loud enough to be a moan, coming from his own throat, almost awakened him, but apparently did not change the nature of his dream. Then a sudden noise that was neither sigh nor moan, and quite outside the dream, did awaken him—and with a start.

He sat up and switched on the light, while the noise continued—a

violent scuffling in the chimney. That was no bird; that was Henry—
Henry surprised and very angry, because he had fallen into the trap
Tom had set for him. Henry seemed to think it a trap anyhow,
though all Tom had done was to pull down the iron flap and thus
close the opening over the grate. Henry had come down, had found
the way unexpectedly barred, and was now swearing at this and at the
difficulty of getting up again. Not that Tom could hear him swearing; but the row he was making showed that he was far from accepting the situation calmly.

Defeat it certainly was, and presently the sounds of scuffling grew
fainter, and at last they ceased. About thirty seconds afterwards a
wild caterwauling burst out from all directions—from the window-
sill, from the garden below, and from the roof above. "Gracious!"
Tom cried, springing out of bed and running to the window. Two
grey shapes that were actually looking in at once vanished, but down
on the lawn there was light enough for him to distinguish other
shapes—at least a dozen of them. And he wasn't the only one to be
awakened either, for he heard a window going up and Daddy's voice
"shooing" at the invaders. There was an immediate stillness, as of
silent parley, but no retreat; the invaders remained obstinately at
their posts—a whole line of them. This was more than Tom could
stand. A martial spirit flamed up in him; he rushed from his room
and down the stairs; grabbed a walking-stick of Daddy's, and hurriedly unbarred the door. Out into the garden he ran, while the
enemy fled before him. In a trice there was not a cat visible; but Tom
continued the pursuit—shouting and flourishing his stick—beating
the shrubs with it, but without raising a single opponent. Next he
heard Daddy's voice calling to him from the porch. Daddy too had
come down, though he had waited to put on slippers and a dressing-
gown.

Tom in a fever of excitement returned to the house. Daddy himself seemed astonished at what had happened, and together they went
upstairs. The light was on in Mother's and Daddy's room, so Tom
popped in his head. "Did you ever hear anything like it?" he spluttered. "And it *was* Henry who came down my chimney. He came
down again to-night; only I shut it before I went to bed, so he got
caught!"

Mother was now sitting up. "Do you mean to say he's still in the
chimney?" she asked. "You must let him out at once. If he's been
struggling there all this time, goodness knows what he'll be like!"

"Oh, he's *out!*" cried Tom. "He's away over the roof; but he had to *climb* up!"

"Are you sure he's out?" Mother questioned unbelievingly. "You'd better open the chimney and see."

"Quite sure. I heard him. But it was he who brought the others. Just imagine it! That's what the place has been like the whole time we were away!"

Tom's eyes were round and shining. Mother had begun to laugh, however. "Yes, dear; don't get so excited about it! I suppose now you'll lie awake for the rest of the night. Dry your feet, at all events, before you get back into bed."

He left them, but he could hear her and Daddy still talking as he returned to his room. He *was* excited, but he also felt justified, and on the whole triumphant. Perhaps *this* would give them an inkling of the truth! At any rate, if they didn't now see what Henry was really like, they never would!

20: HAVING given himself away so completely—for this was no mere outburst of ill-temper such as had led to the scratching of Phemie—Henry, for all Tom could see, might now do the most reckless things. He had shown his hand, or perhaps it would be more accurate to say that an accident had shown it. Henry's cards had all tumbled on the floor face upwards, with a startling display of trumps and aces; and though he might try to gather them up again, in the hope that they'd be forgotten, this hope was a pretty poor one. Or at least it ought to have been poor; only with players so guileless and inexperienced as Daddy and Mother nobody could tell what would happen. They seemed incapable of grasping anything beyond the fact that Henry had made a few friends, and Mother still clung to the idea of birds in the chimney—in pursuit of whom, apparently, Henry had made his descent. That is to say, if he ever *had* made one; for, to Tom's astonishment, next morning saw her provokingly sceptical on the point.

Daddy, it is true, didn't think much of the "birds in the chimney" theory; but Daddy's own theory, that Henry simply had found a way of getting in and out of the house during their absence, though obviously the right one, didn't lead him to the right conclusions. It led him instead to several anecdotes in which cats who had been removed to new homes performed extraordinary feats of pedestrianism in order to get back to their old ones. This was to prove to Tom that Henry in coming down the chimney had merely acted after his kind; the attachment cats conceived for places being notorious. And when Tom reminded him of the army Henry had recruited, he got out of that difficulty too. Such feline gatherings were also in character. Daddy remembered how, when he was a boy, the lawn of an empty house next door to theirs was the recognized meeting-place of every cat in the neighbourhood; so that frequently he had been sent out by his mother to disperse them, just as Tom had done last night. Henry's food and milk, too, left in the porch for him every day by William, might well have proved an additional attraction.

These and similar remarks, made while he and Tom were working in the garden next morning, showed that Daddy misunderstood the entire situation. Tom did not express *his* view, but he did admit that he wasn't particularly fond of Henry, which Daddy thought strange, seeing that he had always shown so marked a sympathy with animals. Daddy mentioned several early examples of this which Tom himself had forgotten. They were childish certainly—things one would conceal from Pascoe, for instance—but Tom found them amusing. On the whole he and Daddy passed a very pleasant morning.

It was a queer kind of day—warm, even close, yet much more like autumn than summer. Daddy said it *was* autumn, and indeed it had autumn's yellow misty look, even while the sun was shining. Some of the leaves were beginning to change colour—especially the chestnut leaves, which were already falling. The creeper above the porch was crimson, the dahlias were in full bloom, and the sweet-pea was over. It was among the pea-rows and bean-rows that Tom and Daddy were at work, cutting down and tidying up. The withered plants Tom wheeled away in a barrow, dumping them down on a bare patch of soil beyond the strawberry bed; and as the heap grew it reminded him of the evening at Aunt Rhoda's—the Yorkshire terriers, Pascoe in Etons, the bonfire. . . .

In the afternoon he was left to his own devices, because Mother and Daddy went out in the car. Nothing further about school had been mentioned in his presence, and he had asked no questions, nevertheless he had a strong suspicion that they had gone to interview Mr. Rouse. Again he thought of a bonfire. William was against it—as usual. William was still collecting rubbish—damp heavy stuff that would not burn easily—and he objected to Tom's using up the more inflammable material, which he said he needed for a foundation. It was William's invariable policy to object. *His* kind of bonfire was one which merely smoked and smouldered for a couple of days. But he was obstinate as a mule, and far more disobliging, so Tom in the end left him, and left the garden, and set out with a vague idea of looking for mushrooms.

He wandered across the dreaming fields, but only found some puff-balls. A few of the blackberries were black, but they were hard and sour, and when he spat them out he discovered that they had mysteriously turned red again in his mouth. Presently, and quite by accident, he came to the lane leading to the old graveyard. He had not been in the graveyard for ages, so he determined to visit it now, and see if there were as many rabbits as William said. He scrambled through the hedge and dropped down into the narrow grassy track.

Mushrooms grew in the graveyard, Tom remembered; but Mother wouldn't touch any that were gathered there, though Daddy said this was mere prejudice, because all the bodies must have crumbled into dust long ago. And in fact, at first sight, it would have been hard to recognize it as a graveyard at all. Not a headstone was left standing in its original position. Some still survived, indeed, but they were propped up against the broken wall that surrounded the whole enclosure, and their inscriptions, as Tom knew, were for the most part indecipherable.

When he entered, through a gap on the north side, the place looked for all the world like some ancient earthworks, except that the surface was everywhere uneven—all heights and hollows, hummocks and tussocks—with a sprinkling of bushes, of whin and bramble. It was impossible to tell where the paths had once been, where individual graves had been; and when you crossed the long tangled grass your feet unexpectedly sank into holes, or sometimes struck against a hidden fragment of stone. Walking over it gave Tom a queer feeling, not altogether pleasant, though this was entirely due to the suggestions of a too active imagination. He trod gingerly, his eyes lowered to watch carefully each footstep, as if he feared he might tread on something he did not wish to tread on. A movement in the grass of frog or rabbit, a flutter of a bird in the brambles, would have made him jump. But there was no movement; the afternoon, which had clouded over, was profoundly still; the air stagnant and heavy. Tom had been gazing at the ground immediately before him, but as he approached the side wall he looked up, and then, and not till then, became aware of something extraordinary. Ranged along what was left of the wall were perhaps a score of tombstones—broken oblong slabs, chipped and stained and lichened—and on each of these stones, seated motionless and upright, was a cat. Tom stood stock still: it was like a scene one might come on in a dream, but hardly in waking life. Not a movement, as Tom stood there in astonishment. The cats might have been asleep, had it not been for their wide-open watching eyes—green eyes, yellow eyes—bright, steadfast, and beautiful. It was the strangest sight he had ever beheld. Each cat had his own stone, and took not the slightest notice of any other cat. There was something weird in their stillness, in their presence in this spot, in the fixity of their gaze. They might have been entranced, or simply lost in meditation.

Tom drew nearer still. "Puss, puss," he whispered, but received no response: the eyes watching him never even blinked. He had a sense of unreality, a feeling that he had strayed inadvertently into an unknown and fantastic world—a world not human, but feline and necromantic. He wasn't alarmed, wasn't even momentarily startled. He realized this and was pleased, though directly afterwards felt a little ashamed of his pleasure, for what was there to be alarmed at? The hint of sorcery in the air was not malevolent, only strange, dreamy, and rather lovely. He passed along the line of cats—cats of all sizes and ages—grey cats, striped cats, orange cats, and black cats—pausing a minute or two in front of each, until he reached the seventh. . . . The seventh cat was Henry.

And Henry knew him; Henry's mouth opened to emit the faintest sound of recognition. And then a stranger thing than any yet happened. For it seemed to Tom that a struggle was taking place in Henry, that he was on the point of jumping down, that he wanted to be stroked and petted, but something was preventing him, an alien influence which had at that very moment entered into him and was fighting for possession. The battle was soon over. There was no palpable difference in Henry; the only difference was in the light shining in his eyes. Tom had seen precisely that light in them when they had been watching a bird.

Presently, while he stood there looking into Henry's eyes, he felt a drop of rain splash on to his hand, and then another and another. Glancing up, he saw that the clouds had gathered threateningly overhead; and there was no shelter here unless he crept in between those furze-bushes and the broken, overhanging wall. After a brief hesitation he did so, and snuggling well in, curled himself up in the hollow beneath the wall, where he could wait till the rain was over. Henry and the other cats would soon go too, he thought, for they disliked getting wet much more than he did. . . .

The rain was taking a long while to pass—or had it already passed? —for he must have been thinking of other things. At the same time it struck him that it had grown very dark, which possibly was why, when he stood up to look everything appeared strange, and vaguely different. It must be the effect of this mist, which had floated up and now hung in a thickening veil over the fields. At any rate he had better go back, for after all he was not much more than a mile from home, and he set off at a trot in the direction he had come from. The rain grew no heavier, it was the mist which had this curious effect on the aspect of things. But it was thinning a little; and soon through it, and down below him, he caught a glimpse of the river. He ran on and on, while all the time it was growing lighter.

Only where exactly was he? He was standing on an upland; beside him was a long narrow ravine, thickly wooded; before him was the river valley. All this he recognized, yet with a swiftly increasing uneasiness. For the scene was not quite as he knew it, and that grey stone house, bare and gaunt, was certainly not his home. The garden, too, was gone. He felt a strange drumming in his ears, and a dizziness. The memory of the garden, the memory of his own house, began to wink and flicker. Instinctively he clung to it, feeling that if his mind relaxed ever so little the memory would go out. And it seemed even now to be very faint, and difficult to keep before him. He bent his whole mind, with a painful concentration, on that wavering vision. The struggle was acute, and it was like the struggle against a powerful anæsthetic. A rapid succession of waves of light and darkness swam before his eyes, through which, very shadowy and dim, the phantom of a garden hovered. Only the great stone house before him was solid and real, and drew him with a fascination that was stronger than his will. Then the struggle was forgotten. . . .

It was winter, and the fallen leaves lay soaked and sodden on the grass. The house showed no sign of being inhabited, except that a dense coil of smoke curled up from one chimney and spread sluggishly against a leaden sky. Tom drew nearer still; he passed round the side of the house. He saw a heavy door, studded with iron nails and ornamented with a design in beaten ironwork. And though the door was shut he felt quite sure that it was not locked, that he had only to push it and it would open. He did not do so; he peered through a window, but could see nothing except a dirty empty vault-like room. Ten yards from the front of the house rose a tree, with black leafless twisted boughs that were patterned against the cold grey sky. By jumping he might just reach the lowest branch, and he did so. Pulling himself up, he clambered astride this branch, and once there, the tree was easy to climb. He climbed till he was on a level with the upper windows, and then, hugging the trunk tightly, he stood gazing into a familiar room. On the bare floor were traced the magic symbols; a fire burned on the hearth; an old man was sitting in a chair, absorbed in a big book which lay open on a table before him—and staring straight out of the window, with fierce hungry eyes, was a huge black cat. . . .

The cat saw him, the cat's tail began to twitch, his mouth opened, and, though no sound reached Tom, the wizard raised his head. Simultaneously Tom half slid, half tumbled down the tree. For a moment he lay sprawling on the cold wet grass; then he was up and running as hard as he could. He ran and ran and ran, till he could run no longer. He staggered a few steps further, but presently, tripping over a hidden ivy root, he tumbled down—lost, breathless, and exhausted.

21: IT had begun to rain again. Tom wriggled in between two whin-bushes growing under a tumbled-down wall. . . .

A wall! And the ground was rough and broken into mounds and hollows: he was back once more in the graveyard.

He had neither looked nor cared whither he was running, yet it seemed an evil omen. A yellow twilight swam between earth and sky, and beneath it the landscape had taken on a livid unnatural hue. A black motionless figure crouched at a little distance.

He was trapped. To try to go home would only be to return to the house he had run away from—the house of his dream, the house the serpent had shown him: how could he ever go home again if his true home was not there?

But if it was not there, where was it? And instantly the answer came to him that it *was* there, only not there for him. Something had happened to him which shut him out. It was there, but *he* was not there. And if he could not get back to it, get back to Daddy and Mother, then neither would they be able to get to him. They might be looking for him even now, but their "now" was not his "now." He could do nothing: he was lost. . . .

For a while sheer helplessness produced a kind of mental inertia; and then, without seeking for it, he saw the flaw in his reasoning, and hope revived. He *must* have escaped—escaped at least from *that*, which was the worst. The proof was staring him in the face: the proof lay just in this ruined graveyard, for *it* could not be in the same "present" as the house he dreaded. Centuries stretched between them. Moreover he remembered the drifts of fallen leaves, the black naked tree, the winter sky—and this was not winter. It might seem to him a long long time since he had set out to wander over the fields, but the season was the same, it must be the same afternoon; he would go back, he must try it again at whatever risk, and this time perhaps all would be well.

Then his eyes fell on the crouching beast, which at the first movement he made had raised its head. Half hidden in the long grass it lay—sleek, with pointed ears—a cat, but not Henry, much larger than Henry, as large nearly as a lynx—as large as the cat in that house. And with this last recognition Tom cowered back again.

He shut his eyes. Some minutes seemed to pass—how many he did not know—perhaps only one or two, perhaps none, merely an infinitesimal interval of silence, not ordinary silence, but a total absence of sound, such as must exist in the unimaginable void of outer and empty space. It was simply there, and then it was gone, though it had been broken only by a ripple of light. But Tom was breathing again, the earth was breathing, and very far and faint, he now heard a positive sound, hardly audible indeed, and yet surely a sound of barking. Again came the drifting wave of light, and this time through the heavy canopy of cloud a thin lance of sunshine pierced—stretched across the graveyard and vanished. Tom lifted his head. The clouds were splitting into two solid masses, were drawing back like dark immense gates between which a hot gush of sunlight swept, spreading over the fields and flooding them. In another second it had reached the graveyard, and the big cat rose to its feet, angry and threatening, but not threatening Tom, for its back was turned to him, and it was watching a young man who had just then come into sight at the edge of the adjoining field. Tom stood up to watch him too. He was still some distance off, but he was moving swiftly, and a few yards in front of him ran a white woolly dog about the size of a sheepdog.

Tom's heart leapt; he dared not shout; but he saw the dog raising his head as if to catch a scent, and directly afterwards he sprang forward at full gallop.

What happened next happened quickly—so quickly that Tom had no distinct view of it. There was a leap, a furious snarling, but there was no battle—the black cat was gone.

And while Tom still stood staring at the spot where it had been, the young man reached the graveyard. Tom heard him and turned round. He had seen him twice before—once as a boy, once as a youth. Then, without quite knowing why, but to hide a deeper feeling that he could not express, he stooped and began to stroke and make friends with the dog.

There were no greetings; the young man simply sat down on the broken wall and Tom sat beside him. The white dog stretched himself at their feet.

It was enough; there seemed to be no need for speech; at any rate Tom felt none. The young man understood; Tom too understood. And merely to sit like this was in itself a happiness, which no words could deepen.

"All the same," Tom thought, "I very nearly forgot to call him." And after a while he asked, remembering the vanished beast: "Where did it come from?"

"From you," the young man said, and so quietly that Tom glanced at him in doubt.

"From me?"

The strangely bright eyes were fixed on his; the young man spoke again. But his voice had not the tone Tom wanted, nor were his words the words he wanted. "In itself it was nothing," he said; "only the image of your fear, which you brought to life."

Tom hung his head; he had perhaps deserved some such answer, but that was not what troubled him. He knew the answer to his next question also, though he could not keep it back. "And when you go away from me again—will that too be all?" Suddenly he felt that it would be very easy to cry, though quite useless—useless unless he could be given the comfort, find the comforter, he longed for.

But the angel did not comfort him, nor did he seem to notice the hand that Tom instinctively half held out and then quickly withdrew. Did not take it at all events, but only counselled gravely: "Do not think about it; it will do no good; because at present you cannot understand. . . . I *am* you; the beast that is gone was you; do not think about it, but go to sleep."

"I don't——" Tom was beginning sadly, when a sudden drowsiness covered up his thought. For a moment, as he tried to grasp it, the thought flickered back into consciousness, or something like it. What he wanted to say was: "Can't you——"

Only somehow he was listening to the waves, and watching them, and lying on the sand at Glenagivney, and Pascoe, not the angel, was beside him. . . .

22: A GRASSHOPPER was singing near the furze-brake. "Tom!" it sang in a shrill thin voice. "Tom—wake up now—Tom!"

The voice grew louder and more insistent; it no longer sang, it spoke—and a little anxiously, for it had become Miss Jimpson's voice. "It seems very strange, Geoffrey! Do you think there can be anything the matter?"

The "Geoffrey" was interesting, therefore Tom hung on a little longer to a now pretended slumber. He didn't even peep, though sorely tempted to, for he was both curious and faintly amused; but he kept his eyes fast shut. Then, like the turtle's, the voice of Geoffrey was heard in reply. "No, Anna, I don't. His eyes are tighter shut than they were a minute ago. He's shamming."

Tom smiled and looked up at them. "I was really asleep at first," he protested, scrambling to his feet. "Honestly."

"But wasn't that very foolish of you!" Miss Jimpson exclaimed. "I'm sure the ground must be damp."

Tom, after the least hesitation, remembered that it *had* been raining, though nothing to speak of. That was why he had got in under the whin-bushes, he told her, and added: "I'm really looking for mushrooms."

Miss Jimpson laughed. But presently she asked: "How long have you been tucked in there?"

Tom hesitated again. He knew he had come out soon after lunch, but how long ago was that? "I'm afraid I've been here most of the afternoon," he was obliged to confess. "What time is it now?"

"It's nearly half-past five," Miss Jimpson answered. "We were on our way home when we saw you, or rather saw the dog."

"The dog!" cried Tom quickly, turning abruptly round. But no dog was visible.

There was a brief pause. "A big white woolly thing," Miss Jimpson then went on in a tone of faint surprise. "He seems to have disappeared. . . . It was he, anyway, who attracted our attention. He looked exactly as if he were mounting guard over something—as apparently he was—so we came to have a closer inspection. . . . Oh! —here he comes."

But Tom had already seen him, and also seen that Mr. Holbrook's face wore a curiously speculative expression. The white dog came trotting up.

"He must be a stray dog," Tom began. "I mean—he's not mine." Mr. Holbrook was still watching him, and now he spoke. "He doesn't seem to be aware of that," Mr. Holbrook observed quietly, and there could be no denying that this was so. The white dog had suddenly planted his two fore-paws on Tom's shoulders and was licking his cheek. Tom's arms clasped him tightly. "I wish he *was* mine," he said.

"Can do, I should think," Mr. Holbrook murmured, while Miss Jimpson looked at them both, frankly mystified.

"There were only cats here when I came," Tom continued, with a glance round at the now abandoned tombstones. "A whole lot of them—sitting like a row of images—but they all seem to have gone."

"And we ought to be going," Miss Jimpson declared. Then she said to Tom: "I shouldn't pet him too much or you'll have him following you the whole way home."

"Yes," Tom answered gravely, "I'm going to take him home. He's a stray dog."

Miss Jimpson was quite sure he was nothing of the sort. "Nonsense!" she said. "No stray dog ever had a coat like that. He looks to me as if he had been washed and combed within the last hour."

"He hasn't a collar," Tom maintained with a hint of stubbornness.

"No," replied Miss Jimpson, "which is a further proof that he's been washed quite recently."

Tom said nothing, but his silence was not submissive, and Mr. Holbrook intervened. "Oh, I shouldn't worry," he told Miss Jimpson.
"The dog can look after himself, I expect. He's by no means a pup,
and if he wants to see Tom home why prevent him?"

"I'm not preventing him," Miss Jimpson answered. "Only it would
be easier to get rid of him now than it will be then, and less disappointing to the dog."

"I don't intend to get rid of him," Tom muttered under his breath.

But Miss Jimpson heard him; she had very sharp ears. "Now,
Tom," she said firmly, "you know very well that you can't take
possession of other people's dogs."

"Not this one—with any safety," Mr. Holbrook agreed tactfully.
At the same time he laid a friendly hand on Tom's shoulder. "He's
pretty conspicuous, isn't he?"

The white dog appeared to be following the discussion, though
not as if it mattered much.

"Dogs are such queer things!" Miss Jimpson unexpectedly murmured. "You can *see* he's taken some notion into his head. . . .
About Tom, I mean."

"Well, he *found* Tom," said Mr. Holbrook. "Found him when he
was asleep—like Moses in the bulrushes—and 'finds' are 'keeps,' I
suppose."

Miss Jimpson supposed so also, and her manner, Tom was quick
to perceive, had lost its slightly dictatorial tone. "What sort of dog
is he?" she mused. "Not a sheepdog and not a poodle. . . . I've
never seen a dog like him before."

"Oh yes you have," Mr. Holbrook contradicted.

"Where?" asked Miss Jimpson, still pondering. "And when?"

"Last Easter," said Mr. Holbrook. "And in Italy."

Miss Jimpson gave a little shrug. "For that matter, I don't remember seeing any dogs in Italy—which, judging from the way they
treat their horses, is just as well."

"All the same, it was there you saw him," Mr. Holbrook persisted.
"A smaller version of him, I admit, and in a picture—several pictures.
My dear Anna, look at his colour; look at those little curls! He's the
dog who invariably accompanies Tobias and his Angel in old Floren-
tine pictures. He's a Botticini."

Miss Jimpson gazed in silence.

"There's no deception," Mr. Holbrook laughed, "it's him."

"He," Miss Jimpson corrected abstractedly. Then suddenly she smiled and looked at Tom very much as she had looked at him across the table in the teashop. She had liked him then, he knew, and he was pretty certain that she liked him now; yet behind this she remained puzzled. "It's a very queer thing to me," she murmured, "that if anything extraordinary happens, it always seems to happen either to Tom or when Tom is present."

"That's the magic in him," replied Mr. Holbrook gaily.

Miss Jimpson smiled at Tom again, but thoughtfully. She sighed, shook her head, and, as if finding reverie to no purpose, abruptly emerged to the practical affairs of life. "Well, magic or no magic," she announced, "I must return to my home. . . . Come along," she added to Tom. "Perhaps he won't follow us after all."

In this conjecture at least she proved correct, for the white dog trotted on ahead.

"He's a white Chrysanthemum," Tom whispered to himself, "and I'm going to call him Caleb."

But he had now time to think of other things, and among them of all the "Geoffreys" and "Annas" he had heard. It was clear that in his absence the "romance" had not stood still. Mother had been quite right when she said that Miss Jimpson would be able to manage her own affairs; and she must have managed them jolly cleverly, he reflected—innocently giving her all the credit both for the original idea and for the efficient way in which it had been carried out. It wasn't a matter, however, that one could very well allude to, so he refrained from comment. "How did you get here?" he inquired instead, knowing that neither Mr. Holbrook nor Miss Jimpson lived near.

"We came in a tram," Mr. Holbrook told him. "After that we walked. This old graveyard of yours wasn't in the programme at all. Like yourself, it was an accidental discovery; we didn't even know that it existed."

But Miss Jimpson—who was obviously in a most unstable mood—had again begun to look thoughtful. There seemed to be something on her mind which she could not quite bring herself to say; though she *would* say it soon, Tom was sure, because it was very evident that she wanted to. He smiled at her encouragingly, and once or twice she nearly spoke, and then at the last minute didn't.

"Why not trust us?" suggested Mr. Holbrook, who also must have noticed the preoccupation. "You're making *me*, at least, extremely nervous."

Mr. Holbrook spoke lightly, but Tom could see that Miss Jimpson was serious. It was queer that they should be lovers, he thought, because really they were very different, and you saw this even more when they were together than when you met them apart.

Miss Jimpson coloured, and next moment Tom found himself blushing in sympathy, which was idiotic, and annoyed him. Then suddenly she said: "It's only that Tom somehow—— I don't know —— But in a way I can't help feeling that he's been connected from the beginning with——" She broke off, and finished almost crossly: "Oh, what I mean is that I don't see why we shouldn't tell him."

Tom looked at Mr. Holbrook, but Mr. Holbrook only laughed and said: "Well, tell him then."

"I should like him to be the first to congratulate us," Miss Jimpson went on. "It's just a—superstition."

"I do congratulate you—very much," Tom hastened to assure her, and Mr. Holbrook laughed once more, and slapped him on the shoulder.

"You're a particular friend of ours," he said. "I imagine that's what we're trying to convey. . . . For that matter, always were of mine," he added half to himself.

Tom felt pleased, though his pleasure was mitigated by an alarming impression that Miss Jimpson wanted to kiss him. Hang it all, she couldn't! Fortunately she herself appeared to be doubtful about it, and had less time to make up her mind than she knew. "This is my turning," he was able to tell them half a minute later, when they had reached the main road. "I mean, I go to the right here, and the way to the tram is on the left."

So they stopped, and shook hands, and the dangerous moment went by. Miss Jimpson didn't kiss him—though he still believed she wanted to, and indeed he might have let her if Mr. Holbrook hadn't been there. He suddenly found himself feeling a little sorry for Miss Jimpson—and understanding her—understanding her better than Mr. Holbrook did perhaps.

Miss Jimpson told him that he would be the first person they'd invite to their new house when they'd found one, and that anyway she hoped she'd be seeing him before that.

"Of course," Tom replied, and thanked her. After which he and Caleb took the road to the right, but they hadn't gone far before it occurred to him that it would have been nicer if he had asked Miss

Jimpson and Mr. Holbrook to dinner. He half thought of running back to do so, only when he looked round they were already hidden by a bend in the road. So he scudded on, with the white dog galloping beside him.

When he reached home he found Daddy pottering about the garden as usual, but abruptly he stopped pottering to stare at Tom's companion. Luckily Daddy was not an excitable person and was always willing to listen to explanations. He listened to one now, without comment or interruption, though at the end of it he announced: "We must ring up the police."

"Yes, I know," Tom hastened to agree. "But if he *isn't* claimed mayn't I keep him?"

Daddy looked dubious, pulled up a weed or two without speaking and finally said that they'd first have to see what Mother thought about it. "You needn't keep on thanking me," he added after a minute or two, rather dryly. "I haven't given you a present and I haven't said 'yes.' You're a great deal too impulsive, and in this case it's only going to lead to disappointment: the dog's certain to be claimed within twenty-four hours."

Tom did not argue the point, but he mentioned what a good dog Caleb was, winding up hopefully with: "Mother will like having him—I mean of course if we *don't* find his owner." After which he sat down on a stone and watched Daddy's slow and deliberate movements, wondering what he would think were he to be told of all that had happened that afternoon. He knew of course that he never *would* tell him, because Daddy, he had long ago found, neither welcomed nor cared for such confidences. But he might tell Mother —particularly now that the whole adventure was over. And somehow he felt that it *was* over—felt this very strongly—so strongly that he didn't believe it would make the least difference whether Henry came back or not. He had even the feeling that it had all been in some way explained, so that it could never trouble him again. It had lost its power to trouble him; it was like an imaginary phantom, which you suddenly discover to be an effect of light and mist. And with this he remembered that he had not written to Pascoe.

He had intended to write; he must write this evening; though Pascoe himself, he was sure, would be returning home at least a day or two before the holidays ended.

How quickly things ended! Tom thought. Nothing lasted very long, and nothing seemed the same when it was gone as it had seemed while it was there. Summer was gone, or nearly gone, and it would be a year very likely before he visited the sea again. Pascoe was luckier; Pascoe had Aunt Rhoda's house always there for him to go to, and Aunt Rhoda herself always dying to have him at any time and to keep him as long as possible. Tom hadn't an aunt even of the most ordinary kind, let alone one who lived in a lovely place like Greencastle. But he had an uncle—Uncle Stephen. What would it be like, he wondered, if he were to go to stay with Uncle Stephen the way Pascoe did with Aunt Rhoda? True, Uncle Stephen didn't live beside the sea; but he lived in the country, which was the next best thing. Supposing he *did* get an invitation from him then, would he be allowed to accept it? And immediately this question became so urgent and fraught with possibilities that he was obliged to put it to Daddy.

Daddy seemed to be more amused than interested. He merely laughed, said that it wasn't in the least likely to happen, and began to tie up one of the rambler roses. Tom felt secretly irritated. How could Daddy *tell* what would happen! For all he knew, Uncle Stephen might at this very moment be writing a letter of invitation. Mother would at least have admitted the possibility and been ready to discuss it, but Daddy's next remark was: "Aren't you satisfied with your mother and me?"

As if that had anything to do with it! Tom felt inclined to say "No." It was meant as a joke, doubtless; yet none the less it closed up the entire subject, so that he couldn't go on without seeming childish and silly. You can't go on talking when the other person is like that. And Pascoe was like that too, though he didn't make jokes.

Daddy must have noticed the silence, and perhaps been surprised by it, for presently he glanced round and observed: "Your Uncle Stephen's a rather strange person from all accounts."

But it was now too late; Tom's desire to talk about Uncle Stephen had subsided; and he only replied, while he stooped down and pressed his mouth against the top of Caleb's head: "Mother likes him." Then he remembered that Daddy had been very decent about Caleb, and that he was very decent in lots of ways, though he was so against what he called "flights of imagination."

"All the same," Tom thought, "it's just because Uncle Stephen

doesn't happen to be his kind of person that he says he's strange.
. . . Like the Blakes—and like me. . . . But he's Mother's kind of
person."

With which he was content until he added: "And so am I."

January 1934
October 1935

Uncle Stephen

O that I might have my request; and that
God would grant me the thing that I long for!

The Book of Job

They were as companions. . . .
Objects which the Shepherd loved before
Were dearer now. . . . From the Boy there came
Feelings and emanations—things which were
Light to the sun and music to the wind;
And the old Man's heart seemed born again.

1: BEYOND the iron wicket-gate stretched an avenue of yew-trees with, at the end of it, four wide shallow steps, dark and mossy, descending in a terrace to the graves. This avenue was straight as if marked out with a ruler. The yew-trees were straight, trim, and sombre, of a dull bluish-green that was not so dark as the shadows they threw on the unmown grass. They stood up stiffly against a deep ultramarine sky, and composed a picture at once formal and intensely romantic.

That is, if it happened to burst upon your vision unexpectedly, as it did upon Tom Barber's, flooded with a light from Poe's *Ulalume*. Young Tom in his new and ill-fitting suit of rough black cloth, beneath which he had sweated freely during the long drive, was for a minute or two rapt by that instant recognition into forgetfulness of the business that had brought him here. It was but a brief respite, however, and he awakened from it guiltily. Certain muffled and sliding sounds caused him to shrink back. *This* was not like *Ulalume*— this ugly varnished brass-handled box covered with flowers. For the flowers somehow increased its ghastliness. Shoulder-high his father's coffin was carried through the narrow gate and down the avenue, while he followed with Eric and Leonard—the chief mourners.

A feeling of resentment arose unhappily in his mind against everything and everybody connected with the funeral. The solemn wooden faces, the formal clothes, the secret indifference which had allowed hired men to bear the burden, depressed and exasperated him. If anyone had really cared! But all this, and particularly those hideous wreaths with the cards of their donors carefully attached to them, suggested neither grief nor affection, but only the triumph of clay and worms, and the horrors that were already at work out of sight.

The burial service began. Mr. Carteret in his starched yet ghostly surplice stood by the grave slightly apart from the bare-headed group who watched and listened to him. It was as if everything for the moment had passed into his hands, and he were, by some mysterious incantation, sending forth the soul, which till now had lingered near its old dwelling, on a perilous and distant journey. Tom felt a sudden desire to weep.

He turned away. Deliberately he fixed his attention on a creamy, black-spotted butterfly who had entered the avenue. The butterfly's wavering flight as he flickered in and out of the bands of shadow and sunlight barring the green path seemed purposeless as that of a leaf in the wind. He, too, was like a little soul newly exiled from the body and not knowing whither to fly. The soul of an infant, perhaps. Then suddenly he alit on a stalk of foxgloves and became at once a comfortable earthly creature, warm with appetites, eager, impatient, purposeful, as he explored cave after purple cave, forcing an entrance, greedy, determined. Tom smiled: he very nearly laughed.

His smile faded and he blushed hotly as he encountered the rather dry and speculative gaze of Dr. Macrory. Dr. Macrory looked away, but Tom knew he had been caught. He felt ashamed and miserable. Furtively he glanced round the little group of mourners, of whom he was the smallest and youngest, but every face was still drawn to an appropriate expression of apathetic decorum. Only *his* mind had wandered, and yet it was his father they were burying. He was only Eric's and Leonard's step-father; only Uncle Horace's brother-in-law: as for the rest, there were even several persons there whose names Tom did not know.

He heard a faint cawing of rooks, like sleepy distant music. If he could slip away now, away from that raw red gaping hole. . . . He heard Mr. Carteret's voice: "to raise us from the death of sin into the life of righteousness; that when we shall depart this life, we may rest in him, as our hope is this our brother doth; and that, at the general Resurrection in the last day . . ." The words fell with a solemn cadence, but for Tom they had neither more nor less meaning than the cawing of the rooks. Any gentler feelings he might have had about death were at present obliterated by its unsightliness. The ugliness of death had been revealed suddenly, much as if he had come on an obscene inscription or picture chalked up on a wall. You didn't hang wreaths of flowers round *that*, or put on your best clothes to mope or to gloat over it. And supposing it was somebody you *loved* who had died—then all this kind of thing would be doubly revolting. . . .

Uncle Horace and Eric and Leonard:—he found himself staring at them with hostility. And at home there was his step-mother, and Jane his step-sister—Jane, who among all these "steps" was the only one he really liked. He *had* liked Eric—liked him more than he would ever like Jane—but it is impossible to go on caring for a person who shows you he doesn't want to be cared for. Eric did not like him, and Leonard did not like him, and his step-mother did not like him. The only difference was that he could see Mrs. Gavney—now Mrs. Barber —*trying* to like him, an effort that faintly tickled his sense of humour, which was as odd as everything else about him. Of course, both Eric and Leonard were older than he was—though Leonard was only a year older, and for that matter Tom knew the question of age had nothing to do with it. They did not despise him because he was young but because he was different. And the worst of it was that in all on which they set the slightest value they *were* his superiors. . . .

Tom's eyes closed for a moment at the sound of the shovelling of earth—the first dull thuds on hollow wood. It was horrible, but it passed quickly: once the coffin was covered there was only a scraping, scuffling noise. And all this squeamishness was not really sorrow for his father. *Was* he sorry—even a little? While his father had been alive he had never felt much affection for him: an atmosphere of spiritual remoteness had, as far back as he could remember, surrounded him. His father had never been unkind, but he had been extraordinarily unapproachable. And after his second marriage—his marriage with Mrs. Gavney, the mother of Eric and Leonard and Jane—he had seemed to think Tom must now have everything he needed—a second mother, companions of his own age. This last advantage had actually been mentioned—during a painfully embarrassing conversation from which Tom had escaped as soon as he could. Well, they needn't think he intended to go on living in that house in Gloucester Terrace, because he didn't. Not without a struggle at any rate! If only he were his own master how easy it would be! In that case he would simply pack up and go; for though he knew nothing of his father's affairs, he knew Granny had left him plenty to live on. His mouth pouted in the incipient and repressed grimace inspired by Uncle Horace's solemn and proprietary gaze at that moment directed full upon him. Uncle Horace! All this "uncleing" and "mothering" had been from the beginning *their* idea! Uncle Horace was merely his step-mother's brother, Mr. Horace Pringle— no relation whatever. If it came to that, he had only one true relation in the world, or at least there was only one he had ever heard of, his mother's uncle—Uncle Stephen. . . .

Tom's expression altered. The freckled face—redeemed from marked plainness by a pair of singularly honest and intelligent grey eyes—became stilled as the water of a pool is stilled. He might have been listening intently, or merely dreaming on his feet. Probably the latter, for when he awakened it was as if the hands of the clock had suddenly jumped on, leaving a little island of submerged time unaccounted for. It was strange: a few minutes had been lost for ever: he had been here and yet he had not been here! . . . *Could* you be in two times at once? Certainly your mind could be in one time and your body in another, for that was what had happened—he had been back in last night. But suppose his body had gone back too! Then he would have vanished! Uncle Horace would have said, "Where is Tom?" and somebody would have answered, "He was here a minute ago: he was standing over there: he can't be far away." Only, he *had* been far away. As far away as last night—and in his bedroom. This odd experience seemed to make all kinds of things possible. Somebody might come to you out of *his* time into yours. You might, for instance, come face to face with your own father as he was when he was a boy. Of course you wouldn't *know* each other: still, you might meet and become friends, the way you do with people in dreams. The idea seemed difficult and involved, but doubtless it could be straightened out. Dreams themselves were so queer. When he had dreamed last night, for example, he was almost sure he had been awake. What he wasn't so sure of was that it had been a dream at all, or at any rate *his* dream. . . .

Abruptly he became aware of a movement around him—an involuntary communication, as of so many simultaneously-drawn breaths of relief—and next moment he found himself shaking the damp hand of a stout elderly gentleman who seemed to know him. Tom's own hand was damp, with little beads of sweat on it, and his shirt felt moist and sticky against his body. Several other people shook hands with him: Mr. Carteret placed his arm round his shoulder. . . . And the midsummer sun beat down on the hard earth.

Eric and Leonard had put on their black bowler hats, and Tom put on his. They began to retrace their path, walking in twos and threes along the yew-tree avenue, at the end of which the cars were drawn up in a line. Tom came last; he did not want to walk with anybody; but Dr. Macrory waited for him.

Coming out of the gate, Tom halted, moved by a sudden desire to escape. The ruins of the Abbey stood grey and ivy-creepered on a low hill, and down below was the lake, its water a steel-blue, broken by immense beds of green rushes. He heard the thin cry of a snipe.

Rooks were still cawing in the distant trees, which stretched away
in sunshine on the right; and beyond the lake the ground rose gradually in cornfields and pasture. The thridding of grasshoppers sounded
like the whirr of small grindstones. Tom instantly saw them as tiny
men dressed in green who went about sharpening still tinier knives
and scissors for the other insects. A blue dragon-fly, like a shining
airman, flashed by in the sun. There were lots of these small airmen,
he knew, among the reeds on the lake, where they bred. He had an
impression of emerging from some choking stagnant valley of death
into the world of life.

Suddenly he whispered to Dr. Macrory, "Let's go down to the lake.
Couldn't we? *You* say we're going. Tell Uncle Hor——; tell Mr.
Pringle."

Dr. Macrory glanced at the smooth back of Uncle Horace's
morning coat, at his beautifully creased trousers and glossy silk hat.
His own coat, like Tom's, appeared to be the handiwork of a distinctly inferior tailor, and the collar showed specks of dandruff. "I
don't think it would do," he said. "You know what they are."

But he rested a friendly hand on Tom's shoulder, which the boy
impatiently tried to shake off. His face suddenly flushed and lowered.
"Oh, damn," he muttered. "I'm going anyway."

The doctor's hand closed on the collar of his jacket and grasped it
firmly, while at the same moment the clear voice of Uncle Horace
inquired, "Where's Tom?" He turned round to look for his nephew,
standing by the big Daimler, holding the door open. Eric and Leonard
had already taken their seats at the back.

"He's coming with me," called out Dr. Macrory, pushing the small
chief mourner, whose face was like a thundercloud, towards his own
two-seater; and when he had him safely inside, "That's all right," he
murmured. "They'll probably take your behaviour for a sign of grief."

Tom stared straight before him through the windscreen. For all
his friendliness, the doctor, he felt, had let him down. He had wanted
to talk to somebody: if they had gone to the lake he could have talked
—sitting by the edge of the water. But he did not want to talk now.
The kind of things he had to say were not to be said in a motor-car
and to a person half of whose attention was given to the road before
him. He might just as well be in the other car with Eric and Leonard
and Uncle Horace. For a moment, among all those people who so
definitely were not *his* people, who were and always would be
strangers, he had turned instinctively to his old friend Dr. Macrory.

Now he felt disappointed in him. Unreasonably, he knew, for what after all could Dr. Macrory have done? With a little shrug he settled down in his seat.

2. THE others had arrived before him, and as he came downstairs after removing the dust of his journey he could hear them talking. They were in the dining-room, so he supposed tea was ready. But the moment he opened the door the voices ceased, and in the sudden silence he stood motionless on the threshold, with heightened colour, his eyes fixed on the assembled faces, all turned in his direction. Then the flash of Uncle Horace's smile, and his rather strident welcome, broke a pause which threatened to become awkward; for Tom still hovered by the door, unconscious of the curious effect his reserve and shyness were creating. His step-mother, looking blonde, resigned, and expansive, in her deep mourning, murmured that everything was ready, that they had only been waiting for Tom, and she told Leonard to ring the bell. "It's raining," Jane announced from the window.

He suspected, and the impression deepened when they took their seats round the table, that a definite policy in regard to himself must in his absence have been argued out and settled. Leonard actually of his own accord passed him the butter:—"Butter?" he murmured languidly:—and Eric asked him what he thought of Dr. Macrory's Citroën. Tom had not thought of it at all; he hadn't even known it was a Citroën; but he produced what he hoped might be a satisfactory answer; and the conversation drifted to and fro, superficially normal, though with occasional pauses betraying an underlying constraint.

It was during one of these that he made up his mind to risk the question which all day had been in his thoughts, but which, he knew not why, he had felt a strange reluctance to ask. Even now he spoke in a low voice and without raising his eyes. "Was Uncle Stephen told?" he said.

Nobody answered.

Tom recollected that possibly they did not know who Uncle Stephen was. "*My* Uncle Stephen—Uncle Stephen Collet," he explained. Then, as the silence continued, he glanced up.

What had he said?—for he saw at once that it must have been the wrong thing. His step-mother's hands, grasping the hot-water jug and the lid of the tea-pot, were arrested in mid-air, and Uncle Horace was looking at her warningly. Tom stared at them in astonishment, but next moment Uncle Horace replied. "I didn't think it necessary to tell him. The announcement was in the papers. As a matter of fact it never occurred to me to write. Perhaps I should have done so."

Mrs. Barber put the lid back on the tea-pot without having filled it. "Why?" she asked stiffly. "Why should you write?"

"Well, I suppose, as the only blood relation——" And again, it seemed to Tom, he flashed his signal of danger.

Mrs. Barber ignored it. "He was no relation of Edgar's, and there had never been any communication between them."

"I meant of Tom's," Uncle Horace murmured.

"He never took the slightest interest in Tom. He cut himself off entirely from his family years before Tom was born; in fact when he was not much more than Tom's own age."

"Oh, I don't for a moment suppose he would come. Still——"

"I think it is much better as it is," Mrs. Barber said, with an air of closing the subject.

For Tom she had merely opened it. "Why?" he asked in his turn, flushing a little.

Mrs. Barber took no notice, and it was Leonard who spoke, fixing his eyes on Tom's puzzled face in a faintly cynical enjoyment. "That's the magician, isn't it? It would have been rather sport if he——"

"Be quiet, Leonard!" his mother checked him sharply.

Tom felt the colour deepening in his cheeks. Enough had been said to show him that Uncle Stephen had been discussed before, and unfavourably. What right had they to discuss him! Nevertheless, he was more bewildered than offended. Leonard's mysterious allusion in particular left him in the dark. He knew it was meant to be sarcastic and to annoy him; but why should Uncle Stephen be called a magician? Where did the sarcasm come in? It was at this point that Jane kicked him under the table—a hint, he supposed, that he was to say no more. He obeyed it. After all, what did it matter what they thought! And he dropped into a detached contemplation of the whole Gavney family, induced by the secret knowledge that he would not often again be seated at their table. . . .

They certainly were a remarkably good-looking lot:—Jane, dark and vivacious, singularly unlike her large-limbed, fair-haired brothers; his step-mother, handsome too, in an opulent full-blown way; Uncle

Horace, always vivid, sleek, and immaculate, no matter what the hour or the occasion. He wondered why he had got on so badly with them —or at least with his step-mother and the boys—if it had been as much his fault as theirs? Of course, he had nothing in common with them, but then he hadn't *really* very much in common with Jane either, yet Jane and he were friends. They quarrelled; they quarrelled frequently; but they always made it up again—and sometimes he thought Jane quarrelled on purpose, just for the pleasure of making it up. . . .

He became aware that Mrs. Barber, after a glance round the table to make sure everybody had finished, was rising slowly to her feet. All her movements were slow. They were like the movements of a cow—heavy, indolent, yet not ungraceful. She even suggested milk! This last reflection was quite free from irony; it simply came to him as he watched her standing by her chair in ample profile. Next moment she turned to her brother: "I think Eric wants to have a little 'confab' with you, Horace. Perhaps you would rather talk here, and join us later."

"Not at all," Uncle Horace answered dryly. "I don't suppose Eric has any secrets to tell."

Mrs. Barber did not press the point, and they adjourned to the drawing-room, Tom loitering behind the others in the hall, for he felt tempted to go to his own room. He wondered if it would do? The fact that Uncle Horace had not gone home to dine, but had returned with them and was evidently going to spend the evening with them, seemed to show that the occasion was regarded as a special one. It was to be a family gathering, a kind of continuation of the funeral. Therefore it mightn't look very civil if he were to disappear, and indeed most likely somebody would be sent to bring him back. Besides, if they were going to discuss Eric's affairs, he supposed he would be allowed to read, or play a game of bezique with Jane.

One glance at the assembled company removed all hope of games. His step-mother looked mournful, Jane and Leonard bored, Eric sulky, and Uncle Horace cross. Not exactly cross, perhaps, but ready to become so. "Well, what is this important news of Eric's?" he asked, and Mrs. Barber, to whom the question was addressed, glanced encouragingly at her son.

"It's about the bank," she prompted him. "Eric has been thinking things over."

Uncle Horace eyed the thinker impassively. "I understood all that had been settled months ago and that he was now working for his examination."

Eric blushed, cleared his throat, and suddenly glared at his Uncle. "I'm going into the motor trade," he announced, in a tone which nervousness rendered alarmingly final.

"It's not that he doesn't appreciate the interest you have taken in him," Mrs. Barber hastened to explain. "But you know he's always had this taste for mechanics, and——"

"I know nothing of the sort," Uncle Horace interrupted. "It's the first time I've ever heard of his having a taste for anything but cricket and football."

Mrs. Barber looked hurt, but she continued patiently, though with an implied reproach. "He put in your wireless set for you. And when the electric light goes wrong, or the bells, as they're *always* doing——"

"Any child could put in a wireless set. He did it very badly, too; brought down most of the plaster, and the thing never worked from the beginning."

Mrs. Barber coloured. "I'm sure the poor boy did his best, and you seemed quite pleased at the time."

"Well, I'm not pleased now," Uncle Horace snapped. "The thing's absurd! Everybody knows the motor trade is overcrowded—all sorts of twopenny-halfpenny firms springing up daily and cutting each other's throats. I've offered to use my influence as a director of the bank, and if he gets in I can look after him and help him."

"I *know* that, Horace. But you won't listen——"

"Who's going to pay his premium?" Uncle Horace asked bluntly.

"Surely, if the boy has a special talent——"

"Special fiddlesticks! It was a taste a minute ago. Anybody has only to look at him to see he hasn't a special talent. If he has brains enough to pass his bank examination it will surprise most of us."

And in truth at that moment Eric did look a good deal more angry and obstinate than talented. He had risen to his feet and now stood before his uncle, with a frown on his handsome, sulky face, and his head lowered, rather like a young bull meditating a charge. Yet it was just this vision of him which moved Tom. Forgotten were all the slights and rebuffs he had received. "He *does* know about motors and things," he burst in impulsively. "He helped Mr. Carteret to take his old car to pieces and put it together again. And the other day——"

"Oh, shut your mouth," said Eric roughly. "I can look after myself without your interfering."

Tom walked to the window, where he remained with his back to the room, looking out into the wet street.

"You *are* a beast, Eric," Jane informed him dispassionately. "I wonder Tom ever speaks to you."

"Nobody was speaking to you anyway," retorted her brother.

Mrs. Barber rose hurriedly from her chair. "You're not *going*, Horace!" she exclaimed, for Uncle Horace was already half-way to the door.

"The children will be able to talk more freely when I'm gone."

"Surely you needn't mind about the children!" At the same time she embraced the entire group in one imploring glance. "It was Tom who started it, though I dare say he meant very well. And Jane said she wanted to show you her poem in the school magazine."

"*Mother*, what a whopper!"

But it was as if with this too emphatic denial the scene had culminated. There followed an uneasy silence, and as it drew out Tom realized that, like himself, everybody had forgotten and everybody now remembered the funeral. Uncle Horace returned sulkily to his arm-chair; his step-mother's face reflected an odd mingling of consternation and bereavement.

"Show him your poem," said Tom under his breath; and Jane went meekly to fetch the magazine.

"Oh, Leonard, do stop!" cried Mrs. Barber tremulously.

The feeble tune, played with one finger, which had begun to tinkle falteringly from the piano, instantly ceased. Leonard got up from the music-stool and he and Eric retired into a corner, where they began to converse together in an undertone. Tom sat upright in his chair. And the minutes grew longer and longer, stretching out till they seemed like hours. Where on earth had Jane gone to? Was she never coming back?

The silence was at last broken by Mrs. Barber, speaking in a half-whisper which perhaps he was not intended to overhear. "Do you think I *ought* to write to Mr. Collet?"

Tom pricked up his ears, but no reply came from Uncle Horace.

Once more his step-mother spoke, and this time her voice had sunk lower still. "The only thing I'm afraid of is that he may say or do something."

"Say or do what?" Uncle Horace grunted irritably, as if he had not yet got over the matter of Eric and the bank.

"Well—you never know. And if he gets any encouragement. . . . Suppose he were to take it into his head that he wanted to *see* Tom!"

"About as likely as that he'll take it into his head he wants to see you."

"You're so *rude*, Horace, when you're cross! Yet you complain of the children's manners!"

"I haven't complained of anything. Even supposing he did want to see Tom——"

"Well, you know the stories there were——"

"I don't."

"And I told you what Elsie said."

Uncle Horace made a gesture of fatigue. "Elsie! Who's Elsie? If you're referring to a lot of servants' gossip—gossip in this case even more nauseating than usual——"

"Nauseating!"

"Well, imbecile then—and libellous—for it was both."

"Elsie wasn't an imbecile. She *came* from Kilbarron, too."

"Naturally she came from Kilbarron, or she couldn't have picked up the gossip."

But Mrs. Barber was not easily silenced. "Some of it may have been gossip," she pursued with a quiet stubbornness. "All the same, there's no smoke without a fire, and you can't deny that he disappeared for *years*. That at least is true, for Edgar told me so himself." She paused, to make her next words more impressive. "What was he *doing* all those years? Even now nobody knows. There was a scandal of some sort, though it happened abroad and was hushed up, so of course at this time it is hard to say to what extent he was mixed up in it. But he seems to have had some very queer friends, and when he came back it was to shut himself up in that house."

Uncle Horace had closed his eyes. He now half opened them. "All this, I suppose, is on the authority of Elsie. I wonder you ever brought yourself to part with her. She must have been singularly ungifted in other directions."

"It isn't on the authority of Elsie. I told you I heard it from Edgar."

"Then you might have kept it to yourself instead of bringing out ridiculous tales before the children."

"The children—I'm sure I've never uttered a word to the children,"

Mrs. Barber was beginning, when she caught sight of Tom's solemn gaze fixed upon her, and stopped.

"You've uttered a good many in the past five minutes," Uncle Horace dropped acidly. "Where do you think Leonard's remark at tea came from? Or was Elsie allowed to unbosom herself to the family in general?" He turned to Tom. "Your mother thinks you've got an uncle out of a fairly tale, Tom; but I shouldn't advise you to build a romance on that. Mr. Stephen Collet is simply a recluse—which is all we know about him."

Mrs. Barber looked first at her step-son and then at her brother. "In my opinion a person who avoids his fellow creatures *must* be——"

But what such a person must be, Tom, to his regret, never learned, for at that moment Jane came back, having found her magazine, and Uncle Horace stretched forth a languid hand to take it. He put on a pair of gold-rimmed eyeglasses, read the poem, and returned it to the authoress without comment.

Jane began to giggle.

"What is there to laugh at, Jane?" her mother inquired severely.

"Uncle Horace thinks it's no good," said Jane.

"And why should you laugh at that? I suppose you *wrote* the poem to give pleasure."

"Well, I'm not going to cry if it doesn't," Jane retorted. "For one thing, I never imagined Uncle Horace would like it, and for another, I don't expect he knows about poetry:—do you, Uncle Horace dear?"

Uncle Horace, however, without even glancing at her, had again risen from his chair, and this time with an air no one ventured to oppose.

3: JANE had whispered to him not to go to sleep, and he lay in the darkness waiting for her. She was extraordinarily fond of these nocturnal conversations. Things she had plenty of opportunity to tell him through the day would be saved up for the pleasure of communicating them at midnight. Tom could see no sense in it. Sooner or later her mother was bound to find out, and then there would be a fearful hullabaloo. But it was just this element of risk which Jane appeared to find so fascinating, and she took elaborate precautions of a kind that increased the danger. To-night, however, was an exception; to-night he wanted her to come; to-night he really had something to talk about. All the same, he didn't intend to lie awake for hours, and had half a mind now to get up and turn the key in the lock. It was useless to go to sleep without doing so, for she would not hesitate to waken him; and he was still considering the matter when he heard the signal she had invented, a scratching on one of the panels of the door.

That too, of course, was silly; but he was supposed to reply to it with a cough, and if he didn't cough Jane would simply go on scratching until she lost patience and came in. So he cleared his throat, and she immediately entered, a dark figure wrapped in a dressing-gown, and plumped down on the side of his bed.

Tom playfully had hidden under the clothes, but he popped out at once when she began to laugh. "Don't make such a row!" he whispered angrily. "You'd think you were doing it on purpose. You might have some self-control."

"Well, it's your fault. You know if I once begin I can't stop."

"Then go away: there's nothing to laugh *at*."

Suddenly his eyes blinked as an electric torch was flashed in his face. "Now I can see you," Jane declared complacently.

"Put that out. Where did you get if from?" He made a grab at her hand.

Jane eluded him, but she switched off the light.

"What is it you want to tell me?" Tom asked.

"Heaps of things. We're going to have a really long talk—longer, I mean, than usual."

"We're not; so if you've anything to say you'd better say it at once."

"I can't unless you sit up. If you don't you'll be falling asleep. I'm going to put on the light."

"No," said Tom.

"But what harm can it do? Everybody's in bed, and it's so stupid talking in pitch darkness."

"I know it is, and I'm always telling you so. If it wasn't that this is very likely the last time——"

"The last time! Don't be absurd! You ought to be pleased and flattered instead of grousing like an old man of seventy."

"Do speak lower," Tom implored. "You know what a scene there'd be if——"

"The only scenes are those you make yourself. You're the most frightful little coward—and frightfully conventional too."

"If I am it's you that put it into my head. I'd never have thought about it except for all your hints."

"I'm an adventuress," Jane admitted. "A dark, fateful woman with lovers."

"Am I supposed to be one of the lovers?"

"Though I'd rather be in the secret service," she pursued thoughtfully.

"What secret service? Your mind's absolutely crammed with rot."

"I must say you're the politest boy——"

"Well, it's your own fault, with your dark fateful lovers."

"I didn't say the lovers were to be dark *or* fateful: they may have sticking-out ears and freckles."

Tom tried to think of a retort, but could not find one. "Was this what you had to tell me? Because if so——"

"I never said I had anything to tell you."

"You did: you kicked me at tea: and you told me afterwards not to go to sleep, because you were coming——"

"Well—so I *have* come. Why don't you tell *me* something, for a change?"

"I was going to, but now I won't."

"You really want me to stay a long time, then?" Jane murmured pensively.

"No, I don't: I want you to go away at once."

"But I've only just come. Tom dear, I can't imagine one single reason why I should be so fond of you."

"Neither can I."

"And yet I'm going to give you a kiss."

Tom moved quickly out of her reach. "Can't you stop fooling," he said.

"I'm not fooling: I'm yielding to affection."

"What have you to tell me about Uncle Stephen?"

"*Uncle Stephen!* Nothing."

"Why did you pretend you had, then?"

Jane drew her fingers softly down his cheek, but he pushed her hand away. "You did: you know you did."

"I'm sorry."

Tom suddenly sat up and clasped his arms about his knees. "Look here, I do want to talk, only——"

"Only what?" Jane murmured.

"I don't want you to make fun of me."

"But I won't make fun of you:—not if it's anything serious."

Tom turned to her doubtfully in the darkness. "You mayn't think it serious," he said.

"Is it about Uncle Stephen?"

"Yes, it is. I've read a book that he wrote. I've got it. I bought it. It's an old book, but Brown's were able to get it for me."

Jane's voice lost its sentimental note. "How long have you had it?" she inquired.

"Not very long: only a week or two. I'd have told you before, but I knew you wouldn't read it. It's all about Greek religion and a lot of it's *in* Greek."

"Why are you telling me now?" Jane asked suspiciously.

"Well——" Tom's voice trailed away.

"Did *you* like it?"

"I liked the bits I understood. There were some bits I didn't understand."

"Is that why you've suddenly begun to take such a violent interest in him? I don't believe it is."

Tom hesitated. "He doesn't know anything about me," he answered evasively. "You see, he was my mother's uncle, and even *she* had never seen him. He's my great-uncle."

"Then he must be as old as the hills," said Jane.

"Not so very old. He's only sixty-three."

"How do you know?"

"I looked it up. Mother had a family tree. *Her* name's in it, and mine. I'll show it to you."

"You put yours in yourself."

"Well," said Tom defiantly—"why shouldn't I . . . ? Anyway, it was Dr. Macrory who told me Uncle Stephen had written a book: but I never thought of getting it till the other day. I don't know *much* about him, but I know something happened when he was a boy, and he ran away from home, and never wrote, and for ages nobody knew where he was or what had become of him. And there were stories told about him. At least I think so: your mother said so to-night."

"What kind of stories?"

"I don't know."

"He *does* sound rather fascinating," Jane confessed. "But of course he may have reformed and become quite ordinary."

"What do you mean?"

"Nothing: and if you're going to be so frightfully touchy about him we'd better talk of Uncle Horace instead."

Tom hurriedly apologized. "Uncle Stephen and I are the only Collets left," he said.

"And you're not a Collet, you're a Barber."

"It's the same thing. Besides, Mother told me I took after her family. . . . Uncle Stephen was very like me when he was young."

"Was he?" Jane asked sceptically. "Did she tell you that too?"

"No, but I've been thinking about it. I wish Uncle Stephen *was* a boy."

"Well, if you're so keen about him why don't you write to him? He might invite you for part of the holidays."

"You saw what happened when I mentioned his name at tea."

Jane's surprise was rather contemptuous. "You mean to say you're going to let a thing like that put you off! Especially when you know how silly Mother is about everybody who isn't exactly the same as herself."

"They said a good deal more when you were out of the room, getting your poem."

"Well, I know *I'd* write, no matter what they said—I mean, if I wanted to. . . . And I bet Uncle Stephen would have written when *he* was a boy."

Tom sat quiet for a little. "I dreamt about him last night," he said softly. He waited for a moment or two, looking back at his dream. Then he went on in the same half-hushed, curiously childish voice. "It was awfully vivid—just as if he was in the room. But it was dark and I couldn't see his face."

"You couldn't have seen it anyway," Jane pointed out, "because you don't know what he's like."

"He spoke," said Tom. "He told me not to be frightened, and who he was. He told me where he lived."

"You knew that already. . . . *Were* you frightened?"

Tom considered. "I think—a little—just at first," he admitted. "That's why it wasn't like a dream."

"People are often frightened in dreams," Jane contradicted. "I've been frightened myself."

"Not in this kind of dream. I—liked it. There was nothing to be frightened about—except its suddenness. He was suddenly there, I mean—in the room, between my bed and the door. And in a dream you're not surprised when a person is there, are you? It doesn't give

you a start. It doesn't occur to you that they *oughtn't* to be there:
it seems quite natural. You're just talking to them, and that's all. This
wasn't like that. . . . Besides, I don't think I'd been to sleep," he
added. "I'd been lying awake, feeling rather——"

He broke off, but Jane divined the unspoken words. "You mean
you were unhappy?"

Tom did not reply.

"It *must* have been a dream," said Jane sharply. "If it wasn't, what
was it? I hope you're not going to be silly about this!" And she
switched on the electric torch to have another look at him. Tom was
staring straight into the darkness.

"If I tell you something," he muttered, blinking and frowning in
the unexpected illumination, which Jane immediately extinguished,
"will you swear to keep it a secret?"

"Do you want to tell me?"

"Not unless you promise."

"All right, then; what is it?"

"You haven't sworn yet."

"I've sworn all I'm going to swear; if you're not content with that
you can keep your secret."

"I'm going to Uncle Stephen," said Tom.

"But——You mean you're going to run away?"

Tom nodded: then realizing that Jane could not see him he
said, "Yes."

There was a pause, followed by a sigh—a sigh which made her
next words the more disconcerting. "What a perfectly heavenly idea!
I'm coming too."

"You're not," answered Tom promptly, his voice, in his eagerness,
rising to its normal pitch. "I'm sorry I told you."

"You'll lend me a suit of clothes," Jane went on as if he had not
spoken. "I'll get my hair cut short, and I'll go as your brother. Uncle
Stephen won't know. You might have as many brothers as Joseph
for all he knows."

"I told you I was serious."

"So am I. It'll be like *Twelfth Night*. You'll be Sebastian and I'll
be Cesario. Uncle Stephen will be the Duke."

Tom said no more, but he felt Jane's arms round his neck, and
her lips pressing against his cheek. "Dear Tom, *do* let me come. It's
the sort of thing I've been dying for all my life. I'll promise to do
everything you tell me. I'll not so much as sneeze without permis-

sion. . . . And I want to sneeze now." She abruptly dived under the bedclothes and was as good as her word.

"You're probably catching pneumonia," said Tom gloomily.

"Well, don't let's talk about it. The question is, when are we going?"

"Of course you can spoil everything if you want to. . . . And you can tell me it was my own fault," he added bitterly. "It'll be perfectly true. Anybody is a fool who imagines he can trust a girl."

There was a silence. Jane withdrew the arm with which she had been clasping his neck. At last she said coldly: "You know very well you can trust me. That part of it is merely sentimental—as well as being a lie. It would be much better to say plainly why you don't want me."

"Because we'd be followed and caught at once and I'd get all the blame."

"That isn't the reason."

"It's one of the reasons."

"And what are the others?"

"I want to go alone."

"Why?"

"Because he's *my* uncle. . . . And anyway I told you. There won't be nearly so much fuss made if I go alone. Very likely there won't be a fuss at all. I should think your mother would be glad."

"Then you'd better think again," returned Jane disagreeably.

"She *will* be glad. She doesn't like me."

"Whether she likes you or not, there's a financial consideration, and she likes that. Perhaps it hadn't occurred to you!"

Tom felt rather shocked. "It oughtn't to have occurred to *you*," he said feebly.

"It didn't till I heard it discussed."

"What!"

"So you see it won't be so easy."

"Of course, I may come back," he mumbled. "Uncle Stephen may send me back."

Jane abruptly altered her tactics. "It's not so bad here, is it?" she asked in her most coaxing voice. "I mean, being with us."

"I don't like it," Tom confessed. "And I think I'll like it less after what you've told me."

"Why?" Jane demanded. "I don't see that anything I've told you ought to make a difference. It seems to me quite right that you should pay your share. You can afford it better than we can."

"It's not that. . . . But since nobody really wants me—except you perhaps——"

"Well, I've explained that they *do* want you."

"Yes, in—in that way."

"I think you're being very unreasonable about it. I never said Mother didn't want you in other ways too. The only thing I ever heard her say against you was that you were precocious."

"Precocious!"

"Mother isn't clever. She doesn't understand you. If you were precocious all round she would understand you better. But in most ways you're just the opposite. It's like a baby coming out with frightfully grown-up remarks."

"Oh."

"I'm not blaming you. As it happens, I like it. . . . I even think you're rather nice-looking. At least, you've got a very nice expression, and——"

"Perhaps you'd better not explain any more."

"What I'm saying is a compliment," Jane persisted. "Or at any rate what I'm thinking. . . . I think you're the nicest person we know. You don't imagine that if you were just an ordinary boy I'd get out of bed at this hour to talk to you. There'd be nothing to talk *about*."

"Nor is there: we've finished," said Tom, and slid down under the clothes again.

Jane had very far from finished. "We've discussed nothing," she went on. "At all events we've settled nothing. When are you going away, and for how long? For ever?"

"I don't know. Very likely Uncle Stephen won't want me either." Tom drew the bedclothes over his ear. "Good-night."

"You don't really think that or you wouldn't be going. You're the very last person to go where you thought you weren't wanted. There's something that makes you think he does want you."

"There's nothing except what I've told you."

"That dream? I don't see how you can trust a dream. It seems to me silly. Uncle Stephen mayn't be a bit like what you imagine. If he isn't, will you come back here?"

"Perhaps."

"That means you won't, I suppose. Where *will* you go?"

"Oh, I don't know. I wish you'd say good-night: it must be fearfully late."

"I don't believe I ought to keep your secret," Jane began, in a new and ominous tone, suggestive of the sudden birth of scruples. "Unless you'll promise to come back here if Uncle Stephen won't have you or if you don't like him."

"You mean you're going to tell?"

"I don't want to, of course."

"No, of course not," Tom echoed scornfully. "Look here; if you do I'll never speak to you again as long as I live. And it won't keep me from going away either, if that's what you think. I wish now I hadn't told you. I needn't have told you, only I thought it would be rotten not to."

Both their voices in the last few minutes had risen, and as Tom finished speaking he suddenly became aware of another sound. He sat up, gripping Jane by the arm so tightly and unexpectedly that she gave a slight scream. "What——?" she began, and then said. "Oh!"

"Now we're for it!" muttered Tom, while they stared at the door, which opened, to reveal in the light she immediately switched on, the bewrapped and imposing figure of Mrs. Barber.

Jane slid off the bed. "You needn't make a fuss, Mother," she began before that astonished lady had even time to frame a question. "And you needn't glare at Tom."

Mrs. Barber glared at Jane instead. "Go back to your room at once," she commanded.

"I'm sorry if we wakened you," said Jane, still rather defiantly. She moved slowly to the door—but her mother answered not a word, nor did she so much as glance at Tom again, but followed her daughter in a freezing silence. There was a click and the light went out: then the door closed and Tom was left alone.

"So that's that," he muttered aloud: but, though he might pretend to dismiss the matter in three words, he lay with his eyes open, staring into the darkness. The sooner he left the house the better. Not that—except to Jane perhaps—he thought what had happened could make much difference. His step-mother was angry, but probably she would be less angry in the morning, and at any rate he would be going away. She was really not an unkindly person, not sulky like Eric, nor sarcastic like Leonard, nor unaccountable like Jane. She had the best temper of them all, and if her affections were exclusively lavished on her own children, there was nothing strange in that. It would have been stranger if they weren't, Tom thought, for he knew well enough that on his side he had neither shown nor felt anything more than civility. He was not much better at disguising his feelings than she was. When it had been possible he had avoided the good-night kiss which from the beginning had been one of the proofs that she "made no difference" between him and the others. He couldn't help it. He couldn't think of her as anything but a stranger—his father's second wife—a dull, good-natured, and rather common person. He had even been glad that she looked and spoke and thought as she did, because it shut her out so completely from the soft clear memory of his real mother.

Clear, but intermittent; sometimes for long periods absent, sometimes returning in a dream, or like a ghost. It was as a ghost now that it glided into the silent room, laying its head on Tom's pillow and taking him into its arms. There had been a time when this ghost had made him cry a little, but now it only made him grave and rather sad. But it still had power to make him wish childish wishes, such as that he could hear its voice. It was strange—very strange—how the sound of a voice had come to be the dearest of his memories. . . .

He knew he was beginning to grow sleepy, which with him at night was unusual. As a rule he was only sleepy in the mornings; at night he dropped asleep without any conscious preliminary drowsiness. But now he knew he was sleepy, very very sleepy, though awake. No voice this; merely the faintest breathing in his ear. "Uncle Stephen —Uncle Stephen." . . . It was his own breath whispering the words. . . . Uncle Stephen, then, was the only living being except himself who had belonged to his mother. Sleepier and sleepier he grew; deeper and deeper he sank into a darkness pierced now by fantastic shafts of dream-light. Yet still he was awake, he knew he was awake, though his spirit had gained a marvellous sense of buoyancy and power. An intense happiness gushed up as from some sunken fount within him, filling his mind, which was no longer conscious either of sleepiness or wakefulness. "Uncle Stephen—Uncle Stephen," he called, half laughing, as if it were a game: and the tall figure dimly visible against the window-blind came noiselessly to his bedside. But in the darkness Tom could not see his face.

"Tom?"

"Yes; I am here."

The faintest grey of glimmering dawn showed in the window-frame. There was a thin awakening twitter of surely the earliest birds. Tom only just noticed these things, sighed luxuriously, and smiled. The freckled, sleep-flushed face turned on the pillow as the small clean body turned between the sheets, and then the drowsy eyelids once more descended. . . .

4: "IT'S all very well," said Jane, "but I don't see how you can go away without clothes. You can't expect Uncle Stephen to lend you things, and anyway, unless he happens to be a dwarf, they wouldn't be much use if he did."

Tom regarded her disconsolately—a not infrequent sequel to their conversations. He was sure she could help him if she wanted to, but this morning she was in one of her least tractable moods.

"It's not as if he had invited you," Jane went on. "Very likely he detests boys. Most people do."

"Couldn't you send some of my things after me?" he suggested humbly. "A small bag would do. And you could address it to the railway station, to be called for."

"If the bag is to be so small why don't you take it yourself?"

"I might be seen."

"So might I."

"But you could wait till some time when your mother was out."

"And I'm to hang about the house—perhaps for two or three days —till she *goes* out? That will be *very* pleasant."

Tom sighed. "I can take my pyjamas and what is absolutely necessary in a parcel. If you help me I can hide it in the yard, and then I'll slip out by the back-door after dinner. I must catch the three-twenty-five. The next train would be too late. I don't know where the house is and I may have a long walk."

"How much money have you?"

Tom coloured. Jane once more had gone straight to the point, and it was this time a point he himself had been alternately approaching and avoiding. She knew it too; he could see that from the stony gaze she had fixed on him. "Not very much," he admitted.

"*How* much?" asked Jane.

"Three-and-eightpence."

Jane's expression grew more stony still. "You're evidently going to walk most of the way," she said unfeelingly. "Three-and-eightpence won't take you far, and you've two journeys to make."

"I can get a through ticket of course."

"For three-and-eightpence?"

Tom waited a moment, but so did Jane. "You got a pound from Uncle Horace on your birthday," he said, "and you can't have spent much of it."

"Oh," said Jane. "*Now* I see why I was taken into the secret!"

"Of course if you like to be a beast about it," muttered Tom.

"Calling names won't do any good."

"Well, why do you say such rotten things then?"

"They're perfectly true things. You mayn't like them, but that's because you're ashamed."

Tom flared up. "I'm not ashamed. . . . You know very well that wasn't the reason why I told you."

"And even if I lent you the money," Jane pursued coldly, "it wouldn't get over the difficulty of your clothes."

"I tell you I'm going to make up a parcel. I'll do it now if you'll stand outside my bedroom door and keep nix."

"It would be better if *I* packed and *you* kept nix."

"No. Somebody might come along and want to know what you were doing in my room. We'd enough of that last night."

Jane, for a wonder, yielded to the argument, and he hastened to take advantage of this compliance. But when five minutes later he rejoined her on the landing she cast a sceptical glance at the parcel. "You don't seem to be taking much!"

"I can't. It has to look like an ordinary parcel."

"Why—if you're taking it out by the back way?"

"I may be seen from the kitchen window."

Jane gave the parcel another glance. She had assumed her most patronizing manner. "Did you put in your toothbrush?" she asked. "Or was that not one of the necessaries?"

Tom controlled his feelings. "I have it in my pocket."

"Handkerchiefs?" asked Jane.

"Yes."

"Well, they *weren't* necessary: Uncle Stephen probably uses them."

Tom repressed a retort: he knew she was only trying to annoy him. "Promise you won't say anything before the others."

"About what?" Jane inquired.

"I mean make allusions—with double meanings."

"You don't mind if they've only a single meaning, then?"

Still he was determined not to squabble. "You know well enough it's the kind of thing you do do," he muttered.

"I think you're perfectly horrid," Jane broke out unexpectedly. "I don't want you to go to Uncle Stephen a bit, though I'm helping you in every possible way, and all the gratitude you show is to call me a sneak, and——"

The sentence ended in an ominous sniff: Now he had made her cry! He felt guilty and uncomfortable, and yet what he had said *really* was quite justifiable. But the weeping Jane had clasped herself to his bosom, her wet cheek was pressed against his, and he could only mumble apologies and tell her he was sorry. He continued to do so, calling himself various unflattering names, until, with a disconcerting shock, he discovered that her grief had changed to amusement.

"I'm *not* laughing," she immediately told him. "At least, if I am, it's hysterical. But, Tom, you *are* a funny boy. No, no—you're a darling. Only I wish you did—even just a little bit—feel sorry."

"Sorry! But haven't I been saying how——"

"Oh, I don't mean *that* kind of sorry. That doesn't matter. You didn't say anything I didn't deserve. I mean sorry about going away. No, I don't mean that either, because of course you're bound to be glad. I don't know what I mean——"

"But I *am* sorry to leave you, Jane. I like you very much. I——"

"Yes;—you needn't strain your imagination. Tell me what I'm to do with your parcel."

Tom breathed the faintest sigh of relief. "As soon as you hear me whistle (I'm going down to the yard now), I want you to chuck it out of the bathroom window. I'll hide it somewhere, and it ought to be easy enough to slip out through the yard after dinner."

"And when I can, I'll lock and bolt the back-door so that nobody will know."

At this so unexpected and reasonable an attitude Tom had a flash of compunction. "You're being awfully decent, Jane. I'm leaving all the worst part of it to you, and you get nothing out of it. But I don't want you to think you've got to tell lies. If you're asked directly, you know, you must tell the truth."

"I can say you talked about running away to sea."

Tom stared. "But I didn't."

"Yes you did; we've talked about it now."

Tom was speechless for a minute. "Oh, well," he said at last, "I think you can look after yourself."

But Jane still held him. "There's something I want to ask *you* to do," she murmured.

"What?" He had hesitated a moment, though only for a moment, because he really wanted to do anything he could.

"You'll think it silly. I think it silly myself."

He waited; and then, "I'll come back when I've hidden the parcel," he suggested, since she seemed loth to proceed further.

"I want you to let me cut off some of your hair," Jane said abruptly, half defiantly.

"My hair?" He looked at her in astonishment. At first he thought she was trying to be funny.

"I can do it so that it won't be noticed," Jane went on.

"But what——"

"Oh, take your parcel," she cried impatiently, "and come back. I'm *going* to cut your hair," she added, as he moved towards the staircase. "If you don't let me I won't help you or lend you any money, so you can make up your mind which it is to be."

"All right; you needn't get excited about it."

"It's because you're so stupid: everything surprises you: the least little thing."

"Nothing that comes from you does," Tom retorted. "I didn't know what you meant at first; I thought you wanted to cut my hair all over. It's the way you said it."

"A scrubby little schoolboy with freckles. I bet nobody else will ever make such a suggestion. What's more, *I* only made it out of kindness. Everything I've ever done for you has been done out of compassion, so you'd better get that into your head."

"It hasn't," Tom replied, now completely enlightened. "And I do understand; I've felt that way myself."

"I don't know what you're talking about," returned Jane loftily. "If you want your wretched parcel you'd better hurry down to the yard, because I'm going to throw it out of the window now—at once."

"All right; I won't be a jiff. And I *am* sorry for being stupid. I think it was because it was about *me* that made me not understand. At any rate, all I was going to tell you——"

"I know what you were going to tell me. You needn't repeat it. Was it Eric's hair you wanted?"

Tom blushed scarlet. "I didn't want anybody's hair," he muttered gruffly. "I wouldn't be such a fool."

"Well, you'd better run downstairs, because I'm not going to wait much longer."

"I'm going. But don't throw it till I whistle: there may be some-body there. And I'll come back when I've finished, and let you——"

"You needn't bother: I've changed my mind," said Jane.

"Well, I'll come back anyhow."

5: THE first part of his journey had been accomplished with comparative celerity, but there had been a long wait at the end of it, and now, on the branch line, the ancient train puffed and panted asthmatically through the summer fields as if quite unused to such violent exercise. There were many small sta-tions, and at each the engine stopped to take breath. Then, with an indignant scream, it would jerk on again, till finally it came to rest where there was no station at all.

Tom, sitting upright on the hard, straight-backed, unupholstered seat of what was little more luxurious than a cattle-truck, with his brown-paper parcel beside him, was neither surprised nor annoyed by the delay. The mood of elation, or at least of expectant excite-ment, in which he had started, was fast ebbing. He had begun to feel nervous, as well as hot and thirsty, but he was in no hurry to reach his journey's end. He was tired of looking out of the window, he had neither book nor paper—nothing indeed to read except the inscrip-tions pencilled on the opposite wall of the carriage—inscriptions of three kinds—religious, political, and improper—though occasionally all three were blended in a single sentence. He wondered why such inscriptions were always the same. Even the prurient impulse seemed incapable of anything but monotonous repetition, and the feeble at-tempts at illustration were still more narrowly limited. He studied the countenance of his only fellow-traveller, a young clergyman who was absorbed in a crossword puzzle. He too had a parcel, obviously a tennis-racket, on the shop label attached to which was typed Rev. Charles Quintin Knox. Tom was interested in names. It seemed to him that people were always like their names. They must grow like them, because of course you weren't *born* Percy or Sam or Jim or Alfred. If he ever had children of his own he would be very careful what names he gave them. What would Charles Quintin Knox be like? Rather stand-offish, rather English public-schoolish, with cold light blue eyes that betrayed not the slightest desire to make your acquaintance. Tom was certain this analysis was not merely the result of his impression of the young man in the opposite corner, though it accorded with it. Would Charles Quintin Knox be good at games? He could tell from this young parson's eyes that he was good at games, just as anybody could have told from Eric's and Leonard's. Perhaps it was only when you were exceptionally good that your eyes had that particular clearness of vision. But his thoughts were interrupted by the sound of shouted questions, and he leaned out of the window to learn the cause of the commotion. From all the other windows people were leaning out, and to his surprise he saw what must be either the engine-driver or the stoker seated on the embankment, lighting a cigarette. Tom had taken the stopping of the train in this secluded spot to be a part of the ordinary procedure, but it looked otherwise, and it was apparently the detached and leisurely attitude of the cigarette-smoker that had excited expostulation.

A grimy oil-smeared person in stained blue overalls came walking down on the sleepers. "There's no use talking," he announced in good-naturedly bellicose tones. "The front's dropped out of her, and ye'll either have to get out and walk, or wait till another engine comes. Jimmy's away to telephone, and God knows how long he'll be."

"What's happened? What's the matter?" Tom's parson had dropped his newspaper and was leaning out over Tom's shoulder.

The man in overalls recognized an acquaintance of a superior order. "It's the engine, Mr. Knox." He squirted a thin jet of tobacco juice in a delicate parabola and with a black hand wiped away the sweat trickling down his forehead. "Sure it was only a matter of time annyway: it's not our fault."

Mr. Knox rejected the excuse. "The engine ought to have been examined," he said. "There must have been carelessness somewhere."

"Ah well, you know yourself, Mr. Knox, the less examining you do on this line the happier you'll be."

Tom laughed, whereupon the man in overalls winked at him and Mr. Knox withdrew.

The man in overalls, after further expectoration, now addressed himself directly to Tom, as the only person who seemed capable of accepting an accident in the proper spirit. "It'll be above an hour likely before they get another engine," he said. "If you're only wanting the next station it would maybe answer you better to walk it: it's not above a mile."

"I'm going to Kilbarron," Tom said.

"Ah well then, you'd have a goodish step, and it's a warm day. . . . But sure it's a lovely view you have there from the window, and his reverence for company."

Whether this hint was sincere or not, it produced an effect. The young clergyman addressed Tom for the first time since he had entered the train. "I'm going to Kilbarron too," he said, rather stiffly.

"How far is it, sir?" Tom asked.

"About five miles."

Tom considered whether he should risk the walk. It was a perfect evening, and though the sun still shone and the air was windless the heat of the day had abated. On the other hand he had never been in this part of the world before and was not very good at following directions.

"I'll walk if you will," he said—a suggestion which appeared to surprise rather than charm Mr. Knox, who answered briefly that he intended remaining where he was.

"I knew he was particular," thought Tom. "Charles Quintin Knox. . . . . And he's got an accent too."

He guessed that his own appearance must be grubby in the extreme: it often was: and to settle the question he wet the corner of his handkerchief and drew it down his cheek. The handkerchief had not been clean to begin with, but on the conclusion of this experiment it was distinctly dirtier. The aristocratic Mr. Knox watched the performance with an air of aloofness.

"I've been in the train most of the afternoon," Tom expained. "I was quite clean when I started."

Mr. Knox nodded. "It's always a dusty business travelling, especially at this time of the year and with the windows open." He again took up his paper and pencil so that Tom could not very well interrupt him by further conversation.

He wanted to: he wanted to ask questions about Kilbarron—questions which must lead eventually to Uncle Stephen. Mr. Knox must know Uncle Stephen. Unfortunately he remained absorbed in his puzzle, occasionally filling in a blank—rather tentatively as Tom could see—but more often chewing the end of his pencil.

Tom re-examined the inscriptions and had another look out of the window, but nothing was altered except that now several of the male passengers were on the railway line conversing in more or less injured tones. Their remarks were uninteresting and their suggestions to the guard futile. Tom took off his cap and rubbed an inquiring finger softly over the top of his head. The result was worse than he had expected. Jane *had* made a mess of it! There was a whole patch near the crown of his head that felt quite smooth. It was well she hadn't done it till after dinner or his step-mother would have been sure to notice. But she must have made an awful mark! Suddenly he became conscious that the young clergyman's eyes were fixed on him over the top of his newspaper. Tom blushed and hastily put on his cap. "Now he very likely imagines I've got ringworm," he thought. "He'll be changing into another carriage."

He decided to explain once more—this time that he was free from contagious deseases. "My sister cut my hair," he said. "At least, she's not really my sister. I expect it's pretty awful. I was in such a hurry I hadn't time to look at it, but she told me it was all right." He hoped Mr. Knox would confirm this view, but Mr. Knox remained dumb. He consulted a gold watch, and then produced a pipe, which he filled and lighted. Tom, after a brief hesitation, produced a crushed packet of cigarettes.

They smoked in silence.

"You're not a scout, are you?" asked Mr. Knox suddenly.

"No," said Tom.

"I thought not."

Tom felt snubbed. But if this parson believed scouts never smoked he must be jolly innocent. He felt inclined to tell him so. His cigarette wasn't half finished, and he had only three more, but he chucked it out of the window.

"Why did you do that?" asked Mr. Knox.

Tom was embarrassed. "I thought you didn't like to see me," he said.

Mr. Knox puffed for a minute or two without speaking. Then he removed his pipe from his mouth. "I rather fancied that was the reason. It was an uncommonly gentlemanly thing to do. If ever you *should* think of becoming a scout I'd like to have you in my troop. But I don't expect you belong to these parts."

"No," Tom murmured, his embarrassment increased by Mr. Knox's approval. "I've never been here before."

"And you're coming on a visit to Kilbarron? I wonder if I know

your name—your surname, I mean—I think I know nearly everybody in this neighborhood."

"My name is Thomas Barber."

"Then I'm afraid I don't know you. Thomas, is it, or Tom?"

"Tom."

"My name is Knox. But perhaps I know the people you are going
to stay with."

"I'm going to stay with Unc—with Mr. Stephen Collet."

The effect of this was delightful. It caused Mr. Knox to look at
him with a vastly increased interest. In fact, he seemed more than
interested.

"You see, I'm his nephew," Tom went on. "Or at least I'm his grand-
nephew. But he doesn't know anything about me. He doesn't know
I'm coming. He was Mother's uncle, and when Daddy died I thought
I'd come to him. I haven't written or anything. I told you I was going to stay with him, but I shouldn't really have said so, because I
don't know yet. He mayn't let me stay: he mayn't even believe I
am his nephew."

Tom poured out this information in an uninterrupted stream,
which ceased abruptly, leaving Mr. Knox looking more surprised
than ever.

"But——You mean you've run away from home—is that it? Or is
it that you now have no home?"

"I ran away from my step-mother's. . . . She's quite decent," he
hastily added. "You mustn't think there was anything—any *cause*.
It was just because—Uncle Stephen belonged to Mother." The last
words came in so low a voice that they could barely have reached
his companion.

That they *had* reached him, however, was apparent in his own
altered tone when he replied, "I understand." After which he paused,
and Tom read in his face a genuine kindness. Indeed he could hardly
have believed it was the same Mr. Knox whom he had watched doing
crosswords, who had rebuked the engine-driver, and who had rejected the invitation to walk to Kilbarron. "I have only spoken to
Mr. Collet once," this new Mr. Knox went on, "but I think it very
likely he will understand too."

"Then you *do* know him?" said Tom, a little wistfully.

Mr. Knox hesitated, but finally, and as if reluctantly, shook his
head. "There's no use pretending. Of course, I have only been at
Kilbarron a little over a year, but I don't think that makes much

difference: I don't think *anybody* knows Mr. Collet. I don't think anybody has been given the chance. Ever since he came to the Manor House—or at least so I have been told—he has kept entirely to himself. . . . A recluse."

Tom recalled Uncle Horace's similar description. "But if he is —so reclusive as all that——" he pondered doubtfully.

Mr. Knox had a further pause. Then he seemed to make up his mind. "Not a bit of it," he replied briskly. "And you won't find him really an old man either. His eyes are as young as yours. They're very remarkable eyes—very deep and blue and clear—extraordinary. . . . I won't say that some boys mightn't be a little afraid of him at first (he doesn't look, and he isn't dressed, quite like other people), but I've a notion you won't be. I rather imagine he's the very uncle for you, or, if you think it should be put the other way, that you're the very nephew for him."

Tom turned to the deepening glow of sunset. "I'm glad you like him," he said softly.

There was just the faintest, faintest stressing of the "you," but Mr. Knox looked pleased. "Ah," he as softly replied, "you *are* his nephew." And then, as Tom's gaze fixed itself on him in a kind of questioning muteness, "Don't bother," he added. "I *did* mean something, but I'm not myself sure what. At all events it had nothing to do with outward appearances, for you aren't in the least like him to look at—even after making every allowance for all the years between you."

"You don't think——" Tom began. "You don't think he'll be angry with me?"

"No. . . . And, if you should meet anybody else—I shouldn't ask questions about him."

Tom gazed, feeling not very sure what this meant. "I don't think I understand," he said.

"I mean, when you reach Kilbarron. Go straight to Mr. Collet."

"Of course," said Tom, though he was still puzzled. "That's what I intended to do."

"Well, that's all right then. You'll have no difficulty in finding your way: I can put you on the road."

"Ought I not to have asked *you* questions?" Tom said, after a longish pause, in which he had been turning the matter over.

"Yes, of course. I only meant——" Mr. Knox, however, found it hard to express what he had meant. "Kilbarron is a small country town," he went on. "With two or three exceptions the inhabitants belong to the semi-educated class, and a good many of them are not even that. Among such people you usually find a good deal of narrow-mindedness and bigotry: also, I'm afraid, superstition. Quite a number of them believe in charms, and fairies, and that kind of rubbish, for instance."

Tom had already picked up the drift of these remarks. *That* was why he wasn't to ask questions. "You mean they don't like Uncle Stephen?" he asked.

"They know nothing about him. It's enough for them that he rarely comes out from his own house and grounds, and that there is something in his appearance slightly unusual:—not that the vast majority of them have ever even seen him. And by the way, it's quite possible, in fact it's practically certain, that you'll find Mr. Collet alone in the house. It's a biggish place, too, with a lot of trees, and it will be dark, I dare say, when you get there——"

"I know," said Tom quietly.

"What do you know?" Mr. Knox's eyes were fixed earnestly on him, but it was, Tom imagined, an expression not uncommon to them. He thought Mr. Knox took things very seriously and would not easily see a joke. He was that kind; but Tom liked him.

"I think that you think perhaps I'll be frightened, and that you don't want me to be, because there's nothing really to be frightened about."

"There *is* nothing."

"Well, I won't be. I mean, I won't show it. It's not that kind of thing I'm afraid of."

"What kind of thing are you afraid of?"

But Tom did not answer. He could not explain to Mr. Knox that he would be afraid of nothing so long as Uncle Stephen was really Uncle Stephen, and that if he should find he wasn't, it wouldn't then much matter what else he was—or matter about the house, or the darkness, or the trees, or the villagers, or anything.

6: ABOUT two hours later they rattled into Kilbarron station where, having got wind of the accident, quite a number of persons had assembled. Tom's arrival thus became a rather public matter. Everybody stared at him as he walked to the

exit beside Mr. Knox, who also accompanied him down the main
street, and then, on the outskirts of the town, pointed out his way.
He was to go straight on for about a mile and a half, when he would
reach a bridge crossing the river. Here he was to take the first turning on his left—Tinker's Lane, it was called—a short cut which
would bring him out close to the house. He would see a wall, and
he was to follow this wall till he came to a wooden gate; he couldn't
make a mistake for there was no other house near.

So along the road Tom trudged, swinging the famous parcel, his
shoes white with dust. The sun had almost reached the horizon, leaving a green liquid sky against which homing birds were black as ink.
And not a soul did he meet till he drew near the bridge, where a
young man stood facing him, with his right arm stretched along the
parapet. It was perhaps the solitude of this unexpected figure which
caused Tom, though only while one might draw a breath, to slacken
his pace. The attitude of the loiterer was graceful and indolent, he
might have been standing for his portrait, yet somehow at that first
glance Tom had received a faintly disquieting impression, which the
dark eyes fixed on him intently did nothing to remove. He thought
of gipsies, for this young man, in his rough homespun jacket and
leather leggings, did not look like a farm labourer, though he might
have been a gamekeeper; but his deeply tanned complexion and the
bright scarlet neckcloth he wore loosely knotted round his muscular
throat were very much in keeping with Tom's conception of a gipsy,
and he wondered if there was a camp in the neighbourhood.

And all this time he continued to advance, though with a growing
embarrassment. For the young man's stare was persistent, and Tom
could not escape from it, even though he kept his own gaze averted.
Nor did he altogether like the brown surly face upon which short
black hairs showed a weekly shave to be nearly due. There was something in its expression to which he was unaccustomed—something
boldy investigatory, vaguely predatory. He himself kept his eyes
fixed on the landscape, nor was it till he was actually abreast of the
figure leaning against the parapet that the latter spoke. "Evening!" he
said.

Tom replied with equal brevity, and had passed on a few yards
when an unaccountable impulse made him turn and ask, "Is this Tinker's Lane?" He pointed to the only lane there was, branching off on
the left, and which he knew very well must be the one he wanted.

And instantly he knew that the young man knew he knew. He did not even trouble to reply, but their eyes met and Tom blushed crimson. Then, with a smile that was only just sufficient to show a gleam of very small and very perfect teeth, the young man asked, "Who'll you be looking for?"

"I want the Manor House."

"Collet's? You going to work there?"

"No," answered Tom, and pursued his way.

He had not gone more than twenty yards before he heard footsteps behind him. He was startled, though there was no reason why he should be, except that the young man on the bridge had presented a picture of a kind of feline laziness not likely to be abandoned without a purpose. Tom's inclination was to walk more quickly, but pride and annoyance prevented him from doing so, with the consequence that in two or three minutes the young man was by his side though not actually abreast with him.

"Beg your pardon, sir: I made a mistake: but there's no offence I hope."

Tom, without turning, replied that it was all right; yet his companion did not drop behind. On the contrary, they were now walking in step together, the young man having accommodated his stride to the boy's. "My mother's Mr. Collet's housekeeper," he said, in a deep, slightly husky voice. "But she doesn't sleep there. Deverell's her name—and mine. Our cottage is across them fields."

This time Tom did not answer. Out of the tail of his eye he could see that young Deverell's face was turned to him, and he had again the unpleasant sense of being subjected to a prolonged and very searching scrutiny.

"I thought I'd better tell you, because unless something's kept her working late you'd maybe be knocking a long while and nobody hear you. The girl—Sally Dempsey—she doesn't sleep in either. . . . You'll be a friend of Mr. Collet's perhaps?"

"Yes," said Tom, quickening his pace.

The young man's stride—noiseless, effortless—still kept step with him: he might as well have tried to outdistance a leopard or a wolf.

"I don't mind seeing you in these parts before. Would the old gentleman be expecting you to-night?"

"No," Tom replied.

"Then he mightn't hear you knocking, and him reading in his books. So if you'd come to the cottage Mother would go back with you."

"I think I'll go on to the house, thanks. Your mother mayn't *be* at the cottage."

Tom spoke, or imagined he spoke, coldly and distantly, but he was not very good at producing such effects, and his companion seemed to notice nothing amiss. He continued to walk close by his elbow. "You'll be staying on a visit with Mr. Collet, likely?" he suggested.

"I dare say. I don't know."

To make it perfectly plain that he wished to be alone, he stepped aside, and began to walk along the grass close to the hedge. But this manœuvre was unsuccessful: he caught his foot in a bramble. He tripped, and would have fallen had he not instantly been steadied by a firm grasp round his body. There was something so miraculously swift in the movement which had saved him that even through his annoyance Tom felt a reluctant admiration.

"It's not easy to see in this light," Deverell said quietly. "You'd best keep to the middle of the road."

Tom, a little out of countenance, accepted the advice. Between the high banks, topped by still higher hedgerows, the light had deepened to twilight. Moths were astir; a white cloudy moon was rising; and when they came to a stile he caught a glimpse of the river, its winding course indicated by a faint mist that hung above it. Tom paused and looked out across the fading meadows, while Deverell waited beside him.

But it was getting late and he stood there only for a minute or two. "I'll take this for you," said Deverell gruffly, possessing himself of the parcel without paying any attention to Tom's refusal.

And they walked on again, now in silence, except that Deverell had begun to whistle softly and in a plaintive minor key. It would be lighter, Tom supposed, when they got out of the lane, which seemed to grow deeper and deeper as they proceeded, that solitary stile being the only gap they had yet come to. The faint scent of briar and meadowsweet was pleasant in the dusk. He kept his gaze fixed on the track before him so that he might avoid treading on the snails.

And by and by he took the paper of cigarettes from his pocket and offered it to Deverell. "You may as well have them: I don't want to smoke any more."

The lane had been bearing all the time to the right, and now began to wind uphill. They must soon reach the end of it, Tom thought, and indeed before Deverell had finished his cigarette they emerged on to a road which he knew was the one he wanted. Along one side of it ran a stone wall higher than his head, and beyond the wall rose the trees of what must be the Manor estate. At this point Deverell stopped and held out the parcel. "I think I'll be bidding you good-night here. The gate's just round that bend."

Tom took the parcel shamefacedly. "It was very good of you to carry it, and to come all this distance out of your way."

"You're welcome," said Deverell.

Tom fumbled with the string of his parcel: he wanted to say something more—something that might make up a little for the suspicions he had shown; but all he could think of was, "My name is Tom Barber."

In the shadow, where they had halted, he guessed, rather than saw, that Deverell's dark eyes were looking at him—guessed really from his attitude more than anything, for he had put his hands in his pockets and was standing, with his legs slightly apart, directly facing him. "What were you feared of?" he asked unexpectedly.

"Nothing," answered Tom. "I thought you were—" He was on the point of saying "a gipsy," but checked himself in time, though he could hit on no politer explanation of his behaviour.

"Still, you *were* frightened, and then about half roads down the lane it stopped."

"That's quite true," said Tom simply. Then he added, "How did you know?"

"I knew well enough."

"You mean——"

"Ay," answered Deverell laconically.

It was not much of an answer, but Tom knew it was all he should get, and for the first time since their encounter he laughed. Deverell did not echo his amusement (he was, Tom guessed, in his own way quite as serious a person as Mr. Knox), but none the less their relation had undergone a modification of some kind when he said. "Good-night, Mr. Tom."

"Good-night," Tom replied.

Next minute he was alone, and the minute after had broken into a jog-trot, for it really *was* very late, far too late to be arriving at a strange house. A most alarming thought occurred to him, that perhaps Uncle Stephen went to bed early. People living in the country often did, and though no doubt he would be able to waken him by hammering at the door, he did not think he should have the courage to do this; he would rather spend the night in the open air. He would be pretty sure to find *some* kind of shelter, and at any rate it was quite warm.

He stopped, and in the brightening moonlight looked at his watch:—twenty-five past ten. Here, anyhow, was the gate—a white wooden gate—very likely the back entrance. But he pressed down the latch with a fluttering heart, for all his misgivings had returned, accompanied by not a few new ones.

In the avenue he had to proceed warily. The moon was not yet clear of the tree tops, and it was so dark that more than once he found himself blundering into the bushes. The black trees towered above him; everything was black and alarmingly still. He was sure now that Uncle Stephen would have gone to bed, and the prospect of spending a night out of doors was much less attractive than it had been only a few minutes ago. He wanted to hurry, but that was impossible. It was difficult enough, even when walking slowly and carefully, to keep to the path, which wound this way and that way, so that there was always a wall of trees directly facing him.

Then suddenly he saw the house. It was there, in the moonlight, dark and solid, and though from this distance he could make out no architectural details apart from two projecting wings and a flat roof, there *was* a light, there were several lights, warm and bright and friendly.

Tom crossed the intervening silver-grey lawn, and on the broad gravel sweep stood still. The porch was wide and deep, but before mounting the two shallow steps leading to it he had to summon up all his resolution. It was a brief struggle, however: he entered the porch, and began to search for the bell. He could not find one, but he found a knocker, and gave two lamentably timid raps.

They were hardly loud enough to have disturbed a mouse, let alone to have waked up Uncle Stephen, yet barely had the discreet sound subsided when he heard footsteps in the hall, and next instant the door opened wide, letting out a flood of light, through which he faced a small, fragile, elderly woman—Mrs. Deverell, he supposed.

"Does Mr. Collet live here?" he was beginning nervously, when his question was interrupted.

"Why, it must be Master Tom! I'd given up expecting you, Master Tom, and was getting ready to go home."

"I know I'm awfully late. I couldn't help it." He stopped suddenly in the bewildering realization that he had been expected. He gazed with astonished eyes at Mrs. Deverell, but the housekeeper had re-plunged into her own explanations.

"You see the master wasn't quite sure which day you'd be coming, and it was only this morning he asked me had I got your room fixed up. And then, even if you came by the last train, I made sure you'd be here by nine o'clock. But your room's all ready, sir, and your sup-per's ready. . . . So you walked from the station! Even so, the train must have been terribly late. And they've never sent on your things: it's just like them! However, you'd better go and speak to the master first, and then I'll show you your room. I kept up a fire, thinking you might like a bath, so the water will be nice and hot. Leave your parcel there on the hall table and I'll take it up. Just follow me, sir."

But Tom had not yet regained sufficient composure to follow her, or even to produce any very intelligible speech, though he did man-age to say the engine had broken down. It was as if he clung to this as the one comprehensible fact in a maze of unreality. Then it flashed across his mind that Jane might have sent a telegram to announce his arrival. But why should she? It wasn't a bit like her to do such a thing. Besides, if there had been a telegram Mrs. Deverell would have known definitely he was coming.

And all this time she was waiting, and had even begun to peer at him rather anxiously. "Uncle Stephen *expected* me?" he said, with an effort forcing his conflicting thoughts into a coherent question. Yet involuntarily he added, "How *can* he have expected me? How can he have known?"

Mrs. Deverell continued to look at him, while an expression of uncertainty slowly deepened in her own eyes. "Didn't you write him a letter, sir?" she murmured. "Or him to you?" Her frail and faded features seemed to beg him to answer "Yes."

"I hadn't time. I——"

"Ah, well," she caught at this as better than nothing, "that's why he couldn't say whether it would be to-day or to-morrow." And her manner struck Tom as carrying an odd note of not wishing to push the matter further. "You'd better come with me now, sir, and tell him you've arrived."

The hall, of whose appearance Tom was only beginning to take in a conscious impression, was square and carpeted; and half-way down it, against the panelled wall, a grandfather's clock ticked with a homely, comforting sound. Beyond this was a wide low staircase, branching off on the first landing to right and left, where it was

backed by three tall narrow windows. From the foot of the stairs
dimly lit passages also extended to right and left, following the lines
of the upper flights. It was towards the passage on the left that Mrs.
Deverell by the gentlest push now impelled him, and half-way down
it she knocked on a door, opening it, however, at the same time.
"Here's Master Tom now, sir," she said in a toneless voice, her thin
hand grasping Tom's sleeve as if to prevent him from running away.

There had been no summons from within, but firmly Mrs. Deverell
pushed him forward, while simultaneously she herself withdrew,
closing the door softly behind her, and leaving Tom, dumb and motionless, on the threshold of what was the largest room he had ever
seen, and which in fact must have covered nearly the whole area of
the east wing of the house.

He had, in his nervousness, a blurred impression of high book-
lined walls, of a soft floating light that dimmed and shaded off into
a surrounding darkness, but above all, though at what seemed to be
an immense distance from him, of a figure seated by a table, a figure
whose grave, kind face and silver hair were surmounted by a black
skull-cap. There was a perceptible pause and an intense silence. The
room rapidly became brimmed with this silence, which passed over
Tom in wave after wave, so that he might have been deep down under the sea. His heart was thumping, his cheeks burned, and all at
once an unutterable misery swept over him. His mouth quivered; he
was at that moment on the very verge of tears; but he forced them
back, biting on his lower lip. At the same time the seated figure had
risen, looking tall, though slightly stooped, in a black costume that
vaguely suggested an earlier period than the present, and showed
only a touch of soft white linen at throat and wrist. But this movement seemed to have the effect of decreasing the distance between
them, and Tom advanced. It was all strange enough, for no word
had yet been spoken, and Tom came forward slowly, step by step,
his arms hanging by his sides, his head drooping a little. He came
on and on till at last he felt a hand resting on each of his shoulders,
and at this he looked up into eyes of the darkest deepest blue he had
ever beheld. His own eyes were misty and again he was biting on
his lip, but he felt a hand brushing lightly over his head, and then
more firmly, so that, obedient to its pressure, he tilted it back a little,
and at the same time closed his eyelids. The hand came to rest, still
pressing lightly on the tumbled hair, and Tom all at once had the
oddest and loveliest impression. He didn't know whence it came—

perhaps out of the Bible—but he knew—and it was as if he had never known anything so deeply, so beautifully—that Uncle Stephen had blessed him.

He felt suddenly at rest: he felt happy: he even smiled faintly —shyly—but contentedly—after a little, rather sleepily. And still he said nothing:—nor did Uncle Stephen. Thus, in fact, Mrs. Deverell found them when she came back. It seemed to Tom as if she had been gone only an instant, though it must have been longer, much longer. She had come to say that Master Tom's room was ready, and that she thought he'd better have his supper now and go to bed, after which she herself would go home.

Tom held out his hand to Uncle Stephen, and they said good-night: then Mrs. Deverell took him off to the dining-room.

He obeyed her in a kind of dream. It had all come about so wonderfully that by now he had ceased to question anything. He supposed he should understand in time, but not to-night—nor did it matter if he never understood. Strangest of all perhaps, was his sense of having plunged into a world utterly unknown to him, but in which he was not unknown, and which appeared to have been always there waiting for him.

And, if he did not understand, he at any rate knew; for this was Uncle Stephen—*his* Uncle Stephen. He had seen him before—twice —though it was only to-night he had seen his face. And he had known the sound of his voice—known it before he had heard it bidding him good-night. Moreover, he thought Uncle Stephen knew too. . . .

"You're dropping asleep on your feet, Master Tom," Mrs. Deverell said as he smiled at her. "And little wonder after the day you've had. The minute you've finished your supper you must go straight to bed."

He had forgotten how hungry he was, but he realized it when he sat down at the table. Mrs. Deverell had prepared nothing elaborate for him, but there was cold chicken and ham, a fresh green salad, and rolls and butter. While he ate she sat knitting, and more than once, when he glanced up, he caught her eyes fixed on him in a mildly speculative gaze, as if she were searching for an answer to a riddle his advent had suggested. She did not tell him that a delicate moustache of milk marked his upper lip, that there was a sooty smudge down one of his cheeks from temple to chin, that his hands were shockingly dirty. Of the last fact, before the end of his meal, Tom himself became conscious. "I say, I shouldn't have sat down like this," he apologized.

"Well, I *was* going to take you upstairs," Mrs. Deverell answered, "but I hadn't the heart to keep you starving any longer. You'd better wash your hands and face though, before you get into bed, or I don't know what the sheets will be like in the morning. I suppose they'll be sending up your luggage first thing to-morrow."

"They won't," answered Tom, his mouth full of lettuce. "I mean, I haven't any. Except that parcel."

Mrs. Deverell suspended her knitting to look at him. "But bless you, child, there's nothing in your parcel except your pyjamas and two or three handkerchiefs and collars and an old pair of flannel trousers!"

"I know. You see I couldn't bring anything that would be missed. I came away unexpectedly."

"Unexpectedly!" Mrs. Deverell resumed her knitting and for a time the clicking of needles and the munching of lettuce leaves provided the only sounds in the room. At last, however, she spoke: "I don't rightly know what 'unexpectedly' means, nor if I'm intended to know, or just to mind my own business."

"You don't even know my name, do you?" said Tom.

"Not your second name," Mrs. Deverell admitted, "unless it's Collet?"

"It isn't: it's Barber; but my mother was a Collet. . . ."

"She's dead," Tom added, after finishing his milk, "and my father died last Friday."

Mrs. Deverell at this laid down her knitting. "Oh, you poor lamb!" she cried. "And me sitting here asking you questions. Now don't you be bothering about anything I may have said."

"But you *haven't* said anything," Tom assured her. "You haven't asked a single question. I ran away, but that was really because I thought my step-mother wouldn't let me come. I mean, I would rather have asked her, only I couldn't risk it."

"And have you told your uncle that?"

"Uncle Stephen?"

"Yes: you must tell him: you'd have been better to tell him at once when you were having your talk to-night, but it will do in the morning."

"All right, I'll tell him in the morning."

"And I must say I hope your step-mother will allow you to stay.

Because your uncle has taken to you: that's very plain. And I won't deny I had my doubts about it beforehand—when he first told me you might be coming. He's never had visitors of *any* sort so long as I've known him. And a boy seemed the last in the world. . . ."

"But I'm his nephew," said Tom.

"Nephew or no nephew. Well, as I say, it's easy to see he's taken to you, and it will do him a world of good to have somebody."

Tom wiped his mouth, brushed the crumbs from his waistcoat, and said, "I met your son on the way here."

Mrs. Deverell looked up without a smile. "Oh, him!" was all she replied, with a slight shake of her head.

"He wanted me to go back to your house, because he thought I wouldn't be able to get in here. He thought you'd be at home."

"You needn't be paying much attention to what he'd think or not think. I suppose he begun asking you questions."

"I asked *him* one first."

"Well, I wouldn't bother your head about him. Mr. Collet wouldn't want you to be making friends with him. I'm his mother, and perhaps oughtn't to say it, but it's little good he's ever done either to himself or anyone else. If you've finished, Master Tom, I'll show you your room, for it's late and I must be going. I'll leave the things here for Sally to clear up in the morning."

Tom jumped to his feet, while Mrs. Deverell turned down the lamp. "Your room's right over this," she continued, as she preceded him upstairs, "and your uncle's is at the end of that other passage." She paused to point it out before opening Tom's door. "Your uncle thought you'd like this room best, it being so bright and cheerful and getting all the sun."

"It's lovely," said Tom, looking round him, "and it must be bright with so many windows," All of them, he noticed, had cushioned window-seats, and he admired the four-poster with its flowered chintz counterpane, on which, looking absurdly small on that immense expanse, his pyjamas were laid out. "I never slept in a bed like this before. It will be like going to sea in a Spanish galleon."

"Well, so long as you don't get lost in it," Mrs. Deverell said. "And you've a bathroom to yourself—through that door there. But you're not to take a bath to-night, after all that supper. There's a hot jar in your bed, though it's such a warm night perhaps you'd be more comfortable without it. I only put one blanket on, so if you feel cold you can spread the eiderdown over you."

"Oh, I won't feel cold: at the present moment I'm boiling. What time am I to get up?"

"The master has his breakfast at nine. But Sally will wake you in the morning. She'll be bringing you a cup of tea, and if you leave your clothes on a chair outside the door she'll take them away and brush them. I brought you a pair of the master's slippers, but I doubt they'll be too big unless you can manage to tie them on. And now good-night, Master Tom, and I hope you'll sleep well. I must be off."

"Good-night, and thank you very much."

But Tom, left to himself, did not at once begin to undress. He first went to the windows and pulled up all the blinds Mrs. Deverell had drawn down: then he made a tour of inspection, opening and shutting drawers and doors. In the big carved rosewood wardrobe there was a mirror in which he could see himself from top to toe. The carpet was thick and soft under his bare feet as he padded about, and at last, having heard the hall-door closing behind Mrs. Deverell, he got into his pyjamas. Now he and Uncle Stephen were alone in the house. Not a sound, not a murmur, either outside or within. It was queer, it was really rather thrilling.

Tom opened his bedroom door cautiously and looked out. The passage was dim, lit only by the light that floated through from his own room, for Mrs. Deverell had taken away the lamp. He carried a chair out and hung his clothes over the back of it; then stood for a moment or two listening. But there was nothing to hear, except the remote ticking of a clock, and he tiptoed—a small pallid figure— along the passage to the staircase, where he hung over the banisters gazing down into the hall. A broad river of moonlight stretched from the landing windows down the central staircase. Tom knew that, according to the way he allowed his thoughts to turn, this silent house might become a place haunted by fear, or by a spirit of extraordinary peacefulness and beauty. But there was no fear in his heart. What actually kept him hovering there in the cool though not cold darkness was a desire to go down to Uncle Stephen. What prevented him from going down was the thought that Uncle Stephen might be displeased if he did. And beneath both the impulse and its repression was the memory of a time when his mother used to come to say good-night to him after he was snugly in bed. That was long ago, but now he wanted—wanted most awfully— Uncle Stephen to come. He remembered his dream. Would there ever be a time when he should be able to talk to Uncle Stephen about it? Why did things never really come right except in dreams? But perhaps they did— here. There had been those minutes—he did not know how many—in the room downstairs, before Mrs. Deverell had returned. . . .

The mellow chiming of the grandfather's clock rose from the hall, dispersing his reverie. "Dickory, dickory, dock," Tom chanted. Then abruptly he was reminded of another clock: but he would not think of those days, and ran back to his room.

7: TOM, wakened by a knocking on the door, opened his eyes drowsily to see another pair of eyes regarding him with a frank and friendly curiosity out of a rounded, fresh-coloured, pleasant face, and concluded that this morning vision must be none other than Sally Dempsey. The vision, the moment he took notice of it, retreated to the landing, only to reappear, however, carrying in first a small tray with tea and biscuits, which was placed on the table beside his bed, and then his clothes more neatly folded than they had been since leaving the tailor's. Sally next went into the bathroom, where he heard her turning on the water.

Tom found such attentions as delightful as they were novel. He ate all the biscuits, and drank all the tea contained in the little china pot with its pink and green sprigs. He lay in his bath luxuriously as a frog. Nor was it a cold bath, as he had feared it might be, and it was so deep that the whole of him was covered at once. He raised and lowered himself from his middle to make warmer waves pass over him, while outside the birds sang and through the open window the sun shone.

But when it came to dressing he looked at his clothes with distaste. He had been obliged to come away in his black suit, and the jacket he *must* wear, since he had no other. But he discarded the waistcoat and the trousers, putting on his flannels. With a clean collar, and his hair nicely brushed, he felt himself to be a much more presentable as well as a good deal more comfortable person than the sticky travel-stained Tom who had arrived last night.

Coming downstairs, he paused on the landing overlooking the hall, where the front door stood wide open. Out in the porch he could see Uncle Stephen, and after a moment of shyness he ran down the last flight to join him. They shook hands, said good-morning, and then stood waiting, Tom supposed, to be summoned to breakfast.

A gong sounded and they went in. Uncle Stephen's place was laid at the head of the table and Tom's at the side. Looking out through the window, he had a view of a man mowing the lawn, swinging his scythe in a slow rhythmic sweep, while the tall grass toppled over and lay still as the blade passed through it. Sometimes a ray of light was reflected from the bright flashing steel on to the ceiling.

Tom was not a great eater—his step-mother accused him of picking at his food, a habit which had much annoyed her—but Uncle Stephen kept a less critical eye upon him, and there being no Gavney boys to create an unfavourable comparison, he did not do so badly. Uncle Stephen, at all events, seemed satisfied, and towards the end of the meal said, "I think, Tom, you had better tell me everything that has happened."

Tom thought so too; but it was difficult to make a beginning.

"I dare say I can guess most of it," Uncle Stephen helped him out, "Only, I should like to know exactly where we are before taking any further steps. And some further steps, I suppose, will have to be taken."

Tom looked out at the summer morning and at the mower; then he looked at Uncle Stephen. Too easily, perhaps, he had jumped to the conclusion that everything was settled; for now he remembered Uncle Stephen really had said nothing about keeping him. The preparations might mean no more than that he was to be a visitor for a few days! He lowered his head and sat there without a word.

Uncle Stephen glanced at him. "What's the matter?" he asked. "What is troubling you?"

"Nothing," Tom replied; and after a moment proceeded to give an account of yesterday's adventure. The account was fragmentary and at times obscure—particularly in all that had led up to the actual journey—but Uncle Stephen did not interrupt him. When Tom had ended he merely asked, "What are your own plans?"

It seemed to Tom that he had made his plans very plain indeed. At any rate he could not express them more openly until he knew they were Uncle Stephen's also, and now he supposed they weren't. For a moment he saw himself returning to Gloucester Terrace—but that at least should not happen. He remained silent. His knife dropped to the floor and he was a long time picking it up.

Uncle Stephen was watching him closely. "Perhaps that was not a good way of putting it," he said. "What I really meant was, that I suppose, until you have given it a trial, you won't be able to tell me whether you would like to stay on here or not. You see, by 'stay here' I mean live with me, looking upon this house as your home. You are bound to find it very quiet—and not only quiet, I'm afraid, but dull; for the quietness wouldn't matter if you had a companion of your own age. Unfortunately there is nobody—at least I know of nobody. There are young people of course, but they're not of your class."

"That doesn't matter."

"Doesn't it?" Uncle Stephen seemed more doubtful. "Perhaps you're right: I don't know."

"Do you want me?" Tom asked, his bright eyes on Uncle Stephen's face. "Please tell me truly."

"I thought you had made up your mind about *that* part of it last night!"

"Yes, I did."

"And what conclusion did you come to?"

Tom coloured. "I thought you wanted me," he said.

Uncle Stephen allowed a few seconds to elapse before he replied, "Well, Tom, nothing has happened since."

"Then you *do* want me?" said Tom with a little sigh of relief.

"Of course I want you, but it isn't only what I want that has to be considered."

"It is—if I want it too," Tom answered.

Uncle Stephen looked out of the window. "I suppose I shall hear from your step-mother to-day," he said. "I shall write this morning to ask her to send on your things. Temporarily, I don't expect there will be any objections made. Unless, of course, the question of school should arise—I was forgetting that."

"It won't arise," said Tom. "I wouldn't have been going back before the holidays even if I'd been at home. The holidays begin next week."

"Even so," Uncle Stephen pursued, "holidays can't last for ever. What we want to reach is a permanent arrangement—something which will prevent the whole question from being reopened in a few weeks' time. You see, if you are to become my boy, I should like you to live with me—all the time—not only during your holidays."

"Yes," said Tom, "of course. I *will* live with you."

"But in that case it will have to be settled properly—definitely. And we must find you a tutor."

"Couldn't *you* teach me, Uncle Stephen? I wouldn't give you any trouble: I'd do everything you told me."

"I don't think that would be a good plan, though we might sometimes read together if you would care to."

"I'd love it."

"But we've got to remember that in two or three years you'll be going to a university, and therefore there should be somebody who can direct your work along the usual lines. I can't. I never was at a university, and even if I had been, my experience would now be out of date. My own training was special and entirely *un*usual. It would be well to have all this part of it as cut and dried as possible. We might speak about it to your curate friend."

"Mr. Knox?"

"I know even less about him than you do: still, if he is willing to coach you, I think his qualifications ought to be sufficient. You don't require a *great* deal, do you: you're clever enough to do the real work yourself?"

"Yes," said Tom.

"So if you called to ask him to come to see me, we might sound him on the point. I've an idea that it would be as well to get hold of him as soon as possible."

"I can go this morning. I know where he lives; he showed me the house."

"The more practical our plans are, the better. That is, of course, supposing certain difficulties *should* be raised."

"Yes." Tom had no very precise notion as to what kind of difficulties were meant, but he had a complete faith in Uncle Stephen's wisdom.

"There's a good deal," Uncle Stephen went on, "about which we are still in the dark."

"Yes," said Tom again, though this time he added as an afterthought, "Is there?"

Uncle Stephen laughed. He pushed back his chair, and Tom slid off his own seat and came and stood beside him. Then he sat down on the edge of the chair, and Uncle Stephen, taking the lobe of Tom's left ear between his finger and thumb, pressed it gently. "You don't believe there will be any opposition?"

"But I'm here now," Tom replied.

"Yes, you're here, and we'll hope that in this case possession will be nine points of the law. It's the tenth point that may be troublesome. You see, Tom, your father must have made a will, and it's quite likely he appointed somebody to be your guardian."

"Uncle Horace?" Tom suggested, though without conviction.

"Uncle Horace perhaps—the particular person doesn't much matter. What matters is that any such arrangement will leave us awkwardly placed."

Tom weighed the proposition for half a minute. "I don't believe there *is* such an arrangement," he declared. "To begin with, I don't believe Daddy liked Uncle Horace. And there's nobody else except my step-mother. Besides, anyway, what can they do?"

"That," said Uncle Stephen, "remains to be seen. I imagine legal proceedings could be taken if I refused to give you up. It would depend on whether they thought it worth while."

"You mean a trial?" said Tom, and the idea amused him greatly.

"Not a trial exactly—though goodness knows what a lawyer mightn't make out of it. You never can tell. We must make inquiries of our own lawyer, who will be Mr. Flood. I'll have a talk with him about it: in fact you might leave a note at his office when you go to see Mr. Knox."

His eyes rested on his nephew's, and there was in them an odd light of half-amused complicity which instantly recalled to Tom the description Mr. Knox had given in the train. "But what can they *do*, Uncle Stephen," he persisted, "even if they do go to law about it?"

"I hope nothing, but I expect they would begin by trying to prove me an unsuitable person to have charge of you."

Tom was unimpressed. The one important thing to him was his acceptance by Uncle Stephen, and in the light of this the hypothetical struggles of Uncle Horace and Mrs. Barber to regain custody of his person struck him as negligible. "All we'd have to do would be to prove you *were* suitable, and I could easily do that."

"Yes. I don't know that your wishes would be exactly the point in question—still, they might have some weight. The real difficulty, Tom—the thing we can't get over—is that during all the fifteen years of your existence I never once showed the slightest concern for your welfare. This *does* give the others a claim. There is no use denying it, and it will be quite open to them to ask why, when I never showed an interest in you before, I should begin to show one now. You might even ask that yourself."

Tom shook his head.

"Haven't you wondered?"

But it was hardly a question; or, if it was, it was addressed to himself rather than to the boy, who however shook his head once more; then thought for a minute or two, and at last seemed to catch at something. "It was because——" He stopped there, trying to read the remainder of his sentence in Uncle Stephen's face.

"Because of what?"

Tom coloured. "Because it wouldn't have been the same," he said.

Uncle Stephen did not reply. Tom saw, indeed, that he was lost in thought. What that thought was he could not guess, but it left his eyes rather stern. A lock of fine white hair dropped down below the silk skull-cap over the delicately moulded temple. Tom noticed the tiny blue vein that ran up beneath it; the curve of the ear, the cheek, the mouth, the nose, the hands. He called up for comparison pictures of all the other people he knew, but there was nobody in the least like Uncle Stephen. That grave and impenetrable countenance, which was only partially turned in his direction, so that he saw it little more than in profile, seemed to him as strange as it was beautiful. But it *was* beautiful: Uncle Stephen really was a beautiful old man. And it was quite certain that he liked Tom, which, so far as the latter was concerned, settled every difficulty. He felt indeed settled for life. He was utterly determined to resist whatever authority, legal or domestic, might be exerted to take him away. If both Uncle Horace and his step-mother were at this moment to drive up to the door he wouldn't care.

"Uncle Stephen," he said, and put his hand on Uncle Stephen's arm, giving it a small pull a bring him out of his reverie. It was odd how he could at once not understand Uncle Stephen and at the same time understand him so well, for he knew immediately that this little touch of familiarity had pleased the old man. "Uncle Stephen, it wouldn't have been the same if I hadn't come to you of my own accord, would it?"

"You mean if I had gone to fetch you?"

"Yes—or if you had written. Of course, you knew I was coming, but even so——"

"Well—even so?"

"If I hadn't come of my own accord you wouldn't have wanted me." Tom had made it all out at last clearly. "My coming the way I did showed you it was all right—that I was right—the right kind of boy for you. It doesn't sound conceited for me to say that, does it? I mean, I hope it doesn't sound as if I thought a lot of myself; because I don't."

"We've wandered a good deal from where we started," Uncle Stephen replied, "which was not whether you were the right kind of boy, but whether I was the right kind of uncle."

He looked at Tom, who immediately answered, "It's the same thing. If I'm right for you, you *must* be right for me. . . . And of course—anyway—I knew last night."

8: WHILE waiting for Uncle Stephen to write the notes Tom went out, but he found the lawn deserted, and attracted by the sound of voices wandered round to the back of the house. The mower was there, having come for a drink, and Sally Dempsey, standing by the open kitchen door, was disagreeing with him, if not actually quarrelling. Her face was flushed and she did not look at all so good-tempered as the person who had awakened Tom that morning. Her companion, on the contrary, turned to him with a broad grin, and a warning that the atmosphere was dangerous. "You'd better keep your distance, Master Tom; she's as cross as a bag of cats because young Deverell come to the house this morning."

Tom looked from one to another doubtfully, aware that he had appeared at an unpropitious moment. "I was talking to him last night," he said. "He walked part of the way with me."

"Well, don't you have anything to do with him, Master Tom. You couldn't trust him; he's sleekit; any time he was round here there was always something missing afterwards."

"Oh now!" the man with the scythe expostulated, but his good humour was wasted.

"It would answer you better, George McCrudden, to mind your own business and not be standing up for an idle young lout that never did an honest day's work in his life but is content to let his mother keep him!"

George winked at Tom. "He was never one for the girls, Master Tom: that's why he's having a bad character put on him."

Sally tossed her head. "It's little any decent girl would have to do with him; and the black looks he'd give you out of the side of his eyes when he'd meet you on the road."

"He knows too much about them," George continued humorously.

"And he knows what the inside of a jail's like," Sally retorted.

At this George ceased to grin. "Come now," he said, "you've no call to be setting Master Tom against him, just because you've been having words and lost your temper. You'll be saying something you'll regret if you're not careful. Poaching isn't anything so very sinful, and that was all they had against him." He turned to Tom and added good-naturedly, "There's Master Tom himself, I dare say, has gone after apples and such, and there's no great difference."

"No great difference! You can say that, and you a man getting on in years with a family of boys growing up that would maybe listen to you! Putting such notions into Master Tom's head, too! Hasn't he his own apples—as many as he wants—without you'd have him stealing other people's!"

George sighed. "I'm not saying——" he began: then gave it up. "Anyways, Master Tom knows what I mean, and that things is sometimes done for sport that wouldn't be done otherwise."

"Well, you'd better be getting back to your work if that's the kind of talk you have. I didn't know you'd got so great with Jim Deverell." And Sally retired into the kitchen, slamming the door.

The discomfited George stood for at least a minute, staring at the spot she had vacated. He drew the back of his hand across his forehead, scratched an ear, and looked at Tom. "I'm not great with him," he announced, "and there's maybe a bit of truth in what she says, though it's just because she's taken a skunner against him. Women's always like that. If she had a fancy for him he might do all the poachin' he wanted an' she'd be at the jail door to meet him comin' out. Not that he's any friend of mine, for he was always dark in his ways, even when he was a young limb—never joining with the other lads when they'd be jokin' the girls, but keeping to himself. An' when he was no more'n a wee fellow he'd be going into the woods alone at night, and his mother thinking she had lost him. Ay, an' I mind him going away with some tramp he'd picked up with. He come back a month after, an' would say nothing, where he'd been or what he'd been doing. The schoolmaster he give him a leatherin', an' the young devil bit him so that he had to carry his arm in a sling for above a week. After that he was always runnin' off and comin' back. Sometimes he'd do a job of work, but he'd never keep a place, and at the latter end few would employ him. I tried giving him a job myself in the garden, but it was no good, you couldn't depend on him. Still, Sally had no call to be sayin' what she did. But you'll never get a woman can keep from bletherin'. They're all alike. What I say is, a man may know plenty, but he keeps his mouth shut. Isn't that so, Master Tom?"

"Well, you've told me a few things about him yourself, you know," Tom replied, anxious to be fair.

"No, Master Tom, I haven't. A man can always keep his mouth shut."

"But hang it all, you gave me his complete family history. I don't mean to say I didn't want you to. But there's no use pretending it came from Sally, because Sally told me nothing except that he'd been in jail."

George looked at him reproachfully. He fumbled in his trousers pocket and produced a black-handled single-bladed knife and a quid of tobacco from which he cut off a portion. This he placed in his mouth before saying a little grumpily, "Well, I gotta get back to my work."

He clumped out of the yard, accompanied by Tom as far as the hall-door. The notes for Mr. Knox and Mr. Flood were ready, and, having inquired from Uncle Stephen what time he was to be back for dinner, Tom set out to deliver them.

For a short while he stood watching George at work. Tiny blue butterflies hovered near the trees, and the scythe passed through the ripe tall grass with a faint swish. A puff of warm soft wind lifted the hair from Tom's forehead: the day was going to be hot, like yesterday.

George was already hot: Tom could see the sweat glistening under his hair. His hands and forearms were brown as oak bark; above the elbow his arms were white. The blue dye of his shirt was half washed out, and had acquired a pleasing tint that harmonized with his surroundings. His trousers were of a neutral earthy hue, and Tom wondered how he kept them up, for he wore neither braces nor a belt.

Leaving George, he sauntered down the dark avenue and took the road he had traversed on the previous night. But everything looked different now, particularly Tinker's Lane, which was deep in sunshine and zooming with wild bees. There was the stile he had looked over, and there the river—no longer veiled in mist, but bright as a snake between its green banks. Not only was there this change of aspect, but the walk itself seemed shorter—no distance at all compared with the tramp he had found it last night.

Mr. Knox was out, so he left the note with his landlady, and was free to do some sight-seeing. To most people sight-seeing in Kilbarron would have proved rather dull. It was an ordinary little country town, without a past and without a future, but Tom discovered attractions. He loitered in the market-place, which was smelly and more or less deserted; he came out into the High Street. He inspected the bank, the town hall, and the post-office, as conscientiously as if they had been buildings of European fame. Lower down the same street he came on the Unionist Club and the offices of R. P. Flood, solicitor (*their* solicitor, his and Uncle Stephen's), where he left his second note; while just round the corner was the Royal Cinema, whose coloured posters he stopped to study in the company of a red-haired message-boy—a butcher's boy, as the parcels in the carrier on his bicycle showed. The butcher's boy was less interested in the posters than in Tom, though this interest partook of suspicion. Eventually, however, a desire to talk of the film overcame distrust of the stranger. The butcher's boy had seen it on the previous night, had in fact seen it twice, and soon they were in the thick of its entanglements. Tom gazed at a distraught female clinging passionately to a cold and aloof young man. "Is she his love?" he asked, for he had these quaintnesses of vocabulary.

The butcher's boy stared stolidly at the lady. "What d'you mean, his love?" he presently said. "She's a tart."

"Oh," said Tom.

"Can't you see he's spurning her?" the butcher's boy continued. "He's got a girl already. His girl's the other girl's sister."

"What other girl?" asked Tom.

"The tart. His girl's the tart's sister, but he doesn't know that, because she calls herself another name."

"Who does—his girl?"

"No, the tart. What would his girl change her name for? Have a bit of wit."

"But why should the tart change hers?" asked Tom, bewildered.

"Ah, you're silly. Tarts always chooses fancy names—foreign names. I don't believe you know what a tart is."

"Yes, I do."

"Well then, what you talkin' about." The butcher's boy gave him a scornful look, mounted his bicycle, and rode away, leaving Tom to pursue his tour alone.

His next pause was before a stationer's window, filled with paper-backed novels showing pictures of masked men in evening dress pointing revolvers at persons of both sexes also in evening dress. Occasionally the man with the revolver was not in evening dress, and then Tom recognized a detective. A small sprinkling of wild-west and idyllic pictures interested him less, though he read all the titles and the names of all the authors, and after he had done so could have given each one of these correctly. With a like thoroughness he worked his way through the dismal vulgarities of a row of comic postcards. There was never a smile on his face; the feebly bacchanalian, or timidly salacious jests did not amuse him in the least; but he accomplished his task. . . . He went into a confectioner's and bought some chewing-gum. Then he asked for a drink of water. . . . He bought a fishing-line and some hooks; he would have bought a rod, only his money—Jane's money, he remembered—was not sufficient. He lingered to watch a young man in difficulties with a motor-bicycle, and when, after a succession of horrible detonations, the bicycle started, he took up a position on a weighing-machine. He did not put a penny in the slot, but his slim brown hands grasped the sides of the machine, while he jerked himself violently up and down, making the pointer on the dial jerk too, until an enraged hairdresser, brandishing a pair of scissors, rushed out to dislodge him. Tom apologized and proceeded on down the street. He came to the rescue of a lady whose dog was fighting with another dog, and when the animals were separated—not without clouds of dust, furious barks, and considerable risk of bites—he decided that it was time to go home.

At the gate he caught sight of Uncle Stephen, who had come out to look for him, and Tom broke into a run. Together they walked up the drive.

"Well, what mischief have you been up to?" Uncle Stephen asked.

Tom told him. He prattled happily of everything he had seen and done. He found Uncle Stephen very easy to talk to. "But Mr. Knox was out so I just left the note."

"In the meantime your telegram has arrived," said Uncle Stephen. "It came an hour ago."

"*My* telegram?"

"A telegram about you."

Tom was delighted. "What was in it? Did Jane tell?"

"That I can't say. It was merely to ask if you were here."

The telegram itself was on the hall table when he went in, and Tom read it. He brought it in to dinner with him and read it again, aloud. "Pringle," it was signed, and Tom accentuated the name, which for some reason he found amusing. Also he saw in it a sign that battle was imminent, and the idea of battle, with himself and Uncle Stephen fighting on the same side, pleased him extremely.

"They won't get your letter till to-night," he said gaily. "Or perhaps to-morrow?"

"To-morrow, I fancy. But I've sent a telegram too. Indeed, Mr. Pringle very kindly prepaid a reply. 'Tom arrived safely am keeping him.' Was that right?"

Tom considered. "Yes," he said, "that ought to do it. At least, it may."

"Do what? Not, I trust, create annoyance."

"Oh, it will do that all right. But 'Am keeping him permanently' might have been better."

Uncle Stephen looked at him. "I've been quite clear about the permanence in my letter," he said. "I've asked your step-mother to send on your belongings—all your possessions—books, clothes, everything."

Tom had a vision of the arrival of this letter, of its being opened by his step-mother, of her face as she handed it to Uncle Horace, who would be standing, fussy and angry, on the hearthrug. The scene appealed to him. If the letter arrived in the morning she'd take it to the bank, though visits to the bank were rarely risked, Uncle Horace having expressed himself strongly on the subject.

After dinner he followed Uncle Stephen to the library. He wondered if he might suggest going down to the river. The river attracted him, and as yet he had only seen it from a distance. On the other hand, Mrs. Deverell had told him Uncle Stephen rarely, if ever, went outside the Manor grounds. Before he could make up his mind Uncle Stephen himself settled the question. "It is just possible Mr. Knox will call this afternoon. I didn't mention any time to him. Do you think you can manage to amuse yourself?"

"I don't mean in here," he went on, as Tom turned to an examination of the bookshelves. "It's far too fine a day for that. Why not go out and explore the place? It's all pretty wild—a regular jungle—but there are paths, and even an old garden, if you can find it."

So Tom went out alone, though he determined to leave the exploration of the grounds for another day, and to go down to the river. There was an easy way to get to it, by Tinker's Lane, but when he reached the gate he decided against this. The bridge at Tinker's Lane was more than half a mile off, and though the river was not visible from where he stood, he was certain he could reach it without going near the Kilbarron Road. At any rate he would try. So he scrambled through a gap in the opposite hedge, and skirting a tract of ploughed land, made for the meadows beyond. The grass was long here —all these fields were hay fields—and Tom supposed he ought not to trample it down, but to keep close by the edge. Anyway he liked hedges, and this was the finest he had ever seen, eight or nine feet high, a double hedge, with a narrow ditch in between, dark and green and cool, having a trickle of water at the bottom of it, which he could hear, though a dense tangle of vegetation—cow-parsley, vetches, convolvulus and brambles—hid it from sight. Here and there the hedge was broken by a beech-tree, its dark corrugated branches showing through the golden-green leaves. Honeysuckle was in bud, and the fresh young bracken gave out its peculiar, cold, slightly astringent perfume. On his left the trees of the Manor woods looked almost blue.

The sun beat down on the wide meadow. The ripened grass, heavy now with seed, trembled, though to Tom the wind stirring it was imperceptible. And in contrast with the green path by the hedge, where he walked partly in sunlight and partly in shadow, the colour of the meadow was a tapestry of infinitely delicate shades—greys and browns, pinks and mauves, gold and crimson, flecked here and there with the vivid whiteness of dog daisies.

Tom had never seen anything so like his idea of a prairie. If he had waded out through it the grass would have reached almost to his thighs. Small blue butterflies like those he had seen in the morning— nearly the same colour as the speedwell flowers and nearly the same as the sky—hovered in the quivering air, close by the hedge. The shrill hidden orchestra of grasshoppers played their ancient Greek melody, through which, from somewhere behind him, the two notes of a cuckoo broke monotonously—the dullest of all bird songs, Tom thought, really not much better than the clock.

Once or twice, as he proceeded, he fancied he heard a sound on the other side of the hedge, but when he peered through the dark trellis he could see nothing. It came, he thought—this stealthy rustle

—from the field beyond, and he stopped to listen. Again he heard it —a sound of movement, but certainly not made by a horse or a cow. This was the movement of a much smaller beast—a dog perhaps, or even a cat—come out hunting—for not a few creatures must have their homes and their runs in this hedgerow—rabbits, birds, mice, and hedgehogs. Tom whistled, but no dog appeared.

He cut himself a rod from an ash-tree, and went on his way. From the beginning he had been ascending a continuous though very gradual slope, and when he reached the brow of this long low gradient he saw the river beneath him, about two hundred yards distant. Tom decided to bathe. He ran down the gorse-splashed hill, which on this side was much steeper; found between two ancient whins an undressing-place; and three minutes later was in the water. The current was sluggish, dragging its winding course by beds of willow-weed, loose-strife, and flowering-rushes; the water was warm on the surface and of a sweetish taste. He was drifting and splashing luxuriously when he remembered the warning, so often impressed upon him, that to bathe within an hour or two of a solid meal was always dangerous, and frequently fatal. Something or other happened inside you and you expired in agony. Was anything happening now? He couldn't *feel* anything. But something *might* be going on inside him all the same. Anyway, it wasn't so nice as bathing in the sea. The water had a slightly oily feeling against his skin—particularly against the tips of his fingers; it was as if he were bathing in milk. And it wasn't only the feeling; it was partly the smell—a sleepy, sticky kind of smell—not a bit invigorating like the smell of the sea. The sea produced sharp little prickles all over you, but the river clung to you like syrup. It, too, was pleasant enough, of course—in a lazy, water-lizard kind of way, and when you got used to the green weeds trailing round your legs, which at first felt slimy. Tom, standing up to his knees in the shallow water at the edge, slowly picked them off his body and limbs.

He lay on his back in the grass, and the hot golden sun licked his body, poured over and penetrated him. He shut his eyes and tried to imagine the sun as a God. Or a God might come to him out of the river. He would not open his eyes until he had counted fifty slowly, and then——

He opened his eyes. . . .

It would be pleasant if the old tales were true—or some of them. He would read Uncle Stephen's book again. Uncle Stephen seemed

to believe, not exactly in the stories, but in something behind them
—powers, influences, a spiritual world much closer to this world than
the remote heaven of Christianity. Was that why Leonard had called
him a magician?

He sat up. The river glistened in the brooding sunshine. He would
come here to fish, he told himself, for *The Compleat Angler* had been
one of his school prizes, and this river reminded him of it. He did
not see any fish, but probably by bathing he had frightened them
away. It *looked* a good place. Only, as he had never fished in his life,
this judgement was perhaps not worth much. What he *did* see were
dragon-flies—bright, strange, metallic creatures, iridescent in the sunlight. And they carried his mind back to the afternoon of his father's
funeral. All *that* seemed now infinitely remote; he had a feeling that
his whole life had changed since then. He remembered he had been
unhappy, but this unhappiness was now like a far-off cloud barely
visible on the horizon. It disappeared entirely when he heard a plop
on the farther side of the river and saw a small animal swimming
straight towards him.

Tom laughed. The God, as usual, was taking a strange form, for
this was a rat. Eric and Leonard had once gone out hunting rats with
another boy and a couple of terriers. That was supposed to be sport.
Why? This rat, at any rate, must have made up his mind that Tom
was not a sportsman, because he landed among the rushes within two
yards of the spot where he was sitting, his hands clasped round his
knees. There was a slight movement among the rushes, a slight rustle,
and the rat was gone. "This place is swarming with wild life," said
Tom.

It was an optimistic view, perhaps, for half a dozen dragonflies,
some water-grigs, and a rat comprised the entire fauna he had as yet
observed. But now he saw a frog, a very small one, reclining on the
leaf of a water-lily. Tom bent down and gazed at him. The frog did
not return his gaze, did not seem to do so at all events, for his black
unblinking eyes were fixed on the sky. He was as still as if he had been
carved in bright stone; yet now and again Tom could see him breathing. And suddenly it struck him with a little shock of surprise that
this frog was one of the most lovely things he had ever beheld. He
was lovely. In his shaping there was a delicacy and a perfection that
could hardly be possible in so large a creature as a human being. Or
was it that most human beings were faulty specimens, did not come
nearly so close to their own perfect type as frogs and other animals

did to theirs? Why was that? He remembered the line of a hymn, "And
only man is vile." So *that* was what it meant! He had known the line all
his life and never guessed its meaning till now. He had always supposed
it to refer to people who weren't religious. But this new meaning must
be the real meaning, the meaning it had had for the author of the
hymn, who quite possibly had been looking at a frog when he wrote
it. Tom thought of another line:—"And every prospect pleases." He
gazed round him, and with delighted recognition saw that this was
equally true. There was not a single thing he could see that wasn't
beautiful. What a fine hymn it must be! As if to put it to further
proof he ran to a spot on the bank, where, beyond a bed of rushes, the
water brimmed clear and cool and still. And there he stood gazing
down at his own image reflected in the stream. The image of man's
vileness! Well, it certainly wasn't much to boast about. Not exactly
vile perhaps, but absurdly unprotected-looking, as if anything could
hurt it. Even a snail without his shell would not look so much at the
mercy of his surroundings. But there were boys who didn't look like
that when they were naked. Eric and Leonard didn't.

Tom returned thoughtfully to his clothes and began to dress. He
was half-way through his toilet when a shadow fell on the grass beside him, and looking up he saw Deverell. Tom was not startled, but
he was surprised. Not only was Deverell there, but he was accompanied by a liver-and-white spaniel, and both must certainly possess
the gift of moving noiselessly as phantoms. Then he remembered the
sounds he had heard before—the sound on the other side of the
hedge. That might have been the spaniel—a little less noiseless than his
master. Tom now suspected that Deverell had been following him
all along.

He was annoyed. He hated slyness. It was so unnecessary too—
and stupid. It annoyed him, moreover, because it reminded him of
what Sally Dempsey and George McCrudden had said. Meanwhile
a smile had been dawning slowly on the young poacher's face. He had
shaved, Tom noticed, and his dark eyes had a much less sullen
expression.

"Nice day, Mr. Tom. You been in for a swim?"

"Yes, I have," answered Tom rather crossly. "I suppose you were
watching me." The spaniel began to snuffle at him with a blunt, pink-
ish nose, and Tom scratched his ears.

"I seen you," Deverell admitted, "but I thought maybe you
wouldn't like me to come down. Would you a' minded, Mr. Tom?"

"No," answered Tom, rather less crossly. "But I do mind being followed."

"I wasn't following you."

Tom looked across the river. "I think you were. I think you were on the other side of the hedge."

Deverell stood without speaking for a minute or two; then he sat down on the bank beside the boy. "Not much doing round here, Mr. Tom, is there?"

Tom looked straight before him. "I suppose that depends on what you want to do. I should have thought there was plenty." The spaniel thrust his head against Tom's shoulder, trying to attract further caresses, but Tom was not pleased.

"Dingo his name is," Deverell went on. "He's made friends with you already. Dogs always knows the right sort."

"The right sort for them, perhaps," said Tom ungraciously.

"The right sort for them *is* the right sort."

"For you?"

"Yes an' for everybody. You ever had a pal, Mr. Tom?"

Tom did not answer. He was on the point of getting up to go home when it struck him that he was making a great deal of fuss about nothing—in fact behaving very much as he had behaved last night in the lane. What if Deverell *had* followed him? Was there any great sin in that? He remembered the way he himself had hung round after Eric in the mere hope of receiving some sign of friendliness.

"You angry with me, Mr. Tom? I did follow you, but it wasn't because I was spyin' on you. I'd have joined you that time you whistled only I didn't like—I didn't know. I knowed it wasn't me you was whistlin' for."

"I'm not angry," said Tom.

"Then why is it you won't answer me?"

"About having a pal? I don't know what you mean by a pal."

"I mean what you mean."

The question was indeed one Tom had often enough considered, and it recalled various attempted friendships—always abortive, always ending in disappointment, usually ending in regret that they *had* been attempted. "Well then, no," he said grumpily.

"You wouldn't be one, I'd think, to choose a pal just because he had fine clothes on him," Deverell continued.

"Nor would I choose him just because he hadn't," Tom replied.

Deverell was silent, and the spaniel, who had been nosing among the furze bushes, suddenly put up a couple of birds, which rose with a loud whirring noise.

"Partridge," said Deverell.

Tom said nothing. Deverell probably knew all about birds and animals and plants. He would like to know about them too, and he took a sidelong glance at his companion. The young poacher puzzled him, although deep below the surface he had a secret understanding. And it was mixed up with that other feeling—not actually of distrust, but such as might have been awakened by the advances, say, of a friendly leopard, who should have strolled unexpectedly out of the jungle. Stranger still, this dubious element attracted him. He even had a desire to see the leopard put out his claws, hear the faint low growl at the back of his throat, see the yellow flame flickering in his eyes. All this was very wrong and inexplicable.

"I suppose they bin giving me a bad character up at the house," Deverell presently muttered. "That's what makes you unfriendly like."

"I'm not unfriendly," Tom protested. "As a matter of fact I never *am*—even when I want to be. I've been friendly with people I detested."

Deverell listened, and then asked simply. "What they bin sayin' about me?"

"What makes you think they said anything? Why should they?"

"Because I know they did. Sally Dempsey wouldn't lose the chance. She as good as told me so this morning. She knows I come a bit of the way home with you last night. There's one thing—she never seen me the worse for drink the way her oul' lad is every Saturday night, and him a sexton of the church."

"Well, let's talk of something else," said Tom. "It doesn't matter what she says."

"It matters to me, Mr. Tom. What call has she to be taking away my character? There's not much difference between characters if all was known."

Tom shrugged his shoulders. This was the kind of thing he hated.

But his unresponsiveness seemed to embitter Deverell. "Yes, some's hypocrites and some's not—that's the difference."

"Then you think everybody is equally good?" said Tom coldly. "Or, I suppose, your real meaning is that they're equally bad?"

Deverell did not answer, but his face darkened. He looked straight before him with sullen unhappy eyes. Then he muttered, "Perhaps you'd a' got into trouble yourself, Mr. Tom, if you'd belonged to a different station of life."

Tom flushed. "You don't mean to say you think I was alluding to *that!*" he exclaimed disgustedly. "You must have a beautiful opinion of me!"

"Well——" Deverell dug his heel into the grass, but his countenance was still clouded over.

"Look here," Tom burst out. "I hate this kind of thing. It never leads to anything, but goes on and on for ever. Why are you so suspicious? I know you've been in jail, but I wasn't thinking of that at all. I'd forgotten all about it. As a matter of fact I don't *care*: not if it had happened fifty times. Also what you say about me is perfectly true: I might easily have got into trouble, as you call it: nothing is more likely. But I don't see why we should be talking in this way— just as if I had accused you."

Deverell tore up a handful of grass. He put his arm round the spaniel, who sat between them with his tongue out and his eyes half shut, except when now and then he snapped at a fly. "You see, I took a likin' to you, Mr. Tom," he said rather shamefacedly.

"Yes, I know."

"It was that made me follow you."

"I know. It was only because you hid I was cross."

"But I told you I didn't like——"

"You didn't hide last night."

"I didn't know who you was last night."

"Well, it's all right now, isn't it?"

"Yes, it is, Mr. Tom. . . . Mr. Tom, I took a great likin' to you."

Tom did not answer, because there seemed to be nothing to say.

"You like me to show you how to set snares for rabbits, Mr. Tom?"

Tom shook his head, and Deverell's voice went on, close to his ear. "There's plenty up there in the old magi—in your uncle's woods. I wouldn't say but I might find someone as would buy them from you too. Keep you nicely in pocket-money, Mr. Tom, not to mention the sport."

Tom shook his head again.

"A shilling each I might get for them, and there'd be no trouble in findin' a score or two."

"I couldn't," said Tom. "I hate killing things. Anyhow, I never heard putting down traps called sport before; most people think it rather beastly."

"But rabbits has to be kept down, Mr. Tom, without you want them to be overrunnin' everything."

"Well, I'm not going to keep them down."

"Perhaps you'd fish, then? I know a place where you might kill a trout or two."

"I bought a fishing-line this morning."

"Well, if you'd kill a fish, why wouldn't you kill a rabbit or a hare?"

"I don't know. . . . I don't believe I'd care for fishing either."

"You just think it over and I'll meet you any time. There's no harm in it."

"The more I think it over the less likely I'll be to do it."

"But if there's no harm——"

"I know you *think* there isn't; and it's not that *I'm* thinking of either. It's really only because I like these things. There was a frog I was looking at before you came. Well, I like it; it seemed to me a lovely thing—now, do you see?"

Deverell appeared to be wrestling with a point of view which remained incomprehensible.

"Hang it all," exclaimed Tom impatiently, "I don't see why you can't at least *understand* it. I understand *you*. Besides, you must have felt sometimes like that yourself. You say you like *me*, and I suppose that means you don't want to hurt me."

"No, I wouldn't hurt you, Mr. Tom, nor let anyone else hurt you."

"Well, there you are then: it's just the same."

"No; it's different."

"Why is it different? There isn't any difference. The feeling you have is exactly the same."

"No, it isn't."

"But it is. I mean, the feeling itself is. The only difference is that I'm a boy and the other animals are frogs and rabbits and hares."

"It's not the same."

Tom's forehead wrinkled. He thought it over once more. "At any rate it's *partly* the same," he concluded. "I know it's not *all* the same, but there's a great deal of it the same."

"But you can't be fond of *everything*, Mr. Tom."

"No," Tom admitted, "I'm not. There are some insects I'm not fond of. Still, I don't think there's any advantage in that. I don't object to wasps, for instance, and it must be much pleasanter to be that way than to jump every time one comes near you."

The young poacher was now smiling at him. He looked wonderfully different. All the darkness and sullenness had passed from his face. He looked quite happy.

"I think, you know, I ought to go back soon," Tom said. "I've been out nearly all day."

"It's early yet; you've plenty of time."

"But I ought to see if Uncle Stephen wants me." He got up, but the young poacher did not stir.

Tom stood for a moment looking down at him: then he said, "Won't you walk back with me?"

Instantly Deverell sprang to his feet. A slight flush had come into his swarthy face, and Tom, with rather mixed feelings, saw that he was extraordinarily pleased. He was glad, of course, that he was pleased; but he didn't want him to be so pleased as all that, because really he had meant no more than a mere politeness.

They returned by another route. The field path Tom knew bore round to the left, but Deverell took him straight on in the direction of the Manor woods. This surely was a roundabout way, Tom thought, unless he actually climbed the wall and took a short cut through the grounds: and he wondered if he might propose doing so.

"Will you be coming down to the river to-morrow, Mr. Tom?"

"I don't know: Uncle Stephen may want me."

"But if he doesn't want you."

"I don't know: I'd rather not make any promise."

"Well, I'll come along on the chance."

"But you mustn't. It's not worth while: I'm almost sure to be doing something else: there are lots of things I have to do."

"Yes, I'll come."

Tom could say no more, and they scrambled through the hedge and down on to the road. The Manor wall faced them, and Tom looked at it and looked at Deverell. "I say, wouldn't it be a short cut if I got over here?" he asked. The top of the wall was some three feet higher than his head, but he could climb it all right if he was given a leg up.

"It might," Deverell replied.

"I think I'll try it. Do you mind?"

"You'll have a long drop on the other side; it's lower than it is here."

Tom could not tell from his manner whether Deverell minded being left or not. It was ridiculous thinking of such things. Why *should* he mind? Nevertheless, it was on the tip of his tongue to say that after all he would go home by the road, when he felt himself suddenly lifted in the young poacher's arms. He scraped with his toes for a foothold, found one, and next moment was astride of the wall.

He smiled down at his companion. "I say, you're jolly strong," he exclaimed admiringly. "I wish I was like that."

"I'll make you like that: all you need's living in the open for a bit; you're tough enough."

"Only metaphorically speaking," Tom replied.

The poacher's sombre eyes were fixed upon him; he really was a frightfully serious person—far too serious for comfort. "You won't laugh at my jokes," Tom said. "I don't call that being a pal."

Slowly—very slowly—a faint smile dawned on Deverell's face. "All the same, I like them, Mr. Tom."

"Then I'll prepare more for next day. . . . Are you sure you don't mind my leaving you?"

"Not the way we are now, Mr. Tom."

"What way are we now?"

"We're friends."

"Yes, of course we're friends. And if I don't see you for a day or two, I'll see you soon. Good-bye."

With this he dropped down into the tangled wilderness on the other side.

9: IT *was* a wilderness. Not a sign of a clearing anywhere. He would simply have to break a passage through. Long streamers of goose-grass attached themselves to his jacket and trousers; he was soon covered with down and pollen and cuckoo-spit, and, to protect his face, was obliged to hold aside the branches with both hands while his feet stumbled among hidden roots and creepers. The branches were tough and elastic, the briars and thistles painful, the nettles stung him even through his trousers; but he was determined not to go back, though very soon he had lost all sense of direction, and when he looked behind him could see how hopelessly crooked was the path he had beaten down. The important thing was to get out of this jungle as quickly as possible, for the

ground was becoming soft and muddy, and in wet weather must
be little better than a swamp. Fortunately there had been no rain
for a week or two, yet even as it was the sticky black mud more
than once rose above the tops of his shoes. He struggled on, now
quite blindly, and when eventually he did emerge into a comparatively open tract of higher ground, he was hot, breathless, and
smeared all over with a protective colouring of vegetable matter.

He cleaned his shoes in the grass and removed some of the less
tenacious dirt from his clothes, but the fact that his trousers showed
several large green stains and his new jacket had acquired a jumble-
sale appearance did not trouble him. More immediate discomforts
were the scratches and stings which seemed to leave not an inch of
him without its own particular smart. And where was the house?
He hadn't the remotest idea. It might be to the right of him or it
might be to the left, but what actually faced him was a low wall—
either a very ancient or a very badly built wall, for there were gaps
everywhere, many with young trees thrusting through them. This
surely must be the old garden Uncle Stephen had referred to—a separate enclosure within the main grounds, cut off from the surrounding
woods for a definite purpose. And in fact, threading his way between
giant boles of trees, he presently came upon what had once been an
avenue, though now a thick carpet of mossy grass covered it.
Whither did it lead, and what was this place upon which he had
stumbled? He had a sense of breaking in upon some private and
secret spot. But not forbidden, since Uncle Stephen had sent him out
to look for it. The intense silence of the woods rose up around him
like a flame.

Chequered bands of golden fire splashed on the moss-dark sward.
A stilled loveliness breathed its innocent spell. Then suddenly
a hare bounded across the path, and the trilled liquid pipings of
hidden thrush and blackbird broke on his ears like the awakening of
life. The music came to him in curves of sound. All the beauty he
loved best had this curving pattern, came to him thus, so that even
the rounding of a leaf or the melting line of a young human body
impressed itself upon him as a kind of music. The avenue turned,
widened, a house was there.

It was long and low, thatched with pale yellow straw over which
climbed trailing boughs of old man's beard. The strangest house
he had even seen, built of wood and thickly covered with a dark,
small-leaved ivy. Up the sides of the porch, looping and twining

all about it, grew this old man's beard; and the roof, jutting out to form a narrow cloister below, was supported by trunks of trees— the natural, unhewed trunks, bulging and crooked—and they too, like the walls, were densely coated with layer upon layer of ivy. The unusual depth of this vegetable growth was what indeed gave the house its strangeness, its at first sight startling suggestion of life. It *was* alive. Watching it intently, Tom imagined he could see the walls—though ever so slightly—swelling and contracting in a slow breathing. The woodwork round the door and windows had once been painted white; the three chimneys were of different heights, and set between them in the straw thatch was a latticed dormer-window, dark and uncurtained. The window was open. Tom saw nobody, yet he had a feeling that someone was watching him, and he never lost consciousness of this, though presently he turned his back on the house. A narrow lawn of moss-thickened grass sloped down from the stained door-steps to a grass terrace, where a further flight of balustraded steps descended to a pool rimmed with stone. On an island in the middle of the pool stood a naked boy holding an urn tilted forward, though through its weedy mouth no water splashed. The fountain was choked. A tuft of grass had found a roothold in the hollow of the boy's thigh; and on one side of him crouched an otter, on the other was an owl. All round the pool were rough grey boulders coated with mosses, dark green creepers, and trailing weeds. Between the stones sprang scarlet and yellow grasses, hart's-tongue fern, and bushes of cotoneaster, barberry, and lavender. His garden must have been blown to the fountain boy by wandering winds, or dropped by passing birds. On the dark surface of his pool floated the flat glossy leaves of water-lilies, and the lonely little sentinel gazed down at them, or at his own black shadow, or perhaps he was asleep, awaiting the spell-breaker.

Tom knelt on the rim of the pool and dabbled his hands in the water. It was warm and viscid, its faint smell not unpleasant. He let it drop from his fingers, and on the back of his hand tiny snail-shells glistened. He wondered for how many creatures this choked fountain was the whole world. The moon would turn it to silver, and the first arrows of the rising sun would turn it to gold. In autumn dead leaves would drift over it; in winter it would be frozen to ice and its small guardian be turned to a snow-boy. Tom's busy mind, and perhaps busier emotions, began to weave a story round the solitary urn-bearer. Being of his own composition the story followed the dictates of his temperament, just as a drifting branch will follow the current of a stream. He was always making up such stories, in which he lived his secret life of waking dreams and sleeping dreams, and the hidden current deepened day by day and year by year, as its soundless flow bore on inevitably to a predestined sea.

Some instinct made him look round at the house, and immediately the web of fancy was broken. For at the open window he saw not a boy in a story, but a real boy, looking down at him through a screen of green leaves. Tom's eyes grew round as O's. He was very much surprised. It had not been this kind of watcher he had expected—of humans he had felt sure the house was empty. Yet this boy was no ghost, he was as real as Tom himself. He was staring straight at him too; their eyes met; and Tom, conquering a shyness which always overtook him at inopportune moments, smiled. He could not be sure whether the other boy smiled back or not, he was gone so quickly, leaving the window blank and dark. Tom wondered if he were coming downstairs or merely hiding.

But the situation was altered. With the knowledge that there were people living in the house Tom bumped back sharply to earth and to the fact that he was trespassing. He got up and began slowly to retrace his steps, casting every now and again a glance behind him, and once, while still within view of the house, pausing deliberately. He waited, just in case the boy he had seen *should* be coming out, but nobody came, and after a minute or two, rather mournfully, Tom decided nobody would. He continued on his way, oddly disappointed.

Uncle Stephen would be able to tell him what this house was and who lived in it. Though it was strange, Tom thought, that he had not already done so, for surely he must know, since the house was in the Manor grounds. He couldn't know there was a boy there, however; otherwise he would not have said there wasn't a companion for Tom. The boy must be a visitor.

But a visitor visiting whom? For Tom knew the house had looked empty—looked, moreover, as if it had been empty for years. He had a sense of something dreamlike and mysterious. True, he had not approached very closely, not closely enough to see inside: but those curtainless windows, those green door-steps, that choked fountain, those signs everywhere of dilapidation and neglect! And not a thread of smoke from any chimney! What kind of people would live in such a place? It would be almost easier to imagine he had made a mistake, had seen nobody at the window. . . . Only he *had*.

And he now, quite unexpectedly, caught through the trees a glimpse of the Manor House. The two houses, he guessed, were really not far from each other, though there was either no direct path between them or else he had missed it. For it was through the shrubbery that he emerged on to the lawn, and at the same time he saw Mr. Knox, on a bicycle, riding up to the hall-door. The curate dismounted, leaned his bicycle against the window-sill, turned round, and catching sight of Tom, waited for him.

"Well," he asked, "how are things going?" But he gave Tom no time to answer before he drew him gently but firmly away from the porch. Mr. Knox, holding him by the arm, led him past the side of the house. "Grass just been cut!" he murmured. "Delightful smell—so fresh! I suppose you've no idea what Mr. Collet wants to see me about?"

He asked the question not exactly in a whisper, but certainly in a voice dropped to confidential pitch, and he still kept his arm firmly beneath Tom's, as if there were a danger of his taking to flight.

"Yes, I have; it's about me," Tom replied. "Only we'd better go in, because it must be nearly tea-time and it will take me ages to clean myself."

"Oh, you're all right," said Mr. Knox. "That'll brush off easily."

"I hope so, for I've no other clothes here."

Mr. Knox pulled out an old and very handsome gold watch, which he wore fastened to a silk ribbon, and which, instead of telling him the hour, appeared to present him with an arithmetical problem. He was behaving very oddly, Tom thought; much less like a parson than a schoolboy who has been summoned, he isn't quite sure why, to an interview with his headmaster. This impression was not diminished when the curate suggested, "Perhaps I'd better slip away and come back later."

"But Uncle Stephen *wants* you!" Tom exclaimed. "He's been waiting for you all afternoon! Besides, he may have seen us from the library window and it will look so silly."

Mr. Knox glanced back at the house. "Yes," he admitted doubtfully.

"Uncle Stephen likes you," added Tom.

This unexpected encouragement caused Mr. Knox to smile—somewhat sheepishly. "At any rate, you're quite the *kindest* boy I've ever met," he said.

And whether it was the kindness of Tom's remark, or something else that influenced him, he altered the direction of their walk. He turned abruptly back to the house, where, ten minutes later, they were all three seated at the tea-table, the curate opposite Uncle Stephen and Tom between them.

To the smallest member of the party it was deeply interesting—this confrontation of his two friends—particularly in the light of Mr. Knox's earlier reluctance to be confronted. But he had got over that quickly, and Tom noticed how, once the ice was broken, it was he who did most of the talking. Uncle Stephen listened. And even in their ways of listening there was a marked difference between them. Uncle Stephen listened with a kind of quiet attentiveness, and always there was a slight but distinct pause before he replied. Mr. Knox's "listening" was much more like Tom's own, charged with a restrained eagerness to interrupt.

It was Mr. Knox who talked, but it was Uncle Stephen who provided subjects. It was like that game in which you scribble a line on a piece of paper and the other person fills it in, making it a horse or a man or a cat or a boat. Tom, as usual, saw it like this, in a picture. He was alert and observant, a spectator, or perhaps still more an actor who was not on in this scene, which he watched from the wings. He had a feeling of being with his own people, his own kind (though Mr. Knox was less his kind than Uncle Stephen), a feeling he had never had at his step-mother's, where all the talk had consisted of a series of statements and contradictions, and everything was either a fact or a lie.

It was not till the meal was over, however, and they had retired to the library, where in a big arm-chair Mr. Knox made himself comfortable and lit his pipe, that the really important subject was broached. Then Uncle Stephen said, "Tom and I were wondering if by any chance we could persuade you to help with his studies. But first I had better tell you our whole plan, because there may be difficulties we haven't thought of."

There weren't—none that mattered, Tom said to himself; but outwardly he sat quiet as a mouse, at the open window, though he had turned his chair round so as to get a view of the room. He could see from where he sat only the top of Uncle Stephen's head above the back of his chair, but Mr. Knox's face was turned towards him, and he watched it closely while the situation was being explained—with certain slowness and deliberation—in Uncle Stephen's low yet very clear voice.

When that voice ceased the curate bent down to the grate to knock the ashes out of his pipe. Then he sat up and looked hard at Tom, as if an inspection of his proposed pupil might help him to reply.

Apparently it didn't, for it was with an air of embarrassment that he turned to Uncle Stephen. "It's awfully good of you, but—well —I don't quite know how to put it——"

Tom's hopes sank. It looked very much as if what Mr. Knox didn't "quite know how to put" was a polite refusal. The ominous silence was filled with his disappointment. And then again Mr. Knox spoke.

"You see, I only got a second, and that was four years ago. I was always better at games than books, though not much of a swell at either."

"Of course I don't expect you to reply definitely till you've had time to think the matter over," Uncle Stephen explained. "Indeed, nothing can be settled till we have heard from Tom's relatives. It was merely the possibility I wanted to discuss. Apart from the point you have raised—and which I don't think we need regard as a very serious one—is there anything that makes you disinclined to accept? —You don't, for instance, find the idea in itself distasteful?"

Mr. Knox shook his head. "Not at all: far from it: I'd say 'yes' like a shot if I'd had the least experience and didn't feel my Latin and Greek to be so extremely rusty." He smiled at Tom, who at this point clambered out through the window, feeling that the further discussion of Mr. Knox's qualifications might be carried on more happily in his absence.

He strolled up and down the lawn, out of earshot, but within sight should he be wanted. He half hoped he would be wanted, but evidently he wasn't, for he waited a long time and nobody called him. Mrs. Deverell and Sally appeared, and he watched them walking together down the drive on their way home. Another quarter of an hour passed, and he was growing very tired of doing nothing, when the hall-door opened, and Mr. Knox came out, followed by Uncle Stephen. They stood for yet a further minute or two talking in the porch; then they shook hands, the curate got on his bicycle, and Tom ran across the grass to intercept him.

Mr. Knox jumped off, but he continued walking, wheeling his bicycle, while Tom paced beside him. He looked pleased, and Tom at once felt that a solution must have been reached. "I suppose you want to know the result of the conference," Mr. Knox began.

"I think that means it's favourable," Tom answered.—"I mean favourable to me."

"Well, we'll hope it will be favourable all round. At any rate, there's to be a preliminary canter—a sort of trial trip. I made *that* a condition. So one of these mornings I'll come over to find out what it is I've actually let myself in for."

"I'll promise to do as well as I can," said Tom. "I'm no good at 'maths,' but I'm tolerable at Greek because I like it. The other things I suppose are about average. When they send on my books I'll be able to show you what I've been doing."

"In the meantime I can teach you your catechism," said Mr. Knox.

Tom received this as a joke. "I know some of it already, I know the bit about my pastors and masters."

Mr. Knox glanced at him. "Yes, I dare say you do—so long as the pastor and master happens to please you. However, we'll see. As for your Greek, I believe Mr. Collet intends to look after that himself: he has views on the subject which make it quite impossible for me."

"I hope that doesn't mean they'll make it impossible for *me*," Tom replied. "It sounds jolly like it."

"No; you possess a natural aptitude—or so Mr. Collet thinks. You'd better remember that you are regarded as much more than a nephew—as a kind of spiritual son. . . . And here's the gate and here we say good-bye. I've got a meeting, and unless I can ride a mile and a half in two minutes I'm going to be late for it. But come to see me soon: it's the first kidnapping case I've ever been mixed up in."

He *was* rather nice. . . . Tom watched him out of sight, standing in the middle of the road, his eyes screwed up a little as he faced the setting sun. He liked Mr. Knox. Mr. Knox was as safe and simple as a glass of milk. Half unconsciously he was contrasting him with Deverell.

Then he turned round and through the gate looked into the green avenue from which he had just emerged. Within *there*, was something not so simple. While he lingered, there deepened in him a strange impression that he was on the boundary-line between two worlds. To one world belonged Mr. Knox and his meetings, and Tom was standing in it now, as it might be on the shore of a pond. It stretched all round these stone walls, but within them was the other, and as soon as he passed through that gate he would become a part of the other. Here he was free to choose, but if he took a step further all would be different. What he should enter seemed to him now a kind of dream-world, but once inside, he knew it would become real. In there was the unknown—mystery—romance: the ruined garden, the stone boy holding his empty urn above the pool, the boy he had seen at the window, Uncle Stephen. As he stood at the gate Tom at that moment was not very far from seeing an angel with a flaming sword guarding it. His body thrilled when the call of a bird rose through the silence. He took a little run forward, tugged at the bar, pushed: and the latch dropped back into place as the gate clanged behind him.

10: "THAT was a near thing!" Tom breathed, only half pretending. But he knew when he had carried such play far enough (because it wasn't all play—not by any means), and now deliberately he tried to shut the doors of imagination. It was the spiritual equivalent to shutting his eyes and digging his fingers in his ears, but it must be done; and as a preliminary he thrust his hands in his trousers pockets, assumed a slight swagger, and raised his voice in the Soldiers' Chorus from *Faust*. What could be more blatant, more idiotic than the Soldiers' Chorus?—yet somehow it was not successful. Perhaps he was making too *much* noise. He stopped singing abruptly and ran at the top of his speed towards the house.

He entered the library breathless, with flushed cheeks and shining eyes. Uncle Stephen was standing by one of the bookcases and there was a pile of books and papers on the floor. He turned to Tom, and instantly all Tom's wandering fantasies and dilemmas were at rest. . . . "I've cleared a table for you," Uncle Stephen said, "and that big cupboard in the corner, and this shelf for your books."

Tom was very pleased. "But you shouldn't," he expostulated, his face lit up with happiness. "I could quite easily have kept my things in my bedroom."

"I want you to use this room:—do your lessons here, bring everything here, make as much mess as you like. Only I don't know yet what you *do* like."

"I like reading," said Tom, "and I like drawing, and I like some kinds of games, and I like making things."

"Is that all?"

"I like gramophones, if I can choose the records myself. But you haven't got one."

"No; but perhaps that means the records will be better when we do get one."

"Of course I'd get some that you liked, too," said Tom.

"They'll be the wrong ones—eh?"

"But you're not musical, Uncle Stephen, or you would have had a gramophone already."

"I suppose so. The idea never occurred to me."

"I know. That's what I mean."

"As for 'making things'—does that refer to carpentering?"

"Yes; though I've only done it with a boy called Pascoe, and I'm not much good at it."

"Well, you can't do *that* very well in here. We'll have to fit up a workroom for you: half the rooms in the house are unoccupied."

"What I'd like to make first would have to be done in the open air."

"Why?"

"Well, it's a raft. I thought of it this afternoon. I'd like to make a raft to go on the river—the way Bevis and Mark did. . . . They're two boys, you know, in a book. I'll lend it to you when my things come. It's about exploring on a lake, and swimming, and camping out."

"Does it tell you how to make a raft?"

"No—not altogether. At least, I'm not sure. But I think I could do it. Bevis made his out of a packing-case."

"He had the other boy to help him, though, hadn't he?"

"Deverell would——" But Tom stopped suddenly. "Uncle Stephen, there *is* another boy," he said.

The silence that followed seemed to lend his words an odd significance. He looked up quickly.

"Who?" Uncle Stephen asked.

For a moment Tom, ever sensitive to the unspoken mood, had thought—— He did not quite know what he had thought, but at any rate it was all right. "I don't know," he said. "I wondered if *you* would know. I wanted to ask you before, but when Mr. Knox was here I couldn't. I saw him this afternoon. He was in that other house, looking out of the window. I didn't know there *was* another house.

You didn't tell me, and when I found it I thought at first it was empty."

"You mean the lodge? Not really a lodge of course, but that was what it was called to distinguish it from the Manor House."

"I suppose so. It's in the wood over there." Tom pointed. "There's a fountain, but it's choked up. The house didn't *look* as if anybody was living in it."

"Nobody does live in it," Uncle Stephen said. "I doubt if it's habitable. There are still a few sticks of furniture, but nobody has lived there for a long time."

"But I saw him."

"And what was he doing?"

"I don't know. Just standing at the window. He wasn't doing anything really, and as soon as he caught me looking at him he went away."

"You didn't venture inside, then?"

"No, of course not. I thought there must be people there. Very queer people too, to leave the place like that. Who is he, do you think, Uncle Stephen?"

"Anybody could get in," Uncle Stephen replied. "I expect most of the window-catches are loose, and I know the back-door isn't locked or bolted."

"Why?"

"There isn't a key. The key is lost."

"You think, then, he may have been a boy from the town?"

"He may have been a boy from anywhere."

"But why had he gone there?" Tom reflected for a moment. "And he wasn't a boy from the town—or at least I don't think he was."

"How do you know?"

"Well, he wasn't a message-boy, or a farm-boy, or anything like that."

"And as soon as he saw you he disappeared?"

"He went away from the window. I thought perhaps he was coming down, and waited a bit." Tom had a further cogitation before he said, "Supposing I see him again?"

"If you see him again you can ask him his name."

"Then you don't mind his going into the house?"

"Not in the least. Why should I?"

Uncle Stephen was busy with the lamp and Tom waited till he had lit it. "Still, it was rather cheek," he said slowly.

"Then you'd better warn him off. I leave it entirely to you. You can do exactly as you like."

"He was trespassing," said Tom.

"Yes, I suppose so."

There was a brief silence, during which Tom was conscious that Uncle Stephen was looking at him closely. He did not know why, but he had begun to feel vaguely uncomfortable. "He *was* trespassing," he mumbled.

"Yes. Well, I've given you full authority to act."

"You know you don't want me to act," said Tom unhappily.

"I know you don't care a fig about trespassing, if that's what you mean."

Tom hung his head. He turned away. "Shall we have a game of chess?" he asked.

"Very well," said Uncle Stephen, and Tom went to a table in the corner, whereon the red and white ivory pieces were already set out.

He carried the table over into the lamplight. He lifted the red knight. It was quite heavy, for these were the largest chessmen he had ever seen. "Are they *very* old, Uncle Stephen?" he asked. "Have you always had them?"

"No, but I played my first game with them."

"When you were a boy—at home?"

"When I was a boy; but not at home. It was in Italy."

"Then they're Italian?"

"They belonged at that time to an Italian, but they've belonged, I expect, to a good many people. There's a name on the box—Nicolo Spinelli. That was some ancestor of my friend's, for his name too was Spinelli. But the chessmen were made in China, and their first owner probably was a Chinaman."

Tom had placed the table in front of Uncle Stephen's armchair: he now brought up a chair for himself and sat down. He looked across the table and suddenly smiled: the tiny cloud had passed.

"Shall I move first?" he asked.

Uncle Stephen nodded assent, and Tom lifted a white pawn. But he held it poised in the air. "Wouldn't it be queer, Uncle Stephen, if all the people to whom these chessmen had once belonged came in now to look on?"

"Very queer. I think we're better without them."

"They'd be ghosts, of course, and we wouldn't know they were there."

Then he stopped talking, and with bright eyes watched Uncle Stephen's move. The game proceeded with a profound gravity. Beyond the clear circle of lamplight was a deepening darkness, and in the darkness the open windows were visible, for the curtains had not been drawn. From time to time Tom looked up from the table and out of the window behind Uncle Stephen's chair. Dimly he could see the black branches of trees. In the distance he heard a corncrake.

"It would be quite possible, Uncle Stephen, that they were watching us, wouldn't it?"

"Quite—so far as I know."

"You see," Tom explained, "I wasn't going to move my bishop at all, and then somebody gave me a hint."

"That must mean he wants you to win," Uncle Stephen replied gravely, "because it was an excellent move."

Tom gave him a quick glance. "He had a pigtail, and long wide sleeves with little sprigs of flowers worked on them in coloured silk."

"That was Fu Kong," said Uncle Stephen.

Tom thought. His face was very happy. "Do you know, Uncle Stephen, I often used to get into rows for saying things like that— I mean about Fu Kong's sleeves."

"While your mother was alive—wasn't it all right then?"

"Yes, but she was like you. My step-mother thinks I tell lies."

The spell of the game was suddenly relaxed, and Uncle Stephen looked across the table at his antagonist. "*Did* you see Fu Kong's sleeves, Tom?"

"I don't know. That's the queerest part of it. I must in a sort of way have seen them or I couldn't have described them, could I? I mean *something* must have put them into my head; or where did they come from?"

"What put them into your head was knowing that the chessmen were Chinese."

"Yes, but—— Somehow I can't ever think of things without beginning to see them."

"Are you frightened of the dark?"

"No. Not often."

"Were you nervous last night—when everything was strange to you?"

"No. Well perhaps a little bit. But it hadn't anything to do with being in the dark. It was more as if—— Sometimes I pretend things, and then all at once they become real. I mean, I begin to believe them."

"And you went to sleep last night at once?"

"Yes. At least——"

"At least what?"

"I went to sleep as soon as I got into bed. But I came out on to the landing first and listened."

"Listened?"

Tom nodded.

"But why? What were you listening to?"

Tom coloured. He did not answer.

"Had you heard anything?"

"Nothing except the clock. I can't explain, Uncle Stephen. Really, I'm not trying to hide anything. I just—— I don't know. It's just that I try to make things happen. No, it's not quite that. I *would* tell you if I could, but——"

"Don't worry. I expect I understand. Everything depends on what things you want to make happen. They must be good things."

"Yes."

"You can make them good things."

"Yes."

"And if you make them good things *always*, the time will come when there won't be any others."

"I think this *house* is good, Uncle Stephen. Don't you think houses can be good or—not good?"

"Yes."

"But it's not an ordinary house."

"Don't you like it?"

"Yes, but it's not ordinary, and neither is the other—the lodge." Tom hesitated. "And you're not an ordinary uncle," he added.

"What is an ordinary uncle?"

Tom had no difficulty whatever with this. "Uncle Horace," he replied.

Uncle Stephen laughed. Tom was pleased that he had made him laugh, though it had been quite unintentionally. Again the game proceeded, and presently Tom moved his queen and said "Check!" But he said it half-heartedly, for a suspicion had been dawning in his mind. "Uncle Stephen, you're not to let me win on purpose."

"Don't you want to win?"

"Yes I do, but not in that way."

"All right."

"You mean you can win if you like?"

"As the pieces are now, I think in five moves."

And so it was. Tom immediately rose and put away the table.

"Does that mean bedtime?" Uncle Stephen asked, glancing at his watch.

"Bedtime! Why it's quite early! It only means that we can play chess again to-morrow."

"And what shall we do now?"

"I don't want to bother you. I'll read for a bit. . . . Shall I tell you what I'd *like* to do?"

"I don't see how I'm to know otherwise."

"I'd like you to show me some pictures."

"Pictures. What kind of pictures?"

Tom had his eyes fixed on a row of tall portfolios. "Any kind. One of these," he said, going to the shelf.

"But my dear boy, I'm sure those aren't pictures—or at least what you probably mean by pictures."

"Which shall I bring, Uncle Stephen?"

"It doesn't matter. I've forgotten what's in them."

Tom carried a portfolio to the table and Uncle Stephen unfastened the tapes that kept it closed. "These are all Greek vases," he said. "We'd better try another lot."

"But I like these," said Tom, pulling his chair round beside Uncle Stephen's. "At least I like this first one. Only I want you to tell me about it. Who are those figures?"

"The two goddesses are Demeter and Persephone: the boy is Triptolemos. They are sending him out on his mission."

Tom bent over the plate. "Tell me how you know who they are, and about Triptolemos."

"Are you sure this isn't just an excuse for sitting up when you ought to be in bed?" Uncle Stephen asked doubtfully.

"Really it isn't. Of course I know who Demeter and Persephone were, but I don't know much about Triptolemos. What was his mission?"

"His mission was to give corn-seed to the country-people, and to teach them how to plough the land and to sow the corn and reap it and thresh it. He later became a half-god, but as you see him there he is just a farm-boy, though a prince of Eleusis. The chariot is Demeter's own car, drawn by winged serpents."

"Was there ever any such person as Triptolemos?"

"Nobody knows. He hasn't always even the same father. But he is always the favourite of Demeter. He is her messenger and it is through him she gives her blessings. Altars and temples were built to Triptolemos himself, because he really was Demeter's adopted son, besides being a very pleasant person."

"What else did he do?"

"He gave the people three commandments—like Moses, except that Moses gave ten. The commandments of Triptolemos were: Honour your father and mother. Offer fruits to the gods. Be kind and just to animals."

"Those are good commandments," said Tom. "I'm going to keep them myself. I think it's far better to keep a few commandments absolutely than to bother about a lot that don't really suit you."

"But, Tom, that's a very immoral doctrine."

"Is it? I'll always keep your commandments, Uncle Stephen. Is there anything else about Triptolemos?"

"Sophocles wrote a play about him, but there are only a few lines of it left. Some say that he was an elder brother of Demophon—the little boy Demeter tried to make immortal by putting him every night into the fire, until his mother interfered. According to another tradition that little boy was Triptolemos himself. Ovid, in his *Fasti*, gives a different version, making the father, Keleos, not a king, but just an old peasant who worked on his own farm, and who met the goddess when he and his small daughter were coming home one evening with a load of acorns and blackberries. The girl was driving a couple of goats, and it was she who spoke first to Demeter, seeing her sitting by a well and mistaking her for an old country-woman— the kind of solitary old woman Wordsworth would have made a poem about. All the Greek stories, you see, were treated in different ways by different writers. They were everybody's property, and the writer when he made a poem or a play out of them drew the characters to suit his own temper. And somehow this makes them all the more real—when you come across them over and over again, different but still the same. They accumulate a kind of richness of humanity. Triptolemos may once have been as real a boy as you. The heroes had strange fates. Some began as mortals and slowly grew divine; some, beginning as gods, lost their divinity and became human. . . .

"You know, we can't possibly go through all these to-night," Uncle Stephen said, an hour later.

Tom sighed, smiled, stretched himself, and got up from his chair. "Is that milk for me?" he asked, looking at a tray which had been set on a side-table.

"Yes, Mrs. Deverell left it for you."

Tom drank his glass of milk and put some biscuits in his pocket. "Good-night, Uncle Stephen," he said, holding out his hand, "and thanks awfully for showing me the pictures."

"Good-night, Tom. Sleep well. I suppose you can find your own way?"

"Oh, yes."

"Don't drop candle-grease on the stairs."

"No."

Tom lit his candle and walked as far as the door. There he stood holding the door-knob, and once or twice he turned it, but he did not open the door nor look back into the room. Then he put the candle down.

He returned to the table. "Let me put this away," he said, lifting the portfolio and carrying it to its shelf.

Uncle Stephen watched him in silence. Tom lingered for another minute or two by the bookshelves, but at last went once more to the door. This time he heard his name spoken.

"Tom."

Instantly he blew out the candle, came back, and stood beside Uncle Stephen's chair.

"What is it, Tom?"

"It's nothing," Tom whispered, putting his arms round Uncle Stephen's shoulder. "Just—I don't want to go to bed yet."

11: NOTHING had come from his step-mother—not even a letter—so after dinner Tom went down to the station to make inquiries. But he did not find his luggage. If it came, the station-master told him, it would be sent out to the house; it might come by the next train; there was one due at 4.30. Tom thanked him and turned homeward.

But he was annoyed, and he was particularly annoyed because it seemed to him so stupid! What good could keeping his clothes do? It wouldn't bring him back. At least they might have sent on a few things, such as shirts and socks and collars—things they *knew* he would require. He hadn't even a pair of slippers, and his step-mother must know that too. In fact, he was sure she had long ago gone through all his possessions to find out exactly what he *had* brought, and Jane would have told her. She simply wanted to make him uncomfortable, and wanted to be disagreeable to Uncle Stephen. He half thought of going into the post-office and telephoning to Uncle Horace. But it would do no good. Let them keep his things if they wished to: they could have them as a memento—the only one they were likely to get.

Both on his way to the station and on his return through Kilbarron he had kept a sharp look-out for the boy he had seen at the other house. Not that he expected to meet him: he thought it far more likely that he lived ten or twelve miles away and had ridden over on a bicycle. He might easily have done that, and hidden his bicycle somewhere while he explored the Manor grounds. It was just the sort of thing Tom himself would have liked to do—though when it came to the point he might have funked it. . . .

That was it:—if you had courage you could do anything. . . . He remembered seeing Eric diving off the balcony at the shallow end of the swimming bath into three feet of water where a slip would have meant a bad accident. It was an idiotic thing to try (he still thought that) and at the time he had begged him not to. All the same he had admired him tremendously—too much even to resent being called a "sloppy little fool" by Leonard, who was waiting to perform the same feat. It was strange how if you were like Leonard or Eric you had to *invent* such exploits; you never *naturally* got into disagreeable positions where courage was necessary and must be pumped up whether you felt it or not. Leonard, for instance, who rejoiced in fights, was never singled out by other rejoicers; he had had far fewer scraps than Tom himself, who was all for peace, and whose nose bled at the slightest touch. *Was* he a coward? It was disgusting to think he was: but can you be a coward in some ways without being a coward in all?—and in lots of ways he was sure he was one. His courage seemed to *vary* so much. He could never count on it; it never seemed to work spontaneously, but had to be manufactured, and there must always be somebody to be courageous *for*. Therefore it wasn't natural—didn't come from his guts, as it should have come, but from his mind—a sort of angry pride. . . .

Tom's self-examination was not yielding much comfort. He had forgotten what had started it. Perhaps this other boy. Beauty, strength, courage—those really were the qualities he admired. And he hadn't *any* of them. The image of Deverell rose before him. Deverell, he supposed, at this moment would be waiting for him down by the river. He frowned. *Purposely* he had made no promise, but still he hesitated. He felt rather mean, and most likely in the end he would have gone to the river had not the idea flashed upon him to leave a note for the trespasser. He could pin it to the door where he would be sure to see it if he came back. The temptation was irresistible, and Tom hurried on.

He entered the grounds and turned aside from the main avenue, keeping by the wall, and skirting the shrubbery, beyond which he caught a glimpse of George, and George's assistant, Robert, a stocky youth of eighteen or thereabouts, whose acquaintance he had not yet made. Robert was shy, and had deliberately kept at a distance. At present he and George were clipping the laurels, though for the moment they had stopped working and their voices were raised in the clamour of religious argument. At least George's voice was raised, which Tom took for a sign that he had been getting the worst of it. He paused to catch the gist of the discussion, but it had already reached its climax.

"Cut them bushes an' houl' yer tongue!" George ordered angrily. "The like of you puttin' it on you to give *me* salvation, that got you your job and learned you everythin' you know except foolishness. If your sins is washed clean it's more than your face is."

"It's into the heart, not at the face, that the Lord looks, Mr. McCrudden," said Robert earnestly.

"Ay—well, it's yer face *I* have to put up with."

Tom moved discreetly away.

Still keeping by the dark stone wall, in whose ancient cracks and crannies a multitude of ferns and climbers, and even an occasional sapling, had found a roothold, he approached his destination through a copse of larch and hazel. Deverell had certainly been right about the rabbits; in every clearing their burrows were manifest, and the white flashing of their little scuts as they dived into shelter at his

approach. He reached the inner wall which surrounded his abandoned house, and passed through one of the gaps.

But hardly into the land of yesterday's sorcery. Not even when he
emerged on to the lawn and saw before him again the low creepered
house, the grass terraces, the ruined fountain with its solitary guardian. It was all lovely and quiet and neglected, but it was somehow
less thrilling, less strange. It was as if a vivid light, thrown upon it
by enchantment, had been withdrawn. Was it he himself who had
broken the spell, or had he really seen it first in a peculiar lighting—
though the hour must have been nearly the same? He only knew that
its beauty was more familiar, less wonderful, that the suggestion of
life had vanished from the house, and that it was empty.

Treading noiselessly on the thick matted grass, Tom went round
to the back. He entered a square, roughly paved yard. He peeped
through a dark cobwebbed kitchen window, then turned the handle
of the door and gently pushed. The door opened and he heard a
scuttle among the litter of old newspapers on the floor. Tom stood
there, still grasping the door-handle, gazing out of sunshine into
twilight. But he did not enter. There was a wooden chair, a table;
the grate was stuffed with rubbish; in one corner a heap of plaster
had fallen from the ceiling. Not a sound now even of a mouse: then
the noisy buzzing of a bluebottle who had flown in over his head.
Fat fussy creature! A feast for somebody! Tom thought; noting the
thick webs, and wondering what spiders shut in here could possibly
find to eat. Or mice either. But the mice doubtless were not really
shut in—had their secret passages connected with the outer world.

The friendly chirping of sparrows in the ivy, and the bright sunshine, held him on the threshold. Inside, it was dirty and gloomy, and
a cold musty smell rose from the paved floor. Besides, he knew
there was nobody there. Tom, who had come to explore the house,
closed the door without entering. He recrossed the cobbled yard;
he would leave his message and go. But when he reached the corner
of the house he put paper and pencil back in his pocket, for the trespasser was there.

Tom stood still. Yes, he was there, kneeling by the fountain, exactly
as Tom had knelt yesterday, his hands plunged in the water, his back
turned. And Tom knew him. Presently he lifted his cupped hands
from the pool. He did not look round; his head was bent over some
captive; and the water dripped down between his fingers on to the

grass. But he must have heard a footstep, for he said over his shoulder, "I've got the biggest water-beetle you ever saw."

"Have you?" Tom replied.

The words dropped rather lamely. In fact, though there was no reason why he should do so, he felt a little let down, like one who has prepared an elaborate surprise only to find it has all from the beginning been regarded as a matter of course. But this check was momentary. "Let's see it," he said, running to the fountain.

The trespasser held out his hands, and Tom surveyed the black, glossy, rather formidable creature, who was making indignant efforts to regain his liberty. All at once his back split open, two wings unfolded, and he whirred triumphantly away.

Tom watched his short clumsy flight as he grazed the top of a fuchsia bush and dropped down among a clump of irises. Then he turned and encountered the dark-blue eyes of the kneeling boy. They were candid yet watchful, with an unusual breadth between them, and the corners of the eyebrows were slightly protuberant. The line of the nose was firm and bold, the mouth just a little pouting, the chin rounded. He would have looked exactly like a young buccaneer, Tom thought, only there was something else there, something that removed him indefinably from that type and from the purely athletic type of Eric and Leonard—a kind of subtle intellectuality.

"Where do you come from? You were here yesterday."

Tom, lost in contemplation, was taken aback. Questions as to *his* identity were not what he had expected, particularly when asked in a tone that struck him as singularly high-handed. "I live here," he answered stiffly. "This place belongs to my uncle."

The kneeling boy accepted the statement, but it did not abash him. "Tell me your name," he said in the same dictatorial tone.

Tom coloured. "Why don't you tell me yours?"

At this the trespasser showed surprise. But he was not annoyed, and after just the briefest hesitation answered, "Philip." A rather longer pause ensued before he added, "Coombe."

"Well, my name's Tom Barber," said Tom.

The announcement brought them to a deadlock. The whole encounter, somehow, had been unfortunate, and very different from the one he had anticipated. But that was always the way. He began to suspect that this boy *was* after all of the type of his step-brother: the arrogance was not so pronounced, but it was there, and he recognized it with a pang of disillusionment. He had looked so pleasant! He did still for that matter: there could not, Tom felt, in the whole world be anything that looked much pleasanter. Meanwhile the strange boy had risen to his feet and they confronted each other. Tom stared as long as he could: then his eyes dropped and he merely stood there waiting unhappily.

He was astonished to hear a quite friendly voice addressing him. "What are you annoyed about?"

Tom looked up. "Nothing."

"Well, you haven't spoken for nearly five minutes."

"Neither have you," Tom said.

"I was thinking—coming to a decision."

"So was I."

"About me?"

"Perhaps."

"You *said* this place belonged to your uncle."

"Oh that!" Tom was relieved to find his real thoughts so widely missed.

"Did you tell him you had seen me?"

"Yes, I told him last night. He doesn't mind. He says you can go into the house when you like. . . . I only told him," Tom added, "because at that time I thought you lived there, and that he might know who you were."

"Well, *you* know now."

"I don't know very much," said Tom.

"You know my name."

"Yes."

"And in a way I do live there."

Tom looked at him uncertainly. "How do you mean?" he asked.

"I mean I'm living there for the present—temporarily. I found the door unlocked. Nobody can have been near the place for ages and I didn't see what harm I could do. I don't do as much harm as the birds: the chimneys are full of nests."

"No, I'm sure you don't," said Tom. "But why do you want to live there? It can't be very comfortable."

"I ran away. As a matter of fact I ran away twice—first from school and then from home. I want to go abroad, but I thought I'd better hide for a while, till they had stopped looking for me."

"Everybody I know seems to have run away," murmured Tom. "At least everybody about here. Uncle Stephen did, long ago: and Deverell did: and I ran away myself to come to Uncle Stephen."

"Well, you can't stay at home for ever," said Philip.

"No," Tom agreed, more doubtfully. "Though if you come to think of it a good many people do—at least till they're grown-up."

"I wanted to go to sea a year ago, but my father wouldn't let me. And I'm not going back to school. Anyhow I don't think they'd take me, because I nearly killed one of the boys with a cricket stump before I left. I thought at first I *had* killed him. I tried to."

"*Truly?*"

"Well, perhaps not quite: but I wanted to hurt him badly, and I did."

There was a pause.

"I like this place and nobody will ever find me here."

"I found you," said Tom.

"Only because I allowed you to. I stood at the window on purpose."

"I would have found you sooner or later without that: I intended to explore the house."

"I shouldn't have been in the house—unless you had come in the middle of the night."

Tom tried another subject. "How do you manage about your grub: I mean where do you get it?"

"I haven't had to get any so far. I only came yesterday and I have what will do me till to-morrow:—bread and cheese, and there's a well in the yard."

"But it must be frightfully uncomfortable. Isn't the place swarming with mice?"

"Only downstairs: they come in out of the garden. Besides, in the hold of a ship there would be rats and cockroaches."

Tom regarded this bold adventurer with serious and wondering eyes. "Were you going as a stowaway? I thought that only happened in stories. How would you get on board to begin with? And as soon as they found you they'd send a message. Nearly every ship has a wireless."

"A wireless!" Philip looked puzzled, but continued his explanation. "I'll not go as a stowaway if I can get a proper job. But I'm going *some* way, and I can't risk being caught."

"I'll bring you your grub," said Tom.

"Will you?"

"Unless you'd like to come and stay at the Manor. I know it would be all right, because my uncle said this morning he wished there was another boy for me to knock about with."

"No," replied Philip decisively.

"But why? You needn't be afraid of Uncle Stephen."

"I'm not afraid of him."

"Why won't you come then? It would be a good deal better than where you are and just as safe. That place must be filthy."

"It's not so bad upstairs. You haven't seen it."

Tom looked at him in uncertainty. "You mean you don't want to come?"

"I can't come. I must be free to do what I like and I couldn't be free if I went to stay with your uncle. Besides, he'd expect me to tell him all about myself."

"I don't think he would," said Tom quickly, "but it doesn't matter."

He looked down into the fountain. He could think of nothing else to say and yet he wished to say something. Philip did not help him, and Tom turned away. "I must be going," he murmured.

"Will you come back again?"

It was less an invitation than a question, but Tom answered, "Yes, if you want me to. Besides, I've to bring you your grub."

Philip kept step beside him. He was at least a head taller than Tom —as tall as Leonard, and of the same clean powerful build. "Are you going to tell your uncle what I've told you?" he asked.

"I'd rather tell him, and I'll have to tell him some of it; but if there's anything you don't want me to tell——"

"I don't mind. You can tell him whatever you please—so long as you make him promise to keep it a secret and not to interfere with me."

"You needn't be afraid," said Tom, "he isn't that kind."

They walked slowly over the thick matted turf, and entered the green avenue. A hare, twenty yards away, squatted down to watch them.

At the gate Philip stopped. "I don't think I'll come any further."

Tom too paused, in indecision. "I wish you would," he said. "I want you to help me to build a raft, and then we could go on the river. Have you been to the river yet?"

"No."

"Will you come with me to-morrow and bathe?"

"Would anybody be likely to see me? Should we have to pass any houses?"

"No. . . . It's over there." He pointed through the trees. "There are no houses near."

"Well——"

"I'll come early," Tom promised eagerly. "Then we'll have the whole afternoon. And I'll bring your food at the same time. I'll come whether it's wet or fine."

"Alone?"

"Yes, of course."

"There won't be any other boys there?"

"No, there won't be anybody except ourselves."

Philip thought it over for a minute or two. "All right," he said at last. "Good-bye for the present."

He was turning away, but Tom stood still. "What is it?" Philip asked.

Tom hesitated. "It's just that it seems rotten leaving you here alone," he murmured shyly.

Philip looked at him with a faint surprise. "You needn't worry about *me*," he answered rather coldly; and the statement was so obviously true that Tom wished he had left his own words unspoken.

12: WHEN he was still about a stone's-throw from the Manor, Tom stiffened into immobility, like a cat, who, in the act of crossing the road, suddenly changes his mind. But it was not at the house he was looking; it was at a car drawn up on the gravel sweep before it, the engine silent. He knew that car. Yes— and he knew that voice too, though the speaker, being within the porch, was invisible. Also he knew the back of Shanks, the chauffeur: the problem was whether to advance or retreat.

Quiet as the stone boy at the other house, he stood to debate it. But what on earth was Uncle Horace kicking up such a row about? Surely they hadn't refused to let him in! *Had* they, though? It *sounded* like it. This was extraordinary!—and whatever happened he mustn't miss it.

But he approached with circumspection, since it was quite possible he might be pounced on unawares and carried off by main force. It *could* be done. After all, the car was there, Shanks was there to lend a hand, and—George and Robert having left off work at five o'clock

—Tom had nobody to call to his assistance. At the same moment Shanks turned and saw him. His wooden face expressed a total lack of interest, but that might be only part of a "plant," for Tom was not yet within pouncing distance. "Here's Mr. Tom now, sir," Shanks called out officially; and then, having carefully turned his back to the porch, he winked.

It was a deliberate wink; there could be no doubt about it; nevertheless, coming from the saturnine and inscrutable Shanks, its significance was ambiguous. It might mean anything or nothing. Tom winked in response, but approached no nearer.

"Hello, Uncle Horace," he said, as Uncle Horace came fussing to the edge of the porch. "What's happened?"

"Nothing has happened except that your mother sent me down to bring you home. But it appears Mr. Collet can't see me. I may say that I intend to wait here until he can."

Uncle Horace, Tom perceived, was not in the best of tempers; his complexion was a shade more florid than usual, and his always high-pitched voice had an unmistakable edge. He did not even ask Tom how he was, but then Tom himself, instead of coming forward to shake hands, continued to hover at a cautious distance.

"Where is Uncle Stephen?" he asked of Mrs. Deverell, who stood, frail but determined, in the background, holding the fort as it were.

"He's in his room, Master Tom, and he left instructions that he was on no account to be disturbed."

"And in the meantime his hospitality extends as far as the doorstep," Uncle Horace said, with an angry flash of his white teeth.

Tom was puzzled. It *did* look rather odd.

"You must pardon me, sir," Mrs. Deverell interposed quietly, "but the master never receives visitors except by appointment; and this afternoon he mentioned particularly that he would be engaged and was not to be disturbed."

"Disturbed!" Uncle Horace echoed impatiently. "My good woman, all I asked you to do was to take him a message. And considering the distance I've come——"

"I'm sorry, sir, but the master's orders were definite; I wouldn't dare to go against them."

Uncle Horace turned from her abruptly. "Then you'd better get into the car, Tom. We've a long drive before us. You can write to your uncle when you reach home. Would you fetch Master Tom's hat and coat, please?" he said to Mrs. Deverell.

As if at a signal Shanks swung open the door of the car and stood in readiness, but Tom retreated another yard or two. There he again halted, very much on the alert, ready to spring away at the slightest attempt to lay a hand on him.

"Is Uncle Stephen in his study, Mrs. Deverell?" he called out.

"I don't think so, Master Tom."

Uncle Horace descended the steps. "Come, Tom," he said, but Tom did not budge. The impassive Shanks, still holding open the door, remained sardonically at attention.

"You know very well, Uncle Horace, I can't possibly go away like this," Tom expostulated. "And at any rate I'm not going at all. I'm going to live with Uncle Stephen. He's adopted me. The whole thing's settled."

Uncle Horace said nothing. He might have been calculating whether Shanks had even a sporting chance if ordered to pursue his nephew, but if that were his thought he decided against it.

"I think, all the same, Uncle Horace ought to be invited in," Tom went on, addressing Mrs. Deverell.

"Whatever you say, Master Tom. I'm sure there's no discourtesy meant, but your uncle's always most particular that his orders should be obeyed. Of course, with you here it makes a difference. Mr. Collet wouldn't wish you not to be polite to your visitors. I could get the gentleman some refreshment, if you would bring him into the dining-room."

"Thank you, I don't want any refreshment," the visitor snapped. "As for you, Tom, you appear to imagine you are going to be assaulted. I didn't bring either ropes or handcuffs with me. I supposed your natural feeling would be sufficient to make you respect your mother's wishes."

"She isn't my mother," said Tom.

"She is in the place of your mother."

"Yes, I know."

"And your father committed you to her charge."

"Did he?" Tom answered softly. "I don't doubt your word, Uncle Horace, but I should have to have some proof of that."

Shanks suddenly coughed, and Uncle Horace darted a furious glance at him.

"My mother committed me to Uncle Stephen's charge," Tom added.

Uncle Horace smiled—the coldest and thinnest of smiles. "I don't think we need to continue the discussion," he said. "It is hardly a suitable place."

"Will you swear you won't touch me?" asked Tom.

"Really!" Uncle Horace broke out. But he checked himself, and an exasperated shrug of his shoulders completed the sentence.

Tom, however, was obstinate. "I won't come any nearer unless you promise."

It was the last straw. "I don't *want* to touch you," cried Uncle Horace, in tones much belying his words. "Your stay with your uncle has been short, but it seems to have had a disastrous effect upon your manners."

This outburst Tom accepted as a promise. "I'm sorry, Uncle Horace. I don't want to be rude to you." And he stepped forward at once. "It's just the way things have happened that is unfortunate. Come in, won't you? I'm sure Uncle Stephen must be somewhere about. You see, it's tea-time; in fact it must be considerably after tea-time."

Uncle Horace glowered as he preceded Tom up the steps and into the hall. Mrs. Deverell hastened to open the dining-room door, but Tom was now anxious to show the visitor every courtesy. "I'll take Mr. Pringle to the study," he said. "Though I don't think Uncle Stephen can possibly be there," he added to Uncle Horace, "or he would have heard us. If he didn't—I mean if he's so absorbed as all *that*, I shouldn't think he'd see us either, even if we do go in." But Uncle Horace received his little joke without response.

And when they entered the room it was to find it unoccupied. All Uncle Stephen's belongings were there, and some traces of Tom also, but not Uncle Stephen himself.

Tom was about to invite the visitor to sit down when the visitor abruptly waved *him* to a chair. "Sit down," he said, and Tom obeyed him. "Now, tell me what is the meaning of this pretty performance?"

Tom looked docility itself, and it was in the mildest possible voice that he asked, "What pretty performance, Uncle Horace?"

"You know what I refer to: kindly answer my question."

But, as he stared into the boy's face, he remembered perhaps something which induced him to alter his tactics, for it was in a less aggressive tone that he went on. "Why did you run away from home?"

Tom did not reply: indeed Uncle Horace hardly left him time to do so before adding, "Why did you *want* to run away? Why couldn't you have said something? Don't you think it was treating your

mother—your step-mother—rather badly? I suppose *that* didn't occur to you?"

Tom looked at him gravely, but without any hint of a troubled
conscience. "It did occur to me," he said. "Only there was no other
way. And at any rate I didn't think she'd care."

"She did care."

"Yes . . . perhaps. . . . I don't know. . . . You see——— I don't
think I want to talk about that part of it: it won't do any good."

Uncle Horace's thin lips drew closer together. "Why won't it
do good?"

Tom sighed. He looked at Uncle Horace in a kind of unspoken
deprecation. "Because———" he began, and then stopped. He knew
so well what Uncle Horace was leading up to, and he wished he
wouldn't. "I think it will be better if you don't tell me she's fond of
me," he said at last, slowly and inoffensively. "You see, I know she
isn't: I've always known. I think it's the kind of thing people always
do know."

Uncle Horace checked him with a quick movement; but he looked
for all that rather taken aback. "You're making a big mistake," he
replied pompously, but without much conviction, and Tom did not
answer.

"Don't you understand, too," Uncle Horace went on, abandoning
the point of sentiment, "that it puts her in a most unpleasant position
—that when people get to know you have run away they will talk—
imagine, and very likely say, there must have been some cause to
make you behave like that?"

There was truth in this, and Tom acknowledged it. "Only there's
no reason why they ever *should* get to know," he persisted.

Uncle Horace took him up quickly. "That's all nonsense: you can't
keep a thing like this quiet. I shouldn't be surprised if Eric and
Leonard and Jane had already been chattering about it."

"Well, I don't see that I'm to blame for *that*," Tom replied. "There
was no need to say more than that I'd gone to live with Uncle
Stephen, or even gone on a visit to him."

"The effect remains, no matter who is to blame. Tell me the real
truth now, Tom. There wasn't any particular *reason*, was there, why
you did what you did? You weren't unhappy—nobody had done anything you didn't like? Eric or Leonard hadn't been teasing you? I may
tell you I've inquired into *that* side of the matter very carefully—it was
the first thing I did—without finding much, though of course I may

not have been told the truth. The boys did admit that now and then they had teased you. There was a book of yours it seems—a particular favourite—*Rudolph the Mysterious*—and they hung it up in the W.C. as—eh—toilet-paper."

Tom laughed. The relaxation was so complete that he could almost have embraced Uncle Horace. "Oh, that was ages ago. Of course I was angry at the time, but I'd forgotten about it. It was a rotten book anyway, though I liked it frightfully then, and read it I don't know how often. That's why they hung it up. But it was only a paper-backed thing, in the *Boy's Companion Library*." He looked half incredulously at Uncle Horace. "Surely you don't think I'm such a fool as that!"

"As what?" asked Uncle Horace, who saw nothing amusing in the incident, and at any rate found these changes of mood singularly unsatisfactory.

"As to worry about a joke. In fact, I think it was quite a good joke."

"But——" Uncle Horace paused. "Then there is some other reason?"

"I wanted to come to Uncle Stephen."

Uncle Horace repressed his irritation. "Look here, Tom: you had never set eyes on your Uncle Stephen in your life: you had barely even heard of him, and what you had heard wasn't favourable."

"Oh yes, I'd heard of him," said Tom simply.

"What had you heard?"

"To begin with, I knew what all of you thought."

"That's just what I say. You knew nothing except that."

"I didn't believe it was true, you see—what you thought. . . . Besides, really that had nothing to do with it."

"Then what had to do with it?" asked Uncle Horace.

"I forget."

It was a far from satisfactory answer, and he knew from Uncle Horace's stiffening countenance that he believed it to be a lie. Of course it *was* a lie, too, but what else could he say? Uncle Horace kept on badgering and badgering till you didn't very much mind what lies you told. And if it came to that, what was all his own talk but a lot of bluff? The chief reason why they wanted him back he hadn't mentioned: he had taken jolly good care not to mention it. How mad they would be if they knew Jane had told him!

He awoke out of these considerations to the consciousness that Uncle Horace's cold, greyish eyes were boring into him like gimlets.

It was the kind of gaze with which a cross-examiner attempts to extract the truth from a prevaricating witness, and Tom resented it. Not because of any reflection it cast upon his candour (for he *wasn't* being candid), but because he could not see what right Uncle Horace had to question him at all. It was none of his business: he was just a cross old thing, who loved interfering—even his own relations admitted it.

"Tell me," said the cross old thing, "had you received a letter from Mr. Collet?"

"No," answered Tom in surprise. But the question threw a new light on Uncle Horace's attitude, and again he felt his answer was not believed.

"No message of any kind?"

"No."

"Had you written to him yourself?"

"No."

Uncle Horace, momentarily baffled, sat back in his chair before beginning a fresh attack, and Tom, in the interval, ventured a question on his own account. "When are they going to send on my clothes?"

"Your clothes aren't going to be sent on: you are coming home with me."

"I'm not." It was the first definitely defiant speech he had made, and it transformed him instantly, as if by magic, into a sullen schoolboy, brimming over with obstinacy. He sat there frowning, but Uncle Horace was not perturbed. Indeed, from his face, one would have gathered that he welcomed the change. Sullen boys he had met before and knew how to cope with.

His satisfaction permitted a brief flash of the well-known smile. "You're coming to-night," he declared.

Uncle Horace was sitting with his back to the door: Tom was facing it and now got up. "I think I'd better go and look for Uncle Stephen," he muttered darkly.

"You'll oblige me by remaining where you are. Mr. Collet, if he is in the house at all, must know perfectly well I am here. Probably he has known from the beginning. All this childish business of wasting my time is either a pose or a calculated rudeness: in fact he is acting quite as I should have anticipated from what I've heard of him."

"You know nothing about him," cried Tom passionately. "And

what right have you to interfere with me? *You're* not my guardian, anyway!"

Uncle Horace had completely recovered himself: he was now master of the situation. "You won't make matters better by losing your temper," he said. "You're behaving at present like a spoiled, self-willed child."

While he was speaking, Tom had turned half round. He stood scowling in mute anger, and then suddenly his whole countenance altered as an expression of relief, affection, happiness, and trust swept over it. At that moment, in spite its of plainness, his face became oddly attractive. Not that Uncle Horace was attracted. On the contrary, turning once more, Tom encountered a gaze of fixed and profound suspicion.

"What's come to you now?" asked Uncle Horace coldly.

Tom's smile broadened. "It's Uncle Stephen," he breathed, as if conveying a secret. "He's there."

At this Uncle Horace also whipped round, and rising abruptly, knocked over a small table beside him.

"What——"

"I must apologize," Uncle Stephen said. "I didn't know anybody was here."

The tall figure still stood in shadow, motionless; and to Tom the black panelling behind it, throwing into relief the silvery whiteness of the hair, made it look exactly like an old portrait in a dusky frame. Uncle Stephen came down the full length of the room; he laid a hand on his nephew's shoulder, and Tom leaned close up against him in a way that annoyed Uncle Horace indescribably. "You'd better introduce me to your visitor, Tom."

"This is Mr. Horace Pringle," Tom replied, with an unconscious trick of mimicry catching the very tone of the clear low voice which had just spoken.

Uncle Horace jerked his head in acknowledgement, but he remained where he stood, one hand behind his back, the other resting on the top of his chair. "This is Mr. Horace Pringle——!" and there had been a glint in his eyes when he had said it. A precious pair! That boy, looking like a tiger's cub in the ecstasy of being stroked and caressed! A precious pair indeed. Uncle Horace's unspoken opinion was cried aloud from every visible inch of him—even from his clothes and buttons and tie and collar, the white frill of his waistcoat, his spats and his slender, highly polished boots.

Uncle Stephen had bowed ceremoniously. "Do sit down," he suggested. "Tom, I'm afraid you haven't been very hospitable. You might at least have got your uncle something to drink after his drive, even if you couldn't offer him a cigar or a cigarette."

"Thanks, I never drink between meals," Uncle Horace interrupted frigidly. "I shan't beat about the bush: I've come for Tom himself."

"For Tom?" Uncle Stephen's eyebrows were slightly raised as he repeated the last words, throwing into them a note of interrogation and just a shade of surprise.

"Mrs. Barber—my sister—wishes him to return home."

"At once? But surely that is a very short visit! My letter, perhaps——"

"Oh, she got your letter," Uncle Horace interrupted. "She ought to have acknowledged it at once, no doubt, but you will receive her reply to-morrow. And in the meantime she thought it would save trouble if I drove down and fetched Tom back with me. She asked me to apologize for the inconvenience his unexpected arrival must have caused you."

"It wasn't unexpect——" Tom began, but a slight pressure on his shoulder made him leave his speech unfinished. Uncle Horace had pricked up his ears, however, and Tom knew he would now be more suspicious than ever.

"His arrival wasn't at all an inconvenience," Uncle Stephen said softly. "It gave me great pleasure."

"I should have thought—with your habits of solitude—it couldn't be anything but the greatest possible nuisance."

Uncle Stephen waited a moment. "Habits of solitude, don't you think, usually mean no more than a distaste for uncongenial society?"

"Perhaps: but the society of a young boy can hardly be congenial."

"That, of course, you have no means of judging. I don't wish to be rude, but you must see yourself that it is so."

"I dare say I can't judge in the present case," Uncle Horace answered dryly, "though I should have said that the first essential to congeniality was the possession of something in common—interests, tastes, experience, age. What can you possibly have in common with a boy of Tom's age?"

"A boy of Tom's age is not necessarily devoid of interests and tastes. Also your list ought surely to include character, a certain temperamental outlook or sensitiveness."

Uncle Horace received these additions with something very like a snort. "Tom's," he said, "is the kind of temperament that makes it desirable that he should not be removed from the ordinary healthy influences of home and companions of his own age."

"You mean the particular home and companions he left behind him when he came to me?"

"Since my sister is his guardian, naturally that *is* his home. . . . I don't know what tales he may have brought you," he went on, with a glance at the possible tale-bearer; "the fact remains that he was well looked after in every way, perfectly happy, perfectly content till——"

"Till what?" Uncle Stephen asked.

"How do I know," Uncle Horace answered sourly. "He's always been secretive. Now there seems to be some particular secret that he refuses to talk about. But I'm convinced it wasn't there a few days ago."

"*Rudolph!*" Tom whispered. "I never knew I was so like him." He was regarding Uncle Horace with inquiring eyes in which brimmed a suppressed laughter. He was unaware of it, but nothing could have been more provocative.

"Your idea, then, is that this secret of Tom's has been implanted by me?" Uncle Stephen went on quietly.

"I didn't say so."

"But it is the obvious meaning of all you *have* said."

"You can take it in whatever way you like."

Uncle Stephen's eyes narrowed for a moment, though whether in distaste for the accusation, or for the manner of its expression, Tom could not tell. To him it seemed that Uncle Horace was merely being tiresome. *His* uncle was not like that; and he rubbed his cheek softly against Uncle Stephen's hand.

Uncle Horace withdrew his eyes from the revolting spectacle. "Are you or are you not going to send Tom back with me?"

"You also forget that he really *is* related to me, of my own stock, whereas——"

"Family affection has meant a lot to you in the past, hasn't it?" Uncle Horace interrupted. "I repeat my question: Are you or are you not going to send Tom back with me?"

"I don't think so," said Uncle Stephen quietly, and Tom experienced a strange thrill of pleasure.

"How long do you propose to keep him?"

"For ever and ever," Tom breathed, but again he felt a warning pressure.

"As long as he cares to stay: I certainly shan't keep him against his will. But I explained all this clearly in my letter."

"Your letter was serious then?"

"Yes. Didn't it strike you as serious?"

"It did not, but my sister was more credulous. Therefore the first thing she did, after showing it to me, was to consult her solicitors. I suppose you understand that you can be compelled to give the boy up."

"We shall see."

"You mean, you are going to fight the case?"

"I don't think there will *be* any case."

Uncle Horace gave his high nervous laugh. "You are optimistic. I can assure you matters won't be allowed to remain as they are now."

"That also we shall see."

Uncle Horace took out his watch, glanced at it, and replaced it in his pocket. Deliberately he seemed to pause before making his next point. "Another thing you perhaps haven't considered. All this must entail publicity."

"Yes?"

"It may become necessary to rake up ancient and buried scandals: —if we have to prove, for instance, that you are not a suitable person to be in charge of the boy."

"If you can do so it will certainly strengthen your position."

"I may add, speaking for myself," Uncle Horace pursued, "that my visit to-day has convinced me you are *not* a suitable person."

At this Uncle Stephen smiled, but gravely, not in derision. "That *at least* is a little unreasonable," he protested. "I should have been here to receive you if I had known you were coming, and I have apologized for not being here. The only other cause for offence you can have found is my refusal to send Tom back."

"I am not alluding either to your refusal, or to your reluctance to admit anybody to your house—or even to the slightly theatrical manner of your own entrance."

"Oh! the concealed door! I assure you my use of it was entirely accidental."

"Most people are content with ordinary doors."

"You think others definitely not respectable? I'm sorry. I can only plead the age of the house and the fact that *behind* the door there is nothing more alarming than a staircase leading to my bed-room. If you are not referring to any of these things, however, what *are* you referring to?"

"To the alteration in Tom himself."

Uncle Stephen, now at all events, showed a genuine astonishment. He looked at Uncle Horace half incredulously. "An alteration?—an alteration for the worse?"

"Most decidedly." And with this Uncle Horace stepped lightly across the room to its more orthodox entrance.

The impulse was irresistible, and Tom made a face behind his back. Unfortunately Uncle Horace, turning his head unexpectedly, had time to catch it. He regarded his nephew grimly, though he said nothing, and Uncle Stephen, who luckily had missed this by-play, rang the bell; then changed his mind and went himself to see their visitor off.

Tom, left all alone, stood in the middle of the floor, waiting for Uncle Stephen to come back, and thinking. Of course, he had heard something—a faint click—it was that which had attracted his attention—but he had unusually sharp ears, and Uncle Horace could have heard nothing. And even for *him* it had been a thrilling moment when he had turned and looked and—Uncle Stephen simply had been there. Yes, and the thought *had* risen in his mind of how wonderful it would be if he really were a magician. He had had a vision of himself going through the streets of Kilbarron, of the women peering furtively out of their windows, and the boys calling after him "Wizard's brat!" . . .

Suddenly Tom hated himself for these thoughts. They were stupid —all wrong.

He was wakened out of his reverie. "I suppose it is going to be war to the knife—eh?" Uncle Stephen had returned.

13: THROUGH the open window, flung wide to the evening air, Tom watched the departure of Sally and Mrs. Deverell—figures in a garden picture, but walking straight out of it. Why should this nightly departure continue to affect him so oddly, like a queer kind of ritual? For no sooner were they lost to sight than he had again that sense of an indescribable change in everything around him. The clock ticked on, the birds sang, the branches waved—nevertheless, nothing was the same. The quiet seemed to deepen; the light, he could have sworn, deepened too; something that he knew was withdrawn, something he did not know drew nearer; it was like dreaming; it was like the approach of sleep.

If Uncle Horace were to return now would he be able to find the gate—or would Uncle Stephen have hidden it by enchantment?

Tom leaned his hands on the window-sill, and the stone was warm. The last sunlight mingled with the shadows on the grass; a wood-pigeon cooed from the ash-tree; Tom felt at peace with all the world.

He turned his head and looked round at Uncle Stephen, who was reading. One book he held in his hands, and three or four others were open on the table beside him. Tom thought he would read also, but as soon as he tried to think of a book the impulse died. He did not really want to read. He glanced at the chessmen and immediately knew he did not want to play chess. He got a stool and placed it beside Uncle Stephen's chair; then, in silence, sat down upon it. In this way he was not interrupting Uncle Stephen, while at the same time he was letting him know he was there, for Uncle Stephen had all day to read and might like to talk for a change.

Uncle Stephen turned a page. The fingers of one hand twisted Tom's coarse, dry, brown hair into little locks, but absent-mindedly, and presently he withdrew them to turn another page. This was not in the least what Tom wanted, so he took from his pocket a feather he had picked up in the wood, and began to tickle Uncle Stephen's hand. The feather produced no effect, and Tom gave the hand a tiny bite. At this the book closed, but with a finger still keeping the place. "Uncle Stephen, I must either disturb you or go out of the room."

Uncle Stephen laid down his book. "What is it to be, then;—chess?"

"No, I want to talk. I have something to tell you. I saw that boy again this afternoon and I spoke to him. His name is Philip Coombe. He ran away from home and he's living in the other house now—hiding there. But he's going abroad, going to see the world. He'll do it too; he's just that sort."

"Where does he come from?"

"I don't know. I don't know the least thing about him. He won't answer questions. But I like him."

"How can you like a person you know nothing about?"

"Well—you can, too. *I* can, anyway."

"You mean you like what you've made up about him?"

"Yes—but I think it's true. . . . I asked him to come and stay here."

"To stay in *this* house?"

"Yes. Was that wrong? Do you mind, Uncle Stephen? He isn't coming, anyway."

"I'd certainly prefer you to tell me your plans beforehand."

"Yes. So I will. I promised to take him food every day while he is there, but that was right, wasn't it? I *ought* to do that, don't you think?"

"I suppose so."

Tom sat pondering for a while: then he began again. "Uncle Stephen?"

"Yes."

"You don't seem very interested in him."

"Interested—in what way? So far you haven't told me anything interesting."

"But you're not trying to be interested."

Uncle Stephen regarded him mildly. "What should you call trying? If you give me a hint I'll do my best."

"Well, you haven't asked me how old he is, or what he looks like, or anything."

"How old is he?"

"I don't know."

"Tom! Tom!" Uncle Stephen stretched out his hand towards his book.

"No, you're not to," cried Tom quickly, catching his wrist and pulling it back. "I only mean I don't know *exactly*. He's a good deal bigger than I am, but I don't expect he's much older—about sixteen."

There was a pause, broken at last by Uncle Stephen. "Well, what's the next point? Am I to ask another question?"

"I'm just thinking," said Tom. "There's *something* about him I can't quite make out—something *different*. Perhaps it's only his way of speaking—but there's *something*."

"His accent?"

"No." Tom's forehead wrinkled. "It's awfully hard to describe. What would you call it if a person didn't always use the words other boys use? . . . But I'm not sure that it *is* that," he added quickly.

"I've no idea. Do you mean he's very prim and pedantic?"

"No, I don't," said Tom. "Just the opposite. I'm far primmer myself: I bet he'd do anything."

"Anything! A reckless, lawless kind of person?"

"Well, not anything rotten, of course. . . . All the same," he went on half under his breath, "I bet he *is* pretty reckless and lawless."

"Apart from the question of his speech?"

Tom waited a moment before saying reproachfully, "It's very easy to make fun of people."

"I'm not making fun of people. I'm only trying to find out what has impressed *this* person. You see, for me that is the most important point."

"What?"

"What I'm trying to discover."

"But I mean what is the important point?"

"The important point is the source of *your* interest."

"I don't think I understand."

"Well, we'll put it in a different way. What quality is it that *must* be there, or at least that you most want to be there, in anybody you regard as a friend? Is that plain?"

"It ought to be—but I'd have to think it over."

"Think then."

Tom sat still for several minutes. He shut his eyes tight; he compressed his lips; he might have been grappling with the riddle of Sphinx.

"Well, have you found it?" Uncle Stephen asked. "Or was this just an opportunity for taking a snooze?"

Tom opened his eyes. "I believe," he said, "I would *have* to like anybody who was faithful—even if the person was bad—really bad —in every other way."

"Faithful to *you*, do you mean?"

Tom thought once more, but this time appeared less satisfied with the result. "I suppose that *is* what I mean," he admitted. "At least, it's the way I imagined it."

"And the 'faithfulness' implied a deep affection. You imagined that too, didn't you?"

"Y-es," answered Tom. "How did you know?"

"I knew you were creating a romantic impossibility."

"Why is it impossible?"

"Because nobody *could* be faithful, and bad in every other way. To begin with, there must be your capacity for affection. Besides, you can't have faithfulness without unselfishness and courage. When courage evaporates faithfulness goes with it. I don't deny you have hit on a good quality, but it isn't one you can recognize at a glance. Therefore I shouldn't be too ready to attribute it to every attractive new acquaintance."

Tom puckered his brows, not in dissent, but not wholly in acquiescence either. "Don't you think there are *some* people you can be sure of at once?" he asked.

"There may be."

"But you must know. You *must* know. Why, the first minute I came into this room—or at any rate a few minutes afterwards——"

"You feel sure, then, about this boy?"

Tom shook his head. "No, I don't. I'm not a bit sure. And I'm not a bit sure that he likes me. Will you come with me to the other house?"

"I don't think so."

"But if *he* won't come here, then you'll never get to know each other!"

"Does that matter?"

"Did it?" Tom asked himself. "Did he want Uncle Stephen to go to the other house?" Deeper and deeper he sank into his thoughts. He supposed it was true that it took a long time really to get to know people, and that he was always in too great a hurry. Certainly he was in too great a hurry to tell them he liked them, and it hadn't answered well in the past. They didn't want to be told. They didn't want—those he *had* told—even to be liked; and Philip, he half suspected, was of that kind. . . . Nor were words ever satisfactory. What you said always sounded either too much or too little. You could hear it yourself—either horribly gushing, or else so feeble and dry that it expressed nothing. The only true communication seemed to be not words at all:—when Uncle Stephen stroked his hair, for instance. Yes, it was that. He wanted to keep Uncle Stephen for himself: he didn't want to share him with Philip. It might be selfish

—but there it was. He wanted Uncle Stephen for his very own. He wanted Philip too, but not in the same way—— He wanted nobody else in the same way.

Tom became more and more doubtful. The room grew darker without his noticing it: he only saw that it *was* dark when Uncle Stephen got up to light the lamp. And how much darker it must be in the other house, with its cobwebbed windows half overgrown by ivy. Was Philip standing at his window looking out? The fountain would be hardly visible. And suddenly Tom felt that if he had to go to that house now he would be afraid. He wouldn't be afraid if he had Philip with him; but he would be afraid of not finding him, of finding the house empty. He saw it with the moonlight glinting on its cold black windows. And inside it was empty—empty and dark. . . .

The vision altered his mood, and into his mind, like rooks returning to a rookery, flocked strange and restless thoughts.

"Uncle Stephen," he asked, "is there really such a thing as magic?"

Uncle Stephen looked at him, and his look, though it was kind, *because* in fact it was kind, made Tom feel guilty.

"There have been people who have thought so, and who have tried to practise it. That is to say, there are the rites and ceremonies invented to accompany magic, and there are books—obscure, pretentious, and fantastical."

"Is it wicked to practice magic?"

"Not the kind of magic you mean: not the magic of fairy stories."

"But I don't mean that."

Uncle Stephen was silent a moment, and Tom felt that a faint shadow had passed between them.

"The other is usually associated with wickedness: certainly I can't imagine any good coming of it."

"But the Greeks believed in it."

"Yes, some of them." Tom had an impression that the shadow had lifted, and he was sure of it when Uncle Stephen went on. "I dare say Homer believed in the magic of Kirké, but I don't think Euripides believed in the magic of Medea. Doubtless there were real women, who, like the woman in the poem of Theocritus, turned a magic wheel to charm back a lost lover. But all that is utterly different from medieval magic, with its conscious evil and depraved association with Christianity. Apollonius of Tyana was called a magician, but he and his master Pythagoras

were really holy men, and if supernatural powers were attributed
to them it was because they were in communion with the Gods,
not with evil spirits."

Tom, with his forefinger, began to trace an invisible design on
the carpet.

"Are you drawing a pentagram, Tom?" Uncle Stephen asked,
and in his voice was that half-bantering affection which Tom particularly liked.

Nevertheless, a strange mood of perversity seemed to prompt
him with questions, which he hated all the more because he knew
Uncle Stephen thought they were innocent.

"Have you ever known a magician, Uncle Stephen?"

"I have known people—unpleasant people—who tried experiments
in magic."

"In real magic?"

"Yes."

"Here?"

"No; not here. Not even in this country. It was many years ago,
and their experiments were not successful—in any way."

"Did you help them—in the experiments?"

"Yes."

"And were they unpleasant too?"

"Not at the beginning—only foolish: but in the end—yes."

There was a hardly describable change in Uncle Stephen's voice,
yet it was perceptible, and still more so when he spoke again. "Now,
tell me why you asked these questions, and what is in your mind,
and who put it there?"

"It—it was just something I heard," said Tom, speaking very low.

Uncle Stephen sat silent. Tom did not dare to look up, but as
the silence lengthened he began to feel it like a coldness spreading
through the room—a cold mist in which he had lost sight of his
companion and friend, which shut him away from him almost as
some palpable barrier might have done. Gradually it became un-
bearable. "Uncle Stephen, I'm sorry," he broke out, clutching the
hand that had not been withdrawn from his shoulder. "I shouldn't
have said anything. And I haven't even told you the truth. It was
really what happened to-day that made me think of it. You know—
when Uncle Horace was here—the things he said. And my step-
mother had a servant—a girl who came from these parts—and she

told some story, though I never heard it. But I'm sorry. Uncle Stephen, forgive me. I know I've hurt your feelings. And I didn't believe it anyway: and anyway I wouldn't care if it *was* true. I'd like it."

"Stop," said Uncle Stephen peremptorily. "You mustn't lose your self-control like this. What is there to get in such a state about? One would think something dreadful had happened. Your whole body is shaking."

Tom gulped: then he said in a queer, choked voice, "It was because I thought I'd offended you."

"Even if you *had* offended me it would be no reason for such an outburst. You mustn't give way to your emotions in this way. Remember you are a man, or at least a boy."

"Yes," said Tom, but with a little sigh of relief. "Then you're not offended?"

But Uncle Stephen's voice was still rather stern. "I can't very well be offended till I know what you mean."

"I didn't mean anything," said Tom, "or at any rate I don't now." Then he added, as if to make a last confession, "I tried to find the secret door when you were out of the room."

Uncle Stephen rose. Clothed as he was, all in black, and with the black skull-cap crowning his silver hair, he would, Tom felt even in this moment of contrition, have made a lovely magician. Yes—and he would have helped him. He watched him now light one of the wax candles which stood in slender bronze sconces on the carved chimney-piece. "Come," said Uncle Stephen, and, a little awe-struck, though filled with excitement, Tom followed him across the room.

Uncle Stephen held the candle aloft, and Tom noticed how firmly and levelly he held it, so that not a drop of wax fell. The flame shone on the dark panelling, and at the corner of each panel was carved a flattened conventional rose. On the centre of one of these roses Uncle Stephen pressed, and it sank inward, releasing a spring. Four of the panels swung back in a single piece, and Uncle Stephen motioned to him to pass through the aperture: then he himself followed.

And after all they were only in a narrow passage, from which a flight of stone stairs ascended to another door, that opened precisely as the one below had opened. Tom stood on the threshold of a room he had never seen before—Uncle Stephen's bedroom. Uncle Stephen entered, and lit a lamp, which in a minute or two burned brightly. He beckoned, and Tom stepped forward and stood beside him.

The room was not large—not so large as Tom's own bedroom —and it was far more simply and sparsely furnished. A low narrow bed in the centre of the floor, a wardrobe, a chest of drawers, a dressing-table, and a single cane-bottomed chair—there was no other furniture than this. There was not even a carpet, only a rug beside the bed; and the grey walls were bare—the whole room had a monastic bareness and austerity, except that, in the open space beyond the bed, there was something wonderful.

It was wonderful because—time-stained, ancient, battered— without arms, and with the legs broken off below the knees—it yet had all the beauty and radiance of a God. Motionless he stood there dreaming, with a lovely mildness in his open countenance. He was a spirit, and Tom felt himself to be in the presence of a spirit—of a beneficent guardian, who had made sweet and sacred this place in which he stood.

Uncle Stephen was watching him. "Who is he?" Tom breathed. And suddenly he felt that this room was different from all other rooms: it was as if merely by his acceptance of it, and by his presence there, that broken lovely figure had made it into a temple for himself and filled it with life. Tom was ready to drop down on his knees.

"Who is he?" he asked again.

"You like him?" Uncle Stephen said. "Well, that is right, because he is, or was, especially a boy's God—Hermes Παιδοχόρος, 'he who cares for boys,' and his statue was put up beside that of Eros in the palaestra, as a kind of symbol of the relations that ought to rule there. You have read of him in the *Iliad*—a 'boy before the down has begun to grow on his cheeks, who is then most lovely.' But he is also Hermes Ψυχοπομπός, the escorter, the guardian of souls. He is the prototype of the Christian Good Shepherd, and you can be his young ram."

"But—— Does he allow you to sleep here?"

"He is the God of sleep and dreams. The last libation of the day was made to him—a kind of 'now I lay me down to sleep' ceremony. The Greeks would have found Doctor Watts's poem quite appropriate:

With cheerful heart I close mine eyes,
Since Thou wilt not remove;
And in the morning let me rise
Rejoicing in Thy love.

It was the custom to put his image in the sleeping-room, and the beds were so arranged that it was the last thing the sleeper looked at before he fell asleep, and the first thing he saw when he awoke in the morning."

"That is how *your* bed is arranged," said Tom.

"The Gods protected those who slept under their shadow. The idea is pleasant—don't you think? It is very like your own idea of faithfulness. Even the animals who haunted a shrine were protected. They were safe, their rights of sanctuary were respected, and Aelian says the Athenians put to death a man who had killed a sparrow in the temple of Asklepios. If you had been an Athenian boy, and were sick, you would have been taken to sleep in that temple. Being a boy, you would have prayed to Asklepios Παîς—Asklepios in his boyhood—and the boy god would have come to you in a dream, or perhaps while you were still awake, and cured you."

"Uncle Stephen, *please*, would you let me sleep here—just once?"

"We shall see."

Tom was still gazing at the statue. "Where did he come from?" he asked.

"From Greece first. But at one time he must have been brought to Italy, for it was in Italy he was discovered, buried in the ground, by a man who had found lots of other things, but nothing so precious as this."

"And he gave him to you?"

"Yes—before he died."

"The same man who gave you your chessmen?"

"Yes."

"He must have been very fond of you, Uncle Stephen."

"I lived with him much as you are living with me."

Tom took Uncle Stephen's hand and drew him a step nearer to the statue. "Was he—once—worshipped?" he asked reverently.

"Yes—or the spirit within him."

"Sleep—the spirit of sleep," Tom whispered. "Haven't even the words a lovely sound?"

"It is more than mere sleep as you know it. It is a road through time—a gateway into a world where time is like space, and you may go backward or forward."

"I have been there," said Tom. "I have gone back till I was quite small, and Mother was there. . . . Uncle Stephen, he *is* alive: I can see his arms and his hands; his legs and his feet: I can see all of him now—quite perfect and whole."

"Yes, I know you can."

"Does he make me see him like that?"

"Perhaps. I don't know."

"If we brought him downstairs, wouldn't he make that room into his temple—just as he has made this?"

"I should not care to move him. He has always been here. I would rather give you this room for your own. You would like it, wouldn't you? You see, all the space between these four walls is now holy ground. Downstairs it could not be the same—with strangers coming and going."

Tom gave a little laugh. "Surely, Uncle Stephen, not a *great* many strangers come and go."

"Perhaps not. But think of that wretched scene this afternoon. It would have been odious. All that you now feel in the air around you would have been desecrated by it. *Don't* you feel it? Like a kind of soundless music. Perhaps to you it is even not quite soundless, for I think you are much closer to these things than I am. And it is stronger now than it used to be. Sometimes—— Well, all *that*, I think, would have gone. It comes from the spirit within the image, and, if that spirit were withdrawn, it would vanish too, like the scent of a flower when the flower dies. But here there are no intruders, no contrary influences, nothing antagonistic. You looked at him and found him lovely, and in doing so your spirit was mixed into his spirit. Your mind reached him, like the sunlight or like a prayer: his power was strengthened, his life was strengthened; you became the unconscious priest and your affection drew him nearer. . . . But most people *would* be intruders."

"Uncle Stephen, was it really true, what you said about people who were sick sleeping in the temples of Asklepios, and about the God coming to them in the night?"

"It's certainly true about the people. As for the God, I told you the tradition. Asklepios was an earth-god, or an earth-daimon, and the sleeper slept with his ears to the ground, so as to receive a healing dream from below. Sometimes the God appeared in his own form,

sometimes in that of a snake, sometimes in the dream he performed
a cure and the patient awoke healthy and sound."

"Has Hermes ever come to you?" Tom asked wonderingly.

"Not in the way you are with me now; not so that I could touch
him or hear him; not even as a ghost. But as an influence—yes: as a
power—yes."

"Do you think on the night I sleep here he will come to me?"

"I don't know. . . . I'm not sure that I should have brought you
here at all. Not now—not yet."

For Tom was standing there with a strange expression on his face.
He might have been listening to some very faint, very distant sound;
and in his eyes there was a peculiar veiled and inward look. Slowly
they were raised till they met Uncle Stephen's eyes, and more slowly
still his words came. "Uncle Stephen—there is something I don't
understand. Tell me—tell me." His voice suddenly broke, and next
moment Uncle Stephen's arms were round him.

"What is it, Tom? What is the matter?" Uncle Stephen was patting
him and consoling him.

"Nothing—nothing," Tom faltered. "I'm sorry. I couldn't help it.
It was just for a minute. I—I don't know what happened. But somehow it all seemed to come over me."

"What seemed to come over you?"

"I mean—you, and him, and Philip, and—even the boy at the
fountain:—it was as if you all were one person. . . . " His face had
grown white and strained, his parted lips trembled. "Uncle Stephen,
don't you love me—really—really?"

"Yes, yes. Don't look like that. I shouldn't have brought you to
this room. I ought to have known. But I wanted you to see for yourself that there was no magic; that it was no magician's den with circles
and triangles chalked on the floor; that there were no rods and tripods
and chalices—nothing, nothing at all, but the broken statue of a God."

"But I never thought there was any such den," Tom protested,
half laughing through his trouble.

"Perhaps not. But a seed had been sown in your mind, and I did
not want it to grow. Now you have seen the whole house, and if
that foolish door worries you, you can nail it up yourself."

"I'm not such a baby," cried Tom.

"You are very young in some ways, extraordinarily young. It is
just as if a little corner of you had never changed at all—and I keep

stupidly thinking of what I was at your age and treating you as if
you were the same, whereas you are not—not at all."

"I think it must have been because I was tired," Tom went on, trying to explain. "So much seems to have happened to-day. I think
I'd like to go to bed now."

But he still clung close to Uncle Stephen, who looked down at him
and stroked his bowed head.

"Don't you want your supper?" he asked.

"No: I'm not hungry: I couldn't eat anything." Tom lifted his
head, his eyes still a little troubled. "But I'd like you to come up
with me."

"To sit with you?"

"Yes: you won't have to wait long: I'll go to sleep awfully soon
if I know you're there. . . . And—and—you won't think any the
less of me because of this, will you?"

"No, I won't think any the less."

"I hope you won't," Tom said ruefully. "Though I don't see how
you can very well help it. I'm not like Philip, am I? *He* doesn't mind
being all by himself at night in that other house, and it must be frightfully lonely and queer."

"I don't want you to be like Philip."

"All the same, I'd hate him to know about this. He wouldn't be as
kind as you are."

"Perhaps not. But don't get it into your head that because he's not
afraid to sleep by himself in an empty house he's a wonderful person.
I've a very good idea of what he is."

They went out of the room and along the passage, Uncle Stephen
holding the candle. In his own room Tom undressed quickly, and his
spirits rose more quickly still, so that by the time he was safely in bed
he was his normal, by no means melancholy self.

"Now, you're not to talk," said Uncle Stephen, for Tom had already begun to chatter.

"But you won't go away till you're sure I'm asleep?"

"No; not if you keep quiet and try to go to sleep."

There was a silence. The door was ajar, and presently from down
below came the soft deep chiming of the hall clock.

"Dickory," said Tom.

"I thought you weren't to talk."

Tom said no more, until he murmured, "Uncle Stephen, I'm getting
sleepy now: will you say good-night."

14:

"MY dearest Tom,

"What on earth did you say or do to poor Uncle Horace? None of us can quite make out, though he has *talked* of precious little else ever since he got back. He came round that very night foaming at the mouth with rage, and there was a most awful scene—entirely apart from you—because he barked his shins against Leonard's bicycle in the hall. You see, it was late and darkish and he was in such a hurry to get in. At first we thought the ceiling had come down; but it was Uncle Horace and the bicycle. However, that doesn't concern you, and I'd better tell you what does.

"To begin with, Uncle Horace says U.S. pretended to be too busy to receive him and that he wouldn't have got into the house at all if you hadn't turned up just as he was going away. Then, after he did manage to get in, there was still no sign of U.S., though really he was hiding all the time and listening, so that, when Uncle Horace had at last persuaded you to come home, he was able to upset every-thing by appearing suddenly through a trap-door. This is the part where Uncle Horace gets so feverish that we simply daren't ask questions, and Tom dear, though awfully thrilling of course, don't you think it *was* a little eccentric too? But perhaps you don't, for Uncle Horace says you've become the *âme damnée* of U.S. (I've been dying to bring that in—it's a lovely expression—and it really *is* what Uncle Horace means.)

"What he *says* is that you're being hopelessly spoiled and that mother isn't to send on your clothes or your books or anything. They sit talking about it together by the hour. At first we were sent out of the room, but now they've got reckless and discuss everything openly. Uncle Horace is angrier with U.S. than with you, though he's pretty angry all round and says you both insulted him and that your manner, once you had U.S. there, became insolent to the last degree. He also says it's mother's duty to get you out of U.S.'s clutches, though when she asked him if any wickedness was actually going on in the house he told her not to be a fool. That's the sort of temper he's in: poor mother has her head bitten off about fifty times an evening. And the worst of it is, it brings him round here *every* evening—simply the pleasure of abusing U.S. He hasn't missed once since he got back, and he finds fault with all of us nearly as much as with you. Everything in the house annoys him, but particularly the drawing-room clock, which at nine and ten has taken to striking thirteen and fourteen, and mother always forgets to have it fixed. They've both been to see lawyers, but I didn't hear what happened, and I don't think you need worry, because Uncle Horace knows he'd have to pay all the expenses if they went to law.

"I got your two postcards, but would much rather have had one letter. By the way, you'd better disguise your handwriting when you reply to this, as I've been forbidden to hold any communication with you. I hope you're having a good time—it sounds as if you were—and send you my love. To U.S., *at present*, only kind regards.

"Ever your affectionate friend,

"Jane Gavney.

"P.S.—*Is* U.S. a magician, and can you bring rabbits out of a hat yet? "P.P.S.—It would be better if you addressed your letter c/o Miss Margaret Stanhope, The Limes, Dunmore Park."

Tom refolded this epistle and put it back in his pocket. They had heard neither from Uncle Horace nor his step-mother, but he had ceased to care whether his clothes came on or not. His measurements had been sent to Uncle Stephen's own tradesmen, and a complete outfit had arrived several days ago, to the delight of Mrs. Deverell and Sally, who had made out a list of his requirements, had gone over everything carefully, had marked his linen and superintended the tryings-on of his suits, while Tom strutted in front of them, endeavouring to appear indifferent to criticism and admiration. Sally had made jokes. She had pretended he must be going to get married, and all questions of taste were referred to a mysterious "She." Mrs. Deverell was not given to joking, but it was rather clear to Tom that they both enjoyed having him at the Manor and enjoyed even the extra work it gave them. It was Master Tom this, and Master Tom that, while George McCrudden and Robert docilely had fallen in with the feminine view. The only drawback was that the women were too inclined to forget he wasn't a small boy. He liked being made much of, but——

He glanced at Philip lying on his back under a beech-tree, and the contrast struck him. It was impossible to imagine anybody treating Philip as *he* was treated by Sally and Mrs. Deverell. Yet Philip was only a year older. It was the self-reliance of his nature, more really than any physical qualities he possessed, that made the difference—though the physical qualities were there too, and Tom was sure the roughest kind of life would not alarm him. He would be able to hold his own either on board a ship or anywhere else; nothing short of positive ill-treatment could injure him; and he was strong enough to stand even a good deal of that. . . .

Just now he was asleep, or seemed so. Both boys had taken off their jackets, and Philip had rolled his up to make a pillow of it. Tom sat beside him, leaning against the broad trunk of the tree and still holding in his hand a branch of syringa he had broken off to drive away flies while they were walking through the bracken. Their beech was on the slope of a hill overlooking the river valley. Between banks of reed-grass, sedges, and wild parsnip, the sluggish water wound in and out, sometimes hidden by overhanging bushes and pollard willows, but its course always visible as far as Tom's sight could reach. The air was heavy, and there was a dark, threatening line of clouds on the horizon. . . .

He closed his eyes. For a minute or two perhaps he actually lost consciousness, but the sudden nodding of his head was sufficient to awaken him. The fire they had lit had not quite gone out; he could still see the red glow of the sticks beneath a covering of grey ashes. He felt a tickling sensation below his knee. He pulled up the leg of his trousers and discovered a furry caterpillar—a Hairy Willie was his name for it. . . . Philip *really* was asleep, he thought. . . .

Tom picked up the caterpillar with the intention of placing it on the sleeper's nose, but instantly it curled into a tight ring in his hot hand, pretending to be dead. He laid it on the moss and looked down at his friend.

His first thought was that if he himself had been dressed as Philip was dressed he would have looked like a boy out of one of Dr. Barnardo's Homes. Yet Philip didn't: his clothes didn't matter. There was a triangular rent in his crumpled trousers; he had no waistcoat, no collar, and his shirt, open on his sun-browned chest, required both washing and mending:—and none of these things mattered. Tom bent down till he could see on the sleeping boy's cheeks and upper lip a faint down composed of minute silken hairs, invisible at a distance, but which now showed like a velvet film on the smoothness of his skin. With the tip of his finger he tested his own skin, brushing it lightly to and fro.

He held the syringa over Philip's mouth, but, though he touched him with the utmost carefulness, the blossom left a golden stain of pollen. Tom moistened his finger and tried to remove it without wakening him.

A lazy voice grumbled, "What are you doing?" Philip had only half opened his eyes, and in the narrow ellipse the dark-blue iris acquired a strange depth into which Tom gazed. As he did so his lips parted and a thrill passed through him. Two words he whispered involuntarily, though it was only after he had spoken them that they reached his consciousness, producing a slight shock.

"You were asleep," he said hurriedly.

"I wasn't, but *you* must have been: you called me Uncle Stephen."

"I didn't. . . . At least, I did," stammered Tom. "I mean, I didn't mean to."

"I hope not. Are we going in for a swim?"

Tom hesitated. He put up his hand and began to loosen the knot of his tie: then stopped. "There's no hurry," he said.

This reluctance was unusual. Every afternoon during the past fortnight they had bathed: the mornings Tom spent with Uncle Stephen. He was not to begin work with Mr. Knox till September, and it was hardly work he did with Uncle Stephen. They read together, and talked of what they had read, but it was more than anything else an introduction into the beauty of a creed, outmoded perhaps, but not outworn, rejuvenescent as the earth's vegetation. . . . And when he read in Homer of boys building their sand castles on the shores of the Aegean, it seemed to Tom as if all time had been only one long summer day. . . .

He looked up to find Philip watching him. "Will you promise to answer me truthfully if I ask you a question?"

"How can I promise before I know what the question is?" Tom said. But he added immediately, "Yes."

"Why did you call me Uncle Stephen—because you did, you know?"

"I told you why: it just slipped out. Besides, I wasn't really calling you Uncle Stephen: it was only that for a moment something made me think of him." To avoid further discussion he began to strip off his clothes as quickly as possible. Then he ran down the hill, and was splashing in the shallows at the edge before Philip had unlaced his boots.

He waited until Philip joined him. Neither boy was a good swimmer, though both, with some puffing and blowing, could manage fifty yards or so, and at its widest the channel actually out of their depth was not more than ten yards across. "This is great!" spluttered Tom. "I wonder how far the river goes?"

"Oh, for miles and miles: they always do. Right up into the hills somewhere."

"Sally says you ought to be careful when you bathe in fresh water, or you may swallow something that will go on living inside you. She says you shouldn't lie on the grass, because an earwig may creep into your ear, and if it once gets in, it will eat your brains. She says a cat should never be left alone with a baby, or it will suck its breath and kill it. She says a drowned woman always floats face downward and a drowned man on his back. . . . I say, suppose we got a canoe and *discovered* the source of the river! The raft would be no good for that. I expect Uncle Stephen would get me one if I asked him."

"We could go by land."

"When?"

"I don't know."

"Why don't you know? I hate putting off things, if I'm going to do them at all."

"It's you who will have to get permission, not me."

"Yes, but there's no use in my asking till we've settled when we want to do it."

These last remarks were made on the bank and while Philip squeezed the juice of a dock leaf on to his ankle, where he had been stung by a nettle. Tom was pulling his shirt over his head when another thought occurred to him. It had occurred to him several times before, though he had said nothing about it, nor was it without a struggle that he brought himself to mention it now. "You did Greek at school, didn't you?" he began.

"Naturally. . . . It's only the juice that really does any good, and there's so little of it."

But Tom was not thinking of the virtue of dock leaves. "Why do you say 'naturally'? Plenty of people don't learn Greek."

"At my school it was compulsory."

"That's queer. Wasn't there a modern side?"

"I never heard of any."

Tom pondered. He wished Philip wasn't so uncommunicative. It made it difficult to ask him even the simplest questions. He had never been told the name of this school, for instance, though he had once asked. He had an idea that it was a good deal more distinguished than his own, but that was all.

"Did you like it?" he said.

"Like what? Greek? No."

This was discouraging, but once he had begun Tom was determined to go on. "Of course, with Uncle Stephen it isn't like school. There's no 'prep,' and he doesn't mind if your construe is pretty wobbly. I don't mean to say that he doesn't put you right, but what he really wants you to do is not to translate but to get the meaning without—to read as if you were reading your own language; and I'm beginning to be able to—a little. And then he tells you things, and he has all sorts of pictures—photographs, you know, and plans and maps. It makes it all true, somehow—talking about it. . . . I mean, that river, for instance—*our* river—it seems different—you begin to think of it differently—to think of it as alive. *Everything* comes alive, becomes in a way the *same* as us, so that you wouldn't be awfully surprised if the river became friends with you, and appeared in a human form, or at any rate spoke. You see he *is* our river—and we ought to dedicate our hair to him as a bond of friendship."

Philip did not answer, and Tom, glancing at him, saw a faint smile on his face. He coloured. What he had said, of course, had been vague and confused—he couldn't put things the way Uncle Stephen did—but still—— For a minute or two he sat without speaking, offended. Then he asked, "*Will* you come in the mornings?"

"To do Greek and talk about rivers? No."

Again there was a pause, but it was broken abruptly by Philip. "Who's this?"

Tom looked up. He followed the direction of Philip's gaze and his face changed. "He's a chap called Deverell," he said uneasily, at the same time half rising to his feet. "I say, let's move on. He mayn't have seen us: I don't think he has."

Deverell was still at a considerable distance. He was approaching along the bank of the river, but he was moving at a sauntering pace, sometimes coming to a standstill, while his dog, with flapping ears, hunted in and out among the sedges.

"Let's go before he sees us," Tom repeated more urgently.

"He has seen us already," Philip replied.

"Well, let's go anyway: we might as well."

Still Philip did not budge. "Are you frightened of him?" he asked. "You seem to be."

"Of course I'm not frightened," Tom muttered in annoyance. Nor was he, for, though he wanted to avoid this encounter, what really troubled him was the feeling that he had behaved shabbily to Deverell —letting day after day pass without ever going near him. Once they had met by accident—or so Tom supposed—and even on that occasion, after five minutes or so, he had invented an excuse to get away. Moreover, he had not given the true reason, for he had said not a word about having to keep an appointment with Philip. He had said not a word about Philip to Deverell and not a word about Deverell to Philip. Now he was reaping the consequence.

Deverell meanwhile had begun to climb the hill, striking a diagonal course which would bring him straight to where they sat. He had given no sign of recognition; he was not even looking in their direction; but that, Tom knew, was characteristic. Philip *might* have come away when he had asked him to! And that was characteristic also. He glanced at him. Philip was sitting bolt upright, watching the approaching figure with an expression of extraordinary coldness. Tom stretched himself on his side, pillowed his head on his arm, and pretended to go to sleep.

He was perfectly aware how these ostrich tactics would strike the boy beside him, and also of their futility, but the minutes passed— perhaps they weren't really so many as they seemed, or perhaps Deverell had turned back. Suddenly he felt against his cheek, first the touch of a blunt cold nose, and then the rapid caress of a warm tongue. Even in his embarrassment he could not suppress a stifled laugh. At the same moment a deep voice growled, "Here, Dingo, come out o' that." The voice assumed its ordinary pitch. "Doin' a sleep, Mr. Tom?"

"Yes," said Tom, opening his eyes.

"Bathin' makes you sleepy like, don't it?"

"Yes," said Tom once more.

He sat up, and saw that Deverell's gaze was directed not at him but at Philip, in a hard fixed stare. "Mr. Tom, he likes to play at peep-bo," Deverell dropped grimly. "Isn't that so, Mr. Tom?"

"No it isn't," said Tom. He smiled up at the poacher and his bright eyes were lit with friendliness. He felt that Deverell recognized the friendliness, that even for a moment he responded to it, and that then, deliberately, he rejected it. And Tom understood this too: it was strange how much better he knew Deverell than he knew Philip: it was as if one similarity of temperament were stronger than all that was unlike. "All the same," he went on, "I think it must *look* extremely like that." He smiled again, and there was in his voice a curious blend of provocativeness, appeal, apology, and mischief. The young poacher's dark eyes rested on him sombrely, but not angrily. Simultaneously Tom became aware that Philip also was looking at him, with a faint and slightly disdainful surprise. But he didn't care. It wasn't Philip's business to choose his friends for him: he would be friends with whoever he wanted.

"Mr. Tom nearly promised to go fishin' with me," Deverell said slowly, "but in the latter end he drew out of it."

"Oh, I never!" cried Tom. "You asked me and that was all. You mustn't say that, really: I mean, you mustn't think it, because whatever else I don't do I keep my promises."

"Well, I won't say you were very keen on the sport of it," Deverell admitted. "Maybe this other young gentleman is more of the sportin' kind than what you are. He wouldn't be any friend of yours, would he?"

"Do you mean a relation? He isn't a relation, but of course he's a friend." It was at this point that he might have performed an introduction if it hadn't been for the frozen expression on Philip's face. Tom gave it up in despair.

"I seen you about with him these last two weeks," Deverell went on, "but my mother says there's no one stayin' at the Manor barrin' yourself."

"Neither there is," Tom answered.

"And I didn't hear any word of him down in the town. Perhaps he'd be coming over from a distance each day?"

"Don't you think you'd better be moving on?" Philip abruptly asked, his eyes as blue as ice and as cold.

Deverell looked at him, thrust his hands into his breeches pockets, then turned and spat before facing him once more. "So that's the kind of talk, is it?" he said softly.

"Yes, that's the kind of talk. Just show me how quickly you can get down that hill again."

"At your bidding, perhaps? Look see, my young cock, if you weren't a friend of Mr. Tom's here, I'd give you a clip on the ear might learn you manners."

Philip rose to his feet. "Clear out," he said. "And don't let me see you molesting Mr. Tom again."

"Molestin'—molestin'—and when was I molestin' him? Isn't it for Mr. Tom himself to choose who he'll——"

"No, it isn't for Mr. Tom. And if I catch you hanging round here——"

"Well, what will you do?" asked Deverell, dropping his voice almost to a whisper. At the same time he advanced a step, and the effect was so suddenly threatening that Tom sprang in between them.

"Oh, I say, stop it," he cried. "What's the sense in all this!" He turned half angrily to Philip. "He's as much right to be here as we have, and I don't see why he shouldn't speak to me. I'm going to speak to him anyway, and I'm going fishing with him too."

Philip remained for a moment quite still. Then he wheeled round. "Good-bye," he dropped over his shoulder, and walked off without another glance.

"I'm sorry," Tom muttered to Deverell, who was standing with his eyes bent gloomily on the ground. But the young poacher did not answer.

"I *am* sorry," Tom repeated half petulantly. "I wish you wouldn't be angry with me. I know I've behaved rottenly, but I'll really go out with you one of these days—if you'll let me—if you want me. I'll send a message by your mother. . . . I don't know why he spoke to you like that, though it was partly my fault, and a little bit yours too, perhaps. I mean he didn't like your asking questions about him. . . . And—I think I'd better go after him now. . . . You see, he *is* my pal (you remember what you once asked me?) though I don't think I'm *his* very much. I mean, he likes me well enough, but—not in the way you do. That's how it is, really, and I can't help it."

Still Deverell said nothing, and Tom, after a further hesitation, began slowly to follow on Philip's track. Presently he broke into a trot, and Philip must have heard him, though he did not stop nor look round. Even when Tom came up with him he continued to march straight on without a word.

"What's the matter?" asked Tom pacifically. "What are you in such a rage about? What have I done?"

Philip stared in front of him and walked on.

"Oh well, if you won't speak—— All I tried to do was to prevent a row. What chance would you have had if it had come to that?"

"Not very much, I dare say, unless you had backed me up: but I exepct that's hardly in your line."

Tom flushed. "If you think I'm a coward you're welcome to do so: I don't care."

"I don't suppose you do, and I'll know another time what to expect."

"What *have* I done?" Tom repeated. "Is it because I told you he had a right to speak to me?"

"Yes, you said that when he was there—after telling me first he'd been annoying you."

"That's a lie: I told you no such thing."

Philip immediately confronted him, blocking the way. "Are you calling me a liar?" he asked, raising his hand.

Tom flinched ever so little, but he stood his ground. "Yes," he muttered, biting on his lower lip to prevent it from betraying him. He waited for Philip to strike him, as he had waited in more than one such crisis at school, but no blow came. Instead, Philip thrust his hands into his pockets.

"I don't think you're a coward," he said, with a kind of angry honesty, "and you mayn't actually have said he had annoyed you; but you implied it; you even wanted to run away from him."

"It wasn't for that reason."

"So I see now. Why didn't you stay with him, then? I gave you the opportunity."

Tom answered nothing, and after a moment Philip once more began to walk on towards the Manor woods, whereupon Tom also walked on beside him.

In this fashion they proceeded, without uttering a word, but Tom was not good at keeping up a quarrel, and very soon his sole desire was to find an excuse for ending this one. "It wasn't Deverell's fault," he began. "It was really mine. It must have looked to him exactly as if I wanted to avoid speaking to him, and I had been quite friendly before."

"A good deal too friendly, I should imagine."

"What do you mean? Why shouldn't I be friendly?"

"He's the surliest-looking brute I ever saw. You seem ready to trust anybody."

It was on the tip of Tom's tongue to reply, "I trusted *you*," but he refrained. All he said was, "You might have done what I asked you to: then none of this would have happened."

"What did you ask me to do?"

"To clear out when we saw him coming."

"That's not the way to get rid of him," returned Philip impatiently. "You've got to take strong measures with a person like that: you've got to send him about his business. He admitted himself he'd been spying after us and asking questions. Do you think I'm going to have a chap like that prying round, or to hide every time I see him?"

"Well, *I'm* not going to send him about his business. I've got nothing against him. It was only because you were there that I wanted to avoid him."

"Yes, I know that—now. You needn't go on repeating it. Have you arranged to meet him to-morrow?"

"No, but I've promised to meet him one of these days, and I'm going to." After which he was silent until he added, "You see, you won't even try to understand. The reason why I wanted you to come away at the beginning was partly because I had broken my word to him, but chiefly because I knew you wouldn't get on together."

"You were right about that at any rate: though you told him you hadn't broken your word."

"Not literally, but I never went near him."

"Why?"

"Because of you, I suppose."

Philip's face did not clear, though he answered less angrily: "Well, if you take my advice, you *won't* go near him."

"Wouldn't it be rather mean if I took your advice?" Tom asked quietly. "After all, I must form my own judgements of people."

"Then you think I'm mean?"

"I think you're unfair and prejudiced. You've taken a dislike to him without any cause—simply because he asked me who you were."

"It wasn't only that. It wasn't even principally that."

"What was it then?"

"It was because I know he won't do you any good; and I *do* know it."

"I don't see how he can do me any *harm*. Surely I can look after myself!"

"Yes, if you wanted to: but you seem to like him."

"So I do," Tom answered.

The statement, nevertheless, did not bring him much comfort, and later, walking home alone, he became unhappier still. The quarrel had ended, but it had not ended like his quarrels with Jane; it had left a feeling of estrangement behind it; there had been no "making up."

15 :　　AS Tom sat up, a single chime—deep, distant, mellow —reached his still drowsy ears. He knew it came from the grandfather's clock in the hall, and it was strange, he thought, that he never seemed to hear it in the daytime. But at night, though he was far away and his door shut, if he happened to lie awake he could always hear it, and if he opened his door, even the slow tick, tock—tick, tock—rose up quite distinctly through the well of the staircase.

He had drawn up his blinds—always so carefully drawn down by Mrs. Deverell—before getting into bed; the windows were open, and the moon was shining into the room. Perhaps it was the moon which had awakened him. There had been a thunderstorm and a heavy fall of rain a few hours earlier, but now the night must have cleared, and Tom, slipping out of bed, went to the window to breathe its freshness. He leaned over the sill, and the garden lay below him filled with light and darkness, black and white like an etching. Motionless trees threw their shadows across the grass. There were shadows everywhere. In spite of the flood of moonlight, Tom thought it would be easy for an enemy to approach the house unseen. . . .

He leaned farther out, trying to view the garden from a different angle, and in doing so his elbow knocked against a book on the dressing-table, which fell with a thud to the floor.

"Damn!" Tom muttered under his breath.

The book was the first volume of *Arabia Deserta*, and he had put it there so as to be sure to remember it next day. It was for Philip. Not that he had asked for it—nor indeed for any book—the idea was Tom's own. He had thought a travel book might interest him since he was going to be a traveller, and Uncle Stephen had said this was a good one.

He thought of Philip and he thought of Deverell. It was because of what had taken place that afternoon. He did not believe Deverell would readily forgive or forget an injury—he would be far more likely to exaggerate one. His temperament was passionate and brooding: and, quite apart from the insult he had received, Tom knew he must be jealous. Suppose he had followed them. They had taken no precautions; they had not once looked round. Nothing indeed seemed more probable than that he *had* followed them; and once he knew Philip's hiding-place, what was to prevent him from going back at night when he would be sure to find him alone?

Tom's thoughts might not have taken this turn in broad daylight, nor even had he lain on snugly in bed, but now, looking out into that mysterious garden, it became increasingly difficult to dismiss them.

Swiftly and silently in the moonlight he redressed himself. He opened his door noiselessly, and tiptoed along the passage and down the stairs. With equal caution he stole along a second and darker passage, branching off on the right from the hall, and leading to the kitchen. The kitchen door was locked, but the key was in the lock and Tom turned it. Then, very gingerly, he pushed open the door.

Not that he felt any ghostly terrors: what he actually dreaded (the result of one memorable descent to the kitchen in Gloucester Terrace) was cockroaches. But cockroaches or no cockroaches he must get his shoes. He lit his candle, cast a rapid glance round the tiled floor, and breathed a sigh of relief.

Having found his shoes and put them on, he returned to the hall. His every movement was made with the utmost carefulness, for, though the darkness told him Uncle Stephen had gone to bed, he might not yet be asleep. Tom opened the hall-door—always left on the latch for Mrs. Deverell in the morning—and instantly was face to face with a white, crystalline world—glittering, treacherous—like a landscape in the moon.

Beyond the shining pallor of the lawn was a black wall of trees. Keeping on the grass, so that his footsteps should be noiseless, he passed the row of dark windows at the front of the house, then broke into a run, and in a minute or two had reached the outer fringe of the wood. He by this time knew his way to the other house so well that he believed the darkness would not matter, but almost immediately he blundered into the bushes and fell headlong. He was not hurt, but it showed him how useless it was to hurry. He lit the candle he had brought with him. Here, in the close shelter of the trees, the flame burned almost steadily, yet the light it cast was equivocal, seeming to illuminate Tom himself much more than his surroundings. It was better than nothing, however; it helped him to avoid overhanging branches, and he moved slowly on. His daily journeys had beaten down a well-marked track, but it was narrow, and even with the light he carried not easy to follow. Now and then he heard a rustle in the brushwood, and once he heard a distant scream that might have been the scream of an owl or of a cat, but he saw no living thing except snails, and the pale-winged moths his candle attracted—creatures fragile and insubstantial as the ghosts of white hawthorn.

When at last he reached the broken gate he blew out his candle. He no longer needed it, for the path was now smooth under his feet, and wide enough between its leafy walls to admit the moonlight. Tom's heart was beating with a strange excitement. He had half forgotten the errand that had brought him here, or perhaps it would be truer to say that he no longer believed in that errand. The avenue curved, widened, ended: he stood still. He gazed at the house, but approached no nearer. Never before had he looked on anything like this. It was as if house and garden and terrace, as if the stone boy and his urn and his owl and his otter, were all sunken to the bottom of a silver sea. An indescribable beauty flooded Tom's mind, and his eyes dimmed, though no grief was in his heart. And on that spot where he stood he dropped down on the cold grass.

When he raised his head in the shadowy air his face was wet. He got slowly to his feet. His face, his hands, his shirt, his jacket, his trousers—all were wet and cold with dew, yet he did not feel cold. He approached the house over the damp sward. He stood below a window and called "Philip," but there was no answer and he did not repeat his call.

He stood there dreaming, his head bowed. Night brooded over him with dusky wings. A faint wind sighed and passed, stirring the lock of coarse brown hair that tumbled over his forehead, and rustling in the ivy. Tom awakened. Perhaps he had forgotten that he had called Philip's name once only, and not very loudly, for he moved round to the back of the house and entered the yard. He pressed down the latch and pushed the door open.

Once more he lit his candle. The moon was shining on the front of the house, but here all was in darkness. He knew the room, however, in which Philip slept; his only fear was lest he might startle him. Perhaps it would be better to go back and throw gravel at the window. But if he went up very quietly and sat down beside the bed and spoke Philip's name or touched him, then he would see who it was before he was really awake enough to be alarmed. So Tom ascended the stairs, being careful to tread on the side of each step to prevent it from creaking. Softly he opened the door; then raised the candle above his head. These precautions were unnecessary, however, for a single glance told him the room was empty.

He crossed to the bed: there was nothing on it but a mattress and a couple of moth-eaten patchwork quilts. Tom sat down. The sudden disappointment, following on his mood of emotional excitement, for a while shut out every other feeling. Then his earlier anxiety reawakened. The thought of Deverell again occurred to him, but he did not see how, even if there had been a second quarrel, it would explain Philip's absence. There was only one thing to do, and, though he felt it to be useless, he made a search of the house and of the garden.

He found nobody. Philip must be abroad on some nocturnal adventure of his own; and indeed, when he looked at it more calmly, Tom ceased to find this surprising. For anything he knew to the contrary, Philip might be in the habit of roaming the countryside every night, especially since he had the whole morning in which to sleep. He folded his jacket and sat down on it beside the fountain to wait.

But his mood had grown less confident. The confidence perhaps had never been very stable. At all events, he did not now believe Philip would want to find him here when he came back. Supposing he was in the habit of taking such rambles, he had breathed no word of them to Tom, and that in itself showed he did not want his company. The hours they spent together in the afternoon were sufficient: they had been sufficient hitherto for Tom himself: what was this sudden fever of restlessness crying like an ancient cry within him? A melancholy crept over him, and the strange unearthly beauty of his surroundings grew sad too. It was as if the whole scene had retreated from him, as if he were no longer in it as a part of it, but only as a stranger from another world. So a ghost might feel whose hauntings were unperceived and unsuspected. The lovely stone boy, though so near, was not conscious of him; his head was bent sidelong as if to listen to the water dropping from his urn, though there was no water. Perhaps he was content to stand there smiling at his thoughts; perhaps, like Tom, he felt lonely. And suddenly springing to his feet, Tom stepped across the basin of the fountain on to his small island and clasped him in his arms. He kissed him passionately;—kissed his cold mouth and cheeks and forehead and hair. He would wait no longer. What was the use of waiting—only in the end to be asked why he had come? How could he say why? He shivered, for he had grown cold sitting without his jacket, and the heavy dew was everywhere. In stepping back on to the grass his foot slipped from the mossy stones, and he splashed knee-deep in the water.

He hurried home. He had forgotten his candle and he no longer troubled about the path, but forced a way recklessly through bushes and undergrowth. Branches whipped his face, brambles tore his hands and clothes. Sometimes he tripped and stumbled, but nothing checked his course, and he even found a relief in the resistance he encountered. When at last he emerged from the jungle, he was plastered with dirt, there was more than one rent in his jacket and trousers, and his face and hands were smeared with blood.

Thus it was that he confronted Uncle Stephen, whom he found standing at the edge of the wood, a lighted lantern in his hand. Uncle Stephen raised the lantern, and its light fell on the forlorn, bedraggled figure, who for a moment stopped, and then approached him with hanging head. But Uncle Stephen asked no questions: all he said was, "I came out to look for you."

The nervous force that until that instant had supported Tom was suddenly extinguished; he felt now only tired. And what he wanted more than anything was for Uncle Stephen to put his arms round him. Then, he felt, he would never go away again. For a minute, until he had regained his self-control, he clung to Uncle Stephen. "I'm sorry for disturbing you," he said, "I didn't think you would have heard me."

Uncle Stephen spoke quietly. "What has happened to you? Are you hurt?"

"No," answered Tom. "I may have scratched myself—it was so dark in the wood: but it's nothing; I hardly feel it. . . . I'm afraid I've torn my clothes."

"You're quite sure you're not hurt?"

"Yes."

They walked on together to the house, Uncle Stephen with his hand on the truant's shoulder. "I had gone upstairs only a few minutes before you went out," he explained. "That is how I came to hear you. I had left my door open because the night was so close. I heard you going downstairs."

"And you knew I was going out?"

"Not till you opened the hall-door."

"But you could have called me," said Tom half reproachfully.

"Yes. Are you sure that at that time you wanted me to call

you? . . . I thought you had gone down to the study to get something and would be coming back. It was only because you stayed out so long that I began to feel uneasy. You have been away a long time, Tom—nearly three hours."

"I'm sorry. I didn't think it was so long."

"And you're shockingly dirty and wet. If the water's hot enough you must take a bath, and if not you're to go straight to bed."

"Yes. . . . Uncle Stephen, I want to tell you about it."

"I wish you sometimes wanted to tell me about things beforehand," Uncle Stephen replied.

"I thought you would be asleep: I didn't want to disturb you."

They had entered the hall, and Tom sat down on the stairs to remove his shoes. Uncle Stephen waited till he had done so; then he said, "You must take off those wet clothes at once. And don't bother about a bath: I'll get you something to drink instead. But I shan't be more than a minute or two, and I expect to find you in bed when I come up."

"All right," Tom sighed, ready enough himself for bed.

The lamp had been lit in his room, and he undressed in a last burst of energy, flinging his clothes on the floor and scrambling between the cool sheets, where he lay blinking at the light, his cheeks burning, and all the surface of his body tingling with stings and scratches. Presently Uncle Stephen appeared, carrying a steaming tumbler.

"You're to drink this—all of it," he said. "Sit up or you will spill it."

Tom sat up and took a sip—a very small one. "What is it?" he asked, wrinkling his nose. "It's pretty awful!"

"It won't be awful after you've finished it. You may be slightly drunk, but you'll be warm and comfortable and sleepy, and it will prevent you from catching cold. . . . Come, it's not so bad as all that." For Tom had taken another sip and made another grimace. "Hold your nose if you like, but drink it while it's hot."

Tom gulped down the contents of the glass—coughed, choked, and cuddled back under his bedclothes. Uncle Stephen was right. There was just a moment of nausea, and then a warm drowsy wave of physical comfort spread through his body. He yawned and began to talk.

"Won't it do to tell me in the morning?" Uncle Stephen interrupted. "You know you're tired out."

"I'd rather tell you now, before I go to sleep," Tom muttered.

"But I can guess: I can guess what happened. And I'm not cross with you, if that's the trouble."

"You're never cross with me," said Tom.

"Well, I don't want you to think that either; because I could be very angry indeed if the occasion arose."

"I don't think I'll ever do anything to make you angry. . . . I know I won't purposely, and I don't think I will even unintentionally."

"Then you know what *would* make me angry?" said Uncle Stephen.

"If I wasn't sure I'd ask you."

"And yet it would have pleased me very much to-night if you had come to my room and told me you were going out."

"Yes. I *would* have come too, if I'd known you were awake. You don't think I'd ever be *afraid* to tell you things! But I hadn't planned this. I'd gone to bed; I'd been asleep; then something must have wakened me, and I went to the window—and then I thought of it."

"Very well."

"But, Uncle Stephen, there was nobody there. I went all over the house and there was nobody. What do you think can have happened?"

"Nothing. If your friend had come to look for *you*, there would have been nobody here either. Don't worry about it."

"You mean, you think he had just gone out the way I did. I think so too, now. Have you ever been to the other house at night, Uncle Stephen?"

"No."

"It was lovely. . . . I mean at first—with the moonlight and the fountain-boy and everything so different. . . . It was like that poem about the boy 'plucking fruits by moonlight in a wilderness.' Do you know the poem?"

"I don't think so."

"Oh, you must know it: it's by Coleridge."

"Well, I may have read it, but I've forgotten."

"Then you can't have read it, because nobody could forget it."

"And were you the boy?"

"No, no. . . . Only he *might* have been there. But there was nobody there except that boy with the urn. I kissed him, and the stone was covered with dew and very cold. . . . Why are you looking so grave?"

"Don't I usually look grave?" Uncle Stephen smiled, but it did not alter his expression.

"No, you don't; not like that."

"Perhaps I was thinking."

"Was it about me?"

"Partly about you. About a good many things."

"But why did it make you look like that—when you're not angry with me?"

"I'm not angry."

"You're sad then—and that's worse."

"I'm not sad—nor glad. I was simply trying, I suppose, to look into the future—your future—and wondering how much sadness or gladness it might contain, for there is always a mixture of both."

But Tom was dissatisfied. "Uncle Stephen, will you nearly shut your eyes, bend down quite close, and look at me?"

"No, I won't: you're to go to sleep. Don't you know it will soon be daylight? I heard a bird just now—and there's another one. You're not to come down to breakfast, but to sleep as long as you can. And don't be puzzling your head about the other house. I'm beginning to be sorry you ever found it. . . . Good-night."

Uncle Stephen extinguished the lamp. But Tom lay looking at the window in the glimmering twilight of dawn.

16: NOBODY having called him, it was after ten when Tom came down to breakfast. Mrs. Deverell poured out his tea, but she made no comment on his lateness. Indeed, there was something unusual about Mrs. Deverell this morning. She looked as if she had not slept—either that or else she had been crying. And she attended to Tom practically in silence. She called him "sir," too, instead of "Master Tom," which he found disconcertingly formal. He wondered if anything had happened and whether he ought to ask her about it. He had just decided in the negative when he heard a sniff. This was dreadful!—and Tom, who happened to be taking a drink, stared round-eyed over his breakfast-cup in alarm. Mrs. Deverell was standing near the sideboard, her back turned to him. He saw her take out a pocket-handkerchief and give a surreptitious dab at her eyes. Then another. Tom put down his cup. He had never before seen a grown-up person cry, and perhaps he ought to take no notice. But how could he go on callously with his breakfast while she wept with her back turned? Mrs. Deverell sniffed again.

Tom pushed back his chair. He wished she would speak. He himself made a timid remark, but Mrs. Deverell answered in so subdued a voice that he did not hear what she said. "Mrs. Deverell, what's the matter?" he asked, and this time there was no reply at all. He gazed at her. Why wouldn't she speak to him? He left his chair and adopted the mode of consolation that came most natural to him, though in a modified form, for Mrs. Deverell wasn't the kind of person with whom you could take liberties. She wouldn't like it. Her manner was mild, but she was a firm stickler for proprieties, and her sense of class distinction was adamantine. Tom was the young master and must behave as such. Nevertheless, he took her hand and patted it two or three times. Even that, perhaps, was overstepping the mark, for Mrs. Deverell withdrew her hand. "If you've finished your breakfast, Master Tom, run along now like a good boy."

Well, at any rate she had regained her composure, and Tom, though he hadn't finished his breakfast, did what she told him. Out in the porch he spied Sally polishing the brasses. The sleeves of Sally's blue and white print were tucked up above her elbows and the morning wind had fluffed her hair. Also she was singing! She sang in an undertone—a song without words—and so far as Tom could make out without tune—but presumably expressive of a contented mind. He approached her hopefully therefore, and put his question. "What's wrong with Mrs. Deverell?"

Sally's song ceased. Her polishing went on, however, and the glance she gave him was frigid. "You needn't ask me, Master Tom. If there's anything wrong I suppose it's the usual thing."

"What usual thing? Do you mean Jim?"

"Oh, it's Jim, is it? I didn't know you'd reached that length in your acquaintance!"

Tom was annoyed and made a grimace at her. "Well, it's his name, isn't it? He's not Charles or Joseph."

Sally disdained to reply, and he went on: "What's he been doing anyway? I saw him yesterday afternoon and there was nothing the matter then."

"Yesterday afternoon's a long time ago. A good many things might have happened since yesterday afternoon—especially where *some* people's concerned."

These pregnant words were followed by a pause, but Tom did not take up the challenge.

"It took me nigh and next an hour trying to clean your clothes, and those trousers may as well be turned into floor-cloths for all you'll ever be able to wear them again!"

So that was it! Tom laughed. "They were my old bags," he said carelessly.

"And what about the tear in your jacket, to say nothing of a big green stain that'll never come out in this world?"

"We'll take it out in heaven, Sally. You shouldn't have bothered."

"I suppose not: and have you running about the countryside the way you'd be a disgrace to your uncle and the whole house!"

Tom wrinkled his nose. "It seems to me everybody's very grumpy this morning. I hope Uncle Stephen is all right. Is he in the study?"

"He is, and there's a gentleman with him, so you needn't go worrying him."

Immediately a transformed Tom faced her. "Who?" he cried excitedly. "Not Uncle Horace!"

Sally threw an instant damper on these hopes. "It's Mr. Flood that's with him," she returned loftily, "the solicitor from the town."

Tom's enthusiasm subsided. "Oh," he murmured, and then added, "Do you think he'll be long?"

"Now how can I tell how long he'll be! What's more, I've my work to do, instead of answering questions."

"Well, it's a very queer time to call. You should have told him Uncle Stephen and I are always busy in the mornings."

"Maybe the first one that asks for you I *will* tell them that. This morning your name wasn't mentioned."

Tom assumed a crushed and humble air. "Don't you like me any more, Sally?" he asked. "You're not going to let a few green stains come between us!"

He took a short run, and slid along the dark and shining floor, while Sally screamed after him, "Stop that, now! And me just after polishing it!" But Tom had already turned down the passage, and next moment was tapping at the study door.

"Come in." It was Uncle Stephen's voice, and Tom entered. Uncle Stephen was seated at the big square table, while at the opposite side of it, with a litter of papers between them, sat a small grey man with bushy eyebrows and gold-rimmed spectacles, who was writing on a stiff parchment with a pen that produced scratching, squeaking sounds. At the noise of the opening door the writer looked up, but Tom, who had not expected to find them occupied like this, stood still, uncertain whether to advance or retreat.

Uncle Stephen decided for him. "Come and shake hands with Mr. Flood. . . . We shan't be able to do any reading this morning. Mr. Flood is going to keep me busy—or rather, I'm keeping *him* busy." And to Mr. Flood he added, "This is Tom, the cause of all our trouble."

The solicitor had risen. He shook hands gravely, but there was both curiosity and a twinkle of amusement behind his spectacles. "I've heard about him," he said. His eyes, in spite of their half-quizzical expression, were subjecting Tom to a close scrutiny, and his next words were addressed directly to him. "My wife declares you came to her assistance in a dog fight."

"Yes," said Tom. "At least I came to somebody's assistance, but I don't know how she knew my name."

"That was feminine intuition. In the first account I heard, you were merely a boy with freckles; but before bedtime you had become Mr. Stephen Collet's nephew."

"Well, it *was* me," said Tom, "though it happened the day after I arrived, and the only person who knew about me was Mr. Knox."

"The day after you arrived everybody in Kilbarron knew about you," Mr. Flood answered, in his dry, matter-of-fact voice. He pushed his spectacles up on his forehead, and had another look at Tom. "Do you know, Mr. Collet, though it may sound fanciful, I believe I myself could have guessed that boy was your nephew."

Tom tried hard not to look self-conscious, while the lawyer went on: "Taken feature by feature, of course, there's not the ghost of a likeness. Or rather, it must be a ghost—just something in his expression. *Is* he more like his mother's family than his father's?"

"That, I'm afraid, I can't tell you. I never saw either his father *or* his mother. In his appearance Tom doesn't remind me of anybody: in other ways, I should think probably he belongs to our side."

Mr. Flood prolonged an examination which was becoming embarrassing. "I have an idea he likes belonging to your side," he said shrewdly.

Tom blushed. It was time for him to clear out, he thought. He shook hands again, said good-bye, and left the room feeling slightly puzzled.

But it didn't matter—even if they were, as he suspected, engaged in some business concerning himself. What he had to do now was to fill in the time before dinner. Lunch, Mrs. Deverell would call it—like his step-mother—the implication being that they dined at some fashionable hour such as half-past eight. . . . Uncle Horace dined at half-past seven, and dressed for dinner even when he was alone, but he was the only person of Tom's acquaintance who lived up to these high standards. . . . Poor Mrs. Deverell! He hoped Sally's explanation of her troubles was not the true one. . . . And there was also the matter of Philip to be settled. Not the matter of his absence last night, for Tom had ceased to regard this as a mystery, and in fact could not now understand his own mood of last night, nor why he had got into such a state about so little. But he wanted to make it up properly with Philip. He would go to him that afternoon and do everything he could to please him. Or everything but one thing, for he was not going to drop Deverell. . . .

He passed out through the front gate and sauntered down the road till he reached a field path, which branched off on the left. He had never been along this path, but he knew it was the one leading to Deverell's cottage. He leaned against the stile for a minute or two, thinking: then he made up his mind and climbed over.

A walk of some three hundred yards brought him almost to the cottage door, but here again he paused, and was still standing there irresolutely when Deverell himself looked out of the window. The young poacher beckoned, and a moment later partially opened the door, though he did not speak till Tom was quite close. Then he said in a low voice, "You want to see me, Mr. Tom? Come in."

A slight pull enforced the invitation, and Tom entered the narrow hall. Deverell immediately shut the door behind them. He pushed Tom firmly, but not roughly, on into the kitchen, where he drew out a worn arm-chair for his visitor, while he himself sat down on the white deal table, his legs swinging, and his back to the window. Between them a silence seemed to deepen, and yet it was not exactly a silence of constraint. The young poacher did not look at Tom; his head was lowered, he was gazing at the tiled floor. Presently he spoke, but still without raising his eyes.

"I'm glad you came, Mr. Tom: I wanted to see you. I wanted to send a message to you, only my mother wouldn't take it."

"What's the matter? Has something gone wrong?"

At this Deverell at last looked up, and his face was dark and determined. "I've got into trouble, Mr. Tom. I must have money to get away."

"What kind of trouble?"

"Nothing's happened yet, but if I don't get away at once it might be bad."

Tom did not ask for further particulars; nor did he reply at all for a minute or two, and then it was only to say, "How do you expect me to have money?"

He saw Deverell get down from the table, take three strides to the door, lock the door, and put the key in his pocket.

Again there was a silence. Tom made no movement, and Deverell watched him with an expression that gradually became troubled.

"You needn't be frightened, Mr. Tom; I'm not going to hurt you; but I don't want you to go till we've settled something. It's not the way I'd like it to be, but it's not my choosing. I could have got money easy enough by playing a trick on you. That gentleman that come down in his car to fetch you—he wanted me to help him get hold of you, but I wouldn't."

"Uncle Horace."

"Ay."

Tom's face had whitened a little; nevertheless, at this, a tremulous smile for a second appeared on it. "What a frightful lie!" he said.

"I could telephone to him now," Deverell went on. "I know his number. I could tell him I have you safe locked up here and all he's got to do is to drive down and he'll find the goods ready for him."

"The goods being me?"

Deverell made no answer.

"His surname, by the way, is Pringle," Tom said quietly. "That will help you with the telephone-book, if there *is* any truth in your story. You will only find the number of his private telephone, and he won't be at home just now, but he lives over the bank and if you ring up the bank you'll get him."

The trouble on Deverell's face deepened. Again he went to the door, but this time he put back the key and unlocked it. "You can go, Mr. Tom," he said. "You're the only one I've ever cared for. I would have been a good pal to you, but it can't be now. I'd have gone straight with you, and this would never have happened, but now it's too late." He sat down on a kitchen chair, his elbows on his knees, his bent head supported between his hands, so that Tom could only see the thick black hair which covered it.

But Tom did not take advantage of his liberty. "I don't want to go," he said, "I came here on purpose. It was your mother—something about her—that made me guess something was wrong."

"Ay, there's always something wrong according to her," said Deverell bitterly. "Always has been. Many a time I've gone out just to avoid the way she'd be looking at me as if I was the cause of all the sorrow in the world. If you'd had somebody grieving over you, Mr. Tom, and mourning and praying over you ever since you was ten, you'd know what it was like."

Tom did know, or at any rate could easily imagine, what it would be like. Mrs. Deverell could be very tenacious: had he not seen her facing Uncle Horace without yielding an inch? But he could also imagine what it must have been like from *her* point of view—with a son perpetually out of work—silent, morose, at loggerheads with all the neighbours—a son who had brought disgrace on her name and who apparently was about to do so again.

"This trouble," he began; and then stopped. There was no use in going back over that. It was done—whatever it was. "Why don't you ask Uncle Stephen to help you?" he said.

"What good would that do?" answered Deverell sullenly.

"I don't know. What good does asking me do?"

"You're the only one I could ask. Even if you refuse me it won't be the way the others would."

"But Uncle Stephen could do so much *more!* What *can* I do?"

"It's no use, Mr. Tom. It wasn't poaching this time. And I'd no luck. I was seen."

"Seen?"

"Seen coming away. I got into a house last night, but I didn't take anything. I thought I heard someone moving and I funked it."

"If you didn't take anything it won't be very bad, will it?"

"It will be bad enough. You see, I been in jail before and that makes a difference. They count that against you. Only—I think if I could get right away they maybe wouldn't bother doin' anything. Not on my account, but on account of Mother."

The last words were a little chilling, but Tom accepted them. He had refused to listen to any warnings against Deverell in the past, and he wasn't going to begin to listen now.

"I wish you hadn't done it," he said. "If you had only told me that you needed money—— I mean, it would have been far easier to help you *before* than it will be now." Then, realizing the futility of such talk, he stopped. Lifting his eyes, he encountered the young poacher's brooding gaze fixed on him.

"It wasn't the money, Mr. Tom."

Tom opened his mouth to speak, but turned away without having spoken. He already had an idea of what was coming—was not, for that matter, even particularly surprised. It had been stupid—horribly stupid—but he could understand. After all, it was only a variation on the thoughts he himself had had last night. "You needn't have been so angry with me," he said.

"No—nor I wasn't either. I was angry for a bit with that young fellow that was with you, for he'd no call to treat me like he did. What had I done on him? But it wasn't that. It was just that I felt the way I didn't care a curse what I did. And then I remembered the one that had give me away first and started most of the trouble."

Tom sighed. All this seemed to him hopeless—and yet very natural. It was muddle-headed, savage, blind—but it was very natural. "Do you want to leave to-day?" he asked. "Are you sure you were seen? Don't you think, if you had been seen, somebody would have been round here before now?"

"There's a reason for that. But I bin keeping a watch, ready to slip out the back way. You give me a start for a minute till I seen who it was. It was James Dunwoody that seen me; him that's doin' night-watchman where they're mending the road up by the station. He maybe wouldn't think much of it at the time, and he'd be going home to sleep before the news would be out. But he'll hear soon enough and he's not one would keep his mouth shut. You see, they don't like me, Mr. Tom."

Deverell had taken a packet of cigarettes from his pocket. He held it out to Tom who took one mechanically, forgetting that he had given up smoking. He lit it from the match Deverell struck, and then Deverell lit his own. They sat there, facing each other, smoking in silence—a rather odd picture for anyone either at Gloucester Terrace or the Manor House to have peeped in upon.

"Of course, when it's found that nothing was taken, it may end there," said Tom.

"How? What way would it end there?"

"Whoever it was mayn't go to the police at all."

"Mr. Tom, what's the use of talking like that?"

"Not very much," Tom admitted. "Don't be angry with me. I'm not really talking; I'm only trying to think."

"Wouldn't you go to the police yourself?"

"Not if I knew the burglar. Was it a shop?"

"It was; and the man that owns it is the same that was always spreading talk about me when I was only a boy like you, and that gave me away the first time I got into trouble."

Tom transferred his gaze from a gaudy picture calendar to Deverell. "Did you break open anything—drawers and that kind of thing?"

"I did."

"It was lucky you heard him."

"Why? You mean he'd have seen me. I don't see as it makes very much difference, Mr. Tom."

"It might have made a difference if he had crept down without your hearing him," said Tom. "I expect you hate him."

Deverell rubbed one hand backward and forward against his thigh. "You mean——?" But he did not develop his idea of what Tom might have meant.

"I'm going to help you if I can," said Tom, "and if I can't it won't be because I haven't tried."

"I know that, Mr. Tom."

"But it will take some time. I'll have to go home first, and then to the town. If my plan doesn't work I'll come back and tell you."

"When?"

"As soon as I can. Quite soon if it's no good: in less than two hours if it is. But I'd better go at once."

He moved to the door and Deverell at the same time sprang to his feet. For a moment he laid a detaining hand on Tom's arm.

"You're mighty good to me, Mr. Tom."

"No, I'm not," said Tom, "I'm just ordinary. But everybody else seems to have been pretty rotten. I think you'd better try to get some sleep while I'm away. I'll knock on the kitchen window."

Deverell shook his head. "I must keep a look-out. I'm not going to let them get me."

"Well, good-bye for the present."

Tom glanced at his watch and saw that it was after one. Without further speech he hurried off. He was trotting quietly along the road when a small car met him and from the driver's seat Mr. Flood waved his hand. Tom waved back. "That's a stroke of luck anyhow," he thought, for he had been vainly racking his brains as to how he might get Uncle Stephen by himself for a few minutes. It would be no betrayal of Deverell to consult Uncle Stephen. If it came to that, he *had* to consult him, had to tell him everything or he would not be able to help Deverell at all. He would just have time before dinner.

On reaching the house he went straight to the study. Uncle Stephen was locking up some papers and had his back turned, but Tom began at once, and in fact, with the particular question he had to ask, it was easier to address his back.

"Uncle Stephen, supposing I wanted fifty pounds immediately, how could I get it?"

Uncle Stephen turned round, but he did not look surprised, only mildly speculative, as he gazed on the flushed, slightly breathless questioner.

"I don't think you *could* get it," he replied. "Certainly not without a great many explanations as to what you wanted it for, each one of which would be met with the firmest opposition."

"This is serious: I want you to take it seriously. As a matter of fact, I'm not sure that fifty pounds will be enough."

Still Tom could see from the way he looked at him that Uncle Stephen was not taking the matter in earnest. "What have you been up to?" he demanded. "It sounds to me very much as if you wanted to square somebody."

Tom did not smile. "I have some money of my own, haven't I?"

"Yes, but not at your disposal. If you wanted fifty pounds of it I'm afraid you would first have to approach your Uncle Horace. *He* might take it seriously, but I doubt if he would give you fifty pounds."

"That's no good," Tom answered quickly. "I must have the money to-day. Uncle Stephen, will you lend me fifty pounds?"

Uncle Stephen sat down in his arm-chair. "Come here," he said, "and tell me all about it."

Tom came over, but with less alacrity than usual: he both looked and felt worried. Seated on an arm of Uncle Stephen's chair he told his story.

And even then Uncle Stephen did not seem very much impressed. Instead of answering directly with yes or no, he began to talk of other things. "It's odd, Tom, how since your arrival this house has become the centre of problems, adventures, and mysteries, whereas previously we never found anything more exciting to discuss than whether it was too warm for a fire in the study, or some question of food already decided by Mrs. Deverell in her own mind. . . . . Tell me, before we go any further, what is your own attitude in this?"

Tom did not reply. He did not quite understand the question he was to reply to, and there was no use telling Uncle Stephen the first thing that came into his head.

Uncle Stephen altered his question.

"What is your reason for wanting to give Deverell fifty pounds? Are you doing it merely because he asked you to? Do you take the slightest interest in him apart from this scrape he has got into?"

Tom still was puzzled. "Do you mean, do I like him?"

"No. We all like for the time being the person we are helping. I want something better than that."

"Then I don't know what you mean."

"Do you think there is any good in him; that he'll ever do any good—ever even become self-supporting?"

"I'm sure there's good in him," said Tom.

"What makes you sure? His mother isn't, you know."

Tom hesitated. "It's just—things. . . . He's been rather decent to me over all this."

Uncle Stephen did not answer. Indeed, the first sound he made was more than anything else in the nature of a slight gasp: but the clear, solemn gaze turned on him caused him to repress it. "Well, Tom," he said at last, "it's for you to judge. Mind you, I don't say you're wrong, though I think you're wrong. But you shall have your fifty pounds. I believe you're going to waste it, and I wish you had discovered a more promising protégé. Still—— Ring the bell, like a good boy; I want to speak to Mrs. Deverell."

Tom obeyed him. He did not know what was going to happen now.

17: MRS. DEVERELL, pausing on the threshold, at the very first glance appeared to take in that she had been summoned for a special purpose. She was nervous, though Uncle Stephen both looked and spoke very kindly to her when he said, "Sit down, Mrs. Deverell."

Tom watched her take a chair close to the wall and sit there stiffly.

He saw that her thin, veined hands trembled before she folded them in her lap; she looked so frail and frightened indeed that he would have escaped from the sight of her distress had not Uncle Stephen motioned to him to remain where he was.

"Master Tom has been to see your son this morning, Mrs. Deverell," he began.

Mrs. Deverell tried to reply, but what she said was inaudible.

"I don't suppose you know all the particulars of this unfortunate affair, but your son told Master Tom about it, and also that he would like to get out of the country before further developments take place. I've no doubt myself that if this can be done it will be the best thing —for you at any rate. For a long time, I'm afraid, you've had more anxiety than comfort from keeping him at home."

"Oh no, sir, it's not that: I——"

"Master Tom proposes to help him by giving him fifty pounds," Uncle Stephen continued.

"I'm sure, sir, he'll pay it back when——"

Uncle Stephen made a slight gesture with his hand, and Mrs. Deverell did not complete her speech.

"Master Tom does not expect to be paid back and does not want to be paid back. He has asked me to advance him the money and I intend to do so, but that is my whole share in the matter; the idea is Master Tom's and the money is his. That, I think, is all."

Mrs. Deverell burst into tears.

Tom turned his back. He had known what would happen, and why couldn't Uncle Stephen have let him clear out before it did happen? He caught sight of the open window and scrambled across the sill before anybody could prevent him.

He did not go far, however, but waited where he had a view of the room, and no sooner had Mrs. Deverell left it than he returned. Uncle Stephen was unlocking his desk, from which he took a cheque-book.

"You'd better tell them to give you a pound in silver and the rest in treasury notes," he said quietly, as he wrote out the cheque and dried it on the blotting-pad. He handed it to Tom, who put it away in the inside pocket of his jacket.

"Thank you, Uncle Stephen."

"You know what you're doing, Tom? If it comes out that we've been assisting a criminal to escape it won't help *our* case. . . . Well, don't look so guilty about it: you've nothing to be ashamed of. I suppose all your time now will be spent in avoiding Mrs. Deverell. It won't be the slightest use, and you'd have done much better to have let her thank you and get it over. Are you going to the bank at once or are you going to wait till after dinner? It must be dinner-time now."

"I think I'd like to go at once, Uncle Stephen, and I'd rather you didn't wait for me."

"Very well. I suppose you won't be happy till the matter is settled."

Tom departed on his errand, but on reaching the bend of the avenue he glanced back at the house and caught sight of Mrs. Deverell watching him from an upper window. "I hope she's not going home," he thought. "And I bet she is. He won't like it—especially when she wouldn't take the message he asked her to. And he'll hate taking the money before her. Really, you'd think she might have sense enough to wait till after I'd been."

So Tom scolded poor Mrs. Deverell for an act she merely looked like committing, but once out on the open road he ceased to think of her and began to run. He could not run all the way, but he ran at least half of it, and arrived at the bank in a moist, breathless, and excited state. He fumbled for his cheque and pushed it across the counter, forgetful of the rule of precedence, so that a lady, waiting to have her own cheque cashed, told him he was an ill-mannered boy, and the cashier stared at him coldly and asked him if he didn't know that he had to take his turn. Abashed, apologetic, blushing, but at the same time hating both the cashier and the lady, Tom took up his proper position.

The lady received five single notes and counted them correctly three times. Then, apparently having forgiven Tom, she bestowed a smile upon him and withdrew.

"A pound of silver, please, and the rest in treasury notes."

The cashier again looked at him coldly, but after examining both sides of Uncle Stephen's cheque, as if he hoped to find a flaw in it, handed Tom the money.

"Count it and see that it's right," he said sharply, as Tom was stuffing the notes into his pocket.

So he had to take them out again and count them—count them twice, because two of the notes got stuck together the first time.

"Wet your fingers," said the cashier, obviously a person of the baser sort.

Tom took no notice.

"Don't be losing it now," the cashier went on, in tones indicating that this was what he expected to happen. "I suppose you're going straight back to Mr. Collet?"

"Then you supposed wrong," replied Tom, who felt there had been enough ordering about.

Out on the road again, he proceeded at a more rational pace. The first act was successfully accomplished; the rest was up to Deverell.

There was nobody in sight when he reached the field path and climbed the stile, but Deverell was waiting for him, and appeared from behind the cottage the moment Tom drew level with it.

"This way, Mr. Tom; the back-door's open."

"Was your mother here?" Tom asked, when he was once more in the now familiar kitchen.

"Yes; she's gone about five minutes."

"I've got what you want: at least I hope it's enough," said Tom, emptying his pockets. "There's forty-nine pounds in notes, and a pound in silver."

Deverell stared at the money on the table. A deep, painful flush had risen in his swarthy face and his head hung awkwardly. A change seemed to have come over him: he looked ashamed, he looked shy, and this altered attitude immediately produced its reaction on the impressionable Tom.

"Mr. Tom," Deverell stammered, "you won't think too hardly of me?"

"No, of course not," said Tom hurriedly. "Why should I think hardly of you?"

He felt now very shy himself, and was thankful that Deverell said nothing more, but began to busy himself with the kettle and a teapot.

"You'll take a cup of tea with me, Mr. Tom?"

There was something in this rather wistful question, a kind of rough gentleness, that made Tom more uncomfortable than ever. He began to feel miserable and knew from past experience that it would take very little more to bring him to the point of blubbing.

"Yes," he said.

They sat down at the table, Deverell eating steadily and methodically, Tom nibbling at a slice of bread and butter.

Deverell's chair suddenly grated on the floor as he pushed it back. His hands, brown and rough and powerful, the nails uncleaned, the fingers stained with nicotine, rested on his knees. "Mr. Tom, I wish I'd known you five years ago."

Tom smiled faintly. "You wouldn't have wanted to know me five years ago. I was only a kid."

"Yes," said Deverell slowly, "I suppose so. It's queer, isn't it, how things is always like that?"

As he looked at the dark unhappy eyes that were turned on him, Tom too had a feeling that human affairs were hopelessly ill-arranged.

Deverell rose and began to clear away the tea-things. Tom helped him. When at last everything was tidied up the young poacher turned to the boy. He laid his hands heavily on Tom's shoulders. From this position they moved round till they clasped the back of his head. And Tom remained absolutely still, his face curiously grave.

"Wish me luck, Mr. Tom," Deverell said at last.

"Yes, I wish you good luck."

Deverell's hand passed awkwardly over his hair.

"You can kiss me if you like," said Tom simply.

Deverell bent down.

"You'd better go now, Mr. Tom. I must go soon myself."

Tom without another word went out into the sunshine, nor as he walked away from the cottage did he once look back.

18: WHEN a whole week had gone by without bringing news of Deverell, it was taken for granted even by his mother that there was no longer cause for anxiety. He had got away, and nobody had seen him go or knew his destination. Moreover, Mrs. Deverell had found out definitely—though Tom did not quite know how—that the police did not intend to do anything so long as the culprit remained in exile. But Tom had his own troubles —troubles which he kept to himself. He had not thought it right to bother Uncle Stephen, because Uncle Stephen was not well. This indeed was one of the causes of Tom's inquietude, though the doctor had assured him there was no need to worry. All morning and all evening he sat with Uncle Stephen: every afternoon he hurried off to the other house. When he was in company he tried to be cheerful; when he was by himself he moped.

One afternoon, half an hour before tea-time, he had gone for a short walk along the Kilbarron road. But he had not proceeded far when he heard somebody calling him name, and looking round saw Mr. Knox. The curate waved his hand and hastened his footsteps: there was nothing for it but to wait.

"It's a long time since I've seen you," beamed Mr. Knox as he came up. "Where have you been hiding yourself?"

"I've been very busy," Tom answered.

Mr. Knox glanced at him, then glanced again, more closely, and there followed a brief pause.

"I called at the Manor this afternoon," the curate said. "I'm glad to hear Mr. Collet is so much better."

"Yes, he felt better this morning, thank you."

"And how are you yourself?"

"Very well, thank you."

With an effort Tom continued the conversation. "Did you see Uncle Stephen?"

"No. I'm afraid I didn't ask to see him. It didn't occur to me that he would want to see anybody while he was still in bed."

And they walked on for another fifty yards.

"It was Mrs. Deverell who told me he was better and hoped to get up for an hour or two to-morrow. As a matter of fact it was partly to see Mrs. Deverell that I called."

"Yes," said Tom.

"Poor woman, she's had a good deal to worry her, but I hope things will be all right now. It must be a temporary relief, at any rate, to have got rid of that blackguard, and I fancy from what I've heard he's hardly likely to risk coming back."

"What blackguard?" asked Tom.

Mr. Knox looked at him in surprise. "Surely you knew that her son had decamped?"

"Yes."

"Well——"

"Did you know him?"

"I can't say I *knew* him, exactly," Mr. Knox replied. "I knew *of* him. I don't suppose I've spoken more than half a dozen words to him in my life: any time I called at his mother's cottage he slunk out by the back-door."

"Yes—he would do that."

"You don't think he was a blackguard?" Mr. Knox said. "Perhaps I shouldn't have used the word."

"No, no; it's not that: you might be right. I don't know what a blackguard is. It's somebody you don't like, isn't it? But then I liked Deverell, so it's different for me."

"You *liked* him?"

"Oh yes. I used to think I didn't—or to pretend I didn't—but I did, and do still."

Mr. Knox looked at him again. "What is the matter, Tom?"

"Nothing. Why?"

Mr. Knox walked on for some time in silence.

"I asked for you also at the house, but Mrs. Deverell told me you had gone out with a friend. I'm very glad you've found somebody of your own age to be friends with. Mrs. Deverell did not seem to know his name, but she said you went out together every afternoon."

Mr. Knox paused, as if expecting a little further enlightenment, but none was forthcoming.

"Well, Tom, I'll not inflict my company on you any longer," he said. "Because I don't think you want it."

Tom's eyes met the curate's for the first time. "That's because I've been rude to you."

"No, not rude—I can't imagine your being rude to anybody—but not very friendly."

"Rather a beast. I know. If I told you I'd been trying not to be, I suppose you'd hardly believe me."

"Yes," said Mr. Knox, "I should. But I can see you're worried about something and would rather be alone."

"No——" Tom began.

"Now, Tom, don't tell me an untruth: it's better to be rude than to do that. So good-bye."

"Good-bye," said Tom.

19: FOR all his determination not to show it, it was a very chastened-looking boy who approached Uncle Stephen's bedside that evening. "Would you like me to read to you, Uncle Stephen?" he asked.

"Presently, perhaps."

Tom sat down on a low chair beside the bed.

"First, I want you to talk to me, to tell me why I've had such a woebegone nephew for the last week."

"You've been ill," said Tom. "Naturally I tried to be quiet."

"Not ill enough to account for *that* forlorn appearance. I've been waiting for you to tell me of your own accord."

"I didn't tell you," said Tom, "because I thought you oughtn't to be worried."

"Then you've been a very good boy; but you need have no further scruples."

Tom looked up at the watching Hermes. "It is only that I don't know what has happened to Philip," he said. "I mean I don't know what has become of him. He has gone."

"He must have gone that night," he continued after a moment or two. "The night I went to look for him and didn't find him."

"And he left you no message?"

"No message; nothing. . . . I suppose it's that that I mind most. . . . I knew he was angry with me. He was angry because he thought I took Deverell's part when they quarrelled."

"Do you mean Deverell actually saw him?"

"Yes. . . . It was on that last afternoon. Philip was with me. We were down by the river. Then Deverell came along and they quarrelled. . . . All the same, I didn't think he'd go away like that—without even saying good-bye. I can't understand anybody doing that. But I've been over at the other house every day. I've waited there all afternoon every day—and he has never come back."

From his present position Tom could not see Uncle Stephen's face without turning his head, and he did not turn. But he leaned his cheek against the coverlet of the bed so that Uncle Stephen, like Socrates, might stroke his hair and twist it into little knots. "Perhaps I'd *better* read to you, Uncle Stephen," he said, after a long pause. "Wouldn't you like me to?"

There was no answer and Tom did not repeat his question. The light was fast ebbing from the room. Soon, in the twilight, he could only see the Hermes dimly. It was as if the marble, which even in broad daylight created a mysterious illusion of warmth and softness, had now actually dissolved, leaving in its place the glimmering spirit of the God. . . .

What influence was there belonging to this room that always affected him so strangely, though not always in the same way? *That* depended a little on his own mood, and to-night he had a feeling of something dream-like and precarious, as if he might suddenly awaken and find he *had* been dreaming—as if everything might change, the walls disappear, the ceiling melt into the open sky, and he, Tom, find himself living in a different time, a different place. . . .

And that God there—the guide, the messenger, the friend—was the God of dreams. He could lead Tom's spirit to the ends of the earth and guide it home again. . . . It must have been in this room that Uncle Stephen had dreamed first—and, awakening in his bedroom in Gloucester Terrace, Tom had known he was there. . . .

Why didn't Uncle Stephen speak? He could not even feel the touch of his hand now. . . . Yet Tom too remained motionless and silent: his eyes closed; he might have been asleep. . . .

It was into this room of darkness and silence that Mrs. Deverell presently entered. She stood near the door, her slight form visible in the dim light from the passage behind her. "Hadn't I better light the lamp, sir?" she asked, with a note of surprise in her voice; and when nobody answered she struck a match. She stood by the lamp till the flame burned clearly and evenly. Then she carried a small table over to the bed. She went out into the passage and returned with a tray which she set upon the table. "I brought up Master Tom's supper too," she said.

Tom watched her as a native of some remote island might watch the rites and ceremonies of his first missionary. It was Uncle Stephen's voice that brought him back to actuality.

"I'm afraid, Mrs. Deverell, you've been kept far too late these last few nights. There's no need for it any longer: Master Tom can look after me."

"Oh, it's all right, sir; there's plenty I can find to do downstairs. But I'll be going now if you're sure you won't require anything more."

Yet she still lingered, her pale eyes fixed as if in uncertainty on her master, and on the boy seated in the chair beside him. At last, with a low "Good-night, sir," she left them.

And as usual Tom listened for the sound of the hall-door being pulled to, for the sound of retreating footsteps on the gravel.

It was Uncle Stephen who spoke first. "Put away that stuff, Tom," he said abruptly. "I don't want it."

Tom rose obediently and removed the tray, with its steaming bowl of gruel, and his own biscuits, cheese, and milk. Then he returned to his seat.

But he did not again propose to read aloud. He had a premonition that something was coming, that Uncle Stephen was going to tell him something—though he had no idea what. He waited. It was something which would make a difference:—he knew that, but he knew no more than that. And he tried to stifle the feeling of suspense which with each moment grew, till it became a kind of reasonless dread of the unknown.

Yet what Uncle Stephen said, after all, was quite ordinary. "Would it make you very happy if your friend came back to you?"

Tom felt an immediate relief. He shook his despondency from him and breathed more freely. It was this room, it was sitting here in the dark without a word, which had worked upon his mind. He was all right now, and he turned quickly to the bed. "You aren't angry with me, Uncle Stephen, are you?"

"Angry! Why should I be angry?" Uncle Stephen asked in surprise.

Tom smiled. "I didn't really think you were," he said. "Yes, of course I'd like him to come back. I'd like to see him *once* more at any rate. I don't expect him to stay. I mean, he always told me and I always knew he wouldn't stay. But I'd like to see him once."

"Even though he left you like this?"

"I think there must have been a reason for it. I'm sure there was. Besides, he was angry with me."

"What reason could there be?"

"I don't know."

"Nobody can have been making inquiries about him, for the first thing they would do would be to call here. Don't you think the most probable reason is simply that this sort of thing is natural to him—that he doesn't think much about other people's feelings? It seems to me to fit in with what you originally told me about him."

"I don't remember what I told you."

"Don't you even remember that I warned you?"

"Not about this."

"Not directly perhaps, but indirectly. After all, he behaved in much the same way to his father and mother. It seems to me that restlessness and a desire for adventure are the main ingredients in his character, and that, once the wander-fit seizes on him, he isn't very likely to pay attention to such trifles as saying good-bye to his friends. If you had been there he would have said good-bye to you, but you weren't there, and he didn't think it worth while to wait."

"But how do you *know* he is like that, Uncle Stephen?"

"Because you told me about him."

"I didn't tell you all that: for one thing, I don't believe it's true."

"Then you're still fond of him?"

"Yes."

Uncle Stephen paused, and it was as if he were carefully weighing his next words, so slowly they came. "He *is* what I say, Tom. There may be, there must be, the germs of something more, but they're not developed: the whole circumstances of his life tended to keep them from developing."

Tom started. There was something in Uncle Stephen's manner which revived all his misgivings. "How do you know? Why do you talk as if you knew? You did once before, too? Uncle Stephen, *do* you know anything about him; and if you do why won't you tell me?"

"What I now know," said Uncle Stephen a little sadly, "is that I should never have allowed this to happen."

"What?" Tom breathed. He had turned completely round and his eyes were fixed very intently and brightly upon Uncle Stephen's face.

But Uncle Stephen did not answer. He was sitting up in the bed, the skull-cap he wore, vividly black against the pillows behind him, his eyes not looking at Tom, but towards the door by which Mrs. Deverell had come and gone: and for the first time Tom saw him frown.

He leaned closer, he was half kneeling now on his chair, but still Uncle Stephen did not look at him.

"Tell me—tell me," Tom repeated.

"Yes, I am going to tell you; but it's not easy. I don't know how you will take it. I wish I did. I wish it had never happened. . . . Tom, there isn't any Philip."

"Isn't——" Tom began, but he stopped short. A flush rose and died in his cheeks. Unconsciously he laid his hand on Uncle Stephen's and gripped it tightly.

"Listen," said Uncle Stephen. "This boy——"

Tom was listening with his whole being, but for the moment he was to hear nothing further. Uncle Stephen only added, "No—I can never explain it in that way."

And suddenly he seemed to withdraw into himself, and his eyes shut.

"Go to that cupboard in the wall, and bring me the box that is there."

Tom sprang to his feet. The cupboard, as he pulled back the door, revealed itself as but a couple of shelves, and on the upper one of these was a flat wooden box, its corners brass-plated, its lid overlaid with a criss-cross pattern in brass filigree. It could not contain much. It was about twelve inches long and a third of that in depth. But it was the only box there, and Tom lifted it from the shelf and brought it to the bed.

"Now give me my keys," said Uncle Stephen, "they're on the dressing-table." And the smallest of these he inserted in the lock, turning it twice before he raised the lid.

As he looked over Uncle Stephen's shoulder Tom's eyes were still and absorbed. The ferment in his mind too was momentarily stilled— forgotten in an intense expectancy.

Yet he saw very little. The box was lined with olive-green silk, and appeared to contain merely a few old letters, among which Uncle Stephen fumbled before he drew out from beneath them a flat leather case, which he opened by pressing a spring. Tom bent nearer. Only his breathing was audible. Within the case was a thin slab of ivory on which was painted the portrait of a boy.

"Do you know him?"

Tom did not answer. He was gazing, not at the picture, but at Uncle Stephen himself. The pupils of his eyes were slightly dilated and his face had grown very white.

"There is a name," Uncle Stephen said, "and a date—there inside the lid. The date is that when the likeness was painted; the name is the name of the sitter, of the boy. Read it aloud."

Tom read in an oddly muffled voice: "Stephen Collet. 1880."

"It was painted three months before he ran away from home."

"It is your name," whispered Tom.

"Yes, my name. And it is the only portrait that was ever made of this boy. At the time it was supposed to be a good likeness, but if you were to see him a year later he would not be quite like that."

Tom waited a moment: then he asked, hardly audibly, "What happened to him?"

"He carried out his plan. If I could show him to you as he was a year later, you would see him among strangers, in a foreign country, living anywhere, anyhow—ragged, more or less homeless, but not starving, not even particularly conscious of discomfort, because the climate suited him and he was strong and healthy. Besides, any squeamishness he may have felt at first had by then disappeared. Not even if things had been much worse would he have dreamed of returning to the country rectory he had left, to the old people, his parents—whom in fact he never saw again. There was nothing romantic about all this, Tom; nothing fine; and the future held no prospect of anything but disaster. It was by the merest accident that disaster was averted—a chance encounter in the street. There are people, perhaps, who possess a gift of instant recognition, or who think they do. At all events, it was this boy's fate, after a brief exchange of perhaps a dozen questions and answers, to be singled out by a stranger—a man of another race—as possessing the particular qualities and faculties he happened to be in search of. The whole thing was sudden; improbable; for all the boy knew to the contrary, dangerous; and therefore precisely of a nature to appeal to him. He followed his master without a moment's hesitation. But though you may think it resembles it, this was no prelude to an Arabian tale, but to long years of arduous training during which, if again I could show him to you, you would see the pupil becoming a disciple, the disciple a collaborator. . . . And when he was once more alone his youth was over. . . . That is all, Tom—all I need tell you now. As for what you want me to tell you—that is nearly as inexplicable to me as it can be to you."

"But that *is* you, Uncle Stephen—that boy?"

"It was—once."

"And it is Philip."

"There never was a Philip, though I took that name when I ran away."

"But," Tom stammered painfully "——then it must really be true after all."

"What must be true, Tom?"

"That you are a magician."

Uncle Stephen shook his head. He looked away. Then he looked back at Tom, and still waited. "It had nothing to do with magic," he said at last. "The first time it happened I myself thought it was an ordinary dream—or if extraordinary, only because of its unusual vividness. And then you came to me with your story."

Tom, leaning over Uncle Stephen's shoulder, was thinking. Strangely enough, his nervousness and apprehension were gone, he was only puzzled. "Was it here that you dreamed, Uncle Stephen?"

"Yes."

"Was it on purpose—I mean, did you try to?"

"No. I will tell you about that too."

"Tell me first, Uncle Stephen, had you ever heard of me before I came to you?"

"I had heard of you—yes—from a friend of your mother's. But it was very little—a phrase or two in a letter. I don't know what there was in it that impressed me, gave me a definite impression which persisted and deepened. For many years I had lived alone, and possibly that may have had much to do with it. I cannot say. I can give no rational account of what happened, but you became very real and very dear to me in imagination. Imagination, I suppose, is a faculty which can be trained; but what had been trained in me for years was more the power of concentration. That is everything, Tom. Before I dreamed that afternoon, I had been thinking of you, thinking too of my own boyhood. Then the scene arose in my mind in which these two boys met. It arose spontaneously: I did not seem to be making it up. At a certain point it must have passed into a dream, for I definitely woke up, and I knew by looking at my watch that the afternoon was nearly over. But I really thought very little about the matter until you came with your story. That seemed incredible, and yet I had to accept it. I knew there was no boy at the other house—besides, what you told me *was* my dream. I ought to have left it at that. Unfortunately I knew exactly the conditions under which this accident—if it was an accident—had taken place. I determined to repeat everything. And you came to me again with your story and this time it had advanced a step. I knew it must be dangerous. Even if some strange connection *had* been established between present and past, I knew it could not be safe. Therefore I should not have gone on, because it involved not only myself, but you. Besides, I had to deceive you."

"I *think*, you know," said Tom slowly, "that deep deep down I must have had a sort of suspicion. I don't even now feel frightfully surprised."

Uncle Stephen turned to him doubtfully, but Tom pursued his idea. "You see, I couldn't have liked Philip so much if he hadn't been you."

But Uncle Stephen did not look convinced. "You have a considerable capacity for liking people," he said.

"Yes," Tom admitted. "I even, in a sort of way, loved that fountain-boy—and Deverell—a little. . . . But this is different. Anyway, you know, Uncle Stephen, I once almost asked you if you were Philip. It was that night, you remember, after Uncle Horace had been here: the first time I was ever in this room. I couldn't understand then, and I was very silly about it—but it was because I felt there was something I *didn't* understand. And one day I called Philip by your name. It was because his eyes were exactly the same as yours. . . . You know, I'd like you to come to the other house just once more. It would be quite different this time, because I'd know who you really were. Everything would be different." He suddenly paused. His eyes were fixed on the broken lovely figure, mild and benign, dreaming, half in shadow, half in lamplight. "Do you think," he whispered, "it happens through the God? . . . I don't want you to answer," he went on quickly. "Don't let us talk at all for a little. I want to be quiet."

20:

THE track through the wood had become a path and was now used by other creatures than Tom. Pheasants, hares, squirrels, a weasel, and a big black fierce-looking cat who had lost an ear—all these he had met at one time or another. The track was used by butterflies, moths, wasps, and bees—in fact, the entire animal world had immediately discovered and begun to make use of Tom's path. He kept it clear, not only by tramping it daily, but also by vigorously swinging a stick; and gradually it was widening. On either edge pressed closely and silently the green, rooted world of vegetation.

This evening he advanced over the sodden ground, sweeping his stick like a sword, and at every blow scattering a shower of raindrops from the drenched leaves. In his left hand he carried a picnic-basket, for Mrs. Deverell had continued to pack one for him daily, though now most of its contents went to feed the mice and birds. The hour of his visit was much later than usual; it was past seven o'clock; and it had been with the utmost difficulty that he had persuaded Uncle Stephen to allow him to come at all. He felt ashamed of his importunity. More than ashamed, now that he had got his own way. It was as if he had taken an unfair advantage. To be sure, he had promised that it would be for this once only—and indeed he wanted no more than that himself. Still, Uncle Stephen had been strangely reluctant— and at the back of Tom's mind there was an uneasiness, a feeling that he had done wrong.

He reached the broken gateway and walked quickly up the avenue. He entered the house and climbed the stairs to Philip's room. It was dark and cheerless, and he wondered if he could do anything to make it less so. He tried to drag away some of the obstructing ivy which looked so picturesque from outside; but it was very tough and he had nothing to cut it with. He knelt down and leaned out over the dark lichened sill. He listened to the knocking of a woodpecker. No other sound reached him. At that moment the sun struggled out from behind the clouds and the whole prospect changed.

It was like a signal, a propitious omen, for it had been cloudy all day, even when not actually raining. The house faced west and the sun streamed straight into the room. Tom did not mind now how long he had to wait: in fact he enjoyed it. Only, sitting on the bare floor was uncomfortable, so he fetched one of the ancient patchwork quilts from the bed, and also the volume of *Arabia Deserta* which he had brought for Philip and never taken home. The quilt was stuffed with flock, but it made a tolerable cushion. Tom sat on it by the low window-sill and turned the pages of his book. But either the style was too crabbed, or his mind just then was incapable of concentration, for after reading for ten minutes he discovered that he had not taken in the meaning of a single sentence. He put the book down and began frankly to dream.

He heard the far-away cawing of rooks, and the sound reminded him of the passing of time. Something unexpected must have happened. He got up and walked up and down the room; he ate two of Mrs. Deverell's sandwiches; he went out into the garden and came back again.

He was determined to wait, no matter how long Philip should keep him. He wondered what would happen when he *did* come! Somehow he could not get it out of his head that this meeting would not in the least resemble their other meetings. If nothing else, Philip would have to admit that his name was Stephen Collet, and, once he knew Tom knew that, he would no longer have any reason for not talking freely.

There were all kinds of questions Tom wanted to ask. Philip would be far better able to answer them than Uncle Stephen himself, because Uncle Stephen must have forgotten heaps. What would he say, for instance, when Tom began to talk to him of Uncle Stephen and of all that had occurred? Would he remember? Tom somehow had taken it for granted that he would, but now he felt more doubtful. It was really very queer and confusing. Uncle Stephen for Philip was the future, *Philip's* future, and of course you can't remember the future. Besides, he had often talked of Uncle Stephen before and Philip hadn't remembered, hadn't known anything about him except what Tom himself had told him. Therefore it would be the same this time. Either that, or he wouldn't *be* Philip. Tom felt a chill of discouragement: he wished now that he had not made this plan, but it was too late to draw back.

Uncle Stephen must have altered a great deal—altered in every respect. Tom was not thinking of physical alterations, but of other things. And the more closely he recalled Philip the more he realized that Uncle Stephen was dearer to him than all the Philips in the world, and the more he wished that he had not insisted on a final experiment.

He wondered if he himself would ever change as much as that. So far, he thought, he had changed very little, if at all; but of course other people might not agree with him. Probably everybody changed —whether it was to become nastier or nicer. He began to think of various grown-up people he knew and to turn them back again into boys. In some cases it was easy. It was easy to picture Mr. Knox as a boy, easier still to picture Deverell: but what on earth had Uncle Horace been like? Uncle Horace must have changed more even than Uncle Stephen. Far more, because there were definite glimpses of a boy in Uncle Stephen, but no boy in the world could ever have been like what Uncle Horace was at present. Where had that boy gone to, then—or was he still somewhere inside Uncle Horace— hidden, shut up as if in a cupboard, frightened to squeak? Tom remembered strange little creatures—caddis worms they were— which he had often fished out of ponds and streams with a net full of water weeds—creatures so thickly encrusted with bits of stick, stone, sand, and shell that you never would have dreamed anything but the protective case existed till the case suddenly began to move. The *boy* Uncle Horace must be like that. Perhaps not a bad little chap either. In a minute or two Tom began to feel an affection for this small and hitherto unsuspected Uncle Horace. Out of a mysterious limbo he had sprung fully equipped and articulate, and was capering about the room, chattering, as lively as a cricket. He slipped behind Tom and clapped his hands over his eyes. Who is it? And Tom knew who it was. It was perfectly idiotic, but he was sure that never again would his relations with the grown-up Uncle Horace be exactly what they had been in the past.

Dusk was falling now, and once or twice Tom's eyelids closed. A white shape drifted noiselessly past the open window. He knew it was an owl, and wished it had perched on the sill and stared in at him, for he was fond of owls. They were beautiful and fierce and solemn, and he had once read, or somebody had told him, that when they mated it was for life. This had impressed him deeply. It was the old quality of faithfulness cropping up once more. He thought of it now and it led to other thoughts. His mind was a stilled pool over which he brooded: then gradually the pool dimmed, wavered, vanished.

21: TOM opened his eyes, but for a moment or two did not realize where he was. Then he remembered and sat up. Outside it was broad daylight; he must have slept the whole night through. He scratched his head, stretched out his arms, turned round from the window and saw—Philip.

He was lying on the bed fast asleep. Tom crossed the room quickly and stood looking down at him. When had he come? Could he have been here all night? He stooped lower and at last knelt beside the bed. His face was within a foot of Philip's face; he was gazing so intently that he held his breath. And in that sleeping countenance he could certainly trace a definite resemblance to Uncle Stephen, though even now, even with his knowledge and his desire to prompt him, he saw far more difference than resemblance. He *knew* it was Uncle Stephen, but should he have known had he possessed only this shadowy likeness to guide him? Would other people—Mrs. Deverell, Sally, Mr. Flood, or Mr. Knox—know? And suddenly he found himself looking into two wide open eyes—blue, dark, questioning.

Tom drew back with a kind of spiritual shock. Though their colour and shape were the same (and it was a most uncommon colour), the expression in those eyes was not Uncle Stephen's. Recognition there was in them, and friendliness; but the recognition and the friendliness were not Uncle Stephen's.

"Philip!" he faltered.

The boy on the bed yawned, swung his legs round and assumed a sitting position. "Hello! Are you saying your prayers?"

Tom got up in some confusion. "I never heard you coming in last night."

"Is that why you were kneeling there staring at me?"

"I wasn't."

"You *weren't!*"

"I mean——" But, having begun his explanation, Tom could not end it, and Philip watched his embarrassment ironically.

"I hope you were praying that you might become a nice truthful boy."

"Why shouldn't I look at you?" asked Tom, defending himself. "I thought you were asleep and I was wondering how you managed to get in last night without wakening me. It *was* last night, wasn't it?"

"Yes, of course it was last night."

"What time?"

"I don't know: it was dark: and *you* were pretty sound asleep. . . . I say, aren't you hungry? What about breakfast?"

Tom hurried to unpack the basket—the more readily in that it gave him time to think and helped him to conceal a growing anxiety.

"I brought two thermos flasks," he mumbled, trying to speak in his ordinary voice. "But the tea in them must be quite cold by now." Having said this, it was as if he were afraid to risk further conversation, for in silence he spread out the contents of the basket, using the napkin Mrs. Deverell had wrapped round the sandwiches as a tablecloth, and drawing the table itself over beside the bed. He knew he was not behaving naturally, probably not looking natural, but he could not help it, he had grown all at once horribly nervous.

He fetched the chair and sat down. "You haven't told me yet what brought you here last night," said Philip.

"No," answered Tom.

But he could not go on like this, and suddenly he blurted out, "There are other things I have to tell you. You said your name was Philip Coombe."

"Yes."

"Well, it isn't."

Philip glanced at him, surprised, but unperturbed. "How do you know?"

"I do know."

"Is that what's worrying you? Coombe is the name of the place I came from:—Coombe Bridge. Philip is the name of a dog, a retriever:—our dog at home. They were the first names that came into my head. There's nothing more in it than that."

"Why did you invent a name at all?" asked Tom.

"Well, I thought it safer, I suppose; and once I had done it, it didn't seem worth while changing back. Your uncle's name was another reason."

"Uncle Stephen?"

"Stephen Collet. It gave me a considerable scare, you know, when you mentioned it; and I knew I'd got to be jolly careful. It isn't a common name, and I was pretty certain he must be a relation though I'd never heard of him. . . . How *did* you find out by the way? I mean, how did you find out that I wasn't Philip Coombe?" He looked at Tom in sudden suspicion.

"I—I guessed," said Tom.

"You must be a remarkably good guesser," Philip answered dryly.

He said no more, but Tom felt that a gulf straightway had opened between them. Nor was he astonished. He was making a mess of everything. He looked timidly at Philip, but Philip did not return his look, he went on quietly with his breakfast. Tom grew more and more unhappy. And to think he had insisted on this meeting! All the questions he had looked forward to asking were forgotten. He did not want Philip now; he had never wanted anybody less; he wanted only Uncle Stephen.

His trouble doubtless was visible in his face, for Philip asked him, "What's the matter?"

Tom was gazing down at his paper of sandwiches, but without even pretending to eat. "I'm not very hungry, I think."

Philip did not question him further. He appeared to be perfectly content that Tom should withhold his confidence, and it was Tom himself who was forced to break the silence, for the unruffled countenance of the boy opposite him had begun to be almost terrifying. "Philip," he said, "don't you remember *anything?*"

Philip shrugged his shoulders. "Why do you go on calling me that, if you know it isn't my name?"

"I can't call you Uncle Stephen," said Tom miserably.

"No; I dare say one Uncle Stephen is enough."

"Stephen, then: what does it matter!"

"Nothing except that it *is* my name and you seemed rather particular about it a few minutes ago."

Tom made a movement, half of impatience, half of hopelessness. "Listen," he began. "You must listen——"

"I can listen a great deal better if you don't get excited," said Philip. "You seem always either in one extreme or the other. If anybody has found out about me I suppose it's your friend the gamekeeper—or whatever it is he calls himself. But if he thinks I'm going to pay him to hold his tongue he's jolly well mistaken. For one thing, I've nothing to pay him with. At least—that's not absolutely true; but the little I have I'll require for myself."

"It's not that: he's not that sort. And anyway he's not here now——"

"Not here? Where has he gone?"

Tom's hands clenched. "Oh, I don't know. What does it matter where he has gone! Philip, do you remember talking about a dream— you called it a dream—a dream through which you got back to the past. Try to remember. It's important. *Awfully*. I can't tell you *how* important it is."

Philip looked at him. "Got back to what past?" he asked.

"To your own past. To—to what you are now."

"Don't you think we'd better change the subject?"

"I knew you'd say something like that," answered Tom bitterly. "I'm trying to make you remember something—something that happened. If I could only even make you realize how much depends on it!" He spoke with all the self-control he could command, but the thought that he might *never* succeed created in his mind a hardly bearable tension.

"I don't even know what '*it*' is," Philip replied, "so I can't very well realize its importance. You seem to me to be talking nonsense, but I know you like to do that and I've no particular objection if it pleases you." He had begun to look bored, however, and Tom's sense of defeat deepened.

"Don't you remember Uncle Stephen?" he asked.

"I never saw Uncle Stephen in my life."

"Philip—Stephen, I mean——"

"I haven't the ghost of an idea what's worrying you or what you've got into your head. That's the honest, absolute truth; and if you can't speak more plainly——"

"Don't interrupt me."

"Well, don't talk so wildly then."

"But I must. I must make you remember. And I'm speaking as plainly as I can."

He paused, and for a minute or two sat with his eyes narrowed and his head turned slightly away from the other boy, as if concentrating all his faculties on some interior vision.

"I want you to think," he began slowly, "of a room—at night. . . . There is a lamp burning. . . . There is a bed—low and narrow —and beyond the bed—at the foot of it—a marble figure, broken, the arms missing, and the legs broken off below the knees—it is a statue of Hermes. There is someone sitting beside the bed—me. There is someone sitting up *in* the bed—you—with the pillows arranged behind you. You ask me to get a box from a cupboard in the wall, and I bring it to you—a flat wooden box ornamented with brass. Out of the box you take a leather case which opens when you press a spring, and inside is the picture of a boy painted, I think, on ivory— your own picture. There is a name on the inside of the lid—Stephen Collet."

"You're right enough about the miniature," Stephen said with a dawning interest. "How on earth did you know? Father got it done as a birthday present for Mother; but I'll swear it's never been out of our house—at least, I shouldn't think so. Mr. Collet *must* be a relation of ours—a cousin of my father's, or something. And they must have written to him about me. Is *that* how you guessed who I was?"

"Oh, don't bother about how I guessed," said Tom desperately. "Think of what I've told you. Of the room. Think—think."

"Well, I *am* thinking."

"What do you remember?"

"I suppose you'll be furious if I tell you, but what I remember is a missionary who once stayed over the week-end with us: my father's a parson, you know."

"Yes?"

"This missionary had had a sunstroke. It happened in Africa, I believe. He recovered all right, but sometimes—— I say, there's no use beginning to blub! I didn't mean anything. . . . Tom!" He jumped up and leaned over the younger boy's chair.

Tom tried to smile. "It's all right," he answered huskily. "Only— only—it's *awful;* and it's all my fault!" He hid his head in his arms which were stretched out on the table.

"What is awful? What has happened? Tom, old man, what *is* the matter?"

Tom looked up wildly. For a moment, surely, though faintly and through a rougher, younger voice, he had heard the voice of Uncle Stephen! But it was only Philip who stood there patting him on his shoulder.

"If you've got into a scrape perhaps I can help you: I'm pretty well used to them."

Tom did not lift his head. He felt too miserable even to say that he had not got into a scrape. . . . Uncle Stephen had warned him of the danger, but like an obstinate fool he had refused to listen. For one sickening moment he felt the full weight of having betrayed Uncle Stephen. If even he had had sufficient strength of mind to keep awake last night this might not have happened: but he had felt sleepy, and so had slept. His bitterness was too great to admit of self-pity: he was no good: he had prated about faithfulness, and he hadn't been able to be faithful to the one person he loved.

"If you like I'll go back to the Manor House with you," Philip— or Stephen—offered. "I'll do anything you want."

Tom sat up. He drew his hand across his eyes, leaving a black smudge, but a glimmer of hope had been created by these words. Was it not just possible that in Uncle Stephen's own room something might happen; the cloud might be lifted; and if it broke for even an instant he believed all would be well.

"Will you, Stephen?" he said slowly. "If you do I'll—I'll—— It's very good of you."

"No it isn't. Come on: we'll go at once."

Tom got up. "I'm sorry I can't explain why I want you to come," he said. "I'm sorry about everything. I would try to explain only—it would be just like all the rest."

"Yes," said Stephen hastily, "don't bother. Time enough when we see Mr. Collet."

Tom followed him from the room, and they passed through the yard and round to the front of the house. Here Stephen abruptly thumped him on the back much as one might thump a dog. "It's sure to be all right," he said, encouragingly. "You never know your luck. Did you tell him you were going to stay all night at the other house—Mr. Collet, I mean?"

"Yes—no—I don't know. . . . Please Stephen, don't talk to me; I want to think."

But all the thinking in the world, he knew, would help them little if this last experiment failed. What would happen then? Nobody would believe him. The whole thing was too unreal, too fantastic. He might call it an accident, but it was an accident which upset every law of nature and made the plain solid earth no better than quicksand.

They plunged out of sunshine into woodland shadow, walking on dark moss, with a green roof above them, and the rustling of leaves in their ears. These tree voices were softer, thicker, and more blurred than they would be in autumn, when the leaves had grown thin and dry. This was the liquid murmur of life—rich, luxuriant. Stephen had begun to whistle, and the clear notes were answered from overhead and every side by trills and pipings that wove a delicate arabesque of sweetness round his common tune.

Tom looked at his watch. It was after ten. An hour ago Mrs. Deverell would have discovered that he and Uncle Stephen were not in the house. . . . Unless Uncle Stephen *was* there—all the time—asleep—dreaming! That had not occurred to him before, and the thought made him slightly dizzy. Better to wait; better not to think: it was all so uncertain. . . .

He hurried on, a slender eager figure, with Stephen close behind him, but when they reached the edge of the shrubbery he stopped. In the distance he saw George McCrudden wheeling a barrow, and the sight somehow was faintly, temporarily reassuring. He gathered from it at any rate that there had been no alarm raised as yet, and from behind the taller, sturdier Stephen, with his arm round him, and peeping over his shoulder, he gazed at the house.

"What's our next move?" Stephen asked placidly.

"We'll go in," said Tom: but he did not stir till George had disappeared. "Thank you, Stephen, for coming with me."

"Oh, that's all right. Only you'd better tell me what you want me to do."

"I—I don't know yet."

So much, indeed, depended on what Mrs. Deverell might already have done! And the first thing was to find out. While they were approaching the house his eyes searched window after window, but all were empty. Nor was there anybody in the porch—or in the hall. Suddenly Mrs. Deverell appeared.

She came out quickly from the dining-room at the sound of the closing door. "Why, whatever has happened, Master Tom?" she cried. "And where's Mr. Collet?"

Tom saw her glance at Stephen, who grinned cheerfully in response. But Mrs. Deverell had no time just then to give to strange boys. Her eyes questioned Tom. "When Sally came and told me there was neither of you in the house I got quite a turn! I never *have* felt easy about leaving the master all alone at night, cut off from everything and everybody, without as much as a telephone in the house. There should be someone within call, even if it was only Robert. Suppose he was to be taken ill; or tramps were to break in!"

"I'm within call," said Tom.

Mrs. Deverell looked as if she thought *that* made little difference. "When will the master be back?" she asked.

It was the question Tom had been dreading. "He won't be back. . . . At least, I don't know *when* he'll be back. . . . Perhaps not for some time."

He tried to make his news sound as ordinary as possible, but the effect was to bring Mrs. Deverell's attention on him in a swoop. "Not for some time!" she repeated. "He'll be back for lunch, won't he?"

Something inside Tom was behaving exactly like a guilty conscience. He forced himself to return Mrs. Deverell's gaze, but his cheeks burned. "No—and I've had breakfast. Uncle Stephen was called away on business—very early. It was important—and—and I went part of the way with him to see him off."

"You mean he's gone by the train!" Mrs. Deverell exclaimed.

"Yes—I mean, no. Earlier than that. . . . He went in a motorcar. The one that brought the message. Very early. A—a little after five, I think."

Mrs. Deverell's astonishment increased. "Why, he's never done that—not in all the years I was with him!" she pronounced half incredulously.

Her voice, her expression, her whole manner, had begun to exasperate Tom. "I can't help it," he answered. "It was quite sudden, or of course he would have told you." Then he added, to get everything over at once, "Philip is to stay with me till he comes back."

"But, Master Tom, your bed wasn't slept in last night."

Tom's face grew sullen. It was just as if she had set a trap for him. "Yes, it was," he contradicted. "I made it after I got up."

Mrs. Deverell did not ask him why he had done so; she said no more; but Tom knew it wasn't because she was satisfied. She didn't *look* satisfied: she looked as if she had ceased to question him only because she saw he wasn't going to tell her the truth. Her eyes turned from him to Stephen, and immediately Tom realized how disreputable was Stephen's appearance. Fortunately Mrs. Deverell already knew about him—the boy at the other house—the boy for whom she had packed so many baskets. "If you would let me have Master Philip's clothes," she said, "I could mend them and clean them."

Tom was filled with gratitude. "That's awfully decent of you, Mrs. Deverell. I *will* let you have them. My things will be too small for him, but he can wear a dressing-gown or pyjamas. Come, Philip." And he hurriedly pushed him in the direction of the study.

They had not gone more than half-way down the passage, however, when Mrs. Deverell called after him, "Master Tom, do you mean that Mr. Collet won't be back to-night?"

Tom turned round. He wondered how many times she was going to ask him this question, but with an effort he answered in his natural voice. "I really don't know, Mrs. Deverell. I've told you all I *can* tell you. We're not to expect him till we see him. It may be some—some days." He faltered again, on the last words, and he knew they left Mrs. Deverell as bewildered as ever. Again he pushed Stephen on in front of him, and opened the study door.

Once inside, he felt inclined to lock it behind them, but resisted the temptation. They stood there, side by side, Stephen looking nearly as puzzled as Mrs. Deverell herself.

"What's up?" he asked. "I thought I was being brought here to *see* Mr. Collet, and now you say he mayn't be back for a week!"

"Yes."

"But is it true? Some of what you told her was lies, and all of it *sounded* like lies."

"I know it did. . . . Most of it was."

"What's the idea, then? What *really* has happened?"

"I—I want you to wait, Stephen:—not to be impatient." Tom's voice was almost imploring. "If you are, I can't bear it. Will you try? Will you try even a little?"

Stephen looked uncomfortable. "That's all right," he answered. "I know you've got something on your mind, and it seems to be something you're frightened to tell."

Tom turned to him irresolutely. "It's not that, but—— You—you don't—— This room doesn't remind you of anything?"

Stephen shrugged his shoulders: then he remembered his promise to be patient. "That's the way you talked in the other house. It's no good. What on earth are you so scared about? Anyone would think you'd *done* something! Even if you have, I won't give you away."

He waited a moment, and at last, as if giving it up, "Hadn't I better let her have my clothes?" he said.

"Not yet: there's something I want to do first." Tom crossed the room and began to move his fingers tentatively over the dark panelling till he found what he sought. He pressed on one of the carved, flattened roses, which sank in, releasing the spring of the secret door.

Stephen, who had followed him, uttered an exclamation.

"It only leads to Uncle Stephen's bedroom," said Tom dully. "I'd better go first: it's very dark—or it will be when I shut the door. I must shut it, because Mrs. Deverell may come in."

He did so, and then, striking a match, began to climb the steps. "Will you hold a light for me, Stephen?" he said, when they had reached the top of the flight.

Another match flared up, and Tom, after some fumbling, opened the second door. This he did not trouble to close, but sat down on the side of the bed, while Stephen, who seemed to be more pleased now with the way things were going, gazed curiously about him.

Tom did not speak. Nor did he look at Stephen, who, after closing and opening the secret door several times, and inspecting much more briefly the statue of Hermes, was now at the window. But even without looking he knew his experiment had failed.

Stephen approached him. "Well?" he asked, with a subdued expectation in his voice: "Is this all?"

"Yes," answered Tom.

"But you must have had *some* reason for bringing me here? What was it?"

"I thought—something might happen."

"To me?"

"But I see now that it won't—unless——"

"Unless what?"

Tom looked up at him. "Unless you sleep here."

"In this room? What do you expect to happen if I do sleep here? What do you *want* to happen? If you'd only tell me that, you know, instead of——"

"I wish you would sit down, Stephen. I can't talk to you while you're standing up and moving about."

Stephen sat down in the low chair where Tom himself had sat when Uncle Stephen was ill. "I'll do anything you like," he said good-naturedly. Then a sudden thought occurred to him and he turned to the smaller boy, who was sitting on his two hands, his toes turned in, staring moodily at the opposite wall. "It's not Mr. Collet who has done something, is it? He hasn't gone away and left you, or anything like that? . . . But of course that's nonsense," he added after a moment.

"All the same, it *is* something like that," said Tom dejectedly, "And it was my fault. . . . I'm going to tell you about it. Will you promise to listen without saying anything till I've finished?"

"I've been asking you to tell me for the last hour."

"Well, I'm going to do it now: I'm going to tell you everything— from the beginning: it's the only way."

But having announced his intention, he still, for a while, added nothing further. Stephen also remained dumb, leaning back in his chair, his legs stretched out, his hands in his pockets.

"The first thing that happened," Tom began at length, "happened before I left home. . . ." And with only an occasional pause, he told the adventure of himself and Uncle Stephen, from the first dream he had had in Gloucester Terrace down to his vigil in the empty house last night.

When he had finished there was a silence. Tom could not read from Stephen's bent head what he was thinking, yet he could see that some kind of struggle was going on within him. Once he glanced up quickly, but he did not speak; and it was a strange glance; it might mean that he believed Tom to be crazy; for beneath its incredulity was a hint of aversion, perhaps of fear. At last he asked a question, in an oddly repressed voice. "What date is this—what year?"

It was a question which produced an electrical effect upon Tom. Why hadn't he thought of it! *That*, of course, must settle the matter finally—at least so far as convincing Stephen went. "Tell me what year you think it is," he asked breathlessly.

Stephen raised his head, but did not answer. Perhaps it was Tom's eagerness, something in the bright intentness of his eyes—at all events there was visible in his own eyes a failure of confidence. Tom, with a hand that shook a little, fumbled in his jacket. He found a letter— two letters. Their envelopes were post-marked. He found a small calendar. "Look!" he said; and Stephen looked.

Tom watched him with parted lips, but Stephen turned from him. "You see!" said Tom.

Still Stephen did not answer. And then, unexpectedly, he flushed— deeply, painfully—which was what Tom had never seen him do before. He rose to his feet, walked to the window, and leaned out.

Tom watched him without a word. Did Stephen mind? He hadn't thought of it like that, somehow, but his heart smote him now, and he too got up. After what seemed a long time Stephen turned back to the room. Whatever he may have been thinking or feeling was no longer visible in his face; the countenance Tom saw was filled only with a half-mocking bravado. "This," he said, walking up to Tom and catching him by the arms, "is going to be the greatest sport that ever was."

Tom gazed mutely while Stephen rocked him, unresisting, to and fro. His eyes grew rounder and more and more filled with consternation. Among all the effects he had imagined as resulting from his story, this at least he had not dreamed of. He gazed up at Stephen in a kind of fascination till Stephen, still gripping him closely, gave a short laugh. "Don't you see," he said—"don't you see that however it goes, we're bound to be up against it? *Nobody* is going to believe such a yarn. Why, I don't believe it myself, though I'll try to make the most of it while it lasts. That is, if it *does* last; for I've an idea I'm going to wake up soon."

"But——" Tom stammered.

"But what? I must say you don't look too pleased about it!"

"But—— It's *real*, Stephen. And—and—everything is still where it was."

"How do you mean, still where it was? Everything is jolly well *not* where it was."

"I mean—you still have to get back."

"Get back! So far as that goes——" Then, as he saw the expression on Tom's face, "Oh Lord!" he groaned, "you don't mean to say you would rather I was that old——"

"Stop!" cried Tom, his cheeks flaming. "If you say another word——"

"You'll hit me, I suppose. . . . After all, I'm talking about myself."

"You're not. You've no right—— I only *told* you so that you could try to get back again."

Stephen released him. "Aren't you asking a good deal? . . . Besides, according to you I *am* Uncle Stephen."

"You're not," cried Tom. "You're not even like him. Uncle Stephen didn't *want* to become a boy again. He only did it to please me. It was all my fault. And I only wanted it just once—just this last time, for a little."

"Well, you've got what you want," said Stephen. "There's no use making a fuss: it's not *my* doing. Besides, if I'm going back I'll go back, and if I'm not I won't. To talk of "trying" is silly. If it happens at all, it will happen as it did before—when I'm asleep. At least, I should think so." A sudden suspicion appeared in his eyes. "Is that why you want me to sleep here?"

"Yes it is," said Tom brokenly.

Stephen contemplated him for a minute or two with a slight frown. His mood appeared to change. "Look here——" But he checked himself and put his arm round Tom's shoulder. "Why won't I do as I am?" he coaxed ingenuously. "Don't you like me? You always seemed to."

"Yes I do."

"Well, then, what's the matter?"

"I could never make you understand," said Tom, turning away.

Stephen looked perplexed. Again he thought. "No, I suppose not," he admitted, with a shade of reluctance. "You're such a queer chap. . . . Of course, I know you were Uncle Stephen's darling. Still—— I say, if I promise to give the thing a chance, will that do? If I sleep in this room to-night? Hang it all, you can't expect me to do more than that! There isn't any more *to* do."

"You *will* do it?" Tom gulped.

"Yes, if I say I will."

"And—and suppose nothing does happen," Tom went on, "you won't go away from me?"

"Go away! Why should I go away?"

"I mean, you won't leave me, you'll stay with me?"

"For how long?"

"You won't go away at all—ever. All that—about going to sea— you'll give that up?"

Stephen hesitated. "I believe it would be better if I *did* clear out."

"No," cried Tom in sudden alarm. He gripped Stephen by the wrist and held him. "Promise that you won't leave me."

"But why?"

"Because you must."

"But I don't see what good it can do. If I'm going to remain as I am now you won't want me hanging about. After all, it's only Uncle Stephen you want. Honestly, I think it would be better if I kept to my first plan."

"You can't," said Tom, "you *can't* go." What was in his mind was that he must be near Stephen—that he must be there when Uncle

Stephen returned—but it seemed impossible to say this, and what he did say was, "If you go I'll go with you."

Stephen welcomed it as the happiest of solutions. "Of course! Why not? You see, it's all very well for us to promise that we'll keep together, but we won't be *allowed* to keep together—at any rate, not here."

Tom stood thinking. "If it comes to the worst——" he began.

"Yes? By 'the worst' you mean me, I suppose:—me remaining as I am?"

"I'm sorry, Stephen. I know it must seem beastly of me to talk like this. . . . But—we must make *some* plan."

"Well, I've just made one. Or rather, you made it."

"What?"

"To go away together."

Tom looked down. "How are we going to live?" he asked. "Uncle Horace won't give me any of my own money."

"We'd have to rough it, of course."

Tom did not reply, but he knew he had small capacity for roughing it; at least, not in the way Stephen meant. To cadge for odd jobs, for food and a sleeping-place—such a prospect might hold no terrors for Stephen, but *he* had not the physique for it. He was far from sickly, but it did not take a great deal to knock him up. One thorough wetting would be sufficient. Stephen might be able to work his way alone—in fact, Uncle Stephen *had* done so—but with Tom as a drag upon him it would be hopeless.

"What I'd like best," he said, "would be for us to stay on here—at any rate in the meantime—if it could be arranged with Mr. Knox."

"What has Mr. Knox to do with it?"

"Well, I told you he was going to be my tutor—after the holidays —and he could tutor us both."

"I see." Stephen's tone was unenthusiastic. "Well—what then?"

"Then—I suppose—we'd be his pupils," Tom replied. But he said it half-heartedly, for he knew himself it was not a brilliant conclusion. Nor could he add that long before the holidays were over Uncle Stephen would have returned, though this was what he believed— what he *must* believe, or else his whole world would be plunged in darkness.

"It sounds all right for you," Stephen admitted, "but it's not particularly like *my* plan. I want to go abroad; to see places."

"But you've *done* all that, Stephen," Tom reminded him. "It's over."

"So *you* say." Stephen knit his brows for a minute; then he said, "At any rate, it doesn't much matter. I think you've forgotten *one* difficulty."

"I know what you're going to say, but would you be willing to try it?"

"Oh yes; perhaps."

"Then that's all right."

"It isn't all right. You needn't imagine your guardians will agree to it. At a pinch, and to save trouble, or out of kindness, somebody might offer to help me in my original plan of going to sea; but that will be the most."

"You mustn't mention anything about going to sea."

"And after all, you can't blame them. Even if this business is true —— Look here, I'm going back to Coombe Bridge."

"Surely you've had proof enough!" Tom expostulated.

"I can't help it. I know I've had proof. At least, there's that calendar you showed me, and the portrait. Still, I can't realize it, and perhaps if I saw the old place, and that it had changed. . . . You know —if what you say is true—my father and mother must be dead," he went on in a lower voice. "Everybody must be dead. I never thought of that. It's rather—— I don't like it."

"We'll go to Coombe Bridge then," Tom promised hurriedly. "We'll go together. . . . Stephen, I'm most frightfully sorry. The whole thing is my fault. But whatever happens I'm going to look after you."

Stephen did not answer. Only he put his hand on Tom's shoulder, and between his finger and thumb pressed lightly the lobe of his ear. Tom started. He drew in his breath, for that particular caress was strangely familiar to him, it was associated in his mind only with one person, and on Stephen's part he knew it had been unconscious. "I mean," he muttered, "that I'll be quite comfortably off later on and——"

But Stephen was not listening; he was looking straight before him. "It's strange," he said, "but I've a faint, faint——" He broke off abruptly, and stood there, his hand still on Tom's shoulder. "No—it's no good. For just a minute I thought——" He awoke from his reverie. "I say, there's not much use in our hanging about up here all day. Let's go out or something."

"It must be dinner-time," said Tom. "I believe I heard the gong. We'd better go and see."

But he spoke so much more cheerfully that Stephen turned to him in surprise.

22: THE day was over—the evening too—and Tom sat alone in his own room. He had put on a dressing-gown over his pyjamas and was turning the leaves of a book Mr. Knox had lent him, glancing absent-mindedly at the pictures. The book was *The Prince and the Pauper,* and since saying good-night to Stephen he had read fifteen chapters of it, a hundred and forty-eight pages. It was now twenty-five to two.

Earlier than he had expected, for he seemed to have been reading for hours. Yet all the time something which had nothing to do with the adventures of either prince or pauper had been floating in and out of his thoughts, and the moment he closed the book this something took complete possession of them.

His face grew troubled. Presently the book slipped from his knee to the floor, and he let it lie there. . . .

What was happening in Uncle Stephen's room? Could he persuade Stephen to repeat the experiment if to-night it failed? These questions he asked himself, and though he could not answer them they led to others. Supposing the experiment *did* fail, how many days could they count on before Mrs. Deverell began to ask further questions? Not many, he thought; and if he tried to put her off a second time very likely she would go to Mr. Flood. It might be wiser for him to take that step himself: certainly it would be well to get *somebody* on their side. But who was there? Uncle Horace and his step-mother were impossible: there remained only Mr. Flood and Mr. Knox, and Tom felt that neither of these would give him the kind of help he needed. The lawyer, though friendly, was dry and matter-of-fact: probably the first thing he would do would be to communicate with Uncle Horace. Mr. Knox might be sworn to secrecy, but——

The chief difficulty, as Stephen himself had pointed out, was Stephen. Even if he resumed the name of Philip Coombe, he still would be asked to give an account of himself—to expain why he had been living at the other house and where he had come from. How could he do this! How could he give any account that would bear examination! As Philip he had no past—no home, no parents, no friends—there was nobody he could refer to, nobody who could speak for him, nobody who had even seen him except Tom, and, once, Deverell. If he said he had run away from home, he would be asked where this imaginary home was, and the first inquiry would reveal its non-existence. Mr. Knox of course knew, just as Mrs. Deverell and Sally knew, that there had been a boy staying at the other house, but that would make no difference. The questions would be asked just the same. "As if it mattered *where* he came from!" Tom sighed. Tobit had not asked his angel where he had come from, nor who were his relations. The angel had appeared and Tobit had taken his hand and they had walked by the bank of the river: and the angel had a fishing-rod and they had caught a fish. Then they had rescued a woman from her demon lover, and cured Tobit's father of his blindness. . . . He could not remember the rest of the story, but he knew everybody had been happy because nobody had asked questions. . . . The earth *might* be a kind of heaven! It wasn't really impossible. Happiness depended on kindness and understanding and—and —on not insisting that everybody should have the same feelings and thoughts. . . .

But these reflections did not throw much light on the present dilemma. *Perhaps* Uncle Stephen would be there in the morning, and in that case nobody outside the Manor need ever know he had left it. It would be sufficient to tell Mrs. Deverell that he had come back after she and Sally had gone home. Tom felt a sudden desire to visit the other room and *see* if he had come back. The impulse brought him to his feet. It held him trembling with excitement, suspense, and longing. It *might* be that Uncle Stephen was there now! He took a step forward and then stopped. He must be prepared to find only Stephen: he must not be disappointed if he found only Stephen. Nor would it follow, because Uncle Stephen had not yet returned, that he would not have returned by morning. The change might take place gradually. It was only three hours since he had left Stephen, and Stephen might have lain awake for a long time. With such warnings he fortified himself, determined not to move until he had gained complete self-command.

He lit a candle, crossed the room, and opened his door. On the threshold he stood for a minute, peering out into the darkness. His naked feet made no sound on the thick carpet. He walked along the

passage till he reached the broad central flight of stairs descending
to the shadowy hall, but here again something seemed to hold him,
and to hold him longer. Noiseless though his movements had been,
he felt they had attracted attention. Not human attention, but that
of the house. It *knew* he was there—knew what he was doing, just
as each evening it knew of the departure of Mrs. Deverell and Sally.
His unwonted activity at an hour when he should have been in bed
and asleep had disturbed it; it knew someone was abroad, that something unusual was happening, and there had been a moment perhaps
when the nature of its response had hung in the balance. Then, as he
had crept on from one to the other of its outspread wings, there had
been a soft sigh of recognition. For it was Uncle Stephen's house,
and it regarded him just as Uncle Stephen's watchdog would have
regarded him—as belonging to Uncle Stephen, as belonging to itself.

He had never been afraid of it. Even now, the necromantic beauty
of its shadowy stair and glimmering window held him only because
it seemed to breathe of Uncle Stephen's presence. The house protected him; it would allow no evil thing to harm him. He entered
the passage which led to Uncle Stephen's room. He reached Uncle
Stephen's door and gently turned the handle. Not hurriedly, but
without hesitation, and holding his candle before him and above the
level of his eyes, he approached the bed.

He stood there for a moment with held breath. He had made no
sound either in opening or closing the door; the sleeper had not
stirred; but the sleeper was Stephen. One arm lay outside the linen
counterpane: Stephen's face was flushed, his breathing low and sweet.
As Tom stood gazing down at him his heart melted. What dreams
were passing through that mind? Probably none: he was sleeping too
soundly to be dreaming: but he looked so young and guileless!

Tom turned away, and the light of his candle floated over the
watching Hermes. He approached nearer till it reached the slightly
bowed head. He took off his dressing-gown and knelt down before the pedestal, placing his candle on the floor beside him. . . .

He remembered the night of his arrival at the Manor. The memory
brought with it a longing that he might again be blessed. Or perhaps
memory itself had been quickened by that longing, which grew
and grew, while with shut eyes he waited. A spirit was near him—
whether the spirit of Uncle Stephen or the spirit of the God, he did
not know. But the response he yearned for washed over him in wave

after wave, brimming the room, holding him closely clasped and breathing into his breath. . . .

He remembered Uncle Stephen's words—that in approaching the God in a spirit of love and worship he became a priest. He remembered that in ancient Greece there had been boy priests. He remembered the beautiful opening of Euripides' play, where, after the speech of Hermes, the young boy Ion decorates the porch of Apollo's temple with laurel branches, drops the lustral water on the ground, and chases the birds away. The scene was infinitely lovely as it floated before him now. It was as if the sunlight of that morning long ago had been caught and imprisoned in the words, to burst out with renewed glory when their spell was whispered. And all this loveliness was eternal. It could never fade until the earth grew cold and dead, or some cloud descended on the world, darkening men's minds until nobody was left who sought for and loved it. . . .

His troubles dropped from him. He believed that the God had welcomed him, and was his lover, his friend. This was Hermes the shepherd, Hermes who, Uncle Stephen had said, guarded young boys, and would guard him. His eyes half shut, and on his face was a strange dreamy expression, gentle and happy. Nobody had ever seen him quite like this, and nobody ever would, for he was more than half out of his body, on the confines of another world. The whole house, he now knew, was the spiritual creation of Uncle Stephen and this God; and here, in this room, he was in its very heart, which was beating in tune with his own.

When he rose at last, his knees were stiff and sore and for a moment he staggered, but it was as if his mind had been bathed in some fresh mountain stream, and he knew that he could sleep. Putting the candle on the table by the bed, he looked down again at the slumbering Stephen. To Tom the whole room was still humming and vibrating with a secret life. This impression was so vivid, indeed, as to produce in him the strange feeling that merely by stretching out his hands he could make the surrounding air break into a flame. But Stephen slept on. Nothing that had taken place had disturbed him. It had passed over him and round him, leaving him untouched, as the fire had played harmlessly over the wise men in their burning fiery furnace. And gradually for Tom too its waves began to subside. His mind grew quiet, and he became all at once aware that his God was pouring sleep upon him—softly, ceaselessly, compellingly. Tom's eyes slid round to him, liquid and dark. The pale, honey-coloured marble was still warm and breathing, but the spirit was only lingering there till Tom himself should be safely tucked in and his eyes sealed. "Sleep —sleep," a faint voice whispered. "Sleep——"

Tom smiled drowsily. He must go back to his own room; but somehow his own room seemed miles and miles away, and to leave his present sanctuary would be like going out into a cold, wet, winter's night.

There was no longer anything but silence. The whisper had died away, but its command was overwhelming. Tom's chin sank forward on his breast. He blinked and opened his eyes: he was dropping asleep on his feet. Stephen had pushed aside one of the pillows, which had fallen to the floor. Tom replaced it: then crept under the clothes and blew out the candle.

23: THE miracle had not happened: Tom seemed to know that even in his dreams, for he heaved a deep sigh before his eyes opened. Instinctively he clung to the sleepiness that prevented complete realization. He put his arms round Stephen's neck and wriggled himself closer till their heads lay on one pillow. He hoped it was very early, and that they need not get up for a long time. He did not want to awake; the day before him, he knew, was going to be full of trouble; he put his other arm round Stephen and buried his nose in the short crisp hair above his ear. He listened to twittering bird notes, he felt rather than saw the drowsy sunlight floating through the open window.

But Stephen would not let him stay like this. Tom might snuggle up against him and murmur that he wanted to go to sleep again, but Stephen was wide awake. He proposed getting up and going for a swim. "I had the rummiest dream," he declared. "At least, it seems so now." He gave Tom a little shake. "Are you listening? Wake up!"

"I'm not asleep," said Tom. But a warm delightful languor was diffused through his body, and he nestled closer.

"You're next door to it. Remember, I don't intend to tell you this twice. . . . You'll be sorry, too, because it's very much in your line: in fact you were in it. . . . All right, I'll not tell you. And please don't breathe into my ear."

Tom slightly altered his position. "Is that better?" he asked.

"Not very much, and I don't see why you aren't in your own bed. You certainly weren't here when I went to sleep last night. . . . It was about your uncle—my dream. I dreamt I was in the room downstairs—the room with all the books—and you were there too."

"Yes?" Tom still kept his eyes tight shut.

"Don't you see?" said Stephen, giving him another shake. "Don't you see how queer it was? Of course it must have been the result of what you told me yesterday, but it was queer all the same."

"Why?" Tom whispered. "I don't see anything queer about it."

"Well, it was: you'll understand why presently. Do lie over a bit: I'm far too hot: besides, you're choking me."

Tom moved grudgingly. "You might be more comfortable," he mumbled. But Stephen had spoiled his own drowsy sensations, and he lay on his back blinking up at the ceiling. "What happened?" he asked.

Stephen stretched out his arms and sat up. He looked down at Tom. "Nothing happened. I was just there: it's not that that was queer."

"Was I in the room?"

"Yes; I've said so already: I knew you weren't listening."

"What was I doing?"

"You were sitting on the hearthrug untangling a heap of string and winding it round a stick."

"I did do that once."

"Very likely. Most people have wound a ball of string."

"What was queer then?" said Tom, with a shade of impatience. "Was Uncle Stephen there?"

"I'm coming to that. . . . Uncle Stephen was there in one sense." He paused deliberately, but Tom would ask no further questions. "He was there in the sense that you called *me* Uncle Stephen. . . . But what really was queer was the way I thought of you."

"Thought of me?"

"Yes. Though I don't mean 'thought' exactly. It was really the way I *felt* about you. I was frightfully fond of you. I didn't know anybody *could* care for another person so much."

To this Tom made no answer, and Stephen after a moment went on. "You see, I've always liked you quite well; but this was a good deal more. In fact, it strikes me now as rather absurd."

"Yes, it would," said Tom.

"Well, hang it all, you're not an angel! You're a pretty averagely bad boy—with faint streaks of a better nature."

Tom buried his face in the pillow. "Is that all?" he asked in a muffled voice.

"Yes, I think so." Stephen kicked aside the clothes and swung his legs over the edge of the bed. He took off his pyjamas—Uncle Stephen's they were—and proceeded to test the muscles of his arms. Tom, peeping out at him, watched this latter performance moodily. Somehow it had the effect of making the return of Uncle Stephen seem infinitely improbable, though last night it had seemed imminent. But nothing could be more remote from Uncle Stephen than this boy light-heartedly parading his nakedness and rejoicing in the strength of his body.

Stephen stood beside the bed, looking down at him and smiling. "Well?" he said.

"Well what?" muttered Tom. "Aren't you going to put some clothes on?"

Stephen smiled more broadly. "Not at present. Aren't you going to get up?"

Tom slowly assumed a sitting posture, and still more slowly put his feet to the ground. Stephen bent down and, half lifting him, pulled him out into the middle of the floor. "Look here," he said, "don't be so frightfully dumpy about it."

"I can't help it," Tom muttered. The pleasanter Stephen was to him, the more difficult everything became. He half wished he would be *un*pleasant—or at any rate that he didn't look so nice. He wouldn't look at him. He put his hand against Stephen's breast and pushed him back almost roughly. "I'm going to my own room. *Your* bathroom is the first door on the left."

"Come and take your bath with me."

"No. . . . Leave me *alone*, Stephen! You're a bully—that's what you are."

"Well, I like that! When a minute ago you were hugging me."

"Yes, and you wouldn't let me." He struggled free, and picking up his dressing-gown, ran along the passage back to his own room.

He got into his bath and let the water run over him. But he did not enjoy it, his mind was too full of worries and perplexities. A few days ago he would have loved having Stephen here! And now, though Stephen was far more friends with him than he had ever been before, he was getting no good out of him, it was all wasted, because he couldn't be happy. While he was drying himself and dressing he tried to review the situation dispassionately. How *could* it go on as it was? Mrs. Deverell would think it strange that there was no letter for him this morning from Uncle Stephen. Perhaps she would expect one herself. And it would be only natural for Uncle Stephen to write her a note to explain matters and give instructions about what was to be done in his absence. Tom wondered if the news of his absence had already leaked out. With Mrs. Deverell, Sally, George, and Robert all knowing about it, it could not be long before it became public property. It was not as if such a thing had ever happened before. It would be regarded as an event, a mystery: Mrs. Deverell seemed to have taken that view from the first. It would be discussed; there would be all kinds of gossip; soon it would reach the ears of Mr. Flood and Mr. Knox, and Mr. Knox very likely would think it his duty to call—not out of curiosity, but just out of friendliness. On the top of this there was the money problem. Tom knew nothing of how the house was run—whether Mrs. Deverell received an allowance for household expenses, or whether Uncle Stephen paid for things himself by cheque. He supposed the bills could be allowed to run on, but he knew George and Robert were paid weekly, for he had seen Uncle Stephen paying them. What was he to do about that? They would need their wages for their own expenses, and it wouldn't be fair to keep them waiting. He would have to borrow from somebody—and the only person he could think of was Mr. Flood. Poor Tom, as he completed his toilet and surveyed himself in the mirror of his wardrobe, looked as if all the cares of the world were on his shoulders.

He went downstairs to breakfast, and instead of sympathy found Mrs. Deverell regarding him with a grim reserve, and Stephen with amusement. True, the amusement was mingled with liking—Stephen had distinctly altered in this respect—but that didn't make it more helpful so far as their problem was concerned. Tom wished Mrs. Deverell a subdued good morning and took Uncle Stephen's place at the head of the table. He began to fumble with the tea-pot, which Mrs. Deverell at once removed from his hands.

"No letter from your uncle?" Stephen inquired pleasantly.

Tom blushed and gave him an angry look, but he was obliged to answer, because Mrs. Deverell was listening. Why couldn't she clear out? "The post isn't in yet," he muttered. "Anyway, I don't expect a letter for a day or two."

He wondered if he could forge a letter. It might help to keep Mrs. Deverell quiet, and he had gone so far that it did not seem to matter much if he added forgery to his other crimes. When the meal was over he and Stephen went on to the lawn. On an ordinary occasion Tom would have been full of suggestions for passing the morning. There was still his raft to be built, there was still the river to be explored. But now he felt too restless to settle down to anything, and at the same time was conscious of a reluctance to go far from the house, though nothing was to be gained by loitering there, and he knew it would be better if he could distract his mind from brooding.

"Did you remember to make your bed, Stephen?" he suddenly asked.

"No. Why? I didn't know I was supposed to make it."

Tom sighed. "It's only that Mrs. Deverell may think it queer that you slept in Uncle Stephen's room."

"Shall I go back and make it now?"

"No, it doesn't matter: she's sure to have discovered it by now. Anyway, I forgot to *un*make mine, so she'll know where we both were."

"Then you didn't go to bed last night after you left me?"

"No."

"What were you doing?"

"I sat up reading till I came to your room."

Stephen laughed. "It seems to me we're pretty poor conspirators."

"It's hard to remember everything," said Tom. "She can think what she likes," he added gloomily. "I don't care."

"Of course not. Anybody can see you don't care."

"Well, I can't help it," muttered Tom. He sat down on a garden bench and stared morosely at a thrush trying to swallow an uncomfortably large worm. But he felt Stephen was right and that he was not showing a proper spirit. It wasn't as if he didn't *know* Uncle Stephen was coming back. There had been more than one sign to encourage him. There had been his vigil of last night. There had been those few minutes yesterday when Stephen had seemed just on the point of recalling everything. He hadn't succeeded; the result had been only two or three unintelligible words; but still—especially when taken with the dream he had told Tom that morning—there had been enough to prove he was not *completely* Stephen. A final state of equilibrium had not been reached; *some* kind of spiritual ebb and flow must be going on under the surface. Of course, it might be that Uncle Stephen was losing, not gaining, power in this conflict, but Tom would not believe that. The chief impediment, he felt, was that the boy who had dropped down now on to the green bench beside him and was gazing idly into the distance, did not *want* to be anything but what he was. He wasn't trying. He was just enjoying himself, and enjoying teasing Tom, and from all Uncle Stephen had told him Tom knew that on those other occasions the will and the desire had been primary agents.

Stephen had become very quiet all of a sudden! And it was not like him to sit like this. Through the cool, bright sunshine there came the sound of Robert whistling a hymn tune. Robert himself remained invisible: he invariably did. He seemed to live and conduct all his labours in thickets and behind bushes: he was the shyest person Tom had ever met. Tom stole a cautious glance at Stephen; but he did not want to disturb him, and remained quiet as a mouse. Robert's tune also had ceased. Tom turned ever so little so that he could watch Stephen's face. What was it that made the chief attraction of a human face? Was it the line or the colour or the expression? Why should the dirt on Stephen's hands, where unconsciously he had been rubbing them against the iron bench, be pleasant? Dirty hands weren't as a rule pleasant. The remarkable reflection occurred to Tom that Stephen would still be attractive—to him at any rate—if he were dirty all over. That was strange, though he remembered he had always found young chimney-sweeps attractive: their dirty faces made their eyes so extraordinarily bright. But this was the kind of thought he had to keep to himself. There were a good many thoughts he had learned to keep to himself. Not that he would have minded telling them to Uncle Stephen. Uncle Stephen was the only person with whom he had ever felt there was no need to conceal anything. He was, too, the only person who had ever loved him as he really was. His mother had loved him, of course, and Deverell too had loved him, but they had only loved part of him, because they had only known part of him. Uncle Stephen knew all—good, bad, and indifferent.

A hideous screech from a motor-horn interrupted Tom's cogitations. Surely it couldn't be a visitor to the Manor! The only possible visitor was Mr. Knox, and *he* rode a bicycle. There was no doubt of it, however; a car had entered the avenue, and Tom in alarm gazed fixedly at the point where it would come into view.

There was another hoot. It was not Mr. Flood's car; it was a big car; and next moment it swept round the corner and sped on to the house. Tom uttered a faint, protesting exclamation. But really it was sickening! For there, in the driver's seat, spick and span in dark-blue uniform, sat the dour and saturnine Shanks. Simultaneously he felt Stephen's body tauten, and turning, saw that his face had lost its absent-mindedness and become intensely alert.

"Don't," he murmured, not quite knowing what he meant, only that he was sure Stephen had become filled with a zest for action and would do or say something irremediable.

"Don't what?" Stephen answered.

"Don't do anything," Tom completed feebly.

At the same time he held out a restraining hand. "It's Uncle Horace and Mr. Knox," he said. "But they haven't seen us."

Stephen had half risen. He shook off Tom's hand: his face was alive with curiosity and excitement. "What's that thing they're in? I never saw anything like it. How does it work? I'm going to have a look at it."

"No, no," Tom implored him. "It's only a motor-car. You'll see plenty of them. *Please*, Stephen, stay where you are."

Stephen submitted, but not without a visible struggle, and meanwhile the car drew up and the two visitors got out. They went straight into the porch.

"What are we going to do?" whispered Tom. "I never dreamt of Uncle Horace coming. He can't possibly have heard——"

"Don't worry; it will be all right."

But how was it going to be all right? Tom couldn't imagine anything more all wrong! "You don't know Uncle Horace!" he said, casting a covetous glance at the shrubbery. "He's far cleverer than either Mr. Flood or Mr. Knox. He'll find out the whole thing in two ticks."

"He won't. You leave it to me. Just tell them what you told Mrs. Deverell."

Stephen spoke confidently, even with a mysterious elation, which inspired in Tom the utmost misgiving. But he had no time to inquire into its source, for Uncle Horace and Mr. Knox had already ended their colloquy with Mrs. Deverell and were now bearing down upon them. The curate waved his hand, and Tom had sufficient presence of mind to wave in return, but he felt a weakness in his stomach as he rose to his feet.

Stephen gave him a shove. "Don't stand there staring at them as if you were stuffed! Go and meet them. What are you in such a pet about?"

But Tom still hesitated.

"I tell you it will be all right," Stephen went on impatiently. "That is, if you don't give the whole show away at the very start."

"I won't," Tom promised, but he felt he would, or at least that it was extremely likely. He followed Stephen's injunctions, however, and advanced to meet his visitors.

Mr. Knox greeted him with extreme friendliness. So, for that matter, did Uncle Horace, who radiated geniality in an astonishing manner. "Good morning, Tom. I suppose you're surprised to see me. But I ran down this time to pay Mr. Knox a visit."

"I'm very glad to see you, Uncle Horace," Tom replied faintly.

"Yes—yes. We've had our little quarrels, but I don't think we're enemies yet. Our last meeting was unfortunate, but I dare say there were faults on both sides."

"There were faults on my side at any rate," said Tom.

"Odious little prig!" he thought immediately afterwards, but Uncle Horace positively beamed. "Your step-mother sent her love to you. I told her I didn't think I'd be seeing you—but there it is. Jane sent hers also: she wanted me to bring her."

"I hope they are very well," said Tom.

"Very well, thank you: very well indeed."

A sudden pause followed this exchange of amenities, and for a moment nephew and uncle regarded each other a trifle self-consciously.

"Did you drive down this morning, Uncle Horace?" Tom inquired, still in the same flute-like tones. "You must have made a very early start."

"No, no: arrived yesterday. But we had a breakdown a few miles out of Kilbarron and were late. So, as Shanks seemed doubtful about the return journey, and the hotel looked passable, I decided to put up there for the night. Shanks wanted to overhaul the car, and that gave him plenty of time."

"Uncle Stephen isn't here," said Tom, lowering his eyes. "I suppose Mrs. Deverell told you."

"Yes. She told us he mightn't be back for a day or two."

"At least," Tom amended.

But Uncle Horace's attention had veered towards the unknown

boy hovering in the background, and Tom performed an introduction. "This is Stephen—Philip, I mean," he said nervously.

"Philip Stephen," Uncle Horace repeated, holding out his hand.

The mistake was instantly corrected by Stephen himself. "No, sir; Stephen Collet. Philip's only a kind of nickname."

Tom drew a quick breath. Luckily nobody was looking at him, for he knew his face had betrayed the shock Stephen's unexpected avowal had given him. "He's my friend," he stammered. "He's staying with me. Mr. Knox knows about him."

The moment he had made this speech he realized that it too was wrong—sounded as if he were apologizing for Stephen, vouching for him. Mr. Knox noticed his embarrassment and came to the rescue. "You're the boy who has been living in the other house?" he said, shaking hands with Stephen in his turn. "Tom hold me about you, but I don't think he mentioned your name. It's an odd coincidence, for I suppose really you are no relation of Mr. Collet's. I remember he told me Tom was his only nephew."

"So he is," Uncle Horace chimed in.

"My father was a relation," Stephen answered quietly.

Uncle Horace looked at him, but made no reply. Mr. Knox's scrutiny was more prolonged and ruminative. "Forgive me for staring, Stephen," he apologized, "but——" He turned to Uncle Horace. "Don't you see a likeness?"

"A likeness?" Uncle Horace hesitated. "A likeness to Mr. Collet, do you mean? Well, I have only met him once, you know." He paused again. "Still—now you mention it—— Yes, perhaps——"

"To me it is striking," said Mr. Knox. "As a matter of fact, I was trying to think of whom he reminded me even before I heard his name. The very unusual colour of the eyes—so dark a blue. And the shape of the forehead——"

"Won't you come in, Uncle Horace?" Tom suggested desperately, but Uncle Horace brushed the interruption aside with a gesture. "Your father, you say, is a relative of Mr. Collet's?" he questioned, his eyes fixed on Stephen's face.

"Yes sir. He *was* a relative; but both he and my mother are dead. My father was Mr. Collet's son."

"His son!"

Tom drew back. Stephen had deliberately done this, and it left him helpless. It was the plan, he supposed, he had concocted a few minutes ago—the plan which was to set everything right! Well, if assurance could do it, the assurance was there. Stephen's gaze was serene and steadfast, his face unclouded. Tom waited in a kind of angry suspense for what would come next, but to his astonishment it came in Uncle Horace's suavest tones. "I always understood Mr. Collet had never married."

"No, sir. My father was his natural son."

Tom choked back the protest that rose to his lips. How could he protest, even though he believed Stephen had invented this story wantonly—because he enjoyed it?

Uncle Horace had turned away. His gaze rested with unusual dreaminess on the quiet sunlit park. Mr. Knox, too, looked only puzzled. Tom's head drooped.

He followed the others slowly, for they had begun to walk back towards the bench he and Stephen had vacated. They reached it, and Uncle Horace and Mr. Knox sat down, before another word was spoken. Even then, Uncle Horace's first remark was more like a continuation of his private thoughts than a question. "Both your parents are dead, you say?"

Tom had squatted down on the grass: Stephen remained standing and facing Uncle Horace, a picture of candid and artless boyhood. "My father died when I was two years old," he explained. "I don't remember him. My mother was drowned only a few months ago—in a boating accident—near Sorrento."

"Very sad—very sad," Uncle Horace mused. "You had been living abroad, then—till you came here?"

"Yes, sir, in Italy. I think it was because it was cheaper there than anywhere else. We weren't very well off, you see, and we never stayed long in one place—I don't know why."

"But you went to school, I suppose?"

"Only for a few months—once—in Rome. My mother taught me. She had been a teacher before she married. She was English."

Mr. Knox, who so far had been as dumb as Tom himself, now made a remark. "I could have sworn you were the product of an English public school," he said.

Tom was startled: he even glanced reproachfully at the curate. It was fortunate that Uncle Horace disliked interruptions. Therefore, instead of encouraging Mr. Knox, he pursued his own inquiry. "Then you've lived all your life abroad, have you?"

"Yes, sir."

"And you came over here at Mr. Collet's invitation?"

Stephen hesitated. "No-o," he replied, drawing out the word reluctantly. "But—he was the only person I *could* go to. I mean—there wasn't anybody else."

"I see. . . . You knew his address, of course?"

There was a slight pause, and Tom waited anxiously. Uncle Horace *was* asking a terrific number of questions—even for him! Tom had never known him so bad before. But he supposed it was because Uncle Stephen was mixed up in the matter, and Stephen himself did not appear to mind.

"No, sir," he said. "I had to find it out after I came over. I mean, I didn't know the exact address: I couldn't write to him—or at least I didn't think I could. I came because I had to do *something*. . . . My mother used occasionally to get work from newspapers—translating English stories into Italian. And now and then she had a pupil for Italian conversation; but even with that we only just managed to scrape along, and I wasn't earning anything. She wouldn't allow me to take the only kind of job I might have got—as a message-boy, or in a shop."

Uncle Horace nodded: he seemed pleased with Stephen. On the other hand, though he hoped he was mistaken, Tom was almost sure that Mr. Knox was *not* pleased. He was looking at Stephen, and there was in his eyes just a shade of—no, not incredulity, incredulity was too strong a word to describe the vague dissatisfaction lurking in the curate's expression. It was as if there were something in what he had been listening to that he did not quite like, that slightly jarred upon him. Tom saw him on the point of making a remark, and then repressing it, and then finally yielding to the temptation to bring it out. "You weren't living at the Manor, were you?" Mr. Knox asked.

Stephen turned quickly, and for the first time appeared to scent an antagonist. His eyes momentarily sought Tom's, who had been watching the whole scene motionless as an image, the tip of his tongue slightly protruding between his lips. "He was living at the other house." Tom broke in quickly. "I told you that."

"Yes, I remember your telling me. Camping out, I suppose. It can't have been very comfortable."

Tom's face darkened. "We only used one room," he replied. "An upstairs room. It was quite comfortable."

The pronoun was not lost on Mr. Knox. He regarded Tom rather sadly. "*You* didn't stay there, did you?"

"Have you heard from your uncle yet?" Uncle Horace interrupted

with a hint of impatience. "Has he told you when he is coming back?"

Mr. Knox immediately withdrew from the discussion, and Tom
answered, "No."

"Where is he?"

"I—— He didn't tell me."

"But I thought you saw him off? The housekeeper said you did."

"Yes, I drove part of the way with him. You see, it was quite unexpected. This man called for him."

"What man?"

"A very nice man."

Uncle Horace looked at Tom and the look was entirely in his old
manner. Tom blushed. It was more, however, from indignation than
embarrassment. Here had Uncle Horace been swallowing all Stephen's outrageous story without a protest; yet the very first thing *he*
said aroused suspicion.

"Don't you even know his name?" Uncle Horace persisted.
"Weren't you introduced to him?"

"Yes." Tom had a sudden happy thought. "His name was Spinelli,"
he declared confidently. "Uncle Stephen knew him long ago in Italy.
They were, I think, partners."

"Partners?"

"I mean they worked together. I've forgotten the word."

"Accomplices?" suggested Uncle Horace grimly.

"Collaborators." But next moment Tom laughed.

"What are you laughing at?" Uncle Horace snapped.

"Well, it *was* rather funny," Tom apologized.

"What was funny?"

"Your joke—the way you said it. . . . You know you do say
things like that, Uncle Horace, and you must know they're funny,
even though you may be cross when you say them."

Uncle Horace gave him another look, but not really an angry one,
and Mr. Knox took out his watch, "I think I must be going," he
remarked.

"Why?" Tom asked. "It's very nearly dinner-time, and Uncle
Horace will be having dinner with us. Do stay."

Mr. Knox wavered, glancing at Uncle Horace, who immediately
said, "I shan't be staying either."

"But you must," cried Tom. "I know what you're thinking, but
you must, all the same."

Uncle Horace flushed, and Mr. Knox involuntarily asked, "What was he thinking?"

Tom did not answer. His eyes were still fixed on Uncle Horace. "Uncle Stephen would want you to stay. He'll not be pleased with *me* if you don't."

"All right—all right," returned Uncle Horace hastily. Then, after a moment, he added, "Come with me for a little stroll, Tom, I want to have a word with you. And at any rate if you're to be my host you ought to show me over the grounds."

Tom got up at once, though it was not without a feeling of anxiety that he left the others behind. Something in Mr. Knox's manner made him uneasy. It suggested either that he had taken a dislike to Stephen or else was not satisfied with his story. But he would hardly continue to question him when they were alone, for he was the last person in the world to try to drive anybody into a corner. Tom had a high opinion of Mr. Knox. He did not think he was clever, but he knew he was a gentleman. That was the difference between him and Uncle Horace. Uncle Horace *was* clever, but he wasn't—— Well, not quite in the sense that Mr. Knox was, anyway.

Meanwhile, Uncle Horace, fortunately all unconscious of these reflections, was stepping delicately over the lawn in highly polished shoes. Tom wondered if his shoes were ever *not* highly polished, if he ever did *not* look as if he were dressed for an afternoon party. "How many suits have you, Uncle Horace?" he asked innocently.

"Suits—suits—what do you mean by suits!"

Tom took Uncle Horace's arm, for somehow he felt he had been stupid about him, and that his bark was worse than his bite. "Nothing," he answered. "But you must have a lot. I mean your trousers never have baggy knees and your waistcoats never go into wrinkles and——"

"I try to keep myself decent, if that's what you're getting at," Uncle Horace replied grumpily.

"Yes, but other people try. I try myself. This suit was new about a fortnight ago, and look at it now."

Uncle Horace looked. "You ought to keep your trousers in a press," he said shortly. "I expect you don't even bother to fold them. . . . But it's not that I want to talk to you about, and you know it."

"I'm quite willing to talk about anything, Uncle Horace; only I'd rather talk about something that—that won't make us angry."

Uncle Horace glared at this peculiar nephew, who was clinging to his arm (in itself a novel experience) and whose odd, freckled face was turned up to him with bright, singularly pleasant eyes. "You know, you're either a most accomplished young Jesuit or else——"

The alternative he left unspoken. "I *do* want to please you," Tom said.

"Well, if that is all, you know how."

"You mean by going back to Gloucester Terrace? Suppose, Uncle Horace, I had come to you, and you had got very fond of me. . . . That might have happened, mightn't it?"

"Um," said Uncle Horace.

"But mightn't it?"

"You're very persistent; how am I to say what might have happened?"

"But you don't dislike me?"

"Well, well—suppose it *had* happened?"

"If it *had* happened, and you had done everything you could for me, wouldn't you think I was rather a—a squirt, if I gave you up just because some other people didn't like you?"

"A squirt!"

"Yes. You must know very well what a squirt is, even if you've never heard the expression before."

"I haven't. I understand it to mean somebody who is ungrateful?"

Tom laughed. "Yes, and a whole lot more. Why won't you let me talk to you naturally, Uncle Horace? That's what I mean by being friends."

"You can talk as naturally as you like, but you know my views on the subject you've raised, and nothing will be gained by repeating them."

"I don't want you to repeat them."

"I came down, as I told you, to have a talk with Mr. Knox, and we had that last night."

"Mr. Knox likes Uncle Stephen, I think."

"So it would appear. He also—— Well, what he said inclined me perhaps to alter my judgement a little."

"Uncle Horace, if I tell you something, will you believe me, will you help me, will you be my friend?"

But Uncle Horace was not to be rushed into making rash promises. "It depends on what the something is," he replied.

"You know what it is."

"Then why do you want to tell me?"

Tom looked up at him gravely. "Because I don't think you—understand it. You think I just want to stay here because I like it better than Gloucester Terrace, but it isn't that: at least, it's much more than that."

"What is it then?"

"It's very hard for me to explain—unless—unless you try to understand." Tom's head drooped, and his voice became husky and uncertain. "I—I love Uncle Stephen. . . . I couldn't bear to be taken away from him. . . . You won't try to do that, will you?"

Uncle Horace walked on without replying. Tom's arm was pressing upon his, but he gave no sign of being aware of it. Neither did he repulse it. Presently he said, "Why are you talking like this now? On my last visit you took a very different tone. Why have you changed? There must be some reason."

"I suppose it's because I haven't Uncle Stephen with me now," Tom said simply.

"That seems a poor reason."

"And it's partly because *you've* been different," Tom added.

Uncle Horace frowned, though not at his nephew. He was looking straight before him at the landscape. "I think the chief trouble is that you're a great deal too emotional," he brought out deliberately, but not unkindly. "All along, that really has been my chief reason for wishing to see you back at Gloucester Terrace."

"But suppose it was you I was fond of, Uncle Horace; you wouldn't think I was too emotional then."

"That's where you make a mistake. I *should* think you were too emotional. A great deal too emotional. Why can't you be like other boys?"

"Like Eric and Leonard?" said Tom doubtfully.

Uncle Horace hesitated. "Well——" He glanced at Tom and left his remark unfinished. He found another. "There's not the least danger of your ever becoming like Eric and Leonard."

"But you'd rather I was," Tom said in discouragement. "I know what you mean. I know I'm—— You see, they're so different in *every* way. At any rate you *have* them, they're your real nephews."

"Yes," said Uncle Horace dryly. "I don't want you to be like Eric and Leonard. I don't want you to be like anybody but yourself. The only thing I do wish is that you were a little more—normal."

"But——"

"There are no 'buts' about it," said Uncle Horace firmly. "It isn't so much of the present as of the future I'm thinking. You won't be a boy always, and you won't always have your Uncle Stephen to depend on. He ought to see that for himself, instead of encouraging you."

"He doesn't encourage me," said Tom. "Once or twice he spoke to me very much in the way you're speaking now."

"Umph," said Uncle Horace.

"But he did! I don't know why you're so against him! *Will* you help me, Uncle Horace? I know I've sometimes been cheeky to you, and——"

"That has nothing to do with it," Uncle Horace interrupted testily. "One would imagine you thought I took a kind of spiteful pleasure in trying to come between you and Mr. Collet!"

"I never thought of that," Tom replied, "but I do think you don't like him."

"Perhaps I don't. One can't like everybody. At any rate, now there is this fresh complication."

Tom for a moment did not understand. "What complication?" he asked.

"This other boy—this Stephen." Uncle Horace halted. "I think we'd better turn back."

"But Stephen has been here all the time," said Tom. "Ever since I was here."

"In that case I don't see why Mr. Collet wants you. Isn't his grandson enough for him? Doesn't he care for him?"

"Of course he cares for him. . . . Only, they haven't very much in common. Anyway, Stephen is only here on a visit: he isn't going to stay: he doesn't want to stay."

"Why doesn't he want to stay? It looks to me as if his grandfather took little or no interest in him. Otherwise he would hardly let him go about dressed as he is."

"That's his own fault," said Tom quickly.

"Where is he going to when he leaves the Manor? Has he said what he wants to do?"

"Well, of course, he won't be leaving for some time—I don't know how long exactly. But I can tell you one thing he wants to do. He wants to go to Coombe Bridge."

"Why?"

"I suppose because his people came from there. I mean the Collets
—they belonged to Coombe Bridge."

"He only wants to see the place, then?"

"Yes."

"Well, is there any objection to his going? Does Mr. Collet
object?"

"No. We were thinking of going while he was away. We were
talking about it this morning."

"You can't get to Coombe Bridge from here," said Uncle Horace.
"At least, not by train. I don't know anything about buses, but by
rail it would be a most roundabout journey."

"Where *could* we get a train?" Tom asked. "Isn't there a junction
where we could change?"

"There's no junction that would be of any use. Coombe Bridge
isn't on this line at all—nowhere near it. You'd have to go back
to town."

Tom thought for a moment. "Will you be going back to-day,
Uncle Horace?"

"Yes, after lunch." But the words dropped rather dryly, as if he
understood what the next question would be.

"Could you take us with you?"

Uncle Horace did not reply, and Tom did not repeat his request.
Neither did he relinquish Uncle Horace's arm nor look offended. It
seemed to him, after all that had taken place, that Uncle Horace had
every right to refuse.

"In the car, do you mean?" Uncle Horace said at last. "I thought
you wouldn't trust yourself with me!"

"*Will* you take us then? I know I oughtn't to ask you."

"It will mean staying the night at Gloucester Terrace," Uncle
Horace warned him. "Even if we start immediately after lunch we
shan't be home much before six."

"I know. Do you think they'd mind putting us up for a night?
Couldn't we go to an hotel?"

"Two nights," said Uncle Horace ignoring the hotel. "You'll have
to break your journey on the way home too."

"Well, for two nights."

"How do you know we won't keep you when we get you?"

Tom looked down. "I think I've been rather stupid about that,"
he said.

"You weren't so stupid. If I'd got you before I *would* have kept you."

"Why have you changed?" Tom asked.

"I don't know. Probably because *I'm* stupid."

"You're not. You're being most frightfully decent about everything, and I won't forget it."

"Well—I wonder where the others have got to. Knox will be thinking he oughtn't to have stayed."

"But wasn't there something you wanted to say to me?"

"I've said it. Or at any rate part of it, and we'll let it go at that."

"Thank's awfully, Uncle Horace. . . . I mean for giving us a seat in the car."

"Yes, I know what you mean. And for the other too, I dare say. I'll get Shanks to send a wire to your step-mother while we're at lunch. One person, at all events, will be on the doorstep to welcome you."

"Who? Jane?"

"Yes; Jane."

Uncle Horace consulted his watch.

"Will you say anything about Stephen in the telegram?" Tom asked as they drew near the house.

"Stephen? No. I can't go into explanations about Stephen by telegram. Besides, it's not necessary; there's only your own room available and he'll have to share it with you."

"I know. But—I don't like going back like this. It seems pretty rotten—just as if we were making use of them. I think we ought to go to an hotel."

"Nonsense," said Uncle Horace. "If there's any difficulty you can stay with me."

24: ON the way home Uncle Horace himself drove: Shanks sat beside him, and Tom and Stephen behind. The rain which had begun to fall before they left the Manor had now increased to a steady downpour; the car swished over the wet road between dripping hedges; but there was little traffic; Uncle Horace must be doing nearly fifty. . . .

Shortly before starting there had occurred a slight awkwardness.

It had been due to Mr. Knox. Just when everything was going well Mr. Knox suggested that Stephen had better change his clothes and put on a collar. *Some* kind of action had been necessary, and the two boys had left the room. "Silly ass, what business is it of his!" Stephen spluttered angrily while struggling into one of Tom's shirts, the sleeves of which were a great deal too short and the neckband too narrow. Uncle Stephen's socks fitted him, but these, and Tom's shirt, exhausted their available resources. Therefore, when they came downstairs again, Stephen's appearance was very little altered. It next transpired that he had not even an overcoat, but luckily Uncle Horace by this time was impatient to set off.

So they had started—more than an hour ago—dropping Mr. Knox at his lodgings—and from the beginning Stephen had been far too much interested in the car to bother about his clothes or anything else. This interest increased as the journey proceeded. He watched every movement of Uncle Horace and asked Tom innumerable questions. His conversation, indeed, had taken the tone of Eric's and Leonard's, lacking only the deadliness of their expert knowledge, so that the smaller boy had begun to look bored and cross.

Suddenly Stephen nudged him in the ribs, a habit Tom particularly disliked. "I wonder if he'd let me drive?"

"How can you drive when you've never learned?"

"All the same I think I'll ask him." And Stephen actually leaned forward to tap on the screen.

Tom immediately pulled him back. "Don't be stupid! As if anybody's going to begin to teach you now! You might have more sense!"

"Have *you* learned? I mean, why haven't you?"

Tom did not reply, and Stephen pursued obstinately: "It looks quite easy. If he'd been *my* uncle I bet I'd have got him to teach me."

"Would you! He won't even allow Eric to touch it."

"Selfish old beast!"

"He's not," said Tom, loyal to his recent alliance with Uncle Horace. "At any rate, everybody who has a car is like that."

Stephen gave up the idea of driving, and looked out of the window. "I hope it's not going to be like this to-morrow," he said. "What'll we do if it is? Do you think I could borrow a waterproof?"

Tom did not answer. To tell the truth, he felt extremely doubtful about Stephen's reception at Gloucester Terrace, quite apart from the borrowing of waterproofs, and even though he was being introduced under the auspices of Uncle Horace. But the house didn't belong to Uncle Horace, and for that matter Tom wasn't at all sure of his own welcome. His step-mother couldn't be feeling particularly friendly towards him at present: there was no reason why she should: for it wasn't even now as if he were coming back to stay. He was only coming back to suit himself, and when you looked at it like that it did seem pretty thick! He wished they were going to an hotel.

There was no use wishing, however, and no use trying to reopen the subject with Uncle Horace. The whole thing was getting more and more difficult. All his relations with people had become difficult and unnatural. His relations with everybody—with Mrs. Deverell, with Mr. Knox, with everybody he knew—had become secretive and defensive.

"For goodness sake, cheer up!" Stephen said abruptly. "We're not going to a funeral."

Tom drew back into his corner. "I didn't know I wasn't cheerful."

"Well, you know now. It seems to me about a year since I heard you laugh."

"I don't see anything to laugh at."

"That's just it. It's a little depressing."

Tom was too offended to reply.

"I've told you it will be all right," Stephen went on, half impatiently, half amused. "We've got to take this as a kind of game—at any rate for the time being. Look how beautifully everything went this morning."

"Not so beautifully as you imagine."

"You mean Knox. What does it matter about Knox? You'd think he was a bishop."

"It's all very well talking like that," Tom burst out hotly, "but there'll be Mr. Flood too. Mr. Knox is too decent to say much, but Mr. Flood knows all about Uncle Stephen."

"I doubt it."

"He does: he's his solicitor: and he'll know very well you weren't telling the truth."

"He may think so, but he can't *know* without making inquiries."

"He will make them."

Stephen yawned. "Well, let him," he returned carelessly. "You're very hard to please. I thought you'd have liked my story, even though parts of it were so sad. . . . Uncle Horace was just a little casual about the sad parts, don't you think?"

The ghost of a smile flickered across Tom's face, and Stephen immediately smiled back.

"All the same," Tom went on, "Mr. Flood *will* find out. He's bound to. He's in charge of Uncle Stephen's private affairs. You'll have to give him proper information—I mean, addresses and that kind of thing—and then he'll write at once, or telegraph."

"He won't. He'll wait first to see if Uncle Stephen comes back. Can't you understand that they *must* think he'll come back? *They* don't know what you know, and they'll leave it to him to decide whether he has a grandson or not. I shouldn't be surprised myself if he had several."

"Then why did you invent all that story? It won't help us in the long run, and I never told so many lies in my life."

"They're not lies—not real lies—they were forced on us."

"They weren't. Not those particular ones anyway. They were made up just for your own pleasure and because you thought them funny. They weren't a bit funny. All you did was to make Uncle Horace and Mr. Knox think Uncle Stephen wicked."

"Wicked?"

"Yes—immoral."

It was his last protest, however, and he did not speak again until he said, "We're nearly there."

Uncle Horace had in fact begun to slow down, for they had reached the outlying houses of the city, and in a few minutes more were on the tram-lines, threading their way through an increasing traffic. It was nearly six, and in spite of the rain the streets were full of people. Stephen glanced about him eagerly.

The car branched off the main road, and Tom too stared out of the window. It was all exactly the same as when he had seen it last. There were the same people coming home from business to the same houses; the same message-boys on the same bicycles; the same milk vans; the same dogs; even most of the advertisements on the hoardings were unchanged; and yet he felt as if he had been away half a lifetime. . . .

The next turning would be Gloucester Terrace. . . . There it was: there was the house: there was the next-door cat on the window-sill.

The car drew up.

But in spite of Uncle Horace's prediction Jane was not waiting on the steps to receive them. Nor was anybody else; they had to ring twice; and then it was Eric who opened the door.

"Hello!" he said, while he stared past Tom at the other boy.

"Go on in; go on in," cried Uncle Horace irritably from the rear. "Don't stand there blocking the way."

"Sorry." Eric drew to one side, and at the same time both the kitchen and the dining-room doors opened.

Through the former emerged Mrs. Barber. "Well, Tom!" she exclaimed, and then she too caught sight of Stephen.

The brief distraction enabled Tom to avoid an embrace: he shook hands instead.

"This is Tom's cousin, Stephen Collet," Uncle Horace announced fussily. He waved a general introduction—"Eric—Leonard—Jane."

Eric and Leonard shook hands; Jane was still hugging Tom; Mrs. Barber, looking very much mystified, seemed uncertain what to do.

"Tom had better show Stephen his room," Uncle Horace went on, taking charge of the situation. "You got my wire, of course." His intention, Tom thought, was to remove him and Stephen out of the way while he explained matters.

He obeyed the hint, and even before they had reached the second flight of stairs he heard the dining-room door closing. He glanced back over his shoulder and saw that Jane had not followed the others, but was standing in the hall gazing after him, her attitude exactly that of a dog who has not been taken for the expected walk. Tom put his finger to his lips, beckoned, and swiftly and silently Jane sped up the stairs.

"Tom dear, it's lovely to have you back again," she murmured, sitting down beside him on the edge of the bed. "And it's nice to have Stephen too. . . . Will that can of hot water be enough for both of you, because if it isn't I'll get another."

"Heaps," said Tom. "Stephen can wash first. I'll tell you what you might do though. You might get him one of Leonard's collars."

"And a shirt," said Stephen, taking off his jacket.

"And a shirt," Tom repeated.

Jane looked a little surprised, but she departed without a word. When she returned Stephen was splashing at the wash-basin, so she sat down once more beside Tom.

"You needn't say anything downstairs about borrowing Leonard's things," Tom warned her. "You see, we had to leave in a hurry. I'll send them back, and Stephen can wear one of my ties: then he'll be all right."

Jane still seemed slightly puzzled, so Tom continued diplomatically: "You didn't know I had a cousin, did you?"

"No; I don't think anybody knew you had a cousin. I must say he's not a bit like you."

"Why should he be like me?" Tom replied. "Cousins aren't often like one another."

Jane did not dispute this, but while she watched Stephen drying himself an increasing curiosity grew more and more visible in her face. At last she gave utterance to it. "What has happened? Why have you come back? Have you left Uncle Stephen?"

Tom frowned. "No, of course not. Uncle Stephen is away on business, and Stephen and I came up because we're going to Coombe Bridge to-morrow. We're only going for the day, however; we'll be back here to-morrow night."

"To stay?" Jane asked.

Tom hesitated. "Well, not exactly to stay. We'll have to leave the next morning."

Jane looked at him. "Then I'll hardly see you at all," she said.

"Of course you'll see me. I'll be here all this evening and part of to-morrow evening."

Jane's face clouded. "*That's* not very long. Besides, the others will be there: I won't see you by yourself."

"You must come and pay us a visit at the Manor."

"I can't help it," he went on, as Jane failed to respond to this not very heartfelt invitation. "We *must* go back the day after to-morrow."

"Then I'll come to-night and talk."

"Come where?"

"Come here. To you."

"You can't. Stephen will be here."

"Stephen won't mind."

Tom began to lose patience. "Don't be silly! How can you go rushing about boys' rooms? You know what happened last time. Anyway, I'll lock the door, so if you like to kick up a row and get caught it will be your own fault."

Jane drew away from him. "I think you've altered," she said coldly.

Tom stared gloomily down at the carpet. He might have guessed how it would be! "I dare say I *have* altered," he muttered. "There's been plenty to——"

"Tom dear, I'm sorry," Jane interrupted impulsively. She clasped her arms round his neck and gave him a hug. "I won't ask any more questions and you needn't tell me anything you don't want to. And I won't come to your room. I wouldn't have come anyway: I only said that to tease you. But it was horrid of me to say you'd changed, because you haven't, not a scrap. At least, not to look at—I've just counted your freckles."

The first notes of a gong rose from the hall, and Tom got up to take Stephen's place at the washstand.

"I suppose I'd better go down," Jane said, "but there's plenty of time for Stephen to change his clothes: that was only a warning. I'll tell them you won't be long."

The door closed behind her, and Stephen remarked, "She seems quite a decent kid." He began to undress, and presently made a second remark. "In fact, I don't see anything the matter with any of them, in spite of all you told me."

Tom wheeled round, the water dripping from his hair, his cheeks hot, and his eyes flashing. "No," he answered with a sudden bitterness. "I expect you'll be bosom friends with the whole family."

Stephen gave him a sidelong look. "Is there any harm in my saying they seem decent?"

"You know very well I always told you Jane was decent."

"Well, what's the trouble then?"

"It's just that you take a delight in siding against me. I'm not talking about Jane. But because I told you the others hated me you at once begin to like them, though you've barely spoken to them. If it was somebody who did care for me——"

"Your gamekeeper?" Stephen suggested.

"Yes; you can sneer! But he was a jolly lot more——"

"Here," said Stephen, gripping him by the shoulders—"don't be a young ass. To begin with, you know I don't care a fig for the whole jing-bang of your relations."

"They're not my relations."

"Well, whatever they are."

"Yes, I do know it; and that's why you needn't have said——" He stopped. "I'm sorry, Stephen. It was stupid. I don't think I'm fit to be in decent company at present."

"That's rot, too," said Stephen. "You're much the decentest person here."

Once again the deep notes of the gong floated up to them.

"We'd better hurry," said Tom. "I suppose they don't know you're changing."

Uncle Horace was still there when they entered the dining-room, but he did not join in the meal. Tom was glad to see him. It was perhaps the first time he had ever known the presence of Uncle Horace to ease off a situation, but it certainly had—for him at least—this effect now. Only, when he *had* waited, he might for once have sacrificed his dinner and eaten with them. His refusal to do so struck Tom as shockingly bad manners.

It was a curious repast. Not the food, but the demeanour of the eaters of the food. He could see that Eric and Leonard, especially, were puzzled by Stephen—that they were inclined to form a favourable impression of him, and were at the same time held back by the fact of his relationship to their step-brother and to the unknown and mysterious Uncle Stephen. He could follow exactly the logical procession of their thoughts. Anybody who was friends with Tom! But possibly he really wasn't friends, and he couldn't help being a cousin—it was a misfortune rather than a fault. . . . If only they knew how obvious all their ideas and feelings were, they wouldn't take even the little trouble they did to disguise them. He could tell, as surely as if they had whispered it in his ear, that on the very first opportunity they would try to draw Stephen away from him and into their private camp. They wouldn't succeed, however: he knew that now. . . .

And Stephen had begun to talk to Mrs. Barber. He was talking of his plan to visit Coome Bridge. Mrs. Barber wanted to know what time they would like to start. "They'll have to start early," Uncle Horace said. "It will take a couple of hours to get there."

"Are there any Collets at Coombe Bridge now?" Mrs. Barber asked, and Stephen replied that he didn't think so.

"It's most remarkable how families die out!" But after a pensive moment she abandoned this line of reflection and asked instead if Stephen had liked living abroad. She herself had never been in Italy, but she had been in France and Switzerland, and neither country had appealed to her as a permanent home.

"Don't you sometimes find yourself talking Italian by mistake, Stephen?" Jane asked.

"Never," said Stephen, and winked at Tom.

It was an outrageous thing to do: anybody might have seen him!

Tom's face was crimson. As if things weren't bad enough without starting to play the fool! "I suppose there's a railway guide in the house," he mumbled. At the same time he frowned at Stephen and received a broad grin in return.

"There should be a guide somewhere," Mrs. Barber thought, and Jane said, "It's in the drawer of the hat-stand."

"At least it *was* there," she added, jumping up from the table.

Tom stared down at his plate. He wasn't going to look at Stephen again. He wished he wasn't sitting opposite him.

Jane returned with a guide. "Rather ancient. The year before last. And a Christmas Number, too."

"It doesn't matter, dear, the trains won't have altered," said her mother—"not to a little place like Coombe Bridge."

"Those are just the trains that *are* altered," Leonard contradicted. "They alter them every month or two."

"Ten-forty. Twelve-fifty-five," Jane read aloud, as she resumed her seat beside Tom.

"The ten-forty will do," said Tom.

"Ten-forty—ten-forty—ten-forty—arrives three-twenty-nine."

"Oh, don't be silly. Here—show it to me."

"Don't *you* be silly," returned Jane, gripping the book more firmly as he attempted to take it from her. "No, that's wrong. Ten-forty —— *Stop*, Tom! How can I see if you keep pulling at it! Ten-forty arrives at twelve-twenty. . . . That's *right*," she declared, still clinging tenaciously to the guide, which Tom also grasped.

"Give it to me," he said impatiently. "I want to find out about coming home."

Jane still held on. "Trains coming home," she chanted. "Let me see. There's one at——"

Tom turned away, putting his fingers in his ears.

"Oh, all right! *There*—take the old thing! Baby!" She dropped it in the middle of his jam.

"Jane!" Mrs. Barber said sharply.

"Well, he thinks nobody can do anything except himself, and he's the very one to get it all wrong."

Tom, having gained his point, was indifferent to criticism.

"There may be a bus," Uncle Horace suggested from his arm-chair, and Tom turned the pages to see—very much as Jane had turned them, but with the satisfaction of doing it for himself.

Uncle Horace, leaving the family group in one of its more characteristic moments, rose from his chair. "Well, it's time I was moving on. I may possibly drop round again later, and if not I'll look in to-morrow evening and hear the Coombe Bridge news. Good-bye, every-body, for the present. Don't get up: I can find my own way out."

But Tom did get up. He was aware that all eyes were turned upon him, and those of his step-brothers with contemptuous dislike. Suck-ing up to Uncle Horace, they would call it. He didn't care. He fol-lowed Uncle Horace into the hall and helped him on with his coat. Uncle Horace accepted the help. He accepted it, too, without im-patience, though Tom got the sleeves mixed up and was not tall enough to be of much assistance. Uncle Horace, having disentan-gled himself, put on his hat, and Tom opened the hall-door.

On the threshold Uncle Horace turned to his nephew and held out his hand. "I don't fancy I *will* be back," he said, "so I'll say good-night to you."

"Good-night, Uncle Horace. And—thank you ever so much—for everything."

Uncle Horace, on the point of stepping out into the street, sud-denly paused. "Look here, Tom," he began, and paused again.

Tom looked up at him expectantly.

But Uncle Horace, after a moment, merely flashed his most bril-liant smile. "All I was going to tell you is, not to worry. Good-night."

25: STEPHEN at the last minute had bought a news-paper, but, to Tom's surprise, he had not read it. He had rustled its leaves, glanced at a few headlines, looked at the photo-graphs on the back page, and offered it to Tom. It now lay on the floor between them.

The train was slowing down. So far it had stopped at nearly every station, and Tom had begun to feel oddly restless, almost excited, though he could not have told what he looked forward to. Coombe Bridge meant nothing to him, nor even so far as Stephen was concerned did he see what benefit could come of their visit. There was nothing to be learned at Coombe Bridge that they did not know already.

The train drew up, and their carriage came to rest directly in front of a group of market-women. Tom guessed what would happen, and got up to help with the baskets. There were plenty of half-filled coaches on the train; most of the women were stout, and all of them were hot; but where one entered the rest followed, and soon they were packed so tightly that for Tom and Stephen only standing-room was left. Stephen let down the other window with a bang.

"Well, if that isn't too bad now! We've been and taken their seats. It's them baskets that takes up all the room."

"Ah, sure, they won't mind for all the distance we're going: it's not worth changing now."

"Indeed I never looked whether there was room or not: they're always in that big a hurry they wouldn't give you time to look round."

The glowing matron who had last spoken, and who had plopped herself down in a corner seat, suddenly pulled Tom on to her lap. She did it without a word, and so unexpectedly that he was there and her stout arms about him before he knew what had happened.

He struggled indignantly away from her and took up a position at the door, very red in the face, while the others laughed.

"My, but he's proud!" exclaimed the forsaken lady. "I suppose even his own ma's not allowed to touch him!"

"I'm too hot," Tom answered through his confusion. "I'd rather stand."

"What'll he do when he's married? He must be one of them that has to have a separate bed."

Another laugh greeted this sally, and Tom, after a moment, smiled himself.

"I'll sit on your knee if you like," he said, "but you won't find it comfortable, because I'm a good deal heavier than you think."

"Divil a knee! But perhaps you wouldn't be so backward in other ways."

She removed the lid from a basket and the other ways were revealed as gooseberries. "Here, hold out your cap, and don't say I'm not a forgiving woman."

She filled his cap, and Stephen, who had no cap, was allowed to fill his pocket. Then she leaned forward and addressed a friend at the further end of the compartment. "Who would you fancy he resembles, Lizzie—the way he wrinkles his nose. He's the very spit of him."

Lizzie turned a meditative gaze on Tom. "You mean my Jimmie?" she said dubiously. "But it's nothing barrin' that trick he has."

"It's the whole of him—the way his ears sticks out, and the brow—I'll warrant this one is good at his books too."

The comparison was pursued by the entire company, while an uneasy suspicion (shortly to become a certainty) grew up in Tom's mind that Jimmie's earthly career had ended several months ago. He was glad when a more cheerful topic was started, gladder still when they got out.

Stephen had noticed nothing, nor did he help Tom and an impatient railway porter with the baskets. With his back turned he hung out of the window, seeming to be absorbed in the landscape, slowly and deliberately spitting out gooseberry skins. From his attitude, from his silence, Tom concluded that they must be drawing near their destination. He wondered what Stephen was thinking, but he could not guess. He spat out his gooseberry skins more and more absent-mindedly; he seemed to have become oblivious to Tom's existence.

"We're nearly there, aren't we?" Tom asked, but Stephen did not look round. Then presently he muttered over his shoulder, "Next station."

Tom leaned back in his seat. He shut his eyes. There was no use trying to feel sleepy, however, so he opened them again and looked at Stephen.

The engine whistled. . . . They were approaching their station. Stephen was again hanging out of the window, but he drew in his head as they passed under a bridge. The brake jarred; they glided up to a platform and stopped.

Stephen had already opened the door. He jumped out and Tom followed. Nobody else got out, and there was nobody waiting to get in. The platform looked extraordinarily empty. And whether it was this emptiness or not, Tom experienced a peculiar sensation, as if the whole adventure had fallen flat.

It was absurd. What had he expected to happen? A porter was at a white wooden gate waiting to take their tickets. He hurried after Stephen. . . .

Coombe Bridge itself was nearly as deserted as the station. To Tom it seemed a moribund spot, even when compared with Kilbarron.

"All these wretched little houses are new," said Stephen shortly.

They turned a corner and were in the main street. At the end of it was a market square, and behind that a church, with a road branching off on either side of it.

"They've taken away the pump!" muttered Stephen.

"Where was it?" Tom asked gently.

"There, on the green—where they've stuck up that awful thing."

The awful thing Tom recognized as a War Memorial, but he said nothing.

Suddenly Stephen stopped before a shop—a draper's and clothier's. "I know this place," he said.

"What do you want to do?" Tom asked, for Stephen had come to a standstill in the middle of the footpath, and was looking back in the direction of the railway station.

"I don't know," Stephen replied. "I wish I hadn't come."

But he approached the shop and pushed open the door, which emitted a sharp ping as he did so. Tom followed him inside.

The interior was cool and dusky after the glare of the street: the shop was empty. The sound of the bell, however, brought a middle-aged woman from some hidden region at the back. Stephen had advanced to the counter, and in a low indifferent voice she wished him good-morning. Her whole appearance was curiously lethargic; she had an air of being not in the least interested either in them or in what they might want; she simply stood there as if waiting for them to go.

"Could you tell me if a Mr. Collet lives here?" Stephen asked.

The woman raised heavy-lidded dull brown eyes. "Here? Do you mean in this house?"

"No: I mean anywhere in Coombe Bridge."

"Collet. I don't remember the name. . . . Wait a minute." She retreated without haste in the direction she had come from, but only as far as a curtained door. Opening this, "Pa," she called listlessly, "you're wanting a minute."

There was a perceptible pause: then various sounds arose from the other side of the door, though none of them verbal. Sounds of a pipe being knocked out, of a throat being cleared, of a chair being pushed back over a tiled floor—followed by a sound of shuffling footsteps accompanied by the sharp tapping of a stick. An old man, bent, white-bearded, with red twitching eyelids, emerged through the dim aperture.

"I'm a'wantin'—who wants me?" he asked querulously, in a thin cracked voice.

"This young gentleman is looking for a Mr. Collet. Is there any Collet lives in Coombe Bridge?"

"Collet?" The old man peered at Stephen. "Collet, did you say?"

"Yes," Stephen answered.

"An' what might a' put the name of Collet into your head, young gentleman?" The old man drew closer. "There's been no Collets in Coombe Bridge—not since the Reverend Henry Collet died, and that must be nigh and next forty years ago. No, there's no Collets left except what's dust and bones in the graveyard. Who might *you* be, if you'll pardon the liberty?"

"*My* name is Collet: I'm Stephen Collet."

The old man continued to blink his eyelids rapidly, while he stood pondering. He was a rather dirty and far from pleasant old man. It was not a pleasant shop either, Tom thought. There was something wrong with it—something decidedly wrong.

"That would be the name of the second son," the old man said cautiously. "I mind hearing about him, but both the sons had left home before ever *I* came to this place. The shop belonged then to my uncle. I was brought up to the farming. I was on the land till I was nigh on thirty years of age, and——"

"Yes, Pa; but the young gentleman wants to know about Mr. Collet."

"Well, amn't I tellin' him," the old man snapped with an unexpected waspishness. "I was well acquainted with the Reverend Collet: not that I was one of his denomination. But I had converse with him when he would be coming into the shop maybe. And he would mention his sons. They had both left home, and Henry, that was called by him and was the eldest, was doing well; but the young one was a rover and they could get no tidings of him. He had the true Collet blood in him, that one, for they were mostly a wild lot—not fearing God or man. You wouldn't be his boy, would you?"

"No."

The old man looked down and began to mutter incantations into his beard—or so it seemed to Tom. Then once more he took a long look at Stephen and broke, rather startlingly, into a laugh.

"The Reverend Henry Collet is buried deep in the churchyard of his own church," he said with a glee that was somehow shocking. "And the last time I seen his grave there was a hare sitting up on it with its ears cocked. Not that I hold with them superstitions—that comes from the devil—or so they say."

"Pa!"

"Is there anybody else who knew him?" Tom interrupted, for he wanted to get out of this shop as quickly as possible.

"Are you a Collet too?" the old man said softly.

"Yes—or at least my mother was."

"Ay—ay—the family's comin' back it would seem. . . . There was something strange about them all—even about the Reverend Henry. . . . The churchyard is no place for hares. It looked at me the way the little gentleman might be looking now, and it never budged though I threatened it with my stick. It was after that the rheumatism took me bad and I was lyin' for three weeks."

"Don't you be heeding him, sir," the woman said in an undertone. Then more loudly, "Pa, the young gentleman asked you a question. Can't you tell him if there's anybody still living here might have known Mr. Collet?"

The old man without turning his head slid his eyes round at her. For a moment they expressed an astonishing malevolence: then he began again to mutter into his beard. "No, there's no one would have known him—no one at all—no one unless it might be Miss Charlemont."

Stephen turned to the woman. "What Miss Charlemont is that?" he asked.

The woman's eyes were strangely still—stupid—stupid and slightly glazed. "It's the lady living in the red house on the hill he'd be meaning—Miss Alice Charlemont."

"Has she lived there long?"

"Ay, she's well up in years. Not what you'd call ancient, like Pa there, but she'd be turned sixty."

"Let's go," whispered Tom, plucking Stephen by the sleeve, for Stephen stood motionless, plunged in meditation.

"Go straight through the square," said the woman, for the first time showing signs of animation, "and take the turn on your right after you pass the church. It's not above half a mile. Keep on till you get to the top of the hill and you'll see the house from the road. You can't miss it, for it's the only house there."

The old man again was peering at Stephen, with an extraordinary mixture of slyness and suspicion. And again he broke into a chuckle; after which he turned abruptly and hobbled back to where he had come from.

"You needn't be payin' any attention to him," said the woman.

"Sometimes he's like that. You'd never know beforehand whether he was goin' to be sensible or not."

Tom thanked her and gave Stephen another tug, this time effectively.

"I don't like those people," he said, when they were out in the sunshine again. "The old man especially."

"He's doting," Stephen murmured absently.

"He may be doting, but I don't like him: I think he has horrible things in his mind."

Stephen shook off his reverie. He smiled faintly.

"And I think they've begun to get out," Tom went on. "That shop was awfully queer."

"I didn't notice anything. Except that it didn't look very prosperous."

"Something is going to happen there," Tom persisted. "I knew the minute I went in. And he hates his daughter—or his daughter-in-law."

"Does he? I wasn't much interested in either of them. The woman knows nothing and the old man is cracked. . . . I was thinking of Miss Charlemont."

"Well, I hope she won't be like them. That is, if we are going to see her."

"Don't you want to go?"

"I want to do whatever *you* want. Do you know Miss Charlemont? Was she here—before?"

"How can I tell? The woman said she must be sixty. The Charlemont girl I knew—Alice Charlemont—was fourteen."

Tom glanced at him. "Would you rather not go?"

"Oh, I'm going, but there's no need for you to come."

"Did you know her well—*your* Alice Charlemont, I mean?"

"Yes. She used to lend me her pony."

"Did you like her?"

"Yes—well enough."

"I don't think you like many people."

"I like them if they're my sort."

"*I'm* not very much your sort."

"Not in some ways, but—— Oh, well, it's hard to explain. There are different kinds of liking. I don't think I'd ever want to be with one person all the time, or to live in one place all the time, or to live one kind of life all the time. You're different, I know. You'd be quite content, wouldn't you, to settle down at the Manor with Uncle Stephen for the rest of your life? But you ought to remember Uncle Stephen had *returned* from his adventures. It wasn't that he'd never had any. According to you, he'd had plenty."

"Uncle Stephen wanted me to stay at home."

"Yes, he would—naturally. He wanted *you,* and of course if you didn't stay at home he couldn't have you. He was an old rascal, you know."

"He wasn't."

"And he was jolly lucky to find you. You suited him as well as if he'd helped God to make you. How many boys, do you think, would have wanted to read Greek with him, to play chess with him, to live in that old house with him? About one in ten thousand. I'd have been fed up with it in two days."

"I don't see how that can be," said Tom. Nevertheless, his brow puckered as he thought it over, for it did actually seem to be true.

"That is the house," said Stephen, catching him by the arm. "There, through the trees."

Tom looked up in time to see it, but almost immediately it was hidden by a turn in the road.

Straight in front of them were two tall iron gates, and beyond these was an avenue, which wound about corkscrew fashion, either with the design of making the grounds appear more extensive than they really were, or of minimizing the steepness of the approach. "If she's at home," said Stephen, "she can't very well not feed us, and that's what we need most at present."

The house, built on the brow of a hill, was square and solid and completely devoid of ornament. It was in fact the very house Tom again and again, in childhood, had drawn on paper—with its rows of windows all exactly the same, its door in the middle, and its chimneys, from one of which the conventional trail of smoke was rising. Not a leaf was allowed to touch the precious bricks, and the steps were so spotlessly white that it looked as if visitors must use the back-door. Tom wiped his feet on the grass, but Stephen was less particular. He rang the bell, which responded with an alarming exuberance. He must have given it a frightful tug!

Miss Charlemont was at home, they learned, but no invitation to come in followed the announcement. They were left standing in the porch while a message was carried to her. Tom stooped down to stroke a somnolent tabby basking in the sun.

Suddenly the door opened wide. "Miss Charlemont will see you if you will kindly step this way: she'll be down in a few minutes."

They were ushered into a bright morning-room, the furniture of which was covered in gaily-flowered chintzes. The paper was gay also, a rose-coloured pattern on a white ground, and all the wood-work was white. The sun shone in through two windows, and there were flowers in bowls and vases. . . . Rooms! Tom fancied he was rather a specialist in them, and this one certainly was pleasant: there-fore so must be Miss Charlemont. The servant retired and came back with a tray on which were wine-glasses and a decanter and a blue china biscuit box. "Miss Charlemont hopes you will take a glass of wine and a biscuit while you are waiting," she said, and then left them alone.

"Very decent of her, I must say," murmured Stephen, filling the glasses and taking a sip.

Tom watched him with pellucid, oddly childish eyes. "What kind of wine is it?" he asked, also sipping. "Port?"

"Port—no: it's sherry." Stephen wavered. "At least I think so. You don't drink port before meals. Anyway, it's quite good. Let's get drunk before she comes down." He hastily emptied his glass and re-filled it.

"Don't be piggy," said Tom.

"Why not? I've never been really squiffy except once—last Christ-mas—staying with a chap called Rockmore. Besides, I expect you'll like me better when I'm tight."

Tom's face flamed. "I don't like you now, anyway," he said. "You'd think you were being beastly on purpose."

"So I am. This visit is having the wrong effect."

Tom had no time to say more, for just then the door opened, and an elderly lady with smooth grey hair, small, and very alert and active, entered. There was something birdlike about her—in her brightness, her quick movements. She smiled at them both, turning from one to the other. "Which of you is Stephen Collet? No; don't tell me." She advanced swiftly to Stephen and kissed him. "*That* question at least was unnecessary."

Tom from the beginning felt out of it. His presence might not actually be unwelcome, but it certainly was superfluous. Miss Charlemont had eyes only for Stephen.

"It's wonderful!" she kept on saying. "It's not a mere family re-semblance: you might be the very Stephen Collet I used to know. He was a friend of mine; a dear dear friend, though we were only children. *That* will tell you how long ago it was. . . . And you say your name is Stephen too!"

"Yes, ma'am."

"Oh, don't be so formal, child! You must call me Aunt Alice. And you too"—she suddenly remembered Tom—"I'm afraid I didn't quite catch your name, dear."

"That's cousin Tom—Tom Barber," said Stephen. "His mother was Henry Collet's daughter."

"Yes, yes. I'm afraid I don't remember Henry very well. He was older than Stephen, and I scarcely ever saw him. But Stephen and I were playmates—when he was home for his holidays." She paused, her eyes rejoicing in the boy who stood there smiling at her. "I don't think I ever in my life got such a surprise as when Annie brought me your name. . . . And, you know, I haven't got you *yet*," she went on—"where you come in. . . . But I shan't bother you now. Lunch is ready; you must explain it all to me afterwards."

Miss Charlemont led the way to the dining-room. She struck Tom as being a somewhat scatter-brained person, though extremely kind. "Isn't it fortunate there *is* lunch," she babbled on happily. "Very often I have nothing but an egg and a cup of tea myself, but to-day by some special providence there is a roast fowl, and I'm sure you're both starving."

They sat down at the table, and Tom, with a shade of uneasiness, watched Stephen drinking another glass of wine—this time burgundy —which had been poured out for him. Moreover, there was a glint of recklessness in his eyes Tom did not like at all. So he signalled a warning across the table while Miss Charlemont was giving an order to the maid, though he would have preferred to get up and remove the decanter which had been placed at Stephen's elbow, and from which he now proceeded to help himself once more.

When the maid had left the room Miss Charlemont returned to personal matters. "You must give me a *complete* account of your-selves," she said; but she addressed Stephen, and it was Stephen she meant. "I've lost all sight of your family for I don't know how long, and one hears nothing in an out-of-the-way spot like this. Of course, to begin with, I suppose you must be Henry Collet's son, or grandson —and that would make you *my* Stephen Collet's nephew, or grand-nephew."

"You've got it all wrong, Aunt Alice," Stephen replied gaily.

"Henry Collet hadn't a son. He had only a daughter, and it is Tom there who is his grandson. Don't you really know who I am? I thought you were only pretending, but now I don't think I'll tell you. I'll give you three guesses."

Miss Charlemont laid down her knife and fork. Once more she subjected Stephen to a close scrutiny: then she nodded her head two or three times and looked extremely wise. Stephen had begun to laugh, and his young eyes met her old eyes boldly. "If I didn't think you were making fun of me," said Miss Charlemont, "and if I hadn't always been told that Stephen Collet was a bachelor——" She broke off, and Tom groaned inwardly. "Now we'll get all the natural son business!" he said to himself; and however lightly Mr. Knox and Uncle Horace might regard such matters, he was sure Miss Charlemont was unaccustomed to them.

"*Who* told you, Aunt Alice?" Stephen questioned playfully.

"Never mind who told me," Miss Charlemont replied. "Well— everybody——" she went on rather vaguely. "Everybody who ever mentioned him." But Tom could see she was becoming more and more uncertain. "You don't mean you *are* his son!" she exclaimed at last. She shook a reproachful finger at him. "That wasn't fair of you. I think you might have told me at once instead of letting me make a goose of myself."

"But I really thought you knew," Stephen protested, laughing. "Particularly when you recognized me straight off like that. And then—well, I was sure you would know who I was, just because I *had* come specially to see you. Of course, Tom came too, but that was different: he happened to be with me."

Miss Charlemont sat silent a moment, and a faint flush came into her cheeks. "So your father sent you!" Her eyes had grown very soft, and she sighed, but it was not from sadness. "Well, dear, that was extremely nice of him, for I thought he wouldn't even have remembered there was such a person after all these years. But why did he wait so long? Why have I never heard?"

"*Is* it long since you heard of him, Aunt Alice?"

"Yes, dear. And the last I heard was that he was living all alone——"

"But don't you see that that explains it?" cried Stephen triumphantly. "He only married shortly before I was born . . . I mean, about a year before," he added, with a quick glance at Tom. "And it was abroad and nobody in this country knew anything about it.

He *has* hardly any friends over here. In fact, you might say he has none—except you. Shall I tell you the whole story, Aunt Alice? I mean all about his marriage, and how it happened. Would you like me to?"

"Yes, dear, of course. . . . And perhaps it is my own fault that I know so little. He went away when he was a boy—no older than you are now—and he never wrote. Afterwards, when I heard he had come back to this country, I thought of writing. I debated the idea with myself many times, but it always ended by my deciding against it. You see, I thought that if he had wished to renew our friendship he would have done so himself, and—and that it wasn't my place to remind him of what perhaps he had no desire to recall. I wish now I hadn't been so stiff and stupid, for I won't deny that his sending you to visit me like this has touched me very much."

Tom suddenly felt sorry for her, and at the same time indignant. It was as if Stephen had invented this graceful action of Uncle Stephen's for no other purpose than to lead Miss Charlemont on to make herself absurd.

Meanwhile the maid had come back into the room, and while she remained there Miss Charlemont spoke of the weather and apologized for having nothing more to offer them than dessert—if she had only known they were coming she would have had a really nice lunch for them. But the moment they were alone again she turned eagerly to Stephen. "I think, dear, I interrupted you. You were about to tell me something."

"Yes," said Stephen, sipping his wine, while his gaze rested dreamily on a picture above Tom's head. "It was about Father's marriage. But I don't want to bore you."

"You won't bore me," Miss Charlemont assured him.

"At any rate I'll try not to," said Stephen, suddenly looking straight into Tom's eyes. "You see," he went on, after this ominous assurance, "it was all most unusual. In a way, you might call it romantic."

Tom glared, but Miss Charlemont sat mutely expectant, an expression of profound interest on her mild and innocent face.

Yes, it was romantic—*and* unusual. Uncle Stephen, it seemed, some seventeen years before, had revisited Italy, and during this visit he had married, and he had married a nun. He had heard her singing in chapel and had fallen in love with her voice. There had been an elopement—more in the nature of an abduction, it appeared, as Stephen added fresh details—followed by a year of perfect happiness. The story grew more and more picturesque as the narrator warmed to his task. Tom glanced at Miss Charlemont and hastily averted his eyes. There she sat, lapping it all up like cream, an absorbed expression on her face. Couldn't she *see* how preposterous it was? But no; she accepted it; and a deeply sentimental sigh escaped her when Stephen ended dramatically: "My mother died two days after I was born."

Miss Charlemont awoke out of her trance. "It's really wonderful!" she breathed. "And you told it wonderfully, Stephen—so sympathetically; it brought the whole thing up before me! It's almost like a novel by Marion Crawford—in fact *very* like a novel by Marion Crawford—I've forgotten its name—but where your father listened day after day to the nuns singing in chapel, and to that one voice——!"

As for Tom, he had sat through this brilliant performance with a darkening countenance. He had known that Miss Charlemont could not be told the truth, but there was a difference between not telling her the truth and mystifying her to this extent. *That* seemed to him as ungentlemanly as it was unnecessary. After all, they were her guests. "I think you've drunk enough of that stuff," he suddenly said across the table, and in a tone that brought Miss Charlemont's eyes round to him with a startled look.

She hesitated, and perhaps something in Stephen's manner did at last strike her, for she murmured timidly, "I think, dear, you *may* perhaps find that burgundy rather heavy on such a hot day. Wouldn't you like to mix it with a little soda water?"

Stephen, his hand still grasping the neck of the decanter, stopped dead, and Tom went on coldly: "If you're going to do all you said you wanted to do we ought to be starting soon."

Miss Charlemont again interposed, and Tom knew from her manner that she resented the way he had spoken. But he didn't care: he wasn't going to have any more of this kind of thing. "You want, I expect, to see the Rectory and the church," Miss Charlemont murmured. "They are both quite near: in fact you can see the church steeple from the window."

Stephen had relapsed into silence: he even had the grace to look slightly ashamed of himself. He glanced deprecatingly at Tom, but Tom turned away. He was really angry, and he would have been angrier still if Miss Charlemont had not been so foolish. But by the time coffee was brought in she had completely forgotten her misgivings. Perhaps she had never felt any, and had only been annoyed with Tom for interfering. At all events, it was perfectly clear when at last they rose to go, that she would have liked to have kept Stephen with her for the rest of the afternoon and to have sent Tom to explore the church and the Rectory alone. She told Stephen she was going to write that evening to his father, and before saying good-bye made him promise he would come and stay with her.

"Sorry," Stephen began, the moment the door had closed behind them.

"You needn't have made fun of her to her face!" Tom exploded. "Especially after she'd been so decent."

"But I didn't. I mean it wasn't really of her I was making fun. It was of the whole thing—of you and me and our explanations and all the rest of it. Besides, I *can't* feel that it matters a straw what I say or what I do. . . . I know it does matter," he added hastily, "but I can't *feel* that it does. And then—— Somehow, I can't think of it as real. I can't think of Miss Charlemont as real. The only person who seems real—besides myself—is you: and that, I suppose, is because you belong to both times."

"So does Miss Charlemont."

"She doesn't. She's no more like my Alice Charlemont than that monument was like the old village pump. Hang it all," he went on half impatiently, "whatever *you* may be doing, *I'm* living in a kind of fairy tale. You ought to remember that. I don't think you'd find it so easy yourself."

"I dare say it's difficult," Tom admitted, relenting a little. "But I'm doing all I can to try to make it less so, and you might help me."

"I'm going to help you. I want to help you—naturally—because I think something must be done pretty soon. . . . I think it was partly coming back to this place made me like that. It was just—— I don't know. . . . But——" He walked on for a few yards with his hands in his pockets. "Don't you see, there's a way I *might* look at it all that would make it pretty beastly. I've tried not to look at it like that; I've tried to make the best of it, and I don't think you're quite fair. I know you want to be, but I don't think it's possible for you to be fair to both me *and* Uncle Stephen. It's quite natural that you should choose him: only—you oughtn't to forget there is this other side."

"I'm sorry," said Tom contritely.

"It's all right," Stephen answered. "You've been as decent as any-body could be. It's not your fault: it's just the way things are."

"I only meant that by talking the way you did at lunch——"

"I know. I'll try not to do it again. I knew at the time you didn't like it."

But Tom felt unhappy. He had not realized this other point of view: he had only realized Uncle Stephen's. He could understand it now. He could imagine what his own emotions would have been had he suddenly been projected into the future. He would not have taken it nearly so courageously and cheerfully as Stephen had. To be alone like that—for that was what it amounted to! And Stephen must feel he was unwanted. The only friend he had was Tom himself, and there could be no illusion in his mind that Tom wanted him. . . . And yet, he *did* want him. It was only that he wanted Uncle Stephen more. . . .

They walked on in silence, but Tom had the impression that their pace was insensibly slackening. It was when the road took a sharp turn, however, that he became sure of it, for Stephen now gripped him by the hand. "That's *our* house," he said. "I'm not going any closer."

He was frowning, and Tom saw that something had begun to affect him powerfully. Yet in spite of his words, after a moment or two he walked on. Thus they reached the entrance to the Rectory and passed it, Stephen with his eyes fixed on the road ahead.

"Shall we turn back?" Tom asked. It was merely a suggestion, for he was now hopelessly in the dark as to what Stephen wanted to do. They were within a stone's throw of the old church, and all around were the quiet grassy mounds and headstones of a country graveyard.

Stephen shook his head. What was passing in his mind Tom could not imagine, but he raised the latch of the wooden gate and they went in.

There were few trees. The place was exposed to whatever winds might blow. The low stone walls, the straggling gorse-bushes and ragged bramble and heather, gave little or no shelter. It must be a bleak spot enough in spring and autumn and winter, Tom thought; yet on this grey, still, summer afternoon, which had clouded over in the last hour, it was beautiful and peaceful. The gravel paths were smooth and black; the place, though it had this lonely appear-ance, was not ill-tended.

Stephen led him straight to a grave near the further wall. Tom saw a plain, rounded headstone, on which names and dates were cut. His own mother was not buried here, nor was his grandfather. The names most recently recorded were those of his great-grandfather and great-grandmother:—Henry Collet, who had died in 1889; Margaret Collet, who had died two years later. They were Uncle Stephen's father and mother: they were the present Stephen's father and mother: the two boys read the brief record, each to himself, and turned away. They sat down on the rough, low wall. In the valley below them, across intervening cornfields, they could see the houses of Coombe Bridge.

For perhaps ten minutes they sat there without speaking: then Stephen said, "Will you come back with me to Kilbarron?"

Tom wakened out of his daydream. "To Kilbarron? But——"

"I know. Will you come with me?"

"To-day? This afternoon?"

"It's the first thing I've ever asked you to do."

"Yes, I'll come," Tom said.

"Then we'll go now."

They got down from the wall and, without another glance at the grave, left the churchyard and started on their walk back to the village.

"Why do you want to go to Kilbarron?" Tom asked, for such a desire, if it were more than a mere whim, seemed to him strange.

"I don't know. Perhaps I'll know when we get there."

"They'll be expecting us at Gloucester Terrace, of course," Tom went on softly. "We told them what train we'd catch."

"Yes."

"And they won't be expecting us at the Manor: it will be shut up for the night. Mrs. Deverell will have gone home, and very likely she'll have gone to bed. We won't be able to get in."

"I wasn't thinking of the Manor," Stephen answered. "I was thinking of the other house: we'll be able to get in there."

But having said this, for a long time he kept his lips closed, and Tom, walking beside him, left him to his thoughts.

His own mood, though it had changed less completely than Stephen's, was not what it had been in the morning. The aspect of Coombe Bridge itself struck him as different. Perhaps it was because the day had altered, and with it the colour of everything: perhaps only because places are always different when you are leaving them.

Stephen broke his silence at last. "I think we'll buy our food here," he said. "I suppose a loaf and a pat of butter will do. We'll have to see if we can get a bus."

It was odd how he seemed to be acting now with a definite purpose, and yet not to know what that purpose was.

"I'm sure there won't be a bus," Tom said.

"There must be some way of getting there, and it's not four o'clock yet. We'll find our way somehow. You don't mind, do you?"

"No."

The grocer from whom they bought their bread and butter could tell them little about the journey, but a stationer proved more helpful. He happened to be a motor-cyclist, and he not only sold them a map and marked it, but also worked out carefully the stages of their route, wrote down two or three buses which would take them part of the way, and assured them that they might expect to reach Kilbarron not later than half-past nine or ten.

This seemed to be all right, and the first few miles were covered even more quickly than their time-scheme had allowed for. It was not till they were more than half-way that they began to lose ground. Then a failure of one of their buses meant a long extra trudge, and it began to look as if midnight was more likely to be the hour of their arrival. Tom had begun to wonder if he would be able to last out the journey. He did not mention this, however; he was determined to keep on as long as he could. Sometimes they got a lift which took them a short distance, but after each of these lifts he found it increasingly difficult to keep up with Stephen's steady tramp. Fortunately, Stephen from the beginning had been silent and preoccupied. When they descended from their last bus ride—either disappointingly brief or remarkably rapid, for it seemed to Tom that it was over in a flash—it was ten minutes to twelve, and they still had, according to the map, a journey of several miles before them.

It was a perfect night for walking—windless and clear, with a full moon to light their way. The country was unknown to them; they were not approaching the Manor from the Kilbarron side; but Tom was too weary to take an interest in his surroundings, or indeed to see anything but the high thorn hedges and the white road. After another mile or two his feet began to drag ominously. He had done his best and he was still determined not to give in, but when he sat down on a bank to tie his shoelace he felt as if he could not get up again.

"Would you like to rest for a few minutes?" Stephen asked. "I don't think it can be very much further."

Tom shook his head. "Resting will only make it worse." He got stiffly to his feet.

Yet, though he could hardly put one foot before the other, his spirit was content. He was happy—happy and tired—very happy and very tired. Ever since they had left Coombe Bridge, though they had scarcely spoken a word, he had felt like this, and as if he were being drawn into closer and closer communion with Stephen. Or was it Stephen . . . ? When he had been asked a minute ago if he would like to rest—was that Stephen . . . ? Yes, of course it had been Stephen: Stephen was walking beside him now. Only—somehow—— It was because he was half asleep, and the pale light was so strange, and everything was so quiet, as if they had the whole world to themselves. . . . He dragged on, his feet white as the road. He hung on Stephen's arm, hung more and more, and this was strange too, because he knew he would not have done so a few hours ago. But now he didn't mind—didn't mind showing how tired he was—felt there was no need to pretend about anything. There had been only one person with whom he had ever felt like this, felt happy in this particular way, this way that left no room for doubt or fear, that was without shadow, because it contained the assurance of giving no less than it received. He was happy, and, because he was happy with this *kind* of happiness, a certain childishness, which was an essential part of his spirit, no longer feared to peep out. . . .

But he *was* tired. He had long ago given up trying to make out what way they were taking: he left it entirely to Stephen. He was not very clearly conscious of anything now except that he was walking beside Stephen down an endless and moon-washed road. . . .

All at once they stopped. It had seemed to Tom that they would walk on and on for ever, and this sudden pause brought him up with a sharp jerk, the effect of which was as much mental as physical. He realized that for the last twenty minutes he must have been in a state bordering on somnambulism. He blinked.

Stephen was looking at him oddly. "Well, don't you know where you are?"

Instantly Tom knew, and when he knew he began to recognize. But he sighed. "Stephen, I simply *can't* climb that wall. You go. I'll lie down underneath it and you can come and find me in the morning."

"The gate's a long way round," said Stephen doubtfully.

"I know. The gate's impossible. Now we've stopped I can't go on again: all the works have run down."

"Come: I'll give you a leg up."

"I need two legs, and two arms: my own feel like melted candles."

"You're a terrible chap: come on now."

Stephen lifted him bodily, and Tom, with an effort that narrowly escaped landing him on his head on the other side, managed to get astride the wall. He stretched down his hands.

"Don't bother," said Stephen, "I can manage all right." And he clambered up beside Tom; then dropped down into the long grass.

Tom dropped also, and Stephen caught him. "Steady—steady!" he said.

"Sorry," murmured Tom.

"We're practically there." He waited a moment and then added, "Look here, I'm going to take you on my back. Climb up."

"You're certainly not," Tom declared, pushing him away.

Stephen yielded unwillingly. "But you look dead-beat. Why didn't you tell me sooner?"

"I didn't know sooner. It's always like this. I can go on for a long time, and then there's a sudden collapse. It's well, isn't it, we didn't start to go round the world together the way you wanted to do?"

"It was stupid of me not to see you were so tired."

"I ought to have been able to do it," said Tom. "It doesn't seem to have affected you much."

"I'm used to tramping. Besides, I *am* tired. And very sleepy too. It will be daylight soon."

Tom began to walk, but with uncertain steps. "Do you know your way, Stephen?"

"Yes."

"Then I'll leave it to you. If you go first I'll follow."

But they had not gone a hundred yards before he stumbled.

Stephen stopped. "Look here, I'm *going* to carry you."

"You're not."

Stephen sat down. "Get on my shoulders. I can carry you better that way than on my back."

"I don't want to," said Tom.

"Well, I want you to. Don't be obstinate."

"It seems so silly."

"It's much sillier to make a fuss about it. If I'd suggested it on an ordinary occasion, simply as a joke, you'd have thought nothing of it."

"Yes, but then I wouldn't have been giving in."

He made no further difficulties, however, and Stephen, grasping him by the ankles, rose from the ground.

"Catch hold of my hair; that will steady you."

Tom fumbled.

"Don't tug it," said Stephen. "Hold my ears instead. You won't hurt me: the least little touch will give you your balance."

Tom took an ear in each hand, while Stephen trudged on.

"You'll be able to guide me that way, too; but don't pull too hard."

Tom gave a small pull, and Stephen moved to the left.

"That's right: you've a better view than I have, so keep a look-out."

"I love you, Stephen," Tom whispered.

"You're not to think of that now."

"How can I help thinking of it when I'm holding your ears."

"Well, think of it then, but don't talk about it: I have to watch where I'm going."

"I mean you yourself," Tom went on, "as you are now. I wanted to tell you, because—I mayn't be able to tell you later on."

Stephen did not reply, nor did Tom himself very clearly understand what he meant. Suddenly, while he was thinking, there was the old familiar broken-down wall before them. Stephen stepped carefully through one of the gaps and over the loose stones. In a minute or two, threading his way between the trees, he had found the path. The way was now easy: a further fifty yards brought them out into the open—into the garden—with the low creepered house before them, and the stone boy watching them from his dark pool. Tom's heart stirred with an unaccountable emotion. He clambered down from Stephen's shoulders and stood beside him on the grass. The silence dropped like oil upon his senses. Every leaf hung as if painted on the air.

Only for a breathing space they stood thus before going on to the house. The back-door was on the latch, as it had always been, and they climbed the stairs to Stephen's room. Stephen lit the two candles he had bought in Coombe Bridge, and set them to stand in pools of grease upon the chimney-piece. Then they ate their supper.

They took off their shoes and prepared for the night. The window was wide open, but so still was the air that outside not a leaf stirred, and the candle flames stood up straight and motionless. The moon had dimmed and there was a faint reflection of daylight in the sky. Stephen blew out the candles.

"We're here at last," he said, "and now do you know why I wanted to come?"

"It's too late to talk," Tom answered drowsily. "Wait till the morning."

He was already on the threshold of sleep, with the door ajar and infinitely alluring. "Good-night," he whispered.

Stephen did not answer. Tom leaned closer. Then he shut his eyes, and almost instantly sank into the dark unconscious world which lay below his dream-world, and in which, from night to night, his life was mysteriously renewed.

26: THROUGH uncoiling mists of drowsiness Tom heard his name called, but it seemed to him a part of the dream from which he had not yet awakened. The dream had been all happiness and he tried to cling to it and in the effort half opened his eyes—sufficiently to see the sunlight on the wall and the shadow of moving leaves. He opened his eyes completely and turned round.

Instantly he tumbled from the bed and ran across the room. "Uncle Stephen!" he cried, and next moment his arms were round Uncle Stephen's neck.

"You're back—you're back—you're back," Tom repeated, rubbing his nose up and down Uncle Stephen's cheek. He did not seem able to say anything else, and it was as if by these words and these instinctive animal movements he were keeping Uncle Stephen with him, making sure of his solidity. He hugged him tightly, once—twice —then became still. . . . "Yes, you're back," he said.

"You've got to tell me everything, Tom—and very slowly and quietly, leaving out nothing. You can begin while we're having our breakfast. And remember your troubles are over—every one of them—and you've nothing to worry about any more."

"But *must* I tell you?" Tom demurred. "Don't you remember any of it? There's so much has happened, and a lot of it must be happening still. I mean, I don't know what they're doing now—

only I'm sure they're doing something—Uncle Horace and Mr. Flood and Mr. Knox and my step-mother and even Miss Charlemont. I expect we're being searched for at this very moment. You see, we were expected back at Gloucester Terrace last night, and we came here instead. Uncle Horace will have telephoned to Mr. Flood, and they'll be making inquiries at Coombe Bridge. If they don't hear anything about us to-day they may even tell the police. There are all the stories we told, too. Miss Charlemont's is a new one, and——"

"Poor old Tom. I do remember a good deal—rather hazily—and for the last hour or two I've been trying to remember more—ever since I woke up. I was not with you, Tom, when I woke up: I was back in my own room at the Manor. I came over here at once. Mrs. Deverell had not arrived—it was too early for her—which simplified matters; but she will have arrived by this time, for I've been here for over an hour. . . . I want you to tell me the whole story in your own way. The *whole* story, remember, because there is much about which I'm not at all certain. It seems to me that between us we've managed to create a pretty kettle of fish. Isn't that so?"

"I'm afraid it is."

"I can remember last night. I think the change, the dream, the enchantment, or whatever it was, had worn pretty thin last night. In fact, from the time we left the churchyard at Coombe Bridge till our arrival here all is clear. I can remember our journey and how tired you were at the end of it; I can remember carrying you: it is of what happened earlier that I am doubtful. There must have been a complete break somewhere. A break in consciousness, I mean —*my* consciousness. It is like this:—I can *think* back over last night, remember what I thought and felt; but of what came earlier I have only vague impressions, as if I had *watched* the earlier scenes."

"You did more than watch, Uncle Stephen. Or at least, Stephen did."

"Yes, I know; but I can't get back into the mind of Stephen. That is where you can help me: by telling me the whole thing as you saw it."

Tom told him. He talked sometimes with his mouth full and sometimes with his mouth empty, but always with his eyes fixed on Uncle Stephen's face. He did not minimize any of the complications that had arisen, nor gloss over the highly equivocal positions into which attempts to escape these complications had landed them. But for him the whole aspect of the adventure was altered now that he had Uncle Stephen back again, and he even could be amused where before he had been nearly in despair. This frugal breakfast was in fact for Tom a very happy one. Perhaps some difficulties remained, but all anxieties were at an end, and his confidence was increased by the unruffled expression with which Uncle Stephen listened. Just so had the boy Stephen taken their troubles: one quality at least remained unmodified by time.

"Well, we now know where we are," Uncle Stephen said, when he had heard the story out. His eyes looked straight into Tom's solemn eyes. "Shouldn't you say, Tom, that it is a situation calling for all our diplomacy?"

"Yes," said Tom, "I should."

"And what does *your* diplomacy suggest we ought to do? What policy, do you think, will be least likely to land us both in the police court?"

Tom looked serious. "The police court!"

"I was only joking. Still, we're not quite out of the wood yet. Our position is that we have eliminated in broad daylight a full-grown boy; and you can't do that, you know, without questions being asked. Moreover, young Stephen appears to have made himself extremely conspicuous."

"I never thought of that!" breathed Tom. "Uncle Horace was frightfully interested in him, and Miss Charlemont wants him to go and stay with her!"

"They'll *all* want to know what has become of him."

"Why can't they think he's just gone away?" Tom protested. "I mean of his own accord. It was what he always intended to do."

"If he had remained Philip I dare say we might have hoped for that, but as my grandson I'm afraid we can't. You say Mr. Knox was struck by the likeness?"

"Not half so much as Miss Charlemont was."

"Miss Charlemont I don't think matters."

"But she's going to write to you, Uncle Stephen; you'll probably get a letter to-day!"

"Even so, I think we may ignore her—for the present at all events."

Tom pondered.

"Mr. Knox only saw the likeness after Stephen had told him his name," he said tentatively. "He *thinks* he saw it before, but he didn't."

"The likeness of course, if he's really convinced of it, might help him to believe the truth," Uncle Stephen murmured half to himself.

"You mean they won't believe he has gone away?"

"It's not that, Tom. I don't imagine anybody will dispute his absence. After all, he *is* absent. But the question will be *why* he went away, and where he went *to*: and, in short, what particular part was played by his grandfather in the matter? I'm afraid we can't make that part look anything but dubious. Let us put it plainly. He arrives here destitute. I do nothing for him, and when he runs away take no steps to get him back again. In other words, leave him to shift for himself, to sink or swim, without friends and without money. It is difficult to put that in an attractive light. In fact, it justifies all the suspicions of Mr. Pringle and your step-mother."

Tom pondered again. He had felt all along that Stephen's account of himself was not going to help them, but he had not foreseen this particular predicament and he could discover no way out of it. "What do you think yourself, Uncle Stephen?" he asked.

Uncle Stephen smiled. "I don't know that I think anything, Tom. But we'll go out into the garden and see if that will inspire us."

Tom got up. In spite of the impasse they appeared to have reached, he felt happy. As he sat on the stone steps in the sun beside Uncle Stephen he came to the conclusion that he also was happy. The problem, in fact, presented itself to Tom now merely as a kind of abstract puzzle. He looked forward with the liveliest interest to the solution Uncle Stephen would eventually find, but that he *would* find one he never for a moment doubted.

And it came even sooner than he had expected. "How would it do, Tom, if we were to make a temporary break with the past; if we left the Manor in charge of Mrs. Deverell for six months or a year, say, while we went on our travels? How would you like to explore the south of Europe? I'd take you over all my old ground, and we'd potter about until we found the right place, and then settle down—probably somewhere on the Italian coast, but there'd be no need to decide till we were both sure."

"I'd love it," said Tom.

"It's what we'll do then," Uncle Stephen answered, and the finality in his voice for Tom settled the question.

Uncle Stephen was thinking; Tom, leaning up against him, waited for his next words. But before he spoke them Uncle Stephen rose to his feet. "I suppose we might as well stroll on to the Manor now: and then I'm afraid I'll have to send you to Kilbarron."

Tom looked at him inquiringly, and as they walked slowly over the grass Uncle Stephen explained what he wished him to do. "I want you to try to get hold of Mr. Flood and Mr. Knox, and bring them out to see me. First, however, you must send a telegram to Gloucester Terrace—a rather expensive one, I'm afraid, for it must explain your return yesterday *with* me. That will relieve the situation there and give us time to make our arrangements."

"Am I to say anything about Stephen?"

"No: they'll take Stephen for granted. But I'll write out the telegram for you when we get home, and then we'll attend to one or two other matters which must be settled before we leave. You see, our arrangement with Mr. Knox will have to be cancelled. Now that we've altered our plans, you won't be able to become his pupil. That is one reason why I want you to bring him with Mr. Flood to the Manor. I'm going to tell them the whole truth, the whole story, though how they'll receive it I don't know. But I think we owe it to them. Besides, even if it proves to be too much for them, I believe they'll still remain on our side—at least to the extent of not standing in our way."

Tom believed so too. "This is my path, Uncle Stephen—the path I made to the other house." He stepped on ahead, for there was no longer room to walk side by side. Presently he said over his shoulder, "I think they might believe it if you were to show them that portrait, with the name and date on it, and take them up to your room."

"I doubt if the room will have much effect, and, portrait or no portrait, their faith is going to be put to a pretty severe test. All the more severe because with neither of them, I fancy, is imagination a strong point."

"I don't believe Mr. Knox ever thought Stephen was telling the truth," Tom said. "I mean about what happened in Italy and all that. If he did he behaved very queerly."

"Perhaps. We shall see. But don't, Tom, begin to make explanations on your own account. I want you to leave this to me. You've done your share."

"I won't say a word," Tom promised.

"You've done a good deal more than your share," Uncle Stephen went on. "I think you must have been very good to Stephen."

Tom coloured. Not until they reached the end of the path, however, and the Manor House came into view, did he speak again. Then, as he caught sight of Sally sweeping out the porch, he turned. "What are you going to tell Mrs. Deverell, Uncle Stephen?"

"I don't intend to tell her anything," Uncle Stephen replied. At the same moment Sally paused in her sweeping, looked up, and instantly disappeared.

"She's gone to give the news," said Tom.

He was right, for Mrs. Deverell was at the door to receive them. "Well, Mrs. Deverell," Uncle Stephen said pleasantly, "here I am back again, and I hope Master Tom behaved himself while I was away."

"Yes, sir—him and the other young gentleman."

Tom looked at her, and instantly knew that the allusion to the other young gentleman had been deliberate. Mrs. Deverell went on immediately: "You're welcome home, sir. Only I didn't know to expect you and I'm afraid it may be a few minutes before——"

"We've already had breakfast," Uncle Stephen said. "But we had it rather early, so I dare say Master Tom would like a cup of tea. You could bring it to the study perhaps. You don't want a full-sized meal, do you, Tom?"

"No, thanks: what I really want is a bath."

"Well, run along then. That will give me time to write a couple of notes as well as your telegram. You're sure to find Mr. Flood at his office, but Mr. Knox may be out."

"And the other young gentleman, sir—Master Philip—Master Stephen?" Mrs. Deverell hinted.

"Master Stephen has gone away," said Uncle Stephen quietly, but with a quietness that closed the conversation.

27: AS it happened, the very first person Tom saw when, about an hour later, he entered Kilbarron post-office, was the curate. He was standing at the counter turning over the leaves of a directory, and when he closed the book Tom was at his elbow.

Mr. Knox was surprised, as he was intended to be, but he did not know how significant was the playing of this small joke. It was in itself an answer to the question he at once put: "Any news from Mr. Collet?"

"Yes," said Tom, "I've a letter for you from him." And he took it out of his pocket.

He handed in his telegram while Mr. Knox was reading Uncle Stephen's note. The curate refolded it and put it away before he glanced rather curiously at its bearer. "Your uncle wants me to come to the Manor this morning, and if possible to bring Mr. Flood. But I suppose you know that already. Have you told Mr. Flood?"

"Not yet. I've got a letter for him too."

"Then I'd better go with you to his office: it will save time. When did Mr. Collet get back?"

"He came with me—last night."

"And Stephen?"

"Stephen hasn't come back."

Mr. Knox seemed about to say something further, but after a moment's thought reserved it for another time, and in silence they went out into the sunlit street and walked together towards Mr. Flood's office which was not more than a hundred yards away. When they reached it Tom drew back. It had occurred to him that Mr. Knox and the solicitor might like to exchange a few remarks in private concerning this unusual invitation, so he took the second letter from his pocket. "Will you give it to him?" he said. "I'll wait out here."

"Well—just as you like," Mr. Knox replied. But he took the letter, and passed through the swing door.

Left alone, Tom strolled on as far as the nearest shop window, where, his hands deep in his trousers pockets, he stood apparently fascinated by an arrangement of tinned meats and fruits, which was the principal feature of the display. But this was not what he saw. Nor was he thinking of either Mr. Knox or the lawyer. In imagination he was standing beside Uncle Stephen gazing at the ruins of the Parthenon, sitting beside him on the shore of the Sicilian sea, far far away from all this, under a bluer sky and a hotter sun. . . . Five, ten minutes passed. Occasionally he glanced over his shoulder in the direction of the solicitor's office, and at last he saw Mr. Knox coming out. Tom went to meet him. "Mr. Flood is getting the car," the curate explained. "The garage is at the back. I suppose we might as well walk to the corner."

They did so, while Mr. Knox added, "I hope we didn't keep you too long. He was waiting for the post. In the end he decided to leave it till his return. Here he is."

Mr. Flood drove up, waved a greeting to Tom, and opened the door for Mr. Knox, while Tom climbed up on to the seat behind.

The car turned into the road leading to the Manor. Tom, perched up behind them, wondered what the other two were thinking about, for they said nothing. He also wondered what they would be thinking an hour hence. He had a feeling of excitement and elation, and enjoyed the short drive, though the dickey was uncomfortable.

The car swung round the bend of the avenue, and Uncle Stephen, who had been waiting near the porch, stepped forward to meet it. "So he did get you," he said, shaking hands with the curate, who had got out first, and then with Mr. Flood. "I must apologize for dragging you here at such an hour. I expect it is the least convenient I could have chosen. It was very good of you to come."

"Not at all—not at all," the visitors replied politely.

"Well, I hope you'll forgive me when I have explained my reason. But come in, won't you? Tom, I think we shan't require you in the meantime, but don't be late for dinner."

Tom promised, and as the others turned to enter the house he walked slowly away.

He crossed the lawn. There was his path, and presently he found himself retracing his steps to the other house. It was more from force of habit, however, than anything else. The other house was now only an empty house to him, and he had no particular desire to return to it: indeed he had a feeling that it would have been better had he never gone there at all.

And while he drew nearer this feeling deepened. There was a moment when, at the entrance to the avenue, he very nearly turned back. For a strange, an almost ghostly fear had suddenly touched him, like a faint cold sigh of autumn wind. He did not yield to it: he walked on: but no further than the fountain, where he stretched himself on the grass. Once only had he glanced at the house, and it was like a hollow shell, empty and drained of life. Yet he knew that nothing could have induced him to go inside and climb the stairs.

He lay there, his elbows digging into the soft turf and his chin supported between his hands. The hot sun beat down on him, but that was what he liked. The world into which he and Uncle Stephen were going he saw as drenched in sunlight. He had built up his picture of it much as a child puts together a jigsaw puzzle—from fragments of Theocritus, from a walk taken by Socrates and Phaidros along the banks of the Ilissos, and from deepest impressions of his own summer woods.

Thinking of Uncle Stephen made him think of the conference which must be going on at that moment in the Manor study. He wondered how far they had got. Uncle Stephen at any rate would have finished his story; there had been more than time for that; they must have been talking for at least half an hour. Would Uncle Stephen tell them all about him, Tom, as well as about himself? He could hardly do otherwise, for the secret must lie really in a kind of collaboration. His desire and his imagination must have acted in collusion with Uncle Stephen's, and this union somehow had produced all the rest. Would Uncle Stephen tell them it had begun even before he had left Gloucester Terrace? For that too was a part of the story. Unknowingly he had sent out a message which had reached Uncle Stephen through the night and the darkness. Their first meeting had not taken place in the Manor study, but in Tom's room at his step-mother's; and this much at least he supposed they would believe—surely it was easy to believe— though the rest was more fantastic. The lawyer, he felt, would *not* believe the rest. On the other hand, he would have to believe *something*. . . . What? That it was a delusion? That both he and Uncle Stephen were slightly mad: only not mad enough to be shut up or prevented from going away together? *That*, after all, was all they wanted, though it might not be a flattering solution. His thoughts sank into a kind of dreaming. They floated over the past and the present, drifting to and fro, rising and sinking, like loosened seaweed on a swelling sea. . . .

"Down—down—down." He dabbled his hand in the water of the fountain, and gazing into the shallow pool, began to sing in an undertone that one word. It was because he was looking down through the dark greenish water: yet there were poems by Sappho —fragments of poems—which contained no more than a word or two, but were somehow beautiful and sufficient, like that broken statue of Hermes. . . .

"And golden pulse grew on the shores. . . ."

All the most beautiful things he knew had come to him through Uncle Stephen. They had been there, perhaps, like anemones in a wood, waiting to be discovered:—still, it was a kind of gift if somebody brought them to you, or brought you to them. And not an ordinary gift, for they were things which could not be worn out or broken. Uncle Stephen was his master and he was Uncle Stephen's pupil. In the old days a pupil had lived with his master. He had that kind of master to-day. . . .

Where was Deverell? If it had not been for Uncle Stephen he might have gone away with Deverell, and what would have happened then? What would have become of him? His whole life would have been different. . . . Why had Deverell loved him? What was it he had loved? Not his beauty at any rate, for he had none. . . . Everything seemed to depend so much on chance. It was by chance that he had met Deverell, by chance that Uncle Stephen was his uncle. And Deverell's chances had all been unlucky. He had gone very likely straight into the darkness. He might find somebody else to love, but it was improbable and—Tom knew there were two kinds of love. "I'll never forget him," he said softly, "but what good is that to him? He won't even know."

He thought of Stephen. Stephen had gone back into dreamland. But dream and reality were hardly distinguishable, for what was real yesterday to-day became a dream. All the past *was* dreamland: it was only the present moment that wasn't. Deverell and Stephen— they were equally near, or equally far. Involuntarily he glanced up at the window where he had first seen Stephen, but the window was empty. . . .

This place was making him morbid. Like the raven in the poem, it seemed, wherever he turned, to beat out one monotonous refrain— nevermore. He would go back. The discussion, favourable or un- favourable, must be ended. He rose to a kneeling posture and then to his feet. He looked farewell at the stone boy watching over his garden. . . . Nevermore. . . . He would take this with him as his last and most beautiful impression of the place. But even as he stood there, letting the picture stamp itself upon his mind, he felt again the impulse to kiss that faintly smiling mouth. He would not. He remembered the last time—remembered telling Uncle Stephen. He turned his back and instantly felt an intense sadness. Why should he not kiss him? What harm could it do? It might be silly and babyish, but nobody would ever know, and it really was the kiss of good-bye. . . .

The stone was warm. The sun had warmed the curved pouting mouth and the smooth limbs and body; but when Tom's lips pressed

on those other lips the eyes were looking away from him, and dimly
he felt that this was a symbol of life—of life and of all love. No,
no—not all—not Uncle Stephen's. Uncle Stephen's eyes were fixed
upon him, looked straight into his spirit, that was why he was
different from everybody else. "Good-bye," Tom whispered into the
delicate unlistening ear.

He hurried from the garden, trying as he went to shake from him
this incomprehensible mood and return to actuality. Surely the
present crisis was absorbing and exciting enough, and the future
was there, beckoning eagerly, filled with happiness.

And it was as if the influence he had felt could indeed reach
only a certain distance, for as he hastened along the wood path
his spirits rose rapidly. He had completely recovered them when
through the trees he heard a low whistle, and knew that Uncle
Stephen was come to look for him. Tom broke into a run.

"Where are they?" he asked, as he burst out into sunlight. "Have
they gone?"

"Yes, but Mr. Flood is coming back. He wanted to attend to his
letters: the post hadn't arrived when he left this morning."

"And Mr. Knox?"

"Mr. Knox couldn't stay."

"Is it all right?" Tom questioned eagerly, his eyes searching
Uncle Stephen's face.

"From our point of view—yes."

"And from theirs?"

"Well, theirs isn't ours, I'm afraid."

Tom was silent.

Uncle Stephen walked slowly on, his hands behind his back, while
Tom kept pace beside him. "I should think Mr. Flood won't be
here for another half-hour," Uncle Stephen said, "but Mrs. Deverell
knows; I told her we were expecting him."

Tom did not ask what had taken place at the meeting. In a way
he was even glad not to know. He wanted to forget the whole
thing, and Uncle Stephen must have guessed this. "To-morrow we'll
start," he said. "That ought to give us plenty of time to pack. Mr.
Flood will look after the closing of the house. You're sure the plan
appeals to you, Tom? You're sure you are quite happy?"

"Yes."

Uncle Stephen laid his hand on the boy's shoulder. He kept it there
while they continued to pace slowly up and down the lawn, Tom

silent, Uncle Stephen talking of their approaching travels. He presently, indeed, plunged into a stream of reminiscence; the prospect of revisiting old scenes and reviving old memories evidently attracted him, though it was not so much the thought of the direct renewal of impressions as the thought of renewing them through the eyes and the intelligence of the boy beside him that lay behind all he said. In that seemed to be his pleasure. They were as companions. Objects which he had loved before were dearer now. From the boy there came feelings and emanations—things which were light to the sun and music to the wind: and the old man's heart seemed born again. . . .

Up and down they walked, waiting for Mr. Flood. And the sun shone, and Sally flapped a pink checked duster out of an upper window, and a thin trail of smoke floated away from the kitchen chimney across the sky, and on the next chimney a rook alit with a friendly caw.

August 1929
April 1931